JENRET SENT HIS MIND SEARCHING THE CITY. . . .

He touched . . . yes! A twinge of recognition, of consciousness, but the infantile mind overwhelmed him with its raw terrors—a crashing jolt that rattled his bones, the din thunderclapping on tiny, sensitive ears. An abrupt temperature shift, too, too hot! *"What is fire? Mama scared?"*

Jenret reeled, dizzy with the effort of reaching out mind-to-mind across such a vast distance. Unable to absorb the baby's raw emotions and sensations, he could only grasp that some dire danger threatened Doyce, and the baby as well. Fire? By the Lady, no, not fire! He tried to tap into the voice again, pushed himself back and higher, not looking or caring what was behind him.

"Doyce!" he screamed. *"Doyce! Hold on!"* Flames surged at him, danced and crackled, fingers of fire licking him, an obscene come-hither. They shimmered and crawled all around him. No! It wasn't real! Vivid streamers of orange and yellow circled, tasting his clothes, flashing and flaring at his hands, his face, singeing. Lungs winced at the superheated air. Higher, hotter—he dove to escape the messages slamming into his mind, as if his escape would liberate Doyce as well. And tumbled backward into thin air as Rawn shouted, too late, **"No farther! Stop!"**

D0802148

Be sure to read all three novels in this
magnificent new DAW fantasy series
from
GAYLE GREENO

THE GHATTI'S TALE:
FINDERS-SEEKERS (Book One)
MINDSPEAKERS' CALL (Book Two)
EXILES' RETURN (Book Three)

Exiles' Return

The Ghatti's Tale: Book Three

Gayle Greeno

DAW BOOKS, INC.

DONALD A. WOLLHEIM, FOUNDER

375 Hudson Street, New York, NY 10014

ELIZABETH R. WOLLHEIM
SHEILA E. GILBERT
PUBLISHERS

First Printing, May 1995

1 2 3 4 5 6 7 8 9

DAW TRADEMARK REGISTERED
U. S. PAT. OFF. AND FOREIGN COUNTRIES
—MARCA REGISTRADA
HECHO EN U. S. A.

PRINTED IN THE U. S. A.

It seems as if the last eighteen months have been fraught with tragedy for many of us with beloved companion animals. Those of you who've followed me through Book Two know that I lost Tulip shortly after her 20th birthday. Tulip's successor, Angel, basked in two months' worth of love before she reluctantly left me. The following list commemorates eleven cats (and one collie) who are also mourned and missed:

Alec, beloved of Betty and Diane D.-D.
Pumpkin, beloved of Helen, Dennis and Stephanie D.
Tristan and Gypsy, beloved of Lori D.
Butch, beloved of Mary Jane H.
Shadow, beloved of Susan H.
Chloe, beloved of Mary K.
Harlan, beloved of Ira S.
Dinah, beloved of Mary and Larry S.
Kisu, beloved of Anna-Liisa W.
Hopper, beloved of Liz W.
Sweetie and Kinko's Mama, beloved of Sue Y.

And most especially to those nameless, lost ones who never received the loving hearts and homes they so richly deserved. Please support your local humane societies and remember that mature animals, not just puppies and kittens, need your love.

"So he who sat upon the cloud swung his sickle on the earth, and the earth was reaped."

—Revelation 14: 16

Exiles' Return

PROLOGUE

She strode purposefully, with the gait of someone confident of her goal, though she lacked a clue, desperate to remember which street came next, whether the dogleg swung her back to city center or not. Walk any faster and the temptation to run would consume her, a mistake, a tip-off that she wasn't who she appeared to be, didn't belong, had no business here. No, a nice, steady stride served best, and her occasional reflection in a store window revealed only a forced but bland smile, a coherence of wrinkles drawing her brows together. The reflection also revealed the blurred shapes of her pursuers, one across the street, paralleling her, two behind about a half-block distant. Now only one behind her—where had the other one gone? Not likely he'd tired of his game, and his abrupt absence made her flesh crawl.

With a determined sigh that made her sound like any one of a hundred other women, tired at the end of a long day, hurrying home, she continued walking, didn't alter her pace. What made her stand out, and her heart sank as she attracted yet another look beyond the normal glance-over of passersby, was her garb: very "country," old-fashioned, the style not right, even for the old quarter of Gaernett where people dressed as they fancied rather than in current fashion. At home her clothing let her fade into the woodwork, unmemorable when she and Orem ventured into town for supplies. Here she was a moth amongst butterflies, her careful drabness singling her out as different, an "other," an outsider.

Orem had been right, the boys were too young to accompany them to Gaernett, Collum only five, and Michael nine, though good, steady lads, obedient at the snap of one's fingers. If not, they'd never have been allowed this much freedom. And besides, Collum had endured a miserable summer, the arch of his foot slashed on a hoe blade Michael had left

wrong-sided. It had severed tendons, required a eumedico to
stitch it properly, and then, almost healed, Collum'd snuck
off to swim in the pond. The nearly healed gash went septic,
and he'd gotten an ear infection as well, aches and afflic-
tions at both ends.

To salve the pain and tears she'd promised both boys—
and herself—a treat when the cooler weather came. A day
trip to the capital, to Gaernett, visit the soaring Bethel,
higher and grander than anything they'd ever seen, window-
shop, the promise of a few gaudy penny toys chosen from
the market stalls. Hadn't she lulled Colly, burning with fever
to match the long summer heat, spinning tales of her two
previous furtive visits to Gaernett, poring over the tattered
guide's pen sketches of cosmopolitan marvels to behold?
Who could blame him if thoughts of freedom, the luxury of
being yourself—however circumspectly—in a bustling,
anonymous place where no one questioned your true identity, made his fever dreams soar. Her own dreams did, too.

The man across the street paced her as if they were
double-yoked, but the one remaining behind her seemed to
have dropped back. The footsteps she heard weren't his, the
inexorably heavy tread that matched and mocked her own
stride, drummed terror into her soul. And where, where was
the third man? How could they know, even suspect? They
wouldn't, couldn't snatch people off the street in broad daylight, could they? Her teeth clenched, an artificial, close-
lipped smile pasted over them, death mask false, people
registering the grimace, looking at her twice. She smoothed
her expression.

Which way, which way now? Two long-ago visits to
Gaernett, the wistful studying of the guidebook's spider-
tracked street map. She'd purposely lured them into the Old
Quarter, the multiplicity of winding, confusing streets to her
advantage, rather than the regimented, gridlike patterns of
the newer city areas. Fool—of course they knew the city better than she, every uncertainty and hesitation playing into
their hands! The Bethel's spire rose in the distance, a bea-
con, but how to get there from here? She scanned the twisting streets and lanes in mounting panic, refused to press a
hand over her heart to still it.

If not the Bethel, then where? She thought she recollected
a tavern, an inn of some sort, had admired its three stories
of wood, each fancifully colored, gingerbread gilding all

around, gay as a fairy-tale dwelling. Myllard's, wasn't it called? Crested leather helmets, the creak of half-armor, a Guardian pair sauntering up ahead, eyes peeled for trouble. Reveal herself, plead for help? At least stop and ask directions? Even that would draw attention, and she couldn't break the inbred habits of a lifetime—never call attention to yourself. Yes, the Guardians were sworn to protect them as they would any other Canderisian citizen, but she couldn't make herself believe. Reluctantly, she let them pass. Nothing could happen in broad daylight.

She crossed Gelder's Alley where it intersected Halfling Lane, then turned right to cross Halfling. Crossing Halfling before the intersection would have set her on the same corner as her follower, two pieces on the same square of a game board. Apparently reading her resolve to make a move, he'd held back, restless, on the far corner, content not to apprehend her yet. Ordinary-looking, nothing to raise eyebrows, soberly dressed except for the silvery flash of a crescent pinned on each collar—a new fashion, perhaps. She took what seemed her first breath in ages, faint hope rising because—yes, Blessed Lady!—this was the way to Myllard's. Not home free, but temporary safe harbor. Her face shed years, became as young as it truly was as she hurried along.

Who had tipped them off, whispered that they visited the capital? A way for their own townspeople to be shed of them, yet leave their own hands unsullied? But that bespoke planning, biding one's time. No, more likely, incredibly bad luck. Colly, when that man had trod on his foot in the crowd? A heavy leather boot with a steel-rimmed heel stepping back, crunching the still-tender foot, not shifting, oblivious to the small boy's screams, indeed, grinding his heel even harder. Orem had yelled a warning, shoving the man from behind to shift him off, all the while apologizing, temporizing, explaining. His face screwed in agony, Colly clutched his knee to yank his leg free, Michael crouching and holding his ankle, ready to help. "What?" the man had boomed, cupping his ear, rocking back on his heels. "What? Under foot?"

Before she could launch a mindslap Colly lashed out, mind writhing with pain, *"Get off me, you deaf old fool!"* The man leaped as if Colly had stuck him with a pin, took off as if all the hells' demons pursued him, rather than one little boy holding his foot, crying with pain. Their followers, the shadowers, appeared shortly thereafter, and they'd shakily launched the plan they'd so often practiced, rehearsed against the possibility of discovery. Orem painstakingly wove the insinuation through the air, the niggling, tingling hint of seductiveness, her availability, her want, her need, and she'd drifted away from husband and sons, sashaying by the first man, letting her skirts brush enticingly across his thigh and groin. It sickened her, but her need to protect was stronger. Orem would fade clear with the boys, hide, take the quickest route out of the city. And she, she would play the mother bird with the supposedly broken wing, luring the predators from her young before bursting into triumphant flight—safety! At least that's how the plan was supposed to work.

After she thought she'd detoured far enough, she'd tweaked their brains again, begging forgiveness to her ancestors for the intrusion, convincing them they'd misjudged her allure, her availability, a plain, harried woman, intent on her business. As she was. But still they followed. Mayhap it bespoke divine justice, retribution for her momentary lapse, for they continued following her as if scenting a bitch in heat.

Myllard's Inn was ahead, she could see the top story, the sky-blue one, the sea foam green roof tiles. They wouldn't dare drag her out of a public place, nor reveal what she was in public, not with the Monitor's sanctions to protect her kind. Faster, faster, and she finally let herself break into a run, never saw the hand snaking out of the gloomy alley to snag her wrist, another hand clamping over her mouth. No, not rape—but worse, their minds promised that. She let her mind scream as loudly as she could, uncaring, concerned only that Orem learn the grim reality. No sense in searching for her, mounting a rescue. Then the dagger slipped up under her rib cage and penetrated her heart. And Canderis counted one less Resonant amongst its citizenry as Leah Fahlgren died.

❖

PART
ONE

❖

PART
ONE

With a sigh and a squirm Doyce Marbon dragged another ancient text to the small space she'd precariously cleared at the desk's center, debated what would happen when she opened the book. The leather was so worn, so stiff, ready to crack and flake at the slightest touch, but, despite herself, she caressed it in honor of what it recorded about bygone times, long-ago days.

This one was small, its covers warped and bulging, and the leather wasn't the worst of it: papermaking back in those early days had been primitive at best; indeed, a wonder that someone had managed it at all. As if in agreement with her thoughts, a corner snapped from one page, a few fading letters staring up at her before her prodding fingers almost disintegrated it. She slid another paper under it, holding her breath, and slipped the whole thing into a glassine envelope. Another fragment from the past, salvaged. Where would it fit?

"I've heard about keeping the past at arm's length," she muttered, "but this is ridiculous!" and held the book outstretched. Hazel eyes squinted, unable to focus at that distance. Mayhap if she slid under the table a bit more? Hunching her way down the cushioned bench, she squeezed her mounded belly beneath the table, bent her elbows, and drew the book closer. Not *that* pregnant, she consoled herself, simply that she was so slight her condition had showed almost immediately. She hadn't blossomed, she'd burgeoned. Better, much better, except for the pain in her back.

With an exasperated growl, she elbowed herself upright, shut the book with a gentle thump. Blast Swan Maclough for demanding she write a history of the Seekers Veritas to commemorate their two hundredth anniversary next year! Much as she might be personally enamored of the past, what she truly craved was reassurance about the present—and the future. A tattoo of tiny feet and fists made her belly vibrate, and tears began to flood her eyes. Hormones, bloody hormones, just what she needed! Remaining rational and collected these days could be a losing battle. A brisk wipe with her sleeve conquered her tears, but not her fears.

There were more important things to do than research and writing—what with Canderis still astir over the discovery of Gleaners, Resonants, in their midst! Not to mention their unexpected rapprochement with their standoffish neighbor Marchmont after so many years, only to discover that Resonants there were an integral part of society. It should have helped, but it didn't, simply made Marchmont suspect in a different way from the past.

People were ill at ease, their ordered world turned upside down by the discovery that Resonants, people with the ability to read minds—perhaps even steal them—had secretly lived beside them in apparent harmony for many years. Except now that any and every problem, past and present—from unexpected illness to bad business deals and marital incompatibility—could be blamed on something, someone, a whole misunderstood group to serve as scapegoats. What happened when the familiar turned unfamiliar? Especially when the "unfamiliar" continued to appear familiar—no way to tell, be sure.

And she—she should be out riding circuit, reassuring people, comforting them, showing them that change didn't mean change for the worse, but could mean change for the better. After all, wasn't the father of her child, Jenret Wycherley, both a Seeker and now a Resonant? So what if she were pregnant—she could still ride, or at worst, travel by wagon, with her Bondmate Khar'pern at her side. But instead, here she sat imprisoned in the library, jotting notes, striving to form the Seekers' history into a coherent whole. Relegated to the stacks because she'd taken her duty too seriously, nursing the Seeker General with every bit of her long-ago training as a eumedico and—she snuffled wetly, tried to be honest—hovering, overhearing too much about the turmoils, putting the worst possible cast on a deteriorating situation. Now Jenret was absent yet again, training at the new Resonant school set up at the Research Hospice in the Tetonords, not here to reassure her, share information with her, and even her Bondmate Khar had temporarily deserted her for the sunny paving stones of the sunken plaza outside Head-quarters.

A wave of self-pity engulfed her again, alone, forsaken, bereft, and then she had to laugh. Alone? Hardly. And an emphatic kick reminded her that for better or worse, she was pregnant, a promise toward the future, however unclear it might seem. So enjoy what she had while she had it, and let tomorrow take care of itself. Time enough to do her part, once she knew what it was.

A discreet scratching at the door distracted her and she shoved the table, gained room to maneuver her bulk clear. Grumbling at her ungainliness, she opened the door to find Per'la there, long, fluffy hair the color of butter cream, peridot eyes staring up at her. But saddest of all, and she forced herself not to let her eyes stray, betray her, was the ghatta's lack of a tail, the nipped stub a forlorn reminder of the long, plumed glory once hers. Gone, gone along with Parse's leg, and so many other things and friends lost as well. The war had not been kind. And in a land unused to war, its shock and pain lingered longer, like a sleeper awakening only to discover the nightmare was reality.

Per'la trotted in, tail stub flicking as Doyce closed the door, old habits about the fear of pinching dying hard. "Well, love?" she asked aloud. "How goes it?" The ghatta sprang to the desktop, sat as if to dangle her tail over the edge, then turned and licked vigorously at the stub. And despite herself, Doyce mourned, "Oh, Per'la!" at the sad reminder, the absence, the loss.

"Will you stop being so polite." She buried fingers in the soft, fluffy ruff, let her thumbs scratch just beneath the ringed ears, the left with its hoop, the right with the ball. *"Mindwalk if ye will,"* Doyce offered in silent mindspeech. *"I thought you too dear a friend to need an invitation,"* she continued, consoling with her touch. Per'la twisted so her chin received the coveted scratching as well.

"Never abandon your manners," she noted with wistful dignity. **"If you lose them, who knows what else you might lose."** Ghatti were notoriously polite when it came to conversing with humans, even another Seeker. Without permission to enter, a human's thoughts remained private, despite the ghatti's ability to read human minds, discern truth. **"Parse's coming. Takes a while, but he's coming. He insisted, and he won't accept any help."**

Despite her resolve, Doyce made a face. The librarian, a retired Seeker, had taken a half-day off; no one here but her to help, and the library was on the third floor of the Head-quarters' east wing. That meant Parse had two flights of steep stairs to navigate, plus the long hallway. And all on crutches, balancing on his one remaining leg. He'd never managed that far alone, and she listened, straining to hear the thump of crutches, prayed she wouldn't hear the thud of a falling body. Ask Per'la to call someone to help? The fact that she hadn't showed she'd taken Parse's resolve seriously, judged it important for him to conquer this on his own. Not up to her to intrude. *"Shouldn't you at least be with him for moral support?"* Her hands tugged restlessly at the sashed tabard that constantly seemed too short in front now, stuck out like a coal scuttle.

"He wants to do it alone. Said he has to cope without leaning on anybody, even me." The ghatta pulled away, licked again at her tail stump. **"He thinks he's lost every-thing, not just his leg. He's pushing me away, he's push-ing Sarrett away, all of us . . ."** Stricken by her own revelation, the ghatta trailed off, miserable.

"Well, he does have to learn to cope on his own, but he may be overdoing it." They both cocked an ear at a thunder-ous curse and a sharp, racketing sound that meant a crutch had fallen, slaloming down the stairs.

"What are we going to do?" Per'la paced the desk's edge, poised to jump.

"Give him a little longer, then we'll go see, if we have to."

"I know what it's like," the ghatta whimpered. **"Nothing seems right anymore. When I jump I feel as if I'm off balance, when I go to sleep there's nothing to cover my nose for warmth. And . . . and most of all,"** she could barely force the words out, her muzzle screwed in agony, **"it was *so* beautiful! Wasn't it?"** she appealed to Doyce.

"Absolutely gorgeous," Doyce agreed. And it had been. It was more than mere ghatti vanity that made Per'la ache with loss, although preening pride was one component, and that—that absence of symmetry and grace—perhaps she could assuage. *"Love, I've an idea."* She began unlacing the pale blue ribbon that closed her undertunic's neck opening. *"What do you think?"* She dangled the ribbon by Per'la's nose, and the ghatta touched at it with a tentative paw.

"**Round my neck?**" the ghatta paused, unsure. "**I don't think so.**"

"*No, silly,*" and Doyce gently tied the ribbon around Per'-la's tail stub, making a bow, adjusting it until the ribbon ends hung even and not too long. Per'la twisted this way and that, examining it from all angles. "*Flick it,*" Doyce suggested, "*see how it feels.*" The ghatta complied, captivated by the rustling sound.

"**Tickles,**" she admitted, "**but I think I like it, at least for,**" and ghatti good humor flickered in peridot eyes, "**dress up. Would Parse buy me different colors?**"

"Buy you what in different colors?" Absorbed in their makeover, neither had registered the sounds indicating Parse had at last conquered the stairs and the long, polished hall. He edged the door open further with his crutch and sidled into the room, red face clashing with flyaway carroty hair.

Dodging her own awkwardness, Doyce sprang to drag a chair toward him where he canted against the wall, chest heaving. He waved her back, irritable, face contorted, eyes screwed shut, his body abruptly rigid with anticipation. At first she felt hurt, rejected, only to realize that Parse labored in the midst of a sneeze, allergies indomitable as always. He exploded, both crutches collapsing from under his arms as he plastered himself against the wall for stability, balancing on his left leg, the pinned right pants leg limply waving. "Naa-choo!" and he exploded again, not daring to lift a hand to cover it and risk disrupting his precarious balance.

Its legs scraping, Doyce slid the straight chair toward him, its back turned so he could grasp the top. Then she bent at the knees to gather the strayed crutches splayed to each side of him. He literally swallowed the next sneeze, let it explode inside, head jerking back as his hands went white-knuckled on the chair back. Propping his crutches in place, she waited for him to drag himself upright. "Care to sit down?" Hauling out a handkerchief, she signaled in front of his face, flagging his attention. He grabbed it greedily.

Crutches pinned in place, he blew, while Per'la exchanged a long-suffering glance with Doyce. "Thank you, no," he managed with what dignity remained. "Though I wouldn't mind perching." He indicated her worktable and began his step-swing, step-swing to it, finally hooking a hip onto the edge, laying the crutches aside. "Didn't she tell you?" He sounded almost accusatory.

"Tell me what?" Per'la stared ceilingward, no help there.

Despite himself, Parse began to laugh. Per'la rubbed against the rigid arm balancing him on the tabletop. "I thought losing a leg was the penultimate indignity, short of death, that is." He laughed again, wiped his eyes. "I am definitely *not* in the Blessed Lady's good graces these days. There're other indignities as well, I've discovered."

"What are you talking about?"

"Oh, Doyce, love. I've boils on my bottom. Couldn't sit if you paid me, couldn't even if it meant my leg would grow back! The eumedicos said my allergies are breaking out in other ways!"

Sinking down heavily, Doyce hugged herself, bent double with laughter, then straightened to ruffle the carroty hair. "Oh, Parse! Poor lamb, isn't there a salve, an unguent that will do some good?"

"Well, good is a relative term. Mostly I've just got to stay the course, though Twylla's promised to brew up some horse ointment she swears might help—said it also works on asses." He turned sober, serious, in the blink of an eye. "Stopped in to see the Seeker General after I visited Twylla at the infirmary. She said you might need some assistance." He gestured around him at the books, her piles of scribbled note cards, waiting to be reorganized, refiled to puzzle sense out of them. "Please, Doyce," he begged, "I've got to do something to take my mind off this, off everything. I'm a good researcher, even Sarrett admits to that." All the humor drained from his face as he uttered the name, his blue eyes suspiciously bright. What had happened between Sarrett and Parse? She'd expected their marriage announcement once Parse was out of danger. But gossip said that Sarrett had volunteered for additional circuit-riding lately, had spent less and less of her brief stay overs with Parse as his rehabilitation progressed. "It's about the only thing I can offer these days. That I'm any good at any more." He drubbed at the table, grim and lost.

"That's hardly the case." Another casualty of the war, not physical but mental—the loss of self-esteem. She wasn't the only one who needed bolstering. "You know the eumedicos and Twylla think you can be fitted with an artificial leg, may even be able to ride short circuits. If you think the Seekers Veritas plan to put you out to pasture, you're wrong! We won't let you—I won't let you, Per'la won't let you, and," she plowed ahead before she could change her mind, "Sarrett won't let you! When are you going to do the right thing and marry her, Parse? Given your moods lately, I'd flee as far as I could if I were Sarrett."

Khar, lazily monitoring her mindthoughts from the distance of the plaza, chimed in, **"Well, you've left yourself vulnerable with that one, beloved. Don't be surprised if he uses the opening you've given him."** Mouth open in a little "o," she belatedly realized what Khar meant.

"Just the way you've married Jenret?" A bitter, retaliatory smile accompanied Parse's verbal dagger. "Harrap's been ready to perform the ceremony I don't know how many times. Yes, Doyce," his lips twitched. "How many times has it been by your reckoning? Jenret's so dejected he's lost count." A double distress seized her heart: that Parse, always so exuberantly cheerful and compulsively curious, had fallen to such petty meanness, an enjoyment of hurting; and that she and Jenret had never quite found the proper time or opportunity to wed, despite sharing the large guest house on Seeker Veritas grounds. Had she been pushing Jenret away, putting him off as surely as Parse was Sarrett? Or was Jenret holding her at arm's-length, constantly traveling, running away from her?

Nervous, she ran fingers through newly cropped red-brown hair—nothing to twist behind her ears now. Her exposed neck burned flaming hot. Lady help her, she was too old at thirty-eight to play those sorts of games, wasn't she? She polished off the excuse she'd proffered Jenret, the others—Mahafny and Swan; innocent Harrap, both Shepherd and Seeker; Arras Muscadeine; her mother and crippled sister, living far away but determined to join the celebration when word was given. "There's been too much going on. Every time we set a date, something crops up. You know that, Parse, you *have* to know that. The world's not the same and priorities are different now. Have to be different." An excuse, an exculpation, but it played with sweet reason to her ears and, she hoped, to Parse's.

"I know," Parse's expression went cold and wintery with self-knowledge. "Cold feet. Or in my case, cold foot." He tossed the next words at her, defiant, daring her to contradict him. "What kind of life can I offer Sarrett as a cripple?"

Emboldened despite herself, Per'la round-eyed with shock as she read the subtext of Doyce's thoughts slightly ahead of the spoken words, she plunged ahead. "Why, the same as before but far more efficient, Parse."

"Efficient?"

"Of course, fewer stockings to knit, fewer stockings to wash, fewer boots to polish!"

She braced herself, waited for him to throw the inkwell, his fist clenched around the cut glass, Per'la poised to bat his hand if he did. Instead, he struggled to swallow laughter. "Oh, by the Lady," he finally choked, "better to laugh than to weep, any day." Shakily, he toyed with the bow on Per'-la's tail. "Badge of honor, hey? But, Doyce, if you're determined to be so practical, so pragmatic, let me suggest something to you: if you get much bigger, I'll suspect twins. Best marry Jenret and quickly—twice as many diapers to change and wash, twice as many nighttime cries. . . ." He cocked a brow, let it sink in. "Now I believe I made you an offer?"

"Perish the thought of twins, Parse, but I'd be delighted to have your help." A sweeping gesture indicated stacks of notes, the books awaiting research. "There's so much to organize, still so much to investigate. Not to mention developing a coherence to it all." If Swan didn't cherish her assistance, her nursing and care, her devotion, at least she could do this—and do it well. And that, like everything else, meant to the best of her abilities. Nothing more, nothing less. No matter the pain of being shunted aside—from Jenret, from her true vocation as a Seeker Veritas, from ministering to Swan. Truth was truth no matter the venue. Perhaps truths lurked in this, just awaiting discovery.

Parse's interest was eager, unfeigned, as he turned over scraps of paper, glanced at their contents.

"The thing is," she tried to push herself back on track, to do what she could without longing for what she couldn't, "is that I really want to start off with a bang, discover what truly happened when Matthias Vandersma first Bonded with Kharm—what was it like to be the first, what was his world like then? Not just supposition, but facts, details. Emotions, too—I'm greedy. So little survived from those first years once the Plumbs began to explode." Another time, another world, so like and unlike her own.

He nodded, eager to tackle the puzzle. "If there's something here, we'll find it." He warmed to the task, considering plans. "If we advertise in the daily broadsides, perhaps we'll find someone with relics from those early days, an old log-book or something."

No sense dimming his enthusiasm, and perhaps he was right. She slid him a pile of letters tied with a faded red rib-bon. "Well, you can start here. It's not all the way back, but these are letters from Magnus deWit to his cousin during the near-insurrection when Crolius Renselinck was almost ousted as Seeker General. It's something we have to cover honestly and truthfully, show both sides."

Slipping the letters into his sash, Parse grabbed his crutches and thumped to an old accountant's desk relegated to the library. Slanted to hold ledgers and perched on tall legs so the worker could stand, it was perfect for him. He caught his elbows on the lip and began sorting, swaying and humming.

They both settled in, Doyce returning to the decrepit book she'd glanced at before. How had it come to be in the Seeker Veritas library, behind the ledgers, dusty, disregarded? Not even a code number on its cracked spine. Blowing, she dis-lodged more dust, prayed her thoughtlessness wouldn't trip off another bout of sneezes in Parse.

The writing was atrocious—printing veering into a stag-gering cursive script embellished with ornate curlicues, wan-dering back to print. Almost impossible to decipher. And the orthography, well, spelling clearly hadn't been this person's strong suit. Somehow she suspected the journal had be-longed to someone quite young. Hardly a fair assessment: education had faltered during the Plumb years, and the flighty, labored handwriting and uneasy spelling could be equally indicative of someone of any age unused to marshal-ing thoughts and committing them to paper. Turning the book to catch the light, she concentrated, speaking under her breath, sounding the words as she realized much of the spell-ing was phonetic.

Granther sayed i shoed kepp a dairy. Ha, ha, i meen diary. Dairys is four kows! I m two right daun wat i want to re-memer, cereous or fun, reel things or things i think of alot. Gess i ken try it. But sum things

are ceekret two me, i woodnot dair put
them daun heer becuz evun tho Granther
sez this kan bee my ceekret book, i doent
allays trust Ryk when he goez nozeing
around. Mower twonite. Must sharepen
sickel, go kut reads now.

Closing the book and sliding it away, she folded her arms
on the table, rested her chin on them. She'd been right, the
diary of a youngster, interesting but not germane. Mayhap
she'd take it home, struggle through a few more pages when
she had spare time. Problem with resting your chin on your
arms like this, she decided, is that you can't yawn properly.
Drowsy, try not to give in to it. From the other side of the
room Parse's humming floated about her like droning, distant bees. Best get all the naps I can now, she rationalized,
because there won't be much chance later. And if Parse is
right about twins, Lady forfend, I'll never sleep again! The
last thought she had as she drifted off into sleep was, I wish
I'd known Matthias Vandersma.

"How much does she want to know?" Yellow eyes quizzical behind half-shut lids, Mr'la lolled against the warmth
of the paving stones, white stomach and blue mackerel tabby
sides bulging. **"I swear these ghatten are never going to
be birthed—they've taken up permanent residence!"** But
her tone rang smug with pleasure.

And well it should be, Khar knew, because Mr'la was one
of the few ghatta to ever bear a third litter. Ghattas were seldom blessed with more than two litters during their long
lives, a combination of the contraceptive powder they voluntarily took to avoid coming into heat and disrupting their
Bond, and the fact they weren't generally prolific creatures.
Having ghatten survive to adulthood was yet another problem. Sometimes they had to be destroyed by their mothers
because of an inherent wrongness, a warping of the mind
that would harm any human they Bonded with. It was so, indeed Khar had destroyed her own first litter several years

past and still mourned the necessity. But Mr'la had produced perfect, strong-willed little offspring each and every time. A blessing.

"**Oh, I don't think they've taken up permanent residence,**" she countered, grooming Mr'la's cheek fur, moving upward to explore inside an ear. "**In fact, once they start exploring on their own, you'll wish you could hold them safe as you do now.**"

Wa'roo gave a falanese moue of agreement as she rolled over, dainty narrow head with large olivine eyes snapping up to check where her female ghatten had slithered off to, stalking a blowing leaf. She rolled again in relief, belly pale gray against the cream paving stones, and the exposure of that soft underbelly made the little male ghatten leap in mock attack, a short-lived one when he recognized the chance to nurse. With a sigh she swept a foreleg over him, protective, encompassing. But despite that, she exchanged a glance with Terl, the eldest ghatti present.

But it was Terl who spoke, mindvoice quavery but quick. "**How much does Doyce want to know, Khar? You never answered Mr'la.**"

Mem'now, all tiger-striped yellow, wended his way into the center of the group, waiting for enlightenment, thick tail sweeping the pavement. The female ghatten launched herself, pinprick teeth and claws sinking into Mem'now's tail tip. "**Yeeouch!**" Mem'now leaped and spun, cuffed the ghatten with both front paws, not a claw exposed, more a wrestling into submission, a tumbling frolic evoking ghatten giggles. "**Twylla may have to amputate it, thanks to you! See if I ever let you listen to another Tale-Telling, missy!**" he scolded. He continued to tickle the ghatten but spoke to Khar. "**What exactly does Doyce want to know?**"

Khar picked her words with care, unsure how the others would react. But if Doyce wanted to learn, Khar would do her best to help, because Doyce was her beloved, her Bondmate, and nothing she wanted would be denied if Khar had a paw in it. "**She yearns to understand our earliest days, about how Matthias Vandersma Bonded with Kharm—what it was like. Sometimes,**" she wondered if she should say it, if it were true, right, but it must be because she was ghatti, and ghatti drank truth from the very air about them, "**the past sheds light on the present. It may be important not just for her, but for everyone to under-**

stand how our joined lives came to be—the obstacles, the
fear and falsehoods that stood in the way of our trust and
our Truth."

With gentle inexorability Mem'now pinned the ghatten
beneath his considerable bulk, crouching to hold her in
place. Excited, she managed to roll onto her back, chew at
Mem'now's ruff. "I hope she Bonds soon, Wa'roo, or I'll
be so bedraggled Twylla won't be able to repair me." He
sprang and the ghatten scooted to her mother. "But, Khar,
you know how imperfect humans are. I swear they can't
remember what they ate the day before. Certainly
Bondmates are a cut above regular humans, but even
they may lack the capacity to understand. Besides, how
can Doyce gain the knowledge she needs?"

"Mem'now, Mem'now," Terl scolded as he worked worn
teeth into a mat of fur on his side, the once-black coat rusty
and faded with age. "You, one of the greatest Tale-Tellers
of us all, have to ask that? We all have the knowledge;
collectively as ghatti we know and pass it on to each succeeding generation. We all know different levels, different layerings of the Truth above all truth as we rise in
the Spirals. But with our joint knowledge, ours and the
Elders combined, we should be able to direct Doyce on a
journey in her mind." He coughed once, ignoring the rising
apprehension on Mem'now's broad face. "If we so choose
to, of course."

Mem'now drew himself to his full height. "It's not something to be taken lightly, you know. And is it wise, in her
condition? What of the ghatten-child she carries?"

Mr'la heaved herself upright, glossy sides tight as a drum-
head. "Pity sakes, Mem'now, she's not some fragile little
creature for all she's a human. Females have managed to
have babies without you worrying about it for eternity.
Not that we don't appreciate the thought." Khar realized
suddenly who had sired Mr'la's litter and caught the shamed
twinkle in Mem'now's eyes. "We have to decide amongst
us all if this is the wisest course to take, but Khar's right,
the times are in an upheaval that's near the match of the
past with the Plumbs' literal upheaval. I say we at least
give her a taste of the past and decide what we should do
in depth when we've all taken council."

"After all, she already has the diary, although she
doesn't realize what she's stumbled upon," Terl pointed

out. "Her reaction will show us whether we should proceed. Remember, the gift we offer is not a small one."

Eyes further slanted by worry, Wa'roo protectively gathered her ghatten close. "Who knows whether in future days they may decide they don't need us, that Resonants are enough. I would not have my ghatten go into a world like that, better they die! We know Truth; the Resonants, skilled as they may be, do not. We must not falter or fail, just as we never have before!" Pride, sorrow, exultation— the way of the ghatti, the way of Truth. And truth they could share—amongst themselves or with others.

But now Khar drew back, afraid, "But to enter into her mind without her leave? We can't do that, you know we can't, not by all we hold sacred!"

"And who said we would," Mem'now groused. "Not when we have the perfect conduit here, my beauteous tale-telling ghatta. We'll spin our tales with yours, and you, you just let her listen."

❖

He fanny-skidded down the bank, digging in bare heels to keep from sliding too fast, the sickle held well to the side with his left hand, honed crescent and lethal point away from his body. Draping legs over the undercut bank edge, he dropped into waist-deep water, feet sinking into oozing muck that sucked at his ankles. Water churned dank by his footsteps, bits of rotting matter floating to the surface, rich, rotting smell strong in the beating sun, he swatted at a rising cloud of biter-flies with his free hand, tight-squinching eyes, nostrils, and mouth. Unfortunately, he couldn't close his ears, and one fly began exploring the inner convolutions of an ear, its hum maddening but not as painful as the anticipated bite.

"Damn all, Henryk! Come on, Ryk, you promised! Swore you'd tend the smudge if I let you tag along." No response, but one squinted eye spotted a ghost movement hovering near the tilted trees with their twisted, gnarled roots dreadlocking toward the water. Well, Granther had ordered him to watch Henryk, so watch he would. "Please, *Uncle* Henryk, dear *Uncle* Henryk," he singsonged. "I won't just be eaten alive here, I'll be carried away!" and continued under his breath, "And if you don't obey, do as you're told, I'll tell Granther, sure as sunrise, and you'll be sorry!"

A pale-skinned boy, alabaster white, almost bald-looking because of equally pale, close-cropped hair, skittered out of the shadows, pressing makeshift spectacles against the bridge of his nose. One lens glowed amber, the other green, their shapes different, giving him a lopsided look. Arms crossed, he rubbed hands up and down scrawny ribs, raised them to cup his shoulders protectively, as if he'd cape his back. "It's too sunny, I'll burn to death. My eyes hurt!" His childish reproaches whined over the stagnant water, eight-year-old uncle complaining to fifteen-year-old nephew. "Poppy's gonna yell at you for going in with your pants on!"

The older boy snarled over his shoulder, "I am *not* going to offer the leeches lunch, at least not there!" Aggravated, incautious where he stepped, he disappeared underwater with a choking glug, bubbles rising, ripples fanning across the slough.

The younger boy hesitated, tiptoed closer to the bank, scrawny white body jittering with impatience. Taking his glasses off, he scanned the water, pink eyes tearing, blinking nearsightedly into the bright reflected light. "Matty? Matty?" He waited, kicking at the bank with a bare foot, faster and harder. At last, a drawn out wail. "Mat-ty!"

Dark hair slicked back from his face, lying limp and dripping on his neck, Matty arose, breathless, amongst a tangle of water lilies, fighting aside the tough stems. Straight brows like two finger smears of ash emphasized narrow, dark blue eyes, the long, thin nose. "Damn it, Ryk-Ryk, you made me drop the sickle! Got to dive for it." Suiting actions to words, he disappeared underwater again as the younger boy started to whimper.

"Baa-wah! Ta-da!" The sickle flashed skyward— miniature replica of the crescent moons that seasonally waxed and waned around Canderis's one unchanging moon—followed by a tanned arm and the rest of Matty's body, mouth spewing water as he shouted. A lethal gesture with the sickle, far too distant to damage Henryk's toes, convinced the younger boy to obediently gather his fire materials near the bank. "Now, Ryk, get that smudge going or I'll bury one of your toes in the rushes for Granther to find. Think he'll rethatch the roof with it or leave it as floor covering?"

"I know. I'm sorry." The younger boy seemed truly repentant, at least for the moment. Serious, he continued, "But, Matty, the sun's awful bright and you know what'll happen to me." He thought further, cracking open his clamshell to expose the smoldering punk, shielding it against his bony chest. "And Poppy'll be mad about the pants, too. We could rinse'm in the stream on the way back, turn the pockets inside out, wash the silt out."

Wading deeper into the reeds, Matty swung the sickle below the waterline, let his armful float free, piled the next load on top and coasted them to the bank, swung them up onto the overhang. The sun burned high and hot, Ryk's marble-pale skin already pinking on his shoulders. "Spend a little time out here, then go back into the shade. Come out when you can, spread the reeds to dry. We'll manage." He frog-legged back to the reeds and lost himself in the rhythmic swish of the sickle, pretending he hacked his way into unknown, unexplored territory with each gathered armload.

The light shone long across the water now, had shifted from its zenith, and he scrubbed at the runnels of sweat trickling down his face, let himself sink underwater, blinking as the silt rose and danced before his eyes like petals of soft ashes before it resettled. It permeated the fabric, dragging his pants down skinny hips, his rope belt stretching but the knot itself water-swollen, no hope of hitching them tighter or higher. Ryk was right, Granther'd have his hide if he ruined these new britches after all his efforts to trade for them. It was just that Matty hated them, despised them was more accurate. The material too heavy, the size too big, and worst of all, Granther's insistence on cutting them short, above the knee for summer, and hemming them. All the other boys, indeed, most of the men of the village, wore them below the knee and unraveling.

Granther had stood him on the stool, pinning away, checking the hang, turning the raw edge into a protective double fold. "Can't take'm in anymore or your hip pockets'd be on top of each other," he'd muttered through a mouthful of pins. "And as for leaving them longer and unhemmed— absolutely not! Come winter we can sew the legs back on." He indicated the cast-off, amputated pants legs tossed over his shoulder. "You'll still have plenty of length and you won't have wrecked the knees like everyone else. Waste of material." Frowning, he'd slapped Matty's bottom to send him off the stool. "Now shuck them, son, I've got sewing to do."

Matty sighed at the memory. And didn't he want above all to be like everyone else? Not have a fey-footed father who wandered the world, unable to cope with what he found? Not have a granther sometimes disliked, sometimes revered, but forever in the public eye for his unstinting service as conciliator-mayor in their little hamlet of hovels? Not have a fey uncle half his age with skin bleached so colorless you could track his veins beneath it, watery pink-red eyes that made him stand out, and webbing between his two final fingers and two final toes? No wonder everyone thought Henryk was jinxed, hexed!

And didn't he, Matty, yearn to be like other boys his age, shooting up, chest broadening, voice deepening, instead of being humiliated by its insane swoops from high to low? He shifted the sickle to his left hand, fisted his right hand to flex his biceps, peered under his arm to determine if any hair had sprouted. Nothing. The only visible sign that something had sprouted—too often at times—was the real reason he'd be damned if he'd be caught reed gathering without his pants. After all, the girls sometimes came to swim and bathe beyond this sedge where the water flowed sweet and smooth and clean over a sandbar.

The fire on the bank had just about smoldered out and he debated wading ashore to restart it. As usual, Henryk had vanished, probably asleep in the shade, safe, he hoped. The child tended to roam the night when the sun didn't hurt his eyes, and sleep during the day. Fewer people were abroad after dark, fewer people to laugh at him, taunt him, toss stones, although luckily no one had ever threatened the child with bodily harm, though he'd caught their murmurings. "Cursed spawn of a cursed planet," they called Ryk sometimes, but not to Matty's or to his granther's face.

A flash of laughter skittered across the water, and he knew without looking who it was. Other tinkling laughter interwove it, but he separated that one voice as surely as if there were but one seductive sound. Taking a handful of reeds, he twisted them around the curve of the sickle, hanging it in place, and began to press his way through the reeds, gauging his motions to match the erratic breeze. Yes, yes! Just a little closer and he could part them, peer out, observe without being observed.

Oh, by the Lady those strange, itinerant Shepherds worshiped, she was gorgeous! And wonder of wonders, she faced his way, thigh-deep in water, laughing back at her friends in the shallows. Lathering herself with a scrap of hoarded soap, delicate iridescent froth foaming across her body, so rounded, so curved, so pink and white. Two rosy nipples stared saucily at him, nothing like the pink of poor Henryk's eyes; her round face, blue eyes shut and turned sunward, made him sink his hands into his pockets, fingers working.

Oh! By the Lady above, she was so . . . so, he groped for a word to describe his ecstasy, groped for something lower as well. So . . . porcine! And to a child, nearly a young man, raised in scrimping want and poverty, hunger generally assuaged but rarely by food he liked, nothing more perfectly, transcendingly gorgeous came to mind than the plump young piglet he'd once been privileged to see, stroke, before it had been spitted and cooked into tender, succulent, mouthwatering goodness. Oh, Vatersnelle, light of his life! His Nelle!

He inhaled through his mouth, didn't realize the sound had carried until it was too late. Should have heard the rustling, should have known, realized, that where Nelle and the others went, the Killanins were sure to follow. Their hoarse, grating chant announced them: "Kill-kill-Killanin! Ya!" Hooting, whistling, and blatting sounds sundered the air as the eldest, Kuyper, flung himself into the river, belly flopping, sending up a wall of water at the nearby girls. Luckily his Nelle was too far away to be splashed. Nothing to do but grit his teeth.

The Killanin boys made up their own little pack or tribe, rowdy, raucous, and utterly amoral. Most everyone in the hamlet and the surrounding areas not only disliked but feared them: Rommel, 13; Willem, 14; and Kuyper, 16. Swaggering, blustering, and big—even Rommel, the youngest, outweighed Matty by a good fifteen kilos. Their limited clothes hung ragged, rents and gashes unpatched, their identical sandy hair crept, dirty and matted, over low foreheads and deep-set suspicious dark eyes that glowed with enthusiasm at someone else's pain. Even their parents had lost the will and stamina to impose any standards of decency on them, while the rest of the hamlet did its best to avoid them. Chastise or punish a Killanin today, and one or all three would lurk till the time was ripe for a payback that could never be proved. Granther had meted out justified punishments, but it was always little Ryk or Matty himself who paid.

The question now was where were Rommel and Willem? Driving his nails into his palms, Matty eased farther through the reeds. The girls shouldn't need his weak support: Nelle and five of her friends should be enough to withstand the bullies, though any fewer and the Killanins would prevail, whether with harmless indignities of lascivious, lip-smacking taunts, sly pokes and grabs, or worse—depending on their mood. Riveted, he watched Kuyper wading toward Nelle, his Nelle even if she didn't realize it, naked but holding her ground. She shifted her feet as if in search of something, never removing her gaze from Kuyper, then abruptly dipped neck-deep in the water, rising with a dripping rock, hefting it in silent warning. *Oh, Vatersnelle Houwaert, thou art bravest and noblest of all womankind!* he breathed silently. "Bash him, Nelle!" he instructed in a whisper.

But a taunting shout from the bank heralded Willem's and Rommel's arrival as they dragged a writhing captive, both boys leaning back on bare heels, stretching the small, pale body between them. *Henryk! May a Plumb open under their feet and swallow them!* he prayed, frozen at the sight. A distant pop floated across the water as he not only saw but heard Henryk's shoulder dislocate. Reaching blindly for the sickle, he realized he'd left it too far behind. No choice but to plow ahead. Taking a deep breath, Matty burst from the reeds. "Ya! Let him go, bastards!"

Water up to his armpits he floundered shoreward, Kuyper angling to follow, intercept him. He didn't know what Kuyper'd do to him if he caught up, didn't care, couldn't bother to worry. Had to get poor Ryk free. The younger boy spied him, a tremulous smile surfacing beneath silent tears at the sight of his hero, until Willem relinquished one arm to let Rommel jam Ryk's head tight against his hip, thin neck squeezed in the nutcracker of his arm. Ryk's face abruptly turned scarlet. The water shallower now, Matty drove his knees higher, pumping to gain speed. "Bite him, Ryk!" he yelled. He'd take any distraction he could get, even a momentary one that might temporarily disable or distract at least one of the taunting Killanin trio.

"Drag'em into the woods, boys! Have our fun with him

there!" Willem and Rommel greeted Kuyper's snarled command with a certain reluctance, the naked bathers taking precedence over half-hearted torture. "Go on! Take Whitey and git!" A belated grab at a fast-moving Matty missed, and realizing they could draw him into a fruitless chase, Willem and Rommel bounded off, Henryk dragging between them.

Bursting out of the water, Matty dashed after them, breathless with fear and anger. Stupid oafs they might be, but they were far stronger than he, and ignorant to boot. This might be the time Henryk truly got hurt—because of what he was and what he wasn't. He spat the taste of fear aside and ran, Kuyper's barking laugh chasing behind him, snapping at his heels. Kuyper was faster, stronger; it was just a matter of time before he hauled Matty down from behind or charged ahead by a different route to join the others in torturing Ryk.

His only advantage lay in knowing the trail nearly as well as they did; he checked it as often as he could to see what the Killanins had maimed or crippled each day with their crude traps or snares. Hunting was a necessity—he couldn't argue with that, did it himself, had to to survive. But the Killanins set traps, forgot to check them for days, left birds and animals half-crazed with pain and fear, ripping off wings, gnawing their own feet to escape. Death was death, but a clean, quick one was preferable to a slow, lingering torment. Which his would be, which Henryk's would be, he couldn't judge, and the slap of forest shade, the breeze on his wet flesh made him shiver.

Footsteps pounded behind him, closing in. He ran harder, steeling himself for the hand clenched in his hair or jerking at shoulder or neck, the unexpected foot snagging his, pitching him forward, defenseless. Gritting his teeth, he risked a look behind and saw Nelle galloping along, meaty, muscular thighs flashing beneath the short, damp tunic she'd donned. Round face pink, forehead furrowed, mouth tight, she pulled abreast, could have passed him without effort, her breathing easy.

"Kuyper?" he managed to spare enough air for the question.

A triumphant smile and she brandished the bloodstained rock clenched in her hand. It spoke more eloquently than any word she could utter. "Come on, then!" And for a moment sheer joy shivered up his spine; mayhap, just mayhap they'd free Henryk before Willem and Rommel tired of teasing their prey, left it broken and bloody.

Almost to the giant oak now, massive hub in a small clearing ahead. Beyond that a barely discernible trail that the rolapin traveled to avoid the clearing, a perfect place for setting snares. He knew, had set them there himself, waited fruitlessly before he'd become wise to their ways.

Up ahead, Willem and Rommel skidded to a stop, flinging Henryk to the ground as they gawked at a sprung snare, leather noose dangling from the sapling they'd set it with. And, hanging by its hind leg, suspended, twisting in circles, a snarling wildcat, front legs lashing and slashing, screams of anguish and absolute fury spitting out of it. Unregarded, Matty and Nelle ran closer, almost behind the Killanins, curious despite themselves. A wave of sick rage swept over Matty; it was what they called a larchcat, strange beasts native to the planet that reminded the settlers of an elusive but overlarge house cat—about four times the size of an average one.

The name came from a corruption, a contraction of "large cat," as in the surprised shout, "Look at that larchcat peering out at us!" For some reason larchcats seemed to enjoy watching people, shadowing their movements, although they, in turn, were rarely spied. This clearly was a nursing female. And from the raw mangling of its swollen hind leg and foot, noose cutting through skin and flesh, it had spent a long, bitter time slowly swinging in the breeze.

Captivated by the vision of simultaneously torturing two creatures, Rommel dragged Henryk up by his injured arm, whipped him within reach of those desperate, slashing claws. Henryk cried and shuddered as the claws slashed across his thin ribs.

Two on two—Nelle and himself against Rommel and Willem, and Matty still didn't favor the odds, though he had no choice. But the woods rustled, echoed with thudding feet, and he caught Nelle's grim smile of satisfaction. "Get'em, girls!" she shouted, and the woods exploded with five female bodies, nubile, scantily clad, and all swept by a grim rush of maternal defensiveness. Matty had never seen anything like the furious charge of Nelle's swimming companions and prayed he never would again, although parts of the picture were pleasantly distracting.

Rommel and Willem were no fools; few bullies are, knowing precisely when, where, how—and most especially which—pitiful souls are ripe for harassment and persecution. Odds definitely against them, they took to their heels, the girls making a show of racing after but gradually letting the distance widen.

The girls halted just at the clearing's edge, throwing stones, branches, shouting hoarsely, making enough racket to convince the two, at least for a while, of hot pursuit. Up over the treed ridge, down its side, and heading for the stream, Matty judged by the sounds, when an awful silence pressed flat and heavy over the woods. A stillness, then a precipitous crack, a roar and rumbling that tumbled them all off their feet, knocked over leaning trees, shot gouts of earth and stones into the air. "Plumb!" they screamed at each other, though there was no need for the identification. It was one of the few constants in their young lives. A constant of death and destruction. Screams of panic, two voices shrieking beyond the ridge, one precipitously cut off.

Picking himself up, limping toward Henryk, Matty watched the larchcat swinging from the snare like a pendulum. "Oh my, oh my," Henryk whimpered, spectacles tossed from his nose, the boy spread-eagled on the ground, clutching it with both hands. Legs unsteady, Matty collapsed beside his uncle, dragged him into his lap, rocking him back and forth, ignoring the rest of the world. Nelle staggered to his side, picking at pieces of gravel embedded in the heel of her palm, her elbow where she'd skidded when she'd landed.

"Have the girls check on Willem and Rommel," he told her, cheek pressed against Henryk's white, scrub-brush hair. No matter how much you hated someone, you never not checked on a person in the Plumb's vicinity. Plumb—Periodic Linear Ultra-Mensuration Beamer—hundreds, thousands of them sunk into the earth of this new planet by his granther and his fellow Spacers when they'd first landed. The wonders of modern science, technology, sensor chips able to "read" the land and what it contained, its minerals and ores, determine any hostile movement of the land. Except the Plumbs had turned into lethal time bombs, exploding without rhyme or reason, unable to be dug up and defused. Some had fled the planet in the few usable spaceships, deserting Granther and the rest. Matty spat in disgust, mouth too dry to make it effective.

Nelle's gloomy head toss countermanded him; he'd momentarily forgotten her presence, locked in a past made eternally, dangerously present. "Did already. It swallowed Willem. Rommel was caught halfway down when the crack snapped closed again. The girls are getting help." Funny, he hadn't even noticed they'd gone, so lost in his own private universe of relief and pain, with Henryk in his arms.

"Would you, would you take Henryk back?" he asked, diffident at asking a favor. "Think his shoulder's dislocated, and we ought to disinfect those scratches."

"Take him back yourself," she shot back. "You're his nephew, after all." Sun-bleached blonde hair wisped and straggled around her sweaty, pale forehead.

"I've got to stay, should be there when the rescue party comes to dig them free. Sometimes they need somebody small to slither into the tight spots." A wash of embarrassment at the import of his words, but it was true, he was much slighter than she.

"It's all right. Won't be forever, you'll grow. Boys are always slow. I'm used to it. Besides," she rushed the next words, "if my other choice is Kuyper and his brothers, I'll take you any day!" Turning away, she squatted, broad at shoulder and buttocks, patient, "Now help get Henryk up."

Few wanted anything to do with Henryk, let alone close physical contact. "He won't hurt you, you know." It mattered that he make it clear to her, as if his revealed love for Henryk would reveal something more. "There's nothing different about him 'cept he doesn't have much color."

"I know," she grumbled, hooking arms around Henryk's pipestem legs, shifting him higher. "Not his fault, but your granther should've known better than to lie with old Mad Margare. Look what comes of it." And with that she stood up with Henryk on her back and trotted off.

What he also didn't risk saying was that he wanted time alone, a chance to put the larchcat out of her misery. After all, Rommel certainly wasn't going anywhere. Reaching as high as he could on the sapling, he dragged it down, forcing himself on top, trying to snap it where it grew thinnest. No knife, nothing to saw through the sapling or to sever the leather snare itself. He wrestled with it, felt it finally crack, not broken through, but crippled and bent, at least, so the animal rested on the ground for the first time in he didn't dare guess how long.

"Hush, love, hush," he crooned, hands groping for the

rock Nelle had left behind. She twisted on her side, fixing
him with green eyes, and again the swollen nipples, fur worn
away from them, dominated his vision. Not only was she
doomed, but so were her kits, if they weren't already dead.
Her emerald, almond-shaped eyes pierced him, made him
flinch, wish he could shield himself. "Just get it over with,"
he grated out loud, as if that would compel him to do it. Instead, he began working shaky fingers to loosen the loop
sunk deep in the swollen flesh, shocked that she didn't respond, claw at him, hiss, bite. Hopeless. In a fury of anger
at everyone, everything, himself included for being so hopeless, so helpless, he chewed at the rawhide, sawing it back
and forth between his teeth. And because, for once, luck
smiled on him, because the Killanins never did anything
right, including tanning leather, he chewed through it.

Emerald eyes still intent on him, the cat began crawling
away, spine twisted, hind legs immobile, front legs drawing
her forward, inexorable. "Wait, please, just wait!" he
begged. "Rest easy! I'll find them, bring them if I can."
Rushing to the stream, he folded a moose maple leaf into a
pouch, scooped water, trickled it into the panting mouth, sorrowing that so much spilled, was wasted. A puffy, crusted
tongue pressed the faintest lick against his trembling wrist,
and she began pulling herself along again. He couldn't do it,
couldn't kill her—but he had to give her that kindness. But
first he'd made a pledge that must be honored.

Casting about, he desperately searched for her denning
place. High, low? No idea, no clue, until he spied a rotting
stump with a round hole burrowed under one of the arched
roots. Feverishly he ran and knelt in front of it, thrust one
arm in as far as it would go, fumbling around. Fur, yes! He
pulled out a limp little bundle, cradled it in his hands. Dead.
Too late, too late! Walking back, heart pounding with the
pain of failure, he laid it beside its mother, watched her lick
it once, then stop, look at him again, commanding. Feet
leaden, he stumbled back, sank his arm in again, wild to
touch something warm and living, something to make this
horror of a day right. Something pulled from his touch,
hissed. He grabbed again, fingers splayed, working blind,
closing at last on a struggling little body.

Out it came, fighting all the way. Amazing that growls so
ferocious could issue from such a small creature, so absurdly soft and—ouch!—sharp. Claws raked his knuckles,

four tiny lines of blood sprouting in their wake. Hurrying, unsure he could contain it with his hands without harming it, he laid it beside its dead sibling. The mother larchcat's eyes dulled, a third membrane sliding across, head wavering as she strained to lick the kit, push it to her side to nurse. At last, realizing its safety, the tiny head burrowed, sucked hungrily, only to protest after a few sucks. The mother had gone dry.

Wanting to console, he laid his hand on the little creature's striped back as the mother sighed, body going limp. Squalling in frustration and fear, the kit spun—frightened, hungry—and sank her teeth into Matty's hand, the tender skin between thumb and index finger. With a screech of pain he jerked away, sucked at the wound, found himself openmouthed, the little kit equally so.

"Kharm! Oh, oh, oh! Matty-mind! Did it, did it! All by myself! Matty Kharm love, inside head. Greatest ghatten of all am I, Kharm!" Hands over his ears, body rigid and listening. *Not hearing this, can't be hearing this inside my head, can I? Crazy, crazy, but true!* Anyone related to Amyas Vandersma was crazy. The old man might be rock solid, but none of his offspring were, that was a fact! And now, at last, he, Matthias Vandersma had joined the fold.

"No, no. Inside each other's minds, hearts. Best way to talk is inside head, silly ghatten-boy." The kit scrambled across his knees, tiny claws catching in the damp trouser fabric. She turned three times and collapsed into a tiny ball, ready to sleep. The striped sides heaved in a sigh. **"Hungry! Feed?"**

And Matthias began to cry, doubled over, protecting the little kit, wondering how he was going to cope, what he was going to do, how he was going to conquer this mad voice inside his head.

Whiskers scrubbed against her cheeks, tickled under her chin, pushed farther until it felt as if velvet-clad rocks thrust her head up, righting her, two damp noses at her throat, one warm, the other cool and moist from outside. **"Wake up, Doyce! Wake up now!"** one voice commanded while the other cajoled, indulgent, **"Sleepyhead."**

She recognized the smug protectiveness of the second

voice all too well. *"Khar?"* she mumbled, half-asleep, barely forming the words. *"When ... you come in? Didn't ... hear you."* Fisting herself upright against the table, she sat up, yawned. *"Pests. Why can't you and Per'la let me sleep?"*

Per'la's eye-whiskers flickered extravagantly as she spoke in their silent falanese language, all twitches and subtle movements. "What do you think you're doing? You can't share Major Tales like that? It could be dangerous!" Her truncated tail switched, the ribbon rustling, peridot eyes glaring. "I didn't think she was going to awake when we called!" Parse, engrossed in his work, humming to himself, noticed nothing of the silent contretemps or Doyce's awakening.

Rubbing under Doyce's chin, Khar, all tiger-swirled, wrinkled her pink nose at Per'la. "It may be necessary. And, no, it wasn't dangerous. Mem'now and Terl, Mr'la and Wa'roo helped, though your help would have been appreciated once you realized what we were doing." The ghatta sat, stared at her Bondmate, who yawned again, rubbed sleep from her eyes. **"Pleasant dreams, beloved?"** her innocence a little too feigned.

"Funny how when you doze off like that the dreams mingle what you've been thinking about with anything else floating through your head." Impartial, she set about scratching both ghatta heads. *"So vivid, so real ... about the beginnings of it all, but I can't recall much more than that,"* she confessed.

"Why not call it a day, love?" Khar suggested, claws working against the tabletop as she shoved against the hand. Best take no notice of Per'la's suspicious expression or she might feel guilty about what she'd helped Doyce dream. Besides, clearly no harm had been done if she could scarcely remember what she'd dreamed. Her ringed ears flashed an eloquent, "So there," in Per'la's direction.

"Mayhap you're right." Rising, Doyce stretched and groaned, the sound and movement at last catching Parse's attention. Pivoting on his foot, he turned, grinned.

"Hello, sleepyhead. Back from slumberland, I see. And who's been doing serious research while you've been napping?"

Dignity destroyed by a jaw-cracking yawn, she glared at Parse. "Thought I'd try to let you catch up with me." Then, more apologetically, "If you don't mind, Parse, I think I'll call it quits for the day. The librarian should be back soon, so you and Per'la won't be alone. And I want to see how Swan's doing."

He frowned, not at her suggestion, but at the thought of Swan Maclough, Seeker General, lying so still, so pale, so thin. Nearly run through from behind by a pike during the thick of the battle, a battle in which she wasn't supposed to take part. The pike had punctured a lung, and the eumedicos had managed to reinflate it, but nothing seemed to be healing properly, despite Swan's denials to the contrary. With winter coming on, Doyce worried about pneumonia or bronchitis settling in the weakened lungs. All too likely. Even a common, garden-variety cold could prove too much to withstand. She didn't care how many eumedicos were on call from the Hospice, how often Twylla was there, how often Mahafny visited—she should be at Swan's bedside, not let another friend slip away.

"Of course," Parse replied. "Visit her, see if you can take her mind off things. All she wants to do is discuss business—as if she's afraid that if she doesn't do it now, there won't be time later." The import of his words struck him, and he bit his lip. Wounded as well, he bore the guilt all survivors suffer for those whose wounds were worse or for those who didn't survive. She knew it from her own experience, the patterns her life had taken that had brought her here. The deaths of her husband Varon, baby daughter Briony, and the supposed loss of her stepson Vesey, all consumed by the fire that had swept their house during that period of time when she was no longer a eumedico but not yet a Seeker. Guilt swept over her that Briony hadn't survived, that this unborn child might not survive for a reason she couldn't begin to contemplate, not in this new world. Somehow, in her mind, Swan's continued survival stood surety for her unborn child's survival.

Almost without noticing, she shoved the little diary, the daybook into her pantaloon pocket, discovered it wouldn't fit. Leave it? Bring it with her to read tonight? Jenret wasn't likely to be back, so she'd be alone except for Khar. "Don't worry, Parse. We haven't lost Swan yet." She shrugged into her maroon boiled wool jacket, slid the diary into the larger patch pocket. Why not? She probably should leave a note for the librarian that she'd removed it from the premises, but she'd return it first thing in the morning. Why bother when it wasn't even cataloged?

"Don't work too hard, steal all my glory, Parse," she flung over her shoulder as she left, Khar'pern following.

Per'la jumped on Parse's slanted desk, waited, patient, while he made a note. **"Khar is up to something."** Waited to see if the conversational gambit would be bait enough.

"Um-hm," Parse extracted another letter from its envelope, unfolded it, "she always is." With an inward sigh, Per'la curled up, felt herself coasting down the pitch of the desk. Vexed at everything, she jumped down, stalked off.

"See if I share anything more with you," she snapped, and the ribbon on her tail crackled, a satisfying show of her indignation at being ignored.

Her boot heels clicked crisply on the flagstones as she crossed the courtyard, sky graying with early dusk, scarlet, orange, and yellow leaves rasping across the path in the breeze. Time these days spun faster and faster, catching her up in its vortex and spinning her around with it, willy-nilly, octants passing, the phases of the Lady's moons changing inexorably. The outline of six of the Lady's moons floated low and faint on the horizon. Had it only been bare spring, just two Disciple moons visible when she and the others had set out for Marchmont to learn why the borders between Canderis and Marchmont had been arbitrarily closed, and what—if anything—they could do about it? Autumn now, winter fast behind it, and with it the turn of a new year and the baby's birth.

She shivered, pretended it was the breeze after the stuffiness of the library. No need to go outside and around from the wing that housed the library to reach the Seeker General's suite, but she'd craved the hiatus, a pause for fresh air, fresh thoughts, a chance to reorder her mind. Except whatever order she chose, she always came back to the past. What she'd become embroiled in that spring was war, and love, and confusion. Martial? Marital? Amazing what a transposition of letters could do, and each equally confusing and injurious to one's well-being. Despite herself, her feet halted at the bronze statue of Matthias Vandersma and Kharm, first Bondmates, first Seekers Veritas of them all. A surreptitious, superstitious touch for luck at Matthias's bronze, bent knee and at the ghatta Kharm's head, both worn smooth and slick from generations of such touches. And for some reason tonight Khar'pern sprang onto the statue, vibrant fur alive against metal as she rubbed against both frozen figures, purr rumbling in her chest. What had gotten into the ghatta now?

"You're coming with me to see the Seeker General, aren't you?" Worried, she waited until Khar unwreathed herself and caught up. "You'd like to see Koom, wouldn't you?" Truth was she didn't want to face Swan Maclough alone, see the beloved face strained with pain, the once plump, paunchy body gaunt, ceaselessly shifting to find a comfortable spot. And her reaction, she knew all too well, might be to burst into hopeless tears. So much for her training in self-control as a eumedico. Her previous, almost-constant exposure to the Seeker General's debility during the early days had temporarily inured her, but these occasional flying visits threw Swan's increasing weakness into her face, the wasting freshly painful each time.

"**Not exactly uplifting and cheery for the patient,**" Khar finished for her. "**You know, she may want you to acknowledge her condition, admit it, so she can admit to it herself. Each time she has to cheer you up, pretend things are fine, she's forced to carry not only her burden of pain but yours as well.**"

She wheeled on the ghatta, almost spooking her at the unexpected move. "Khar, she's . . . she's not dying, is she? She *is* going to get better? I know she's weak, there are so many things that could steal her from us, but we're *not* letting that happen, are we? Not Mahafny and the other eumedicos, not any of us."

Khar stared at the path, head dipped, shoulders slanted and supplicating, at last raising her head, the white around her mouth and nose emphasizing the broad aspects of her expression. "**Did you ever think perhaps she longs to go? Craves permission to leave this life but doesn't dare while anyone needs her? Remove or share some of her burden and she could choose her time when she's ready.**"

"But Koom! What about Koom?" she begged, grasping at straws. "Koom won't let her leave, can't let her go." Koom had loved and lost a human Bondmate once already, many years ago, just when the Seeker General had lost A'rah. The two survivors had meshed without the formal Bonding, refusing to be disloyal to the memory of their previous mates, but creating a close, sharing relationship that still baffled some who'd believed such a thing impossible.

"Koom will know when the time's right. His burdens weary him as well." Brushing against her pantalooned leg, Khar trotted for the door, Doyce following, mouth grim, brain working frantically.

As protocol demanded, she rapped hard at the heavy oaken door, waited for it to swing open. A tall young woman, lanky and with wide shoulders highlighted by the green tabard edging that indicated she was a Novie, still in training for the Seekers Veritas, hauled open the door, leaning on her heels and swinging it with a balanced grace. An equally rangy but undersized ghatt with a wide cinnamon muzzle and nose peeked around the door, eyes wide, one paw swiping at its newly gained ear hoop and earring, still acutely aware of their presence. He bristled defensively as Khar marched inside, then thought better of it, taking his responsibilities too seriously.

"Thank you, Cady. Thank you, F'een." Doyce good-naturedly threw her own weight against the door to help close it, the younger woman's strong muscles turning to water in Doyce's presence. "Just as heavy as always. Still squeak and groan before a rain?" Just as it had when she'd first come to join the Seekers Veritas, just as it had when she'd first met Oriel and his Bondmate Saam.

Shyly, the young woman bobbed her head. Propelled by a rising wave of hope and crashing fear, she stammered, "H . . . how'd . . . you know my name? I . . . I . . . haven't done something . . . have I?" The last words a wretched wail of insecurity. The ghatt, a tiger with almost diamond-shaped markings, as if he'd sheltered behind a lattice fence being painted, sprang into her arms and buried his head under her chin, glowering at the intruders who'd worried his beloved Bondmate.

"Lady bless!" Doyce exclaimed, half-amused despite herself. "Mindwalk if ye will," she directed at the defiant ghatt. As the permission, the invitation, sank in, he stared from Doyce to Khar, dumbfounded, grassy green eyes widening, mouth agape.

"Isn't it just wonderful to be fearless—or fearsome—heroines of song, story, and legend?" Khar smirked, sharing her thought on the strictly intimate mode. **"So fulfilling, being larger-than-life role models for the young and credulous. And you,"** she paused significantly, **"certainly are larger-than-life these days."**

Controlling an overwhelming urge to smack the side of her boot against Khar's satiny backside, Doyce tried to retrieve the situation. "Cady Brandt, Seeker-in-Training, stop fishing for compliments. All Seekers are aware of the new trainees and generally have some idea how they're progressing." She tapped her foot, letting the tapping continue, just a touch ominously, while she paused. "And you and F'een are doing very nicely, although you both need considerably more self-confidence. Remember, you're as good as anyone here, or will be, soon enough."

A deep flush further darkened Cady's olive skin as she set F'een on his feet, and tossed off a crisp if belated salute. "Thank you, Seeker Marbon, and welcome. May we assist you with anything?"

"No, I'm just going to stop in and see the Seeker General if she's awake and receiving visitors." And with a casual wave of her hand she and Khar started off down the white and black squared marble hall. "Remember, self-confidence!" she threw over her shoulder. *"Lady bless and keep us,"* she mindspoke Khar, *"is that what we're sending out into the world, wet-behind-the-ears, unable to control herself, let alone a crowd? How can they ride circuit, give the populace the confidence they need?"* she continued, close to fuming out loud. *"I swear, Khar, they're getting younger every day!"*

"Well, you may not have been that young," Khar shot back, **"but you certainly weren't any more self-confident."**

"And you were, I suppose?"

"No," the ghatta stopped dead in front of her, amber eyes reminiscent. **"But I believed in my love for you, even when you didn't believe. And we've muddled through so far, haven't we?"**

Kneeling, she cupped the ghatta's head, let her thumbs trace the stripes radiating out from her eyes. *"Yes, love, yes, we have."* Nothing to do but grin. *"But does it ever get to be less of a muddle?"*

"No. You humans make life more messy and tangled than a ghatten with a ball of yarn. Do you know how

tiresome it is straightening it out and rewinding it? But do you ever learn? No." And for that the ghatta gave genuine thanks. To always be loved and needed was a wondrous thing, and she needed Doyce as much as Doyce needed her.

Pushing off the floor with her knuckles, Doyce tugged her tabard sash into place, although in her condition she didn't know whether to wear it high or low, and belatedly realized they'd reached the Seeker General's door. Giving a little snort to bolster her courage, Doyce knocked, heard a childish treble shrilly overriding a weak command to enter. "Who's there? What do you want?" the childish voice demanded, mouth pressed to the crack by the door. "The Seeker General is resting now. Run along!"

"It's Doyce Marbon and Khar. We just wanted to say hello, but we can come back tomorrow if the Seeker General's too tired." The small "dragon" so zealously guarding the door was Davvy McNaught, a twelve-year-old Resonant raised in the cloistered security of the Research Hospice in the north. And the reason he'd assumed the role of watchdog stemmed from his guilt over Swan being wounded riding in search of him when—overcome with battle fever, war cries resounding in his ears—he'd fled from behind the safe lines into the thick of battle. The banners, the swirling horses, the badly outnumbered Marchmontian royalists luring their brethren into the arms of the waiting Canderisian forces had filled Davvy with a glorious awe—but he hadn't intended for Swan to ride after him to save him. Admittedly she liked the boy, full of all the quirks and foibles and flaws of a child desperately stretching toward manhood, but it struck her that Davvy had become entirely too officious toward her since she'd left Swan's bedside for the library.

"He thinks you've deserted him as well as Swan, and he's decided he's totally responsible for her. And you're just a little bit jealous of that."

"Wonderful. That explains his dragonish tendencies, not to mention my reaction. Sometimes I wish you weren't quite so all-knowing—and so willing to share it."

"Oh, it's you." A round face with heavy brown bangs to eyebrow level peeped around the door, now open a crack. "S'pose it's all right if you come in for a bit. But don't tire her or rile her up." The last at a whisper, a stage whisper that carried all too well.

"I'm not deaf, Davvy. Let them in or I'll tan your hide."

He waved them in while shouting back, "I'd like to see you try!" The battle of wits and wills, albeit a good-natured one, had obviously been in full swing for some time. The thought of Davvy as a "nursemaid" was a bit hard to accept, but they seemed to suit each other just fine.

Koom, blocky and ruddy-furred, arched into a stretch at the foot of the bed, nose crinkling. A little dance in place revealed his delight at the visitors, and Khar jumped up beside him, companionable, rubbing his flank before moving pillow-ward to greet the Seeker General. A thin hand stroked her, and Khar paraded beneath it until the Seeker General captured her tail and shook it. "Mindwalk if ye will," she pronounced the formal greeting, only to be overcome by a wheezing cough.

But Davvy materialized with a cup of water, easing her into a sitting position, piling pillows behind her. Feeling ineffectual, Davvy's quick ministrations showing up her own slowness, Doyce sat beside the bed, waiting for Swan to recover. At last the Seeker General spoke. "Cha, Davvy, if you would. The warmth helps." The lad darted off, obedient, but with a rolling eye to indicate he wasn't fooled, that he knew he was being politely shooed out of the room.

"More omnipresent than dust mites, and Mahafny swears they're everywhere in numbers we can't comprehend," Swan noted as she fingered the satin blanket edge, "but I confess I enjoy having him around. Most of the time." Her twiglike hand clasped Doyce's, and she wanted to throw her arms around the Seeker General, but one didn't embrace one's superior, nor did a eumedico embrace her patient. Foolish—if that were called for to effect a cure. Reining in her emotions, she chafed the cold hand between her own before freeing it.

"Nothing can be caged forever, not even for its own good," Khar murmured.

"Koom, how's she faring?" Doyce appealed, ashamed to ask Koom such a personal question in Swan's presence.

"Not much better. But thankfully, not much worse." The ghatt circled once and resettled at the foot of the bed, placid half-lidded eyes staring into the distance, camouflaging their private mindspeech. **"Just when I think she's a little better, she slides downhill again. And just when I believe she'll continue sliding, she crawls toward the peak again. Except she'll never gain the pinnacle. I know**

that," he paused, "**and she knows that as well. It's just a matter of time.**"

"**As is everything in life,**" Khar soothed.

And it was time, Doyce realized, to pay attention to Swan. Or make it patently clear she was the subject under discussion. "What's the word from the Monitor these days?" Hardly an idle question, indeed, she'd been so immersed in her research that she couldn't always keep abreast of Kyril van Beieven's and the High Conciliators' latest decisions. Some of it Jenret told her, but he'd been absent so much lately she'd heard only bits and pieces. Momentarily angered that something as unimportant as a Bicentennial History held sway over her, she cursed herself for the distraction. Truth be told, sometimes she simply didn't want to know, as if not knowing meant nothing could or would change, the world couldn't collapse at her feet. As far as she knew, the question of what to do about the Resonants in their midst still hadn't been resolved. And the wary waiting, the nervous suppositions drove Canderis to look over its collective shoulder as if in mounting fear of the thumps and bumps and bogeymen who haunted the night.

Swan rubbed parched lips. "Well, one faction is proposing amnesty. A reasonably nice thought, but what are Resonants guilty of that they require amnesty, I might ask? Their only fault is their ability to read minds, something they're born with. Do you grant them amnesty and insist they cease doing it?" Doyce couldn't help smiling at the absurdity.

"Of course, a small but vociferous faction demands they be hunted down, rounded up, and deported to the Sunderlies. How they expect to capture them without a struggle, I don't know. Volunteers aplenty until it's time to form a posse comitatus, I suspect."

Doyce shifted, uncomfortable at Swan's phlegmatic ability to tick off options. It wasn't an abstraction, a textbook case. Any of these solutions would affect Jenret, little Davvy, very probably the child she carried, others as well, and when abstractions gained distinct, individual faces, it became all too complex and too intensely personal. Just like the faces blooming like fireworks in her mind after she'd conquered her stepson Vesey, with his twisted Resonant skills, and nearly forfeited her own sanity. But so few were like Vesey, or Marchmont's Prince Maurice and Jules Jampolis, warping minds to gain a throne they didn't deserve.

Swan's voice overrode the chilling memories. "A third group, supported by some High Conciliators, thinks Resonants should be allowed to remain in Canderis and take part in daily life, but they should be tattooed—some nice, clear marking on their foreheads—so no one can ever mistake them for nice, normal people. Nothing as mundane as a badge that might be removed. And if permanently marking them doesn't make them second-class citizens, I don't know what does. Any of these ideas appeal to you so far, Doyce?" A low, breathless wheezing told Doyce that she'd let Swan talk too much, had best shift some of the conversational burden.

"And what we don't know, we fear. We don't even have an accurate assessment of their numbers, but I suspect we're closing that gap. Some have voluntarily revealed themselves. And, correct me if I'm wrong, but I suspect every Seeker pair on circuit is alert for possible Resonants." She paused, a sense of betrayal overwhelming her, shaming her. "And forcing the ghatti to do a general mindsweep in each village, reading human minds without permission to discover if anyone is a Resonant. Breaking our oaths." A bitter thought, made more bitter by Khar's defensive stiffening.

"Are the other options more palatable?" Koom broke in wearily. **"And there may be even worse alternatives."** He now straddled the Seeker General's thin legs as if to protect her from Doyce's outrage. Yet his yellow eyes radiated nothing but compassion toward her, as if she were too naive, too innocent, that issues of such magnitude could only be objectively contemplated by those already at the brink of the abyss. Well, she'd stood there as well—more than once.

"And we simply can't coexist?" Yes, she *was* naive. "If there were no reason for them to hide their talents, we'd know who was a Resonant and who wasn't. It's worked in Marchmont for more than two hundred years, why shouldn't it work here? So they're different, so what?" Almost sputtering now, angry at everything and everyone, even herself, for so often fearing, doubting. "We don't discriminate against someone who's left-handed, or who has one brown eye and one blue eye!"

"And perhaps if the general populace discovers something good, something necessary about Resonants, they'll be accepted. But it's almost as if they must give the performance of their lives to prove it," Swan interjected.

"Performance of their lives, how apt!"

The door opened and Davvy cased inside, cha tray balanced, face screwed with concentration as Doyce hurriedly cleared the small bedside table. Miracle of miracles, the tray wasn't awash in cha. She did notice, though, that one of the buns on the plate boasted a crescent bite, the childish act of greed a relief after their discussion.

Davvy fussed, handing things around, spooning honey into Swan's cup. "Not so fast," he admonished as the Seeker General tilted the cup to her lips. "It's still too hot. Hurried fast as I could." Satisfied that Swan obeyed, he turned to Doyce, fists clenched at his sides. "I'll help, help any way I can! Show them that we're normal, nice as anyone else."

"Eavesdropping again, Davvy?" Swan rubbed his back.

Perching on the edge of the bed as if to separate Swan from Doyce, he shook his head. "Is it worse to eavesdrop or to listen with your mind? But I don't have much choice, do I?" His mouth twisted in a silent cry. "I *have* to know what's going on! I have to! It's my life at stake! All I want is to be like everyone else! I can't help the way I am, I can't change it!"

Swan wrapped her arm around his midriff, hugging him close against her wasted frame. "No, you can't, Davvy. But we're going to do everything in our power to make things right. And you can help too."

But how Davvy could help, Doyce had no idea. And a part of her wished the boy back in the circumscribed safety of the Research Hospice in the north. Literally and figuratively out of sight, out of mind. The baby within her kicked once in emphatic agreement.

Cha cups rattled against each other as Davvy piled the tray and he grabbed desperately, only to make them clink worse. "Oh, smerdle!" he hissed under his breath, sure that he'd awoken Swan. His brown-eyed gaze danced in her direction, skittered by to pretend he simply searched for other clutter to straighten, but it was all right, she'd fallen fast asleep after Doyce had left. Too much excitement, too much worry. The conversation had upset him as well, no two ways about it. Fish out of water here, the only Resonant in a building full of Seekers. No one to talk with in his mind, except when Jenret Wycherley came by, or Faertom or Darl Allgood, though he'd been specifically forbidden to contact Darl, told to pretend on pain of a paddling—or worse—that Darl was a Normal, not a Resonant. And he'd been warned to steer clear of any other random mindcalls he might hear in the city, to evoke the protective coloration of a normal boy, give no one reason to doubt him. At first it had been fun to pretend, but now it wasn't. He was lonely—and scared. The unknown woman's mindshriek of death a few octs past had chilled him to the marrow.

"Smerdle." He tried the word again, whispering it. Swan was dead-set against swearing, but had no objection to fashioning a personal vocabulary to fulfill the purpose. He began to grin, giggled, and pressed his arm over his mouth at the memory of the day Swan had reared back in bed and told the Monitor, "Kyril, you can go farfel in your queep if you think that plan will work!" Swan had told him later it meant absolutely nothing except what the listener brought to it, and from the look on the Monitor's face the connotation had been less than pleasant. "Smerdle" was Davvy's own first step toward creating words with hidden meanings to express his own frustrations. He tried it again, decided it served his purpose. Of course, a great deal depended on the emphasis, he decided and rolled the word over in his mouth.

"Smerdle!" And smerdle Doyce for wearing out the Seeker General like that. One more napkin to locate and he could remove the tray, come back and sit by her bed in silent watch. He began casting around, hunting, wondering if Doyce had tucked it up her sleeve and left with it. At last he found it, kicked under the edge of Swan's bed, and retrieved it soundlessly, Koom barely opening an eye in his direction.

He sat, folding it between his hands, turned it into a rolapin with its long, floppy ears, silently crushed it in his fist. The more pregnant Doyce became, the more nervous Davvy grew around her. He hadn't seen many pregnant women in his life, still wasn't entirely sure how they got that way. The bare facts didn't seem enough to explain it. But that mystery wasn't the worst of it. Restless, he stood, hanging over the back of the chair, spinning the napkin between his fingers as he tried yet again to determine if what he'd done—was still doing on occasion—was wrong.

Well, they'd told him and told him not to contact any outsiders, hadn't they? So he hadn't. Well, Doyce wasn't an outsider, even if she wasn't a Resonant. It had been a game at first, a way to pass the time when they'd been nursing Swan through those first tentative days to this plateau of partial-health. He knew from Jenret that contacting Doyce by mindspeech would be at his own peril, but no one had said anything about contacting the unborn baby. Well, had they? No. A self-righteous snap to the napkin. And it stood to reason that with Jenret for a father and Doyce, with her Resonant skills dammed inside her, the mother, that the baby would possess Resonant powers. And he'd been right. So there!

It had been fun, a challenge at first to delicately insinuate himself into the unborn baby's mind, although the conversation had been limited—more a wash of emotions than anything else. He could perk up the baby, make it kick and shift, or soothe it with the thoughts he projected. Just as he'd seen the outward evidence of the baby's activity in Doyce's pained expression, her hand abruptly seeking her belly right before he'd left, although he wasn't sure whether the baby had been reacting to her upset or his own distress. Even he'd seen her tabard jerk from the power compressed within her.

But there was more than that to it now. Should he tell or not? And if he didn't tell Doyce, did he have any right to tell anyone else—Swan, or Mahafny on one of her visits, or Jenret? Today he'd been absolutely sure that there really were two distinct personalities contained within Doyce's swollen abdomen. Twins! Oh, smerdle, what to do? He could distinguish two unmistakably different personalities and, more than that, bits of actual conversation, words, although they still revolved around emotions, comfort, or discomfort.

Maybe he shouldn't have done it, should never have contacted them? What if he upset them, made them come early? Could that happen? And if it did, it would be his fault, another reason for guilt. First Swan being hurt, and now this. And what if Doyce were hurt having the babies? He'd heard about that sometimes. His mouth quivered. How in the Lady's name did they ever get out—and two of them, that big? All in all, the best he could do was resolve to see as little of Doyce as possible from now until the babies' birth. And if he did see her, he was never, ever going to contact the babies again. "May I lie in smerdle if I do," he promised, solemn with concern.

"Davvy," the voice came faintly from the bed, "you're making faces worse than a cow with gas."

He jumped. "Smerdle! Swan, you scared me!"

❖

"Morning, Baz."

"Good morning, Bazelon."

A bashful head bob artfully disguised the following look of a young beauty crossing the street, but Baz widened his smile to encompass her, warm her heart for the rest of the day. Cost him naught but a momentary muscle contraction, cheap enough price to pay. And the profit—plus interest—would accrue for him to collect later. Wherever he went Bazelon Foy registered how their eyes sought him out, and why not? He'd cultivated their regard assiduously enough, making himself noticed and noticeable, from handsome looks and an open disposition to hard work and community service. Approbation, that's what he sought, and the accolades he'd receive for the unselfish service he secretly performed. A labor of love, not for Canderis alone, though ultimately they'd revere him as well, but mainly to convince one man, one single man, his idol, his ideal, to salute the full, unstinting measure of his worth.

Baz Foy sauntered down Wexler's main street, making sure the sun caught him from behind, a glowing halo that highlighted his dark, curly hair, enhanced his soft olive complexion with its rosy undercast from the furnace heat at the glassworks. His smooth cheeks, his silklike forearms were always rosy from the near-constant proximity to the furnaces, his full mouth kissably puckered from the blowpipes that formed the handblown glass. Mid-thirties and already renowned as one of the best glassblowers in Canderis, despite his location in the wine province of Wexler. Wasn't business booming now that he had Tadjeus Pomerol and three others drumming the country for orders?

Oh, true enough, most of his income resulted from the lucrative molding of bottles—no great skill there—but he created more than that both for utility and sheer beauty. Delicate decanters etched with spindrift designs that gained life and movement from the tint of the wine inside. And pieces of spun artistry, painstakingly hand-formed, molten glass stretched and crimped with tongs, looped and laced,

more intricate than a snowflake under a magnifying glass.
He cast dreams with his breath and hands, relentlessly on
guard against impurities, polishing and polishing to remove
any flaw that might distort. These days almost everyone suffered from distorted vision, but not he, he saw it all so
clearly. After all, if you must set yourself a task, set the stiff-
est one you can find and accomplish it.

"Baz! Morning to you."

"Morning, Baz."

Oh, yes, they acted as if the sun rose and set with him.
Ha! Mayhap he'd try that on for size next. He stopped to pat
a child's head, made sure to greet the child's dog as well, exchange pleasantries with the child's mother. Yes, see and be
seen, concerned, caring. Oh, people knew Baz Foy exhibited
a hot temper at times, almost uncontrollable, but surely he
was a hot-blooded man, an artist who felt with his heart.
Well, let his apprentices mutter about his flare-ups, screaming rages when glass was smashed, his own masterworks
and their inferior efforts. Everyone admitted his apprentices
received rigorous but superior training. Clearly they might
not be overfond of him as a boss, but when they ventured
out on their own, rare was the man who'd say a word against
him—he'd made sure of that. Another task he'd set for himself, and not as difficult as many. Unspoken fear worked
wonders, as did a word in the proper ears.

No, he'd come out today to check on something, drop by
at the Chief Conciliator's. That position had cried out to be
his when Darl Allgood was called to the capital to become
High Conciliator. Hadn't his passionate caring won him that
right? Hadn't his every action outside the glassworks been
aimed at earning the people's trust and respect? Yet when
the elections came, the secret ballots with their mute, blank
line for each man and woman to enscribe the name of the
person they most trusted to judge their lives, hold them ac-
countable for their actions, Elgar Eustace's name had been
written in, not his own. How could they not see his worth?
No warning, no inkling the elections were due, and he'd
been absent on business, no time for a subtle emotional appeal.

The loss still rankled, clawed at his assessment of himself.
And Darl, Darl, the man whom he'd wanted to love him like
a son, take him to his heart, had apparently done nothing to
take his part. Well, his time would come, and when he ac-

complished this task Darl would be even prouder of him, would admit how wrongly he'd been overlooked, shower him with the recognition he deserved.

He gained the Conciliator's building, its granite lintel with the official seal like an eye mocking his longing, and halloed as he entered. No, no Seekers Veritas today. He knew their schedules as well as Elgar with his shy pansy-brown eyes, the outward example of his inner softness. It took guts and determination to judge your fellow citizens, find them wanting, and pass judgment, just as his grandfather had once, taking the matter into his own hands. " 'Lo, El?" The man came hurrying out, his white shirt with its seven parallel bands on the diagonal, the black embroidered trim at the shoulders, bringing a lusting want to Baz's heart. His, it should have been *his* by all rights. Why hadn't Darl bruited his name about, talked him up as his logical successor? Heir in spirit if not in flesh.

"Cold in here," Baz shivered at the chill the limestone held inside. "Come out into the sun, El."

"You're too used to the furnace heat, Baz," Elgar protested but followed obediently. Amusing, that—how he enjoyed having such weak, malleable souls at his heels, yet felt nothing but contempt for them. Tadj Pomerol was equally pliant to his will.

They lounged against the hitching rack, basking in the sun, watching the light glint off Leger Lake and the vineyards terraced along its slopes. "So, seems as if the capital gets crazier every day. If you read the broadsides as gospel truth." A seeming afterthought, "Poor Darl must have his hands full."

Elgar squinted against the sun as if it pained him. "Aye. Those Resonants cause no end of grief, not by any wrongdoing but simply by being who and what they are. Lucky we've had no cases pop up here, but I live in dread of it— mutilation, murder." The words caused a delicious icing along the fine hairs of Baz's arms. "Having to judge one of my neighbors for a crime he utterly believes to be right. But even Resonants don't deserve to be slaughtered for living and breathing."

"Be easier all round if Resonants would just disappear, but I doubt that'll happen." Baz made his face sad.

"Aye, though some are willing to make that happen. Darl wrote, said people are organizing, planning to eradicate all

Resonants. Call themselves Reapers, no less, and Reaper groups are springing up all over, like mushrooms after a rain. Shouldn't wonder if there aren't some here in Wexler."

"Oh, I doubt that," Baz consoled. Well, the man wasn't as innocent as he'd thought, but he was still blind. Of course Wexler had its Reapers, but here he'd ensured they didn't openly sport the silver crescent pin and wheat sprig. "Good that you can call them Resonants, not Gleaners. My tongue slips more often than not. Old habits die hard." And some habits shouldn't have died at all; his grandfather had had the right of it.

"I know. Suppose they wouldn't call themselves Reapers if it weren't for the old word of Gleaners."

"Wonder what they'd call themselves to match Resonants?"

But Elgar was clearly restive. "Who knows? Trouble enough without thinking about that. Darl says they're well-organized, yet no one knows who heads them."

"Funny, that," Baz said to be agreeable, but was secretly thrilled. "Well, I confess a part of me applauds his humanitarian efforts, even if they're misguided. We need peace, stability, our old lives back without looking over our shoulders in fear."

"Not likely." Gloomy, Elgar looked toward his offices. "Well, work to do. Always paperwork. Nice talking with you, Baz, drop by again sometime." And the Chief Conciliator slapped his hands in a dismissive gesture, as if to brush Baz away, and Baz felt the familiar burning inside.

"Oh, I don't know," he tossed over his shoulder as he strolled off, "Miracles do happen, El. Miracles blossom by believing hard enough and working hard enough toward a goal. Positive thinking, you know—any goal is attainable."

Back to the glassworks, stop, chat with anyone he passed. Always make time for them, make them feel wanted, and he'd gain their support, already had garnered support across the country. Cheerful as he entered the furnace room, he smiled, complimented one of the apprentices as he passed through to his offices. Door firmly locked behind him, he went to the cabinet, opened the doors, and removed the wooden plaque inside. Mounted on it was an old sickle, the one his grandfather had used to personally kill two of the Fifty. Well, not the actual sickle—he'd been fifteen before he'd realized that a convicted murderer would hardly be allowed to bring the murder weapon into exile with him. Still, a symbol, and he'd see that more than two met their death, had seen to it already. Safe in his pocket a little sack of silver crescent sickles to reward his followers. Silverwork wasn't his talent, but you could master any craft if you applied yourself properly.

"Yes, Darl, I'll make you proud of me. Save you so much grief and weariness. I've killed to honor you before, killed to sever the ties that would have kept me from meeting you. I wonder how I knew. You've got to understand—for once you're not right. I promise I won't let you be misguided again. I'll come see you, help you understand."

"Wycherley, hold up! I'll ride with you." Toe in stirrup, ready to swing into the saddle, Jenret Wycherley checked himself and cursed, back rigid until the genuine bonhomie in the request overrode his reaction to what he'd interpreted as an imperious command. Equally impatient, the midnight-hued ghatt Rawn paced on his pommel platform.

Lady bless, Wycherley *was* tired and out of sorts. The only thing that made his eyes brighten, his tired face break into a smile was a mention of Doyce. Not easy learning to be a Resonant, and Faertom had nineteen years of living with it, while Jenret had only a few octants. Faeralleyn Thomas, already aboard his faithful Twink, watched the interaction with unfeigned interest as the larger man ran down the Research Hospice steps, gesturing at a groom for his horse.

The contrast between Arras Muscadeine, with his luxuriant dark mustache and his full-sleeved shirt, crimson slashed with yellow on the sleeves, a lavender sash, versus Wycherley's somber black that set off his pale complexion and his strikingly long-lashed, gentian blue eyes made Faertom feel like a pallid wallflower. Never could he match either man in confidence or in the ability to command others. Outwardly different and yet inwardly so alike, each equally stubborn and strong and uneasy at sharing the same territory. Frankly, in a contest of wills, he'd be crowded out of the picture. Just as well. Best not take sides since he liked them both, but it wasn't restful being around two such robust, indeed, ardent personalities.

"Why?" Wycherley shouted. "You're heading to Marchmont. The last time I noticed, it's in the opposite direction from Gaernett. Training sessions are done for now." And implicit in that was the fact that beyond Hospice walls, Jenret no longer acted the pupil and Arras the teacher when it came to instruction in Resonant skills. Obedience was no longer necessary. Faertom, obedient for most of his life to the higher necessity of never revealing his Resonant powers to outsiders, Normals, reveled in the vicarious thrill of friendship with someone who flouted authority, could be disobedient when it suited him. Wycherley swung onto Ophar, reining him around until the stallion faced south to make it clear.

Mounted as well, Arras Muscadeine wedged his horse between Jenret's and Faertom's. "I need your help, both of you," Muscadeine appealed, intimate and confiding.

Faertom's chest swelled with pride that a man as distinguished and commanding as Arras Muscadeine, a fully trained Resonant and the new Defense Lord of Marchmont, would enlist the aid of a nineteen-year-old Transitor, on leave from his roadwork duties to receive the training his raw Resonant skills so richly deserved. Frightening to publicly admit what he was, but he had, and so far the repercussions hadn't been as severe as he'd expected. Except ... except ... he wished he'd hear from his family, but their caution was only to be expected—he'd make it right with them when he could. He wasn't fool enough to believe that the cloistered world of the Research Hospice matched the world at large. He knew what Canderis was like far better than either Jenret or Muscadeine could, one just beginning to test its depths, the other a Resonant in a land that respected and esteemed them. It wasn't like that, never had been in his lifetime and in his land. Still, a chance to make a new start, change people's minds. And by change minds he meant show his worth, earn his place, not use his mindpowers to force people to accept him and his kind. Stop maundering about saving the world, he ordered himself, and see what Muscadeine wants. Truth be known, Muscadeine wanted Wycherley's aid more than his, but to be considered part of the group gave him a heady sense of belonging.

"Why not call out your troops for help?" Jenret inquired, pulling Ophar aside before he challenged Muscadeine's stallion, too near to Twink for the black steed's liking. "I'd best get home before Doyce thinks I've deserted her."

Muscadeine cheerfully slapped him on the back. "And when are you finally wedding the fair Marbon, eh?" but refrained from twisting the knife any deeper, totally serious again. "And I *would* call out my troops, but that wouldn't be politic on your side of the border—would it now? No, what's needed is circumspect observation and, perhaps, more than that, though I hope not."

Glancing to see that the groom had gone, he continued. "It's reached my ears," and a conspiratorial wink indicated that it had reached his mind, that he'd heard through his mindpowers, "that there may be a somewhat . . ." he groped for the word he wanted, "troubling, or mayhap only troubled, individual living nearby with the potential to cause *us*," clearly he meant Resonants, and Faertom's heart thudded, "a great deal of heartache, or worse."

He'd done it again, hadn't he? His worries projecting so loud and clear he might as well have shouted them from the highest tower. He'd exhibited better mastery, more self-control when he'd known less, because he'd lived daily with the desperate need for self-preservation, as automatic as breathing. Without it, one would be deprived of breath—and life. Now that he'd "come out," his reckless sense of relief had rendered him heedless, indiscreet. But what danger could spring from that poor woman eking out an existence on that miserable croft an afternoon's ride southwest of them? That *had* to be whom Muscadeine was referring to! When he'd stopped to ask about watering Twink she'd reacted peculiarly to his presence, but he'd assumed she reacted thusly with all strangers, despite his niggling discomfort.

"No, lad, what made your hair hackle was deeper than that," Muscadeine mindspoke, expanding his mental converse to encompass Jenret. *"Your subconscious sensed tangible anger, hatred emanating from her, a crazed, twisted fear of anyone with mindpowers. Your consciousness did as well, but you denied it. Oh, you didn't identify yourself as a Resonant, but she responded to it, may be a touch sensitive herself."*

"Besides, you told her where you were headed, didn't you, Faertom?" Jenret asked. *"Even if you didn't, odds are good*

that anyone heading for the Hospice has something to do with Resonants."

Shamed, Faertom hung his head, the mane of tawny hair shielding him from their concern and pity. Fool, fool! Triply a fool! His father'd have had his hide for being so gullible, so open with "outsiders" like that woman. He dragged the words from the depths of his fears, *"What are we going to do? Spy on her? What?"* His stomach pressed higher, tighter against his heart, crushing it. Would—did Resonants kill to protect themselves? Not break the strictures? Would he? And if they did, didn't that give credence to the suspicions and buried fears of so much of the Normal world?

With a lurch he realized the others had ridden ahead and halted, gifting him the space and privacy to steady himself. Drumming his heels into Twink's barrellike gray sides, he coaxed her into a canter instead of her usual amble. He'd never keep pace with them, mentally or physically, given Twink's usual sedate pace. Fool, Faertom, fool! he chided himself bitterly.

"Perk up, lad," Muscadeine spoke as if he gentled a frightened horse being broken to the saddle. *"We need to know if she's a menace to herself or to anyone else. Help if we can. Nothing more. But we have to be sure."*

He nodded, unsure whether to believe or disbelieve, as he caught up and they rode into the afternoon sun and down the steep Tetonord trails toward the main thoroughfare to Gaernett, traveling single file toward the unknown. Speech hindered their thoughts, silence a welcome privacy, and to Faertom the time passed in the blink of an eye as they drew into a sheltered, brambled dip just below the rotting, tilted fence that served as demarcation line between a house and the encroaching woods. In the other direction he could just make out the roadway when he squinted. A shabby cottage, tilted with age, a faint smoke thread, more a shimmer of diminished heat, danced in the sky, chimney canted toward the road, but there was no hint of the woman who lived there.

Ashamed of himself, shamed for his friends, he whispered out loud, as if speech emphasized their community, their common bond with everyone, Normal and Resonant alike. Or was that worse, pretending to be what they were not? "But what excuse, what reason do I have for stopping by again? She made it clear she doesn't enjoy visitors. What are you going to tell her?"

Muscadeine leaned against his horse, arms comfortably crossed on his chest, while Jenret stood at a little distance, as if unaligned with either. Not judging, Faertom suspected, but assessing, assessing which way the wind blew, where his loyalties would lie. "I'm not telling her a thing, lad, because Wycherley and I aren't coming. Three unannounced visitors might frighten her. She's seen you before, so you won't be as much of a threat." He turned, working at the buckle on his saddlebag and delved inside, pulling out a wrinkled paper sack exuding a fruity, rich scent that made everyone, most especially the horses, involuntarily follow it. "Custables," he swung the sack in his fist. "While she may manage a few apple trees this far north, it's usually impossible to grow custables. Harrap liberated a few from the courtyard espaliers where they're sheltered long enough to ripen. A peace offering, so to speak."

Faertom nodded, numb. Despite a lifetime of self-protective tricks, deception for protection, his brain would never match Muscadeine's nimble strategies. "But what're you doing if you're not going inside with me?"

A flash of teeth beneath Muscadeine's mustache reminded Faertom of a predator, a well-fed one. "Why, listening, Faertom—to everything that's said . . . and unsaid."

Jenret slapped his reins against his palm, distaste clear on his face. "What right, Muscadeine, what *right* do we have to do that? How often have you drilled us not to enter another's mind unbidden?" he reached to stroke Rawn. "Even the ghatti sensed from the very beginning that such a thing was wrong."

"Don't be so moralistic, Wycherley. Every sailor knows to trim his sails to the winds before he's driven off course. Don't parrot my lectures back at me if you can't comprehend the deeper significance of the rules, what they're for."

With a conscious effort that left him trembling, Jenret mastered his emotions, conquered the urge to spring at the larger man, pound sense into him. As a Seeker Veritas he adhered to a stringent code of honor, and he'd assumed as a neophyte Resonant that similar strictures would apply. Must. That, indeed, made it almost palatable to acknowledge his Resonant abilities, that codes, rules, structures existed to contain him, channel his gift, not let him trample over others as his elder brother Jared had once done so long ago and to such disastrous effect.

Rawn nudged him, black whiskers tickling just above his collar. **"Our rules are fewer than you believe. After all, our ultimate commandment is to Seek the Truth. And you know as well as I that in times of danger the privacy rule is void if someone's life is in jeopardy. Why else have we ghatti been asked to search minds to identify Resonants, regardless of whether that human takes part in a formal Seeking?"**

"Yes, I know why," he snapped. *"To protect foolish innocents, myself included. But I don't have to like it, do I?"*

"No, but some graciousness might be in order. If you can't win, at least grin."

"Sanctimonious ghatt!" He exhaled heavily, forced his features smooth, squared his shoulders. Never would he consider Muscadeine his superior except, perhaps, during the training sessions, and perhaps this should be viewed an extension of that, but he wasn't convinced.

"Call it a 'field trip,' if you must."

"Then you'll have no objection to Rawn listening in as well?" And enjoyed seeing Muscadeine taken aback. Strangely enough, he caught a flood of relief emanating from Faertom, as if a share of the burden had been lifted. Ghatti were scrupulously impartial.

Thrusting the sack of apples into Faertom's big hands, Muscadeine smothered a foxy grin. Easier to lure in Wycherley than he'd thought, even if it was for his own good. Fine sport to joust with Wycherley like that, and rare sport he'd make of him until he finally wed Doyce Marbon.

The door's warped planks rattled, moaned under the hammering, and at last she rejoined the present, reluctant to admit more than the random shudders of the wind buffeted this, her refuge. She shivered, the morning's meager fire long burned to ashes, remains of the past, as was she. The one warmth against the empty cold in her heart was a ball of white and tan fur on her lap, imprisoned against her rib cage by arms rigid with fear at the burning memories that now refused to remain in the past. Barnaby, the terrier, squirmed, whined to alert her to the presence of strangers. Not that she needed his warning. Somehow she knew—had always known—long before their eyes torched her soul.

Setting the dog on the floor where it dashed in circles between her and the door, she rose without hurrying and checked the mirror, eyes flat and gray as slate casting back their reproach at her, once fine blonde hair overwhelmed with wiry, curly gray poking in all directions as if she'd sustained a lasting fright. And perhaps she had, Hylan Crailford decided as she pushed both palms back from her temples, imprisoned the hair with a yarn remnant she'd wrapped round her wrist. Yes, a lasting fright that had always enshrouded her, would always enshroud her until the end. But the end loomed soon if she had her way, if she resurrected the courage she'd buried these past fifty years. Hadn't she scourged herself in penance for her weakness before? Now was not the time to quail or falter, and the grim crosshatching of torn, scabbed-over skin on her back reminded her of her resolve.

A flurry of knuckles, more tentative, and a hesitant, husky voice. "Mistress, be ye in?"

Ah, too bad, too bad, the young man who'd stopped for water a few days ago, the one who'd made her heart stop dead at his resemblance to the long dead Terranova Owensdatter—friend, idol, betrayer. Beyond doubt he served as an emblem, a reminder and a reproach to her cowardice, harbinger of change, whether he knew it or not, and over his innocence hovered death, death for so many if she didn't act—and soon. Terra had betrayed her once and Hylan had lived, but she'd never let herself be so betrayed again. "Hush, Barnaby, hush," she consoled the dog, prayed she wouldn't have to whip him, though she would if necessary. In cruelty is kindness, beyond pain, redemption. Terra had taught her that, or rather her death had. "Who's there?" she asked, and her voice, if nothing else, held a remnant of eager youth. "What do you want?" She craved a suitable answer, but it never came, never would, no matter how long she'd listened for it. Instead, she opened the door. Time to create her own answers to those fearful questions.

Handsome—Terra's broad, open features sat better on a man—and young, scarce twenty, she judged as Faertom stared at her. "Well?" Watched him step backward, nervous, as he held out the crumpled paper sack.

Secrets swarmed behind his open face, although the broad brow appeared serene, untroubled. Ah, already he'd learned how to dissemble, fabricate—so like Terra. Still, what choice did he have? What choice she? "I . . . I wanted to thank ye for the water the other day. Twink was powerful thirsty, as was I. I . . . I brought ye these . . . for enjoyment's sake." Resolute, he stepped forward, not too close, and laid the sack in her outstretched arms. When had she stretched them out as if she longed to embrace him?

Curiosity overcoming fear, Barnaby burst from behind her legs, shrill barking splitting the air, as did his switchlike tail. He mock-growled and scampered around Faertom's legs, ears perked, waiting to see if someone might play. Even the dog, even the dog wasn't always to be trusted. Faertom bent to rub his ears, toss a wind-fallen stick for him to chase. "I don't glean much enjoyment from anything," she commented, drawing his attention back to her, "or require much. But I thank you for thinking of me, no matter how misguided it may have been." She opened the sack, peered inside, hefted a gold-green globe of a custable. "Still, a change in diet is always welcome." Why did the lad still hold his empty hands in front of him, as if beseeching her for something? What she had to give he wouldn't want. Only the believers would and they were few and far between. Could she convince him to repent? Doubtful, especially if he had Terra's strong will in addition to her looks.

Angry at herself, she whistled the terrier to her, shoved him inside with her foot, and began to shut the door in his face. His mouth opened as if to say more, but she hushed him with a finger to her lips, turned it into a tentative farewell wave. Through the cracks in the planking she could see him standing, dumbfounded, before he finally convinced his legs to obey and move off. Such a waste. But then, wasn't much of life a waste?

Yes, she would scourge the madness from her body, from her mind, from the very land itself! If nothing else, she'd save the land from these marauders. There was Then and Now, a Before and an After, although she wasn't really sure there was an After. Worst of all was Before Then. There had been something there once, faint as yesterday's cook fire smoke. Ah, if she could only retrieve it, breathe on yesterday's coals and fan them to life, life Before the intangible danger that clouded her visions.

Eyes leaking with a sadness he couldn't begin to identify, Faertom staggered toward the dell where the horses were hidden. Saw Muscadeine frantically gesturing to him to hurry, mount up, and ride. Jenret's face frozen with shock, hands wooden on the reins. Strange, strange that neither spoke aloud or mindspoke him. He got as far as a querulous "*Why . . . ?*" when Rawn hissed him into silence. The chill he'd buried tight trickled down his spine, his hair rising along his neck and forearms.

The lanterns, the particolored ribbons and streamers hanging from wagons arranged in a crescent, a fire at the center where people gathered, clapping hands in time to the tune squeezed from the old concertina, made it a festival, a carnival of celebration. At least judging by six-year-old Hylan's jubilation level it qualified, as she dashed from person to person, tugging on sleeves, aprons, being hugged, patted, fed sweets. After all, she was their mascot—Terra had gifted her with that honor. "You're the Fifty-first, love. Our extra lucky one." And, of course, children were lucky, all children blessed, Terra had shared that secret with her. That and so many more—had even promised her a special Lady's Medallion like the ones Corneil had given the others, with its special secret etched on the back, the outline of a human brain. Some wore them openly, others secreted them at home in their velvet-lined boxes. If she had one, she'd wear it proudly, though she'd rather it had a flower on the back, not the inside of somebody's head.

At length, tired and satiated on treats as four Apostle moons partnered the Lady in the night sky, she settled under a wagon, held a spoke, cheek resting against it as she peered between them. The tune came unbidden, a set of words she'd heard and liked the sound of: "HO-se-A BA-ze-Lon, HO-se-A BA-ze-Lon, HO-se . . ." and a yawn. She'd venture out when Terra was free to play, but right now she talked intently with Corneil and Wim. Lucky, lucky Terra to have two such beaus, or so she deemed them with the romance of a child. Some said Wim liked Shoshana Garvey, the quarry master's daughter, but she rarely could get away, absent again tonight. Naturally Wim would prefer her Terra to Shoshana, didn't everyone? Terra stood up for her, and she'd stand up for Terra.

Wim Jonk acted so intense, so darkly scowling at times but passionate for everything. Nothing touched Wim lightly, but Terra always teased him out of the worst of his excesses. And Corneil Dalcroze, almost as new here as Hylan, so sunny, open, blond hair bleached blonder by the sun, that she found him equally enchanting. Especially the way he spoke, a lilting syncopation of words that danced and frolicked like a stream cascading over stones. A strange depth there as well, something more sensed than understood on her part. Once he'd turned to Terra when he'd thought she ranged out of earshot and said, "She's a wonder, a pet, but it's not right for her to be here. We know the risks we run by gathering, but she has no idea." Wim had come then, argued against Corneil as he so often did, and sided with Terra that Hylan should stay. She'd been touched by Wim's support, but the concern in Corneil's voice left her shivery, unsure. Had she done something bad again? Didn't deserve to be part of them?

The spoke hurt her face, so she pillowed her cheek against the hand clutching it, toyed with the ribbon woven through them. So pretty. And so was her Terra, Terranova Owensdatter, her cousin. Eighteen, with a braided crown of tawny hair, a queenly, deeply curved figure, a bosom to comfort, console, when she laid her head against it, desolate at being away from home, lodged with strangers, though Terra was a stranger no more.

Hylan sighed, sucked at a knuckle, refusing to stick her thumb in her mouth. "Too old for that," Terra had chided, and worked to break her habit. More proof she was bad. But the longing returned when she thought about her mother, anxious how she fared. This pregnancy was a hard one, her mother bedridden, unable to cope. And no matter what Hylan had done, how much she tried to help, she only got in the way, her father's temper already short-fused with worry. She'd been whipped more than once, briskly switched, for the things she'd broken, spilled, burned in her attempts to help, until she was convinced she was intrinsically bad, worthless, and beatings her just deserts.

"Evan, she's trying so hard," her mother had protested one night when she thought Hylan was asleep, awash with tears and shame after the last whipping. "I know, lass," her father had replied, "but I'll either beat the goodness into her or the evil out of her, one way or the t'other."

"There's no evil in the child, it's your own frustrations, your own fears that you've pinned on her. Evan, best we send her away for a while, till the baby's born. Then you'll have just me to worry about. Me to beat if you need someone to whip."

"Never! Never have I laid a hand on you! But children need to be castigated, disciplined for their own good when they do wrong."

"But you can't expect of her what you'd expect of an older child, an adult. You make mistakes, you try, you grow, you learn."

But her father had ignored that, mulling over her mother's earlier statement. "But where can we send her? Who'd have her? Your family's dead and gone, and mine's too far."

"Nay, not all my family. My cousin Owen Edricsen and his family live two towns over. We're not close, haven't seen each other much, my grandfather saw to that. Said if Owen's pa didn't want him, he'd have no truck with them, stock or limb. But Owen and I've always gotten on the few times we've met. He's a good man, keeps himself and his family to himself on the farm. Let me write him, please!"

So that was how Hylan found herself living with Terra and her family that summer, eager for autumn and the birth of a brother or sister to end her exile. She'd prove to her father how good she was then. Without Terra she'd have died of loneliness, convinced she'd been abandoned because she was bad. But Terra persuaded her otherwise, tucked her under her wing and, wonder of wonders, Hylan stopped breaking and spilling things, gained confidence.

The concertina music ceased, supplanted by the plaintive conversation of two flutes. Hylan lived for these rare nights, these furtive gatherings when Terra slipped out of the house, smuggling her along. Terra's father Owen didn't approve, and it sent chills down Hylan's back that she dared defy him like that. Maybe she and Hylan were alike after all. Gradually the group had grown to contain fifty members, mostly young and single, about Terra's age or a bit more, though a few were older, gray-haired, their families long grown and gone.

The music, the laughter and gay talk tonight was an exception. Often it seemed they met in dead silence, yet the air buzzed, electric with unheard sound. She'd strain and strain her ears to hear, its pitch beyond her. Mayhap her father'd been right about things not meant for children's ears, though how did her ears know not to hear—from being boxed so many times? So she'd play with her doll, serve cha in tiny

acorn cap cups, content to be near Terra, near Wim, who'd
carved her a willow whistle, and Corneil, who'd sweep her
onto his shoulders to admire the view. Wim scowled whenever Corneil spent too much time with Terra, or even with
her.

Wim and Corneil argued louder and louder now, Terra trying to mediate. "At least mindspeak," she pleaded, "the
whole group doesn't have to be privy to your disagreements."

"And mayhap they should!" Hands on his hips, Wim stood
darkly passionate, face stormy over the sky blue tunic. Even
from behind the wagon Hylan could see the knot in his brow,
prelude to the headaches that often incapacitated him. "Besides, silent argument's too damn civilized, too polite, and we
barbarians are anything but that—untrained, uncouth savages
that we are! So provincial, so utterly gauche! And now a for-
eigner, a stranger from a land that rejected us as worthless
comes to shed his beneficence on us, show us the truth and
the light, save the voices crying in the wilderness."

Corneil held out his hands in appeasement, striving for
calmness. "I've explained again and again. We didn't know,
we honestly didn't realize. Venable Constant took the best, or
so he thought—" he smote his brow. "That was the wrong
thing to say, the wrong way to say it. I mean—"

"You meant to say you left the dregs behind. And who appointed you to play missionary, slip into Canderis from
Marchmont and convert us lost souls?" Wim had taken a step
closer to Corneil, and he was taller, bigger, his wrath enhancing his size.

"We didn't know you were lost, truly," Corneil continued
to placate, "but now you're found. Let us rectify an error
perpetrated by ignorance so many years ago, train you to
your full powers, give you a place in the world. The opening
exists, all you have to do is fill it. The eumedicos *don't* have
mindtrance skills, *can't* read people's minds, discover the internal origins of an illness. You know our countries have
been distant, to say the least. We only recently discovered
that they'd mythologized their lost traditions. You can fill
that role, rise to a respected place in society. Resonants
make the best eumedicos, even yours knew that, though they
weren't able to replicate the talent."

"And so we come crawling, saying 'please, eumedicos,
find a use for us, give us a place in the world?' Why should
they admit their faults, cede us power? Well, gift it may be,

but it's also a weapon to defend us as we fight for our rights, our safety, no more calculating where to run and hide so we won't be discovered, judged to be different, a danger. Yes, we *can* be dangerous, and that's what I'll have us be—able to protect ourselves!" He ripped the Lady's Medallion from around his neck. "I'll take no gifts from you to mark us as one of your own! Why not notch our ears like prize sheep? I know my kind without a badge!"

Despite her best intentions Hylan crammed her thumb in her mouth, listening, not understanding. With the piercing protest of a sharp flute note, the whole camp had fallen silent, everyone frozen, listening to the angry voices, faces unsure, some frightened, some elated. And then people began to shift, align themselves behind either Corneil or Wim, Terra still centered between them, the polestar that gave them direction.

"Must it be completely one or the other? Battle lines drawn to separate us from each other when we've already severed ourselves from most of the world? The eumedicos need us, the people they treat need us—why deny them our abilities? But shouldn't we muster some of Wim's pride? Even a dog must sometimes remind his master of his fangs. And we're not dogs to be trained by people who've feared the worst of us for years.

"You've got to understand, Corneil, we exist on society's margins, scrambling to touch its hem. Whatever happens won't happen overnight. We have our dignity, what little remains, and we won't willingly relinquish it, not even for the promise of gaining a greater role." Breathless, Terra appealed to them. "We must find common ground amongst ourselves, be united before we approach outsiders."

Hylan knelt now, clutching the wagon wheel's rim, in awe of and in love with her cousin, her Terra, brave, canny, reaching a hand to each man, the bond welding them to one purpose. She wanted to run, bask in that love, hug Terra's waist so fiercely she'd never let go. Wasn't she their mascot, after all? She deserved a place at their sides. She started up, only to falter, foot asleep, prickling pins and needles, and almost cried in frustration.

And then in the darkness beyond the crescent of wagons, torches flared, shattering the night sky with avenging brightness, dazzling her eyes. So many torches, why? Screams, yells of rage, pulsating wrath that drubbed her with its fury, buffeted her back beneath the wagon as she stoppered her ears. But she could still hear, "Glean-ers! Glean-ers! Reap you from the face of the earth, let the earth drink your blood. Blood! Blood! You'll not glean our minds any longer!" The words clashed, finally strung themselves into coherent sentences in her mind.

The torches charged ahead, followed by a press of bodies, more than Hylan had ever seen, more than she could count. Bodies wielding farm implements, rakes, shovels, sickles, scythes, and the deadly mowing commenced. Bodies toppled like reaped wheat as her friends screamed, ran, tried to fight back.

Wim grappled with two men, Corneil rushing to his aid, beating one off with the concertina, its bellows sobbing and screeching. Wim's full attention centered on his remaining foe. He pressed his hands to the man's temples, ignoring the hands locked round his throat, and concentrated, brow clenched, eyes squeezed closed. The man went slack, hands falling from Wim's neck. "Fight back!" he screamed, vocal cords rasping, "Fight any way you can. They're armed, we're not. Our minds are our weapons! It's justified!"

Reeling in shock at Wim's reckless exhortation, Corneil stumbled away, leaving Terra standing alone. A scythe swept into her chest, its point biting under her breast, the curve caressing her ribs. Hylan screamed, began running, tripping over fallen bodies, slipping in the blood-soaked, battered meadow grass. Terra! She must reach Terra! So few were standing now that she knew, faltering and falling even as she watched; the others were strangers, though she'd seen some of their faces in the village, including the man her father'd introduced her to, the man whose name created her song, "Hosea Bazelon." He'd looked young, with dark, curling hair, moist red lips, sallow smooth skin, but his dark eyes had been ancient and unforgiving. The rest nameless, unlike the people crumpled dead on the grass. Wim spun toward the man who'd struck Terra, lips pulled back in a wicked snarl as a scythe hooked at his throat, blood fountaining from a crescent wound as feral as his smile.

Bad! Bad! They must have done something evil, been bad for this to happen. Wasn't her father always right, you get what you deserve? But Terra—bad? Wim, the others? She must be bad as well, but not as bad as the others or she wouldn't be alive, could redeem herself. Oh, Blessed Lady, please, I'm sorry!

She collapsed on her knees again, crashing into Corneil's body. He grabbed her, hand over her mouth, pinned her beneath him, began crawling in retreat, dragging her toward the wagons. Blood from an oozing temple wound mingled with sweat, drenched her face, shielded against his shoulder. He gained the wagons' shelter, breath hot and harsh, eyes deep pits of agony. He checked around, gauged an opening, and burrowed through the high grass toward the waving fronds near the pond. Cradling her in his arms, he sank them both into the smelly, duckweed-speckled water until only their noses remained clear.

It took most of the night, frenzied revelry counterpointing the weeping for the victors' wounded and dead, the avengers, whomever they might be, before the area was deserted. The raw, gagging smell of kerosene drenching everything, the sky lit not with sun but with fire as the pyred bodies of her friends flamed high. She'd watched the dancing, soaring flames while Corneil dozed, holding his head clear of the water, raising her own enough to see. The flames were butter yellow and orange, the surrounding pond water a rusty, seeping red, and the duckweed greenly freckled Corneil's pale face.

They'd fled finally, furtive, clinging to the remnants of the dark, shying at every sound, hearts hammering as they hid, dashed for ditches. At last she recognized the path through the back pasture that led to Terra's father's farm.

Corneil held her against him, long fingers light against her temples, and she struggled in terror. She knew what that meant, what it did, had seen Wim do it. Bad and now she must pay. "Hush, child, hush." He leaned down, swaying with exhaustion, kissed her forehead. "Forget, child, forget," he crooned. "It's all I can offer you, the gift of forgetting."

They must have done something bad . . . or they wouldn't have been killed. I will block my ears like the viper against their charms. Scourge the memories from my mind. Hadn't her father held her tight in relief when he'd hurried to get her, saying, "Thank the Lady such evil didn't leave its mark on you—did it?" Hadn't known what he'd meant, knowing only that Terra had vanished. Bad girl to want Terra, so bad, so sinful. But Daddy's whip would redeem her because he only scourged the ones he loved, could save. And the pain would make her few fragmented memories of Terra and that night of terror vanish. Forget, forget . . .

... And so she had, until now. Even those you loved must be scourged from the earth to save them. No, she hadn't understood Terra and her friends were Gleaners, not until now. And that made her even more determined to save herself—and to save them—from the danger they represented. In cruelty was kindness.

Full evening now as Doyce left Headquarters and trudged the path that wound through the grounds to the guest house in which she and Jenret had been billeted. The rationale behind such favoritism was to afford them privacy, unavailable in the barrackslike dormitories which lodged both the curious and well-wishers. Seekers though they might be, they were unsatisfied with just one recounting of Doyce's and Jenret's, Khar's and Rawn's various exploits, whether in tracking down Vesey or, more recently, in averting full-scale war with Marchmont and putting its rightful ruler on the throne.

"And of the Seekers," she grumbled to Khar, who'd paused to consider a windblown leaf, "I don't know who's worse, humans or you ghatti." Like their smaller and distantly related cousins, house cats, ghatti were insatiably inquisitive, eager to unearth the truth about anything and everything, despite their inscrutable expressions.

Padding back with the leaf in her mouth, Khar dropped it, then pounced when it crackled invitingly. **"Well, at least we don't embellish. After all, the truth is the truth. Once we capture that, we're satisfied."**

"And speaking of satisfied, I'd be satisfied if Jenret were home to meet me." Doyce retrieved the leaf, absentmindedly shredding it as she continued along. "I'm ... lonely." The admission hurt. "I'm blessed by your company, love ... but you know what I mean."

"I know. And Jenret does cook better than you do."

"What a resounding vote of confidence! I suppose we could eat in the dining hall tonight. Didn't check the board to see what the special is, though." But as they entered the brick walk, lights gleamed soft-gold from the rear of the guest house, the kitchen area, and her heart skipped a beat. Khar's ears perked as well, though she hesitated to disappoint by telling the truth. Company of any sort might take her mind off Jenret's absence.

Flinging her coat on the entryway rack produced an unlikely thump as the coat swung against the wall. Puzzled, Doyce patted at pockets she'd deemed empty, scolded herself as she pulled the leather-bound diary free. Carry it around and forget it's there, would she? Still, she carefully set it on the hall table. With luck, she'd remember to return it come morning.

Humming under her breath, tremulously happy at the prospect of seeing Jenret again, of being swept tight in his embrace, she didn't notice the black ghatt with a white forehead star, a short white boot on right foreleg and a long white stocking on the left, until he brushed a welcome against her shin, startling her. Not Rawn. Her hopes plummeted—if not Rawn, then not Jenret. Green eyes somber, filled with a deep, far-reaching sadness, the ghatt momentarily brightened as he greet-sniffed Khar.

"M'wa, greetings! Mindwalk if ye will." She babbled to hide her disappointment. *"How's Bard? He's here, isn't he? How's he doing? How are you doing?"* And then noticed with a quivering foreboding that M'wa was bereft of his Seeker earrings, the gold hoop in the left ear, the ball in the right. Earrings removed only when one of a Bond pair died. Hand at her throat, she sagged against the wall, the room blurring before her eyes. *"Lady, no! Not that!"* She ground the back of her hand against her teeth, welcomed the pain.

Not lose Bard, too! Too much, too much to bear. Bad enough that Bard and M'wa strove to cope with the loss of their twins, Bryta and the ghatta P'wa, but now M'wa stood totally bereft, orphaned yet again by the severing of his other Bond. Oh, Lady take him to Your bosom, but wouldn't it have been kinder if You'd let that Marchmontian's broadsword kill all four that day, let them ascend to the havens together, never wrenched apart, separate, and alone?

"What?" M'wa sat, clearly puzzled. *"Humans do overreact, don't they?"* he asked Khar as Doyce's panicked thoughts wove through his brain. *"So much easier if they could read the truth as we do."* He licked a paw, scrubbed at a bare ear, then jumped to the hall table to sniff Doyce's frozen face. One foot landed on the diary and he halted, momentarily distracted, fixing Khar with a look of concern.

"What's that?—as if I didn't know. And what's it doing here?"

Balancing on her haunches, Khar nosed Doyce's cold hand. "Later," she apologized. "Best you explain yourself now before she passes out."

"Bard's fine, truly," M'wa 'spoke Doyce. "Truly. He's in the kitchen, come see for yourself. We have an idea for the earrings. He'll explain. Thought Bard'd be right behind me so you wouldn't jump to conclusions like that."

Legs like jelly, Doyce tottered through the living area into the kitchen where Bard stood at the sink, scraping carrots with grave deliberation, completely involved in his work. He aligned them on the chopping board and began rocking the knife, minting carrot coins. His skin glowed taffy gold in the lamplight, tight, tiny curls the color of maple sugar. Always tall, always thin, even thinner now, worn with grief, shoulders slumped over his work.

Wordlessly she came from behind and locked his waist in a fierce hug, even though she knew how he hated emotionalism. She couldn't help herself. His hands overlaid hers for a moment, then he unwrapped himself with unflustered dignity, pressed one palm against her belly. "Light must be bad, mistaking me for Jenret like that." He registered her paleness, eyes dark with shock, and hooked the kettle off the iron stove. "Think I was a ghost? Here, a cup of cha calms. Your hands are like ice."

M'wa leaped onto the drainboard, flicked a carrot paring into the sink, clearly in private communion with his Bondmate. Doyce sat at the kitchen table, legs outthrust, mug balanced on her stomach, the warmth penetrating, soothing. Amazing that the baby hadn't registered her panic, reacted as well. "If I've had a fright, it's your fault." Hoped he heard only the petulance, not her underlying fear. "What . . ." she almost couldn't bring herself to say it, "what . . . have you done with your earrings? Does it mean you've decided not to be Seekers any longer?" And now, despite herself, anger flared. "You can't quit just like that. Once a Seeker, always a Seeker, so long as your Bond shall last."

Adding the carrots to a tin dish already containing potatoes, brussel sprouts, and onions, he dribbled oil, stirred until they were coated and slid them into the oven to bake. "Mayhap, mayhap not," he answered at last, still peering into the oven. "Oh, our Bond's intact. It's the only thing

that's kept us minimally sane since . . . they died. And no
matter what Mahafny may say, what skills she thinks I have,
I don't want to be a Resonant. I don't *choose* to be, do you
understand! The mindlink Byrta and I shared was ours alone,
a private connection. I *don't* choose to hear what other
minds think. I'm not sure I want M'wa to share what he
learns from other minds." Rare for Bard to speak at such
length—almost as if he'd rehearsed it, his first truly solo
declaration without Byrta to share the dialogue.

He wheeled to face her. "In short, M'wa and I are taking
a leave of absence, sanctioned or not. As to the earrings,"
his hand rubbed his earlobe, daring her to stare at the nakedness, "well, I think I've found a better use for them."

M'wa interrupted, hasty to smooth over Bard's abrupt-
ness, near rudeness. **"When Byrta broke her leg last fall,
a little farm girl helped her. A brave child who challenged the Gleaners when they attacked P'wa and Byrta
to steal their brains. Bard and I arrived in time, but
without her we'd never have driven them off."**

"And what she yearned for, Byrta told me later," Bard
took up the story, "was jewelry, something to bedeck and
adorn herself with. The family's poor, no extra money for
indulgences. We thought to give her our earrings as
thanks—in remembrance of her bravery. Have someone else
cherish the memory of Byrta and P'wa." He swallowed. "It's
only jewelry, and jewelry can be replaced more easily than
. . . other things can be."

"Now, if someone would peel these apples for the pie, we
just might have dinner ready for Sarrett. The chicken's roast-
ing." He unceremoniously thumped a scrap pan in front of
her and placed a paring knife beside it. With as much good
grace as she could muster, Doyce attacked one of the wind-
falls piled in the pottery bowl at the table's center.

"Bard, just don't stay away too long," she pleaded. "We
need you, we need you both. There's no one I'd trust more
than you and M'wa out riding circuit, quelling rumors,
learning the truth before innocent people are hurt." Her eyes
blurred, making it hard to thin-peel the apples. She continued working by touch, feeling the knife blade approach her
thumb, bite too deep and fast for her to stop it. "Ouch!
Please, Bard!"

Blinded by tears, she let him lead her unresistingly to the
pump, the plash of cold water on her hand bringing her back

to herself. *"Khar, talk to M'wa, tell him how much we need them. I know there's sorrow, pain at the loss, but make them understand they have to work through it, you can't run from sorrow and grief."*

Khar and M'wa exchanged glances at what had already been set in motion. Best Doyce not know for her own safety's sake. Even Bard didn't yet know the role he'd been assigned to play, a part of a tale that the ghatti couldn't rewrite although it hadn't even happened yet.

Dinner concluded, all chicken scraps suitably disposed of—in the bellies of three hungry ghatti—Khar waited for Sarrett and Doyce to start on the dishes as Bard sat back and smoked a pipe. Sure at last that the humans were properly occupied, Khar motioned M'wa and T'ss to join her at the door. Aware something was afoot, although he didn't know what, the white ghatt with the black stripings and bright blue eyes jittered with youthful impatience. Without realizing it, he anxiously merowed aloud.

Pushing gilt-pale hair off her forehead with damp hands, Sarrett laughed. "Impolite beast," and scolded as she opened the back door. "All you had to do was ask, and not aloud! Others teaching you bad habits, are they?"

Scarcely chastened, T'ss butted her leg before dashing out the door after the others.

M'wa checked his flight with a rough but good-natured shoulder bump. **"Exquisite vocalization, I'm sure. Now behave, you're too old for that."**

Slipping through gusty autumn darkness toward the plaza in front of Headquarters, they saw they weren't the first to shelter around the statue of Matthias Vandersma and the ghatta Kharm. Other ghatti streamed toward them, some clearly visible in the moonlight of the six Disciples, others shadow-wreathed, near invisible as they padded closer. Since the plaza served as a traditional ghatti communal spot, no one would pay them any great heed, comfortable with such comings and goings, their flocking together at this place. At length twenty ghatti of all ages sat or stretched at length around the statue.

"Birds of a feather flock together," Mem'now chuckled

from the statue's base. **"A glee of ghatti, T'ss. Welcome all."**

Khar settled at a polite distance. **"You know what I would ask tonight."** So curiously formal, almost demure, but he could read the aching want within her, wondered, not for the first time, if this course wound crooked or straight. Well, they'd know soon enough.

"Yes, but others here and nearby may not. May I link all in the mindnet?" With her permission he could direct his thoughts to any distant ghatti within range of his powerful mindvoice, sustained and enhanced by the individual strengths of the nearby ghatti. Ghatti over near-half of Canderis could participate, though never had Mem'now attempted a linking of such magnitude, but these were strange, unsettling times. **"As many as possible should know, share in the decision. Indeed, I ask those at my mindvoice's limits to contact those beyond, join in our communing tonight."**

Needful, yes, but a demeaning exposure. A little shudder rippled her fur, a naked vulnerability at revealing her quandary so far and wide. Couldn't Mem'now just get on with it? And while ghatti etiquette demanded this collective asking, a still higher power was mandated. The Elders must be convinced as well. Was she strong enough not just to contact them but to truly hear their answer? For Doyce she'd attempt anything, do anything that might help, because she dared this not only for Doyce, but for the land and the ghatti themselves, their place in the land, their role in society.

The voices homing in, floating outward touched gentle, curious, unraveling the innermost truth of the situation. Never, ever before had they agreed to commingle so deeply with a human mind, to reveal a part of their private heritage to a human. No surprise, then, to hear first Rawn's familiar bass mindvoice, followed by Saam's; Rawn reassuring, admitting he and Jenret ran late, and Saam's distant voice from the Hospice urging, **"Try. All we can do is try. Believe and you can do anything."**

"I can try, but I can't do it alone," she confessed to the assembly at large. **"My wisdom lacks depth unless I'm accompanied by someone with greater experience on the Spirals."** Eight turnings, eight spirals of ascending knowledge encompassed each ghatti life, some gained early, some not at all, despite the age of the individual ghatti. True in life as well, some never learned completely, accepted and matured to their full capacity and capability. Still, impolite to question any individual as to the level of attainment in the collective Mind Spiral, past and present, of the wisest ghatti of all, the Elders. Khar herself had painstakingly progressed to the Fourth Level on the Spiral and that, she feared, might not be enough.

Mem'now harrumphed, treaded his front feet uneasily. **"I can't spiral *and* keep the mindnet intact. One or the other, I'm not a juggler, you know."**

"Nonsense! I distinctly remember once seeing you toss two voles simultaneously. Such dexterity, such paw work!" Khar recognized Terl, the night damp turning his mindvoice as rusty as his once dark coat. **"I'm slow, not as agile as I once was, but mayhap we could support each other through the turnings, take heart from each other, boost each other along the way, my beauteous Khar'pern."**

Unable to directly acknowledge his generosity, she took a deep breath and began the upward gliding, secure in her following, letting him set the pace. Upward, ever upward, gliding through the first Spiral, swooping into the second, Elder voices, some near, some far, chiming in her ears. Distant yet soothing, past wisdom and present combined, nothing lost or omitted, nothing forgotten or set aside as useless, if she had wisdom enough to hear and comprehend.

"Ah, little Khar'pern, welcome! And welcome to your guide, oh puissant Terl! So long since either of you've ventured here we thought you might have forgotten ..." the voices chuckled, lapped away in an ebbing tide, **"forgotten us. Amazing what they re ... col ... lect ... lect when they wish a favor, isn't it?"**

Unperturbed, Terl swept on, Khar drawn in his wake. The top of the Fourth Spiral, her limit, and she prepared to wait, gasped as she smoothly drifted up yet another. **"Didn't even realize you'd accomplished it, did you, girl?"** Terl asked. **"Should make *you* lead. Such modesty."**

"Modest Khar'pern. Curious Khar'pern." Ripplings of laughter, indulgent, sprinkled over her until she was stardusted. **"At last ready to listen to the past, eh?"**

With a surge of relief she halted at the Fifth Spiral. **"To listen to the past and to share it with another, to share the truth so that past mistakes don't live on."**

"**Mistakes? Surely never?**" A hint of anger seething through the collective voices in a low, bubbling boil. "**Always truth! Never untruth!**"

But Terl's voice floated to her, implacable, from some loftier vista. "**Set Doyce Marbon, Bondmate of the ghatta Khar'pern, loose on the path of the past. Let her learn, profit from our wisdom, that is what we ask.**"

"**A mere human, fond of her as we may be?**" The voices, haughty now at being prodded, and Khar feared a sudden slide down the Spirals, smooth as a banister, unable to catch a claw to halt her descent.

"*My* **human, Elders! And perhaps our hope and salvation, unless you'd relish communing strictly amongst yourselves. If ghatti have no place in this strange new world approaching us, you'll learn naught of the future, of the frailties and foibles of humankind, their thoughts withering and dying, uncollected, because we cannot report to you. Unwanted, unloved, unneeded!**"

"**Rambunctious, undisciplined, overzealous as ever,**" an Elder sniffed.

"**And right on target,**" Terl shot back. "**What good is the past if it's forgotten, unloved, unwanted, and we cannot learn from it? What hope without a future?**"

Aggrieved, "**What do you propose to tell this human? How much of our tales shall she hear?**"

"**The First Spiral, the First Major Tale, of how we came to be a part of each other.**" Greatly daring, Khar placed her request. "**I'm not sure why, but I think it's important they understand the similarities and the differences to what we face beyond tomorrow's shadows.**"

"**Ah, she would hear the resonances, then? Not just the Resonants?**" a hint of mockery to the words. "**How will she cope when unknown, misunderstood fears tinge her mind, counterpoint the real ones around her? Is she strong enough for that?**"

"**We had** *all* **best be strong enough for that, just as Matthias Vandersma and Kharm were, despite their fears,**" Terl interrupted. "**We thank you for your consideration, but we, who humbly lack the Elders' wisdom, can only hope for the best. After all, are we not your children?**"

"**So tell her, then.**" Mindvoices grumbled in distant thunder. "And remember, you reap what you sow. Just so no untruths are heard."

Khar nodded, unable to speak, unsure whether to be relieved or frightened. "Not in an especially charitable mood tonight," Terl remarked. "Ruffled their collective fur, we did," as he began to descend, nudging Khar ahead of him. "Oh, won't that be something to tell the ghatten about!"

Appalled at the enormity of what she'd done, what she'd asked, Khar trembled. "Doyce ... Doyce won't be hurt, will she? They wouldn't allow that, would they?"

"There're all kinds of hurt, all kinds of pain, and some are salutary, as well you know. Now move along, I need a warm fire to soak their mindchill out of my old bones."

Silence shrouded the study where Sarrett and Bard traded canny stares across the chessboard while Doyce, hands clasped behind her neck, sank back in her easy chair and observed the fire. Or as much as she could over her mounded belly. Not bored, exactly—she wiggled her toes—but restless. The lack of conversation didn't bother her, good to have companionship without needing small talk. Enough of that and more at dinner as they'd touched on past and present sorrows, hesitantly mapping the future. Or rather, others' futures, not their own—a taboo topic tonight. As if they could mold it to their whims!

Ears cocked, hoping against disappointment, she half-listened for Jenret's footsteps on the brick path. Instead, a faint scratching at the door and Khar's mindvoice tickled her. "In, please!" Levering herself up, she wandered in stocking feet to the front door, glad of the ghatti's company as well.

Khar, M'wa, and T'ss marched through the door, although T'ss bounded as if a mini-demon rode his tail. No matter his age, T'ss would always be an overgrown ghatten. The other two looked smugly satisfied but tired. Despite her resolve, she opened the door wider, staring into the dark. No, no sign of Jenret and Rawn, though both would be near invisible against the night, Jenret with his black pantaloons, tunic, and tabard, and Rawn so ebony black.

The shabby leather book she'd left on the hall table diverted her as she latched the door. She swooped it up, held it for comfort. Perfect! Just the thing to occupy her mind, diminish—if not demolish—her preoccupation over Jenret's return. Let the others play chess as long as they liked. And reading, she couldn't help grinning, beat knitting booties. Knitting ranked as one of the most boring things imaginable—mainly because the garment never grew fast enough to hold her interest. For that much finger-twisting, stitch-counting effort she demanded immediate gratification.

The three ghatti strung themselves along the hearth, M'wa and Khar compact and loaflike while T'ss sprawled, feet treading air. Pouring a glass of water from the carafe, she settled it on the arm of her chair, squirmed once for comfort, and cracked the book open with care. Before she dove into it, she glanced around the room, stared into the fire, a hypnotic swirling of flames capturing her attention. A part of her registered that all three ghatti now sat, alert, staring almost through her, as if willing her to reach through the patterns of the fire. Khar's amber eyes widened to swallow her, narrowed, widened again, and she was engulfed, adrift in the reflected images. She touched the coarse paper of the page, and gasped, hand crushed against her mouth.

The book forgotten in her lap, she continued to stare, watching as the flickering scene gained shape and definition.

Matthias Vandersma huddled near the fire, the larchcat sprawled across his lap while he stroked it. Purring ripples vibrated its body, transmitted themselves to his hand, and he could sense them going ragged, slow-fading as she drifted toward sleep. And sleep, he prayed, would end the ceaseless, inquisitive cataloging of his mind, every thought inventoried, inspected, while her brain dashed on to embrace the next, and the next, many he wasn't even conscious of until she revealed them, proud as a kitten depositing its first kill in front of its human. Fright crushed his chest like a vise, though he tried not to show it, rhythmic shudders washing over him despite his efforts to remain still. Best not catch Granther's attention now, give him something else to worry about.

Done tucking Henryk into bed, the old man turned to place the boy's spectacles on the stool beside the bed. The mismatched lenses, one yellow, one green, sparkled jewel-like in the firelight, as they must have long ago, warning lights on the Spacers' navigation console. The white of Ryk's sling glowed dully white against the boy's pale body, livid scratches on his torso painted with wide streaks of red-orange disinfectant. Pulling a worn afghan from the back of his rocking chair, the old man draped it across Matty's shoulders, wrapped it around him, deft and tender.

"Ye cannot keep her, Matty." He sat heavily, a hand on the boy's shoulder. "We've been over it again and again. She's a wild thing, a wild beast. Needs to be with her own."

"I'll take care of her, Granther," he pleaded. "She won't be any trouble, I won't let her be! She's too little to be out there alone without her mother to look after her. She'll die if I let her go!" And something within him would die as well. How did he know that? How could he say it?

"Living and dying is nature's way, boy, and it's not up to us to interrupt it or circumvent it. Can't anymore—the high tech's gone."

The ghatten, Kharm, he'd named her, or more accurately, that was what she'd named herself, half-rolled in his lap, tiny belly distended from milk and a thin mash of cooked vegetables and meat. What did "ghatten" mean? Tiny claws pricked his bare chest, demanding his attention. He shushed her, shielded her from his granther. The voice echoed in his mind and he jerked, almost convulsed.

" 'Fraid? Afraid of me. Why?" And seemed to answer her own question. "Not always enough food. True. Can hunt my own! I am Kharm, mighty ghatten, clever ghatten. Oh, no!" she continued as if responding to another question, "won't hunt, won't hurt, won't steal what isn't mine, silly furries in hutches, squawky scratch-feet. Not take unless given!"

Matty felt dizzy, as if he heard her answer two conversations, unheard within his grandfather and the other within him where the ghatten's voice resided. Now, rather than feeling chilled, he was flushed, wave after wave of feverish heat radiating from his body, the afghan stifling, sticking to sweaty skin. "Bad luck? Silly, silly! Super . . ." she stumbled over the new word, "super-squishious? Super . . . stitious. Best luck in the world to share with one of the ghatti, best luck for both of us. True? Truly!"

He felt her arguments as a prompt, priming him with the answers, rehearsing him in some strange way. Manipulated as easily as the Killanin boys manipulated him, but what he *did* absorb was an overwhelming love, not hate. Love surrounded him, cocooned him, made him safe and secure, except for the headache pounding at his temples. His lips silently mouthed her words, clamped down on any stray sounds trying to escape.

His grandfather's face swam into focus in front of him, sad blue eyes—so much like his own—above the full white beard. A hand rocked his shoulder and he allowed it, his body boneless. **"Matty, Matty,"** the voice crooned inside him, then more insistently, **"Matty! Talk to him. No wobble! Too limp, too scary!"**

He stiffened against his grandfather's hand, halting the movement. Best say something, anything, distract his grandfather's worry, the fear swamping his eyes. What he yearned to ask was "What's truth, Granther? How do you know what you hear is true? How do you know what you say is true, not just what you believe is true?" But he didn't dare ask, couldn't begin to explain why it mattered so much. Blinking as if he'd been almost asleep, he licked his lips, smiled at his grandfather. "What's love, Granther? Why does it hurt so much?"

He took refuge behind the question, a part of what he wanted to ask—why had he come to love and need this larchcat so much in such a short time? To weigh in his heart and soul the essential rightness or truth of their connection, even though fearing it. An unknown like so many other unknowns, a way of proving him different when he wanted to be like everyone else, not provide another damning reason to judge the Vandersmas as "touched," "odd," "queer in the head" in some mysterious, indefinable way.

His grandfather's eyes cleared, his body relaxed. "Love? Is it the little Houwaert girl, that little Nelle who toted Henryk back to the house? A fine, well-built girl, that Nelle." A tiny lip smack of innocent pleasure, the hint of a wink.

"Think I like her," he muttered, dipped his head under the afghan to check on the ghatten and used the opportunity to side-glance his grandfather. "Think she might even like me." The warmth surged up his chest and neck, across his face to his hairline. No way she could ever like him, not ever, not when she knew about Kharm.

"Love is strange, eh? Well, love is a lot like an afghan—

amazing that something with so many holes in it can keep you toasty warm. Too solid and you'd have no space to breathe. Why, I remember when I courted your grandmother just after we'd landed, I used to shake and quiver, sweat and feel clammy all together, trip over my own oversized feet . . ." and the reminiscence wound on, safe and sane, secure and solid, no shifting ground of uncharted emotions to baffle him. The ghatten dozed, and the boy half-listened, wondering, wondering so many things.

The ghatten strained backward, coarse twine loop chafing under chin, clawed feet splayed in the dirt, neck trapped by the length of twine tethering her to Matty's hand. Eyes yellow-green as pine needles, circled by an edging of black, then pale buff, reproached, but Matty's mind remained silent, his own. He tugged again and her neck elongated, ears folding forward where the loop had risen, threatening to slip over her head. Her body didn't budge.

Henryk squatted, pinned spectacles to his nose with a dirty finger, fiddled with the bow behind one ear. "I don't think she likes it." Red-pink eyes peered over the lenses. "Fact is, I kin tell she doesn't like it, look at her ears." He picked at his sling, tucked his free arm inside to comfort himself.

Mouth slashing a parallel line with set, dark brows, Matty increased the tension on the twine. A contest of wills. "Granther said I couldn't take her out unless I leashed her, said she'd upset people, dash around, get into trouble. Can't afford that."

Utterly serious, Henryk's bare heels dug divots as he pivoted from one polarity to the other, measuring their willpower. "Mayhap if you asked her? I mean, *asked* her to come, she would. Nobody likes being dragged along, not having any say."

"Come on, Ryk-Ryk. She's an animal—and she's *got* to learn obedience." Still, despite his grandfather's words in his ears, he couldn't but wonder if Ryk traveled the right track while he floundered in the mud, mired by his own beliefs as to what was right and proper. Or what Granther deemed right and proper. Always the need for seemliness, propriety, especially as a Vandersma. Granther might not exhibit the taint, the oddities visited on his offspring, but Matty was all too aware of them. Not to mention the position encumbent upon him as grandson of the village mayor, purser from the Spacer *Antigua,* and Earth citizen. No wonder the village respected, looking up to, and even feared Granther at times.

"Come on, little one," he encouraged, trying to talk to her as she talked to him, without speaking aloud, littering the sharp, early morning air with their sounds. *"Please, I've got to show them there's nothing to fear from you. Or from me,"* he continued pleading silently, not expecting her to pay any heed. *"Make me proud, love. My perfect little striped Kharm-kitty. Act wild and they'll think it's true."*

"Silly!" the ghatten sneezed, sat down hard and began to scratch under her chin with a hind foot, digging at the loop around her neck. **"Silly them! Silly you!"** Rolling onto her back, she began to bat at the leash when it slackened above her head. **"Asking better than ordering. Why fear me? Why fear you?"**

Backing off, he pulled lightly at the leash. *"Then you'll come along?"* he asked inwardly, added a little tongue-clicking sound to entice her. *"Let me show you off. Show them how good you are, how clever."* An inspired pause. *"And how beautiful."*

"May ... be," she teased back but snapped to her feet, following at his heels as he began a slow, dignified walk down the dirt path that divided the village's hovels in half. Ryk capered in circles as they approached the central well that served the community of seventy-four souls. Matty caught his breath. There, drawing a second bucket of water, stood Vatersnelle Houwaert, sturdy bare legs splashed and glistening, feet muddy, as she swung the leathern bucket to the well's lip. Pressing the twine into Henryk's good hand, he rushed to help Nelle wrestle it clear.

With a jealous squawk at his desertion, the ghatten bounded after him, pulling the twine from Ryk's lax fingers. Before Matty knew it, the ghatten was clambering up his pants leg, tiny claws digging through the material, pricking tender skin. Unsure what else to do, he scooped her onto the narrow shelf of his shoulder where she twisted, finding her balance before settling to survey the view. Her claws stung, and he wished for a shirt for protection, better yet, a leather vest.

Nelle leaned near, nearer to Matty's face than he'd ever

had any right to dream, and cooed at the ghatten, traced a finger along Matty's neck and shoulder, teasing her. The ghatten pounced, and Matty winced with pain, a pleasure since it provoked Nelle's nearness. "She's so cute! I heard you'd found one alive. Are you going to keep her? What's her name?" she demanded. "I don't see how anything as little and sweet as that could be bad luck!" Her indignant face pressed next to Matty's. "You sweet thing, you," she crooned, lips practically touching his ear. His knees shook.

"Khar ... mmmm," he breathed back, stretching the "m" into a hum of contentment before ending on a rising inflection. "Kharm—that's her name." He hadn't told anyone else, not even his grandfather, not even Henryk.

She cocked her head, tried it out, working to elongate the last sound. "What does it mean?"

And Matty found himself at a loss, had no idea what, if anything, it meant except that the ghatten had shared her name with him. Did it have a meaning? He wasn't sure. But Henryk charged to his rescue. "It means 'O beauteous beast whose stripings mimic the shifting shadows and sunbeams that dance across the forest floor.' " Pale, near-invisible eyebrows shot skyward, daring contradiction. And Matty didn't, because somehow Henryk had the right of it, even if he hadn't realized it before. He nodded beneficently, as if to confirm Henryk's dutiful memorization.

The larchcat now draped like a fur collar, soft paws dandling his chest, Matty groped to prolong their visit. "Help you carry the water home?"

"No, I can ..." then she nodded, overwhelmed by shyness. "I'd like that. Mayhap I won't slop so much and Mama won't yell."

Intent on showing off his manliness, Matty caught up a bucket in each hand, sure his knees were going to buckle, his shoulders wrench out of their sockets. How could she manage this morning, noon, and night? But Nelle already stood beside him, large freckled hand clasped on the rope bail next to his, Henryk on his other side, his good arm trying to lift the other bucket. It helped—minimally. The three struggled, adjusting their strides, balancing the buckets level, and started down the main walkway, swinging wide to the right-angled path leading to the Houwaert hut.

The third one back, farthest from the main path, almost solitary from the other huts, and none of them noticed when

Rommel and Kuyper Killanin loomed in their path,
Rommel's ribs ringed with purplish-red and black bruises
where the earth had snatched at him, nearly devoured him as
it had Willem. That was why the hamlet felt so quiet this
morning, drawn in upon itself, mourning one of their own,
even if no one much cared for him. Later a collective sigh
of pent-up relief might ruffle the air that one less Killanin
existed, but for today, grief at the loss overrode pragmatism.

Kharm trilled deep inside Matty's head, a note of warning,
not quite fear, that jerked his eyes from Nelle's hand so
close beside his. **"Bad ones! Bad ones here!"** How could he
have forgotten the Killanins, forgotten that Willem lay dead?

Kuyper fingered the lump on his head, legacy of Nelle's
rock, and stood well away, though he still eyed her, smacking his lips, eyes rolling suggestively. Rommel planted
himself foursquare in their path, hands on hips. For once
both boys looked reasonably clean and combed. "Pa said to
remind yer granddad service'll be at sunset. If he ain't
nothing better to do, Pa'd 'preciate him givin' the words."
He hawked and spat, barely missing Matty's foot. His face
twisted, low brow knotting, mouth sour with the next
words. "And Mam says I'm to thank you for helping save
my life." A sullen half-glance, as if to judge whether someone watched from the hovel that served as the Killanin
home. His hand shot out, practically jabbing Matty in the
stomach.

Wonder of wonders, the hand was outstretched, not fisted,
but the stiff fingers just missed spearing him beneath the
ribs. Without breaking eye contact, Matty set down the buckets, brought his unwilling hand forward, and shook, debating
what to say. Damned if it'd be, "Sorry about Willem," when
he wasn't in the least, but some words of condolence, consolation were required. That was what being adult meant, swallowing the truth and saying the needful thing to keep the
social fabric intact. "Know you'll miss Willem, both of you.
Hard to lose a brother like that."

Inside his head words rang, cruelly chiming, reverberating,
**"Hate ya! Hate ya! Gonna get ya! Hadn't been for you
and your stupid white-belly uncle taunting us at the river,
none of this woulda happened! Crazy stupid Vandersmas
spread trouble, disaster, wherever they go. Oughta run ya
out of the village, not let your troubles, your craziness**

flood the rest of us! Well, beware! You're in for it now,
You'll pay for Willem's death!"

Spine prickling, the larchcat heavy-warm around his neck,
his mind jolted at the realization that Kharm plucked their internal thoughts and planted them inside his head, unmasking
the truth behind the offered hand he clasped, the seemingly
sorrowful face. The hairs on the back of his neck rose high
enough to mow. Worse, his own piously neutral platitudes
rang equally false. Starship shit! Kharm hadn't told Rommel
and Kuyper, had she? "No, no, no," the voice wreathed itself
inside his head. "Show you poison thoughts, fair outside,
foul within. Kharm always knows the truth, helps you
know the truth."

They towered over him, hands reaching, and Matty fought
not to take an involuntary step backward, betray his fear as
their hands dove at him. But to his amazement they each
grabbed a bucket, water slopping, and trudged toward the
Houwaert house with their burden. Kuyper swung back once,
a crest of hair climbing down over his low forehead. "We're
even now. So beware." Matty sought for Nelle's and Ryk's
hands. Somehow Ryk was crammed between them, burrowed
there for safety.

As if they played crack the whip, Nelle pivoted, swinging
Matty and Henryk around and away, voice urgent. "Come on,
come on! No sense giving them another opportunity. 'Less
you plan serving yourself to them on a platter."

"Platter-Matter! Matty on a platter!" Nerves high-pitched,
Henryk crowed as he pulled Matty after him. "Gardens?
Plenty of grown-ups there." And because Henryk constantly
searched out safe havens, Matty didn't resist, the larchcat
dangling around his neck, burdensome as the true thoughts of
the Killanin brothers.

They scuttled back to the square, ignoring those at the
well, and dashed right on the cross path toward the communal
fields planted between the town and the river. But there was
one more danger to avoid, and clearly many other townsfolk
had felt the same through the years, because a small, beaten
path wound off the main trail and its final house, aloof from
the rest of the village. The path swooped behind it, not a
shortcut but a longer way, albeit a safer one for not passing
by the front door.

Henryk sought the path instinctively and with good reason,
to Matty's mind. Mad Margare inhabited the final house—

trader in tattered, tatty odds and ends ("Trash or treasure,"
she'd cackle, waving the object aloft), beer brewer, mad-
woman, and sometime prostitute—though those reckless
enough to pay to be bedded showed true desperation by seeking oblivion in Marg's arms, safer to seek it in her beer—and
finally, Henryk's mother. Granther, he suspected but had
never dared ask, hadn't paid for Marg's services. Had lain
with her out of some strange, sorrowful compassion for her
"touched" mind, her craving for comfort and consolation as
great or greater than everyone else's. Some said she'd gone
mad because of the Plumbs, mind shaken lose of its moorings
the day of her precipitate and early borning, induced by the
explosion that had killed her parents. Others that she'd been
touched by the strange, inexplicable longing afflicting so
many of the planet's firstborns: the searing knowledge of two
perfect worlds lost—one far distant, the other here beneath
their feet, taunting with childhood memories of before the
Plumbs. One distant world they'd never see, not now, not
with the Spacers gone, and a world they tentatively lived in,
never sure if or when it could be put right. Why not give up,
go crazy, or decide everyone else owed you a living?

Although he'd been only seven, Matty distinctly remembered the morning Mad Marg had thrust her way into Granther's house, pushing him aside as he'd opened the door. Her
dark hair writhed and twisted around her shoulders, her face
swollen with tears, nose dripping as she bawled and screamed
like a mooncalf. Behind her she towed a makeshift child's
wagon, cobbled together from the odds and ends she'd found,
liberated, or collected and traded. Balanced on the wagon was
a willow basket, and inside that a tangle of rumpled sheeting,
cast-off clothes. And against the dirty rags a whiteness unlike
anything he'd ever seen, a white so pale he could almost stare
through it, trace tiny threadings of deep blue and red. Worst
of all then, the whiteness ghosted, shifted, opened a raw pink
mouth to scream, then relaxed weakly, tiny eyes like pink car-
nelians popping open. A baby! A boy baby, the strangest he'd
ever seen.

Granther had dropped the biscuit pan, scooped the child
into his arms. "Margy, Margy, are you all right?" he demanded, dandling the baby against his chest, narrow infant
shoulders lost behind the span of his hand. "Is it . . . he . . .
all right?"

"Your fault! Yours!" Marg's bare, dirty feet beat a tattoo

on the floor as she spun round in a desperate dance of expiation. "Paler than death! All *his* hopes, all *mine,* washed out! Washed clean away! Told you not to make love under the light of all Her moons, but you said no, 'twas superstition! She brings all sorts of bad things—the Plumbs, this! All gone wrong! Again!" Her breath hooted in great gasps, sobs wrenching her body. "Just keep him far away from me!"

And that was how Uncle Henryk had come to live with them. An icy ball bounded inside Matty's belly as they scurried along the path, Henryk shielding himself behind them. Nelle stroked his fine, old-man's hair, pulled the boy close to her sheltering side. And just as Matty thought they'd passed undetected, Mad Marg bustled out the back door, pan of wet clothes in hand, ready to hang them.

Never be rude to Margare, never taunt her, never rile her. She is what she is, and she can't help it. He'd heard Granther's words, obeyed the rules, the ones that allowed both Marg and the townspeople a modicum of dignity in any daily converse they might have. She has her place in life, you have yours. He plastered a smile on his face, willed his feet faster, the larchcat perched on his shoulders, watching the world flash by. Not another confrontation, please! Weren't the Killanins enough for one day?

But Marg spied them through the canebrake she cultivated to protect her backyard from trespassers, bulling through as if the brambles didn't scourge or sting her skin. What Matty vaguely recollected as a distant, disheveled beauty had long fled or lost itself in fat, loose flesh swinging from arms, unbound breasts momentously swaying beneath her loose dress. Mayhap, just mayhap, she hadn't spotted Henryk yet. Mayhap the larchcat would distract her. "Hurry!" he hissed. "Get along! I'll stay and talk with Marg!" But Henryk had already pulled Nelle into a trot, her youthful face distressed, unsure whether to stay or go.

"Morning, Mistress Margare." She stood, peering through the final layer of brambles, chewing reflectively on a split twig, one of her impromptu clothes-pegs. "Pleasant day, isn't it?"

A humming buzz arose from her throat, vibrated her lips. Please, he thought, don't let this be one of those days when she's forgotten how to talk. She hummed some more, then her mouth dropped open, the clothes-peg falling free.

"One less Killanin scum." Her face split in a sunny smile.

"Too bad the earth wasn't hungrier for the other ones. Indigestion, mayhap." She licked her lips to taste the thought. "Evil reaches out to evil. Oh, yes, that's why Marg's always so good!" A finger the size of a sausage darted in his direction. "What's that?" she shrilled, "What's that around your neck? It's alive, isn't it? It caught you, oh, oh!" She plunged onto the path, brambles bending, snapping, brandishing her fists as if to sweep Kharm off his neck, stomp her into the ground, and dance on the bloody shreds.

Unconcerned, Kharm jumped from his shoulder and he seized her in mid-flight, but she squirmed free and landed, a tiny ball of striped fur prancing toward Marg. And wonder of wonders, a bashful smile shimmered, her eyes seemed to clear, take on life, consciousness. Squatting, she dangled arms between ponderous thighs, urging Kharm forward with wiggling fingers.

"Poor twisted mind, poor clouded mind. Such sadness, so much fear masking such goodness. Can't help, oh, can't help enough, just smooth her as she smooths me." The ghatten let herself be cupped in those hands, cradled against Marg's heart, and a wild purring broke forth, Marg ecstatically swaying as if to a lullaby.

"Lost, alone, no Mama. Ah, I know how it is," Marg crooned between the pointed ears. Afraid it might go on forever, Matty didn't know what to do. Worst of all, he kept overhearing bits and pieces, stray thoughts that Kharm transmitted into his head from Marg's. Starry spaceships, would he end mad as she? A wave of taunts flooded him, threatened to swamp him, echoed and reechoed, trapped in his head. What Marg endured on an almost daily basis, what he'd sometimes heard directed at himself at a distance or at Henryk closer up. How could she stand it? Wisps of conversation . . . "Mad Marg, butt like a bullock, brain buzzed as a bee," right to her face, as if she didn't understand or care. How could he escape it all?

As if sensing a kindred sympathy, Marg rose with ponderous dignity, gravely handed Kharm back, touched his cheek with a finger. "How's my . . . boy? My Henryk?" A tear startled loose, carved its way down her face. "Take good care of him for me." And Matty backed away, nodding, smiling, more frightened of the new Marg than of the old one.

"New things, new thoughts are scarier than old ones. I

know. No ghatti's ever done what I've done," Kharm told him, but he didn't find it reassuring.

I daun no how much mawr of this i kin stand. How do u xcape it? How do u xcape the sounds inside yer hed? Or is that why Marg went mad? I love Kharm with al my hart and think mayhap i cld git usted to her beeing in my hed. But hauw did all the others git inside me? Evreone inside me— Granther, Ryk, Nelle, the whole village weather i want to here them or not. Wear can i go two xcape them? Must i wander in xile?

Matty ruminated over the words he'd written two octants past, paged forward through more recent entries, sparser than he liked, but all an equally repetitive refrain of fear. The world hadn't changed, had it? He'd been transmuted, transformed into something else—but what he still wasn't sure. If he'd pictured himself the odd one out before, the loner, outsider, that had been nothing compared to the dissonances clashing within him now.

"Not so bad, beloved, not so different." Kharm wreathed around him as he huddled on the floor in the corner of their hut. Almost half-grown now, long and limber, scrawny with rapid growth, kittenish antics and clumsiness mingled with the sure-footed stealth that was the hallmark of her breed. **"Don't you *want* to know what they *think*, not just what they say? Better to be warned, hear everything."**

"I don't want to know everything!" he 'spoke back, used to the outward silence that cloaked his inner turmoil. *"Besides, it's rude to hear their thoughts when they don't realize you're listening!"*

"Rude?" she pondered the idea. **"Rude to listen to every**

forest noise, sounds in the fields, in the sky? Any sound, every sound, could cry danger! If I didn't listen, I might not hear the fox's jaws snapping at my neck!" Front paws on his clasped knees, she stretched her cinnamon nose to touch his.

Irritable, he pushed her down, only to relent and scratch her ears. *"But you have to ignore things, at least we have to. If Ryk listened to each slight, each curse he heard, he wouldn't survive!"*

"Might survive better if he did! Not be hurt so much." He shook his head, lips tight. *"Oh, he'd have fewer bruises, but his soul'd be bruised even worse."*

"Rather pretend everything is pretty-seeming? Fox pretty-seeming, cheery red color, handsome white teeth in foxy smile. Fair without, foul within."

"Most of us humans are, love, as I'm sure you're discovering." He paused, tried to explain it. *"Just don't tell me everything people think unless you truly believe I should know. That it's a matter of life or death."*

"Matty? Are you in there, boy?" His grandfather stuck his head inside the door, squinting in the dimness. Guiltily, Matty squirmed and shoved the diary into the crack between floor and wall where it stayed safe from prying eyes.

"See what happens when I don't warn you?" Kharm crowed.

"Yes, Granther?" He rose reluctantly, tucking shirt into trousers. Weather grew much colder, his grandfather'd be sewing on the bottoms of his trouser legs soon. The trousers weren't as loose-waisted as they'd been at the beginning of the summer—a good sign. Mayhap he'd grown some after all. Or mayhap the shirt helped fill the waist. A wonder he hadn't shrunk, been reduced by the often unpleasant, even frightening thoughts Kharm shared.

"Coming to the meeting, Matty? Always proud with you at my side, and you've a right to a place since you reached fifteen." The door opened wider, Granther's large figure blocking the setting sun. "Should be a short one, that's why we decided to get it done before dinner." Still the eternal optimist, Matty thought sourly, even after all these years of loss and disappointment.

Lagging behind, Kharm at his heels, he followed his grandfather to the bonfire at the village's center, fully aware of the other figures already there, waiting for them. Thirty-nine adults would be the maximum turnout, although only slightly less than thirty had gathered; all ready to voice and vote on tonight's problems, accept Granther's word as law. That was all the law they had, based on the rules of confrontation and conciliation from Spacer life, although that assumed a higher authority on a distant planet or a higher-ranking spaceship. Here, the entire burden was theirs, each to care for the other, each responsible for the other, including the meting out of punishment, from censure to fines of reparation to death.

Matty sat cross-legged, as unobtrusive as possible at the rear. No sense having Granther accused of favoritism if he pushed any closer. His age earned him this space. Besides, he enjoyed it back here now that mosquito season had ended, darker, easier to concentrate on both the external and the inner voices Kharm relayed. What troubled him was his increasing inability to clamp down on his tongue when he heard an egregious falsehood, an out-and-out lie, whether intentional or something wrongheadedly believed. Spacer's glory, he tried, but sometimes he couldn't contain himself, the falsehood unbearable, so he stood and waited diffidently to be recognized, asked a leading question, desperate not to reveal the wrongness of a person's statement. Often an innocent question or two lured others onto the track that had been laid, the scent of falsehood carrying them on. Never yet had he directly confronted anyone, stood toe to toe with them and called them liar at these council meetings.

Worst of all he was building a reputation as a canny young man, a youth with a ripe head on his shoulders. Ripe as a melon and ready to split, more likely. And while this new reputation should have pleased him, evidence he wasn't like his spoony-loony father or his odd little uncle, he felt set apart. Set apart by knowledge that he shouldn't have, didn't deserve, illicit knowledge from Kharm that made him a phony, a cheat. That they could hail him as a young man on the rise, one of their best, one of their own, only pointed out how truly different he was.

Wrapped in three shawls, Josee Killanin stood, waiting for recognition, a drab, washed-out woman who looked incapable of having borne such strapping, healthy, and mean specimens as Rommel, the late Willem, and Kuyper. Appearances deceived, because she harbored a bitter meanness the way a dull, dingy little viper harbors its poison. What her placid, stay-at-home husband, obviously at their own hearth cooking dinner, had contributed to the boys' personalities was unclear.

A reluctant nod from Amyas Vandersma, and she spoke. "Don't ye think it right and proper Mad Marg move along to another village now? Them as have the 'evil eye' shouldn't be allowed to settle too long in any one place—best they wander, spreading their evil thins it out, makes it bearable." When Amyas opened his mouth to interrupt, she overrode him. "Oh, I know some don't hold with such things as evil eyes, but some do believe. Many," she emphasized. "Whether Marg means it or not, is one thing, but 'twas her caused Spence's cow to calve too soon this spring, a calf we couldn't afford to lose. And we've all seen her squinting, muttering time and time again since spring. How long're we to wait for worse? Burrowing round like a groundhog and hiding things. How long afore she digs up a Plumb, sets one off, and another of my sons dies?"

Hands on hips, she played for the crowd's support. "Well, share and share alike, I always say, and it's time some other village took her in, took care of her. Winter soon, and you know what that means," a pregnant pause designed to let the women grasp her point.

What it meant was that with the coming winter and time on their hands, some of the men and older boys would start frequenting Marg's hut, drinking, dicing, indulging in a slap and tickle with Marg. Most of them reaped a slap from her, but a few, a very lucky few received a tickle instead.

"First of all, Miz Killanin, her name's Margare Wyngate, not Mad Marg." Striving for neutrality, Amyas ventured a mild reproof. "Secondly, most of us accept bad luck for what it is—bad luck—not the result of some mythical evil eye. And finally, Miz Wyngate always supports herself, earns her own keep, whether you approve of her methods or not. None of us has to have dealings with her unless we so choose. The few times she couldn't support herself, we've all pitched in to help, just as we've helped others caught in the same pinch—yourself included."

Kharm butted Matty's elbow, **"Want to know? Want to know or not?"** Come to think of it, the larchcat had been remarkably circumspect so far tonight, but his own thoughts crowded so thick he'd scarce noticed. Without waiting for an answer, she burst out, **"Jealous old shrew! Greedy, too!**

Pushing Marg out of her nest, wants to claim it herself. Easier than making her own nest winter-tight. Doesn't care if Marg finds another place, dies in the snow or not! Hopes she does!"

The woman had the grace to color at Amyas's carefully chosen words, not a full blush because she was too worn for that, but flushed patches stained her cheeks, as if Amyas's retort had stung like a slap. "I'm worried about the morals of our young ones, most of all. How can they resist if she sets her eye on them, fills them with perverted thoughts? All well and good to have her here for a time, but seems her time must be up. Eight years is long enough!"

Though he didn't want to, Matty had risen, waited until she turned to gauge who would support or deny her plea. "Miz Killanin, Miz Wyngate has many good points, although they're sometimes a trifle hard to appreciate at first glance. Look at what a tight, cozy cottage she's built all by herself. No evil eye could help do that. Why, I'm sure she could offer sound advice on improving your cottage, what with winter coming on. If you don't start soon, the snow'll be sifting through your roof and the wind whistling through your walls before you know it. Late in the season to build a new one, and it's not as if we have any empty cottages to spare."

A guffaw rang on his right, a smothered chuckle farther along. Maxwell Denster waved to be recognized. "Marg brings us to repentance sometimes, but it's our fault for drinking too much of her beer. Can't blame a hangover on the evil eye. What say we get up a work party with Marg Wyngate in charge to winterize the Killanins' house? After all, you don't need a license to live anywhere, your license is that you're a productive member of the community, and that Miz Wyngate is." Amyas called for a show of hands and it was quickly settled.

Head buried in hands, Matty sat quietly through the rest of the meeting, praying nothing more would interest Kharm. He was fast approaching a decision, had sensed it building but had refused to acknowledge it.

"And now that Miz Killanin—as well as her boys—has taken a hatred to you, it might be just as well."

This time he accepted the truth, because he'd finished arguing in his head, was sore weary of it. No sense arguing with the ghatta as well when she was right. *"I'm scared she or the boys'll take it out on Ryk to spite me. Maybe with me gone they'll find someone else to torment."*

"Where are we going?" The ghatta sounded excited.

"Don't know. Anywhere, everywhere. Mayhap look for my father. Look for someplace that respects the truth, is willing to hear it, no matter how much it hurts—if there is such a place."

"If there isn't, we could make our own, couldn't we?"

Men and women streamed by, clutching papers, precariously balancing stacked folders. They, at least, looked purposeful, as if they belonged. It was he and his fellow petitioners who looked out of place, drifting, eddying into each other's paths, struggling to claim comfortable places on the benches along the walls, or crowding the tables where they left their names. These were the outer waiting rooms to the High Conciliators' offices, shared waiting rooms at that, Bazelon Foy realized. A mate to this one stood across the hall, and from the hollow footsteps overhead, the stair traffic, another matched set occupied the floor above him. Four waiting rooms, twenty-four provinces, six provinces congregating in each room, all eager to press their own individual requests, pleas, permissions, favors. Tadj stirred nervously beside him, protective of the straw-stuffed wooden box sheltered between his feet.

"Get along with you, find something else to occupy your time." A hand under Tadj's elbow levered him to his feet, the younger man rising with a smoothly compressed tension that garnered more than a few admiring looks. "It's going to be a long wait. I'm sure you could put it to better use elsewhere, but be circumspect." Baz's lips curved in a cherry-red smile, richly rosy, well aware of the contrast they made, his olive complexion, sleek-curved features, and mass of curly dark locks against Tadj's pink and white sharp profile, his carefully combed, fine blond hair pomade-slicked but fighting its confinement.

"If you're sure . . ." the younger journeyman hesitated, fingers playing with a high collar marred by two tiny punctures barely visible in the navy fabric. "I don't mind waiting, would hate for you to be bored." For Baz bored was likely to be Baz dangerous, mercurial, ready to erupt with joy or wrath depending on the occasion, the cause. But it was all worth it in the end, for he'd never met anyone with Bazelon Foy's charisma and magnetism—such beauty, such strength of purpose, his single-minded ability to conquer a problem. Ever since that first day at the glassworks, Tadj's devotion was absolute, both to the man and to his cause, their cause. He ventured, "You're a close friend of Darl Allgood's. I can't believe he's making you wait this long." Tadj was outraged at the thought that anyone could deny the demands of this bronzed god whose wisdom and actions soared so high above most shallow, unenlightened human planes. And now Baz was encouraging him to test his own wings, giving him more latitude in the cause, as long as he met his sales quotas.

Baz tucked the wooden box safely under his seat, rested a heel on the edge. "I am, but good friends don't presume, push themselves forward, cry for notice. All the High Conciliators have constituents to hear when they're not in meetings, council sessions. It's part of the price they pay. Darl'll get to me when he can. After all, I'm only here to tender my good wishes." It sounded convincing, even to himself, and it was mostly true, but the waiting rankled. Taking off a rich cocoa velvet jacket that denoted his stature, a prosperous member of the Artisans' Ward, he folded it across the back of the bench, pushed up his shirtsleeves to reveal smooth, muscular arms. "So go along with you, drum up some business. And remember, there's business and there's business, and you know which is more important."

Tadj nodded and slipped through the crowd like a child released from lessons. Thoughtfully, Baz tapped his lip with a forefinger, kissing it as he noticed a shapely young woman watching him. Pennington Province, he'd bet a copper on it, by her garb. Send Tadj Pomerol there to drum up sales? No, north or northwest might be better. Harsh mountain land bred equally harsh, uncompromising individuals, who didn't relish change, disruption. He smiled at the woman, a secret, inviting smile that made her tremulous, and then sat back, let his mind wander, sick and tired of the seething humanity, the waiting and wanting that clogged the air with need. He didn't *want* anything, he only wanted to *give* Darl something, something very precious.

Pillowing his head on an arm folded behind him, he lazed against the hard bench. To have advanced so far—literally

and figuratively—to have journeyed to a new land and reclaimed his heritage, to have risen so high in the world so
quickly, and he had Darl Allgood to thank for much of it, for
inspiring him, guiding him along the right paths. That other
life, that earlier life, a squalid, oppressive nightmare. . . .

The baby's cry came high and demanding, splitting the air
as Baz knelt beside his grandfather's pallet, sponging the
lined face. Not a breeze stirred the fronds of the hut, the air
weeping humidity, filming everything with moisture. Methodically he dipped the cloth and wrung it, wiped the face.
Funny to add water to something already damp with sweat,
but his mother said the evaporation cooled. He wiped his
own forehead with the rag but couldn't feel a difference. The
wailing rose another notch, thin and querulous—and constant. "Baz! Do something about the baby, will you?" his
mother called from outside where she stirred a boiling pot of
corn mush, looking so limp that she herself might melt into
the pot.

"Ya," he called back, although he didn't move. Damn
baby always squalling because of the heat, body prickly pink
with rash. Damn baby. His grandfather needed him more, the
fever and chills almost entirely immobilizing him, weakening the already weak legs. *He* didn't cry and bawl, complain,
appreciated whatever Baz did for him. He worshiped his uncompromising grandfather, hated to see him laid low in this
pitiful thatched hut village, some perched on stilts by the
river's mouth, others looking like haystacks dumped on
marshy ground. Damn Sunderlies, damn them for being
here. Was the whole world like this soggy, steaming, heat-
plagued place? Not Canderis, according to his grandfather,
but his grandfather had willingly given that up to do what he
thought right, had acted on his convictions even though it
meant exile to the Sunderlies. The Sunderlies were all that
Baz had ever known in his ten years, all that his mother had
known as well, born here two years after his grandfather, her
father, had been deported, left to survive on these shores as
best as he could.

"Baz, the baby!" He jumped guiltily, racing from his
grandfather's hut and into the only marginally larger one that
housed his family, mother, father, and four children, including Baz. He snatched the baby from its basket and bundled
it against his sweat-slicked chest, the baby flailing in a paroxysm of gassy pain, kinking like a slippery eel, fighting ev-

ery gesture of comfort. He patted the rash-covered bottom
and the baby howled louder, tiny fists pounding and shoving
as he eased him higher on his shoulder. The baby drew spindly legs tight to its belly, shoved against Baz's ribs, and to
Baz's shock the infant arched backward over his restraining
arm, landing with a thud on the packed earth floor.

The cries ceased, the thatched hut silent except for the
rustle of lizards and insects, tiny hopping rodents roaming
the thatch. He touched the baby's head, the soft spot his
mother always warned him about; it felt softly ripe, like a
crushed melon under his fingers. He hadn't intended it,
hadn't meant it to happen, but he was glad. Another reason
gone why he and his family couldn't make the arduous trip
back to Canderis, even if it meant abandoning his grandfather. But that was what his grandfather wanted for them and
Baz would obey.

"Ma, Ma, I think the baby hurt himself," he called outside, and shoved thoughtfully at his brother with his bare
toe, composed his face for grief.

No, he hadn't intended the first death, a fortuitous accident, but after the first death it was easy. And they were better off dead because they sapped his strength of purpose, his
and his grandfather's purpose, the triumphant return to the
promised land. After all, one crushed mosquitoes so they
wouldn't feed off you. His little sister, only three, conve-
niently wandered behind the spavined mule while Baz cur-
ried it, just happened to rub the raw gall spot that made the
mule lash a hind hoof like a crazy demon. He'd cried when
they buried her, his tears for the mule that his father had
beaten to death in his grief. They'd needed the mule more
than his sister. As for his eight-year-old brother, drowning
was simple enough; Baz affixed a short length of rope to the
sunken coral in the lagoon and enticed his brother to dive
with him to see what it was. What the noosed end captured
was his brother's ankle, stranding him beneath the surface.
The water churned blue-green, bubbles rapidly billowing,
frothing, until at last they subsided, smooth and calm. Easy
enough to dive to him, slide the noose free, let the body pop
to the surface for the tide to bring home.

It had taken longer, though, to decide how to separate his
parents from their spendthrift, lazy, carefree life, though
abruptly less carefree with three children suddenly dead.
They lacked ambition, drive, the desire to get ahead. Work—

whatever for? Each paltry project they undertook fell to pieces for lack of planning, follow-through, concentration. Their haphazard attempts at betterment left him writhing with shame, his grandfather cursing their feckless ways under his breath. They couldn't manage themselves, let alone money. Each octant his grandfather carefully doled out his pension, his share from the Samranth glassworks partnership, to cover his care, his food, and shelter, and his daughter squandered it in a flash. His grandfather put it down to an excess of Sunderlies blood in his daughter and her husband, and Baz lived in terror that it had infected him as well, though his grandfather swore Baz resembled a younger version of himself. How the old man ranted and railed, wished for strength to return to Samranth and his old life.

His grandfather had given him some cullet, glass scraps from the old works, to play with, but Baz had carefully saved them in a pouch, treasure of things past, a promissory note to the future. But he willingly sacrificed the cullet to a greater end: the removal of his parents. All afternoon in a secluded mango grove he patiently rolled a cast-iron pipe fragment back and forth over the cullet, crushing the glass smaller and finer, finer and smaller, until it resembled powdery sugar. With the side of his hand he'd gently brushed it into the folded scrap of paper salvaged from the hut. He'd hated to take it, crease it, because it announced his grandfather's coming to the Sunderlies along with others convicted of the same crime: the premeditated murder of fifty Gleaners in Canderis. His grandfather had sounded very brave and righteous, a leader of men was Hosea Bazelon. He'd scraped the side of his hand sweeping the glass powder onto the paper, hoped the blood smears wouldn't obliterate too much of the story, despite the fact he'd committed it to memory.

His parents thanked him profusely for the berries he'd collected that night for dessert and the sugar so thoughtfully earned, a neighbor's payment for chores done. Baz refused the berries, saying he was full, and his grandfather refused because they gave him the grippe, so all the more for his parents. They spooned the sugar on, spooned down the berries and sugar with greedy delight. A shame the racket they made that night as they writhed with pain, vomiting blood, doubling over with cramps. And Hosea Bazelon said nothing as he hobbled around, helping Baz clean up after them, wash and shroud the bodies. Soon after that they'd stuffed their few possessions into baskets and sacks, hailed an outrigger to sail them downriver to Samranth, the capital on the coast. Though a wide sea still intervened, he was that much closer to Canderis.

Back in the present, back in the waiting room outside the High Conciliators' offices, Baz squirmed, set ankle across knee and tossed his arms over the bench back, totally comfortable, at ease and immersed in the past. Those pains and privations made for pleasurable recounting since he knew the ending was happy, so right, so richly deserved. And he deserved so much more, as did the man who'd helped him rise. The number of people waiting had thinned, the slant of light at the windows showed it was late afternoon. Yes, Darl would see him soon. Good friends didn't presume on each other, and after Darl understood what he offered, he'd never have to wait again. Darl would be as indebted to him as Baz was indebted to Darl. Eyes drifting closed, he slid into the past as gently as he'd slid back under the waves of the lagoon to retrieve his brother's body. His cherry-red lips formed a silent giggle.

The Sunderlies: home of Canderis's castoffs, the violent and murderous, the recalcitrant who could not or would not obey the nation's laws. Such misfits faced deportation to the Sunderlies; and Canderis congratulated itself on its humane treatment of criminals, not demanding a life for a life as it had during the early settlement days. What the native Sunderlies thought of this influx of less-than-model citizens was never recorded, but since most of them lived deep in the jungle and beyond along the vast grazing plains, only those on the coast learned to adapt and thrive, interbreeding and learning lawlessness at the same time.

A certain amount of trade sprang up between Canderis and the Sunderlies, a demand for native crafts, intricate wood inlays, metalwork, with deported convicts and their offspring serving as the merchanter middlemen. A few hearty Canderisians eager for adventure and profits came voluntarily, set up stores or manufactures. And it was with Namrath Gilden, a voluntary exile, who'd originally partnered Hosea Bazelon in the glassworks before his grandfather had retired, sold his share. Namrath had handled the glassmaking, and Baz's grandfather saw to the accounts, sought out profitable sales opportunities.

Despite his recurrent fever fits, Hosea Bazelon was welcomed back as a limited partner, and Baz discovered the first real happiness he'd known. The mysteries of glass—from its liquid, flowing potentialities to its crystalline final form, strong yet fragile—captivated him and he quickly mastered its intricacies. He equally enjoyed the rigorous precision of accounting, the subtleties of salesmanship his grandfather taught him. With these distractions Baz could almost forget that they languished in the Sunderlies, postpone his desire to go to Canderis, because he'd finally realized that his grandfather could never return. *That* was the depth of his sacrifice for acting to save his land.

On Baz's fifteenth birthday his grandfather died, the first death he truly mourned—perhaps because he'd had no control over it. For the first time he felt truly empty, hollow, no one left to hate or love. Namrath had offered him Hosea's position, but Baz had rebelled. Namrath served as an end to a need—and most of all he couldn't bear losing his bond with glass, so malleable to his efforts. And each malleable, liquid flow expanded into a thing of wonder in his hands—so it should be with all things.

"I don't mind selling, but I'm not giving up my blowpipe," he'd told Namrath, wearing his singed leather apron and his leather furnace gloves like a second skin.

Sometimes Namrath's features seemed to swim amongst the large pores on his face, gray-blue eyes watery under the sweatband. "Could really expand, have the orders roll in if you'd set your mind to selling, Baz. Not just the expates, but think of the natives, who don't even know what they're missing. Jars with ground glass stoppers to keep the moisture and bugs out of their rice and cornmeal, bottles to hold their liquor, glass ornaments to bedeck themselves." His eyes had a greedy, faraway look. "If your grandfather hadn't retired that first time, that's what he'd planned to do. Too sick to do it when he came back."

He contemplated seizing control of the glassworks if something should happen to Namrath—his skills, his force of personality, his drive—it was possible, despite his youth. But Namrath had something else worth bartering, whether he realized it or not. "I want to learn everything I can to create beauty, that's what I truly want. You're good, but you lack the artistry, the imagination to soar. Namrath, I'll make you a bargain, find me a place in Canderis where I can learn, a place to stay, and a bit of money to live on until I get my feet under me, and you can have my share in the works."

Namrath had rolled a pontil between his palms, thoughtful, greed slackening his jaw. "Law of Return says any convict's offspring has the right to reside in Canderis, if so desired, as long as the person doesn't bear a grudge from the past. Don't want to lose you, but want you to be happy," and Baz could tell that Namrath was somehow afraid of him, in the same way he'd always been covertly fearful of Hosea Bazelon. Those here voluntarily never forgot they dealt with convicts and the offspring of convicts. "My niece just married a young man in Wexler. He's been elected as Chief Conciliator, no less. The glassworks in Wexler won't teach you everything, but it'll start you learning some things you don't know. Could write and see if Annette and Darl would board you."

❧

"My Foy, Mr. Foy, the High Conciliator will see you now." The young woman in clerical garb reached for his shoulder, as if drawn to his beauty, yes, how he knew the reaction, but he smiled and stretched, deflected her hand with his. The direct contact provided a deeper thrill.

"Thank you." He rose and stretched expansively, let the thin lawn shirt stretch across his chest, hint at the olive skin, the sprigs of dark chest hair beneath it. She was fumbling for the box under the bench, but he beat her to it, lifted it protectively. "Don't tell me old Darl's such a hard taskmaster that he makes you fetch and carry packages, too?" and watched color rise from her throat to the roots of her undistinguished, ill-cut sandy hair. "But you will lead the way, won't you? After all, I'm a stranger, a provincial, and in need of your guidance. And perhaps later . . ." he left the thought delicately unfinished as he followed her down the hall.

"Baz!" Darl Allgood pushed away from a battered deal desk, high-stepped over piles of paper as he made his way to the door. Bazelon Foy stood stock-still, anticipating the embrace that would reassure him he was loved, for finally he'd encountered a man he respected and adored, a man who replaced a weak father, brother, and almost, even, the commanding presence of his grandfather. Arms tight around Darl's shoulders he rocked, comforted and comforter. Darl, who saw only the good in him, forced him to be better than he thought he could be. Darl, who ignored the dark places in his heart, or spontaneously forgave them without digging at them. Absolution. Not that he needed absolution, for he'd done nothing wrong, everything was done for a reason, a righteous reason that assuaged his wants and needs. But still, if those dark places existed—as Hosea Bazelon had insisted they did in every man's soul—Darl Allgood turned them into light with his unaccusatory, nonjudgmental ways. Strange, when judgment was his calling.

He hugged tighter, frightened by the thinness, the slack flesh, finally leaned back to examine the face, so careworn in so short a time. What did this job demand of this man? Overwork, no exercise, shoddy eating habits, mental distress. That burden he could ease. "I could count off more reasons than the Lady has Disciples, Darl, why it's good to see you." He pounded lightly on Darl's chest with his fist. "You ran off to take this job without even saying good-bye, and I've had no chance to come to Gaernett to congratulate you."

Darl motioned him to a chair, cleared a corner of his desk, and hopped on it, perching as he was wont to do. "Things came up rather suddenly, Baz. And is it my fault that you're such a prosperous businessman—no, artist extraordinaire— that you spend too much time away from Wexler, promoting your genius? Did I complain all those times you deserted Annette and me while you made your rounds to drum up business?"

"I know, and I had no right to think your home and hearth would always be there to welcome me, no matter where I wandered or for how long." Momentary panic seized him, searching, scanning. The wooden box! What had he done with it? It must have slipped from his grasp when he'd hugged Darl—had he dropped it? It sat beside the door, and he breathed a sigh of relief. It looked intact, as if he'd set it down unheeded in the emotional turmoil of greeting Darl. "I brought something for you, something to honor your new position but remind you of your past." He flourished a circular penknife with a crescent blade and cut the ropes, pried the box open, straw spilling out. Reminded him of that secretary's hair, just as untidy and stiff.

Darl watched with the wholehearted anticipation of a child, and Baz adored him for that. Always curious how something worked, be it machine or mind, how things were constructed, even if he had no idea how to do it himself, always willing to listen to his complaints and joys when Baz pondered a problem at the glassworks, a new technique that had failed or shown unexpected consequences.

The decanter's body was a long, sleek ovoid, tapering into a graceful neck. Grape leaves etched the sides, a meandering thread of glass forming its stem, the veining of the leaves. The four balloon goblets stood pure, unadorned except for a leaf etched on the bottom of each balloon, visible only when the drink had been consumed. Darl took one with reverence, held it to the light, its sides so thin he appeared to look through air, no flaws or imperfections there to refract the light.

"Baz," Darl's awe was genuine, unfeigned, and it warmed Baz's heart, thawed the lonely place, almost erased the abandonment. "It's peerless, absolutely incomparable. Your finest work. Breathtaking." He rolled the stem between his fingers. "To drink from this is almost like having nothing between you and the wine."

"And speaking of drinking," Baz rummaged in the corner of the box, reverently presented the bottle in both hands, "I hope you haven't traveled so far from your roots that you no longer keep a corkscrew around. We need to toast your new position."

Filled glasses in hand, they sampled one of Wexler's finest vintages, savoring it, savoring the companionship. Despite his resolve, Baz couldn't help bringing up the subject, probing at it like a sore tooth. "I confess, in a way, I thought I might be elected Chief Conciliator in your stead. Although Elgar's certainly competent," he hastened to add. "Somehow I thought you ... that you, well, you know, might put in a good word for me, mention my name ... but I suppose you didn't have time before you left." The dark, liquid eyes revealed hurt, almost imperceptible betrayal. But oh, his willingness to forgive, he let it shine out of him, hopeful.

The half-glass of wine had relaxed Darl, moderated some of his strain and worry. He played with the glass, holding it to the light, beaming at its perfect balance. "It's not up to me to influence the voters and you know it, that would have been an abuse of my position." He shifted, cast a sidelong glance at the younger man, assessing him. "Besides, the position of Chief Conciliator is a full-time job. I can't believe you'd give up your art—or your commerce. It's always astounded me how you juggle both so gracefully, not have one overwhelm the other."

"I'd have given it up in the blink of an eye to follow in your footsteps, be like you." Pain, passion, and pride in the words.

Darl sat straighter, relaxation gone, posture uncomfortably formal. "Thank you for the compliment, but you're not like me, Baz, we're very different people. Very different," he emphasized as if depths existed that Baz could never plumb. Ah, try me, he wanted to cry. "You have a certain reputation for caring and compassion," he swallowed, "most of the time. But you also unveil a temper, a consuming rage on occasion, no matter how you try to hide it. You're impetuous, subject to strong emotion, determined to have your own way, no matter how 'oh-so-politely' you go about it. It's not often, but when it happens, people notice, mark the shift. And that absolutely won't wash for a Chief Conciliator. A Chief Conciliator must be neutral, unswayed by emotion, capable of enforcing the letter of the law equitably." He appealed to Baz, "Don't you think you might find that a bit . . . taxing at times?"

Baz had the grace to look guilty, a simulation he'd learned to master well. "I suppose," his reluctance clear, "because I know when I'm right, and it takes a passionate man to listen to his own heart, not be swayed by the petty proprieties that rule others." He shrugged. "Well, you're probably right," and let it drop with an easy wave of his hand, as if he could dissolve it in the air, and changed the subject.

"So, how does it stand with the Glea . . . Resonants, Darl?"

Now it was Darl's turn to withdraw, the lines around his eyes, between his brows, deepening. "It won't be easy, it won't come fast," he took a deep breath, "but we have to make them an integral part of society, accepted by all."

"Accepted by all?" Incredulous, Baz splashed wine as he refilled their glasses. "Accepted by none is more likely. Lady sustain and guide us, Darl, be careful about thinking thoughts like that!" Hitching his chair closer, intimate and confiding, "I travel, Darl, I see and hear what people are feeling, and it's not acceptance, believe me. They remember trade being cut off with Marchmont; they remember their fears on discovering that Marchmont boasts Resonants. And the final straw was discovering them hidden in our midst. Best be rid of them completely, then people could breathe easier."

"And how do you propose we accomplish that? Resurrect your grandfather's zealotry, Baz?" Flooded with disappointment, Darl fought it, swallowed it whole, his throat raw at the effort. "I thought, I hoped I'd dissuaded you from such ugly biases, convinced you to be tolerant and nonjudgmental until you knew a person. That's what a Chief Conciliator must do. Do you *know* any Resonants?"

Despite Darl's attempt at calmness, the vehemence of his words, the implied reproach assailed Baz. Never before had Darl brought up his heritage, thrown it in his face like that. Hosea Bazelon's memory was sacred, a hero who did what had to be done, no matter the cost to him. So, the true gift he'd brought to Darl with all his heart to lay at his feet was unwanted before he even unveiled it—that he, Bazelon Foy, had already put into motion a plan to rid Canderis of Resonants. Relieve Darl of his worries and fears, sweep the land clean. It could be done, the culmination of his grandfather's dreams, and he'd already begun the task. He opened his mouth to speak, but no words came.

"Well, do you?" Darl pushed unmercifully, his words hammering at him, "Do you?"

"But you're here as a High Conciliator to protect us!"

"I'm here to protect both sides, all Canderisian citizens. And we don't even always know who's Us and who's Them, who's a Normal and who's a Resonant." Darl looked drained. "Don't you yet understand that you can't judge by your own moral code, that your code isn't everyone's?"

Baz's chair scraped as he meticulously set his glass on the desk, fought the urge to break Darl's for sullying it. "No, but perhaps it should be. There are times when being impartial isn't enough, Darl, when you have to be a partisan for a cause, when that cause is just." He walked to the door, refused to look back. Ah, he'd misjudged, misjudged Darl all along while worshiping him. So wrong, and turbulence built inside him, destroying the walls of love he'd constructed around his hero, leaving him naked to the winds of change.

At last he trusted himself enough to say as he left, "I wish you well, Darl, and pray the blinders drop from your eyes."

Hard to see through the haze of grief and burning hurt enshrouding him, emotions almost palpable, craving release. Thankfully, the day's business was almost over, the halls and waiting rooms practically empty, except for a bobtailed ghatta and a frizzy, red-haired fool stumping along on crutches. Baz's momentum swept him into the cripple's path and he crushed him in a bear hug to keep him upright. A reason to explode—the idiot'd walked right in his way—but he'd not prove Darl right. "My apologies, sir." He strangled on the words, "Bazelon Foy regrets the inconvenience," and made sure the man was steady before rushing on. Somehow he reached the doors without brushing against anyone else, giving him a reason to detonate, release the upheaval inside.

Tadj was waiting patiently outside. "Did he listen to you?"

"No." His tone slashed at his assistant.

But Tadj was familiar with his superior's emotions. "Then we'll have to give him a reason to believe, won't we?"

With short, panting breaths, Baz labored to control himself, but the litany running through his mind sang, "I'll show him, I'll show him—see how he likes it to be called a Resonant!" The need to hurt back for being hurt pounded in his veins, set his skin tingling. "Tadj," he asked, nostrils flaring with the effort to draw air into his lungs, "how'd you like to write a letter for me? A very special letter." Yes, let Darl *experience* the distress he'd caused him, wallow in the hurt of misjudged motives. Be misjudged, suffer as he'd caused Baz to suffer. Under most circumstances he'd prefer something shorter, quicker, more decisive, but this . . . just might be a fitting repayment for betrayal, for the destruction of love.

Jenret Wycherley sprawled in an easy chair, wishing someone would order more cha. Anything to stimulate him after that harrowing all-night ride with Faertom from the Research Hospice. The detour to Hylan Crailford's house and the ensuing arguments had given them a late start. Only his promise to Doyce had forced him on—and now this, this ridiculous delay in the Monitor's office!

How could they dawdle with everything so crystal-clear?

His eyes felt gritty, permanently narrowed from squinting through the night, face raw from a gusting east wind that had almost propelled them sideways at times. His clothes, his crisp, black tunic and pantaloons plus the black sheepskin tabard, Lady bless, they should be line-hung and beaten for days before he even considered washing them. Dirt, untidiness set his teeth on edge, gave him something to concentrate on instead of what was—or wasn't—happening around him. Best get used to dirt, a baby by its very nature was untidy, messy, leaky. And he smiled. From where he sat on the bench, Faertom didn't look any better served than he, head lolling against the wall, eyes almost closed, the rest of him no more easeful than Jenret felt.

What had possessed him to ride directly to the Monitor's offices, rather than hurrying to Doyce? He'd pay for that, no doubt about it, until he convinced her of the importance of his news. There'd been no choice, the precedence clear in his mind. Except his mind wasn't Doyce's, and he had yet to truly ken how hers worked. He managed a dry, hard swallow. And still, and yet, the desire for more cha eclipsed every other worry and doubt, betrayed by bodily weakness. Parched, so thirsty he longed to stick the spout of the near-empty cha pot between his lips and pour the dregs down his throat. Obsessed by cha! With a groaning stir, Faertom stretched and gave him a wink. "If you don't mind, sir," he offered in the Monitor's direction, "I'll see if I can't find a servant, have more cha brought up. We had a powerful dry ride."

"What? Oh." The Monitor, Kyril van Beieven, scarcely stirred, eyes downcast, clasped hands resting on the desk in front of him, mired in deep thought. The other member of their early-morning foursome, Darl Allgood, one of the High Conciliators, shot a brisk, dismissive nod in Faertom's direction and he slipped out.

"Kyril." Again Allgood tried, more insistent, "Kyril! If you've more questions for Wycherley and Faertom, ask them. Don't sit there in a brown study. If not, dismiss them, let them eat breakfast and go to bed." The unassuming man with his hairline fast creeping back on both sides of his forehead had a compelling voice, energizing Jenret, making him marshal his own exhausted thoughts. He'd not expected van Beieven to be up so early, the sun not even risen, let alone Allgood beside him, but the two had been working when they'd arrived. Perhaps they'd never even been to bed. By now the rising noises throughout the Monitor's Hall indicated the morning had progressed, everyone else was up, starting their day. What was it about Allgood—nothing sinister, nothing like that, but something that left him supremely uneasy, as if secrets were stockpiled within, though he didn't dare pry to loosen them.

Rawn stretched fore and aft at his feet, a black lightning bolt on the carpet. **"Don't worry about Doyce."** Jenret jerked upright, his preoccupation with Allgood had driven Doyce from his mind. **"I 'spoke Khar as soon as we were close enough for my mindvoice to reach. When she awakes, she'll know you're here. Khar wanted her to sleep as much as possible. She's been restless lately, can't get comfortable. She'll be in the library when you're free."**

"Thank you, old ghatt." Grateful, Jenret rumpled Rawn's ears and the black ghatt reciprocated by gnawing on his knuckles, bit down too hard. His "Ouch!" came out loud, sharper than he'd intended.

"And that's for thinking anything's odd about Allgood. He's fine, perfectly trustworthy. His difference is not your concern."

Jenret's pained exclamation had roused the Monitor more effectively than Allgood's entreaties. He sighed, leaned back to examine the ceiling, and Jenret was amazed at how much the Monitor had aged since spring. He'd always had the fine, crinkling lines around the eyes, from weather as much as from age, a legacy from his years of farming before he'd been elected Monitor. But now the blondish hair hung lifeless, the blue eyes faded, too old for a man in his late forties. He was well into the eighth and final year of his octad-long term, and not for the first time Jenret wondered who would win the next election. Many possible candidates had surfaced so far, but each represented a faction, a special interest, not a decisive majority.

"So you and Arras Muscadeine are convinced this woman—this Hylan Crailford—is a threat?" A sidelong glance shared with Allgood. "I didn't receive quite the same impression from Faeralleyn Thomas. She worries him, clearly, and he fears her, but at least he acknowledges she's only one woman. How much danger can one woman be?" Entreaty in the pallid blue eyes.

Jenret whistled softly; he'd not reckoned on Faertom's internal conflicts over spying on Hylan Crailford, or his degree of innocence. Faertom's hesitant descriptions coupled with the Monitor's desire for reassurance hadn't bolstered Jenret's more bleak assessment. For the first time, he cursed the fact that Arras Muscadeine hadn't come with them, instead hastily penning a note for the Monitor before returning to his duties in Marchmont. Clearly the note hadn't carried enough weight, either. But support came unexpectedly as Allgood responded to the Monitor before Jenret could explode with the righteous anger slowly building inside him.

Perching on a corner of the Monitor's desk, he laid a calming hand on van Beieven's shoulder. Or a restraining hand—which? Jenret wondered. **"Or sharing his courage,"** suggested Rawn. **"Governing is hard, lonely work."**

"Hylan Crailford has the power of her convictions, and in someone like her, those beliefs sear, purify with an almost unholy sense of mission and virtue. I've encountered her kind before, though rarely. Depending on how she's perceived by others, she could be ignored as a mad, holy fool or she could sweep people off their feet with the fervor of her convictions, an army of true believers trailing in her wake." Somber, he looked from one to the other, inviting comment. With an effort, Jenret held his tongue, relieved that someone else recognized a viable threat and curious where Allgood headed.

"She has the potential to destroy the Resonants, cause the land to rise up against them at terrible cost to both sides. But," he continued heavily, and Jenret's hopes crashed, "until she makes a move, leaves her little cottage, there's nothing we can do."

"Nothing? Nothing we can do?" Jenret surged to his feet, hands splayed wide as if to coax them to his side. "Now's the time to act, while we still have a chance, before she makes a move!"

"And on what legal grounds, Jenret? As long as she stays to herself, she's within her rights!" The Monitor had risen as well, the muscles on his neck corded with anger, the desk a frail barrier between contending wills. "If she chooses to travel, she's within her rights, the right of any citizen to free movement. Doesn't that mean anything to you—that right? All Resonants have that right as well, and will continue to have it while I govern! She has the right to talk with people, convince them of her beliefs—if they choose to be convinced. But unless—or until—she's guilty of incitement, fomenting a rebellion, there is absolutely nothing that can be done! No law that she's broken. Do you understand?" He sank behind his desk as Faertom returned with a large copper cha kettle, obviously purloined from the kitchen.

Faertom's stunned glance encompassed the passionate figures, although no words passed his quivering lips. Instinctively, he moved until Allgood shielded him from the tension thickening and clogging the room, as asphyxiating as smoke. Allgood gave him a gentle smack on the side, just as one might calm a spooked horse.

"The Monitor's right, Wycherley, and you know it. Those are the laws. Hylan Crailford's but one problem—one of many—that we're coping with right now regarding the Resonants. She'll be watched as best we can." The Monitor nodded emphatic support to Allgood's statement. "But while you've been training at the Hospice, other problems have reared up as well." Questing fingers again massaged the receding hairline, but only the fingers betrayed the man's nervousness, his voice steady. "It seems more Resonants are anxious about our continued ability or commitment to protect them—"

"With good reason!" Jenret broke in, lip curled, eyetooth exposed like a dog about to snap.

But Allgood ignored the provocation. "And have left their homes, their livelihoods, and fled to the deep woods out of concern for their safety. Oddly enough, it's not yet a mass exodus to Marchmont, where they might feel safe, welcome. Instead, they hide, although the Erakwa may have sheltered some. Insofar as we know, mindspeech has little or no effect on the Erakwa. Faertom," he patted Faertom again, compassion muting his words, desperate to inform without frightening, "I don't know if they sent word, conventionally or mentally, but your parents and brothers have left their island and their boat-building business and taken to the woods."

Faertom sank to his knees, hands covering his face, leaning against Allgood's thigh, his shaggy mane of hair helping shadow his hurt from their view. Appalled, Jenret felt like a voyeur. This was reality, not an abstraction.

Van Beieven picked up the conversation. "What that translates into, Wycherley—at least to some of our more credulous populace—is a panic that Resonants are secretly mustering their forces to attack the rest of us, just as the Fifty supposedly did some years ago." Jenret looked blank at the reference, but the Monitor pressed on without explaining. "Now do you see why I can't worry about one lone woman? If we don't convince the Resonants to return home, to their lives here in Canderis, how can we persuade the Normal populace they bode no danger?"

"Well, how *do* you propose to convince either side no danger exists?" Jenret paced, torn between a world he'd assumed he'd belonged to for so many years, and by a Resonant world he was just coming to understand and respect. Fulminating over the injustice of it all accomplished nothing, not given his hard-earned wisdom of the past year or so. Oh, not always wisdom enough, but more than he'd had before. Past time to lay aside the abrupt enthusiasms, the equally sharp angers. But his mental lecture couldn't stopper his mouth. "Somebody, someone must reason with them, make them return, guarantee their protection until things settle down!"

Everyone present except Jenret Wycherley divined where his thoughts headed, and his heart as well, but the Monitor forestalled him before he could say it. "What you're about to blurt out is ill-advised but well-intentioned, Wycherley. Yes, we desperately need volunteers to search out our wandering Resonants, return them to the fold. But you have a double duty here: you're a Seeker Veritas as well as a Resonant. Before you jump to volunteer, think about it, think it through, talk it over with people." A certain heavy emphasis, "And most especially with your wife-to-be, Doyce Marbon, since she *is* carrying your child, or had you momentarily forgotten that."

It stopped Jenret cold. "Thank you for that reminder. You're right, I'll think on it. And on a number of other things as well." A savage, precise bow indicated the depth of his turmoil, his anxiety to leave the Monitor's presence, and he was already out the door before permission was granted.

Faertom heaved himself to his feet, face expressionless, fears banked within like coals. Loyalty counted, and loyalty to Jenret Wycherley was his only claim since his family had fled and Allgood continued to deny him. "They'll be all right, lad," Allgood whispered, "your family will be fine."

He nodded once, blindly, at Allgood and in the Monitor's general direction and bumbled toward the door. Despite his own pain, he hurt for Allgood even more. When would the man ever acknowledge who and what he was? Admit he was Resonant as well as High Conciliator. How could he be so craven, remain silent about his own abilities when it might help?

"Because it's too late to acknowledge the truth, Faertom," Allgood's sorrow reached his brain. *"Don't you know what the Monitor would think, what everyone would think? I'd be seen as a 'plant,' some sort of spy. That I've been here all along, advising the Monitor, cajoling the other Conciliators to my views. I have more use as I am, as a Nothing, a Normal, than I do by admitting what I am."*

"It's not true, and you know it!" Faertom shot back. *"It can't be true!"* and as he stumbled into the hall, the black ghatt Rawn was waiting for him. *"It can't be true, can it?"* he begged for reassurance, but the ghatt, as usual, remained silent to his pleas. He always listened, though, Faertom was sure of that.

"Break!" The shout sank from topside, the "k" sound bouncing between the rock walls like a stubborn stutter, "k-k-k-k." Somerset Garvey nodded, waved so the distant figure on the quarry's lip would know he'd heard. But before taking his break, Garvey rechecked the ropes and harness on the granite slab, far bigger than a double bed. Satisfied, he retrieved his lunch bucket, glad again he'd brought it with him, not left it topside. One of the few good things that could be said for Polter was that his wife packed a hearty lunch. Yawning, eyelids heavy—too early to be so sleepy—he misjudged, tripped in the runoff channel carved near the wall and wrapped in the same shadows that cooled the lunch bucket and the stoneware water bottle. A menace, bleeding ankle-turner, the damn thing was. Polter had more trouble with standing water after snow or rain than did most quarry owners; to rectify it, he'd cut drainage ditches on each level of his workings, slanting downslope to carry the water to the bottom, thirty meters below. Garvey scooped a granite chip, tossed it and counted, waiting for the distant splash below. Groundwater seepage plus runoff, that.

No reason to climb up and socialize with Polter and his sons, all of them packed with muscle instead of brains between their ears. Almost impossible to tell the sons apart without numbering them. Usually he didn't worry, brawny they might be but thought themselves too good for honest labor—that's what hirelings were for. Garvey waved genially again, an exaggerated arm sweep as if to invite them to his level. No enjoyment working Polter's quarry, but money talked and they'd begged his help for this final order for the season. Didn't follow he had to fraternize with them, didn't much care for jaw-flapping. Still, being a good, though distant neighbor was the price you paid to be left in peace at your own little quarry most times. Nobody asked his help overmuch, but when they did, he didn't begrudge it.

Forty-nine years he'd lived beside his quarry, born there and no hankering to leave it. Besides, straying far wasn't wise, especially when he'd been a boy—Mam and Granpa had made it clear by what they didn't say, wouldn't answer. Learned early on not asking the wrong questions meant fewer strained silences. The Garveys cut from one of the few green-black granite sites around, strictly a family operation, always was, always would be, unlike Polter who hired out, ripping his pit wider, deeper to hustle more business. Had to, way those grown sons of his spent. Yes, Garvey quarry provided enough for him and his two boys and the sons after them when they married. Comfortable and steady.

Yeah, he had it good, must have, or Polter'd not have tried to buy him out on occasion. 'Course the work was hard, dangerous sometimes, and your body showed the abuse. He'd broken all of his fingers at one time or another, pinched off the tip of his left little finger when a wedge popped, rock snapping back like jaws. Not to mention the stone chip that had extracted his front teeth, mouth sunken in now, nose hooking toward chin. He unwrapped his lunch and spread it on the slab, finicking the napkin smooth underneath—sausage on thick slices of dark bread, pot of hot mustard on the side, a cup of slaw, and, glory be, a slab of marble pound cake for dessert. Quarry humor and it struck him as funnier than usual, laughter almost giddy and light-headed. Must be coming down with something, explained why he felt so draggy today. Even the water bottle didn't refresh him when he'd paused to drink.

He hoped his own sons, Waite and Wim, weren't attempting shortcuts, trying to do the work of three whilst he was away. Shortcuts got you hurt, best not to mar Waite before his betrothed arrived. Hadn't he worked the quarry alone

after his grandfather died and before the boys were grown?
Mam had helped some, but she'd had her hands full with the
boys after his wife died birthing Wim. Still didn't like the
name Wim, but Mam had begged him for it, confessed it had
been his own father's name. First he'd ever heard it—Wim.
Wim Garvey, but no, couldn't be that 'cause Garvey was her
father's surname and hers. Wim Somebody. Only time she'd
ever mentioned anything about his father.

Funny, Wim so artistic, couldn't fathom where he'd gotten
it from. Mayhap Wim Somebody. Every winter when the
quarry closed, he was the one messing with scraps, barely
eating or sleeping, totally engrossed as he chiseled figurines,
even some strange, free-form vases or some such thing, half
raw stone, half polished. Couldn't quite fancy them, understand what they expressed, but they sold well. Could sell
more if he let Wim do it full-time. Some sold as far distant
as Marchmont, and that tickled him no end, proud even if he
couldn't judge his son's artistry.

Lady bless, his mind was rambling and winding back on itself today! Eating methodically, he looked around, enjoying
the granite rising in stages, like giant steps where they'd
quarried it. Not his beloved green-black granite, but a nice
tan, one vein of pink on the far wall. Just like Polter to insist
he could cut such giant slabs. He shifted on his seat. Getting
each one out intact was murderous. Almost four meters long
it was, and three wide, and 'bout twenty-five centimeters
thick. Build a fort with the bloody things.

Stuffing the napkin in the bucket, he took a final swig from
the stoneware bottle, made a face. Off-taste to it the longer it
sat, odd. Long afternoon ahead, being so tired, muzzy-
headed. He rose, dusting the seat of his trousers, silly considering the stone dust coating him at day's end, but that was
habit for you. Waved up top to indicate he'd finished and
checked the ropes again. The block and tackle hung from a
tall oak pole, almost like a ship's mast, socketed into one of
a series of holes each bored a meter deep. He tamped more
rubble into the hole to make sure the pole was wedged solid,
yawned, rubbed his face. He could hear the oxen being
brought around, so he untied the tackle and the heavy steel
hook from the pole, snapped it into the harness center ring.

"All ready?" Funny, looked like Lemrick, Polter's oldest,
not one of the hired men. Lemrick, whomever, whatever, the
Number One Son if he wore a number. Could paint numbers

on the back of their jackets some night, make it easier. It struck him as uproariously funny.

"Right, bring her up easy," he shouted back and retrieved the long pole with its leather-padded crossbar to maneuver the slab as it rose overhead, like a shepherd with a crook. He yawned again. Not good to be sleepy, wits foggy for something like this. He lurched, leaned on the pole for support. If he didn't wake up, he'd pitch himself into the drainage ditch, sure as anything.

As the oxen moved forward, the block and tackle hoisted the slab straight up. "Fine! Hold!" he instructed as it reached surface level. Now just shift the behemoth with the pole, press and release, let it pendulum, each swing taking the front of the slab closer to the edge and the rollers. Hard to budge at first, but once he moved it a bit, momentum helped. It swung back, then forward again on its own, farther than the first time, and he leaned into the pole to coax it ahead. Once it hit the first rollers, someone up top would snag the hook that brought the second team of oxen into play, dragging it forward on the rollers.

He heard the clink of the metal hook hitting the eye sewn into the harness. "Forward and steady! Back the pulley team for slack." Oxen didn't need a tug of war, one pair trying to raise the slab higher while the other tried to pull it away. Normally such instructions were unnecessary, men who worked together depended on each other, but with Lemrick in charge, Garvey took nothing for granted. Even more so if his thick-headed brothers Pierce and Elnathan were helping. Where the deuce was Polter? He should be supervising. And the other hired men—still on break?

What he heard wasn't the "Forward" command, but "Back!" shouted at the wrong team. The slab, front end resting precariously on the first roller, began to tilt, a giant sledge poised on a downslope of air. "Back!" The shout came again, this time to the team on the block and tackle. Both sets of ropes slackening, the slab came slicing down at Garvey, a shout strangling his throat as he ordered his feet to do something, anything while his eyes locked on the stately, ponderous descent.

But his feet dragged and scraped, legs rubbery as he strove to think over the blur and buzz of his mind. Something wrong here, something desperately wrong, not just stupidity, not just his tiredness. The slab was falling at an angle, rear lower than its front, not flat like a palm slapping the table, and that was good. At last Garvey convinced his feet to act, dove headlong toward the wall and rolled desperately into the runoff ditch as the slab landed on top, coffin lid slamming, a hollow boom of judgment.

He barely fit, arms extended straight in front to trim his shoulders, face pressed sideways in the ditch. The reverberations slowly ceased, but his body kept quivering, trapped beneath the slab, encased by granite on all sides. Living tomb. That's why he always pit mined, couldn't bear tunnels. Couldn't hear, stone muffling every living sound. They, yes, they'd be coming, rushing down, feverishly working pry bars once they realized he lived. Have to shout, relieve their fears. Did till his lungs emptied, scarce room to draw a full breath.

But ears still ringing, he couldn't hear a response and reluctantly cast outward with his mind to determine what they were doing. Not that he'd mine much sense from any of those Polter boys' thick skulls. But his Gleaner skills could magnify the words spoken topside as they gathered around the edge. Belike they were stunned, too frozen to move.

"Smash him, did we?" Lemrick, Garvey thought.

"Course, don't see him, do you? Dead hit, not even an arm or a leg peeking out from under the slab."

"Mashed flat!" Pierce, the youngest.

"Best leave him there all winter. Make up some excuse, tell Da that Garvey left suddenlike. Emergency."

They'd done it on purpose! Why, why kill a man like that? It made no sense. He strained harder.

"If others want to reap them, we can be millers who grind them. Good thought, Lem, that sleeping potion in his water jug."

The pieces fit now, made a sick, demented sense. Garvey lay still, wondering when it'd dawn on their thick brains that the slab straddled the runoff ditch, a slim chance at survival. Without other options he slept nightmarishly, waited for dark, the pitiful rectangle of light at the end of his tunnel dimming. Then he painfully scooted along, shoving with his toes, pulling with his fingertips, until he eased free, a turtle, naked after leaving its stone shell behind. Naked, vulnerable—that's how you felt when you asked questions, didn't like the answers. Didn't dare take his horse, so he legged it home, took two nights, praying he'd arrive before the Polters decided Waite and Wim were expendable as well.

Lady's blessing that Shoshana Garvey lay in her own grave these past ten years, because he thought she'd heard this sort of answer before, had tried to protect him from it.

With a shivery purr of satisfied anticipation, Khar sank her claws into the leather corner of the desk blotter. They came at last! Closer and closer, Jenret mounting the stairs to the library as silently as Rawn. Her ears swiveled, a telltale gesture, and she righted them, although the hoop still swung. Tempting to inform Doyce of their approach, but that would cancel the surprise and wonder on her face when Jenret burst into the room. Her claws kneaded once, twice, eyes slitted to endure the wait.

"Khar," Doyce tapped a white paw with her pencil. "Stop it! You'll ruin the blotter. Trust the head librarian to see it's deducted from my Seeker pay."

A lightning-fast paw swatted the pencil to clatter on the floor, back foot curling in satisfaction as it rolled away. **"You could deduct it from mine,"** spurious generosity on the ghatta's part. **"Except, of course, I'm not paid. Why's that, I wonder? It's never seemed fair to me that we ghatti, who do all the work,"** she paused, **"*all* the work, don't receive a penny. There are things I'd like to buy. Per'la'd like to buy her own ribbons, wouldn't you, Per'la?"**

Per'la grinned from across the room while Parse industriously scribbled, lost in research. This morning her tail stump boasted a far from crisp red ribbon, a leftover from some long-ago present Parse had received. **"If I had my own money, I wouldn't have to wait for Parse to take me shopping."**

"I doubt the shopkeepers would be enthusiastic about hearing you order directly." Balling a piece of foolscap, Doyce tossed it at her, but the ghatta lazily deflected it. Parse, irritated, made a shushing sound and knocked the balled paper clear, uninterested in how or why it had manifested itself in the middle of his desk. *"I might remind you both,"* Doyce shifted to mindspeech, embarrassed at disturbing Parse, *"that the illustrious Kharm, beloved Bondmate of our own Matthias Vandersma and ancestress of you all, never felt the need to be paid. After all, how can you put a price on Truth?"*

Funny, she'd constructed a vivid image of Matthias Vandersma and Kharm in her mind's eye, as if she'd absorbed some hidden, intimate essence of the man. Or, she corrected herself, the boy he'd once been. Almost as if she'd sat beside him and Kharm, privy to their tangled thoughts during those first few lonely octants as summer changed into fall. Now, if she could only find facts to support her intuitions, make her history of the Seekers Veritas come alive! And with that, a niggling sensation of guilt: Damn! Forgot to bring that old diary back this morning. Not that she'd made any headway reading it—she'd started woolgathering about Matty and Kharm as she'd stared into the fire.

"Khar, why didn't you remind me to return it? And why," she chucked the ghatta under the chin, Khar's head wedged into the open V of her thumb and forefinger to let both sides be rubbed, *"am I so wrapped up in Matthias's life? I know it's hard to leave your work behind when you quit for the day, but it seems to me I've other things to occupy my mind. Including wondering where Jenret is."* And though she'd tried to push his delay out of her mind, it returned with a vengeance. How could he leave her alone like this? Anger warred with hurt, betrayal.

Khar slid her head sideways, the better to hear while pretending to want her ear scratched. **"Pregnant women indulge in the strangest fantasies sometimes."** Closer, closer! Just outside the door! And that meant she'd eluded discovery for now, wouldn't have to confess her role as dream-intermediary, bearer and sharer of a Major Tale. Bless the Elders for her reprieve!

The faintest creak of the door, but neither Parse nor Doyce registered it. Finger to lips, Jenret ghosted across the floor, embraced Doyce from behind. Taken totally unaware, fueled by unacknowledged anger and a burst of pure panic, Doyce sagged between the imprisoning arms until she could twist and lever a hip into her unknown assailant's lower abdomen, yank one arm over her shoulder, and launch her attacker into the air. Nonplussed, Jenret arced over her, landed on his back on the desktop. Vacating the landing pad just in time, Khar sniffed in Rawn's direction, **"A tad too much surprise, don't you think?"**

Rawn's muzzle wrinkled with suppressed laughter. **"I**

**wouldn't have had to score Jenret's buttocks if she'd re-
membered how to do that on a certain night back in
Marchmont."**

"Hell of a greeting, woman!" Jenret panted, air knocked
out of him. And found himself even shorter of breath as
Doyce kissed him, all thoughts of Matthias and Kharm
driven from her head.

♣

Making no attempt to smother his yawn, indeed, making
it as widely ostentatious as possible, Jenret threw himself
against the pillows, sighed. Rawn radiated sympathy from
the foot of the bed where he snuggled beside Khar. He
placed a hand on Doyce's thigh to attract her attention.

Abstracted, she brushed it off, shifted the lapboard on her
knees and crossed out two lines, crossed them out again, and
began rapping her pencil faster and faster against the board,
as if she were building up to something. "I *have* to get this
straight in my mind, Jenret, before I can go to sleep. I'm
sorry." Whether she referred to the Bicentennial History
chapter she worked on or to their conversation earlier that
day, he wouldn't have taken any bets. Clasping hands behind
head, he strove for patience.

So much for three days of blissful togetherness without
one precipitous conversation on their part. A near-record,
and one he'd smashed by finally telling her his decision.
She'd said nothing. Still, despite tinder-dry emotions on the
other side of the bed, not such a bad feeling being together
like this, like an old married couple. And then it hit him—
they weren't. Not yet.

He wanted so badly to touch her mind but dared not intrude without permission. At least then he'd know what
worried her: the immediate concerns of the chapter—and she
could be a bear about getting everything organized, logically
laid out—or something else. She could be just as obsessive
about the chapter as anything else. His argument didn't convince him. Or using it to calm herself. A crumpled piece of
yellow foolscap joined the pile of white and yellow pages already discarded, balled on the bed. He took one up, began to
rework it, crumple it tighter, tease it open, concentrating on
not tearing it. Too bad other things couldn't be smoothed so
easily.

No, so far since this reunion he hadn't mentioned a thing about when they'd marry, had he? That must be it. *"Did I?"* He checked Rawn for confirmation. *"Should I? Khar, what do you think?"*

Rawn rolled into a stretch that extended from one side of the bed to the other, impossibly long. **"No, you haven't— yet. Doesn't it strike you that informing her—and I say *inform* because I didn't hear any discussion—that you're leaving in two days to seek out Resonants in the Lower Tetonords might leave her wondering if you've any time for marriage, let alone her?"**

Stung by the ghatt's censure, Jenret tried to cover his dismay. Even Rawn doubted his sincerity when it came to taking marriage vows. *"But it's my duty to persuade those Resonants to return home, become a true part of Canderisian life! Who has a better right than I? They're my people, my own kind!"*

Khar chimed in, **"And she isn't one of your own, your kind?"** Disgusted, she sat up, the better to fix him with a baleful amber eye, Jenret decided. **"Oh, come on, Rawn, I'll be dizzy if they circle-dance their emotions again. I'm going to the kitchen—I have an incredible craving for some nutter-butter."**

The final sentence reached Doyce, as intended, and she glanced up in time to see Khar jump off the bed, followed by Rawn. "Khar?" She'd been meaning to ask Khar something lately, but she hadn't gotten around to it, and now the ghatta was already out the door. Mayhap she was just being forgetful, but she couldn't recollect Khar asking for any of her 'script recently, the contraceptive drug all ghattas took to avoid coming into heat. Of course, she'd probably asked Jenret for it when he gave Rawn his related dose. Yes, that probably explained it.

"I thought Khar didn't like nutter-butter," Jenret mumbled. "Rawn, yes. But Khar, no."

"Mm-hm. Probably doing it more for Rawn." So much said, but often the wrong things—and so much unsaid. Whose fault? She crossed out another line, drummed the pencil, and slumped back, extra pencils quilled behind her ears. "Damn, can't get this to read smooth." Pulling her smock above her belly, she began to rub the stretched skin, ruminating on the words she wanted. And what words did she want?

What I want is. . . . What I *want* is for him to want to stay with me as much as I want him to stay, but she buried the thought inside her, prayed he hadn't read her mind. Or worse, that her vulnerability, her need was printed across her face, as naked and easy to read as the words she inscribed on paper. I promised you time to find yourself, not to look for everyone else. Think of yourself first, think of me. You deserve it, I deserve it! She felt a tear welling, hoped he wouldn't notice as she dragged her sleeve across her face.

But Jenret was engrossed in folding bits of yellow and white paper into strange shapes, pressing her discarded scraps against his knee in sharp folds. In fact, several of his earlier constructions adorned her belly, barely balanced on the curve. They looked like little, upsidedown hats, or tiny, open birds' beaks. With infinite care he set two more pieces, one white, one yellow, on her stomach. "What are you doing?" Had he lost his wits? Here she was convincing herself to talk openly and honestly with him, not lock it inside, and he proceeded to adorn her, although adorn was hardly the right word, with tiny paper hats!

"Visual pun. Can you guess it?" He leaned on one elbow, mouth serious, but gentian blue eyes sparkling with some secret humor. His one recalcitrant curl had sprung over his forehead and he tugged at it, trying to hide a quickening grin.

Mustering her patience she examined the scattered pieces of paper around her belly button, finally flicked one with her finger. He drew back in mock dismay. "Oh, direct hit! Now the forces are uneven!"

"Jenret, what are you talking about? What visual pun? Or I'm going to punt you out of bed." She scowled, torn between indignation and the potential of shared laughter. Oh, to truly share something, even laughter.

"Navel engagement!" he crowed. "Naval engagement, don't you see it? All my little ships having a 'navel' engagement!" He blew them aside, kissed her swollen stomach as she cuffed his ear. "Ooww! Beat the father of your child, would you?"

Her tears fell in earnest, as she clutched his head tight against her stomach, the child within her kicking and stirring, and she hoped he could feel it as well. "Jenret, Jenner, love. Please, please don't leave me! I'm afraid, afraid of this new world changing around us. I'm even afraid of the child

I carry because I don't know what he or she will be, what place the baby will have in this world, what its heritage will be!"

"Our child will have the place we create for it, Doyce, with our labor and love. I promise you that!" Fiercely, he held her, shifted up until she was in his arms. "That's why I have to go, do what I *can* do, the *best* I can do."

"And I'm supposed to stay at home, tending the fire, knitting, waiting? I thought this was to be a partnership of equals, sharing everything! How can I share when you make decisions without me, leave me here to worry if you're all right?"

"Doyce, Doyce," he patted at her back, awkward, ineffectual, wondering why it didn't soothe. "I've talked with everyone I could, including Swan, the Monitor, the Major General and his Guardians. I even had Rawn contact Saam and Mahafny. I wanted her word that you were fine, not likely to deliver early, and she assured me you were as strong as a horse." He beamed. "I've been patient, thought everything through, I promise you. I'm too old, too mature for rash, impetuous decisions now that I have you and our baby to consider."

"*You* thought it through, *you* consulted, *you* decided! Well, you're not alone anymore, Jenret, the only one with the right to make decisions!" She pushed herself off his chest, her fists a barrier between them. "You consulted with everyone except *me!* Damn you, Jenret, how could you be so insensitive?"

"I didn't want to worry you until I had to. Mahafny did say you were a bit broody lately, but that it was only to be expected."

"And if you go—or rather, I should say—when you go, how am I supposed to get word to you if anything goes wrong? How am I supposed to know if you're safe, well?" Hazel eyes had turned a dangerous bluish-green. "You wouldn't want me to get any more broody, would you, now?"

"Then let me share my thoughts with you. No matter how far away I am, I promise each night, we'll pick a time right now, and I'll do my best to send back to you." A reasonable solution, clearly, but with a shock he realized she was shoving him out of bed, fists and feet pummeling him relentlessly.

"And what makes you think I'll be waiting patiently, ready to listen? Why should I commit myself to that when you won't commit yourself to me?" She gasped, fists and feet still working at him. His bottom hung over the edge of the bed and with an unexpected suddenness and finality gravity took over.

The thud above their heads made the ghatti in the kitchen look upward. Rawn paused, paw hovering over the crock of nutter-butter, and winced at a crash and scrambling sounds denoting thrown objects and a hasty exit from the bedroom. **"Jenret's right. If she'd only speak mind-to-mind with him as we do, everything would be much simpler. Less room for misunderstandings."**

The paw swipe came so fast he had no time to duck. He sneezed nutter-butter out of a nostril, wiped at sticky whiskers plastered against his face. **"What,"** he projected injured dignity, **"did I do?"**

"You can both sleep downstairs tonight, and I hope your superiority keeps you warm!"

✤

PART
TWO

✤

PART
TWO

Without shifting his gaze from the window Arras Muscadeine reached blindly for Mahafny Annendahl's shoulder, aware he dared greatly in touching the eumedico, striving to comfort. Despite her advanced years, she was still an elegant woman, and Muscadeine suspected she'd been striking in her youth, though no less daunting then than now. Truth be known, he wouldn't have minded some consolation himself, but few attempted such familiarity with a leader and lord, just as few dared it with the eumedico. Well, so far his hand was still attached to his wrist. They both continued their vigil as the wheaten-robed figure grew smaller in the distance, a crazy-quilt marked ghatt capering at his side. A flash of black and orange and white caught the sunlight as the ghatt leaped, tagged the carved knob on the figure's sturdy walking stick.

"His heart is greater than his girth," Arras whispered. Now his hand was shrugged from her shoulder, as if she'd just registered his intimacy. He waved a final farewell, though he doubted Harrap could see them framed in one of the top windows of the Research Hospice.

Turning her back to the window, Mahafny shoved hands up her sleeves to hide the palsy. A flow of blue-gray steel melted off the adjacent window ledge and Saam padded beside her, yellow eyes searching her heart . . . and her mind. She still wasn't easy with it, wasn't sure if she'd ever be, but she was learning. The ghatt had lost as much or more than she through time—his Seeker Bondmate Oriel Faltran, once Doyce's lover, brutally murdered; his desertion by the Erakwan lad Nakum, now ensconced high in the Marchmontian mountains with his great-great-grandmother Callis, devising ways to save the sacred arborfer trees. And what had Saam gained in recompense for those losses—her? Hardly a fair trade to her analytical turn of mind.

"**But not diminished returns, you know.**" A sneeze of amusement as she jerked to attention at his mindvoice. "**I always choose well, even if not with the longevity I might wish.**"

"Have you set your sights on someone after I'm gone?" His answer mattered more than she cared to admit; so few in her life she loved now, or even risked caring about. A wasteful, weakening thing, love. And now two of her weaknesses, Harrap and Parm, had gallantly marched off on an uncharted journey. Oh, the road might be clear, but not the travails they might face. *"I don't want you having false illusions—I certainly don't."*

He rubbed her knee, cajoling her to remove a traitorous hand from her sleeve and reach gnarled fingers to stroke his head. "**You're lying to yourself again. You know what you have isn't fatal, but you wish it were. You just can't abide being useless. Your usefulness lies in your mind, not in your hands. I think you'd better reconcile yourself to having me around for a long, long time.**"

"A poor bargain on your part, then, though I take comfort in it." Straightening, she saw that Muscadeine had sat down beside her desk, his mustache twitching. As a Resonant he was familiar with strange gaps or changes in the conversational flow, the internal dialogue of his own kind, or Seekers mindspeaking their ghatti. Only a eumedico, not a Seeker, but still she'd been chosen as Saam's companion, a gift beyond price.

"You're absolutely sure this is necessary?" she spoke aloud now. "And that Harrap and Parm are the ones for the job?"

He steepled his hands in front of his lips, schooled himself to restraint. Oh, he had doubts as well, but if you let doubts paralyze you, nothing could be accomplished. "You know we've had Hylan Crailford watched for the last two octs, ever since Jenret and Faertom and I sought her out. The Monitor's people have kept her under surveillance as well, though not as closely as I might wish. My reports say she's readying herself for a journey, where, we don't know. She's left her chickens and spoilable goods with a neighbor, shuttered her house, and started packing a cart." He swung round, dark eyes challenging. "Would you let her wander without supervision? A mind like hers endangers her as well as others."

"But Harrap and Parm? A man who's still unsure if his stronger allegiance is to the Shepherds and his Blessed Lady or to the Seekers? And a ghatt with the personality of a court jester?" Even love couldn't blind her to Harrap's and Parm's flaws; after all, they knew hers just as clearly.

"And when you journeyed to Gaernett last oct to visit Swan, she gave you permission to command Harrap and Parm as you saw fit, have them take on this task if it proved necessary, didn't she?"

A blandly polite expression masking her face, she shook her head, neither agreeing nor disagreeing but rather as if waging internal war with herself and her thoughts. She stopped, suddenly self-conscious at his look. Damn, was the palsy betraying her here as well? She forced herself back to the conversation. "But Harrap and Parm are so innocent!" And hated herself for sending them on such a lonely, precarious mission, nothing and no one to counterweight their innocence. Why not herself, irascible, skeptical, ever on guard? Or Muscadeine, strong, assured, wise in the ways of intrigue and war?

"And in that innocence there's wisdom, compassion, and wit. Things too many of us sorely lack." Had he been reading her mind? No, she doubted it, simply that his thoughts had traveled the same path of regrets hers had.

"And mercy, most of all."

"Yes." He smiled, made ready to leave. "You'll have Saam stay in contact with Parm as long as he can? After that, we'll have to pray other ghatti are near enough for Parm to reach."

Saam leaped to the desk, sprawled across her papers as if to barricade her from Muscadeine's expectations. **"You know, someday we ought to give him a taste of a verbatim transmission from Parm. All that lovely subtle wisdom interwoven with 'oops' and 'by the way' and digressions enough to make his head spin."**

The idea appealed, she had to admit it. But Parm was no laughing matter. She poked Saam between the shoulder blades, raised her eyebrows at Muscadeine. "But of course. We'll see to that." Belatedly reassured, he left, abandoning her to her own thoughts and worries.

❖

"Hullo! The Lady's Blessing on you!" Sandals flapping, Harrap strained to match strides with the woman pulling the small two-wheeled cart behind her. She'd almost crested the hill when he'd caught a glimpse of her in the distance, quickening his pace, galloping up the hill as she surmounted the top and started down, momentum and the cart's weight speeding her descent. He drew a hand over his tonsure, wiped it on his robe, made a face. A hot and sweaty way to meet someone. Exertion had overcome the nip to the fall air, left him radiating warmth like a stoked furnace.

Parm had outrun his greetings, indulging in a skittering dance around the cart where a white and tan terrier perched atop the load. Head cocked, one ear perked, the terrier gave a shrill yip. "Hark!" the woman commanded, and the dog ceased, crestfallen.

"May I give you a hand with the cart?" Harrap puffed along beside her, skipped once, almost adjusted his pace to hers.

"No." With barely a look in his direction, she stared straight ahead, ignoring his presence.

He caught her rhythm at last, Lady's Medallion swinging on his broad chest. "Mind if I walk with you a ways?"

"Yes." Arm and neck muscles strained as she struggled to control the cart's downhill speed, gravity almost stronger than she. Concentrating, apparently absorbed in maneuvering around a wheel rut, she launched a complete sentence in his direction, made him stumble with its unexpectedness. "Barnaby doesn't like cats."

"But Parm doesn't mind dogs, rather likes them, in fact. And he isn't a cat, he's a ghatt." No, this wasn't going to be easy, gaining her confidence, discovering what she had in mind. He chastised himself for meekly agreeing to befriend her, watchdog her movements, determine what danger she presented. False pretenses—a sin. He'd not been sent to give aid and succor as a Shepherd should. And as a Seeker, his role eluded him even more, despite instructions from Mahafny and Muscadeine, who knew even less about being a Seeker than he. Eyes screwed shut, brows beetling in dismay, he chanted a brief prayer, lips moving silently so as not to offend the woman beside him.

"I know." Sweat darkened her serviceable gray work shirt in a wide line front and back, her pantaloons dusted with road grit. For a moment he panicked—what did she know?

Found out already, his cover blown? "Too big for a cat." Harrap exhaled a sobbing sigh of relief. "Don't particularly hold with Seekers, prying into minds like that. Or Shepherds preserving the status quo . . . 'if not in this life, perhaps another,' " she twisted the sacred phrase until it sounded like bogus cant. "In other words, be satisfied with what you suffer here on earth. Always promise the candy, but dangle it out of reach." She swiped at her face with a sleeve, surreptitiously studying him, he realized with a start. He shifted the leather pack strap from one shoulder to the other to grant her more time.

"Think her curiosity's about to come to a boil." Parm had scampered ahead, lolling in a patch of shade as the cart rolled by. **"Wish I could ride."**

"So, how'd you come to be a Shepherd and a Seeker?" More urgently, "How do you choose which to obey? Don't they conflict?" Lady guide him, she was earnest, as if his answer bore a shrouded significance, might help her comprehend other things.

He played for time; his duality still caused him discomfort, distress, this constant stretching between polarities, both of goodness and rightness, but so very dissimilar at times. "Sure I can't help with the cart?" His big hand reached for the closer shaft. Surely it had been meant as a goat cart, but she no longer owned a goat to draw it.

"No!" She strode ahead, firm in her isolation, her determination of duty. Accepting his help would subtly shift the boundaries of their relationship, but it pained him to see someone suffer so, refuse to share her burden.

"It *is* a conflict at times. Perhaps that's why I'm on this journey, to refresh my spirit, wrestle with what I am and what I'm not. Most things can coexist, if you let them—"

"Impossible!" she nearly spat the word at his feet. "Some things, some people, can *never* coexist, shouldn't even share the same world—" and broke off as a cart wheel balked, then rolled over a rock. The cart swayed and tilted; she tried to muscle it back before it overturned, but it was too top-heavy. The dog's claws scrabbled as he slid down the tarp and hit the ground.

"Here, let me." And, without waiting for her permission, Harrap threw his weight against it to level it. She gave him a grudging look of gratitude and he continued holding the shaft, drawing the cart forward. "Easier with two," he added, her hesitant smile and nod of agreement more precious than anticipated.

Jenret sidled along the trail, anxious not to brush against branches, not scuffle or worse, slide and fall on the slick carpet of wet leaves, treacherous after last night's drenching rain. The rain had dislodged more leaves, improving sight lines, but keeping track of Addawanna was a daunting task. Whatever the conditions, the terrain, she melded with them without a betraying trace, almost as if she were part of the land itself. The elderly Erakwan woman moved wraithlike, checking for tracks, beckoning them along with an imperious hand. He paused, intent on Rawn's mindvoice as the ghatt prowled the undergrowth, while Faertom's impatient breath steamed the back of his neck.

"Anything?" Hope soared in Faertom's voice and Jenret wondered sourly how he remained so optimistic after all this time. Easy, he supposed, because each day dangled the lure of locating Faertom's relatives, reuniting them at last. Well, Faertom still hadn't found his relatives, and what did Jenret have to show for fourteen days of drudgery? Nothing, not a single confirmed sighting.

"No," disliking himself for his cursory response, but he was tired, very, very tired of dragging the anchor-weight of Faertom's hopes. His responsibility. Not to mention the rest of them ragtagging through the woods at his behest: Yulyn Biddlecomb and her husband Towbin, with Sarrett and T'ss bringing up the rear. Two Resonants, one Seeker, one Seeker-Resonant, one Normal, and an Erakwan guide whose goals didn't coincide with his—at least not from the results so far.

"Perhaps she's not so sure she wants them found," came Yulyn's comment, then a hesitation. *"After all, the Erakwa don't seem to object to the Resonants' presence in their 'backyard,' so to speak. That's more than I can say about Canderisians in general. Perhaps she feels if they're doing no harm, they shouldn't be bothered."*

"Well, she agreed to help us search."

"And she is, but she can do it on her terms, not ours."

Irritated, Jenret snapped back, *"I don't remember dra-*

gooning her, conscripting her into our service, did I? I asked for help and she volunteered."

Faertom stretched his arms as if to reach out to both of them, connect them. He sounded strained. *"Please, please,"* he tried again, *"don't bicker! Set your minds free to do their work, that's why we're here! How can you project reassurance, reconciliation, when we're squabbling amongst ourselves? Even if they can't hear us, they can sense our annoyance. Anger carries farther than our mindvoices. Project, and listen for them to respond."* Sadness weighted him as he concluded aloud, "If they're here at all, anywhere near."

Surprisingly enough, Tobwin strode to his side to offer solace, although as a Normal he'd missed most of the conversation. His pockmarked jaw worked as he searched for the words. "Don't give up, lad. Between them, my Yulyn and Addawanna can find anyone. Yulyn's had the most Resonant training of you three, no matter how she came by it. If there's a Resonant to hear, she'll hear him. And Addawanna can track where yesterday's beetle crawled."

But Sarrett began shooing them along, urging them to speed up. "T'ss wants us to hurry. Addawanna's found something . . . someone, but we must move quietly, not spook them."

"We can reassure them from here that we mean no harm!" Faertom cried, wilted hopes blooming.

"But our physical presence, unarmed, will prove we mean no harm, not pretty mindspeeches. The one thing you Resonants don't have," Sarrett emphasized, "is the ability to discern the truth. Only the ghatti can do that. That's why T'ss and I are along, as well as Jenret and Rawn. You may have lived without the need for Seekers, but surely even Resonants know our reputation for truth-speaking."

They hurried after Addawanna, aware they'd never match her preternatural silence, her earth-bonded communion with the very land itself. Jenret and Faertom crawled up a shallow rock slope mantled with sodden leaves, T'ss and Rawn already poised on its edge, peering over. T'ss's tail swept once, while Rawn remained motionless. **"Approach slowly, raise your hands over your head,"** Rawn instructed Jenret, **"and tell the others to stay well back unless we instruct otherwise. Especially Faertom."**

After a whispered colloquy, Jenret complied, his heart

sinking. So, they weren't the only ones seeking, searching, and it looked as if they'd been found first. A horrible thought, others searching for Resonants, stalking them like wild game. Still, jumping to conclusions did no good, and Rawn hadn't indicated anything either way. He dug toes into the loose shale, surging upward, unsteady without the use of his hands. As he rose higher, he caught sight of Addawanna at the center of the clearing. She stood, hands on hips, foot tapping. "You wan be meetin' Gleaners, Res'nants, you meetin'em den. Sorry I not introduce you, but for one of yours, he look like he know what hatchet for. Figger you younger Addawanna, *you* test and see. Not what I here for."

Her raised chin and bittersweet smile made Jenret trip as he looked where she pointed, at last puzzled out the shape of a tall young man dressed in greens and gray-browns, blending with the fir trees behind him. He held a hatchet poised to throw, a second one ready in his other hand. Just beyond he glimpsed the rigid line of an arrow, jutting as no branch would. How many were there? The strangers held the higher ground, could pick them off as they crested the knoll. Battle was the last thing he wanted, despite Sarrett's ability with a sword. So what now—a battle mind to mind, Resonant pitted against Resonant? But that wasn't why he was here, indeed, the exact opposite. Did Resonants perpetually live with the fear pricking at him now—of constantly being outnumbered, the minority, backing down, retreating despite their superior skills? Damned if he'd back down.

"My tabard proclaims me a Seeker Veritas," he pitched his voice to carry. "I must speak with you, see if we can't find alternatives to this senseless running." He made the transition into mindspeech without pausing, *"What you can't judge from my outward appearance is that I'm a Resonant as well as a Seeker."*

He waited, but no one rose to his bait. Were they Resonants—or hunters, foresters, surprised, wary at their unexpected, unexplained presence? "Where's your ghatt, then? Anyone can don a tabard, play Seeker." The hatchet never wavered, although Addawanna had sat, doughty and clearly bored. The hidden bowman still targeting him left Jenret less sanguine. A squelch of wet leaves behind him as Rawn called **"Coming!"** and sprang to his right for easy visibility. But a loud crash resounded leftward, and the bowman stepped clear of the maze of branches for an unhindered shot, bow bending as he drew it.

"Faerbaen! Baen, don't hurt them! It's me, Faeralleyn!" The bow jerked, arrow flying wide of its mark. Faertom, more accurately Faeralleyn Thomas, spun toward the arrow's source. "Faerclough, you never could hit anything smaller than a barn door!" But the next arrow landed neatly between his feet.

The words lodged in Faertom's brain with searingly accurate intimacy, perfectly targeted, as only one Thomas could with another. *"They haven't compelled you? Compulsed you?"*

"No!" Their suspicion baffled him.

"Then why'd you expose us, reveal us as Gleaners for all the world to see when you dropped your Transitor-cover, trotted off like a besotted fool to join the Research Hospice? Were you crazy? Everyone knows why people go there now. With you in cahoots with them we might as well have posted the island: 'Gleaners Live Here'." Faertom's mouth dropped at his elder brother, Faerbaen's, bitterness.

"But, Baen, I never meant ..." he wailed, but a short, grizzled man appeared at forest's edge, gesturing to Faerclough and Faerbaen to lower their weapons. "Father!" A wellspring of eager supplication in that one spoken word as Faertom began a clumsy run, cast himself at the man's feet, glowing with relief.

"Get up. Go back to them, they're your people now, not us. You made your choice." The order gruff, irrefutable. Faertom staggered up, arms imploring, unsure which way to turn. His hurt smote Jenret, the same hurt he'd lived with ever since his own father had tried to disavow his younger son's potential, kill the child to ensure he never attained his brother Jared's perverted skills. Now his father had naught but a dry husk of a mind, a gaping emptiness. If only his father had believed there were other ways, that it was a gift, not a dangerous taint. Opposite reasons for paternal anger, but the end results were all too similar. And for the first time Jenret foretasted what his own relationship with his unborn child might be at some future day.

"Faeraday, wait!" From behind the shielding trees a tall, statuesque woman joined them, clear where Faertom and his brothers had inherited their height and coloring. "You swore we'd talk first, not condemn out of hand!" She didn't so

much dwarf her husband as diminish him, his fiery disposition and sharpness tempered by the honor and goodness emanating from her.

"At last someone wid common sense." Addawanna
rubbed her hands together, "Woman, whad else? 'Lowed
bring od'ers up to talk? Not left like scaredy badger huddlin
in hole?" He'd completely forgotten the others, Sarrett and
T'ss, Towbin and Yulyn, still massed below the slope, able
to hear but unable to see what transpired. Without a doubt
Sarrett had split them into defensive positions, attempting to
shadow their movements by their voices.

With a look that cowed her husband, the woman called
her agreement, Jenret retreating until he could glance downward, gesture them forward. Not a word of mindspeech had
he heard from their captors, shut out, not fully accepted as
one of them. Which side did he belong to, where did he fit
in, caught between two worlds?

"By the havens, Faeraday, can't we at least sit and discuss
this rationally?" The woman greeted Jenret and the others as
they surmounted the rise. "I'm Claudra Thomas. My husband Faeraday, and my two elder sons, Faerbaen and
Faerclough." She motioned them close, a son on either side
of her as she stood behind her husband, hands lightly resting
on his shoulders, so balanced and complete a picture that it
appeared no room for Faertom had ever existed.

Their closed solidarity was emblematic of the meeting as
a whole. No matter how Jenret and Yulyn pleaded, argued,
persuaded, nothing convinced the Thomases of their goodwill, the good intentions of most of Canderis. Less than no
help at all, Faertom hovered in the background, biting his
lip, ill at ease, unable to scale the barriers walling him out.
And in her turn, Addawanna remained scrupulously neutral,
her silence a weight, refusing to tip the balance for either
side.

"We're *not* going back." A pounding fist on palm reiter-
ated Faeraday's determination. "We've left everything behind, what choice have you all given us?" And Jenret knew
"you all" included him, no allowance to be uniquely himself. Sides had been drawn before he'd learned the rules of
the game, let alone the name of it. All stood stiff, uncomfortable at the mounting tension.

"We've tasted fear before, our own fears and the fears of
others, and we worked so they'd find no fault, no reason to

direct that fear toward us. Now it's all over, all out in the open—thanks to Faeralleyn, here—at least for us." He glared at his youngest son, but Faertom's eyes were fixed on his feet. "Never satisfied, never happy with what you were but that you had to go wishing to be something more. Satisfied now, boy? Satisfied we've had to pull up stakes, start over somewhere else?"

A snap of the fingers, the toss of an empty hand dramatized their loss. "The boat business, gone. The house, the island, left behind as if plague-ridden. But we're the plague, aren't we? Liable to infect anyone our minds touch. Havens! Why would I want to 'speak a Normal mind? We don't know for sure if Marchmont'll welcome us as refugees—untutored, untrained, scum! That's how they've always viewed us before—why alter that view now?" The flood of invective dizzied Jenret. Why would Marchmont think that of them? How much did Marchmont even know of the Gleaners' precarious existence? After all, Venable Constant had believed he'd brought all the Resonants to Marchmont, safe from the Plumbs. If they'd known some had been left behind, why hadn't they helped before this?

"It doesn't have to be like that, not if you don't let it," Yulyn persisted, not ready to yield. "Canderis may be frightened of what we represent—what they think we are—but they can learn. But only if we're willing to show them our decency, our potential to improve their lives. Any group harbors good and bad, we know that. Would we have Vesey Bell seen as our exemplar? Our actions must repudiate what he stood for, the pain he caused, because that was never our way. Nor do the Reapers stand for Canderis as a whole, they're a distinct minority."

Uncomfortably aware that he and Sarrett represented all Normals, Towbin looked funeral-somber, careworn. "You take getting used to, you know. Considered fleeing far as I could when I discovered what Yulyn was, but I couldn't outrun our love, even if I didn't understand how her mind worked. Scared the living daylights out of me time and again. Has its advantages, though," and a ghost of a smile flickered at one corner of his mouth. "Lets your wife mentally caress you in public, with no one the wiser. No censorious looks. No flouting of decency laws. Scandalously sexy!" A dimple flashed on Claudra Thomas's cheek, but her husband scowled, red-faced with mortification.

"Two octs, that's all I ask," Jenret took their silent challenge. "Stay here at camp for sixteen days before you push on to Marchmont. I can't ask for longer, winter's coming. If other Resonants are hiding nearby or passing through, ask them to wait, hear me out when I return. I'll broaden our search as much as we can, try to find stragglers, direct them to you."

"And what can you promise by then? That Normals will magically come to terms with the idea of us, let alone our reality? That we won't be corralled together, imprisoned, ghettoized? We've heard rumors of a bounty for each Gleaner discovered." Faerclough spoke now, the middle son, as tall as the others, but more slightly built and more fiery tempered, his father's son.

"Then 'truth will out,' as they say. That's what we Seekers Veritas have always stood for, truth." Jenret spoke evenly, cloaking his despair. Sixteen days! Too short a time, you fool! Too short a time to negotiate with both sides for some sort of agreement, a face-saving compromise. Where to begin? Why had his stubbornness, his pride, led him to this impasse? But any truce was a start.

"Never could credit the ancient history books talking about 'endangered species' on Olde Earth, all kinds of different creatures lost because they couldn't survive a changing environment. Now I do." Faeraday Thomas ignored Jenret's outstretched hand. "Mind, though, I don't plan for my offspring to become extinct. I'll break the old rules to make sure of that. See that the terms hold." Not a threat, but a calm explication of what could come. What old rules? And again Jenret felt lost, at sea, wondering what was meant?

"We'll wait, Seeker, we'll wait," Claudra Thomas stated it as a fact, not simply a promise. "We've waited, fearful of discovery all our lives, all our parents' and grandparents' lives and beyond. Waiting sixteen more days won't hurt. Now I think it best you go."

As they readied to leave, the Thomas clan sliding away, canny as forest creatures eluding the hunter, Jenret at last heard a mindvoice. *"We'll wait, Seeker. And take good care of my boy, my youngest. Yes, he's impetuous, but he may just have the right of it. Old ways have to change, have to grow, or we will become extinct."*

Overwhelmed by the scale of the task they'd set for themselves, they settled around the fire at a deserted Erakwa camp that night. Addawanna's chuckle broke through their silence. "Now you know true what it like be ou'cast. Dey don' wan you, an you see any od'er Erawka 'cept me here? Erakwa don' wan you ed'er. Oh, I don' mind you, used to you, used to sharing after so long, but don' need share ev'ryting wid you!" Her innocent mirth seemed particularly mocking in the chilly night air, flaying their petty pride. Despite his genuine liking for her, Jenret glared back, defiant but unsure what he defied. Addawanna bridged two cultures, had ever since her liaison with a trader who, in truth, was Prince Ludo of Marchmont, father of her child, Nakum's long-dead mother. If Addawanna could bridge two cultures, so could he, Jenret thought, his respect for her growing.

Faertom stayed, face down-tilted, peeling thin strips of bark from a twig. Any desire to communicate had dwindled, died since his abortive reunion with his family, all his emotions, all thoughts barricaded inside his brain. Jenret yearned to ease his hurt but hadn't a clue where to begin, contented himself with patting his shoulder. It had comforted him when Darl Allgood had done it. But Faertom gasped at Jenret's alien, awkward touch and bolted from the firelight, crashing through the undergrowth.

Embarrassed by his reaction, Jenret started after him until Yulyn's soft command halted him. "Leave him be. You know what ails him, don't you?"

"Well, it should be fairly obvious, or should I say Faeraday, Faerbaen, and Faerclough obvious." Yulyn shoved hard at her husband's knee, angry at Towbin's whimsy.

"Well, that's enough, I agree, but there's more to it than that." She turned to include Sarrett in the conversation. "Any ideas?"

Sarrett propped herself on her elbows, T'ss on the blanket beside her. "I think so. All sons have to challenge their fathers at some point to prove their manhood."

"That's obvious. So?" He remembered his earlier thoughts about his father, his father's fears for what his younger son might be, but Jenret had been too young to challenge him. Jared as well, though his untrained Gleaner skills outstripped his youth. And if there wasn't a father to challenge, as there really hadn't been in his case when he'd reached adulthood, you chose a surrogate. He stiffened, realized he hadn't thought of it that way before. Syndar Saffron, his mother's lover, had played that role for him.

Sarrett sat up to emphasize her point. "How did he act when he first saw his father, Jenret? We weren't there to see."

"He busy watchin hatchet, bows an arrows, no bad idea right den," was Addawanna's rejoinder.

"I saw enough—eager, anticipatory. It didn't look like a challenge to me. And then blank, so blank you'd scarcely have known it was Faertom."

"Don't you see?" Yulyn shared a secret smile with Sarrett. Why had he expected that? If he still couldn't understand Doyce, did he have any chance of understanding Yulyn and Sarrett? Was this *another* bridge he'd be responsible for building—the one connecting men and women? Unfair, since he was hardly the first to discover the crossing tenuous. But Yulyn went on, "Conflict is one thing, it's to be expected. But he's not being allowed the battle he needs. By denying him that, by denying *him,* pretending he doesn't exist, Faertom's lost his way. Without them, who is he? Who or what is Faertom?"

"He's not a total innocent," Jenret protested, on the defensive for both himself and Faertom. "He's been out in the world, more so than his family. After all, he spent several years as a Transitor on road and bridge surveys."

Yulyn pressed home her point. "But did his work define him, the way it does for many people? Did he live it, eat, drink, and breathe it, the way many people do?"

"Like Seekers?" Sarrett needled.

"Or was he always a Resonant wearing the mask of a Transitor? He gave up that mask, revealed himself to take training at the Research Hospice. And now his relatives won't acknowledge him."

He was beginning to grasp Faertom's plight, but it was an imperfect understanding at best. After all, he was still a Seeker, no matter what else in his life had changed. "So Faertom's doubly doomed? He can't be what he was—that innocence is shattered—and he isn't sure what he is, without the battle to prove it?" He shared a look with Towbin, saw that he had no plans to enter the discussion. A wiser man than he'd realized—or more used to Yulyn than he. "Ah, I see," though Jenret wasn't entirely sure he did, and let the discussion drop.

A life so circumscribed that real life loomed impossibly large and elusive was almost beyond Jenret's ken, but pondering it wasn't going to do any good, he decided. Not when he had more pressing problems—such as reassuring the Resonants of his group's honorable intentions on their behalf. He dug out his leather writing case, licked a pencil point, and began to marshal his thoughts. If only he could convince the Monitor of what had to be done. He hoped, selfishly, that Faertom would reappear, at least by morning, so he could carry the letter to Gaernett. Haste was needed. And putting some distance, physical and emotional, between Faertom and his family wasn't a bad idea for a few days, at least.

Dismounting and tying his horse to a post, Bard scanned the barnyard nervously. Simply too much bustle and life for his liking, and he fervently wished he could mount and flee the commotion, the dust, the debris, chickens squawking as a cockerel challenged a rooster, geese hissing and flapping at his horse from their protective ring near the scummy watering trough.

"Plenty of activity, that's for sure," M'wa remarked from the safe vantage point of his pommel platform. **"Easy to get mislaid in it all."** A piglet squeezed under the fence, ran at his feet and butted, eager to have its ears scratched, for all the world like a puppy. Someone clearly treated it more as a pet than as a prospective dinner, and he prayed it wasn't Lindy.

"Byrta and I used to get misplaced in a similar bustle when we were little, shunted to the side because we looked different, acted different. At least we had each other amongst all the cousins and cattle," Bard noted absently as a diaperless child burst from the house, a pigtailed girl in hot pursuit. "Hallo, Lindy." The girl skidded to a halt, stood, one bare foot on top of the other, eyes large, the tip of a braid shielding her mouth.

Two quick back steps, one hesitant step forward, edging around him to see M'wa on the pommel platform. "You be the twin, the brother. How is she, how's my Byrta? Did her leg heal? How's P'wa?" Blue eyes devoured him, ready to swallow his good news whole, as if its digestion would soothe a craving inside her hungry for word. A man stood at the barn door, arms folded across his chest, expression too distant to read. A taller shadow behind him, sun glinting off the prongs of a raised pitchfork, and Bard winced at the recollection.

M'wa had sprung down to rub against the girl's shins, diverting her while Bard considered what to say, uneasy, hand crushed around the velvet bag in his pocket. **"You'll have to tell her sometime,"** the ghatt commented, allowing small hands to caress his neck and head, his ears with the familiar earrings removed.

He knew it, had known it all along, but had always avoided this part in his mind, jumping directly to his gifting her with the velvet pouch containing Byrta's and P'wa's earring sets, two gold hoops and gold balls. Had concentrated on Lindy's gratitude, her thankfulness for his largesse. Bard the laconic, honoring his sister by honoring the child. When one of a Bond-pair died, the survivor's earrings were removed—and hadn't he and Byrta been more of a Bond-pair than he and M'wa, she and P'wa? Wordlessly, he thrust out the pouch, almost dropped it on M'wa's black head with its white forehead star.

"Lindy," came a shout from the barn, "you don't be taking no presents from strangers," and the man was walking fast, each stride a judgment condemning Bard, ready to scoop the child out of harm's way.

The girl spun in a semicircle, both hands clutching the pouch, unsure of its contents but recklessly pleased with it, charmed by the deep blue velvet pouch itself. "But, Da," she protested, "it's not a stranger! It's the other twin pair, the Seeker brother Bard and his ghatt M'wa! How could ye not recognize'em? Like peas in a pod, she told me."

He'd interposed himself between Bard and the girl, the shelter of the house behind them. "Why, so it is, Lindy, so it is." His mouth relaxed marginally, but Bard was too intent on his own thoughts to pay much attention. "Why don't ye thank'em for the gift and scoot back to the house? Yer mither's wanting ya, I'm sure."

"No, wait!" Bard swallowed, but the lump remained, lodged like rock-hard bread, able to go neither up nor down. He felt light-headed, sick, bereft, head empty of everything except M'wa's comfort, Byrta's voice vanished, gone so long now. "She should . . . she should . . . know." Down on one knee, both to see the child's eyes and to steady himself, he clasped both hands over her own on the pouch, totally unaware of how exotic his honey skin and hair looked next to the homespun child. He gently loosened her grip, poured the pouch's contents onto the palm of his hand. "Not gems, because you're all your father's gems and he's no need of more, but a bit of jewelry. Byrta and P'wa wanted you to have them."

The girl's mouth opened slightly, not in mounting excitement, but rather with dawning apprehension, reading the unsaid words on his face. "W . . . wanted me . . . to have them?" But she pressed on, and Bard admired her resolve, though the next words dug a trench through his soul, "Why . . . why couldn't she give them to me herself? Is she . . . ?" She shook her head once, "She's . . . dead, isn't she? P'wa, too?"

No comfort in her speaking the dreaded words instead of articulating them himself. Indeed, coming from an outsider they hurt more than the private litany he'd devised, the constantly whispered reminder, *"She's dead, she's dead, she's dead,"* that echoed in the void her mindvoice once inhabited.

"Lindy! House! Now!" And strong hands propped him against the water trough, fanned him with a straw hat. "Simon, get the boys to scrub out the trough, damn geese've been swimming in it again." The words prosaic, homey, wonderfully distracting, as was the screeching protest of the pump, the splash of water in an old tin mug. "Didn't recognize you at first. Should have, but wanted to block that episode out of my mind, out of Lindy's mind, more likely, if I could."

"Out of Lindy's mind," Bard parroted, holding the mug like a sacramental chalice during Bethel services. Not that he and Byrta had often attended services, he thought irrelevantly, against his Sunderlies grandfather's wishes, against the old religion. M'wa smashed his head under his hand and splashed the mug's contents across his face. He gasped in shock.

"Deal with it, cope with it. I remember her with every heartbeat as well, so sleekly soft, my other half, my twin-

**sib P'wa, gone. But we have each other, self to self, not
enough perhaps, but it's all we have."**

Blankly Bard thrust out the mug for more water, and the
farmer obliged. It dawned on him that he didn't know the
farmer's name, thought of him only as Lindy's father. "I'm
Bard Ambwasali. My Bondmate M'wa. There wasn't much
time for pleasantries when last we met." He stuck out his
hand, only to grasp the refilled mug.

"Might try drinking it this time. Marlin, Japeth Marlin."
He toed the piglet aside as it struggled into Bard's lap.
"Warned her again and again not to make such a pet of it.
Have to eat it, you know, sooner or later." Bard shook his
head in agreement. "So, what did she die of? Leg get infected before it could heal proper? 'Twas a bad break." He
shifted his concentration from the piglet, dying sooner or
later, for food, not for love, and realized the man spoke
about Byrta.

Pulling himself up the water trough, he dusted himself off,
ran a hand through the close-cropped hair, tiny curls colored
like maple syrup shavings, heritage of his mixed Sunderlies-
Canderisian parentage, as was the honey-gold complexion,
the smoke-haze eyes. Neither dark mahogany like their father, nor blonde and pale like their mother, he and Byrta had
been unique: in their coloring, their twinness, their secret
speech unchallenged by others. Upright now, less chance to
pity a man who stood on his own feet. "No. No, the leg
healed fine. She died in the wars up north this spring,"
couldn't bring himself to say more, to say she'd been be-
headed, and hear again his inarticulate cry of grief as he'd
caught the severed head, pressed his lips to her mouth. Nor
speak of P'wa, head crushed and bloody, lifeless.

"Ah." Marlin shuffled his feet. "Sorry. More lost there
than most of us realized, had other things on our minds
here with tall tales of Gleaners and what like. It explains,
though, why Lindy's dreams have been getting worse and
worse."

"Dreams? Worse?" Conversation seemed beyond him, the
mere repetition of words the safest course.

"Aye. It's been over a year now, nine octants, belike, since
we sheltered Byrta in our barn waiting for you, waiting for
the eumedicos. Late summer, almost autumn then, now it's
autumn, near winter. We can't do a thing about those dreams,
the wife and I, though we've tried. Wakes up screaming in

the night, most every night, wakes up all the other childers as well." He shrugged, a vaguely pleased gesture, "And we've a brood of those as well as all the animals you see here."

"Find out more about the dreams. It might be important."

"What does she dream about?" He didn't want to know, didn't want to share the knowledge. No more sharing.

"First she just replayed the attack in her mind, but come spring, things got worse. Didn't surprise me when she swore she saw Byrta's head in her dreams, blood streaming from it. Overactive imagination, begging your pardon."

Bard stood rigid. **"No, you didn't tell him how she died, no way he could know, or Lindy."**

"I wish, wish we could get her away somewhere else, send her someplace different, mayhap a change of scene would take her mind off it." He sighed, apologetic. "Can't exactly pull up stakes here, decide to farm elsewhere. Offered to send her to my sister's, two towns over, but she wouldn't have a thing to do with that, kept saying it was too close to the hospice there. None of us has got a full night's sleep for so long now. Half the time I can't fall asleep waiting for her to scream." Picking at the straw hat's brim, shredding it, he confessed, "Feel like I've failed. Fathers are supposed to be big and strong enough to chase away the night terrors."

"We must help. She aided Byrta and P'wa without thought of her own life, now we have to help her." The ghatt's words stung his soul, shaming him. What could he do, how could he help, and why, why should he ever involve himself with another human being? **"Didn't Byrta say the girl had a knack for dealing with little ones, children? Used to dandling them, diapering them, and training them on the pot?"**

"So?" he 'spoke back. *"Since when do we know any children who need a nursemaid only half-again as high as they are?"*

"Well, isn't Doyce going to need additional help, an extra set of legs to run errands, do simple tasks, watch over the infant at odd moments?"

"But you can't just snatch a child, haul her to Gaernett, and put her in the house with Doyce! I don't know anything about Japeth Marlin and his family, and he knows naught of me. I could be stealing his child for all he knows!" But Bard had a strange feeling a decision had been reached, whether he

and Marlin knew it or not. What set his mind shying was that earrings were part of the traditional bride-price, as if he'd purchased the child, buying her just as his grandfather had bought his three wives before their trek from the Sunderlies to Canderis with their precious cattle. Just as he'd sent back jewelry, gold, and cattle to buy Sunderlies wives for his other sons, Bard's uncles. Only the twins' father had fought tradition, earned his bride with love. *"You can't buy a human being."*

"You're not buying her. You're buying time to let her heal and a new environment in which to do it. She's not property, but she *will* be your responsibility until she comes of age, decides what she wants to do with her life."

Diffidently, Bard looked at Marlin. "Would you consider loaning one of your gems to me, sir? A new setting for it, perhaps, and a chance for her to earn her keep, send a bit back here?"

Maroon felt bedroom slippers whispering secrets to the carpet, the Monitor belted his robe more snugly, shuffled over to poke at the fire he'd just coaxed to life. And didn't he know what would coax it to life even better—some of those damned letters over there in the tray for starters! Paperwork, paperwork, more bloody correspondence to read, digest, answer. Why had he bothered to drag it all into Marie's little sitting room instead of just girding his loins and taking his place behind the desk in his office? Ruddy light reflected against the blue and white tiles framing the fireplace, and he scuffed to the window, lifted the white cotton curtains with their eyelet lace edgings that Marie kept so scrupulously starched, even with servants here to help her. Even missed the ironing, if she were to be believed. A gradual lightening, as if the sun might consent to rise. At least some things were still constant in life, he decided as he puffed on the glass, watched his breath mist. Overcast again today and that suited his mood.

The real reason he'd sought refuge in the sitting room rather than ensconcing himself in his office was because it still felt so empty with just him there, working through the dawning until it was time for official business to begin. "Oh, Aelbert, I miss you," he whispered to his ghost reflection in the windowpanes. And N'oor, too, the poor little ghatta who had loved too well, though not too wisely. Gone now, gone forever, and had he ever truly known either of them? Obviously not. Aelbert, so efficient and so self-effacing, a Seeker whose special uniform marked him as part of the Monitor's staff. Why did you have to yearn for what couldn't be yours, strive for it in a way that could only harm you?

However justified Aelbert's dreams, they'd been unrealistically grandiose—a rankling desire for full acknowledgment as a scion of Marchmontian royalty, a place amongst them. And capable of working with Prince Maurice's perversions to succeed. This, this hadn't been the young man he'd cherished, depended upon, and he, he'd had no idea what seethed in Aelbert's brain. But then, why should he? He'd treated Aelbert as useful, necessary, indispensable, but hadn't viewed him as a human being fraught with his own longings and needs, hadn't treated him like the surrogate son he'd longed to be. If he had, would it have stemmed Aelbert's other desires? He'd failed again ... by omission. But, by the Blessed Lady Above, what was he supposed to be—miracle worker, mind reader?

In the adjacent bedroom Marie sighed dreamily, the bed creaking as she shifted, resettled. Listening to make sure she'd fallen back asleep, he touched a spill to the fire and lit the oil lamp. Spreading the papers on Marie's sewing table, he surveyed them with mounting disgust. Reports from this, reports from that, summary papers from each High Conciliator recounting what had transpired in his or her province each octant. And the letters—from Canderisian citizens urgent to make their voices heard, their views count. Concerned citizens fearful of Resonants, airing their grievances, their woes; and a few from Resonants as well, attesting to their fears, their desire to have their voices heard and counted. Many of those were anonymous, and with good reason, he knew, but a few showed defiant, scrawling signatures as if they'd emblazon their names across the sky and be damned. "This is who I am," they seemed to cry, "like it or not."

He worked as rapidly as he could and still remain thorough, gave each piece its due, though many were due a great deal less effort and interest than they believed. Scribbling notes in the margins, at the bottom for his secretary to decipher and send responses. Both justified and unjustified complaints needed soothing; many could be turned over to the Seekers Veritas to determine the truth of the matter. Still, it was one thing to rationally know you were wrong, misguided, and another to actually believe it in your heart and soul. Fears festered, perceived injustices rankled. The sky outside turned lighter, though not especially bright and he could hear the servants beginning their kitchen fires, brewing cha. How he needed it, that first steaming cup when he'd slip back in bed beside Marie to sip it, feign a sleepy wakening that wouldn't fool his wife, though she'd conspire with him to pretend she did. Of such indulgences, of such shared little lies is life made.

Damn all, how'd this letter land in that folder? Should have remembered it had arrived. He'd known Faertom had made a hurried trip back to Gaernett with this, Darl had told him so. Should have been on top of the pile, who'd shifted it? Probably himself in the shuffling of papers. Scratching his scalp vigorously with his pencil, he pursed his lips as he read:

Dear Monitor:

I've spoken with such Resonants as I could find and who were willing to reveal themselves to me. Precious few, I might add, but luckily I stumbled on Faeralleyn Thomas's family. I've begged them to give us time, two octs—though 16 days is hardly sufficient—to demonstrate our sincerity in including Resonants as an integral part of our society. Without such reassurances, I fear they may either emigrate to Marchmont, which may not be prepared for such an influx, or remain sequestered in the forests, letting justified anxieties fester into anger and very possibly rebellion.

They will no longer be content as lesser citizens of the shadows, grateful for the bitter dregs a shadow existence offers them, but want to quench their thirst for equality. The stakes are high: we need them and their abilities, although not everyone realizes how much they have to offer. I hesitate to speak out of turn, but it's clear to me that they have much to share with the eumedicos. You may not be aware, though all Seekers are aware, that eumedicos no longer possess their vaunted mindtrance skills, the inner "sight" that plumbs mind and body to seek out ailments. It's possible certain Resonants can assist in training our eumedicos to regain that skill, perhaps become superior eumedicos themselves. Please speak with my aunt, Mahafny Annendahl, about this, for she, at least, is likely to be pragmatic about the situation and not dissemble about the lack.

The Monitor was amused by Jenret's assumptions. "Give me *some* credit, Wycherley, I wasn't born yesterday." He liked and respected most eumedicos he knew, Mahafny most of all. In fact he'd worship at her feet if she could devise a way to accurately identify Resonants. Interesting to think Resonants might know something about mindtrances, only the gullible believed in such eumedico hocus. Not that he'd ever take Mahafny to task for her eumedico rituals. If it worked for most of the populace, who was he to gainsay the practice? Mahafny'd often said half the healing comes from the mind itself. But Jenret's point was well-taken. He went back to the letter.

Finally, we must have an edict, a proclamation, some sort of law unequivocally stating that Resonants are equal. This may seem overdone, unnecessary, because we know all citizens are equal. We need more than mere lip service to what we know as truth. Further, that any discrimination will not be tolerated and will be prosecuted to the fullest extent of our laws. Perhaps we need new laws granting special protections to this group, spelling out the rights and responsibilities of all citizens so that no one group usurps the rights of another—Normal over Resonant, or Resonant over Normal.

Your speedy response will be greatly appreciated
as time passes more quickly than we realize.
I remain, faithfully yours,
Jenret Wycherley
Seeker Veritas/Resonant

And is there a mountain or two you'd like me to move
while I'm at it, Wycherley? A raging torrent to swim? Postpone, ameliorate, that was the best he could do. He couldn't
even whip the High Conciliators into a cohesive group. So
delay, dance and delay, and preserve the status quo. Don't
make it worse, but don't make it better. The Monitor
scrubbed at his stubble. Well, let's see, I *could* make sure the
applicable sections of the laws are printed and distributed,
along with emendations that explain in crystal clear, indisputable language that the laws offer equal protection to
Resonants.

That was within his powers without a vote. Possibly an innocuous resolution of some sort where he could bluster and
cajole, arm-twist to gain a simple majority, thirteen out of
twenty-four High Conciliators' votes, that's all he'd need.
Darl would help with that, help him think up what the resolution would resolve. He smiled, tested the phrase. "This
resolution hearby resolves, this declaration declares . . ." He
waved Jenret's letter as if graciously acknowledging a
throng of people. Bet the King of Marchmont does that all
the time.

What was stuck to the back of Wycherley's letter—
another piece of paper? He pried it loose, rolled off the bit
of pine pitch with his finger before he studied it. As was
his custom, he quickly glanced at the signature to see if the
name gave a hint of the problem. Anonymous, blast, blast.
Pinching sticky finger against thumb, he scanned the printing, almost prissy neat, each letter perfectly aligned. Well,
surely not a eumedico, never could read their writing. More
likely some sort of very precise, fussy individual, a
Transitor or an engineer of some sort, they wrote like
that.

Dear Sir:
I regret to inform you that you unwittingly harbor

a Resonant in your midst, one who has insinuated himself into your trust and the trust of the people. Indeed, for too long he has perverted the people's trust and respect, serving first as a Chief Conciliator and now as a High Conciliator, putting himself and his ilk first against the needs of the majority of Canderis. Darl Allgood is a viper nestling in the bosom of Canderis. Do not let him spread his perversions, work his wiles with his tainted skills. Cut him down, cleanse your house before it is too late! Reveal him, shame him, destroy him and his kind before you are tarred by the same brush. Protect him, and you, too, may face the just punishment awaiting him.

Sincerely,
A Concerned Citizen of Canderis

A shiver ripped through his body and he ground his teeth to conquer it, tried to let the letter drop, but the pitch worked against him again. At last he shook his hand violently and the paper sailed free to land on the carpet, its white outline smugly self-righteous, its black print like loathsome, disgusting tracks of slime. Rubbing his hands together as if to cleanse them, he strove to calm himself, to quell the rising nausea flooding him.

Poppycock! Unabashed, unadulterated poppycock! But the word wasn't powerful enough to efface the filth he'd let enter his mind. Oh, he'd read worse anonymous rantings in his time, but . . . but. . . . His mind boggled. Not Darl, not after he'd come to know and respect the man, consider him a friend. A deep breath, and he held it, finally exhaled.

If it were true, did he like or respect Darl any less for being a Resonant? But if it *were* true, he was angry at Darl for not being forthright about it. After all, keeping him on as High Conciliator would show the Resonants they were trusted enough to be part of government. And that was exactly the sort of thing Wycherley was looking for, something in earnest. He worried it through again, found solace in the fact that the few Resonants he knew, Faertom and Jenret,

Yulyn Biddlecomb, that man he'd briefly met—Fahlgren claiming his murdered wife's body—had made no mention of it. Surely *they* would have said, given some indication. Ergo, Darl Allgood was *not* a Resonant.

The letter was nothing more than a foul, corrupt piece of garbage, slanderous lies. Body limp with relief, he got up and walked to the fireplace, stirred the fire higher, and used the poker to impale the treacherous letter that had temporarily shaken his faith in Darl Allgood. The sound of it crackling, the sight of its edges curling as it burned, made him feel better. Done, stirring the pieces of ash into the coals, he left the sitting room and reentered the bedroom, crawled into bed beside Marie, warmly drowsy and welcoming.

It never occurred to Kyril van Beieven that not all Resonants knew each other or even of each other, so sheltered in their own little enclaves that safety meant not knowing one soul more than one had to know. Because knowing might mean inadvertently revealing one of your own.

"I tell you, it's unbelievable! Absolutely knocked me off my feet, my foot, when I heard!" Parse waved one crutch in extravagant celebration, nearly spearing a passerby, then stumped to catch up with Doyce. Walking through the brick-streeted maze of Gaernett's old quarter, they breasted a sudden freshet of students pouring out of school, their scholars' robes the iridescent shade of a mourning dove in the afternoon sun.

Preceded by her stomach, Doyce tried not to crowd Parse off the narrow walkway, let alone others coming from the opposite direction. Sometimes, especially in cramped quarters, she feared she'd sweep aside everything in her path. A shift leftward gave Parse more space to wield his crutches. Except—where had that man come from?—the one she'd nearly pinned to the wall. He glowered, then gave a mock bow, an "after you" gesture on noting her condition. The decorative pin on his high collar caught her attention as he bowed—a crescent moon shape, or perhaps a scythe, pinned over a piece of wheat. Rather like the rank insignia the Guardians wore.

"Parse, what does the pin indicate?" she whispered, grabbing his shoulder. Parse pivoted back to look and his brow furrowed, his mouth tightened.

"Don't you know? You've been locked in the library too long. They call themselves Reapers." Per'la and Khar drew closer behind them, vigilant, Per'la's new tail ribbon fluttering in the cross-breeze from intersecting alleyways. "Reap what was sown, and Reap thoroughly till not a gleaning or a Gleaner is left. That's supposed to be their motto."

She shivered. "Are you saying what I think you're saying? How can the Monitor allow them to wear those pins as a badge of pride? Do they meet openly?"

"Better to be able to identify them than not—that's the Monitor's theory. And as long as they do nothing wrong, they have every right to meet." Parse speeded up as if to outrun his thoughts. "I don't like it either, but that's the way it is."

How could he act so blasé? Did everyone take the Reapers' existence as a matter of course? Or had the world indeed changed while she did her research? As she continued on, her gaze swept over each person she passed, ceaselessly searching for more insignia, another mark of madness, ready to deny a segment of humanity its existence. After a time she managed to put it into perspective—almost—and acknowledge that there would always be those who disagreed with something. The question was whether they'd be content with simply disagreement or decide to take more decisive action. What would poor Harrap, with his Shepherd's ways, think of all this? Tell her to love them despite their flaws? She sniffed in derision, concentrated on Parse's forced but cheery prattle, appreciating his attempt to distract her.

She'd half allowed herself be swept along by Parse's news but refused to let her enthusiasm get out of hand. A retired Seeker 103 years old living in the Elder Hostel and she hadn't been aware of it. Amazing! And not claiming retired Seeker status and benefits, but living as a private citizen. Still, she'd checked the old records herself before leaving and had found Maize Bartolotti's name and that of her ghatta An'g. A brief four years of service before the notation of An'g's death. "Parse, best not get too excited. At 103, we don't know what to expect." Possibly the woman was still alert, interacted with the present on a daily basis, but hardly likely.

Parse negotiated a broken piece of pavement, concentrating on planting his crutches. A satisfied grin flashed when he dared look up, eyes merry. "Think I'd have dragged you out of your musty, dusty library lair without checking? Though frankly, Per'la and I are convinced you need fresh air, more exercise."

"You're mother-henning me worse than Swan and Mahafny, and she's a eumedico. Do this, don't do that. It's a perfectly natural process, and it's not my first time, you know." Though it *had* been years, another life since Briony's birth and her subsequent death at Vesey's childish hands. That longed-for pregnancy, that birth, had restored at least a limited confidence after her failure as a eumedico, as long as she didn't dwell on the torment after that. A completely separate issue, a completely separate tragedy. Or were there other Veseys to threaten this baby? What if hatred were like a coin: Vesey's perverted Resonant skills on one side, and on the reverse, a Reaper capable of slaying a child who inherited Jenret's Resonant powers?

"Firstly," Parse chattered on, oblivious to her distant expression, the protective hand on her belly. "I checked with the Matron about Maize Bartolotti's condition—and it's astoundingly good. Secondly, if you'd looked at her service dates more closely, you'd have made the connection that she served as a Seeker Veritas during Magnus deWit's final days. You know what that means, Doyce."

She whistled. Magnus deWit and his ghatt Ru'wah had challenged Crolius Renselinck, Seeker General at the time, and his ghatta V'row, for control of the Seekers nearly 150 years ago. Some correspondence existed from that period, material she'd given Parse to study, as well as later commentaries, written well after the fact from an historical perspective, but this, *this* was a chance to reach out to history, to almost touch it. Although Maize hadn't been born when the actual incident took place, she had, perhaps, heard firsthand from deWit what had happened. Very possible, since Maize had worked in the infirmary far more often than she'd ridden circuit. Possible, if deWit hadn't been senile by then.

"Well, at least the story's been handed down only once," Khar sniffed. **"Not told to someone who told it to someone who told it to someone until it becomes the stuff of myth and legend, less the truth than a shadow of it."**

Per'la chimed in, trotting into Parse's path to attract his attention. **"Remember, Ru'wah was long dead by then,**

not there to remind Magnus of the truth. It's possible that after brooding on it in his own mind for years, he created his own version of the story."

Parse halted, panting but triumphant. "True, true, but you're forgetting my precious, that if Maize heard the story directly from Magnus deWit's lips, likely An'g heard it as well, judged whether he lied to himself or not." Jubilant at quelling both Doyce and the ghatti, Parse huffed on, picking up speed, reckless with anticipation.

A sunny, small courtyard, the last roses of the season climbing its low walls, beckoned them off the street. No mistaking this place: elderly residents sat on benches or lay on lounges, basking in the sun, some aware of their surroundings, others clearly not, whimpering, rocking, conversing with nonexistent visitors. Shame seethed within her as she patted the crumpled letter in her pocket. Their mother wasn't well, Francie had written, but she couldn't, she mustn't be ready for a place like this. To be abandoned in these final years, infirm of body or of mind, or both. Waiting, simply waiting—for the next meal, the next activity, the next nap, or for relatives who never came. But the real visitor they were always alert for—some with happiness, some with fear—was death, the final caller.

Although not terribly common in Canderis, Elder Hostels did exist for those without close relatives or with relations unable to assume the burden of caring for an aged family member. They were, she lectured herself sternly, a necessity, not an admission of defeat. Indeed, given her sister Francie's crippled condition, could she properly care for their mother when that day came? Given her own career as a Seeker Veritas, how could *she* cope, make a home for them when she so rarely *was* home, barely had a home of her own? The choices narrowed before her eyes, closing her in, binding her with shame. And how to make a home for the baby? Hadn't she thought any of this through?

Throat constricted, forcing herself to focus on inanimate objects not people, she let Parse chat with the Matron as they stepped inside. The smell, faint as it was, assaulted her nostrils: disinfectants, antiseptic cleaning smells so familiar from her time as a eumedico, the heavy aroma of vased roses, pine boughs hung over doorways all lightened but couldn't entirely dispel the other scents—urine, decaying bodies, steamed food, and most of all, the stench of hope-lessness.

They traversed tiled halls, the tiles, she noticed, etched with textured waves to afford elderly, slippered feet better purchase. Not as easy to scrub and disinfect, but far safer footing. Worn but polished handrails at two different wall heights offered support and balance. There was no time for more exploration because the Matron stopped and tapped at a closed door, and Doyce wondered, hoping against hope, what awaited them inside.

A pause but no response, and the Matron tapped, louder this time but without impatience. "Miz Maize," she spoke distinctly without raising her voice, "Don't try hiding under the bed, it's not the eumedico, I promise! It's the visitors I told you about, the Seekers. Ghatti, too!"

"You'd best not be fooling me, girl! You're a nice young thing, but you've stretched the truth before," came a voice through the door. "Always promising it's for my own good, but that's debatable, in'it?" A scrambling noise, then the creak of a rocking chair. "Well, come in, and there'd better be ghatti. Not right to lie to an old woman, get her hopes up, her heart a-racing."

The Matron swung the door open, and Doyce hovered on the threshold, almost loath to enter the world of the elderly, Parse peering over her shoulder. Uninhibited by her reserve, the ghatti had already glided inside, inspecting the petite fig-ure ensconced in the rocking chair. "Oh, pretty ghatti," Maize Bartolotti breathed. Large-knuckled hands twisted with excitement, suppressed joy as both Khar and Per'la planted front paws on chair arms, stretching so she could reach their heads. "Sleekest tiger stripes I ever did see, such a perfect pink nose," she crooned as she traced the markings on Khar's head before shifting to Per'la. "And that tail rib-bon, absolutely perfect. Wear it with pride, as a badge of honor, I'm thinking, am I right?" Her face gleamed with a hectic gaiety, a restrained longing. "Too much to ask, after all this time, but . . . mindwalk if ye will." And leaned back, stiff with resignation, not daring to hope.

"**But of course, revered one,**" Per'la purred. "**Why should we hide our voices from one of our own?**" Despite herself, "**Do you really like the ribbon, not too gaudy, you don't think?**"

"**No need for loneliness while we're here. Your wel-**

come was assured, why not make it known you desired companionship? You would have honored us." Khar had jumped into the chair, straddling the frail body to avoid pressing her full weight on the woman.

"I know, I know, too prideful, mayhap. And what I once shared is long past, long done." Bird-bright black eyes tore themselves from the ghatti to inspect her human visitors. "Well, sit, sit. Hurts my neck craning up at you like this," and her head tilted in exaggeration. Doyce complied, sitting on the foot of the bed, hands jammed in the pockets of her overvest to wrap it around her stomach. What had possessed her to choose something pumpkin-colored? As if she needed that particular comparison! A brief moan took her mind off her lack of fashion-sense as she realized Parse was debating what to do. Lady bless, she'd forgotten his problem, hadn't asked for days how he fared. Apparently Twylla's salve had offered no salvation as he reluctantly hitched his hip on the cluttered nightstand beside the bed.

The black eyes regarded him, head cocked, assessing his behavior, his obvious discomfort. An embarrassed shift, a squirm, and Parse grazed a small, framed portrait. "Easy, boy, easy," Maize rescued the tarnished silver frame. "Let me guess, let me guess. Don't mean to be personal, like, but what is it? Boils? Bed sores? Not been up on those crutches all too long by the looks of your maneuvering. Spent too long in bed, belike?"

Parse nodded, shamefaced. "Boils, most likely allergic. I'm allergic to lots of things."

Rummaging in the nightstand, she extracted a capped jar, squinted at the label, put it back, dug farther inside, as if excavating. The second jar pleased her. "Here, try this, this instant. Likely you're allergic to the soap they wash the sheets in, too much disinfectant. Wouldn't be the first time it's happened." Parse clutched the proffered jar. "I said now, boy, dab it on now. Hide in the corner if you're bashful, but I doubt you've nothing I've never seen before, your friend here either, given the state she's in."

Struggling to remain solemn and, worst of all, desperate not to follow Parse with her eyes as he stumped into the corner, Doyce interrupted. "I do apologize. I don't believe we've offered our names, although the ghatti have introduced themselves. My red-haired friend, the pantless one,"

Parse grumbled at her description, "is Parcellus Rudyard, Parse for short, and I'm Doyce Marbon."

The rocking chair picked up speed. "Well, well, war heroes, both of ye. I read the broadside every Acht-dag when it comes out. Wait by the door to get it first, else it's all mauled and food-stained, drool, too. Welcome, welcome, though I don't know what brings ye here."

Too lively, too sharp to be immured in an Elder Hostel, although she didn't know what infirmities or ailments of old age the woman might suffer. **"Haven't you realized? She can't walk more than a few steps at a time. Didn't you notice the crutches by the door, the outline of braces under her dress?"** Her heart thumped once in understanding, sadness. No wonder Maize empathized with Parse's plight.

But before pity could swamp her, Maize continued indomitably. "So why visit an old lady like me? Not much use to anyone these days, I'm feared." But her black eyes glowed, expectant, yearning, despite her disclaimers.

To Doyce's amazement, Parse joined her on the bed, shifting his weight delicately, wondrous relief washing over his face. "Numb, blessedly cool and numb. Lady bless you! I don't know how long the effect lasts, but it's stupendous!"

Where to begin? How to build a connection from the here and now to the past? How to show Maize she was still wanted and needed—not only for the past stored in her head, but to actively involve her in the process of discovery? Could Maize discern implications of the past in the present? Or was it too much to hope?

But Parse burst in, no gainsaying him. "We're immersed in a project, Doyce and I, or rather, she's writing it and I'm helping with research. A Bicentennial History of the Seekers Veritas, isn't it a grand idea?"

"Wasn't a Seeker very long," Maize sounded dubious, the chair slowing as if they'd both run down simultaneously. "Spent longer at other things. Only four years of my life, not much to tell. You've both served longer than I, and if I added your ages together I'd guess it would come out, barely over half my years. Think you'll play Sixteen Questions, test the old lady's memory? Just like the eumedicos— 'Who's the Monitor? What did you have for dinner last night?' I asked one what he'd eaten last night and he couldn't remember!" Something, something had made her pull back, distance herself, whether she misered her thoughts, her memories, or whether she honestly doubted she had anything of value to share.

Khar, half-curled, half-crammed beside Maize, flicked her tail, offered them a key to the locked memories. **"Ask about her ghatta."**

"It hurts to lose any of the ghatti," and memories of Chak, P'wa, and poor, desperate little N'oor crowded her head, "but to lose yours so early, in the prime of life, your shared beginnings. What was she like?"

The tarnished silver frame now rested against Maize's rib cage, near her heart. "My An'g? My An'g." And despite the fact that Doyce had mentally spoken the name when she'd read the records, she'd not realized it was pronounced with such a soft sound, more the "g" in "angel," rather than the hard "g" in "angle."

"You needed to hear it with love from her own lips."

"So much beauty, so much beneficence, so truly clever but always so frail. Her body never thrived, though her brain was so incisive. I worked in the infirmary as much as I could in hopes I'd learn something that might help her." A wavering hand thrust the portrait in their direction. Rescuing it, Doyce studied the small oil portrait of An'g. A thin, triangular face with large, almost translucent pink-white ears, slanted eyes the color of citrine. Snowy white with a gray cap and tail and the hint of three gray patches on her lower back.

"Beautiful," she breathed, blinking unshed tears, and remained lost in those prescient citrine eyes, almost jealous at sharing the image with Parse. Why hadn't she ever had Khar's portrait painted?

"Because my stripes would dizzy the artist. And you'd be cross if any were missing or misplaced."

Somehow mollified by their silent homage, Maize snatched the picture back, fingertips caressing the frame. "Aye, the best part of me and for too short a time. After that, somehow didn't matter that I married, had children, created another life for myself far longer than the one I'd shared with An'g. Everything was pleasant, nice, but nothing ever quite lived up to that brief time. And after losing An'g, even losing my own child and grandchild didn't seem any worse, any more painful than that. Horrified some when I said that, but it's truth. Perspective, I guess. Different perspective, different values after that. Even makes living here palatable enough. I guess." She returned the picture to the nightstand.

"But I think I know what you came for, not to hear an old woman's maunderings about her long-dead Bondmate, but to hear about Magnus deWit. Only thing that makes sense. Am I right?"

Parse bounced on the bed, boils either forgotten or truly painless. "Oh, yes, yes! If you could—anything, please! He died shortly after you left the Seekers Veritas. I've been reading some of his old correspondence, piecing the story together. But to hear anything he might have told you about it, even so long after the fact, could be priceless in evaluating the situation."

Caught in the grip of his enthusiasm, Parse managed to come to a halt while Doyce tried to gauge her reaction. Maize had been absolutely correct—no, they weren't here to discuss *her* life, but to hear what she remembered about another's life. Not exactly flattering, viewing Maize as the vessel carrying that information.

"Might consider it, oh, might consider seeing what's stored in this old brain of mine. But tit for tat, you know." Maize turned shrewd, weighing their need, their willingness and intentions. "Might be what you can do for me," she wheedled, "if ye be willing."

So, still canny enough to remember how the game was played. What was the bargaining chip to be? Hardly money, Doyce thought. Her own chapter, or perhaps An'g's own chapter in the book? A promise to visit again? But she'd already promised herself that Maize would be receiving more visits from Seekers and their ghatti Bondmates. Her service, however brief, no longer overlooked.

Per'la rolled peridot eyes, swished her tail ribbon. **"It's not much to ask, you know. An expedition, just a little expedition. Fresh air, sunshine, new vistas and remembered scenes."**

"Hardly too much to ask," Khar chimed in. **"And merrily we'll roll along."**

❖

Merrily we'll roll along is a pain in the fan-danny! Doyce inwardly fumed as she heaved and shoved the wheeled chair across grass overdue for mowing, dips and hollows lying in wait to trap the wheels. Naturally their goal was the far end of the Seeker burial grounds, several acres distant from Headquarters where the earlier graves lay. Parse's assistance was minimal, not that she'd expected much, but just when she relied on him to brace himself, help push the chair over a rut, one crutch or the other would sink into the lawn, bringing him to a screeching halt until he could extricate himself.

Per'la nosed at one of the punctures. **"It looks like moles attacked the lawn."**

"I know. Even managed to burrow a bit back there. Have him nail pie tins to the bottom of his crutches, give him a broader base. Not a bad idea, actually," Khar considered, sat, and scratched.

"Leftward, sharp now," Maize commanded and Doyce, sweaty and tired, pushed her scabbard out of the way and complied. The wheeled chair resembled an oversized version of a baby's carriage, front wheels slightly smaller than the rear ones, the front pair incapable of independent action, their axle anchored straight across, not set on a floating pivot. What they did with frequency was jam. Cornering was not its strong point either unless she tilted the chair, shifted her weight, practically lifting one rear wheel clear while she swiveled the chair on the other. Surely Parse, with his love of puzzles, could create something superior to this overgrown wicker perambulator with its unwieldy wheels. Perambulation was hardly an apt description for such grueling labor.

"Over there! I can see it! Shame they haven't mowed more recently." An imperious arm now pointed right, and Doyce sighed, heaved her weight in that direction. Her shoulders ached—and her back. Impossible to put her whole body into the effort with her belly constantly in the way. "Now! Stop here!" At last Maize called a halt.

Not sure how she'd haul herself up, but not particularly caring, Doyce flung herself on the grass, Parse collapsing beside her. Joy and rapture, now she'd have to pull him up as well! She peered at the small white stone, its incised lettering blurred by moss and lichen, an old wreath from the Annual Remembrance Day dried and faded at its base. "An'g—Beloved Bond of Maize Bartolotti. 146–150 AL." Parse stretched to retrieve the flowers Maize clutched in one shaking hand, the other crushing a handkerchief. Levering himself across the grass with his good leg, he arranged the flowers at the stone's base, saluted respectfully.

"Wasn't what you think it was like, back then, not a bit of it. Don't know if you can credit what it meant to be a Seeker back then." Maize's voice cracked and she bit her lip. "Oh, I wouldn't say you've got it easy now, but things are more regulated, regimented, almost a regular job rather than a vocation."

The words stung. "Hardly a job," Doyce protested. "It's still a vocation, a calling. One you're called to with no warning, no say in the matter, but to serve and serve your best. There's no backing out when you're Chosen. You don't 'choose' to be a Seeker, study for it, pass some examination." She certainly hadn't—already convinced she'd been a failure at everything she'd tried. Her failure as a eumedico, unable to accept the necessary lie that the emedicos' vaunted mindtrance truly let them "see" the illnesses within their patients. Her failure as a wife and mother—bereft by husband's and infant daughter's deaths at the hands of her stepson, Vesey. Naturally she'd expected to fail at being a Seeker Veritas.

"Except for the examination we subject you to before we choose you," Khar corrected, bringing her back to the present. **"Fail our test and you're free to become anything you want, except a Seeker. You *are* glad you passed, aren't you?"**

"Yes, love. And in eternal training, according to you," she 'spoke back.

"It was all so silly, you know, ultimately childish." Maize shook her head, staring off into the distance before twisting to look behind her at Headquarters. "They didn't even have a real Headquarters then, not while Crolius was Seeker General. Oh, had the idea for it, wanted and needed it, but Seekers were leery about settling in one place. Most they had was a stone house they'd built a few years before, someplace for the records, a place for the Seeker General to hold meetings and off duty Seekers to gather."

Parse rolled onto his stomach, chin cupped in hands, grass stem bobbing from his mouth. "You don't mean the old stone guest house? Doyce, the guest house where you and Jenret are living."

She'd presumed it was old, but had no inkling it was that

old. Had Matthias Vandersma ever stayed there? No, silly thought, it was built well after his time.

But Maize continued, implacable once she'd begun, and Doyce feared she'd missed something. "Changes, changes were coming, and people don't always get along with changes. Think they want something new and different, yet in their hearts they want things just as they've always been. You see, Crolius and V'row had already been making changes, had a vision of the way they thought things ought to be. Not easy having visions, ideas nobody else has thought of yet." She began to tick off points on her fingers.

"Formalized training for newly chosen Seekers, not just serving a 'catch as catch can' apprenticeship, riding circuit with a seasoned Seeker. Drew up formal circuits, schedules so Seekers would know when and where they'd work and for how long, and be entitled to time off. Not wear themselves out young for the good of others. Convinced the Monitor and the High Conciliators that Seekers were an essential service, deserved to be paid, not live hand to mouth like mendicants, dependent on others' largesse for food or clothing, shelter or transport.

"But to Magnus's and Ru'wah's minds, all this organization, this formal structure, meant the Seekers were becoming soft, losing their purpose, their goal of serving all without fear or favor when it came to the truth. No, Magnus and Ru'wah weren't alone in mistrusting these changes; others did as well, though not as many as Magnus might have liked, but enough, enough."

Maize looked through them, straining to recapture another era. "Even in my day things were more open, more candid communion amongst Seekers and ghatti—as if we were all a part of one big happy family. Rare to say 'Mindwalk if ye will.' Who needed privacy? We were all part of the same family, and in Crolius's and Magnus's time it was an even smaller, closer-knit family. They'd experienced some of the fears, the taunts people threw their way when it came to believing, to trusting an animal to read the truth in their minds. Nothing like what Matthias Vandersma suffered at the beginning, but there was still worry—probably still is." Clearly, Maize hadn't forgotten, was perceptive enough not to assume all doubt would fade with time. Skeptics, the fearful, always existed.

"Now in any family there's generally a bit of grumpiness,

arguments, and feuds. But the resentments of the traditional-
ists, Magnus and his cohorts, turned to backbiting, and then
worse—to an open contempt for the changes Crolius was so
painstakingly instituting, easing into place. He realized he
couldn't change things overnight.

"It all sounds so petty now, and perhaps it was even then.
The few times Magnus spoke of it in his old age he'd bluster, sound defiant and yet almost embarrassed, shamed
somehow. It's said that Ru'wah died of shame, of having adhered to the truth so rigidly he blinded himself to the greater
Truth.

"All in all, the cha pot boiled over when old Henryk
Vandersma came visiting, promised Crolius the money to
build a Headquarters worthy of the Seekers, but only if he'd
guarantee a statue of his nephew received pride of place in
the central plaza."

"Henryk Vandersma?" The name rang a bell, but she
couldn't think where or how she'd heard it. "Nephew?" The
statue in front of Headquarters was of Matthias Vandersma
and Kharm.

"Yes, Henryk. 'Frog-belly pale,' Magnus called him,
'whiter than a winding sheet and with pinky-red eyes.' Even
after all those years, Magnus acted uneasy when he described Henryk, Matthias's uncle, though Henryk was seven
years younger than Matthias. Henryk had commissioned architectural renderings of how he envisioned the new building, what it should be constructed of. He loved that mottled
rose-gray granite, and it came from the quarries he owned.
Once the Plumbs had stopped exploding for good, apparently he'd gotten rich from all the major building going on."

"Mottled rose-gray granite," Parse echoed dreamily.

"Mottled is right!" Maize snapped. "Like a rash according
to Magnus! The building plans, the materials to be used, the
statue—it was the final straw for him. Well, I'll tell you, that
'rash' itched him worst of all!" Despite herself she began to
giggle, immediately sobered.

"What you forget nowadays, discount, is that remnants of
different social classes still existed. The technicians who
came over on the ships, who monitored all the mechanical
devices now forbidden us. Some said it was their fault the
Plumbs had begun exploding, though they'd done their best
to figure out why it was happening, how to stop it. Then
there were the artists, the folk who'd paid for the expedition

to this new world—a world of raw materials waiting to be carved, sculpted, molded. Folk forced to abandon their creative dreams, their artistic visions, just to survive. And, of course, Magnus was descended from temperamental artists, while Crolius was pure logic, technician-stock all the way. Talk about the twain never meeting!"

Doyce shifted, intent, envisioning what it must have been like with two such headstrong people, each convinced that he, and he alone, had the right of it. For a moment it seemed all too much like her relationship with Jenret. "If Magnus didn't like the marble, I'll wager he hated the architectural plans as well."

"Right you are, my girl." Maize beamed at her. "The plans were unaesthetic, horrid, ugly, and he made no bones about using those words, and worse, to describe them. Lady bless, he didn't even approve of the Bethel—said the love of our Lady didn't translate into natural artistic talent. Well, I know my spirits soar when I go in there, and it's not just from being nearer to our Lady." The Bethel was beautiful, and so was Headquarters, Doyce thought as she caught a glimpse of its cupola beyond Maize. Homey, right, somehow. "And strangely enough, Magnus disliked the idea of the statue even more. '*We* are Matthias Vandersma's and Kharm's living memorial, the Seekers Veritas, not some cold, bronze-cast statue that can never capture what the two were truly like,' he told me time and again."

Restive, Parse prodded, "So what happened? Headquarters got built, no doubt about that."

Maize fixed him with a gimlet stare. "Lad, you've muddled your dates, or worse yet, never bothered to notice. Cornerstone says 135 AL, 135 years After Landing. They didn't break ground until the year I was born! Didn't complete it till ten years later. We'd almost outgrown it before it was finished, so the wings were added twenty years after that."

"What happened? What took so long?" Parse sat up, his chewed grass stem dropping onto Per'la's head. "I'll bet Magnus had something to do with it," he concluded triumphantly.

"Aye, that he did. You see, Henryk Vandersma had left gold to pay for the building. Magnus had Ru'wah eavesdrop on Crolius and Henryk, find out where the gold was stored.

At least that's what Crolius and V'row had to assume when it vanished without a trace."

"Magnus took it? Like a common criminal?" Parse exploded in outrage. "Seekers Veritas don't steal!"

"Parse, that's not the worst of it," Doyce broke in. "Don't you understand? Magnus and Ru'wah purposely listened in on a conversation they had no right or permission to hear!"

"Well, Maize said things were more casual back then, people not always bothering to give permission, say, 'Mindwalk if ye will.' "

But Per'la took Parse in hand before Doyce could argue. **"It's one thing to join in a casual conversation amongst Seekers without permission. But never, never, do we *purposely* eavesdrop, listen to what isn't meant for our ears or minds to hear. It's wrong, as if you hid and listened to Doyce and Jenret talking privately."**

"All right, I'm sorry." Scarcely chastened, he dangled a fresh grass stem tantalizingly near Per'la, tried to restore her good humor. "But I still think stealing is just as bad."

"Well, Magnus and Ru'wah didn't consider it stealing, simply liberating the gold from going to an unworthy cause. And never did they admit they'd taken it as the years went by."

"Crolius and V'row never pressed them about it? Never did a formal Truth Seeking?" Too obvious, and Doyce had a feeling she'd missed something, but what? "You mean Crolius let his dreams go up in smoke, gave up just like that? How did Henryk take the loss of his gold?"

"An'g could never figure that out either, why Crolius and V'row were so forbearing. Had all she could do not to probe Magnus's mind for the answers. What she did gather was that Ru'wah had also told Magnus something else, something beyond the gold's location that gave Magnus a hold over Crolius. Sort of a tit for tat, 'You accuse me of taking the gold, and I'll tell the world that . . .' " Maize trailed off, face wrinkled with the same perplexity she'd undoubtedly exhibited on first hearing the story. "All I know is that Henryk didn't make a fuss, either."

"What could it have been?" Parse's love of puzzles came to the fore. "Something about Crolius, or about Henryk, or," he rushed ahead, "even about the sainted Matthias Vandersma and Kharm?"

"Ah, hit it right on the button, lad." The old Seeker

hunched forward in her chair, as if drawing them in closer to her. "What An'g and I always wondered, and I ponder it even more lately, is if . . . if. . . ." She shared a glance with Khar, her mouth grim, then sat back, sinking into herself like a snail retreating into its shell. "Doesn't matter what I think, no good spreading slander, lies, after all this time if I'm wrong."

Overtired? Or still afraid after all these years to utter whatever it was she'd deduced? What could she need protection from now? And Doyce found she hadn't a clue. "So how did Headquarters finally get built?"

Relieved to be back on safer ground, Maize continued. "Magnus and Ru'wah were marginalized, ostracized after what happened, because everyone knew what they'd done. Most of his supporters dropped away, and Crolius found it easier to institute his changes. But it wasn't until Crolius was on his deathbed that the gold 'magically' appeared, shall we say? As if it were Magnus's final peace offering to a long-term yet respected foe. Crolius never had the satisfaction of seeing the new buildings, but at least he died knowing they'd be built. And the building of them gave Magnus a place to die, a peripheral part of what he'd tried to spurn. Sad, isn't it? Crolius at least got what he wanted, but I'm not sure Magnus ever did."

Maize's voice had run down, her story done, as much told as she'd dare tell. She shivered once as the sun began its final descent, the burial grounds already shrouded in early dark, marble tablets and pinnacles strangely luminescent, ghostly shapings against the tenebrous shadows of dense yews, twisted oaks. A corresponding shiver coursed through Doyce, as if she, too, bore the guilt of knowing more than she told, though she had no idea what. They'd dragged a 103-year-old woman from the safety and comfort of the Elder Hostel, prodded her to relive the past—and all without so much as a lap robe or a cup of cha to sustain her, keep her warm. Forced her to relive memories she might not have wanted to recapture. Didn't she have enough of her own like that? "Time to get you back." Hating the falsely brisk efficiency she projected, she clambered to her feet, back and arms strained and sore, legs rubbery. A groan at the thought of fighting the contrary wheeled chair back through the burial grounds. She kicked a crutch in Parse's direction, futilely sought its mate's hiding place.

"Aye, time." Maize looked tiny, remote, against the cushions. "I'll have enough time here soon enough."

"Don't worry. Per'la and I took the liberty of calling for assistance," Khar consoled. Both ghatti had piled into the old woman's chair, warming her, comforting her with the sensuous touch of their fur.

"For Maize, or for Parse and me?" Doyce stretched and bent, tried to recollect when she'd had a waistline, gave it up as a lost cause. A more likely lost cause made itself apparent: the baby pressed on her bladder, hard. Either a rapid retreat was in order or a quick but embarrassing trip behind a grave marker.

"Well, we didn't ask them to bring two more chairs," Per'la sheltered her mouth with a paw, hiding a grin at Doyce's predicament. **"I bet Parse could figure out a better chair. I wonder . . ."**

The young Seeker-in-Training, Cady, and her ghatt F'een, herded Davvy ahead of them, shooing him along each time he veered off course, leapfrogging grave markers, dawdling to read inscriptions. Apparently Swan had insisted her "dragon nursemaid" get some exercise and fresh air, and appointed poor Cady as dragon-keeper. Finally focused on their task, Davvy fussily competent and concerned, they wrapped Maize in a woolly afghan, thrust a metal cha flask into her cold hands. The two manhandled the chair around, Parse hopping in and out of their path, shouting instructions and commands. Taking advantage of the distraction, Davvy jogged to Doyce's side, held his hand palm-down over her stomach, waiting for permission to stroke the curve. A brusque nod and his hand touched, moth-light, the baby arching like a trout breaking water, then settling. Davvy fled behind the chair, grinning nervously.

"Don't need you escorting me if I've these fine young ones to push me along," Maize offered stoutheartedly. The barest wink in Doyce's direction. "You've that look, you know. Can't hold quite as much as you did, heh? Eyeballs about ready to float out of your head."

"I'll walk you back, Seeker Bartolotti," Parse announced. "Someone'd better explain your absence to the Matron, or she'll fear you've been abducted."

"Eh! Long's you don't plan to hitch a ride, start spooning!" Black eyes snapped coquettishly.

Doyce waved them out of sight, tried to decide which

route would return her to Headquarters quickest. Except she didn't want to go back. Somehow staying here made the legends, the myths, the histories, more palpable, more intimate.

Khar had jumped from the jouncing chair, rejoined her. **"A tale at only one remove. Ru'wah was long gone, remember, so Magnus could have reinvented the tale, emphasizing some parts, diminishing others. And since then Maize may have rearranged the story, emphasized the parts she remembered best. But,"** the ghatta thought it through, **"for the most part, I don't think so. She has a memory almost as fine as one of the ghatti."**

"But what isn't she telling us? She clammed up all of a sudden. Any ideas?"

Amber eyes shifted, then settled to meet her own. **"Oh, nothing, nothing of importance, I'm sure. Are rumors anything but rumors, even after all this time? But truth is always truth."**

"Sleeked yourself out of that one, didn't you? Or should I say 'sneaked'? Fine, never mind, then." It struck her now that the baby had shifted again, the pressure on her bladder less urgent. Mayhap if she walked slowly, thinking, things would fall into place, the said and the unsaid. A detour to Oriel's grave would be nice, a tribute to things past, a way to honor his memory, not forget it. Perhaps even sit on the bench there for a bit and recall those days, what might have been. Oriel had been nothing like Jenret. Mayhap someday she'd be like Maize, reciting the past to an anxious scholar seeking truth.

"*. . . take foot . . . out of ear!*" "*Ouch! Finger in eye!*" She whirled, wondering at the echoes of childish voices. The way they carried on the early evening air, floating away in the distance. Well after dark, they should be inside, safe, loved. Distracted, she looked for Khar, found her perched on the bench she'd halted beside, pink nose planted on the curved swell of her belly, amber eyes almost crossed with concentration.

It suddenly struck her. "Khar, do you know where Matthias Vandersma and Kharm are buried? We've a memorial here, but I don't think it's the actual grave, is it?" She sat beside the ghatta, hoping for an answer. Always so many questions about Matthias Vandersma.

❖

I m goin twonite no mater whut. I cannot
stand there faces waching mine and there
woneduring becuz i no whut thayre thinking. Thay jest doent no that Kharm nose
two, tells me. Hope Granther an Ryk
unnerstand an doent worry. Mi letter saze
i m sorry. I shell miss my Nelle.

Diary entry completed, he'd debated scrawling his fare-
wells on his slate but wanted it to be more lasting, as if by
saving the letter Granther and Henryk could save a part of
him. Much as it hurt, he opened the diary to its final blank
page and tugged, praying he wouldn't rip the delicate stitching. Finally, he tore the paper at the top, near the binding; it
gave with a protesting RRIIP loud enough to wake the dead.
Guiltily he swung around, but Granther was snoringly
asleep, and Henryk's bunk revealed its usual lump of limp
boy, buried in blankets and pillows.
    The pencil was short and stubby, lead worn to a bluntness
that favored his broad strokes, his lack of control in making
precise letters as his thoughts ran ahead of his spelling ability. Henryk spelled better than he already, but then Henryk
had learned earlier. Besides, given Henryk's poor eyesight,
reading was a delight, the printed page in front of his nose
clear to his vision.

I m soary but Kharm an i r going. I doent
feel rite heyer nee-more. Maybe its time i
set out on my own. Maybe i will go louk
four Da, spend time with him. Doent
worry bout me. I louve yu bothe. Telle
Nelle I louve her.

With care he stowed the diary in his sack, pocketing the pencil stub rather than letting it vanish in the sack's vastness. The ghatta stretched at ease on the hearthstones, but her eyes had been following his slightest movement, ever alert, skin twitching with impatience. Or, mayhap fleas, Matty supposed. He scratched an ankle reflexively.

"Both," Kharm admitted and nipped at her spine, burrowing through the fur to rout the small invader. **"Are we going now? Are we ready?"**

"Almost." He stood, gathered his sack tight, though what could rattle, he wasn't sure. One wool scarf, a pair of knit stockings without shaped heels, better he keep outgrowing the worn spots, Granther said. A clean shirt. A cracked clay mug wrapped in the scarf, stuffed in the dented tin pot with its bale so it could be hung over a fire. Some old twine and leather laces for snares and, the thing he'd hesitated over taking—that made him cringe with guilt, almost like a thief—Granther's second-best knife. An old jacknife, its pearl grip missing on one side. But a knife was a necessity. Considering, he opened the sack and fumbled through it, retrieved the knife and stuffed it into his pocket along with the pencil stub. If he lost the sack and its contents, at least he'd have the knife. Taking anything more would deprive Granther and Ryk of things they needed to survive, and Ryk would soon enough grow into the few clothes he'd left behind.

His feet had rooted in place, and he shuffled the overlarge boots. Feet shifted inside boots, but he couldn't bring himself to lift one, take the first step. **"Come on!"** Kharm cajoled. When had she moved to the door, taken the first step? A shallow breath, and when he exhaled he felt an unexpected lightness, as if he could float out a window, or even up the chimney with the smoke. **"Things to see, things to do!"** So there were, so there were.

Hugging the sack close, he eased the door latch free, muffled it with his hand until he found the thumb press outside and slipped round the door without fully opening it. Now, pull up on the door handle and gently close it, less chance for the hinges to creak. There, closed!

The cold air hit him. Killing frost tonight, he could smell it, taste it in the sharp air. Still, everything that could be harvested had been except for the more hardy cabbage and kale, turnips and carrots, earth banked around them. Stars spangled above him, his breath steaming whiteness into the night air as he set off down the dirt road leading away from the village center and the well. Only one true light burned that he could judge, the other minor glows revealed banked fires, a faint, bloody translucence shivering the thin, scraped hide windows. Soon winter shutters would block even that amount of light.

He'd passed the Killanins' house, struggling with himself not to find a rock and heave it through their window. Tempting, more than tempting to strike a final blow, then run like the blazes. **"But not very responsible. If you're going to fight, let them know who they face."**

"Why? They'd ambush me if they had a chance, just as they do Henryk. And anyone else they can catch." The ghatta's rebuke left him sullen, upset because she'd caught his meanness of spirit. *"Don't you ambush creatures when you hunt?"*

"Of course. But we aren't enemies as you and the Killanins are. We're all part of the chain of life. I need the lesser creatures to survive, and they need me to survive. Otherwise too many might breed, overrun what food they've stored for winter." A ghatta chuckle. **"Besides, I don't think they'd willingly march up to me if I sat and waited."**

"True. Nor would I willingly march anywhere near the Killanins. However, I do think they're one of the lesser links on the chain of life, despite their size." Everything he discussed with the ghatta forced him to think, reassess things, even when they bantered, and now their banter had carried him almost to Mad Marg's house.

Something white and ghostly reared out of the tall grasses at road's edge. Spaceship shit! A Killanin! Dropping his sack, Matty took to his heels in terror, hair hackling on the back of his neck until he recognized the pale, slight figure of his Uncle Henryk.

"What are you doing out so late? Granther'll skin you alive," he hissed, skidding to a halt.

Ryk screwed up his face, naked somehow without his tinted glasses, unneeded with the dark to shelter his sensitive pink eyes. "Are you finally going?" As usual, his hands nestled under his armpits, arms crossed protectively over his chest, shoulders hunched. A wail of reproach, muted not to carry in the night, but still clear, "And you didn't even say good-bye!"

"How'd you know? Are you going to tell? I'll tie you to a tree if you're going to tell!" A useless threat, he knew, but irresistible to vent his anger, his needless shock at the apparition.

"No, you won't." Ryk thought hard, head bent, then gave a hopeful upward glance, mouth quirked with delight. "Though if you want to, I'll let you. Tell'em the Killanins did it!"

But after Kharm's earlier lecture, Matty banished the thought, appealing as it might sound. "No. They can make trouble on their own, they don't need our help." He hefted the sack again, debated, then slung it over Ryk's shoulder. "Come on, you can walk with me a ways. Know you like being out at night." True, darkness provided Henryk with at least minimal safety, the freedom to enjoy the world without looking over his shoulder for danger, human danger. Whatever might stalk him, harm him in the night was natural, a risk, but a risk to be savored without fearing the superstitious malice of his fellow humans.

Ryk shrugged until the sack rested comfortably on his back before starting down the road, pausing for Matty and Kharm to catch up. "Saw you sneaking things, found where you'd hidden them. Could tell you weren't real happy, worried about Kharm. If I was big enough, I'd run away, too."

Lulled by the easy comfort yet implicit sadness of their conversation, Matty gave a start. Without noticing, they'd pulled almost level with Mad Marg's house. What had Henryk been doing so close?

As if in answer to his unspoken question, Henryk shivered, peeked surreptitiously at the house. "I like to watch sometimes. Wonder what it'd be like if she loved me. I love Da, I love you," and almost defiantly, "and I could love her if she let me."

Matty trailed a consoling hand on the nape of Henryk's neck. "I know, Ryk-Ryk. She does love you, but she can't admit it to herself or to you. Think of it as a buried treasure and mayhap someday you'll both discover it."

With a gasp, Henryk threw himself into Matty's arms, face plastered against his chest, arms wired around his waist, and Matty looked up to see Marg looming in front of them. Though not as ghostly pale as Henryk, her stealthy, si-

lent movement was even more frightening, should have been
impossible, given her bulk. *"Why didn't you warn me she
was here?"* he threw in Kharm's direction as the ghatta
closed the distance between the two boys and Marg. *"Were
you going to let her ambush me?"*

Kharm gave an indignant squeak. **"She wouldn't ambush
you, silly. She's been standing there patient as can be
while you two chattered like chipmunks, not noticing a
thing in the world. If you can't see a boulder in your
path, it's not my fault."**

"Here." Marg thrust a cloth-wrapped bundle in his direction, rested it on Ryk's head as if he served as a convenient
shelf, nothing more. "Forgot food, didn't you? It's the obvious things in life that men and boys forget." The smell of
fresh baked bread reached his nose, plus the ripe scent of
cheese, the sweetness of dried fruit. His mouth watered; he
hadn't eaten much dinner, throat constricted, stomach tight
as he'd planned for the night.

A brusque nod of thanks, and he unwrapped a cautious
hand from around Henryk to take the bundle, wondering
how to slide it into his sack. But Henryk had scooted behind
him, arms still locked around his waist, thrusting the sack in
his hand and letting Matty stand as his bulwark in front of
Marg. "You knew, too?" Incredulous, his voice slipped up a
notch, turning question into accusation. He'd believed only
he held the village's secrets, but now someone knew his as
well. It made sense that Ryk had found him out; those in
constant danger always watch closely. But Marg? He saw
her so seldom.

Marg swiped at her face with a handkerchief, and Matty's
nose wrinkled at the pungent smell, astringent, faintly alco-
holic. Witch hazel, he guessed as she pressed the cloth
against her temples, half-shrouding her face. "Of course.
Breezes talk to me, whisper secrets. I'm trying not to listen
now. Those as are different always have to seek their way."
Lowering the handkerchief, Marg nodded with utter seriousness, the moonlight highlighting her once fine features,
forcing him to remember how beautiful she'd been.

"Everything talks to Marg." She shifted conversational
tracks again. "I put in a bit of dried fish for that larchcat of
yours." Her body seemed to deflate, spread as she stooped to
stroke the ghatta. "Always hearing tiny, distant voices, but
they never hear me. Funny, though, couldn't hear the

eumedico at all when she came, try as I might. Mayhap if I'd had a cat like this to share my thoughts, I wouldn't be the way I am."

"Mayhap you're right, Mistress Margare, but it's a burden all the same." How could she know! Did she know? Breath shallow, he steadied himself. Poor Marg fantasized about anything and everything.

The ghatta cradled against her ample bosom, she looked up, almost shyly. "Don't harbor any thoughts about going to Marchmont. Venable Constant and his ilk have no use for us—the likes of me with the little I glean, or the likes of you. You're too different from what they know. Now, follow downstream far enough, you'll hit the River Vaalck. Might still be a trade flatboat or two this time of year, but won't be much longer. Where the river goes, I don't know, but that's up to you."

He wanted to protest that he couldn't influence the river's direction, but dimly realized that wasn't her point. "I thank you for the food, for the advice." He already knew enough not to go to Marchmont, why journey to a land of outcasts? He swallowed, longing to beg one further thing, a favor, but it wasn't wise to rile her. Regardless, he opened his mouth to ask, and she put a finger to his lips.

"Yes, I'll see he gets home safe." The word "he" was more of a grunt and a chin thrust beyond, behind him.

Half-turning, he captured Henryk in a headlock, the bristly white hair stiff as he pressed his lips to the crown of the boy's head. "Be good, Ryk-Ryk. Be well and," he whispered the last few words, "be brave. I'll be back someday. Take care of Nelle for me. Promise!"

Henryk's grip around his waist eased, the boy dropping back behind him. "Promise," came the echo.

"Don't look back, just go. There's nothing more to say." Marg ceremoniously placed the ghatta in his arms, and he set her on her feet, began walking faster and faster until he was running. Don't look back, don't look back! But he broke his vow once, thought he was distant enough that one final glimpse wouldn't matter, couldn't hurt, and saw two backs: one large and one small, each on opposite sides of the roadway, as separate from each other as they could be yet still somehow remain linked. The tears started in earnest, his feet stumbled, but he continued running. Running from Coventry where he'd been born, but where would he be buried?

What far town or city, what distant place? Alone? Unloved?
Unmourned?

"Better live first, then die."

Matty leaped for the pier, caught the hawser that Solange
threw to him, snubbed it around a piling. By the time he'd
finished the hitch and done the same with the stern rope,
Kharm had paraded halfway down the pier, drawing glances
and comments from the dockers on the adjoining landings
who were repairing cracked pilings and splintered boards.
Tail high, sauntering along as if she owned the pier, she
stopped to sniff here and there, exploring canvas-draped
boxes and bales, hitching a claw into a loose flap to see
what lurked underneath.

Busy double-checking the ropes, sliding the plank
walkway out to the raft, Matty lanced a mindthought in
Kharm's direction. *"Easy, easy! Wait up and don't go exploring until I've finished here. You know the rules."* Oh, she
knew the "rules," but sometimes they seemed to float right
out of her head, curiosity conquering common sense.

"Aren't my rules," Kharm countered, **"they're *your*
rules. Didn't ask me when you made them."**

"And if I had?" he huffed, sliding the planking farther until the crossbar on the underside butted against a similar
crossbar on the pier. Absurdly pleased with the ease with
which he'd accomplished it, at his gain in strength in just
two octants on the river, he preened and flexed, proud of his
hard-earned muscles. But the vision of the ghatta wandering
alone, viewed by strangers as dangerous, wild, spoiled his
private posturing. *"Kharm, we don't know anyone here and
they don't know us. We need to winter over someplace, river's about ready to freeze, and Gilboa's as good a place as
any. If you don't muck things up,"* he added dark-humoredly.

Carrying on simultaneous conversations, one internal, one
external, and not entrapping himself in either one to the ex-
clusion of the other was still an ordeal. Mostly if someone
noticed his conversation fading or faltering, it was viewed as
distraction or woolgathering, hardly unusual in a teenaged
boy. It almost happened now, but he was already bouncing
along the walkway when Gheorghe shouted, "Ye need an invite, Matty-lad? Let's git unloaded."

Without paying any overt attention to the ghatta, he shot a parting admonition her way. *"Now, just sit and wait for me."* He didn't bother watching Kharm plunk herself on the pier, tail wrapped around toes, its tip flickering, her mouth prim. She was close to full grown now, weighed nearly ten kilos, but was still prone to exhibit the actions and reactions of a ghatten as she referred to herself, more often than not.

So they'd both grown. Not a bad two octants, all in all, other than the continually increasing cold and ever-dampness of the river gnawing at his fingers and toes, chapping his cheeks. Some early mornings with gray scum ice webbing their moorings, he'd thought his fingers might crack off as he hammered ice loose. No sense waiting for the sun to melt it when the work always warmed his fingers enough to flex. Good thing.

He'd journeyed southeast that first runaway night, following the stream that flowed into the River Vaalck, had continued tracing the river course until he'd found a likely spot on the bank for a raft tie-up. Nothing for it but to sit and wait, shivering with nerves and the dampness of exertion. A light rain began to fall, dripping off his nose, slithering down his collar. Sat with Kharm draped across his lap, wondering if his granther or anyone followed him. Didn't know if he'd be glad or sad to be found, forced to return home. Kharm's silence matched his, but her purring soothed, convinced him he'd done the right thing. Only once had she spoken, **"Right thing, wrong reason?"** but he'd refused to be drawn into that discussion. And after a long, rainy day of lonely waiting, at dusk he'd sighted a raft sliding down the river, its stately progress broken as it was poled diagonally to coast bankward. A grating thump as it nosed the mudbank, and he wiped a damp sleeve across his eyes to see better.

Solange and Gheorghe Aadestok had been reluctant to take him on, but Gheorghe's accident had made it necessary, his right hand cocooned in bandages, smashed when he'd tripped and fallen while skip-footing across a boom, his hand jamming deep between two logs as they'd shifted and resettled. Ultimately Solange had insisted Gheorghe take him on. "Pay?" he'd inquired in his best adult voice, concerned about his earning power.

Brown eyes hooded, Solange had pouched her lower lip, thrust it out as she studied him and he'd studied her back, daunting to bargain with a woman who looked as hard and

as solid as the sweep oar on which she negligently leaned.
First salvo to her, "No pay. Food and shelter, more clothes
if ye need'em. Works out, a bonus at the end when we tie up
for the winter. Assumin' trade's been good." Did that mean
it hadn't been good thus far?

"No pay?" Incredulity and a sinking heart. Food, shelter,
additional clothing were blessings not to be denied, but how
could he put money aside for lean times? Not that much
money circulated in Canderis, most things were bartered,
traded. Truth be told, he'd seen little money, actual coinage,
in his life, but the concept appealed to him, the idea of earning it, saving it, counting it, buying what he wanted. Well,
he and Kharm would survive, one way or another.

"No pay," Solange repeated. "Think to be bringing that
larchcat along with you, too?"

A bargaining chip he hadn't counted on, and one to her
advantage, not his. "Well, of course!" he'd almost squeaked
in indignation. "She goes where I go!"

Gheorghe fiddled with the wrappings on his hand, long
black hair falling over his forehead to hide his expression.
"Another mouth to feed, boy. And a useless one at that. Mayhap even worse than useless, destructive, belike. Clawing at
bales, scratching at cargo, who knows what else? Wild creature like that can't be trusted, has its own ways. Raft's no
place for a larchcat."

He'd sensed his chances slipping from between his grasping fingers. Yet again he digested the bitterness of what it
meant to be saddled with Kharm—rejected, outcast—and
they didn't have an inkling about her mindpowers. Spurn
her? Cast her off? Impossible! He squared his shoulders, wet
jacket clinging, molding to him. No sense whining, pleading,
he had to convince on rational grounds.

"First, she'll eat a share of what I get, and I won't beg or
steal more for either of us. Second, she can hunt for herself
when we tie up each night. Third, if she destroys anything,
claws and damages something," he took a deep breath, because Kharm did enjoy clawing things, and even the logs of
the raft itself presented a temptation, "I'll go without food
the next day." His belly growled at the thought; he'd been
cautious about eating too greedily from the limited supplies
Marg had given him, not sure how long they'd have to last
him. "Finally, I'm small, neither of us will take up that
much space, but I'm strong." A slight exaggeration, but not

too great a one, he'd hoped. He'd do what he had to do, learn how, no matter what. Besides, hadn't Granther always said, "Work smarter, not harder."

Gheorghe had mulled it over. "A more immediate saving than saying 'take it from a bonus' you may or may not receive." He'd grinned, showing twisted, gaping teeth. "An bein' small has its advantages. Ye planning on growing much?"

It took Matty several heartbeats to realize it was a joke. "Ah, let 'em come, Gheorghe," Solange relented. "Worst can happen is we try'em for a few days, kick'em ashore or into the river if'n they deserve it."

Now Matty's worries blossomed. Should he, could he trust them? They were hard-bitten, strong, implacably adult in the way Granther was but his da had never managed. The decision had been tossed back into his lap. But Kharm had decided for him, springing aboard, shaking damp fur as if she were a dog. **"They're good, they're true. Think I'll even eat leftovers, scraps."** With a deep breath, he'd stepped aboard as the raft rocked against the shore, had shaken hands, wondering what he'd gotten himself into, but content to wait and find out.

It hadn't been so bad, Matty reflected. Kharm *had* behaved herself and he'd learned as well: how to read the river, its snags and deadheads, its currents, how to spot the ragged, flapping flags that signaled cargo to be shipped. And cargo consisted of most anything, from livestock to salted fish to iron kettles. For the most part they floated down the Vaalck, the current doing the work, although three times they'd poled like the possessed against it, retracing their route to deliver something of importance upstream for double pay. Medicine it had been once, though they'd done that trip gratis.

And once, one night just two days past, he'd been scared witless when the Vaalck reared up and ran backward, lifting them willy-nilly, heaving them upstream as if a giant watery hand refused to let nature take its course. Distant thunder preceded the watery shock wave, yet the night sky was clear, the moons bright. A deep rumble, then a chain of sympathetic answering rumbles as he'd watched the waves reverse their lapping, race toward them. "Tide tripper!" Gheorghe had screamed, "Unlash the stern lines, Matty!" while Solange had run for the bow, not waiting to untie the mooring ropes but severing them with an ax. He'd whipped out his knife and sawed away at the lashings, Solange thrusting him aside, ax striking hard at the pitiful fraying he'd accomplished.

The raft floating free, they'd ridden the reverse tide nearly a kilometer, the raft dipping and plunging, bobbing like a wood chip. Clinging to each other, to anything they could grasp, at last they slowed, the raft beginning to drift back, retracing its normal course as if nothing had happened. Unsteadily, the three managed to pole and paddle the raft around so its minimal prow faced the right way. "What was that?" he'd asked, concentrating on pushing debris away with his pole.

Balancing her own pole in its rest, Solange had looked somber, afraid. "Plumbs, lad. I'd say a string of them popped jest above where the Vaalck merges into the Kuelper, jest afore they runs into the sea. When the earth shifts and heaves, the water backs up, the ocean surges in, runs in ways it shouldn't, sometimes floods the banks if it's bad enough."

"Wonder where it hit, how much damage it did," Gheorghe mused from the rudder sweep. " 'Bove or below Gilboa, d'ye think, Solly?"

"Below, I think. But no doubt Gilboa's damaged. Piers are rickety enough, the town not much better."

"Thinking we should winter in the middle of a pile of tossed toothpicks, woman?" Gheorghe spat into the river.

"I'm thinking if that many Plumbs went off, belike they won't have any more 'sploding for a while. Be needing hands to repair the damage. Why not us? Matty here? Kin live in the raft hut if'n we have to, though it'll be mighty cold once the river freezes and the wind whips 'cross that ice. Or mayhap find a hut on land. Nice to be on land again."

"Least till spring comes and you get the itch again, eh, woman?"

That, Matty reflected as he helped Gheorghe roll barrels across the walkway, emptying the raft of cargo, was how they'd decided to winter in Gilboa.

And how, as the sunset came and the wind picked up, gulls screaming in salt marshes, hovering over the tidal flats, he found himself with money in his pocket. Not much, but some, plus some bartering goods in his sack, and Kharm by his side, walking down the pier, waving good-bye to

Gheorghe and Solange, striding off into the world again.
"Toes cold," Kharm complained. **"Hungry."**

*"Well, you napped all afternoon, nice and snug under that
canvas. I saw the lump you made."* His own fingers
throbbed, cold, stiff, and bruised; one foot ached where he'd
inadvertently rolled a barrel over it in his haste to unload.
"We'll find someplace for dinner." Where, he couldn't say,
but a place as big as Gilboa, so much larger than Coventry
where he'd grown up, had to boast a place to eat. Not that
he'd ever been inside such an establishment, but he'd heard
about them.

**"Rather stay snug with Solange in the hut. Pea soup
tonight."**

The thought of pea soup, of the stuffy, companionable
warmth, did sound inviting, more so than he wanted to admit, and he shivered, not from cold but from the unknown.
Instead, he tucked his scarf tighter around his throat. *"Come
on, Kharm. It's an adventure. No one knows us here, knows
what you can do. And I want it kept that way, do you hear?
Don't tell me what I don't need to know!"* His mindvoice
snapped and stung more cruelly than he'd meant, but he had
to impress the need on her. Had to have a chance to be his
own person, his own, not Kharm's. Mayhap even fit in here,
find a new home.

The ghatta sulked, lagged behind. **"Only tell you what
you need to know. Afraid of the truth?"**

"Sometimes." He clutched the sack tighter, unsure what
awaited him. *"Yes, sometimes, truly."* Especially when he
wasn't worthy of knowing it, didn't know why he'd been entrusted with it. A burden, one heavier than his sack, and his
shoulders sagged under the load.

"I'm hungry. We've missed dinner, I hope you realize."

"Wha . . . ?" Doyce's head tossed almost wildly, confused
as to where the comment came from. Why, in the name of
the havens, was she sitting on a bench in the burial grounds?
Dark out, too, and she flexed her hands, fingers swollen and
cold, callused and rough as if she'd been pressed into heavy
manual labor in the raw wind and damp. "Khar, what are we
doing out here?"

A white paw patted at her hands, convinced her they be-

longed to her again, warm, well-cared for, a hint of callus
where she'd hold the reins, nothing more. Well, the swelling
still persisted, and her feet pinched, tight in her boots.
Hardly an unusual occurrence, given her pregnancy. At least
she wasn't suffering from terminal bloat; it only felt like it
sometimes. The paw tapped again, insistent, on her hand,
then feet on her shoulder, a warm nose, tickling whiskers
scrubbed her face. A tongue rasp under her nose brought her
fully awake. "Ooh, sandpaper! Khar, don't do that! You
know I hate having my nose licked!"

Her brain clutched scattered facts, the expedition with
Parse and, most of all, with Maize. Their visit to the burial
grounds where Maize's Bondmate An'g had been laid to
rest. Her own detour by Oriel's grave, and apparently she
hadn't journeyed any farther—but to daydream for so long?
And why did Khar remain balanced like that, eyes interlocked with her own?

"We missed dinner, did we?" No doubt about it, her
empty stomach agreed. "I take it no one missed us?"

**"Why should they? Sometimes we eat at Headquarters,
sometimes we don't. You aren't very predictable about
meals anymore,"** and Khar concealed her deeper worry at
Doyce's newfound protean ability about when and where
and how she could imagine Matty's life. It had to be Khar's
fault, failing Doyce, failing the Elders. Wasn't she controlling things properly? Or had Matty's past assumed a life of
its own, relived through Doyce? Neither possibility made
sense, but at least Doyce hadn't suffered from the experience.

Sliding her forearm under Khar's forelegs, Doyce tilted
the abstracted ghatta from her shoulder. "Well, if you'd let
go, I could get up, see about doing something about
dinner—for both of us. I feel incredibly hungry, as if I'd
been doing stevedore work all day! Nothing like heavy
dock work to make you famished. And I definitely have to
go to the bathroom now!" Rising, she smoothed her
overvest, began to move cautiously through the dark, dim
white shapes hovering phantasmagorically in the periphery
of her vision. Over there a small, frightened boy, here an
implacable, bulky woman, and there the striped afterimage
of a ghatta.

Too real, too similar, Khar moaned inwardly, one life
blending with another! Distract her, find an excuse, make her

fixate on Now, on us! **"Of course, wheeling Maize and that chair through this jungle wilderness might have something to do with it, especially after Parse insisted on leaving the path and heading cross-country!"**

"True, all too true!" Doyce hesitated, waiting for Khar to lead the way as always. "Dinner at the mess must be done, but I'm sure we can snag some bread and meat, some fruit, from the kitchens. Eat it there? Or take it back to the house?" The thought of the Headquarters kitchen, bright with lantern light, fires, the muted rattle of clean up, sloshing dishwater, and setting up for tomorrow's breakfast, appealed. Surely someone would have time to chat. Other Seekers, especially Novies, were prone to slip in for snacks. Going home to the empty house, their final quarrel still resounding from the walls, was too painful to contemplate. Which one of them was more stubborn? Well, Magnus and Crolius hadn't resolved their differences either, not exactly a comforting thought.

"I'd rather go home." Amazing that Khar could consider that empty house as home. **"Build a fire, just us two sharing dinner."**

"Easy for you to say, you've never built a fire in your life," Doyce scoffed.

"Please? All snuggly in the easy chair, feet toasting, just us two, just like before?" Khar wheedled. **"Go to bed early?"** She yawned ostentatiously, triggered a matching yawn from Doyce. **"I'm so tired!"**

And presently Doyce found herself back at the guest house, a plate of ham and cheese sandwiches on the arm of the chair, stocking feet propped on a hassock. One hand fumbled blindly for the sandwich while the other hand balanced the old book on the pinnacle of her stomach.

The Plum wuz scary. I didn't noe water culd run the aposite way like that. Hope not miny people wer hurt. Gheorghe an Solange an i will wintur in Gilboa. I hope Kharm liks it and that i doent have two worry whut she tells me and i hope i make new frends. It wood bee nice to shair wit

**someone what its like to noe what Kharm
tells me. Awfull nice.**

Shaking her head to clear it, Doyce squinted at the scrawling lines. Lady bless, reach for a sandwich and lose her
place! But it was so difficult to decipher that each time she
picked it up her mind drifted toward other thoughts, an on-
going fantasy she'd been having about Matty and Kharm.
Somehow she knew far more than her research had told her,
conjuring up the textures and details, the emotions and times
more deeply than her scant facts indicated, as if she'd taken
a preliminary sketch and expanded it into a full-color pano-
rama. Strange. Entirely too suggestible, just because she
thought she'd made out the name Kharm in the diary.

Paw poised to snag the cheese overhanging the bread,
Khar stiffened. Trouble! Best act quickly or she'd have some
explaining in store for her, impossible since she couldn't explain it herself. **"It's probably short for Carmen, especially given the way that person spells—you complain all
the time. She sounds a bossy sort."**

Doyce munched the sandwich, set the book aside and
shared a bite of meat and cheese with Khar, compactly
mounded on the other chair arm. "I give up. Just when I
think I'm getting the hang of the spelling, I get distracted."

"Bed now?" Innocently, Khar swallowed the treat, butted
her head into Doyce's arm in hopes of dislodging another
bite. When it wasn't forthcoming, she padded to the foot of
the stairs.

"If I go to bed so soon after eating, I'll have nightmares!"
Doyce protested. "Better to stay upright and digest." But the
food, the warmth, made her logy, ready for sleep. Finishing
the last of her milk, she convinced herself no great virtue ac-
crued from washing dishes.

**"You won't dream, I promise. I'll be there to guard
your dreams."** And Khar would do everything in her power
to ensure Doyce's sleep flowed dreamlessly tonight, no
monster sandwiches chasing her through the burial grounds,
or anything else, let alone another episode from Matthias
Vandersma's life. Not until she discovered how and why
Doyce was able to override her control.

Hylan slung the dripping bucket onto the cart's tailgate, began untying the tarp shielding its load. Pretending to concentrate on her task, she let her eyes dart guiltily, hoping against hope that Harrap remained where she'd left him, stirring the evening's porridge. The dog, Barnaby, whined once, fretful at her worry, then splashed in the stream, muzzle darting as he snapped at a minnow. The slope sheltered her from prying eyes, no reason for Harrap to watch her. After all, her excuse rang genuine: wash the dust off the wagon, soak the wheels so the spokes would swell, tighten from the water. The old rackety goat cart had taken a pounding on the dirt roads, deep rutted from the harvest wagons.

Dragging off the dirt-encrusted tarp, she eased two burlap-wrapped bundles free and plunged them into the bucket. Could almost hear the hungry sucking sound as they absorbed the water. Most of the leaves had dropped, and she fingered one regretfully. After all, it *was* late autumn, that— not to mention the trauma of the move—explained it, but a few hung tenaciously to their spindly twiglets, still green but curling around the edges.

The best time of year to transplant; let them settle into their new homes, lie dormant through the winter, and burst forth with new foliage in the spring. Each a promise, a future hope, a way of culling Gleaners from normal, average folk. A salvation, a promise for the future, a future free of Gleaners, of Resonants, or whatever fancy name they might call themselves, and no chance, no hope they might someday contact the stars, call mind-to-mind to any Spacer ships that wandered into their purview. No, it was her sacred duty, her obligation to liberate Canderis and the whole of the planet Methuen from any taint from space. They'd survived this long without it after that first abandonment, nearly 250 years ago, and nothing, nothing was going to change it if she had her say. Her penance, her sacrifice to erase those last memories of the Fifty who had come so close to seducing her as a child. She was not a child any longer.

She gently grasped the two precious bundles by their thin trunks, much the size of a switch for whipping a recalcitrant child, let the excess water drain from the balled burlap and reverently returned them to the cart. Took two more bundles

and repeated the process before scooping a fresh bucket of
water. They thirsted, just as she thirsted for the assurance
that everything would continue safe, well, unchanging. After
a moment's thought, she positioned herself between the
shafts and backed the cart deeper into the water, let it soak
hub-high. Harrap would notice if the wheels weren't wet.

Were eight saplings enough? She hoped and prayed they
were. Lucky to root eight, have them live through four
years. Four years since that horrific yet miraculous night
when the sky had plummeted at her feet, a relic of what existed out there to harm. Others had died, bark winter-
stripped by hungry rolapin, or roots never setting deeply
enough—these eight the strongest. Even some of the righteous always died. Well, eight it would have to be, a lucky
number—put it on its side and it indicated infinity. Funny
that eight meant so much to Harrap as a Shepherd, the Eight
Mysteries, the eight Disciple moons of our Lady. Yes, eight
could encircle, a protective litany—one each at Alkmaar,
Ruysdael, Coventry, Gilboa, Waystown, Neu Bremen, Free
Stead, and home again to Roermond. Insurance for the future.

Her pantaloons dragged wet and muddy at ankles and
shins. A minor inconvenience, a very minor reminder of the
trials and tribulations she faced, the discomfort, the pain.
Pain that had been, pain that would be, but it was all worth
it, would be worth it if she could save the world. She'd
never asked for that role, oh, no, not in her wildest dreams,
had been content with her solitude, eking out a meager living. Always someone in need of a dowser, able to search out
water, precious lost objects, her pendulum of needle and
thread swinging to determine the sex of a child in the womb.
The vibrations always told her, minor skills, but skills all the
same, something her family'd had down through the generations.

But she'd had been called, chosen, the night the sky had
fallen, a star flaming across the heavens, burning bright, a
lurid false dawn. Had she been the only one awake to see it,
tremble with awe at its blazing, seductive majesty? Been the
only one to rush out, quailing, eyes shielded from its dangerous, devouring glare, certain the world was ending, would
explode in a mighty burst of flame? Oh, yes, sinners burned,
burned forever. Harrap might not believe that, protest the

Lady was kind, always ready with another chance, but she knew better.

Brighter, brighter, a soughing of wind that lifted the hair off her head, made it lash her face, stinging, a searing heat arcing downward in a flaming, rending sword stroke. Huddling on the ground, Barnaby crouched beneath her, she'd sheltered herself and him from the blinding vision. A crashing eruption, the scent of charring wood, and all was blessed darkness again. Except for the spangled lights that played before her eyes and made it hard to focus. Barnaby had quivered so hard beneath her she'd feared he'd shake himself out of his skin. Realized she was shaking as well. When she'd dared open her eyes, before she could even see properly, she'd followed her nose, followed the stink of burning. Had crossed the back pasturage to the stream and seen the old witch hazel tree quivering, leaves dropping, a black, scorched scar blasted down its middle. Embedded in its trunk, a piece of glowing metal, piercing to the heartwood. It looked like a tiny stabilizer fin, the outer edge of one, anyway, the same shape as the ones in the drawings of a spaceship. Warned, yes, she'd been warned that space was a garbage midden, could cast its debris their way. Her father had ranted how their ancestors had corrupted not just the land with their technology, but the very skies themselves. But who had ever believed before this heavenly sign? And the heavens, the starry firmament was hellish.

Why the tree hadn't died from that trauma, she could never surmise, but the next spring it had bloomed a cascade of yellow, threadlike petals, thrived, grown fuller, faster, invigorated by the near calamity, the metal still embedded in its heartwood. She'd taken a forked cutting from it, was stripping the leaves, trimming it into a dowsing rod when the two had arrived. She didn't know them, though she'd seen them before on the roadway beyond the house sometimes, the man with the ropy, twisted scars up the side of his face, often accompanied by the lovely, elegant young woman who wore a white coat, who worked as a eumedico in the Research Hospice farther on. As far as Hylan was concerned, good neighbors left each other alone, and she'd always scrupulously done that. Had no truck with eumedicos, their faltering skills, their lies brought sorrow. What right did they have to invade her property like this?

Gripping the forked stick in her hands, she'd willed them

to be gone, leave her be. And to her surprise the stick had risen and dipped, vibrating up and down without her knowledge, without her help, as if seeking and scenting what it had before it. Her hands trembled as she tried to hold the rod still.

"Look, Evelien, I think she's decided she's found an underground stream in you," the man had laughed.

"Well, it's trembling, pulling more toward you, I'd say," the woman called Evelien responded.

"Of course, still waters run deep." The man bowed in Hylan's direction. "I'm sorry if we're trespassing, just out for a walk. Spring does that, makes you want to ramble sometimes."

She hadn't trusted herself enough to speak beyond a bare "Aye." Something clawed at her brain, unloosening old memories, old fears . . . a night, a night, a night of laughter, song, sharing . . . and then sorrow. Torches, the deaths, her mind vibrating like a tuning fork. Ah, grant me the strength of the deaf adder who stoppeth her ears, who refuses to hear the voice of the charmer, charm he ever so wisely! In self-defense she raised her hands to her face, leaned her forehead into the fork of the rod, the branches shielding her temples. And glory to the Lady, the pain eased!

Head cocked to one side, mouth twisted quizzically, though she suspected it always did that, given the scarring, the man backed away, pulling the woman with him. "Think we should be going, Evelien, we've obviously frightened her."

No, she reflected, she hadn't known then to whom she had spoken, but she'd learned shortly after. Had not sensed power like that since . . . dead, dead, gone . . . had spawn survived? Vesey Bell, the notorious, twisted Gleaner, and Evelien Annendahl Wycherley, Gleaner and eumedico both. Hylan pulled the goat cart forward, turning the wheels to let the top halves soak. It paid to be patient, thorough. Blind before, but now she could see, just the barest premonition of a premonition. They'd come again, would win this time. But she could identify them. Else why had she stuck that freshly cut dowsing rod into the moist ground, cut other twigs and planted them round, hoping they would take root?

And now that premonition was coming to pass. But what to do about Harrap, not to mention that blasted ghatt with him? What did they represent? A part of her plan or an an-

athema? She worried at the thought, set another two balled
saplings to soak. She liked the man, and that was a danger.
How long would he continue with her like her faithful
shadow? He seemed content enough to follow along, keep
her company. What had he said? That his soul was hungry,
that he was on a pilgrimage to visit as many Bethels, large
and small, as he could? But the few stops he'd made had
been perfunctory at best, always rushing to catch up with
her, breathless, face florid with fear that she'd disappeared.

But he wasn't just a Shepherd, he was a Seeker as well,
and Seekers bore a passing similarity to Gleaners. Still, perhaps their skills were natural, unperverted—the ghatti native
to the planet, best not harm something that belonged here, at
least until she could decide, be sure. She longed for the sting
of the supple rod on her shoulders, her back, scourging the
doubts from her mind, scourging the answers in. And that
was denied her with Harrap along. Grunting, she towed the
cart clear of the water, dropped the shafts, and rubbed her
palms. How they itched for the scourge.

In a few days they'd reach Schuylkill, two more days and
two nights to decide. To see if Harrap would persist in accompanying her, if she could convince him to travel on
about his own business. Little enough time to do what she
had to do, make the circuit, planting at the major stops.
Eight weren't enough, but it was the best she could manage
to erect a barricade against the voices that might shout to the
skies, and what would follow would be answering voices
form the starships.

Barnaby whined, pawed at her sodden pantaloon leg. Returning to the present, she saw Parm watching from the rise,
perky and curious and all-knowing, his motley markings a
ludicrous blur of colors. He gave a chirp of greeting, rolled
on his back, all four feet pointed skyward, opening himself
to receive danger from above. Barnaby galloped to meet
him, shook water all over, and terrier and ghatt began to
wrestle, romping and rolling. No, the ghatt had no portent,
was only a ghatt. Nothing dangerous about Parm, but about
Harrap she'd have to reserve judgment. Not that he was intrinsically dangerous but that, despite his best intentions, he
might present a danger to what she had to accomplish. Must
accomplish.

Too often each day melded into the next, research and write, write and research, don't think about the baby, don't think about Jenret or Swan, don't think about the future. At times the tidy progression of Seeker history could almost obscure her daily life, swamp her concerns about Swan each time she visited, mask the passage of her pregnancy. Except when the baby fluttered and shifted, swayed to its own inner music. Everything in neat, precise black-and-white—except for her gray thoughts. Being busy meant less time to worry, so she stockpiled them until later. She'd have whole winter's worth to sustain her by the time she finished.

Rawn and Khar conversed through the ghatti mindnet, carried word to her from Jenret, circumspect, flavorless messages, filtered through too many minds concerned for her well-being. Several times Doyce had startled, strained, almost swearing she could hear Jenret faintly in her mind. Yet no matter how hard she tried, she couldn't relax enough to grasp the sense, the words of the message, each effort blocking her tighter and tighter. Unlikely, anyway, fool's fancy. Why bother to listen, why should he send? How foolish to deny him, deny herself the comfort. Besides, what did she expect? She wasn't a Resonant. Mayhap someday, mayhap never, and each possibility boasted its own inherent fears.

Repenting her vow not to listen, this night she tried again before bed, sitting by the open window, bundled in an old navy robe of Jenret's to ward off the chill. With her eyes shut she could pretend he wrapped his arms around her, the closest she could come to him these days. For a moment her mind eased, and she almost believed it. Already curled at the foot of the bed, Khar squinted a sleepy eye at her, and she hoped when she finally gave up and went to bed the ghatta would cuddle close. Except then she'd be forced to leave her arm outside the covers, and goose-bumped at the thought.

"I'll warm both of us." Khar shifted, yawned pinkly, propped a paw over her nose.

Feeling her way to bed along a path of moonlight, she snuggled the covers close—her neck always got cold— wrestled an arm free as Khar slithered up. Soon, sooner than expected despite her aching loneliness, her breathing began to slow, to match Khar's rhythm, and she drifted into sleep.

Her waking came like a detonation, abrupt, shocking, her senses swimming. Bells pealed, not in measured tones to announce the passage of night, but in a frenzy of tolls, clanging across the city, outshouting each other. A strange brightness writhed, glowing against the far wall, not morning light but something almost alive, moving. Why was the light moving? Stock-still, hands clutching the sheets, she sought her bearings, concentrating on making sense of the clamor before venturing up. But Khar wedged through the window she'd left open a crack. Head through, Khar heaved the sash higher, the screech abrading Doyce's senses, her nostrils dilating at the whiff of smoke. She hugged the sheet to her mouth, gagged.

"Fire! Maize! Hurry!" the ghatta balanced on the sill, face shadowed through the glass. "Arm yourself!"

Arm yourself to go fight a fire? Without elaborating, Khar dashed off, but her command jolted Doyce into action. She dredged up her pantaloons, boots, slung Jenret's old robe around her as an overcoat. At least it covered her long bed shift, half stuffed into her waistband. Fire? Maize? The Elder Hostel on fire? Not fire, please! A harried poking around the darkened bedchamber finally unearthed her sword, its leather sheath dusty beneath her fingertips. The belt mocked her, unable to cinch around her waist when she attempted to buckle it on. Hissing with frustration, she slung it across her shoulder and pounded down the stairs and out the door.

Lights flashed in Headquarters windows, and in the distance she could make out other Seekers piling outside, running toward the brightening sky to the west. The acrid stench of smoke and burning taunted her lungs even at this distance. Praise the Lady, there was no smell of charring flesh as yet! Nothing to do but set her own pace, belly swaying rhythmically, and pray her jog trot would carry her there in time. The streets rapidly filled with clots of people, late-night revelers, half-awake, half-clothed citizens tumbling out of houses, wanting to know what was happening. Others joined her in running, passing her, colliding with her, and now the streets became further clogged, bottlenecked as people ran in the opposite direction, fleeing the fire. She slowed, a stitch crimping her side, was almost shouldered off her feet, slammed against the wall. Drawing shuddering gasps of air she calculated—a risk, yes, the streets less well-lit, more roughly cobbled and potential ankle-twisters, but if she cut through the old quarter she'd make better time by not having to fight the crowds.

As she pounded by Myllard's Inn, a wagon pulled around the gaudy building, sweeping wide as Myllard lashed the horses, his nightgown-clad wife Fala standing in the wagon bed behind him, steadying herself against his shoulders. The wagon looked jumble-loaded with blankets, buckets, other necessities. Somehow Fala caught her trembling outline in the shadows, yanked at Myllard to haul up, and Doyce tumbled up beside him, breathless but relieved. Of course Myllard would throw himself into the thick of things, an honorary fire chief, and with good reason, given the flammability of his three-storied wooden inn.

"How," she gasped, "are you going to force the wagon through? It'll be a madhouse the closer we get."

He concentrated on handling the team, urging them along dark streets, around tight corners, through narrow alleys. Fala, nightdress gleaming white beneath Myllard's old coat, hair in braids down her back, answered for him. "Back delivery door. Everyone always tries to come through the front. Only firemen note other possible entrances and exits. And tradesmen who deliver ale at the back door. You," a cuff stung Doyce's head, caught her by surprise, "should have stayed put. In your condition! Think you're birthing a firebrand?"

Giddy from the blow and the wagon's sway, she spun on her hip and shouted at Fala, "Much as I'd like it to happen as soon as possible, I doubt you'll be tending a birthing tonight. Just give me plenty of space to maneuver and I'll be fine." Sheer bravado, a patent lie, and she was relieved Khar wasn't there to catch her out. Not fire again, even if it had cleansed Vesey's soul.

Closer now, the fire's heat already beating on hands and faces, the light too, too bright, seductively familiar. Luckily, the wind carried most of the smoke away, so breathing wasn't too difficult as yet. Still, the horses grew restive, panicky about moving nearer.

Khar's mindvoice jolted her thoughts. **"Hurry! These louts are reaping with fire and sword! A rumor that the Elder Hostel shelters a Gleaner set them off!"**

Reining the team short at a hastily erected barrier across the street, Myllard gave a bellow for the firefighters to pass him through. Doyce hushed him, groaned inwardly at the profusion of collars boasting silver crescent sickles, winking fiery orange-red in the light. Not firefighters, but the foe, Reapers. "Keep them talking," she hissed at Myllard, and rolled off the tailgate without being seen, she hoped. Blocking their view as much as she could, Fala began a vociferous argument, distracting attention.

Edging along the alleyway, Doyce at last spotted the back kitchen door ajar, a beckoning vertical slice of gold against the dark walls, surmounted at roof level by smoke swirls spinning in the updraft. Flames danced and surged out of upper windows. Dangerous to open the door further, cause a bigger draft, suck in air to fan the flames higher. Exactly what had happened the night she and Varon had rushed home to find their baby Briony in jeopardy from Vesey's childish revenge. Apostle moons protect me, but I need a way in. Maize is inside, Khar as well. This time I'll save them!

Setting her shoulder to the door, she pushed, prayed her body would block the draft, pushed harder, the door balking, partly jammed. Her sword dangled under her arm, clunked against the door, reminding her she'd never drawn it, and she began to fumble it free as she leaned her full weight against the door. From the street front she could hear streams of water surging, arcing from the hand pumpers against the building, playing over the roof, steady and hard, then a sucking hesitation as a pumper ran dry, was dragged clear, and replaced by another.

Mesmerized by the flickering, shifting lights playing deep within as she wedged herself through the door, she ignored the murkiness beneath her feet. Stepped on something solid yet yielding, foot nearly twisting beneath her as she squinted at the shapes of two bodies, no, three. Her penchant for accuracy made her giggle hysterically. One appeared to be garbed in white kitchen gear, while the others wore darker clothes. Bending, she patted and fumbled at collars, the sharp point of a miniature sickle lancing her finger, keen answer to her fears.

Something slammed her behind the knees and she buckled, tumbling forward, gasping in shock, arms rigid to break her fall, protect her belly from smashing into the floor. The air whooshed above her, exactly level with where her head had been, and she sensed the racketing trajectory of a broad, heavy object propelled by ferocious strength and equally strong arms. A sound, half-clang, half-thud, like a berserk gong, vibrated in her ears and the door pinched hard on her extended leg.

"**Head cook has a powerful long reach,**" Khar leaped over her, landed with back arched, tail fluffed defensively until she appeared twice her size. She held the pose, allowing herself to be identified. "**Best identify yourself as well. Jenret's robe isn't as professional-looking as a tabard, you know. Hurry, I deserted Maize to rescue you!**"

A woman of flour-barrel girth and massive arms hefted the large cast-iron skillet as if it were light as a pancake flipper and cocked her wrists, ready to swing again. "Seeker Veritas Doyce Marbon and her ghatta Khar'pern at your service, ma'am." The skillet sank marginally, not toward Doyce's head, but toward the woman's shoulder in a modified rest position.

"Puny reinforcements. Ye'd best get inside and help. Me and Trenchard," she indicated the body in white on the floor, "been holding the back door against those murtherous spawn. Knew you wasn't one of the fire boys, but wasn't sure what ye were. There be wimmen Reapers, too."

Jerked to her feet by an assisting hand, Doyce plowed through the debris of a kitchen fight, smashed crockery mashed food, scattered pots and pans, some dented and crushed. A final backward look showed a meat cleaver sunk deep into the door casing.

"Pleasure to make your acquaintance, ma'am. Guard well, but take care, other friendly souls may try the back door." She struggled free of Jenret's robe, wrapped its bulk around her left arm. *"Which way, Khar?"*

"**This way! Maize's upstairs.**" The smoke still rankled and stung the back of her throat, her eyes watery, but the heavy smell of doused wood, soggy ashes, and wet plaster told her the worst of the fire was under control. The halls were hazed, wreathed with smoke that made it hard to see, but she glimpsed a few elderly bodies collapsed along her route, some almost peaceful-looking, as if they'd drifted off to sleep, others contorted, faces cyanotic blue, a few charred bodies. Hostel workers collided with firefighters and Guardians, evacuating residents, coaxing them from behind barricaded doors. She counted four bodies with the silver sickle crescents pinned over wheat sprigs, dodged a firefighter feinting his ax at a cornered man, defiant with a club.

Where was Khar leading? Her mind blurred the Hostel's layout as much as her stinging eyes; she'd not absorbed the sense of it on her previous visit to Maize Bartolotti, too intent on journey's end, rather than the route there. Up the stairs. She took them cautiously, charred wood crunching beneath her feet. The shifting shape of a ghatt awaited her on the top of the stairs, two other ghatti faintly visible in the gloom and hanging smoke. More ghatti, in fact, wherever she turned.

"Maize sounded the distress call. Begged any of us within hearing distance to come to her aid." Paw poised in mid-step, Khar halted in concentration and tilted her head toward the sunroom, strangely cavernous and foreboding. It spanned the whole west end of the house, its glass panes shattered, glistening like ice fragments loosened from a tree by the sun's heat after an ice storm. Plants lay broken and battered, spilled dirt and crushed greenery underfoot like a dying jungle, the smell sharp with battered, bruised leaves, almost pleasant, though somewhat overcooked.

As she skirted closer, the darker shape of figures took on definition at the far end of the sunroom. A Seeker Veritas, weaponless and wounded, held his ground beside Maize Bartolotti, protecting an old man huddled on hands and knees, blood stringing across his face and scalp. Three Reapers—the sight of one of them brandishing an actual sickle made Doyce's hair rise with an atavistic fear— jockeyed to gain ground, kept at bay by two ghatti, claws as lethal as the sickle as they flowed in and out of the smoke, disappearing and reappearing where least expected. Alternately threatening and blustering, the three stumbled into each other's way more often than not.

With a piqued hiss, Khar launched herself into the fray. **"Humans are *so* impossible sometimes! Absolutely no interest in a Seeking to determine the Truth. That would be *too* simple, might convince them they erred."** Sharp ghatti teeth punctured an unsuspecting Reaper's unprotected calf. Panic-stricken, the man screamed, tried to kick loose, Khar's jaws still latched tight. Not easy to levitate a ghatta weighting almost twenty kilos who'd now wrapped all four legs around his. Wavering, he grabbed his comrades for support, and Maize's arm shot out, the crook of a purloined cane lifting his other foot off the floor. Too easy, almost unfair, and Doyce let her sword point caress his throat as he lay flat, stunned. His two comrades required no further invitation to depart as quickly as possible. **"Others'll scoop them up,"** Khar promised.

Other supporters, Seekers, firefighters, and Hostel attendants poured into the sunroom, chasing after the escapees as Maize collapsed into the remains of a chair. "Took you long enough. Not as spry as you once were, eh?" Maize wheezed, coughed black phlegm, her face and nightshift soot- and dirt-streaked, wet spots exhibiting a midnight black muddiness. "Still, not too bad, any of you, 'specially this young'un here." The tall, wounded Seeker Doyce had assumed was male turned out to be Cady Brandt, pale-faced, pinching together a deep sickle gash in her upper arm. "She tossed two over before they ganged up on her." An affectionate pat as high as Maize could reach grazed Cady's waist. "Wasn't sure if anybody'd come when I sounded my distress call, but the . . . ghatti remembered." With that she fainted.

The cleanup, the succoring of survivors, the removal of the dead consumed the rest of the night, Doyce helping until she was drained and numb of spirit at the wanton, senseless destruction. At last Myllard and Fala pulled her away and frog-marched her to their wagon, now set up out front as an impromptu aid station, dispensing bandages, hot cha and sandwiches, blankets, and odd pieces of clothing to half-naked but still upright senior residents.

Fala thrust a cha mug into her hands, then pressured her shoulders until she sank onto a rug-covered crate serving as a bench. Wiping Doyce's face thoroughly with a damp cloth as if she were a child, Fala instructed, "Now drink up. That's an order."

The cha scalded, tasted smoky, the predominant taste and scent of everything, including the lining of her mouth and throat. The next sip tasted better, the added honey soothing. "What happened?" she pleaded. "I still don't know what really happened. Everyone's been too busy to ask, even Khar." And Maize was beyond asking as well, unconscious, gently carried outside on a makeshift stretcher piled high with blankets.

Myllard hitched his suspenders higher, tucked his night-shirt into his trousers where it billowed in the back. "Pays to be on good terms with the fire boys." Well-pleased, he tugged at his side whiskers to restrain himself and thumped Doyce on the shoulder, began to rub her back. Myllard tended to be a tactile man, and tonight, this morning, whatever it was now, she relished his touch, leaned into the massaging hands. "From what I can gather, about a dozen young toughs broke in well after midnight, overpowered the night duty attendant. Began running from room to room with torches shouting for Max Lewinton. That if they didn't find him, they'd burn the place. Began to live up to their word.

"Some poor old souls were too petrified to unlock their doors. Wasn't meant to provoke the Reapers, 'twas simple fear. Reapers kicking down doors, throwing torches inside, sometimes they'd drag the resident out, sometimes not. Smoke took some, others died of fright." He stared into the distance, wrapped an arm around Fala, "Neither's a good way to die, whether you're young or old."

From the shelter of his arm Fala added, "When you think how many couldn't see or hear well, walk well, you could hardly expect them to march out meekly and prove they weren't Gleaners." Her voice broke. "All they knew was that they were scared, weren't sure what the ruckus was about, best stay safe in their rooms. Safe indeed!"

"Apparently a few, led by your friend Maize, put up some resistance along with the other night duty attendants. They may not have been strong, but they were canny. They lured the bulk of the Reapers away while Maize hid in the sunroom with Lewinton." Myllard looked admiring. "Once the fire boys doused the sunroom, she figured at least they were safe from the fire."

"Is Lewinton a Glea . . ." she stopped herself, "a Resonant?" It didn't matter whether he was or not. A brutal, bestial act had been committed with no concern as to the larger outcome. But to murder innocents along with the purportedly guilty?

Myllard continued rubbing the back of her neck. "I gather that he'd claimed bragging rights on it recently, now that being a Resonant might be good, or at least interesting, but the attendant said he bragged about anything, loved to bask in the center of attention whenever he could. Tall tales." He shifted gears suddenly.

"And speaking of tails, attendants didn't understand what brought the ghatti running, but I set them straight on that." He whisked a bedroom-slippered foot in Khar's direction; Doyce hadn't noticed her return.

"How's Maize? Any change?" If anyone knew, Khar

would, but she asked aloud to include Myllard and Fala in the conversation.

"Didn't Myllard tell you?" Khar stretched her length up Myllard's leg, nosing at the pan of water being poured. **"Still unconscious, but the eumedicos think it's overexertion, nothing more. She's resting at Myllard's Inn."**

"Tell you, did she?" Fala beamed. "Thought you'd like that for your friend, and better for her if she didn't wake up in the hospice, sure the end was nigh. Once they think that, it's often true. Those as needed it have been admitted, but we've been trying to place the other residents in temporary homes nearby, make them part of a family for a bit."

Doyce sank back in relief, head lolling. Lady above, she hadn't realized the depths of her exhaustion and dread, or how afraid she'd been. Myllard and Fala grabbed her arms and boosted her into the wagon bed. "We've done enough here, all we can do tonight. Now we're going home and you'll pass the night with us. No sense going back to that empty guest house."

" 'Nother surprise there for you as well," Fala announced boldly, and Doyce glimpsed Myllard's face as it darkened, then relaxed, wistfulness mingled with pride. "Claire and the baby are visiting. Just visiting," she emphasized in her husband's direction. "She's not going to apologize for marrying that peddler, and you won't apologize for making her run away to do it, so you can leave it lie, Myllard.

Claire, too? It sounded wonderful, Doyce thought muzzily as Khar jumped in beside her and curled against her side. The wagon began its excursion across town. **"You smell like a smoked ham,"** was Khar's final comment as Doyce fell asleep, lulled by the rocking journey.

She sat in the corner where the Seekers traditionally congregated at Myllard's, forearms resting on the table, hands clutching a tankard of weak cider. "Barely had time to turn," Fala had assured her, "scarce no alcohol at all." Sleep had been equally sparse in the remains of the night; after being ensconced in the Inn's marvelously pink porcelain bathtub, soaked and scrubbed clean, she'd tried, but to no avail. On top of everything else it brought back memories of her last bath in this extravagance, the night she'd learned of Oriel's death, discovered she wasn't pregnant with his child. It seemed so long ago, far distant—had it truly been only a little over a year ago?

The Inn was nominally closed, but a steady stream of weary firefighters, Guardians, and citizens who'd helped control the blaze wandered about, breakfast plates stacked high. Others, too spent, too smoke-sickened to eat, sprawled on benches—one snored on the floor—still caught up in the companionship, the brotherhood engendered by overcoming a disaster, and the opportunity to relive its dangers with those who grasped the risks entailed.

She'd spoken briefly with Maize as dawn broke, but the woman was still too weak to comprehend much. Indeed, Doyce suspected there wasn't a great deal to comprehend; few had the scope to understand such a heedless, vicious act. But Maize was adamant that Max Lewinton was no Gleaner, no Resonant. "Never a hint in all the years I've known him. Never." And the look she'd fixed on Doyce was acute despite the exhaustion dulling the once lively eyes. "I think Seekers are more sensitive to it than others, don't you? Always had an inkling about certain people, something a bit peculiar about them, An'g and I did. Or rather, An'g did, though she'd seldom say more." Her burned hand shifted, stroked the ghatta on the bed beside her. "Ask Khar."

A discomforting idea. But none of the ghatti had ever specifically identified a Resonant, ever pointed one out through all the years, except recently, when they'd been so ordered. Puzzling. The ghatti had been innocent about what Arras Muscadeine and his kind represented when they'd visited Marchmont.

"**Of course we didn't know.**" The ghatta's fur stood up in spikes from the damp toweling Claire had given her, scrubbing off as much soot and smoke-smell as possible. "**They never opened themselves to us, not until Muscadeine permitted M'wa to search his mind. Even so it almost surpassed belief if it hadn't been the truth.**" The fur around her face looked especially sleeked, as if she'd been caught in a heavy mist. "**But occasionally through the years as we ghatti Sought as part of the ceremony, we've run into a mind with potential, sometimes witting, sometimes not. If the mind posed no threat to the person harboring it or to others, why say a thing? Their minds are theirs, not ours.**"

"Not even a hint?" Doyce had countered, frustrated.

"No. If anything, we suspected a person with Seeker potential. After all, there are more of you than there are of us, so some of you are always wasted, destined to go through life without Bonds."

The thought took her aback. *"At least they don't know what they've missed."*

Although Maize couldn't hear them, she acted faintly wistful, as if it had occurred to her as well. But then, she knew what a Bond was like, and had experienced the emptiness without it far too soon.

Doyce sighed as Claire poured more cider into the mug and passed along to serve others. A relief, she didn't really want to talk now, didn't even want to think about the thousand and one things they could discuss about motherhood, pregnancy, the joys and terrors of infant-raising.

"Infantry?" Khar inquired from under the bench.

She wasn't in the mood for the joke, not with the somber thoughts that crowded her mind. *"How many years, Khar? How many years can hate persist? Senseless, vicious hatred of innocents? No wonder they've kept themselves well hidden. But what makes it suddenly fester like this?"* Equally tired, the ghatta dragged herself onto the bench, rested her chin on the edge of the table, hazel eyes meeting amber ones. *"How many years can hate go on?"* she repeated more vehemently.

"Eight times eight times eight. Octad times octad times octad or more. You brought it with you when you came to this world, prideful at being a citizen of a specific country, a member of a special group. Factions meant more than the whole to you. Hatred, the fear that the first Spacer telepaths were responsible for the Plumbs, drove Venable Constant and the Resonants to escape to Marchmont, not just his desire for kingship. Or animosity between technicians and artists, like Crolius and Magnus. And now mistrust of Marchmont, of Resonants, rears its ugly head again, even if it's dimly remembered, like fairy tales of old."

Khar's lecture was hardly encouraging. Far from it. *"Does it ever stop, ever end?"*

"Everyone needs someone less 'worthy' to project their anxieties and fears on, and the more similar people are to

each other, the easier it is to fixate on one small peculiarity, one tiny difference."

One tiny difference—the ability to read minds. She pushed the bench back hard, nearly overturning it, the scrape attracting everyone's attention as she rose. *"Khar, I want to go home!"*

"Where's home?"

A fair question; what was the answer? Her old spartan room at Headquarters? The house she now shared with Jenret when he was here—and where was he, by the Lady, why hadn't he gotten in touch with her? The house she'd once shared with Varon and Briony and Vesey, burned as well? A shudder wriggled under her skin. Strange, once she'd dashed into the thick of things last night she'd locked her terror of Vesey's final pyre in a far compartment of her mind, refused to let it battle free. A good sign or not?

Still pondering, she crossed the taproom. Was home the little village near Ruysdael where she'd been born, where her mother and sister still lived? This was how Matthias Vandersma and Kharm must have felt during those long years of wandering. Well, she and Khar couldn't hold a candle to that first great Bond-pair. Downright presumptuous, vainglorious to measure herself against the founder of the Seekers Veritas.

Khar blocked the doorway. **"You're just broody, looking for a place to nest. It'll pass,"** she comforted.

"Don't I have a place here in Gaernett?" Mayhap Khar had the right of it, mayhap she *was* just broody, hormones surging, searching for security, feeling utterly abandoned. A shamed downward glance thrust her into the present: she wore a clean nightshift and robe of Fala's, nothing more. "Were you going to let me go out like this?" she sputtered. Out loud, apparently, because Myllard turned in her direction.

"Can if you want—if you dare!" the ghatta taunted.

And just to have the last say, she stalked out the door, fuzzy knit slippers on her feet. Thank the Lady it was early morning still, and few around to view her like this. The baby kicked and the robe billowed. *"Well, come on. I'll go get changed and head for the library."* It was the best interim home she knew.

❖

PART
THREE

❖

PART
THREE

Jenret cursed, cursed himself and the darkness with impressive fluent dignity. Alone in the forest in the middle of the night following a half-witted scheme. Addawanna had rejected his proposal outright, laughing at him. Sarrett, Yulyn, and Towbin had indignantly refused to leave the comfort of the campfire; Faertom had merely shrugged, as withdrawn as usual. The swathing darkness of the woods obscured the Lady moon and her Disciples, made them equally distant and uncaring. Well, the others'd had the right of it. Fool's errand. But today marked the conclusion of the two oct period of waiting he'd agreed on with the Resonants. Sixteen days, and he'd heard nothing more from the Monitor.

When Faertom had returned with the Monitor's response, Jenret's heart had pounded with anticipation at the thick packet—but the only thing of substance had been the letter's size. No new proposals or plans, simply a reiteration of every pertinent law and regulation, how it was being enforced, how the population was being reminded of each applicable law and the penalities involved for breaking it. Van Beieven had closed by promising to send word if the High Conciliators did anything more. Not enough, not nearly—a sop to the Monitor's conscience. Jenret felt as if a pledge had been broken, but had he had any right to make it to begin with?

"Scare dem more, you loomin in dark at dem. Not very comfort-makin if you wan gain der confidence. Come morning, hot head will cool," Addawanna had urged. Yet he refused to fault his reasoning—small, secluded campfires would stand out in the dark, and that was why he'd hiked upward, scanning the valleys and beyond. Nothing, not a fire beyond their own beckoned. Did it mean no Resonants hid out there, or that they'd cold-camped, taking no chances on being spotted?

Still, being out here with Rawn let him balm his battered

ego in private, afforded him another opportunity to
mindreach Doyce. Each time he'd tried, he'd fallen back,
beaten, bruised, as if he'd collided with a glass wall. So
close tonight, he could almost see Doyce on the other side,
wrapped in his old bathrobe, her palpable longing for him,
her suspicion that yet again he'd broken his trust. But her
mind remained shuttered. Whether she did it consciously, or
whether it reflected his imperfect skill, he couldn't judge. He
should have asked Yulyn.

"It's not really you and it's not really her," Rawn placated. **"Oil and water don't mix, and that's what you're
trying to do."**

Cold comfort at best. He sat on a fallen log, propped head
in hands. *"I wonder, I wonder,"* he mused, losing himself in
the times he'd placed his hand on Doyce's belly, felt the
baby stir at the sound of his voice, his laughter, his songs.
Could he somehow reach the unborn child, the child both he
and Doyce shared, a part of them both? Not alarm it, but
simply send reassuring thoughts for the child to transmit to
Doyce. *"Do you think so?"* he asked Rawn, sure the ghatt
would deduce what he meant.

"It's possible, I suppose," Rawn's tail switched uneasily.
**"But be careful, very cautious. When do babies develop
their own mental signatures? Will it understand you?
The last thing you want is to pitch Doyce into early labor
if you overexcite it, overstimulate it."**

It stopped him cold. But he strove to think it through,
measuring what was best for everyone, but most of all for
the unborn child. He suspected a son but wasn't sure.

"Girl children are nice, too."

A warning? A hint to prepare himself for a daughter?
Well, he'd settle for either, a healthy, laughing child. His intense blue eyes with Doyce's brown hair, red highlights
sparkling in the sun? His dark hair, her hazel eyes, sometimes tender, often tough, framed by his long, curved lashes.
At last he ventured, *"I think the child already knows me,
knows my voice. Lady knows, I've crooned at it out loud and
in my heart. If it were a stranger, an unborn stranger you
might be right."* He stood, backing up the incline until he
balanced practically atop the cliff scarp, wanting the world
to hear his mindshout that he worshiped Doyce, adored his
unborn child, and that all was well with him.

He concentrated, sweat beading his brow, envisioning the

bedchamber where Doyce would be sleeping. Touched a gaping emptiness, almost rocked off his feet by the enormity of it, then relaxed as he confirmed the emptiness signified her absence, not death. Overreacting without reason, surely, but where could she be at this time of night? Jenret sent his mind searching the city, heard Rawn instruct, **"Spiral from the center, the bedroom, work outward. Less chance to miss them."** And obeyed. It seemed the wise thing to do.

Touched ... yes! A twinge of recognition, of consciousness, and he soothed it, crooned to it, but the infantile mind overwhelmed him with its raw terrors—a crashing jolt that rattled his bones, the din thunderclapping on tiny, sensitive ears. An abrupt temperature shift, too, too hot! The oxygen coursing through the placenta thinner than it liked. *"Too bright, too bright, even in here!"* Oh, ouch, jouncing!" *"Ow, toe in eye! Stop!"* *"Hold still, I'll shift!"* *"What is fire? Mama scared?"*

He reeled, dizzy with effort, rising fear strangling him, clawing at his throat, unable to absorb the raw emotions and sensations, the voice—voices?—he heard, but grasping that some dire danger threatened Doyce. The baby as well. Fire? By the Lady, no, not fire! Not like Vesey's demise! He tried to tap into the voice again, pushed himself back and higher, not looking or caring what was behind him.

"Doyce!" he screamed. *"Doyce! Hold on!"* Flames surged at him, danced and crackled, fingers of fire licking him, an obscene come-hither. They shimmered and crawled all around him. No! He would not—he viewed it in his mind's eye, it wasn't real! Vivid streamers of orange and yellow circled, tasting his clothes, flashing and flaring at his hands, his face, singeing. Lungs winced at the superheated air. Higher, hotter—he dove to escape the messages slamming into his mind, as if his escape would liberate Doyce as well. And tumbled backward into thin air as Rawn shouted, too late, **"No farther! Stop!"**

A backward somersault, and he was rolling, bouncing and crashing like a string-slashed puppet down the steep cut of the ravine toward the stream far below. Water, at least, would quench.

❖

The world reared up to meet him, drove the breath from his lungs, the sense from his head, as a tree stump slammed his midsection. For an eternity of moments he hung, paralyzed. His eyes shifted marginally, surveying the weathered bark up close, unable to move any other part of him, unable to blink, unable to make even his lungs work. Lungs were supposed to work whether you were conscious of them or not, weren't they? Why couldn't he—why couldn't they—draw a breath? Why? Why couldn't he twitch even a finger? What he could do was listen, hear while he hung limply defenseless the sound of dead roots ripping free, giving way, readying the stump for the final slide into oblivion. His body hovered halfway there, his mind drifting between consciousness and oblivion, blackness washing across his vision as his whole system craved oxygen.

Just as he thought he'd black out, die, for all he knew, he managed to crack his jaws open, draw a shuddering deep breath. Slowly, the infinite delight of sensation returned, fingers flexed, clenched at his command. That relief, however, couldn't nullify the sounds of the roots tearing free from their precarious rocky hold.

Rawn slipped and slithered to his side, clawing to stop his momentum. **"Phew! Ouch! Down's always faster than up."** A black paw tapped Jenret's thigh, claws pricking to restrain any further movement. **"Break anything?"**

Hard to tell in this splayed, rag-doll position, spitted by a stump canting toward the cliff face, but he thought not. *"No, but infinitely bruised. Like an overripe fruit that's been used for kick ball."*

"Well, you took a hit to the solar plexus. Leaves you rigid as a plank. The stump saved you from falling all the way, though."

"How are we going to get out of here?" Did he dare sit up, test things for himself? No, not yet. Could he move? Most important, *where* to move? Nothing to do but continue hanging there, draped over the tree stump, arms and legs straddling it, hair tangling with the half-exposed roots. Beyond that, empty air.

"Good question. Wish I had an answer." The ghatt shifted sideways on the narrow outcropping. **"If you want to dismount, scrunch backward. Don't think about sitting up until you do."**

He slithered backward, the stump complaining under his weight, roots rearing higher as he untangled himself. **"Sit**

back now, you can't go any farther." He did, leaned
against the cliff wall, the stump still between his legs, feet
dangling over thin air. A close escape. And then the cause of
his predicament swamped his senses, left him quivering with
consternation. His rising panic at hearing the terror in the
baby voice . . . voices? The crystallizing knowledge that
Doyce and their unborn child were in jeopardy, the flames so
perilously close, a transmittal of terror so real he'd been engulfed by it, unable to separate his own truth from their reality. Now that all contact had fled, he couldn't sense what
was happening to them, whether their terror increased or diminished. He bit his lip until the pain brought him back to
himself; surely he'd feel a corresponding but far worse pain
if they'd perished? Wouldn't he? He trembled, drew Rawn
into his lap.

"Rawn, promise me something." He hugged the ghatt
fiercely, rumpling the velvet ears, fingering the earrings.
"Promise me!"

"What?" A delicate snuffling around his ear, the nose
shifting to his eyelids, blotting the tears. **"What, my
Bondmate? Speak."**

Never, ever had he borne a sorrow so oppressive, so all-
encompassing, devouring his heart. Not that he feared death,
had never feared it before, but if he died now, Doyce would
surely believe he'd failed her again, didn't love her enough,
didn't love their child. Loved himself and his dream for the
Resonants more. *"If . . . if,"* he stammered, *"a . . . any . . .
thing happens to me, if I die, don't journey with me. Return
to Doyce, make sure she's all right, that the child is all right.
Watch over them, guard them for me if I can't be there."*

Dipping his head under Jenret's chin, the ghatt butted him,
furiously rubbing. A tall order, and one he momentarily
didn't wish to obey. Life without Jenret was death. Without
a doubt, Saam had balked as well when assigned the same
untenable task by his now-dead Bondmate Oriel. The selfsame task: protecting Doyce from harm. Far better to die
with one's Bond—as Rolf and Chak had, Rolf taking that final step over the cliff, cradling the dead Chak in his arms.
Together, still together wherever they dwelt now. His ears
swiveled, testing the faint noises at the clifftop, judged them
promising. **"Well, I can't honor your request."**

A tensing, chest and stomach muscles rigid beneath him,
arms gripping like iron bands, as if they'd strangle him for

his refusal. *"Oh, yes? And why might that be?"* the beloved voice hissed hot, naked anger in his ear.

"You refused to let yourself or Parse die lost, abandoned in Sidonie's underground passages, and you have the strength and the courage not to die now."

"Well, when this stump breaks loose, it'll take most of the ledge with it. I don't have much choice!"

Rawn radiated smugness. **"Don't fuss any more than you have to. Rescue's coming from above."**

The tail of a rope snaked down the rockface, too far away to catch. Jenret couldn't see it, could only hear its slithering passage. *"Towbin and the others?"* Hope surged, drove the fear from his body. He would live! Rush back to Gaernett, to Doyce's side, never abandon her or the baby again, protect them both against everything, including his own fickleness! Towbin and Faertom could pull him up from here without breaking into a sweat, especially with Sarrett, Yulyn, and Addawanna to help! Easy as jerking a fish out of a stream, especially a fish that wanted to be caught! And he wanted to be caught and hauled to safety so badly.

"No, not exactly," Rawn allowed. **"You *were* out searching for Resonants, you know. Strange how they seem to find *you* without any trouble."**

The sound of creaking rope, scraping noises, rock splinters breaking free and crashing past his head, grunts of exertion. *"But I didn't call for help. Didn't have time. Wouldn't have known whom to contact other than Yulyn or Faertom, how to reach them without a signature."* A body hovered above and to his right when he tossed his head straight back, strained to see. Or rather, a dark shape, more a lump really, against the lighter rockface, spidering toward him.

"I think your distress shouted unconsciously, rallied anyone nearby. Anyone with the mind to hear."

"Then Yulyn and Faertom should have heard." That made sense. *"They should be coming, too,"* he insisted.

"If you wouldn't hold me so tightly, I could breathe better," Rawn mentioned in passing, and at last the iron grip eased. **"No doubt they are, but they have farther to come, don't know exactly where you are. So other company's arriving first."**

He considered shouting, hailing the descending figure, but feared a sharp sound might dislodge additional rocks and stones as well as the man. The Thomases had refused to mindspeak him—would this man? Flaunt it in his face that he hadn't proven his worth? He reached deep inside for all the neutral goodwill, gratitude he could muster, nothing to frighten or startle the dimly visible man. *" 'Ware the out-cropping. It's sharp enough to saw the rope."* He should know, had slashed himself against it on the way down.

"Right. Saw it. Now stow it. Enough to concentrate on without ... magpie ... chattering." The figure sideslipped, gained toe-purchase on a slender fault line and eased side-ways, swinging his rope to the right. He continued down, wall-walking, letting the rope bear his weight. *"How much ... room ... beside you?"*

Jenret groped the dimensions of his impromptu perch. Its greatest depth was where he sat, with the tree trunk project-ing inward like a thorn in flesh. To his right, the man's right, he judged it ran about a meter long. The greatest problem was that the farther away it ran, the more it tapered, until he could touch only a sliver of a narrow lip. *"You're too far to your left. You won't be able to reach the ledge from there. It's mayhap a meter long, but at the far edge it's no more than two fingers deep."*

The mindvoice cut in acerbically, *"Then why tell me to shift away before?"*

Perplexed, Jenret replied, *"Because it would have slashed the rope."*

"Frayed it, sure. Just climb faster than it frays."

Hardly a comforting thought. *"Can you reach?"*

A hawking, spitting noise, the realization that a globule of liquid sailed by his head. **"Not very comforting when you can't hear it land,"** Rawn gulped. **"A long way down."**

"Sure. Climbed worse."

And amazingly, centimeter by centimeter, the man shifted, embraced the wall, hugging himself to it. Once or twice the metallic chink of a pick rang out, shattering the silence. A leg swung over, foot sliding sideways, testing the widening lip. Finally, the other leg followed. Jenret tilted his head, saw ripped woolen trousers and a heavy canvas smock, the bare sketch of a face above that. *"Seeker Veritas and Reso-nant Jenret Wycherley at your service."* A stupid thing to say, considering his predicament. *"Or rather, awaiting your service, I hope."*

A hand braced against his shoulder and the figure turned until he faced outward like Jenret. *"Somerset Garvey. Wasn't planning on a night stroll down a scarp. Still, you called for help. Not right to ignore or deny one of our own.*"

Jenret found himself pulled to his feet, scabard dragging against the wall, Rawn still in his arms. Nowhere now to set the ghatt unless he pinned him between his feet. *"How do I climb? I need a hand free to hold the ghatt."*

"Figured he'd cause trouble." A rustling from under his smock was followed by, *"Wrapped a gunnysack round my waist. Pop him in. Tie it to your belt."*

"No! Not helpless like that!" Rawn squirmed and sputtered. **"I'll stay and starve to death before I willingly crawl into that sack!"**

He lacked the heart to blame Rawn but couldn't fathom any other choice. *"Rawn, it has to be. Trust me."* And brought his attention back to Garvey. *"Are we climbing up together or one at a time? Will the rope hold us both?"*

He could see Garvey's head swivel, realized he was shaking his head in disgust. *"Nother rope anchored topside."* A soft whistle, and the rope came, uncoiling as it went. *"Side by side, that way I kin help if you hang up. Wall-walking's an acquired habit."*

Rawn growled, caught his attention. **"How much do you value your hide?"**

He strove to soothe, suspected he failed miserably, betraying the ghatt by forcing the indignity of the sack on him. Pride versus life. *"It won't take long, Rawn. What do you mean 'how much do I value my hide'?"*

"I mean, enough to forgive some inadvertent shredding if it's necessary?" Claws dug deep into his sheepskin tabard as Rawn clambered onto Jenret's shoulders. **"I'll cling to the tabard, that's what it was meant for, but if I slip, I'll sink my claws into any available part of your anatomy,"** he warned.

Garvey ignored them, fashioning a harness from the rope end. Putting a hand up, Jenret steadied the ghatt. *"Rawn, it won't work. You won't stay stable on my shoulders. I'll pitch you off."*

"I am planning on sinking my front claws into your shoulders, driving my teeth into your collar, and hooking my hind claws into your waist sash. Consider me as a ghatti knapsack, the latest fashion." More urgently, almost apprehensively, **"Please, humans drown kittens in gunnysacks. If the bag falls into the stream below...."**

other human being, even on pain of their own death. It speaks of incredible self-control."

"Or incredible fear," Doyce chimed in, still staring at the ceiling. Ah, so she *was* listening. "Fear of revelation, of exposing themselves and their families for who and what they are. Look at the consequences."

"Been told it's an ingrained habit, not to reveal themselves under the threat of torture or death." Abandoning her view of the ceiling at Dykshoorn's utterance of what he swallowed as gospel truth, Doyce sighed. Everyone was an instant expert. The man's pale blue eyes popped more than usual tonight, his long face seemed even longer, as if a sculptor had positioned his fingers on the cheekbones of a freshly molded clay face and squeezed in, then dragged downward.

"Been told by whom, Shoorny?" The Monitor snapped waspishly, wanting to wound, to hurt something, someone. An unworthy thought, but he yearned so badly to lash out.

Writhing as if strapped to a hot seat, which he was, metaphorically speaking, Dykshoorn stammered, a soldier, a doer, reduced to the panicky state of a private enduring a dressing down by an officer. Used to giving commands, not receiving them, it didn't improve his powers of recall. "I . . . er . . . well . . . ah . . . well . . . everybody knows that, Monitor, always have."

"Old wives' tales, old men whittling in the sun, trading big fish stories—is that what you've based your knowledge on, Dykshoorn?"

"Let him be, Kyril. We're all guilty of believing what we want to believe these days, whether or not it's rooted in fact. Believing in something is better than not knowing what to believe, and I, for one, don't know what I believe anymore." With effort Swan ran fingers through her clipped white hair, spiking it against the pillow. "When that happens, you start from scratch, with zero assumptions, and build on what little real knowledge you have, search out more facts." She didn't like the way Doyce looked at her out of the corner of her eye, back to pretending interest in the ceiling after examining the Major General as if to measure his face. Her expression was almost petulant, teeth sunk into the corner of her mouth as if to hold the words in. Close to erupting soon, Swan'd bet.

Van Beieven rejoined the circle, sank heavily into his

chair. "There has to be a way for us to identify Resonants!"
Silence followed his words, ripened and grew. "You don't
understand, I can't have any more lives at risk, theirs or
ours." If only he could expunge the guilt that he hadn't done
enough, could never do enough to heal the breach threatening to sunder Canderis. He'd lacked the courage to contact
Wycherley again, admit there was nothing further he could
do. Not on a deadline like that, not and acknowledge his im-
potence.

"Who's Us and who're They?" Doyce feigned wide-eyed
innocence. Blast the woman, Swan thought, and muffled a
chuckle. "They and Us, as you so quaintly put it, are all full
citizens of Canderis, native-born, or as native-born as we
can be since all of our ancestors emigrated from another
world—unlike the Erakwa, or the ghatti. If you look at it
that way, we're all aliens, Resonants and Normals alike, offspring of alien invaders."

"Doyce, don't twist my words," the Monitor pleaded, "I
know that as well as you. We have to discover how to unmask them, discover whom to protect. I swear I'd intern
them all if I could, if it meant guarding them from the hotheads, the Reapers, and safeguarding the rest of us from
those idiots as well. It wouldn't be difficult to gain support
for it, you know, a significant majority of the High Conciliators champions the idea. If I lean in their favor, no doubt
some of the undecideds would shift, provide a majority."

Dykshoorn sat forward, eager to contribute to a problem
he could understand. "Easier to round up those Reapers, sir.
Imprison them, convince them of the error of their ways,
or—if worse comes to worst and they won't adapt—ship'em
off to the Sunderlies, let'm squabble and kill each other."

"Solutions are never that tidy, Dykshoorn. Any group,
even Reapers, has a legal right to free assembly. I can't order their arrest *before* they commit another crime, unless we
have evidence a crime may be committed," the Monitor's
forbearance was wearing thin. "The clues in other cases
have been perilously scanty. We can't question everyone
without a cause.

"Oh, I've no doubt the Reapers we captured last night will
be sentenced to the Sunderlies. We've evidence and wit-
nesses aplenty. But the Seekers questioning them can't discover who leads them because they don't know. All they
know is their immediate leader, and we can't find him.

They're too organized not to have a leader, as much as they act as if they spontaneously combust."

"More like spontaneous generation. People thought that's how maggots were created, once upon a time."

Ignoring Doyce's gibe, the Monitor refused to be baited, attention still fixed on Dykshoorn. "But beyond marooning the Reapers in the Sunderlies, have you thought how to re-educate our whole populace, convince them their fears are groundless?"

Chastened by the complexity of the problem, Dykshoorn subsided as Doyce spoke. "Have you considered some sort of peacekeeping force, bringing in a neutral group to keep order?"

The Monitor scowled from under lowered brows. "Surely you're not suggesting that I . . . ?" he let the words trail off. Impossible to be so credulous, and her a Seeker. "Find a neutral group," he mouthed under his breath, "bloody well likely!"

"I wondered about a force from Marchmont."

"Doyce!" The protest from van Beieven's chair was equally loud as he slammed it back, seeking distance from such a radical idea. But Dykshoorn beat him to a response, bulling in ahead of him, "Seeker Marbon, might I remind you we've just fought them. Conveying Marchmontian troops here in force would be construed as an invasion, as if they were the conquerors."

"Nobody conquered anybody else, Major General, given the givens of that abortive war, though all too many died," Swan pointed out. "But your comment's well taken."

"And besides, what would their force consist of—all Normals, Normals and Resonants, all Resonants?" Having recovered his voice, the Monitor attempted scorn but found his curiosity piqued. The suggestion had flabbergasted him, but then, he was *that* desperate for a solution, wasn't he? Even the unsavory tastes delectable to a starving man.

Sprawl forgotten, poised to press home her point, Doyce looked levelly around the room, daring objections. "You're all taking it too literally. Think about it, think! What if we show them harmony in action? I suspect Eadwin believes he owes us a favor or two, given that we helped him attain the throne. What about a royal procession, some sort of royal progress to thank the people of Canderis for their contribution? Have him and a large entourage, a *very* large entourage, journey from town to town, illustrate how Resonants and Normals hold equal stature. That, in fact, Resonants hold higher stature in some instances. Give our people a goal to strive for, a standard to emulate."

"Aye, and all we need's for their king to be assassinated by one of our hotheads." Dykshoorn's long face grew even longer than before, mournful with worry. "We'd be stretched thin guarding a group of that size day and night. You can make assumptions about how an army'll move, where it'll fight, but you can't outguess a few zealots who don't fear anything except failure."

"I don't know." Van Beieven vacillated, certainly not convinced but not dismissing it out of hand. Had there ever been a time when answers, solutions were clear-cut? He seemed to remember such a golden time, not all that long ago. Fool's paradise? That's what Darl Allgood would remind him. "I just don't know. Would Eadwin come? Can he leave Marchmont so early in his reign, while he's still consolidating his own power base? Oh," he threw up his hands in defeat, secretly relieved, "ask him, why not? It never hurts to ask, see what he thinks, if they have any better ideas. We don't have to worry about protecting them unless they come," the last as an olive branch to Dykshoorn before turning to Swan, "but I want Mahafny here as soon as she can come, thought you said she'd be here tonight. I want to know if she's any farther along at discovering a way to unmask Resonants."

And didn't *she* want Mahafny here as well? Not for her healing gifts or for her answers, but for the sweet comfort of kinship. She quashed Kyril's anger and her own with the sweet voice of reason. "Kyril, she's due shortly, just a little late. Can't make her give anything a rest, so she's always behind schedule. Ever know a eumedico who wasn't?" Doyce snickered. "We'll see if she's uncovered anything that might help." The slightest wintery smile frosted her face. "Of course, how you plan to test *every* Canderisian citizen, I'd love to know, Kyril. Oh, yes, I can just see them lined up across the country, no shirkers, no slackers, everyone waiting patiently to prove they're garden-variety Normal, not a thought in their heads but what should be there, or hidden Resonants."

"I'll be first in line, Monitor," Doyce added. "I'd love to know myself."

Khar crouched beside the statue of Matthias Vandersma and Kharm in the plaza, the wind chilling her ears, wafting the heat from her body. Brr! Cold paving stones on fanny and feet, and tail-wrapping did just so much good. Nicer inside, but the tensions wouldn't be any less. Doyce's meeting was important, but this was more important still. Besides, Koom would report anything of significance to her—she'd exacted his promise—not stand on his status, invoke his relationship with the Seeker General. Too nice a sense of propriety about Koom sometimes, but she supposed it went with his position, especially his lack of true-Bonding. He'd never betray Swan's best interests, or the best interests of all Seekers, so *his* best interests—his need for sharing—weren't often served. Rarely had the brick-red ghatt faltered or failed, revealed what he shouldn't, even when his burdens were pressing. It just wasn't someone else's business to hear.

She'd debated as well whether to invite the other ghatti tonight when she described to the Elders how Doyce's life seemed to be merging with Matthias Vandersma's at times. How a simple tale-telling, a revelation of their shared past, ghatti and human, had transmuted into something vastly different and disconcerting. Overlapping now, beyond the merely informational, a commingling of experiences. And Doyce'd absorbed the last one strictly on her own, hadn't required the old diary or Khar's delicate insinuation to key herself into the past. So far no harm had befallen her, but Khar wanted to know how and why it occurred. Most of all, whether it should be allowed to continue like that?

Did she wish the other ghatti absent because she cringed at revealing her shame that things had gone awry? Oh, a hint of that, why deny it? Khar'pern the Clever, Clever Khar had thought it so simple, such a brilliant idea to share their past, find solutions for the future facing them. True, the Elders were ever indirect, elusive to understand, but the burden of failure was hers alone. No, a ghatti burden, but she'd urged them to shoulder it, beseeched the Elders for it. She'd have to be the one to see it through.

Could she attain the Fifth Spiral alone? Had she rightfully gained it, or had it been loaned her through Terl's intercession? Well, one way to find out—try. So why were her ears

flattened with dread? Because most of all, she mustn't harm
the ghatten she herself carried or Doyce's ghatten, although
Doyce didn't yet realize she bore twins. She wiped a paw
across her face, erased a self-satisfied smile. Twins for them
both. Would all these surges of story, nourishing them in the
womb, alter them? Make them the wisest of the wise, she
hoped. Nothing wrong with ghatti pride when it rang true.

Amber eyes fixed on the constellations, picking the patterns to guide her, the circling within circles, she commenced the mental climb. Oof! Heavier than she'd realized,
although she didn't show much yet, Doyce unsuspecting of
the parallel pregnancy. Not that she physically climbed, but
the weight, the knowledge of what her body protected restrained her, yet she forged ahead. Hmph? Extra stability
from the weight?

She purred as she progressed, elated by her new steadi-
ness of mindpurpose, recognizing her goal, spanning the distance. Wisdom appeared different at each level she attained;
she'd never noticed that before. Higher didn't make for
smaller, but sometimes small things grew more visible, more
sparkling clear, while larger worries shrank proportionately.
Was that the wisdom of the Fifth Spiral? Surging around that
final bend, she waited to be cast back, discover she *did* need
Terl's assistance to scale that final curve. But no, she arched
around it, tail floating behind, lofted on starlight, whiskers
pollened with stardust.

The voices tickled and swarmed before she was ready.
**"Well, well, Khar'pern, glowing like a comet in the night,
eh?"** **"Night ... night ... night,"** other voices scintillated
around her. **"Star Khar, stardust bright!"** Embarrassing to
be caught preening like that.

"My apologies, oh Elder Ones." Her eyes squinting in
humility, she wished she could roll over, expose her belly to
indicate submission. **"Sometimes I grow a bit fanciful."**

"Oh ... roll ... roll over!" **"Show us ... show us ...
show us...."** **"Your white belly, let the starlight caress
... car ... ress ... sss ... sss the ghatten inside."**

Possible to do mentally? Never had she heard a command
like that before. She attempted it—aware in a small compartment of her mind that she remained physically seated on
the ground by the statue—flashing her white belly to the
heavens, laving it in the starlight, the moonlight. **"Car ...
ress ... sss ... sss ... bless ... sss ... sss...."**

Pierced by starshine, she rolled back reluctantly, awed by the sensation. A boon, but not why she'd attempted the Spirals. **"An honor beyond deserving, beyond my imagining,"** and she bowed low in homage. **"But my honor will wither to ashes from disgrace if I cannot accomplish what I promised to do—help Doyce discover the meaning of our past."** She groped, unsure how to explain, if it would make sense to them, if they'd care that the memories, the past inextricably merged with Doyce. She'd wanted Doyce to *know,* but she hadn't wanted Doyce to *become* the past, and she dared not try again until she comprehended what was happening, was going to happen.

"She's journeyed ahead of me, ahead of us. She doesn't understand, but she's gathering it to her without our intervention. Unless," and the thought struck hard as a blow, **"unless you've been encouraging it on your own?"** Accuse the Elders of meddling? So unapproachable, so difficult to reach, to extract an answer from—or at least a usable answer?

"Ah, Khar'pern, so much like me ... but much more white trim, very handsome. You've carried our stripes through the generations, you know." Sentences, complete, logical sentences! But the voice, though she'd never heard it before, left no doubt as to who spoke, and she shrank in obeisance, eyes shut, ears tacked back, timorous, waiting for the voice to do with her as it would. Anything, anything the voice commanded must be implicitly obeyed for the good of all ghatti—for the voice was of the Foremother of them all, Kharm! The voice supporting all Elder Voices, the Voice heard by so few in their lifetimes, but ever informing the ways of the ghatti! Her offspring blessed by the Mother of them all!

"And blessed be your Bondmate's offspring as well. Twinkling twins you shall both have." A faint chuckle, an encouraging purr. **"And so boldy striped—"** Khar stiffened in shock, claws spreading. **"Yours, that is, not hers, don't worry."**

Dare she push? Did anyone dare push the Mother of them all? **"But Doyce? I think, I think that Matty,"** how dare she utter such a familiarity? She gulped, made her heart subside back down her throat. **"That Matthias Vandersma, Blessed Bondmate, has intertwined his life with Doyce's.**

I fear she'll be lost between worlds, unable to distinguish which is which."

"You mean that in the middle of one of his adventures, Matty'll be highly surprised when labor starts?" Aghast, Khar's hackles rose at the impropriety of the comment. "Oh, peace, Khar'pern, peace," the voice continued, chucking Khar under the chin. "But it *is* time to teach her to tap into the past on her own. She possesses the power, power for that and more if she's ever able to unleash it. You must teach her which is which, to come and go between past and present unimpeded until she learns what she must learn. And she's always been a good pupil, hasn't she?"

Khar managed a nod. "Help her ... ? Teach her ... ?" she quavered, couldn't think how she could possibly teach this.

"Yes," the Great Kharm continued. "Don't you think she should go away? Abandon her fears and distractions, return to her roots? She's needed here, but she needs to learn more. A country excursion, perhaps, away from this new world a-borning. You can do it. Koom and Swan will help, if you like."

"So very ... generous," the best she could manage. Was she being dismissed? A tentative backward slide down the Spiral.

"Ah ... eager, are we? Even if we aren't completely sure we know where we're going, what we're doing? Commendable."

"Com ... mend ... able." "Oh, so ... so very...." "Commendable ... very ... very...." The voices splintered and prickled, mocking, friendly, unhelpful, or incomprehensible, she was never sure which, or if they encompassed everything. Never had she slid down the Spirals so rapidly in her life, with no desire to linger, savor what she'd accomplished by gaining each turn. Out, out, back to where she belonged, and she'd decipher it later. She must! She landed with a thump inside herself, kicked experimentally behind an ear, hind claws digging into the soft fur. It felt good, felt real.

"But oh, Mother Kharm, if you cherished us true, surely you'd reveal...." No point in finishing. She *had* been shown, now she merely had to determine *what* to do.

She dug harder in frustration. Not just what, but how as well.

✦

"How convenient you arrived just after Kyril and Dykshoorn left." Swan waved away the glass of water that Davvy coaxed her to drink and glared at her cousin.

"Yes, isn't it?" Mahafny agreed blandly, looping her navy cloak over a chair and stalking to her cousin's side, hand almost steady as she traced the curve between Swan's neck and shoulder, the most she could muster in an outward show of affection. "I'm not an oracle, after all, and that's what van Beieven wants." She hadn't known a meeting'd been planned, suspected Swan purposely hadn't mentioned it when she'd told her she was coming to Gaernett. Well, once they'd arrived, late as always, Saam hadn't exactly eavesdropped on the activity inside the Seeker General's suite. No, not at all, but she'd grown adept at using him as barometer, his oblique actions and reactions like isobars connecting equal pressures. She'd gladly agreed that they should check the kitchens for a snack. Now she knew why. Of course, Doyce's presence caused unseasonable highs and lows as well.

Without Khar to chide her, Doyce bared her teeth in an almost smile, nearly scaring Davvy witless as he gathered drink glasses, tidied up. Contrite, she lumbered over to help, affording Swan and Mahafny a small measure of privacy for their reunion.

"Best clear out now," Davvy whispered. "I have to help Mahafny examine Swan." The officious little dragon was dead serious. "I can tell her the bits Swan can't or won't say, things she doesn't always know. I sense what her body's feeling inside."

The glass clunked against the black lacquer tray harder than she'd intended, outwardly revealing her shock. "Mahafny agrees with your . . ." she forced herself to say, "diagnoses?"

"Sometimes. Sometimes she's righter 'cause she understands what it means when I see hidden things." He folded his arms across his chest. "Don't understand, do you? Thought you might, though. Sort of like Hide the Thimble,

Nana Cookie used to play it with me when I was small. For me the 'thimble' shouts its presence loud and clear."

"What's the thimble?" Assuming it had ever existed, was this the long-gone trance skill eumedicos pretended to employ, the ability to "see" internally?

"Hurt places, festering places, spots where germs," he pronounced it "grr'ms," and she corrected him. "And them, too," he countered, "but Nana Cookie calls 'em grr'ms." He'd tilted his chin chestward so his bangs shielded his eyes. "Can even see what's going on inside you."

"Funny," Mahafny kept the flow of conversation low, lulling, despite the change of topic, "I guess he'd be about the same age as her daughter, if she'd lived. Mayhap a tad younger."

Swan's fingers flashed the eight-point star. "Pray to the Lady nothing like that happens again."

"She should deliver fine, she's disgustingly healthy."

"It's the afterward that concerns me. Briony's death wasn't from natural causes, as well you know. Let's pray no other unnatural causes stalk this topsy-turvy world."

"Nothing's certain. The only certainty is uncertainty." Chiding herself, Mahafny wondered when she'd become so pessimistic. "At any rate, I'm here to see you. How're you feeling?"

Swan stared at the wall so long she seemed to stare through it, and Mahafny found herself speculating on what Swan envisioned. A world at peace, a world without pain for everyone? Did she allow herself a place in such a world? "I'd feel a lot better if I were six feet under."

Mahafny leaped as if scalded. "You don't even know what it means, that term's so archaic!" If only scoffing would make it so.

Steepling her fingers to hide a weary smile, Swan recited, "A foot: a unit of measurement, three of them comprising a yard, a yard being slightly less than a meter. Translation: to be buried a shy two meters deep. Unless you'd literally interpret it as resting under six feet—specifically your two plus Saam's four, dancing on my grave."

"Don't even joke about that in passing!"

Saam pushed between them on the bed. **"Would you prefer a ghatti gavotte or a falanese fandango? Or something more stately? Should I start practicing now?"**

Mahafny began to laugh despite herself, but the tears she

surreptitiously wiped away weren't from laughter. "Oh, Saam," Swan choked, "laughter is better medicine than anything Mahafny can offer. And the end is coming whether she'll admit it or not."

But Koom had interrupted, 'speaking her privately, excluding the others. Whatever his message, Mahafny watched her cousin steel herself, as if for some ordeal ahead. "Well, we've still business to attend to, even if you thought you'd escaped the brunt of it." Voice raised, she called, "Davvy, clear out and go to bed—now! I promise Mahafny won't examine me until tomorrow when you're here to help. Indeed, she swears she can't do it without your assistance."

Hip prodded by a hand under the covers, Mahafny nodded. "With the training you absorbed at the Hospice, you're already halfway to being a eumedico." Looking somewhat mollified at his dismissal, Davvy rushed to kiss Swan good night, held Mahafny's hand in both his own, concentrating, then met the eumedico's eyes.

Unconsciously flexing and straightening her freed hand, Mahafny watched him out the door, lips pursed in thought. Did she want to know what Davvy could tell her about her hands?

"Doyce." Her attention commanded, Doyce swung round as the Seeker General fumbled behind her pillow. "A letter regarding you came today. Your sister wrote, begs me to excuse you to return home." Doyce's mouth opened in protest. "No, sit. Your mother's had a slight stroke. Not serious, but a warning to slow down, a reminder that things from the past remain unfinished, deserve an airing, perhaps an ending. Your sister wrote me directly in hopes I'd intercede. It seems you ignored her last letter."

The paper crackled and trembled in her fingers as she took Francie's letter, scanned it. "She's not as ill as . . ." and bit her tongue to stop herself.

"You're not being a traitor by admitting the truth." Koom held his ground, forced her to find hers. **"Just admit all of the truth, don't use one part to shoulder aside the other."**

Khar traced Koom's habitual route up through the thick ivy coating the building's east side, judging from the scratches, the scents that she was right. Oh, other ghatti scents come-hithered as well, for Koom wasn't alone in using this handy entrance or exit when ghatti patience ran thin with humans too busy to open doors. The branching of his scent reassured her that she headed for the right window, feeling pitiful and careworn after her encounter with the Elders. Doyce still remained in Swan's room, thus Khar yearned to be there, beside her Bond.

She scratched at the window, essayed a brief "Merow?" The effort of mindspeech was more than she could bear, made her want to regress to ghattenhood, be cuddled and cossetted, fussed over—if Doyce weren't too preoccupied. And Swan usually had various tidbits of food around, leftovers that her less-than-enthusiastic appetite hadn't been able to stomach. Koom, she hoped, wouldn't mind sharing. It penetrated her senses at last that Saam and Mahafny were also present, unsure if that boded well for her cause, though she was always relieved to see the steel-gray ghatt.

Again she scratched, harder this time, satisfied at the earsplitting "skreek" of claws on the windowpane. There, that should make them notice! Huddled in the sharp, clear night air—colder than the heights she'd so recently spiraled—she waited, saw their shadowy outlines through the window and its curtains, arguing, intent, Koom transfixed by the interplay. At length he shook his head as Saam 'spoke him, glanced toward the window and the dark outside, face comical with surprise as he realized who peered in at him. A bound, a rapid crossing of the floor, and he alighted on the windowsill's narrow edge, ghosted behind the curtains. His body heat radiated through the pane at her.

"Why didn't you say something?"

"I did," and leaned her head against the pane where his breath fogged it.

"You didn't mindspeak. There's so much going on in there that it's a wonder Saam heard you."

"A visit with the Elders sometimes takes its toll," she allowed with a certain unwillingness.

He stretched against the window, checked its fittings, nosed around. "I know," a certain admiration and awe echoed in his tone, but he became immediately pragmatic. "Too tightly latched for me. Should be refitted for ghatti paws. Have to ask Doyce for help."

How much did he know? Could he have learned already?

A puzzlement. Miserable, she waited, contradictorily content to wait, yet yearning to be inside. 'Speaking Doyce, uneasy at what she must tell her Bond, sooner or later, was something she didn't relish. Still, it was her task. Hadn't the Great Mother of them all told her so? Of course the Great Mother didn't have to worry about Doyce boxing *her* ears—or worse!

Curtain rings jangled along the rod, almost making her start with fright as Doyce appeared at the window, put palms on the sash, and heaved upward. Khar struggled through the gap before it widened enough to be comfortable, wanting to be inside more than anything else in the world, rash though she might be. She pressed her cold nose against Doyce's cheek.

"Welcome, glad you could drop by, even if a bit late." Khar's skin twitched at the heavy sarcasm. Definitely *not* a good evening to convince Doyce to drop her Seeker research and quit Gaernett for her childhood home. Would the promise of learning more about the Seekers' very beginnings be incentive enough? A paltry lure if ever there was one.

"Oh, it's not as bad as all that." Koom licked her face, and she tilted her head, let herself be cleansed. **"I've had my marching orders and informed Swan of hers."** Her earhoop in his teeth, he gave a little tug to make her concentrate. **"Actually, the timing's not that bad. I think Swan's relieved by the idea."**

"Mahafny agrees, if that puts your mind at rest," Saam winked.

"You mean ... ?" Unbelievable! The Elder Mother of them all *had* 'spoken Koom, had left nothing to chance. Perhaps, perhaps it might work after all. She allowed herself a shred of hope, heeded an enticing bit of cheese Swan waved in her direction, nicely warm and aged, just the way she liked it.

"I hope you mean the cheese, and not my Swan," Koom teased, **"though she's nicely warm and aged as well. Shall I tell her that?"**

Amber eyes comically wide in appeal, Khar trotted after the cheese, determined to devour it before Koom followed through with his threat. Yes, good. She sniffed but caught no scent of nutter-butter, vague disappointment welling within her. Saam licked his chops, **"Sorry. Wasn't any. I checked."**

"Well, what brings you to join us?" Foot tapping, Doyce waited while Khar tried to work the cheese from her teeth. Not that a full mouth would hinder mindspeech. *"I wanted you here this evening for support, but no, you found something better to do, didn't you?"*

Unfair! Totally unjust! If Doyce only knew what she'd attempted tonight, she'd have been petted and praised as the "most prescient, clever ghatta in the world."

"They don't know about the Elders, and that's the way of it. Nor do we want them to know," Koom reminded her, **"so stop feeling sorry for yourself."**

"I'm sorry, beloved," she ringed Doyce's legs, willing her to sit. **"There were things tonight that needed doing. I had no choice."** Relenting, Doyce sat, and Khar ingratiated herself onto the little of Doyce's lap that remained, shoving under her arm, peeping out in appeal.

"Ghatta, my dear, you're radiating guilt about something." Her grudging laugh loosened after a moment. "You haven't acted this way since ghattenhood. You dove off the wardrobe and went skidding across the table—knocked off my good mug, broke it into a million smithereens. I hope whatever you've done this time mends better than that."

"Leave the poor thing be, Doyce. Swan and I haven't finished arguing with you yet. One thing at a time and don't take out your aggravation on Khar." Bless Mahafny for interrupting, but what had they been arguing about? No help from Koom or Saam. "In fact, let's ask Khar, an impartial bystander uninvolved in our dispute until now."

"Khar, you be the judge," Swan appealed, and Khar shifted beneath Doyce's arm to read Koom's face, chart which way the winds blew. His muzzle and mouth flexed, tightened to make the corners up-curving, reminiscent of a human smile. Doing it on purpose, was he? **"Stormy."**

"Khar, wouldn't it do Doyce good to get away from the capital, leave Gaernett for a time? Things are entirely too tense here lately, whether she acknowledges it or not." Swan shifted, coughed, sought a comfortable place against the pillows. So easy, too easy to forget the evidence before one's eyes that Swan was a very sick woman, her voice, her manner always so commonsensical, unconcerned. "And I should note that firefighting this far along into one's pregnancy is probably not a wise thing to do. Brave but not very wise."

Oh, carefully, carefully, she counseled herself. How to

straddle both sides of the line? Yes, the Elder Mother *had* 'spoken Koom, and Koom had clearly primed Swan for this attack, preliminary feints begun long before her arrival. Any ambushes? How much to prevaricate, cloud the issue, make it appear it wasn't her idea? How could she lie, speak un- truth? **"Leave Gaernett?"** Surprise—never a bad opening gambit. **"What about Doyce's research? How can she fin- ish her history if she leaves?"** An approving stroke from Doyce. **"Where would she go, where would we go?"**

"Oh, anywhere you choose," the Seeker General waved an airy hand, as if the whole world eagerly awaited them. "As you can see, I'm answering your questions back to front, Khar." Khar's admiration grew at the artful conversation. "And I don't see why she can't bring her research materials along, write wherever she is. Parse can continue his research here, send along updates. Even visit to deliver new material. About time we got him on horseback."

"Depending on the state of his sensitive posterior," Koom chimed in. Parse's condition was something of a gen- tle joke amongst the ghatti, although any teasing raised Per'- la's dander to dangerous levels, inflamed Parse's allergies.

"But I'm a Seeker, this is my home. I'm needed here." Not defiance but grim resolution, and the unspoken "aren't I?" rang all too clearly, a sharp chime of desperation. Doyce sounded as if she suspected she was being slowly outmaneu- vered, pressing for reassurance.

"Always," Swan agreed. "But you know where you should go, who needs you more right now."

Mystified yet greatly daring, Khar suggested, **"What about visiting your mother and sister?"** That explained the tight knot clenched deep inside Doyce, closed from her sharing.

And almost got dumped from Doyce's lap for her pains. "She's not that sick, she can't be, not as sick as . . ." and stopped, face flushing, pinned again by the treacherous ac- knowledgment, hemmed in by Swan's and Mahafny's non- committal expressions. "That . . . I couldn't . . . they don't . . . need me." "Want me," she'd almost said. Khar touched the old guilt from years ago, the guilt she'd never quite grappled with, when at sixteen Doyce had abandoned her mother and sister, gone off to train with the eumedicos. Doyce had believed they'd needed her then, unable to exist at more than subsistence levels without her there to partner in the weaving, her sister too crippled to be of much use. It hadn't been true, but the old guilt was still useful for self-flagellation, and now a new guilt burned as well, raw with denial.

"They need you, now most of all. And they've always wanted you," Mahafny pressed home her point. "You don't have to persist in suffering over an argument that faded too long ago to matter."

But Doyce had risen, tilting her hips forward, letting her figure speak in mute appeal. "Is it wise for me to travel this far into my pregnancy?" Surely this served as a valid petition, an excuse from her duties?

"Don't play it for more than it's worth, Doyce," Mahafny warned. "You're healthy, and I'll check you over thoroughly before you go. Coventry isn't that far from here, although I want you to take it in easy stages, that much I'll grant. There are eumedicos there as well, and I'm sure you'll be back long before your due date. Another octant, isn't it? After all," and she tossed the phrase back with casual precision and more than fair mimicry, "pregnancy isn't an illness, simply a natural occurrence."

Strange to admit, but she *did* want to go home, be part of a family again, renew her links with the past, her heritage, her future child's grandmother. There might not be another chance, and the thought chilled her heart. Few active-duty Seekers had children; there were fewer women outside the Seekers she could comfortably talk with about pregnancy, childbearing. Claire had been one, but she'd missed the chance to ask so many questions, her mind still mired in the aftermath of the fire, including Maize's near-escape that night.

"Maybe ... it wouldn't be ... so bad." She tasted at acceptance, half-convincing herself. "But I can't leave everyone here, leave the Seekers like this! How will Jenret know where to find me?"

"I think that can be arranged," offered Khar soothingly.

"I want you to go as a favor to me, Doyce. Not just because I'd rather you were clear of Gaernett and its strife, but because I need your help. Please, take Davvy with you! He's still too young, too much a Hospice-trained Resonant to realize the need for concealing his skills as well as he should. I could send him back with Mahafny, but I'd rather totally remove him, seclude him in the country. Would you,

, except in a dis-
ent as a forester, a
n revitalizing
rees with ironlike
hmont's northern

k his trees as se-
inded himself of
t discovering he
n, the late Queen
d solely because
Eadwin's mother.
late Lord of the
on claiming the
nant powers. Ar-
t Hru'rul batted
With his broad
ul was truly th

ved with pain and
him. I don't need

and Mahafny was
he bed, turning her
lung.

the Elder Mother
ng a little haliday,
except for his mel-
his beloved second
a."

countered, a deep
he first part of her
ion. But what to do
now.

an elbow on the table,
board. "Checkmate!" A
ck suppl   ing chess with Arras
ed the   If he'd ambitions to win.
off   Arras lofted his king across
              the   d from under the table.
              chmont's newest king, "Hardly
              on." A lanky black dog with ex-
scrambl   ears, and   long, slim muzzle
eyes. He   ss and   ach flooding his brown
Bondmate   o   what Hru'rul, the king's
til it skitte   ing the discarded king piece un-
What d   drunkenly across the floor.
deine   an 'poor Felix'? What about 'poor
              ou choose me as your Defense Lord and
              advice? And make me sacrifice my king,
there was one." He shoved hands through
hed at his extravagant mustache, shaking
as he studied his ruler.
outh, but a man of near thirty with clear
y grin, his brown hair and short beard
hite streak, the outward scar of his
the arborfer observatory, forsaken by
spicuously lacking the easy grace of
royalty and command, Eadwin'd

had no hint he stood to inherit the throne
tantly related way. He'd been deeply conte
graduate of the agricultural college, bent
dying arborfer, those strange coniferous t
properties that were indigenous to Marc
reaches.

It took getting used to—a king who too
riously as he did his subjects. Arras rem
that and more: Eadwin's consternation a
was the bastard offspring of Prince Maarte
Wilhelmina's younger brother, and bastar
Maarten had died before he could wed
Fabienne, desperate, had married Maurice.
Nord and Defense Lord, a man intent
throne as his own with his perverted Reso
ras walked slowly to where the giant gha
the king piece, daring Felix to snatch it.
feet, luxuriant ruff, and tufted ears, Hru'n
epitome of the fabled larchcat of yore, a w
Hands on hips, Arras bent one knee in mo
finally meek, "Yield me my king?" he ask
Hru'rul lazily swiped at it, bouncing it
leather boot.

"I yield to my king," he bowed in Eadwin
your decision, your right, my lord," he swali
I deny that sometimes. If you deem it wise w
as they've requested, we shall, but I'm not
idea." At ease behind the chessboard, Eadv
but frank, open as always, chessboard, Eadv
what Eadwin felt. Pray that the none read
better school his thoughts, even fro ould s
Muscadeine.

Rearranging the pieces on the board, p
complex, private pattern rather than setting
Eadwin concentrated, shifted a white piec
cocked his head to judge the effect. "You
advice, Arras." He smiled again, that o
his late father's, and Arras cursed himse
blind to the resemblance. Equally can
the world in microcosm instead of
Maarten had. "And I hope you note
most," he emphasized, "of the time

to—I'm learning as I go along, and I'm the first to admit that."

Hru'rul jumped on the board, indiscriminately knocking over pieces, flopping on his side and stretching out, sending more scattering. **"Go to Canderis? Seeing Doyce and Khar? Seeing T'ss? Play? Ignore black Rawn."** Hru'rul's pronouncements tended toward the succinct from his delayed Bonding, but Eadwin understood; Hru'rul bore little fondness for Rawn, nor Rawn for Hru'rul after the frightened ghatt had escaped over Rawn, trouncing him into the dirt. **"Learning more from Khar on Seeking?"**

A boot on the andiron, Arras stared into the fire, then turned back to his king. "You're hardly a fool, Eadwin." A smile of relief at the use of the king's given name, the habit of so many years. It felt more natural to them both, but Arras continually reminded himself that the relationship had changed, the balance forever altered, something he must constantly recall with every breath. And he'd been responsible for that alteration by overthrowing Maurice. "It simply is *not* politically expedient to journey to Canderis. You're still consolidating your power here, your citizens learning to trust and respect you both as man and king. I don't think there's any danger of an overthrow while you're absent, but I do think it best you consider your own first, not Canderis."

The younger man came to his side, a perfectly nice, adequate man, totally average compared to Muscadeine's physique, leadership qualities, and political acumen. "And there was no need for a Canderis, a Marchmont, until Venable Constant spirited our Resonant ancestors here for safekeeping." A hand on the older man's shoulder. "Arras, I owe Doyce and Khar, the Monitor, and all of Canderis a debt. Without them and without you, I'd never have escaped Maurice, attained the throne." He added as an afterthought, "And for that you owe me—a perfectly good agricultural degree going to waste!"

Muscadeine hadn't given up, not yet. "Reports indicate a subtle slippage of control in Canderis. I've no way to guarantee your safety, even if I'm by your side every moment of the day and night. They *don't* like us there!"

And Eadwin understood some of that baseless dislike, for both he and Arras Muscadeine were Resonants, anathema to many Caderisians. "*Some* of them don't, the rest of them don't really know us, invent the worst. That's precisely why we must go, show them that we live in agreement and accord, that we couldn't envision our world without Resonants, or if we could, it wouldn't be the richly varied world we have."

"And you think they *want* our world?" Bitterness tinged Arras's voice. Without volition, Doyce Marbon's face swam into Eadwin's mind, the revulsion on her face when she'd discovered he was a Resonant, though one with blocked abilities, another of Maurice's little jests at his expense. But she *had* overcome it. And Arras, he suspected, remembered Doyce as well, had been more than smitten by her, but was too honorable to come between her and Jenret Wycherley, despite the opportunities presented.

"I doubt they'll willingly embrace our world unless we can convince them it's viable, that we enhance each other, Normal and Resonant alike, that we take no liberties with such special gifts. Our healing skills alone should make them welcome us."

"Think that last statement through, Eadwin," Arras warned, just as he had so many times before, striving to make the younger man broaden his thinking, weigh the positive and negative, and never, ever assume.

"Healing gifts, healing gifts . . . ?" the king rubbed a thumbnail over his lower lip, deep in thought. "That they don't . . . ? That we . . . ?"

"The position papers the Bannerjee twins prepared for you?" he prompted. Reinstated as Public Weal Lords, the Bannerjee twins, Dwyna and Wyn, had provided copious details on Marchmont eumedico training and abilities and their differences and similarities with Canderisian knowledge. A very large report.

Eadwin groaned, eyes shut in concentration as if rereading each page in his mind. "Hru'rul?" Since all ghatti could seek out the truth in a human's mind, Hru'rul had proved an unexpected bonus for Eadwin, able to winkle the forgotten answer to the surface of his brain. "Differences between Canderisian and Marchmontian eumedicos, please?"

"Pretend. Good eumedicos, but can't see inside. Ours can."

He assimilated the prompt, remolded it to match Muscadeine's question. "Then we would . . . expose them, reveal their lies to the populace?" Arras's nod showed him he was right, but he'd already bounded one step ahead, "But it's something they could have if they allowed their Resonants to train as eumedicos! That's a benefit!" He slowed, considering, "But anyone entrenched in the old ways may not always welcome new ones.

"Merciful havens, Arras! How could I have forgotten? It's Corneil Dalcroze and the Cinquantes all over again! Isn't it an anniversary of sorts—fifty years ago? But this could be different: Corneil's actions were totally unsanctioned, he was guilt-driven about our history, was right that the wild Resonant abilities had flowered and flourished in ways we didn't know. But he tried to right wrongs by himself, atone for the past. What we have to do is win some of the eumedicos to our side! Mahafny Annendahl and some of the others, have them acknowledge not that their eumedico skills are based on years of lies, but to bruit it about that their mindtrance skills are fading, that they've requested our aid in regaining them! Makes our visit even more reasonable, don't you think?"

Yes, he was learning fast, discovering logical sequences, creating a plausible scenario, an outward justification to placate nervous Canderisians. Damn him for remembering Corneil to bolster his argument when that debacle should have pointed out the error of his plans. Well, one final piece to play, and he played it, prayed he hadn't taught Eadwin too well, could still outflank him, his knight to Eadwin's king this time. Let him counter this move if he were so skilled! "There's one other thing, sire," and hoped his mustache camouflaged the fleeting, gloating smile he couldn't conquer. "You've no heir, sire. You haven't yet married and fathered an heir, or fathered one without benefit of marriage, to my knowledge." Eadwin's ears crimsoned. "And you've named no interim heir. Something we must seriously consider, weigh potential candidates."

Eadwin's face twitched, he began to laugh, harder and harder as if he couldn't control it, didn't want to control it. "Naming an heir is easier than you think. In fact, technically I don't have to—there already is one." He felt rich enjoyment at Muscadeine's discomfiture and confusion, his brain scrabbling to decipher Eadwin's meaning. He'd stumped him, he couldn't believe it!

"What! Who?" The man was sputtering, almost livid, baffled.

"Arras, dear fellow, loyal adviser, think!" Fun to needle back, almost irresistible, though he lacked vindictiveness. Hardly a failing when he thought of his stepfather, Maurice.

Took pity at last. "My dear cousin Nakum, up north with Callis monitoring the arborfer. Yes, he *is* Erakwan, but he's also the grandson of my father's younger brother, Ludo. My cousin, illegitimate as well, but definitely of the blood royale, no two ways around it!"

Serious now, before Arras could catch his breath. "We *are* going, Arras. That is my decision. I'm going to repay my debt in full, make up for Corneil's misguided, disastrous efforts as well. Besides, I'm sure Ignacio and Ezequiel will be thrilled at the idea of arranging a royal progress through Canderis. Should keep them on their toes, stretch their ceremonial skills to the limit, because I plan to shine, Arras, *shine!* Glorious as the sun!" His sober modesty and good humor broke through. "Oh, not me personally, but what I represent as a Resonant. That, above all, must shine in all its glory."

Arras Muscadeine knew he'd been beaten. A relief to discover the king had uncharted depths, but he still wasn't pleased.

Lindy wrapped both arms around Bard, jammed her chin into his spine as she surveyed the sky. She wished she could ride in front, but M'wa's platform was bracketed there, and she judged he had the right of it, just as her older brothers and sisters took precedence over her. The sky was *so* blue, and she sighed with pleasure, welling excitment at riding with Bard, riding to new places, new things to see and do. Away, away from the bad dreams plaguing her since Byrta's accident and death. They wouldn't know how to follow her, would they? She compressed her lips, refused to cry over Byrta again, not betray her hurt, because he hurt even worse.

She shook her head cautiously, chin rubbing Bard's back through his jacket, her new earrings swaying and swinging. Her mother had pierced her ears the night before they'd left, sending Jo into town for a precious shard of ice wrapped in sacking and sunk into a bucket of sawdust to keep it from melting on the way. A delicious shiver trembled down her spine as she relived the icy numbness against her ear, the pressure, and then the pink of sharp pain through the numbness as her mother jabbed the heated needle through her earlobe. Once in the middle of each lobe, and once again higher up. Four earrings, two balls and two hoops, and she had sat steady and still four times, gripping her father's and Bard's hands. Not a flinch or moan, although the tears had seeped from under her lids whether she willed it or not.

The earrings had been slipped in, and she'd rushed to the mirror, longing to see what they looked like, what she looked like, so mature now, so elegant with real, true jewelry of her own. And she had looked and looked, head tilting from side to side, then held steady while she stared in absolute amazement and shock, mouth falling open in dismay as she wailed, "They're *not* even, my ears aren't even!" How could she never have noticed that her ears weren't level? And now, and now, everyone would see, would notice—if they hadn't before but been too polite to say—that her ears didn't match, she was unbalanced! All because she'd been vain!

But Bard had slipped up behind her as she stared horrified into the mirror, rested his chin on top of her head so his face reflected above hers. "Nobody's features are perfectly even and regular, didn't you know that? Look!" He raised a finger to one of his eyes, then up to the eyebrow. Right? Left? Looking into the mirror mixed her up. She stared hard, obedient, concentrating on spotting a difference. Impossible with those wondrous tawny gold eyes with blue-hazed edges, the honey-gold skin, the tiny, tight curls of hair. She looked harder, determined.

"That one slants up more, doesn't it?" Her discovery amazed her. "It's cocked just a little higher. Not that anyone would notice!" she continued in a rush, whirling to look directly at him, to judge from this perspective. Breathing through her mouth, she considered it further, saw a mirror image, "But Byrta's slanted on the other side, didn't it?"

His hands tightened on her shoulders before he mastered his emotions. "Yes, hers did. So don't be worried that your earrings aren't even . . . or your ears."

She wasn't worried now, just awed by the honor of having them. She wasn't sure where they were going, when they would get there, but she didn't care. They might travel the long way back to Gaernett and the woman she was to meet, help tend her baby once it was born. Her satchel bulged with carefully folded infant wear, faded and soft from much washing and wearing. Hadn't Mam said, "Take it, Lindy. Its absence will remind me not to have more!"

But the trip in-between was meant for fun, he'd promised, to explore the country, savor new sights, do new things. And since she'd never been farther from home than the adjacent town, she ached with expectation, anticipating things she couldn't even begin to imagine. An adventure, what an adventure! Everything brand new and peculiar ... and probably not level! She giggled, then mashed the tip of her braid in her mouth so Bard wouldn't hear.

Right now she didn't mind leaving home, leaving Mam and Da and all her brothers and sisters, but she'd miss them soon enough. Stood to reason if Bard missed Byrta, but this couldn't be that bad. How much it would hurt, she wasn't sure. As if at a signal the longing tendriled, but she fiercely ordered it to shrink back, not spoil things yet, not so soon, so early. That was what being grown-up meant. Conquering hurts and going on, just as Bard did with the hurt rubbing him. Had thought beyond himself to her and what she'd like. Now she'd do the same for him, help him stop grieving over Byrta, and she had the whole journey for that.

Cheek nestled against Bard's back, wishing he still wore the soft sheepskin tabard, she fell asleep, pillowed against him, legs bouncing bonelessly against his.

"Tuckered out. Too much excitement." M'wa sniffed at the hand anchored in Bard's belt. Bard reached to retrieve the dangling arm, wrapped it around his waist, and she clutched his jacket without realizing, knuckles poking warm against his ribs.

"Yes. Amazing how easily children fall asleep, despite the distractions around them. When they're ready, they're ready." He waited, hoping the ghatt might say more. When he didn't, he continued, *"M'wa, am I doing the right thing? It seemed right at the time."*

"Oh, very likely, very likely," the ghatt reassured. **"But I confess I never thought I'd travel in the company of children, although she acts the proper little old lady, overresponsible."**

"You could mend that flaw, give her back a little childhood."

"I'm too old to chase a string, bat a ball around." M'wa sounded distinctly huffy.

"Proper little old gentleman ghatt, are we?"

"No ghatt or ghatta does beyond ghattenhood."

"They do for someone they love. You've played, acted silly

for me when I've needed cheering up. Mayhap you'll love her, too, a little. She needs more than I can give."

❖

A growl rumbled low in Rawn's chest, growing in intensity as Jenret's captors moved closer. **"Kill them! I will kill them! Not rescue but a ruse!"**

Jenret's very soul froze at the ghatt's despairing anger, the rage to fight against all odds. How to make the ghatt see reason before he threw his life away, got them both killed? *"Rawn, easy! Hush!"* he commanded urgently. Make him think, reckon the odds. *"You're brave—not foolhardy. Do you have a death wish? You can't tackle—how many?"* Desperate, he remained submissive, flat on the ground, counting feet without raising his head. *"If you attack, I'm helpless, pinned by the first sword thrust."*

The ghatt continued rumbling, his tail whip-lashing Jenret's thighs. Not unlike being flogged, though rather softer. **"Eight. I could make Garvey pay dearly."** Rawn strove for control, tail slowing. **"If not fight, then what?"** A snarl and hiss as a boot connected with flesh, Rawn kicked clear of his back. Breathless, Jenret anticipated an explosion, minimally relaxed when Rawn maintained his self-control. Almost exploded himself when heavy rope, the rope he'd trusted in scant moments ago to lift him to safety, roughly trussed his hands behind him. Self-control, dammit, don't let Rawn down!

"Play for time, Rawn. Our only choice until the others come." They'd come, they had to. Faertom and Towbin, Sarrett and Yulyn and Addawanna would rescue them. If his earlier mindshouts of terror had been too scattered to penetrate, he could contact them now, warn of the danger. Bound hands were no obstacle to that. Scant comfort, but some.

"Won't work, you know," Garvey's voice insinuated itself inside his brain.

"Oh, really? Why not?" Of course it would work; the camp wasn't that far away, child's play to reach Yulyn or Faertom.

Rough hands rolled him over, bent him into a sitting position as easily as if they modeled clay. Folded him at the waist, head pushed low toward his splayed legs so he stared downward again. *"Because we can . . ."* the man methodically hunted down a descriptive word, " 'crash' mindvoices. A necessary skill. Discovered how to send out a stronger mindvoice to crash or deflect a weaker one."

"The way a hawk strikes its prey?"

"Exactly! Doesn't necessarily hurt, but it's needful with children still learning their abilities. Get overexcited, angry, lash out with their mindvoices to contact someone they shouldn't, some Normal. Every adult knows to be on the lookout, crash it if need be. Sort of like slapping a child's hand away from a hot stove. It hurts, but not as bad as the consequences of that unconsidered action. Go ahead, try if you'd like."

The dare resounding through him, Jenret threw restraint to the winds, concentrated all of his power on one lightning stab of mindspeech keyed to Yulyn. Sent it soaring, triumphant, until a sting tingled his mind, radiated through his entire body, vibrations turned back on him, rebounding off their sender. "Ouch!" Unable to contain his spontaneous exclamation, he used the distraction to try again. The sting tingled harder, his mind a hornet's nest of stabs and pricks, his body throbbing, the pain refusing to fade as easily this time.

"Care to try again? Slaps get harder each time." Garvey acted mildly amused. "Doubt those Marchmonters know that trick."

The comparison eluded him, then became plain as day, a terrifyingly pragmatic kind of sense in retrospect. Marchmontian Resonants had no fear of their skills, lacked reason to hide them. Oh, a child might be disciplined for an uninvited foray into a stranger's mind, but it wasn't a life-or-death matter as it would be here.

Rawn extracted the essence of Jenret's swirling thoughts and added his own interpretation. **"Most people don't like us in their minds, aren't enamored of it even when done by invitation, as part of a formal Seeking. Imagine how people would react to a Gleaner slipping into their minds, especially when they didn't know any Gleaners were around?"**

"Resonants, Rawn, Resonants," Jenret corrected automatically.

"Are you sure the same word can really describe two such different groups? I think our people have Gleaned whatever skills they have, pieced them together from left-

over knowledge, old taboos, not to mention trial and error."

Well, Rawn had a point, and Garvey's offhand demonstration had canceled that hope for rescue, unless the others had traced his earlier plea. But could they realize he now needed rescue from something infinitely more dangerous, something that threatened them as well? Could their captors monitor Rawn's mindvoice? Somehow he didn't think the "frequencies," if that was the word he wanted, the "channels" were one and the same, or at least weren't unless the ghatti chose to merge them. Parse had said that Roland d'Arnot had contacted T'ss and P'wa when they were swimming the river to enter Marchmont undetected, but that it didn't work the other way round unless the ghatti decided it would.

"*Rawn, can you contact T'ss?*" he hesitated, hoping his share of mental converse couldn't be eavesdropped on, either.

"**Have been, you fool, ever since you swan-dived over the edge.**"

"*And?*" An ominous pause after his one-word rejoinder.

"**T'ss is delighted you've provided some entertainment. However, the humans are having a little trouble finding their way in the dark—Addawanna won't let them light torches. She's told them if they trip and fall one more time she'll leave them behind.**"

The whole situation puzzled Jenret. Why simply remain here? Let him sit quietly in their midst? Not seek safer ground? And why, for that matter, had they taken him prisoner? It couldn't hurt to ask, so he did, speaking aloud, hoping their conversation might carry, give the others a better fix on his position.

"Why have you taken me prisoner? Have I wronged you in some way? Done something to make you retaliate?"

Garvey squatted at eye-level with Jenret, his rock-scarred hands dangling between his knees. "Belike 'prisoner' isn't the word, more like 'hostage,' I'd call it."

"Hostage for what!" The idea left him indignant, incredulous.

"Hostage for good behavior."

"Whose good behavior?" Nothing made sense.

Yulyn's mindvoice interrupted, calm but infinitely colder than the night air. "*You're holding one of us prisoner, why? What is the meaning of this?*" She stepped into view, hands raised to show she was weaponless. Straining beyond her shadow shape, Jenret looked for the others, couldn't spot them.

"Rawn, relay everything I'm saying to T'ss, have him tell Sarrett. Don't show yourselves. Don't reveal there're fewer of us than them, and most of all, don't reveal your positions unless it's absolutely necessary!" he lectured, aware that Sarrett and Addawanna, Towbin and Faertom exhibited sense enough for that. Faertom's earnest zealousness worried him, though.

"Figured we'd draw company soon," Garvey let his voice carry in deference to those who couldn't comprehend mindspeech. "Was just about to explain that selfsame question to him, here. Come closer if ye like, no intent to harm or hold you—yet."

Yulyn moved closer as a lantern was lighted and held to guide her, electrifying her coppery hair, copper penny eyes in a pale face. It ringed Jenret in a halo of brightness as well, brilliance that hurt his eyes, made them water. A hand brushed his hair off his forehead, slid softly down his face to tilt his chin to the light. "Are you all right? A nasty fall, it had to be." Yulyn's shiver transmitted itself to his flesh.

"Bumps and bruises," he acknowledged. "Whatever bark that stump had left on it imprinted my ribs, I think. Scaled like a reptile."

The others in Garvey's party ringed them, backs turned to the three, ever-vigilant, alert for any outside movement, any attempt at rescue. Garvey cleared his throat. "Could we get on with this, do you think? We've word to get out." He struck a pose, and what should have appeared silly, over-stated and self-conscious, shifted into deadly seriousness.

"We're holding you hostage. You asked why, but never heard me out, so now I'll explain, and once only. We know what you been doing in the forest, seeking us out, trying to convince us to go back. Nice gesture, considerate, maybe even noble—but wrong-headed all the same."

"Wrong-headed?" Jenret spat the words back, "Wrong-headed to want to save you from making a terrible mistake? When running is proof positive to many that Resonants are guilty of something, have something to hide?"

"And we don't need to hide, if only to protect ourselves? Think we should march back like docile little lambs when you can't control the wolves out there? Well—can you?"

Garvey laughed disgustedly, the humor forced. "We need a hostage. Convenient you dropped into our hands."

"But he's a Resonant, one of *us,*" Yulyn interjected, clearly as confused as Jenret.

"And he's a Seeker Veritas as well as the son of a respected Merchanter family that's traded across Canderis and Marchmont—he's known. You still don't see, do you?" Anxious now, Garvey pressed home his point. "He's our hostage, not for ransom, not for money, but his life stands surety for ours. His life will be forfeit if any more Resonants are hunted, hurt, killed. And any other Normals as well," he paused, emotion choking him. "Doubt you know, but four were killed tonight in the capital, Elder Hostel torched to flush out a Resonant who didn't exist. A contact ventured near enough to check, sent word."

Jenret strained at his bonds, alarms ringing in his head, the clanging discordance of bells tolling to announce danger. Fire? The jumbled words and images that had overloaded his senses, Doyce and his unborn child in danger? But why would Doyce be at an Elder Hostel? Wouldn't she avoid fire like the plague? But then, when had she ever avoided trouble? Not when she felt it her duty.

His throat grated, clogged by anticipated sorrow. "Do you know who was hurt? I think my wife," and Lady Bright, what fragile claim had he to that word

A sheathed sword sailed out of the darkness, landed hilt first. Clearly it hadn't been tossed with intent to harm. Sarrett sauntered into view as casually as if she walked Gaernett's streets, open hands at her sides. "Then it might up the ante with two hostages, say another Seeker Veritas?" She broached the encircling guards like gold overwhelming dross and sat beside Jenret.

"You fool!" he sputtered, "Never give anybody more hostages."

"Why not, if it's a good cause?" she whispered as T'ss sniffed Jenret's bonds, bumped Rawn's shoulder.

Towbin, deep and reassuring, sounded out. "Yulyn, which side you want me to choose? Not worth much for name or fame, but I'm a Normal, another pawn to hold."

She wheeled at his voice, a tiny smile breaking like an errant wave. "Of course they'd need someone very special to guard you, thwart your escape. Someone you can't work your wiles on." A glance in Garvey's direction. "Would you take me as one of your band, or grant me neutral status? Your choice—as long as Towbin stays with me."

Overrun with confusion and by unexpected, distrusted comrades-in-arms, Garvey stood openmouthed, finally drew himself up. "Didn't know we was holding a membership drive. This goes on we'll have to set up a dues-paying struc-ture of some sort there." He shifted back and forth, obviously caring if trees lashed him, stones reared up to trip him. His eyes were swollen with unshed tears, the skin across his face stretched hot and taut, as if it would split from the force inside. Banned, shunned! Cast off! Who would want him? Who would hear him out? His family had shunned him? Even his mother? That he couldn't believe, didn't want to believe. He wailed low and long like a wounded animal, the hurt resounding inside, leaking out in gasps that did nothing to relieve the pressure. Shunned! But Jenret needed him to rally help—needed him as a friend, an equal, a fellow-Resonant, not as a pet dog. Somehow that fragment of insight offered a precious shard of sanity to cling to, rebuild his dignity. Jenret and Sarrett, Yulyn and Towbin counted on him.

He slowed, staggering, leaned into a tree and hugged it to keep from falling, thinking hard. Darl! Reach Darl Allgood, that was the best hope they had. Did he dare reach out to Darl from this distance? Would Darl, for all his years of care and caution, be open to receiving mindspeech?

A hand on his shoulder nearly lofted him straight up the tree, so convinced was he of being totally alone, bereft of all human comfort and contact. "Nex' time Addawanna wan new trail blaze through woods, she hire you," the Erakwan woman scolded. "Take deer many seasons wear trail deep'n wide as whad you done."

Resting his chin on his chest, panting, he listened to the chiding, grasping the lifeline of connection it offered. "We have to return, tell everyone what's happened quick as we can," he pushed away from the tree, rubbed pitch from his cheek with sudden resolution. They needed him and he wouldn't fail!

"Yes," she agreed. "Mebbe we find Seeker on way, big khatt kin spread word. You no be doin foolishness, however you do it, shouting 'help! help!' in mind." He spun to face her, wondering how she could possibly have known, read his thoughts. "You young, ebry-ting you tink show on face. Dis best said out loud. Very loud."

Parm sat in the deepening twilight, a bit chilly but content, knowing he'd be more content with supper very shortly. The faster winter approached, the earlier supper arrived each night. He faced northwest in the direction of the Research Hospice and let his mind float, wing free to seek 'speech with Saam, as promised. As much as he cleaved to Harrap, touching another ghatti mind gave a sense of familiarity, homeyness, the comfort one absorbed from conversing with one's own.

"Hel-lo? Here we are again, nightly report." Well, almost nightly, since most nights he didn't have a jot to report. Hylan journeyed aimlessly along, dragging her goat cart, undoubtedly clear as to her destination but never bothering to enlighten Harrap or him. Luckily, Harrap waxed content with little, as did he, and the journeying wasn't unpleasant, traveling at a walking pace, scuffling with Barnaby, examining things nose-to-nose. The fuzziness of a red-and-black-banded caterpillar bespoke a hard winter. Had Saam noticed any?

"And about time. We've been waiting. Anything new? Anything different?" A hesitation after the last question, a hopeful hesitation.

Parm mulled over a hundred new and delicious discoveries, but suspected Saam wouldn't chitchat about woolly bears. The distant mindvoice made him ache with loneliness. **"Noooo. Not really."** He paused, hoping for a comment, anything to prolong the conversation, actually make it a dialogue, not a dry report. **"Ah ... oh? I told you about the trees, didn't I? The saplings?"** Hylan's carefully packed cargo consisted of saplings, each one's tender root system balled in dirt and burlap. **"Isn't it nice she wants to plant trees?"**

"Has she planted any yet?"

"Well ... no." A distracted shoulder lick. A distinct possibility Barnaby had fleas. **"I would have said so, wouldn't I?"** Well, of course he would have. He wasn't a blockhead.

"No, you're not a blockhead, but you do take your own sweet time in telling us what's happening."

It stung, although Parm had weathered such complaints before. The fact that too few took him seriously was to their detriment, not his. After all, Harrap bore the same problem without complaint. **"I might remind you, Saam, that we don't know what we're looking for, what might be important—if anything. Hylan keeps herself to herself, has done nothing suspicious. All I can do is keep an open**

A sheathed sword sailed out of the darkness, landed hilt
first. Clearly it hadn't been tossed with intent to harm.
Sarrett sauntered into view as casually as if she walked
Gaernett's streets, open hands at her sides. "Then it might up
the ante with two hostages, say another Seeker Veritas?" She
broached the encircling guards like gold overwhelming dross
and sat beside Jenret.

"You fool!" he sputtered, "Never give anybody more hostages."

"Why not, if it's a good cause?" she whispered as T'ss
sniffed Jenret's bonds, bumped Rawn's shoulder.

Towbin, deep and reassuring, sounded out. "Yulyn, which
side you want me to choose? Not worth much for name or
fame, but I'm a Normal, another pawn to hold."

She wheeled at his voice, a tiny smile breaking like an errant wave. "Of course they'd need someone very special to
guard you, thwart your escape. Someone you can't work
your wiles on." A glance in Garvey's direction. "Would you
take me as one of your band, or grant me neutral status?
Your choice—as long as Towbin stays with me."

Overrun with confusion and by unexpected, distrusted
comrades-in-arms, Garvey stood openmouthed, finally drew
himself up. "Didn't know we was holding a membership
drive. This goes on we'll have to set up a dues-paying structure for the privilege." He shifted back and forth, obviously
uneasy. "Who's left to carry word back?"

Faertom and Addawanna were still unaccounted for,
Jenret thought, a Resonant and an Erakwan. Still, they'd be
believed if they went to Swan Maclough or the Monitor, de-
tailed the situation.

He saw Faertom had finally revealed himself, hanging on
the periphery with a nervous anticipation, intent on being
noticed and acknowledged. Noticed he'd been, but so far totally ignored.

Garvey shied a rock in his direction, an intentional miss
but close enough to make Faertom jump, nearly break and
run. "You're shunned, lad. Word's gone out from your da
that you're formally cast off. Don't want you here, can't
have you here. You broke the rules, the strictures. You want
to be the Normals' lapdog, that's your choice, but people tire
of pets sometimes, abandon them, kill'em if they be too
much trouble."

And Faertom was running, stumbling down the slope, not

Garvey laughed disgustedly, the humor forced. "We need a hostage. Convenient you dropped into our hands."

"But he's a Resonant, one of *us*," Yulyn interjected, clearly as confused as Jenret.

"And he's a Seeker Veritas as well as the son of a respected Merchanter family that's traded across Canderis and Marchmont—he's known. You still don't see, do you?" Anxious now, Garvey pressed home his point. "He's our hostage, not for ransom, not for money, but his life stands surety for ours. His life will be forfeit if any more Resonants are hunted, hurt, killed. And any other Normals as well," he paused, emotion choking him. "Doubt you know, but four were killed tonight in the capital, Elder Hostel torched to flush out a Resonant who didn't exist. A contact ventured near enough to check, sent word."

Jenret strained at his bonds, alarms ringing in his head, the clanging discordance of bells tolling to announce danger. Fire? The jumbled words and images that had overloaded his senses, Doyce and his unborn child in danger? But why would Doyce be at an Elder Hostel? Wouldn't she avoid fire like the plague? But then, when had she ever avoided trouble? Not when she felt it her duty.

His throat grated, clogged by anticipated sorrow. "Do you know who was hurt? I think my wife," and Lady Bright, what fragile claim had been that word when they'd not yet married, but she *was*, with or without benefit of a formal joining, "was at the scene. She's ..." a strange reticence overtook him, a desire to share, an equal desire not to exhibit weakness, vulnerability, "... with child."

For the first time sympathy twisted Garvey's homely features, protuberant chin and beaked nose nearly touching in sorrow. "Far as we know, the dead was all old'uns. Doesn't make it any better. They had the right to die at their appointed time, as do we all."

He nodded, faintly relieved but still haunted by thoughts of Doyce giving birth in the midst of a conflagration.

"So where does this leave us?" Yulyn asked. "If you hold him hostage, I assume you want the fact known. Holding him in secret does no good."

"Aye, we're depending on you to pass the word, see the news spread. Likely a long stay with us, because we demand more than pretty speeches and platitudes, reassurances full of hot air."

raised to show she was weaponless. Straining beyond her shadow shape, Jenret looked for the others, couldn't spot them.

"Rawn, relay everything I'm saying to T'ss, have him tell Sarrett. Don't show yourselves. Don't reveal there're fewer of us than them, and most of all, don't reveal your positions unless it's absolutely necessary!" he lectured, aware that Sarrett and Addawanna, Towbin and Faertom exhibited sense enough for that. Faertom's earnest zealousness worried him, though.

"Figured we'd draw company soon," Garvey let his voice carry in deference to those who couldn't comprehend mindspeech. "Was just about to explain that selfsame question to him, here. Come closer if ye like, no intent to harm or hold you—yet."

Yulyn moved closer as a lantern was lighted and held to guide her, electrifying her coppery hair, copper penny eyes in a pale face. It ringed Jenret in a halo of brightness as well, brilliance that hurt his eyes, made them water. A hand brushed his hair off his forehead, slid softly down his face to tilt his chin to the light. "Are you all right? A nasty fall, it had to be." Yulyn's shiver transmitted itself to his flesh.

"Bumps and bruises," he acknowledged. "Whatever bark that stump had left on it imprinted my ribs, I think. Scaled like a reptile."

The others in Garvey's party ringed them, backs turned to the three, ever-vigilant, alert for any outside movement, any attempt at rescue. Garvey cleared his throat. "Could we get on with this, do you think? We've word to get out." He struck a pose, and what should have appeared silly, over-stated and self-conscious, shifted into deadly seriousness.

"We're holding you hostage. You asked why, but never heard me out, so now I'll explain, and once only. We know what you been doing in the forest, seeking us out, trying to convince us to go back. Nice gesture, considerate, maybe even noble—but wrong-headed all the same."

"Wrong-headed?" Jenret spat the words back, "Wrong-headed to want to save you from making a terrible mistake? When running is proof positive to many that Resonants are guilty of something, have something to hide?"

"And we don't need to hide, if only to protect ourselves? Think we should march back like docile little lambs when you can't control the wolves out there? Well—can you?"

over knowledge, old taboos, not to mention trial and error."

Well, Rawn had a point, and Garvey's offhand demonstration had canceled that hope for rescue, unless the others had traced his earlier plea. But could they realize he now needed rescue from something infinitely more dangerous, something that threatened them as well? Could their captors monitor Rawn's mindvoice? Somehow he didn't think the "frequencies," if that was the word he wanted, the "channels" were one and the same, or at least weren't unless the ghatti chose to merge them. Parse had said that Roland d'Arnot had contacted T'ss and P'wa when they were swimming the river to enter Marchmont undetected, but that it didn't work the other way round unless the ghatti decided it would.

"Rawn, can you contact T'ss?" he hesitated, hoping his share of mental converse couldn't be eavesdropped on, either.

"Have been, you fool, ever since you swan-dived over the edge."

"And?" An ominous pause after his one-word rejoinder.

"T'ss is delighted you've provided some entertainment. However, the humans are having a little trouble finding their way in the dark—Addawanna won't let them light torches. She's told them if they trip and fall one more time she'll leave them behind."

The whole situation puzzled Jenret. Why simply remain here? Let him sit quietly in their midst? Not seek safer ground? And why, for that matter, had they taken him prisoner? It couldn't hurt to ask, so he did, speaking aloud, hoping their conversation might carry, give the others a better fix on his position.

"Why have you taken me prisoner? Have I wronged you in some way? Done something to make you retaliate?"

Garvey squatted at eye-level with Jenret, his rock-scarred hands dangling between his knees. "Belike 'prisoner' isn't the word, more like 'hostage,' I'd call it."

"Hostage for what!" The idea left him indignant, incredulous.

"Hostage for good behavior."

"Whose good behavior?" Nothing made sense.

Yulyn's mindvoice interrupted, calm but infinitely colder than the night air. *"You're holding one of us prisoner, why? What is the meaning of this?"* She stepped into view, hands but from what she knew about Seeker Bondmates, something must be done about him as well. Just in case. Would it work on a ghatt? If so, how much? As to whether Parm liked it or not, he licked his chops, rose on hind legs to sniff, rubbed against her thigh.

Starting to hand over the plate, she halted, pretending to have forgotten something. "I've something you might enjoy with it, some dried herb seasoning that livens it up, heightens the flavor." A suggestive eyebrow cock at Harrap to see if he'd agree. He nodded and she reached back into the cart, found the leather bag, sprinkled on the dried flakes. Pinched a smaller portion on the ghatt's dish. None for Barnaby, naughty dog, so fickle.

"Aren't you having any?" Harrap inhaled with pleasure as the plate came his way again, wooden spoon at the ready.

"No, the taste of plain smearkas is enough for me. I prefer the seasoning on meat, myself." Liar! Even the thought of the word seared her tongue as if someone had thrust a red-hot coin between her teeth. If he could swallow, so could she, no time for pity or regret. Would he notice, would the ghatt notice? If she could but once have them consume it, it boasted an addictive power, enough to ensure future doses would become easier and easier. Until by the end they'd beg her for it, willing to lick it off her fingers, off the very roadway itself, ignoring dust and dirt. Anything for more. Not her own craving, but she understood it.

She spooned at her own plain share of smearkas, forced some into her mouth, swallowed. It's the only way. They won't leave me alone otherwise. Someday they'll understand, when our world is secure again. Always someone, something, must be sacrificed. That was a given. Not her greatest sacrifice yet, but it would come, she knew. Pray she'd be worthy of it. She knew, as well, that there'd be no acknowledgment of her efforts until after the fact. Those in power always ignored, denied, were blind. But then, she'd never asked for thanks—or expected it—in all her life. Why start now? A monumental task, but at least she could begin the scourging so necessary to save Canderis.

❖

"Well?" Marius van Mees growled, half-shielding her behind him, the partway open barn door further obscuring her

so that Hylan Crailford stood in dimness, barely visible to
the revelers, the passers to-and-fro at this ostensible naming
day celebration for van Mees's youngest son. She gripped
the forked witch hazel rod tighter between protesting fingers
already indented by its shape. Sweat beaded her upper lip,
her whole face filmed with sweat, greasy with trepidation.
The sound lurching up in her throat a barely articulated
"No" in response. More a keening "nnn," indicating defeat
once again.

He'd assured her most of the village would congregate
here tonight, either for the naming party or to admire his
new heifer, bought at lavish expense to improve his herd.
Human fodder for her inspection, to cull who passed from
those who didn't. Somehow she'd recognized him in that
pasture, three days ago, when he'd been admiring his new
purchase preparatory to claiming it from the breeder. Not
that she'd known his name or who he was, but she marked
the pursed mouth, the darting, distrustful eyes that nearly
singed whatever they viewed. Let them come in contact too
long with your flesh and you'd be sorry. The aggressive
stance, almost a fighting readiness, yet the quick withdrawal
from close contact with a stranger, this and more, almost the
rabid scent of him, had whispered to her. Yes, this, this, this
was a man ceaselessly vigilant when it came to detecting
Gleaners. A man keyed to the tightest pitch to insure the
welfare of family and loved ones against outsiders, any and
every one a threat if their beliefs deviated from his.

The way he'd taken her measure as she'd tramped through
the field, desperate for a hedge to shelter her while she did
her business, not realizing his presence at first, so intent on
her bodily needs. That he'd suspected *her,* popping up almost out of nowhere like that. The distant sight of the Shepherd, standing patiently in the road by the cart, waiting, had
offered some reassurance, gave a modified relaxation to his
stance, though his eyes still glowed like two burning coals
of suspicion. How to approach him, snare him into
helping?—for in doing so he'd be helping himself. How to
be one of Us, not one of Them, she who had so little truck
with humanity.

"A bit leery of strangers in these parts," he'd offered in
wary apology as she stripped a handful of leaves, clenched
them tight. Dry, ready to fall, but the best she'd have when
she regained her privacy.

"Aren't we all?" The leaves crackled in her hand, she opened her fingers, watched the pieces float and fall. "With good reason. Half-feared myself to travel so, but when needs must, you must."

Van Mces had smiled with self-satisfaction. "Nothing's safer than staying home with people you know and trust, though I swear these days I'm not sure of some of them any longer. They can hide anywhere, be anyone. You must have . . . strong needs."

"Ah, feared that I'll find . . . *Them*. Feared that I won't."

"Feared that you *won't?*" It nearly burst from him. "Bless the Lady every day you don't! That we've held Them at bay a little longer!"

"No, you don't understand." Had she caught him up with her, made him complicitous?

Anger now, and a challenge, face thrusting at hers. "Then explain it to me. What *are* you doing? What's your game?"

Tongue tucked over front teeth, sucking thoughtfully, she'd held her ground, made it clear she was assessing him, his intent, his strength of character. At last, "I'm a dowser . . . a *diviner* . . . but what I divine now is Gleaners. Can always tell." Never let him guess her uncertainty, only her faith guiding her, and that one fateful contact with Vesey Bell and Evelien Annendahl Wycherley to point the way before she'd known, understood what they represented. The harbinger of her skills. Now she must hone them, perfect them. Otherwise, what sense in planting?

"You be sure of that? Fantodding sure?" Nothing left but to reel him in, his desire as overpowering as her own. "What's it get you, gain you?" More cannily, "Do ye charge?"

"What I earn is salvation, the satisfaction of erasing, expunging, one more Gleaner from this world. I've been called to do this, it's my mission." The vague fears enshrouded her again, entwining themselves in her mind, whispering, shrieking that she wasn't strong enough, brave enough. Made her panic at the seduction she attempted. No, not seduction—he stood more than willing on his own. "There's so little time!" She'd almost whispered, a plea, a confession of her need for allies. "So far to travel, so many to search out, accord their just deserts."

"Then I might be able to help us both. I swear we've been harboring a Gleaner in town, but mayhap my sight's been clouded by my fears. Hate to accuse anyone unjustly, but hate

more to let them dig in deeper, gain a hold over us." And
he'd begun to rapidly sketch out his plans for his son's naming day three nights hence, if she wanted to attend, tune her
skills, satisfy his curiosity. Avid curiosity that danced around
him like heat waves.

And now here she stood, sheltering behind the door. "No,"
she repeated again, forcing confidence into her voice. "Not
them," she indicated the last group of four who'd walked by,
tossing greetings and good-natured japery at van Mees that he
thought more highly of his new heifer than of his newborn.

"That's good," he replied unperturbed. "They're all old
friends. 'Twould have hurt."

Another party fast approaching. "Sure you've the stomach
for this?" Asking herself, asking him? Damned if she did,
damned if she didn't. One success to bolster the confidence
worn down by the long road, then word would spread, fire-
fast, people rushing to meet her as she traveled, following behind and ahead of her, rejoicing. It had to be. Van Mees
glimpsed only part of what was at stake, his smoldering eyes
scouring the earth, not the skies for the havoc the Gleaners
would bring with them from above, destroying a way of life.
She gripped the forked twig harder, readied herself.

"No, nor them either," she whispered again, faintly miffed.
Was this some silly joke van Mees played on her? Parading
Normal after Normal back and forth in front of her? The evening continued in that vein, her senses heightened for the
merest twitch from the dowsing rod. Nothing, absolutely
nothing. Failure.

He eased her to a bench outside the barn. "Everyone's
come who's coming." Scratched his head. "Not a one? You're
sure of it?" Miserable, she nodded as a man edged their way,
waiting patiently to be noticed.

"What, Thorstyn?" van Mees shouted over his shoulder.
"Didn't think ye'd be by. Just bringing the sheep down, aren't
you?"

And she jerked to her feet, the wand dipping and waving, vibrating through her hands, practically keening a high-
pitched song of hunger that resonated through her entire
body, feet to hands to head. It bobbed and dipped as if alive,
almost scenting the man, Thorstyn, who remained beyond van
Mees in the shadows.

"Dogs'll hold them steady till I get back. Listen," he
twisted an old beret in his hands, ceaselessly circling it.

"Heard you had a water witch here tonight. Wanted to ask her hire for a day. Well's dry again. Plenty of sweet water down below, but pipe ain't driven in the right place, hit hard pan or some such thing."

She could almost feel her hair fanning out, each strand alive with an electric power, feared her fingers and eyes glowed with nascent light. Yes, yes, yes! He was it, he was the one! She held van Mees's gaze, saw that he'd caught her strange, rapt demeanor, sensed his surprise and rising approbation.

"Well, Thorstyn, ask, she's right here. But let me show you something first. Lovely Janus-bred heifer in the barn I want your opinion on." Van Mees death-gripped the visitor's elbow as they headed into the barn, toward the two or three who waited, entrusted with van Mees's secret.

A dull thud, the next sound a sharper crack. The sound of a shovel blade striking blunt-side first, then its edge, slicing into a skull. The faintest moan, quickly tapering. Van Mees hurried out, wiping his hands on the beret, face almost lascivious with satiation, relief. "I thank ye!" He pried one of her hands loose, pumping it. "Always wondered, always mistrusted him keeping himself to himself like that up in the hills. Too bad he lives alone or we could have exterminated a whole viper's nest!"

"Only him, no others." Each word distinct and painful, throat muscles straining. "That I'm sure of."

"How can I thank you? What can I do for you?" He dug into his pocket.

"No, there's no bounty on each Gleaner head. My bounty is free." And merciful, she hoped. A mercy to save them from themselves.

"There's nothing . . . ?"

Tired from the strain, she arched her back. "Tell them, those you trust. Make the word known, discreetly, of course. I need help if I'm to cover as much ground as possible, hunt out as many as I can. Have your friends pave my way. Others may start tracking me soon." Her eyes bored into his. "Guardians, them you can fool. But if Seekers come, be circumspect, give them no reason to request a formal Seeking."

He nodded, his Adam's apple rippling like a mouse trapped in a stocking. "Mum's the word when it comes to them. Lady bless you. Lady and her Apostles bless you!"

"By the New Year," she blurted, "we should be saved by

the New Year. Have faith until then!" And walked away, cutting across the fields to where she'd left her cart and, she hoped, Harrap snoring sonorously, mind floating through muddled, happy dreams, the ghatt as well. Barnaby would guard them, keep them safe for her, his bark shrill enough to wake the dead, though not poor misguided Thorstyn, might he rest in peace.

❖

"Come on, Alyse, I'll give you a leg up." The Monitor cupped his hands, ready to help Alyse DeVanter into the saddle. Legs spread, he braced himself, but Alyse was lighter than expected, her swirling cabbage rose-printed pantaloons, the tented, nubby jacket only hinting at ample weight within. A false promise, though, Alyse's overripe succulence had withered with age.

"Rather someone'd give me a leg up on Zander Nugent—preferably on his backside," Alyse DeVanter fumed, glowered more as Darl Allgood worked to hide a smile.

"Now Alyse," Kyril van Beieven swung tiredly into his own saddle, "just turn Zander Nugent and Fleur Massoon over your knee. Administer a good spanking. Don't get all grandmotherly and coddle them. Discipline them. They both need Merchanter services."

While Alyse looked for all the world like someone's rosy-cheeked, twinkly-eyed grandmother—and was, twelve times over at last count—she currently headed the Merchanters' Ward, elected for a two-year term to supervise and administer the rules governing all Merchanters. Two years was all anyone could afford, since those two years meant neglecting one's own enterprise for the good of others—in Alyse's case, as a Merchanter of fruits, one of the most perishable of commodities. No wonder she preferred trading in dried fruits, usually had a pocket of samples.

"It's not as easy as that, and well you know it." He certainly did know but wouldn't let on to Alyse, wouldn't confirm her suspicions. Even with her back turned, she could spot a transgressor in the next town, had caught out her sons and their best friend, Rilly van Beieven, more often than he cared to remember.

He'd been invited tonight to mediate amongst three Wards: Merchanters, Growers, and Artisans. Alyse had been trapped neatly in the middle of tonight's verbal free-for-all. The Artisans' Ward, headed by Fleur Massoon, fretted over increased trade with Marchmont, certain their goods were flooding the market, driving down prices on similar Canderisian articles. They were asking for protection, quotas, complaining that members would be driven out of business without it. The Growers' Ward, headed by Zander Nugent, a wheat farmer, wanted no such thing, his members prospering as trade boomed with Marchmont, a kingdom cursed with a shorter growing season because it was so far north. Poor Alyse DeVanter and the Merchanters were dependent on both, her people trading in all commodities, some wanting restrictions, others opting for open trade. A contentious meeting, full of finger-pointing, and unlikely to be resolved without negotiations with their Marchmontian counterparts, including Lysenko Boersma, Lord of Commerce. Fleur Massoon couldn't grasp the basic "tit for tat" concept: put a quota on a Marchmont product and they'd surely slap one on something from Canderis, most likely agricultural.

The meeting had finally adjourned, Alyse riding with Kyril and Darl, a Guardian in the lead with a torch, another following behind. Kyril hated having an escort. Never before had it been necessary, but these days he wasn't so sure. Anything could happen. Hadn't that anonymous letter hinted at that? Lady help him, if he took every gimcrack, garden-variety threat so seriously, he'd be paralyzed. Well, Anonymous was wrong about Darl, but that didn't make the danger any less acute. Any innocent citizen could be adjudged a Resonant, too many already had been.

Alyse and Darl chatted away. More accurately, Alyse indulged in a barrage of babble. It was her specialty: wear an opponent down, wait till his eyes glazed, and then nail him with a demand. Darl, however, seemed to be holding his own, actually shoehorning trenchant observations into Alyse's monologue, making her stop and reconsider her point. From what he could hear, Allgood was being scrupulously neutral despite a tendency to side with the Growers, Wexler being a grape-growing province. Most of Darl's Grower constituents were also winemakers. That had been his reason for coming to listen tonight.

"Alyse, isn't your throat dry from all that? Mine is—just from listening to you," the Monitor interrupted. "Let me buy you an ale at Myllard's. You can fill me in on the grandchildren's doings, not business. I've heard all I want for tonight." Though it was late and he hated to lose sleep, he just didn't feel like going straight to bed. "Agreed?" At her nod, he shouted to the lead Guardian, watched him change course.

He listened, as understandingly as he could as Alyse changed gears, pattering on about the various goings-on of her two daughters, two sons, and twelve assorted grandchildren. Marie listened to this sort of thing better than he, but he *did* care. Alyse had changed his own diapers often enough, he'd half-grown up at the DeVanter house. Darl quickly untangled whose children were whose, chuckling at the right moments. Strange, he didn't know whether Darl had children or not, had never heard any mentioned, had never asked. Come to think of it, he barely knew Annette, Darl's wife—pleasant but excruciatingly shy, bookish, he thought. Had seen her once or twice with Marie in the sewing room, but she'd been as attentive a listener as Darl. Perhaps it went with the territory; undoubtedly the wife of a Chief Conciliator, now a High Conciliator, learned things from her husband best not spread through gossip. Circumspection, a deliberate and prudent regard for not spreading stories, was paramount.

They were passing through a narrow street of shops, shuttered and dark, when Darl spotted lights in a saddler's at the far end of one of the pocket hanky-sized squares that dotted the area. Only the smaller merchants had establishments here; larger, more ambitious ones demanded broader streets, heavier traffic to attract customers. Shops here were either elite, attracting a discerning, select clientele willing to go out of their way, or down-at-the-heels, eking out a genteel subsistence. Darl pointed out the light seeping around the shutters, the sounds of voices, raised sometimes. "Late for customers, isn't it?"

"I know. And if it's a burglary, they're not exactly subtle." Van Beieven gave a whistle, brought the lead Guardian swinging round as their rearguard caught up with them. "Probably nothing, Gelthaart, but check that out, please. Knock on the door, make sure nothing's amiss. At the least we can't be faulted for ignoring possible trouble, showing our concern." It should stand him in good stead when word got out that the Monitor himself was ever-vigilant, concerned with his citizens' safety and livelihoods.

Dismounting, Gelthaart knocked, torch held high in one hand, his other dropping to his sword. From behind, Kyril heard Jollis partially unsheathing his sword, alert for trouble. To one side of him Darl looked merely curious while Alyse munched at some dried apple slices, somber and watchful. Nothing to be concerned about, it couldn't be.

The door flung open, Gelthaart jumping back to avoid being hit, keeping his torch at the ready much as if it were a weapon. They burst out of the shop as if they were a pack, incapable of independent action but deriving communal cunning and strength from the group. As near as Kyril could count, nine men and three women bunched in a wedge, the man at its point folding his arms across his chest, chin thrust forward pugnaciously. "Just checking," Gelthaart soothed. "Are ye the shop's owner, sir? We were worried about the lateness of it, lights, activity. Most are home abed by now."

Darl Allgood shifted uncomfortably in the saddle, and Kyril followed his gaze, blessed the farsightedness of middle years. Tiny at this distance, obscure except for the glint of torchlight at the same place on each collar. Silvery crescents catching the light, winking obscenely. Blessed Lady preserve and protect them, they'd stumbled across a Reaper meeting!

"Yes, this is my shop. Name's Corliss Singletary."

It seemed to Kyril that every one of the twelve had fixed Darl Allgood with a cold, implacable eye, assessing him. An ominous forward milling from two or three of the most bold, as if they'd rush out, drag Darl from his horse. The Monitor felt faint, trepidation turning to grinding fear. Wanted to scream, "Darl, run. Escape!" Didn't dare the exposure, acknowledge Darl's guilt.

Singletary took a step, arms still crossed. Not a young man, at least the Monitor's age. Taller, trimmer, no excess settling around his gut. "Well, well, our esteemed Monitor Kyril van Beieven and . . ." he squinted in the torchlight, "Mistress Merchanter DeVanter and . . ." slowed further to savor the name, "High Conciliator Darl Allgood, Wexler's finest." He turned to survey his followers, ignoring the Guardian beside him, swung back, an insolent smile playing across his face. "Concerned citizens, van Beieven, that's what we are, merely concerned citizens having a meeting to discuss our views, assembling to address our concerns. Nothing wrong with that, is there?" He threw out the words like a challenge.

Van Beieven discovered he couldn't take his eyes off the man, his throat constricting, pulse pounding. Felt totally impotent, unable to cope. It wasn't true, it couldn't be true! Not Darl, not Darl! How could they know, how did they know? And how could Darl sit there, reins loose, and not be trembling in terror? Except he wasn't a Resonant, no reason for him to be frightened beyond the obvious tension anyone would feel at an unexpected confrontation. Take yourself in hand, van Beieven, he ordered himself. But the guilt lodged in his heart for even thinking that about Darl.

He forced his gelding forward to face Singletary, mouth dry, hands shaking so much he held them out of sight, one folded over the other on the reins. "If you've concerns, Mr. Singletary, bring your concerns to your Chief Conciliator, your High Conciliator, to me, if need be. We're always ready to listen, to help." His voice sounded high, strained, even to him.

"And your concern's appreciated as well, Monitor." The saddler unfolded his arms and van Beieven jerked his horse to an abrupt halt, sensing a threat. "But it's late and I think we've discussed all we need to for one evening. Might as well be on our way. Much to do on the morrow, and the morrow after that as well." With a wave of his hand, Singletary's followers began to drift away, some arrogant, pressing much too close, forcing Darl's and Alyse's horses back, others flitting along the square, putting as much distance as possible between the Monitor's group and themselves.

Gelthaart hurriedly took his place, whispered with Jollis as they pressed closer to their charges. The Monitor wavered in the saddle, dizzy, weak. Moisture trickled inside his pants legs—had he shamed himself that way, too?

"Kyril? Are you all right?" Alyse grabbed his hand, chafed it. "You're white as a sheet. Don't wonder the way they were all staring at you, practically licking their chops as if you were a tasty mouse and them a dozen starving cats."

"Staring at *me?*" he repeated blankly. "Me?"

"Well, of course every eye was fixed on you—you're the Monitor, after all."

They'd been staring at Darl, he knew it. How could Alyse

not have realized? He wiped a hand across his eyes as if it
would help him see more clearly.

Darl was beside him now on the other side, hand on his
arm, solicitous. "Gelthaart thinks it's safe to move on now.
We should pick up the night watch at the next block. Good
job, Kyril, good job. But I think we all need brandy, not ale.
You appeared perfectly calm, but I'll confess—they gave me
quite a start."

The Monitor kept shaking his head, mouth partially open,
words beyond him. Staring at Darl, staring at him? Did it
matter or not? All he knew was that he'd been petrified, near
craven with terror, and it was a feeling he never wanted to
experience again.

"Blast all, Saam, why would they put my valise down
here?" She hadn't begun to rummage in earnest yet, had
contented herself with picking her way through the narrow
aisles between benches and tables, piles of strange equip-
ment she couldn't put a name to or identify a use. An overriding smell of damp masonry and seeping stone, a whiff of
mildew and rot, and dust, dust enough for her to write her
name in ten times over.

"An exaggeration." Saam angled by her, tail accidentally
swiping a low shelf beneath a tabletop. He stopped, sniffed
fastidiously, debated licking but decided to shake it clean.
**"But only a slight one. At least gray on gray doesn't
show. Much."** He ducked under the shelf, surveying from
ground level. **"As to why down here, you told the servant
to put it away, out of your sight, and that if you tripped
over it once more ..."** He let her finish the thought for herself.

"That meant in the closet, under the bed, someplace like
that. I didn't think the blasted fool ..." she caught his faint
"ahem" of reproach and emended, "the misguided servant
would interpret me so literally. More fool I."

Where to begin baffled her. Asking for help would be sen-
sible, but this gave her something to do, a place to poke
around, ignore the summons she'd received earlier in the
day, asking—no, demanding would be more accurate—that
she return to Gaernett immediately. And hadn't she just been

spite everything, Farnham didn't appear to be in pain, rather an intense ecstasy, a pleasurable arousal.

Her arm flagged as she stared at him, the circling movements slowing, the sparks between the balls fading, finally dissipating, leaving a pungent smell to the room, fresh and sharp. Electrical storms left the same smell.

"Mr. Farnham, are you all right?" A wave of anxiety overcame her as she rushed to his side, checked his pulse, rolled back an eyelid. He heaved a repleted sigh, tried to gather himself together. It made no sense, she'd experienced no similar reaction, just the staticky tension of the air whip-snapping between her and Saam.

One hand on the floor to steady himself, he managed to rise, brushing off the knees of his trousers, straightening and retucking his shirt. A slow, almost flirtatious wink in her direction gave her an urge to slap him. "Bottle it up like that and it feels so good when it lets loose again." Another heavy sigh of satisfaction. "So good, makes you feel you're alive, able to think."

"What?" She still had no idea what he meant.

Saam pushed between them, eyes ablaze. **"Don't *ever* do that again when I'm here. It freezes my mindspeech so I can't communicate. Tried to warn you, but wasn't fast enough. Worse than the Seeker General's private office."**

"What?" Her conversation was taking very unoriginal turns, utterly baffled by each revelation, puzzle pieces aplenty but without an inkling where they fit.

"Look what it did to Farnham here, though I'm not entirely sure *what* it did. *He* seemed to enjoy it, but then Resonant brain waves aren't the same as ours."

"Sorry, Saam," she apologized automatically, mind sprinting in a hundred different directions. "Mr. Farnham, do you think you could carry that gadget upstairs for me?" and tripped over the valise when she least expected it, didn't care, scooped it up by its handles, more concerned with the strange machine she'd discovered, its peculiar effect. "Don't drop it, Mr. Farnham," she begged. "If it's too much, we'll get someone else to help you."

"Nay, 'tis fine. Just awkward, not heavy." He huffed and puffed, trying to see over or around it, judge his footing, shift clear without sweeping other mechanicals off tables and shelves. "Mayhap you'll do me again?" his face hopeful.

"Mayhap, mayhap," she responded, mind desperately working as they climbed the stairs. *"Saam, would you send word that we will be accepting the Monitor's 'invitation' after all, but a day or two later than expected. I think I'm onto something!"*

That sharing of minds left the steel-gray ghatt singularly unenthusiastic about the possibilities.

"Baz! Baz, I've some special orders from the north, more than anticipated!" Waving his notebook, Tadjeus Pomerol barged into Baz's office, his inner sanctum, dirt-stained and triumphant.

Bazelon Foy repressed a fastidious shudder at his journeyman's disarray, evidence that the man had ridden long and sleepless, if he rightly judged the puffy lids, the purplish circles under the blue eyes. Not nearly as battered, disheveled, and dispirited as the first time he'd encountered Tadj two years' past, a definite improvement, actually.

He sat the man down, forced himself to touch the blond hair, road dust adhering to the scented pomade, traced the curve of the pink and white ear with a finger, tried not to notice the smudge he picked up from it. "So, your work went well?" Checked to be sure his office door was shut tight, came back and skimmed through the orders, then studied them more attentively, mouth parting as he relaxed. Business and business, best know how business fared, pass the orders on along, get the apprentices and masters working. Besides, it gave Tadj a chance to catch his breath. "Go wash while I'm reading." He motioned to the ewer and pitcher, his own private one, on the stand against the far wall. He loved the curves of the white porcelain against the mahogany paneling, saw Tadj struck speechless by the contrast as well.

He sighed. Tadj had an incredible—and innate—sense of beauty and absolutely no ability to create it. But he *was* a superlative salesman, his task a hundredfold easier given the growing renown of the Foy glassworks. Yes, an especially large order for decanters and glasses. Nice, very nice. An especially lucrative and artistically challenging order for one of Baz's unique handblown creations, the rest for cut-glass and molded. And of course the ubiquitous orders for bottles, jars, molded drinking glasses, tankards. Poor Tadj as well, to have to deal with such mundane objects.

He'd found Tadj in a back alley behind one of Wexler's wine shops, crying, sniveling, ineffectually struggling as four sailors attempted to turn him into custard. Pettibal sailors, he was fairly sure, not the lake-traffickers here in Wexler. Must have been traveling overland from the Pettibal to the coast to sign on for ocean trade. Baz wasn't sure what had started the fight, but he had a pretty good idea, with the emphasis on "pretty." Because that's what Tadj was— somehow just a little too handsome, not quite effeminate, but someone who shouldn't sit too near real masculinity. His clothes and his color sense were just a tad precious, although Baz learned later that Tadj had clerked for an upscale tailor in Eremont who demanded that his help serve as walking mannikins for the latest fashions. What the sailors had thought Tadj wanted of them hadn't been sex, because Tadj didn't realize it himself, but the opportunity to bask beside hard-bitten masculine attractiveness.

Rescuing the lad had been a chore, and he'd shown the sailors that not all fetchingly handsome men, including himself, thought or fought that way. He'd been bruised and bloodied by the time he'd fought them off, and Tadj had been unconscious. Easy enough when Tadj came to, full of gratitude, balmed by Baz's good looks, to insinuate that the sailors had been Gleaners, had wiped Tadj's brain until he couldn't remember the evening or its aftermath. Easy enough too, to discover Tadj's skills, his golden tongue for sales, his infallible eye for beauty. Tadj was pliant and pliable in the face of beauty—inanimate or animate, male or female—would sell his soul for it. Why shouldn't Baz be the buyer? Tadj also lusted after the comely attractions of Baz's precision plans to rid the world of Gleaners to get back at those sailors who'd so nearly marred his looks.

Glowingly clean, face and hands at least, even the blond hair reslicked, Tadj sat, hands folded, face eager. "And what of our other business?" Baz finally asked when he'd determined Tadj was about to burst. "Any luck there?"

"Some. Some," Tadj drew it out, reluctant yet excited. "Not as much as I'd anticipated, because someone was there before me."

"Before you?" It made no sense. Tadj had been assigned the north, had one of his other followers mistaken his instructions? Or was someone else poaching, drawing off the support he needed for the cause, channeling it to something else? Nothing could be more important. "What do you mean?"

Tadj bounced in his seat. "I think it's someone special, Baz. Someone we can mold. A visible figurehead we can use to rally people without exposing ourselves any more than necessary." He sounded almost breathless with excitement. "Plus, she has a talent we can only dream about!"

He was seething now, almost ready to slap Tadj, force him to make sense. Was Tadj's eye for talent as discerning as his eye for beauty? He was trying to help, Baz kept reminding himself, make Baz proud of him—just as Baz had wanted to make Darl proud of him. He suppressed his frustration, his failure. No, Tadj might disappoint him, but he'd never disappoint Tadj. "What do you mean?" he repeated again, spacing the words with even emphasis.

"She can . . ." Tadj caught Baz's raised eyebrows, backtracked. "A woman named Hylan Crailford. She can identify Gleaners! They project some sort of vibration she can feel, just as a dowser looks for water. Except her dowsing rod responds to Gleaners!" He'd V-ed his hands in front of him horizontally, demonstrating, homing in on an invisible target.

"Have you actually *seen* her do this?" If this were another of Tadj's odd enthusiasms, he'd have him pumping the bellows in the glassworks for the rest of his life. Let him find beauty in that!

Tadj nodded, solemn. "Saw her. Wasn't supposed to, but I did. The woman I was selling to that day took me along to a naming day celebration she'd been invited to. I saw Hylan Crailford in action, though I wasn't meant to—saw the rod bend and leap in her hands!"

"Did she see you?"

"Yes and no." Tadj considered, trying to explain. "She saw me as much as she 'saw' any stranger that night, took no notice of me because I wasn't what she was searching for. I've seen her since, talked with her, but haven't admitted I was there. I've seen her do it twice again. She doesn't kill them, leaves that for others to do. Her only role, she says, is to identify them."

Baz found himself pacing the narrow office, mind crammed with possibilities—if Tadj weren't exaggerating. But if he weren't, they'd been handed a priceless gift—a mind attuned to their own desires to rid the world of Gleaners. Yes, the harvest was plenteous, but the laborers were few. Let her identify them and they, they would be the ruthless arm that would harvest them. "What sort of person is she?"

"Strange, passing strange," Tadj admitted. "For some reason she's worried about Spacers, fears they'll return to Methuen after all these years, inundate us with technology as destructive as the Plumbs. She thinks the Gleaners will call to them mind-to-mind, direct them here. Totally convinced of it."

"Sounds like an old-fashioned, revivalist upbringing. That Spacer malarky won't help, but her hatred of Gleaners will." He'd come to a stop now, ignoring Tadj. "That's what we must play on."

"She's got a Shepherd and a ghatt with her as well. Following her along meek as lambs."

"What! What's a Shepherd doing with a ghatt?" That tore it right there. What if Tadj had been found out—and through Tadj, himself? "Have they been doing any Seekings?"

"Not likely!" Tadj laughed, sharp face shiny with delight. "She's got them drugged. Resourceful woman, to say the least. She thinks they may be the sacrifice necessary to stop the Spacers from returning. Why not, if it makes her happy? Who am I to say? She's a holy fool in the grip of her passion, to save the world from the Spacers. Luckily for us she has to destroy Gleaners to accomplish it."

"Is she with anyone we can trust now?"

"She's already attracted believers, or at least they believe she can identify Gleaners. I've got two of our people mingling with her followers, but nobody knows our two for what they are, as yet."

Was it too good to be true? Too much to believe that Hylan Crailford had been given into their hands? Well, the only thing to do was to wait and see. He sat opposite Tadj, let their knees almost touch, leaned forward to whisper, though it wasn't really necessary. "Play with her if you like, see what develops, what you can develop. Manipulate and mold her, just as I mold glass. It's your opportunity to create a thing of beauty to enhance our cause." Tadj nodded, lips pressed tight in excitement, watching Baz's cherry-pink lips form the words. "But be careful. I don't want to jeopardize what we already have. I'll not have my people torn between me and her. See how much farther you can insinuate yourself with her, into her group.

"Keep order for her. Guide her. Give order to her cause and her followers will look to you for direction. Do you think you can do that?"

Tadj's head bobbed eagerly. "Yes, oh, yes!" He leaned back, momentarily disconcerted, a moue of distress on his face. "I just wish she weren't so ordinary, almost ugly-looking. Woman hasn't taken care of herself for years. And I think the dog has fleas."

"A dog, a ghatt, a Shepherd—what do you have there? A menagerie?" He laughed. "Any dancing bears?"

"Oh, I think the Shepherd can serve for that."

"Well, what are you waiting for? Get back there. Remember her true beauty is in her utility to our cause. Let me know what happens."

❖

Doyce sulked, straightened her legs against the surrey's dashboard until her seat back protested, furiously finger-tapping in time to the horses' hooves. Davvy galloped Lokka in a loop around the surrey, Khar on the pommel platform, angled along Lokka's neck to catch the breeze. And *she* wasn't supposed to ride! Lokka boasted a perfectly smooth gait when she wasn't playing hellion under Davvy's tutelage. Of course, riding the whole way wouldn't be comfortable, but a short ride would be beneficial, make her feel in control of her fate. Cady Brandt, the Novie Seeker handling the reins, had already refused her a turn at handling the carriage horses. Said she'd been instructed to convey Doyce there safe and sound! Doyce drummed her fingers faster. Was the whole world conspiring against her having any fun, any distraction to take her mind off her conflicted decision to return home to her mother and sister? Blast Swan for playing on her guilt!

Cady's Bondmate F'een fixed her with an expectant stare, more than a little awestruck—as was the girl, if Doyce chose to admit it. This was *not* going to be a pleasant journey! Ir-

ritable, she shifted, scooted down in the seat, and tossed one
ankle over the other. Nothing was comfortable, let alone her
bottom, and she stifled a groan of frustrated boredom.

The surrey slowed, Cady heaving on the reins, casting a
wary glance at Doyce's mounded abdomen. "Are you . . . all
right, ma'am, Seeker Marbon?" The girl's eyes looked like
a scolded puppy's. "You're not . . . going into labor or anything belike that?"

"No, Cady. Trust me, I'd be the first to notice. Not you."
She pushed upright, attempted to muster some charity in her
heart. Well, if it were better to give than to receive, why not
see how Cady did with that? "Your arm must be hurting."
Caught the girl's reluctant nod; Cady'd been wounded protecting Maize and Max Lewinton from the Reapers. "Best
not to aggravate it. Why not let me take over for a stretch?
I've handled a team before."

"But not in a long time," Khar taunted as she and Davvy
whooped by. **"Any team your mother owned was so old
and well-broken that a Plumb exploding underfoot
wouldn't have made them amble."**

"How would you know?" Cross, she fanned a hand to
shift the rising dust.

**"Saw it in your mind. May have been high adventure
to you when you were little. But think on it, would your
mother have let you drive otherwise?"**

"No." Realized that to Cady she'd answered her own
question about relinquishing the reins. Davvy pulled Lokka
parallel to the surrey and wobbled as he stood on the saddle,
Lokka obediently slowing when his aerial acrobatics commenced. Khar glared at the boy towering above her, arms
winging the air for balance, mouth screwed tight with concentration. He took a step to compensate, stabilize himself,
and his foot slammed on the platform, grinding Khar's white
paw.

With a screech, Khar levitated skyward and, as the sorrel
mare moved beneath her, landed in Davvy's flailing arms.
The outcome preordained, they both crashed to the ground,
Lokka dashing to safety beside Doyce and the team. *"I don't
blame you, old dear,"* she commiserated as Cady halted the
surrey, she and F'een darting down to assess the damage.
"Khar, how are you? How's Davvy?"

"I have been mashed," Khar intoned with deflated dignity, not to mention a hint of malice, "between a rapidly growing boy and the ground. How do you think I am?"

"Ouch!" she offered back. *"No bones broken, just bruised pride?"*

"Ghatti are *never* awkward. No bones broken on the boy, either. Though I hope he packed additional pants. A fresh breeze on his backside where they split."

Doyce swung down to survey the damage as Cady hauled the boy to his feet and dusted him off. Davvy was winded but basically intact, discounting his britches, eyes gleaming with triumph. "Smerdle! Almost had it that time, just have to remember to—"

"Never try that again in my presence or on Lokka. That's what you'd best remember," she interrupted, straining for severity, instead breaking into laughter at his dust-streaked mien, bangs sweat-spiked like tiny horns. He had the grace to display momentary abashment before giggling as he rubbed his bottom. "Now it's my turn to ride. And but me no butts, interpret that as you will. That goes for you as well, Cady. Davvy, you'll ride with her for a while."

Had Lokka grown higher, wider? The effort of mounting worse than scaling a high wall, and the obstacle wasn't the mare but her own girth. She almost beached herself on the pommel platform until Cady boosted her upright. Still, marvelous to be back in the saddle, it provided perspective on things, and perspective was sorely lacking about now. That, more than anything else, explained her moping, torn between worry for Swan and for her mother, fear of how she fared, plus her own insecurity, the nagging doubt that her choice was wrong—rekindling old ties best left as they were. *"Khar, come on!"*

Khar nestled close to Lokka's neck, almost crowded off the pommel platform. *"Khar, I know I'm taking up more than my share, but I swear you are, too. You've been gaining weight, you rascal, haven't you?"*

The ghatta evinced rapt interest in the passing scenery. "The sedentary life, you know," she offered at last. "At least that's what the Seeker General always said."

"Sedentary? I'd sooner say it's sediment settling around your middle!" She tickled the striped sides with the reins while Khar sulked, fretful and indignant as she pawed

Lokka's mane. And then it dawned on Doyce. How could she have missed it? *"Khar, you're pregnant, aren't you?"* No response. *"Well, aren't you?"* Damn all, she'd been right, the ghatta *hadn't* asked for the 'script that controlled her fertility cycles. She hadn't been absentminded—Khar hadn't asked, had obviously planned this.

"Love, I think it's wonderful. Truly." And let her mind flood with fond images of Khar, Khar with ghatten, a sleeping baby with a ghatten or two curled beside it. What she desperately wanted to ask but was too reticent to do so, was who had fathered them?

"You'll see." Amber eyes dreamy, Khar leaned into Doyce's stomach, forehead flattened against her as if she communed directly with the child. A jerk backward and Khar grimaced. **"Kicking again. Nailed me right on the nose. There's something I've been meaning to talk to you about."**

"Poor little pink nose," she consoled. *"I should think so. Khar, why didn't you tell me sooner?"*

Loud purring as Khar leaned against her again. **"I don't mean that, though I'd planned to tell you. There's something ... else."**

"What?" She couldn't imagine what Khar alluded to, where this conversation would lead. Suspicion, fear, captured her heart in a lock-hold. *"Not Jenret? It doesn't have anything to do with Jenret, does it?"*

The ghatta reared back, anxious. **"No! I'm sorry. Nothing bad, my honor on it. Truly!"** She resettled, licked a front paw. **"You know how you've been searching for anything you could find about Matthias Vandersma and Kharm?"**

Relieved but still at a loss, Doyce grasped a white paw, shook it gently, held it trapped. *"I should hope so! I wish more material existed, firsthand sources. Sometimes I feel as if I'm fabricating things, pulling them out of thin air to create or re-create his world. Daydreaming with what little I know and then embellishing it."* She laughed, self-conscious. *"Overactive imagination. If it isn't real, I'll make it real."*

"Except that it is," the ghatta pressed along, **"real, that is. Haven't you wondered why you're daydreaming? Who actually wrote the diary you've dipped into now and again?"**

"Well, the diary's of that period, I've no doubt. It probably puts me in the right frame of mind, in the mood."

"Er, not exactly. The diary's the one Matthias kept." Khar took a deep breath. "You just haven't read enough to realize. Haven't you noticed that when you pick it up you become preoccupied, start daydreaming after just a few words? And the daydreams aren't exactly daydreams. We've, that is, we ghatti ... especially the Elders ... are giving you special insight into those earliest days. We've been threading one of our Major Tales through your mind, unwinding it as you watch."

Doyce's hands jerked convulsively on the reins, Lokka snorting and tossing her head in surprise. *"Khar! By the Lady above! What right have you to do that? You know ..."* she shivered, a chill racking her, *"how much I hate being manipulated like that! It's too similar to what Vesey did to my dreams, manipulating them, twisting them inside-out, with me unaware, helpless to do anything about it! How could you?"*

The accusation stung. "But these are true seeings, not distortions. We took the responsibility on ourselves because we hope the past can guide the present. If you understand what Matthias and Kharm went through to gain acceptance, perhaps it will guide us, help Canderis learn to cope with the Resonants."

"Can't we just leave the past alone? We've enough on our plates with the present."

"No, please! You have to continue, have to search for a way to help. It's not just your world that's changing, but ours as well. What sort of world will our offspring inherit if you don't?"

"Well, what am I supposed to do? Let you trance me, let that world wash over me while I passively absorb it?" Anger now, anger at being used against her will. Well, let the ghatti see how much they could cram into her now that she was aware of what was going on!

"That's exactly it," Khar supplicated. "You *can* do it yourself now, you have been, though you didn't realize it. You can do it with your own willpower, without our help. Choose when to enter and relive what Matthias—"
"Matty," Doyce corrected without even realizing it. "Matty and Kharm suffered to found the Seekers Veritas, take

their place in society, not be viewed as different, as outsiders."

"Are you sure this will help? That the past holds answers for today?" Hadn't she complained that leaving Gaernett was akin to fleeing danger? Well, danger stalked all around her, even in the countryside. If she didn't fight it, what would happen? And what would happen if she did? She rubbed at the knot between her brows, tried to push the headache away.

"I can do it myself, when I want? Not wait passively until you decide to spoon-feed me more whether or not I'm ready?"

Hope shot through Khar. **"Yes, I'll show you, show you how to float backward in time and yet remain separate, not let it suck you in."** A gamble, but she took it. **"Besides, it might be nice to have a mental escape, elude your family if things become too much for you. Temporarily trade one past for another. After all, you always daydreamed as a child."**

A certain seductive logic to the thought, remain physically present yet mentally aloof if her reunion became strained. *"Could I try it now?"*

"Yes, but I'd advise practicing from the rear seat of the surrey rather than on horseback. Just in case you become overinvolved. Besides, it'll reassure Davvy and Cady if you're there, quiet and apparently resting."

"We won't reach Coventry until tomorrow at this pace. I guess anything is better than wondering about the reception I'll receive after all this time." She managed a grin. *"But Davvy is not going to ride Lokka for the rest of the day!"* An anticipatory excitement overcame her . . . what was Matty doing now . . . or rather, then?

Matty finished sweeping the packed earth floor with a twig broom, removing the previous night's debris—bits of food, manure from half-scraped boots, the usual odds and ends that constantly sifted from people's pockets or sailed off tables with an expansive arm-sweep. Nothing worth saving, so he gathered it on a shingle scrap, tossed the collection out the door.

"Never know unless you check," Kharm thrummed from where she dozed on a table, tail dangling. **"You've found coins before."** Her head dipped as she caught sight of her disembodied tail below the table and swiped at it as if it belonged to a stranger.

Well, more coins would be nice, but he'd hoarded a fair amount regardless. Not much need to spend them, but having them made him secure. Matty began to scoop up handfuls of dried pine needles from the bin and scattered them on the floor. Jurgen swore it sweetened the air; anything masking the stink in this airless, overheated sod tavern would be a blessing. Spring! Would it ever come? Would the river ice ever break? Waiting, stir-craziness raised to a fever pitch through this long, dismal winter, snow storm after snow storm hemming them in, an ice storm for variety.

Matty'd begun in Gilboa helping with the repairs and rebuilding required after the Plumb's destruction. Almost everyone needed assistance to beat the winter storms, and few free hands were available. He and Solange and Gheorghe had found eager bidders for their work. Some undertook the painstaking rebuilding of permanent structures, snapping their fingers at fate, convinced the chances of another Plumb exploding nearby were slim. Others contented themselves with repairs to their jerry-built, semipermanent structures, cobbled out of the flotsam and jetsam that the confluence of rivers and the sea tide deposited at their doorways. Someone's old door transformed itself into another's porch roof. Sod walls or rough timbered frames patched with whatever came to hand, including old Spacer ship scraps for the lucky ones, passed from generation to generation.

He'd been eager and willing, the work hard but exhilarating, his size and lightness an asset in tight spots or heights incapable of bearing a full-grown man's weight. Kharm would scamper a ridge pole to test it, and then he'd follow, easing along, securing rafters or roofing material.

The basic problem was determining a scale of payment. The barter system prevailed, and he'd no place of his own to store his earnings, not to mention the time consumed in bartering for something he did want—not another smoked ham, three smoothed ax handles, a precious plexi pane slightly larger than his face. At last he grew bold, insisted on coinage, and even that was an education to calculate each piece's

value as he tallied his earnings. Nearly forty years of exploding Plumbs had ruptured the civilization being painstakingly built on the planet Methuen: one of the first casualties
the minting of any sort of currency or coinage. Money now
consisted of whatever odd coins from distant, off-planet fed-
erations that the Spacers had pocketed as keepsakes—Parims
from the Pacific Rim, Reus from the Russian-European
Union, Canusas from the Canadian-USA group, and
Censoams from the Central-South American federation. Plus
a few commemorative coins minted shortly after landfall.
Not to mention dead circuit chips, plexi dial covers and
gauges, twists of copper wiring (prized beyond fiber optic
cable) from the ship remains—in short anything small and
portable that could be assigned an arbitrary value.

Well, he had his stash of all of those, had even unraveled
the values of the copper wiring with its plastic coatings—
dependent on diameter and length and valued as to the color
of the plasti-coating. When the construction boom slowed,
he'd hired on at the tavern Robey and Jurgen ran, no cash
but a loft to sleep in and food to fill his belly and the
ghatta's. Given that winter had set in with a vengeance, he
thought it a fair trade. How Solange and Gheorghe could
survive in their raft shack he didn't know. Not enough blankets in the world to block the winds racing across that river
ice.

He began stacking wooden trenchers, arranging wooden
spoons in a fanned half-circle, the orderly arrangement that
soothed Jurgen's persnickety soul. Not that anyone would
notice the presentation once the night's trade started, but
outward appearances mattered to Jurgen—if he were starving to death, he'd make sure his clothes were clean, his hair
combed. Jurgen obsessed over order, neatness, a dour man
who owned a half-share of the tavern with Robey. Everyone
teased Jurgen about his ways, and he was the less popular of
the two owners, but strangely enough he served as counter-
man, apportioned food and ale, collected the payments, always faintly disapproving of everything under his nose. To
Matty's mind, the division of labor ought to have been re-
versed. Genial and outgoing, a back-slapper, friend to all,
Robey concerned himself behind-the-scenes, ordering the
ale, dickering for the white lightning and occasional wine
that came his way, wine that enterprising women put up—

those who knew how to get a kick to it, not some nose-holding tonic of dandelions or other herbaceous grasses. Robey cooked as well, trading for the wild game and limited domestic meats available, constantly scouting out extra potatoes or carrots or cabbage for sale.

Sure Jurgen was preoccupied, Matty tickled Kharm with a wooden spoon, tapped her between the ears, while she squinted her eyes in sleepy exasperation. "Look out," she warned as Jurgen fussy-bustled around the counter. Looking critically for ghatta hairs, Matty blew on the bowl of the spoon and sleeve-polished it, put it back into place. "Jurgen's not in a good mood tonight, wife's not well again." Matty sighed, the sadness emanating from Jurgen clinging like a damp fog of self-reproach, constant concern for his sickly wife, worry at being away yet again. Sometimes he wished Kharm wouldn't share these outside emotions since he wasn't able to sympathize in return—first because of Jurgen's sparse mentions of his wife, other than that he had one, and second because Jurgen abhorred any appearance of human need. Thankfully, Robey was less complicated.

Given that everyone's temper had been honed by the winter's privations plus Jurgen's heavy mood, Matty wished he were somewhere, anywhere else. Best send Kharm to the loft soon before some fool tied something to her tail and then complained at being scratched. It wasn't only that, he told himself, trying to be fair, Robey and Jurgen had grown as heartily tired of him as he was of them. Sometimes he just blurted things out, things he shouldn't know—mostly in dismay, indignation at some inequity or wrong, not so much to him as to another—Kharm constantly feeding these things into his mind. All it gained him was a muttered, "Self-righteous little prig!" or worse as he elbowed by with fresh ale.

Oh, to be home with Granther and Henryk, see Nelle, discover if she'd mourned his absence, missed him? The ache of it all burned his very soul. Everything was so unjust! And worse, people didn't want to hear about injustice, know the truth!

"Not true. You just haven't discovered how to apply the truth to people's advantage." Kharm rubbed at his ankles, drew back politely as Jurgen passed to light the lanterns. The tavern was beginning to fill, the canvas flap constantly pushed aside, gusts of men and cold air forcing their way in, the peat fire smoldering and glowing. Already too crowded and close with smoke and sour body smells, not to mention the sour thoughts that Kharm transmitted, setting his teeth on edge like sipping vinegar. Everything was just too much! The room started spinning and he forced it to stop, stopped heeding his crybaby sorrowings, concentrated on seeing who needed what, anticipating their demands to help Jurgen keep abreast of serving. Flustered, he'd turn snappish, angry, most likely at Matty. He didn't belong here, didn't know *where* he belonged!

Robey breasted his way from the kitchen, red and sweaty and good-natured with heat, bent to whisper to Jurgen. Frowning, Jurgen retrieved the cash box, misered it open. "How much?" he asked again in disbelief, pushing his thinning hair askew. Robey'd been engaged in protracted haggling over a side of beef, an unlucky cow having broken her leg on the ice. Whatever barter or cash the owner received for the meat wouldn't begin to compensate for the loss of a good milk cow and the calves she would have produced through the years.

Robey's face shone sunny-wide and innocent, crestfallen at Jurgen's testy, disbelieving response. "Best I could do, my friend, best I could do." Jurgen's lips sealed tighter than a purse as he doubled-counted the wire bits and coins.

It hit Matty with a wave of indignation, the words ringing in his head courtesy of the ghatta, as Kharm's ears rose, alert. **"Sure, five for the seller, and two for me. Same's always. Even if you hand them the money direct, they'll see I get my share. Or they won't trade here again."** Not content with half the profits from their partnership, Robey was taking money on the sly! So that's why Robey always worked out back with the suppliers, not out front with their clientele, why Matty'd seen money changing hands the wrong way a few times.

Just let it pass, keep still, he instructed himself, but his mouth wouldn't obey. "Jurgen, want me to confirm the price for you?" Why help one over the other, why make it his business? Why care? Except from the loft he'd heard Jurgen mumbling the accounts each night after closing, mounting expenses wearing him down, striving to put aside enough to hire someone to nurse his wife. The regret shone through him as if he were translucent each time the profits stacked thinner than he'd believed. So little to show for the hard work, the prolonged absences.

He dashed back and returned, shouting over the din, "Likely Robey misheard. Five'll do it." The cow's owner hadn't dealt with Robey before, obviously didn't know Robey's system or that Robey had tacked his own bonus to the agreed-upon price.

"You're sure, Matty? Then why'd ye say 'seven,' Robey?" Jurgen sat tense and still, fingers clenching the coins, suspicions rushing to the fore. Although he hadn't shouted, the tavern went silent, each person hanging on the next words, sensing something was brewing, wanting it to brew and bubble and explode in compensation for their own hard-won control through interminable, boring nights when even loved ones and best friends grated on the nerves. The smallest slight could spark an explosion.

"Ye been cheatin' on me, Robey? Cheatin' on me all this time? Equal partners you always swore. Share and share alike. Seemed like goods cost too dear. Wondered sometimes why I could nose out a bargain and you swore it was dumb luck. Why, Robey, why?" he pleaded. "Your da served under my mum when the Spacers landed. She stood for you on your naming day. We've known each other all our lives, grew up together. You stood beside me at my wedding."

Backing as far as he could until the press of bodies pinned him in, the heat of Jurgen's sorrowing anger burning before him, the crowd's heated expectancy behind him, Robey finally halted, unsure whether appeal or defiance would work. "You niver understood, Jurgen. Wheel, deal, that's the way it's done. Nothing has but one price. We don't charge our customers just what that beef cost us when we serve up a steak, a bowl of stew. Everything gains in value if you improve it. You deny me my value keeping me out back. Up front I'd make everyone easy, laugh more, drink more, jolly them along. Spend more! But you have to gimlet-eye everyone, not lose your control. Well, I just wanted the extra value I deserved now." Pale with rage, Jurgen sprang across the counter, thrusting the cash box in Matty's hands.

"But it's *me* you're cheating! Me! Fair charge on the beef

and we'd botha made more on the meals. Why'd you have to skim it off the top?" His fists were clenched. "Is there a reason, Robey? 'Cause if there was one, a good one, I'd have loaned you money if you needed it, even though I'm saving to get help for Tasha."

"Just wanted it," Robey swaggered with forced bravado, glaring at the smaller man. "Deserved it and wanted it. So I took it."

Jurgen launched himself at the larger man with a vengeful scream, practically foaming at the mouth, pummeling him. Wrath endowing him with strength far beyond his size, Jurgen swept Robey off his feet, the two rolling on the floor, fists pounding, kicking, biting, gouging. The crowd dodged, hemmed them tight, intent on every blow, crude chaffing and cheers, yells of encouragement for one or the other, wagers being laid.

Breathless, Matty crouched on the counter, unsure when he'd taken refuge there, clutching the cash box, the hard corner jammed in his ribs. Kharm had dashed rafterward, clear of the fray, he hoped. He'd started it, all his fault, again. He'd spoken without thinking, without weighing the consequences. He gasped as Robey grabbed a knife, the blade pressing closer and closer to Jurgen's neck. Unable to lever the arm back, Jurgen did the only thing he could do—sank his teeth into Robey's wrist, hanging on like a snapping turtle. Robey screamed and cursed as teeth ground deeper into flesh.

How to stop it, how? No one else would willingly, no one cared, applauding and shouting at the entertainment. Shout that he'd lied, that the price truly had been seven? Not good enough, Robey had already acknowledged his guilt. He threw the cash box with all his might, hitting Robey on the back of the head, the box splitting open, coins, dials, wire bits scattering, decorating the crowd's feet. The money melted like snow on a hot griddle, vanishing as greedy hands grabbed, some retrieving it for its rightful owners, others intent on their own rewards.

With screams and oaths Jurgen and Robey separated, Jurgen spitting blood, and both men crawled about, united in collecting their money, shoving feet aside, scraping at the dirt, rooting under tables. Jurgen rose unsteadily, cash box cradled against his skinny chest, stuffing his random gatherings inside as Robey added his own contributions. "You little troublemaker!" he snarled. "You be out of here by morning! Don't need your kind here, you and that damn larchcat of yours!" Speculation dawned in both men's eyes, a strange, growing surmise not to be credited. "How does he know what he knows? Always something about him that discomforts you—if not him, it's that damn cat staring at you."

But Matty hadn't waited, had already scooted loftward, tumbling his belongings together, checking for his own pouch of hard-earned coin.

"Going now?" Kharm slithered out of the shadows. "Best we do, I think. Spring's coming."

Now she scratched against the little dormer window, shuttered tight against the cold. He could hear shouts below, bellows of complaint, camaraderie, stamps and cries for more ale. Things progressing toward normal and business booming, to boot. Whether they'd ever again look on him as part of the normality was questionable.

He scraped out the window, waited for Kharm to leap on his shoulder as he steadied himself on the window frame below. From there to the back door's overhang, then slide down the post. Awkward with the ghatta and the tote sack, but he did it. Down the road now, jog-trot quick as possible before anyone left the tavern, wondered where he'd gone. Where he was going.

Where *was* he going? He didn't know but made his feet move faster, strangely exhilarated. Up the river, not the Vaalck, but the Kuelper. As he trotted along the beaten down track beside the river, he heard a sudden growl and crushing crunch, a pregnant silence, then another rumble. His face lit with joy. No, not a Plumb, but spring, the frozen river was breaking up, heaving itself into new life!

She lounged in the back of the surrey, eyes downcast on the floorboards, her feet, content to ignore the countryside changing around her, becoming more and more familiar. Each farmstead, patchworked rolling hill, crossroad, the clustered houses of the village brought a pang of recognition. Had she been the only one to change? *"It shouldn't hurt so much to come home,"* she mindwhispered, *"I didn't think it would be like this."* Ever since they'd left the inn this morning she'd refused to take more than a covert interest in her surroundings, as if denying their presence repudiated their reality. Now she swore the surrey's wheels revolved faster, hurtling her into the past, Cady and Davvy innocently and unwittingly conducting her backward to another life.

"Think about Matty and Kharm, where they'll go after Gilboa," Khar urged as she met F'een's aware eyes looking back at them. She wasn't sure how much the ghatt understood, still so young, so untried in the Spirals, but his empathy poured over her, striving to ease her distress.

Doyce swung her foot up, let her heel thunk down on the boards, Davvy startling in surprise. *"Don't want to. I've got other things on my mind right now!"*

"I know." Khar was wearying, tired of playing the game of distraction she'd played all morning and into the afternoon, including convincing Doyce to eat their hurried picnic lunch. A reminder of an inescapable truth: she was hungry again. Worth a try? **"I'm hungry,"** she announced, half-crouched to flee under the front seat in case she'd guessed wrong.

"You're always hungry!" Doyce groused. *"I swear being pregnant has made you hungrier than before, if such a thing's possible."* She reflected on it for a moment. *"It* is *possible, I know. Sorry."* A hand slipped from the coat pocket where it had been hiding, tightly jammed, for most of the afternoon. Cradled in it was a crinkled, oiled paper packet, and a variety of smells assailed Khar's nose, made her lick her chops at two of the smells. The briny, garlicky scent she ignored, hoping it hadn't permeated the other tantalizing odors—cheese and, yes, nutter-butter! Unwrapping the package, Doyce began to munch the pickle, pried two sandwiched crackers apart so Khar could lick the nutter-butter and cheese. The ghatta did so, enthusiastically. And aware, as well, that she'd distracted Doyce a bit longer, diverted her from noticing the scene ahead.

A mantis-thin figure propped on two canes like vestigial limbs stood silhouetted on the rise to their right. A hitch and a shift, and the figure hung one cane over the crook of her arm, shadowed her eyes with her free hand to stare in their direction, into the setting sun behind them.

"Hello, the wagon!" The voice rose high, pitched to carry, and two shy mourning doves burst from cover, wings clattering their dismay. "Doyce! Is it you? Is it really you?" Clambering onto her knees on the seat, Doyce strained upward as much as possible without hitting the surrey's roof. She jammed the last of the pickle into her mouth to muffle an inarticulate cry—of happiness, of distress, Khar couldn't decide. Neither, apparently, could Davvy or Cady as she brought the team to a halt, both of them looking over their shoulders.

The figure bolted down the rise, hunching and bobbing clumsily yet making good time, sure-footed despite her appearance. As she neared, Khar observed one hand jammed into a leather sheath that secured her grip on the cane. The leg on that same side acted equally recalcitrant, dragging, then swinging in an unbroken line as if braced from ankle to thigh. "Francie? Francie!" And Doyce had jumped from the surrey, running equally awkwardly toward the advancing figure. They collided in an embrace so tight that Khar cringed, thinking of her own swollen belly.

With Davvy's and Cady's help they boosted Francie into the surrey, leaving the braced leg angled out, resting on the sideboard. "Straight ahead until you reach the elm," Francie instructed belatedly, "then follow the wagon ruts. Sorry it isn't worn smoother, but we don't get out much." All her attention was directed on Doyce. Khar studied this new person, this person with so much of the same makeup as Doyce and pondered what she saw.

The hair a darker brown, fewer red highlights than Doyce's, as if the sun had had little chance to burnish it, but grayer, chronic low-grade pain leaching the color from it. The oval face thinner, much thinner, cheeks sunken, a thin neck and deep hollows at the collarbones peeking from the open neck of her jacket. But the eyes, the same level hazel ones the ghatta knew so well, yet etched with an equal but different sort of suffering, cross-hatched with humor lines at the corners. All in all, a good human being, Khar decided, and as flexibly tough as a piece of old, well-cured leather if need should arise.

Nervous, Francie babbled, her faulty hand freed of the leather cane support, waving and gesturing, Doyce wincing, drawing inward each time she focused on it. "Are you really staying for a while? And the others as well? We've already decided how you'll sleep. Tight quarters, but glad to have the place full again. We've been bustling ever since we received your letter."

"How's Mother?" Doyce ventured at last, twisting uncomfortably away from the hand.

"Better than she has a right to be. Gave us both a scare, me more than her, I think," then stopped, suddenly. "I . . . you'll see the changes . . . of old age, if nothing more. I suppose I see them, but they register on me differently, more gradually since I'm with her every day. Seeing her after all this time, well, don't be shocked. It happens to all of us." Her good hand stroked Doyce's arm to comfort.

Doyce's face tightened; she rubbed at her forehead as if it pained her. "We've all grown up, grown older, Francie. What I meant was how's Mother taking it that I'm finally returning after all these years?"

Francesca Marbon was not a stupid woman, nor an unsympathetic one. "It was a shock—at first. But a good one," she emphasized. "I think the stroke panicked her, made her really think about her life, not just her fear of failing me. Your coming home gave her the will to fight the fear of another stroke, and that fear can be as lethal, as debilitating as a stroke. She sat there the night the letter came and rocked back and forth all evening, clutching the letter. Sometimes she'd list every task, big or small, we had to do to get ready, other times she'd just stare into the distance." Francie plowed ahead, anxious to explain, "She's happy you're coming, you know. We both are. She only saw you for such a short time when you were ill last new year, staying with the Wycherleys. She swore you didn't recognize her, didn't know she was there, and it ate at her heart. She wanted to stay and nurse you, but she was torn—didn't dare leave me alone. No convincing her I can cope without her. But she was so afraid for you.

"And now this!" Francie reverently cupped Doyce's stomach. "It's as if you've gained everything, finally, everything she wanted for you, prayed for so much. That we've both prayed for you." Keen eyes assessed Khar as well, and the hand shifted, held palm down, fingers curled inward, for sniffing. "And not the only one pregnant, I see. This is the first I've met Khar. Greetings, beauteous ghatta." Khar purred her welcome, nudged the hand. Did Francie like nutter-butter, would she share it?

And now they arrived, the old house standing weathered and slumped from the years, no longer quite as tall and strong and proud as she'd remembered. And smaller as well from an adult perspective. One and a half stories, deceptive because half the interior opened straight to the roof to accommodate the largest loom, its upper windows shedding light straight down on it. Otherwise there was only a combined kitchen/sitting room downstairs and two snug bedrooms upstairs—one that she'd shared with Francie, the other her parents'.

"You'll need a shoehorn to make us all fit!" she grinned, aware it was lopsided, uncertain but desperate to postpone the inevitable meeting with her mother.

Francie gestured back, beyond the house. "We've been dusting and cleaning Father's old work shed. Got two neighbors in to help. Not perfect, but it's tidy and warm, even scoured the woodstove, soot aplenty and three birds' nests in the chimney pipe!"

She nodded, strangely numb, hearing but not hearing, relieved at least one thing had been neatly settled without argument. Where was she? Where was Mother? Doyce kept staring toward the house, and it stared blankly back at her. Simply enter as she always had, as if she'd never left? Or did she require an invitation to do so?

How she could have missed the eyes boring into her from the side opposite the house, she never knew. Should have registered their intensity and nearness immediately, their yearning as she'd pivoted to stare at the house. "Ma'am," Cady said politely, and Doyce whirled around.

Even with Francie's warning, her mother's altered appearance shocked Doyce to the marrow, the tiny figure dwindled away, small as a child's oversized doll. But arms and hands made strong and wiry by years of loom-work reached for her, spilled her sideways into a fierce hug. Maybe, just maybe, it would be all right. And she began to cry with relieved joy against the familiar bosom.

Talk flooded the old kitchen that night, talk that battered and eroded, nearly foundered her with waves of conversation she hadn't journeyed here to have. Better to wait, let them come naturally over time, or let them crest now even if they swamped her?

"Force it and everyone may drown—yourself included." Khar dabbed a paw into the nutter-butter crock, now empty, except for the smears she licked off pink toe pads with gusto.

"I'd rather let the storms rage, have it done with, know where I stand." Stubbornly, she glared at the ghatta, at the smear on her nose where she'd tried to jam her head into the crock. Wooden scraper in hand, her mother bent laboriously and reclaimed the crock, Khar mewling in disbelief until she scooped around the insides with the flat blade and wiped the residue on the rim for Khar's tongue to reach.

"Thank her for me!" Khar almost groaned with delight but her tongue was too busy. Despite her rapid progress, she aimed a final mindthought Doyce's way. **"There's something you should discuss with her and Francie. Davvy, you know."**

For a moment all her own private demons of loss and regret paled in comparison. The enormity of her lapse of judgment, what she'd sequestered here in this isolated hamlet made her doubt her own sanity. Yes, she owed Swan, and, yes, she owed Davvy the chance to live in safety. But was there safety here? Safety anywhere? Or merely an illusion of security, a lulling danger that could threaten them all? Worst of all, Davvy lacked savviness, like a wild animal reared in captivity, gentle and without fear, sure everyone would always nurture him, only to be abruptly returned to the wild, unsure how to protect himself, blithely unaware of who or what presented a danger to his welfare. And she'd brought this innocent into the middle of her own home, perhaps placed them all in jeopardy because of his presence.

Davvy and Cady now slept in the workshop, the Novie Seeker scarcely older than the boy, and both exhilarated and exhausted by the journey and the new environment. Would Cady know what to do if rumors of Davvy's presence reached the wrong ears?

Using the bench to lever herself up, her mother rose slowly from Khar's side, seemed aware where her younger daughter's thoughts wended. "No stranger, no traveler, has ever been stinted by the Marbons—whatever food we could spare, shelter, whatever needful that we could supply." She swallowed hard, her throat constricting, "But I got to know for certain, Doyce, satisfy my own mind, what we're harboring here. Is he . . . what I'm thinking he is?"

Francie stirred, smothered a sharp exclamation as the needle pricked her finger. She glanced between them, assessing the situation, the two figures poised on the verge of speech but both curbing their tongues, but then, both of them were near phobic about openness. Their mother finally continued, "Inez, I said when I read the letter, the girl's tiptoeing round, wanting but not quite willing to say it straight out. Always that way, hugging her secrets to herself as if saying them aloud would shatter them." An almost baleful look in Doyce's direction. "Just like ye never could 'fess up right till the end that ye yearned to be a eumedico. Had to rub my face in the fact that you'd snuck off and gotten accepted, won scholarship money as if you didn't need me or my help!"

Oh, Blessed Lady, it was swelling now, poised to break over her, pent-up years of anger pouring like a millrace, things she'd wondered about, dared not acknowledge, submerging the hurt inside. Pacing the kitchen, fists tight, head jutting forward, Doyce claimed her place in the fray. "You'd never have let me go! You always swore you needed me to partner in the weaving after Da died, or you and Francie couldn't earn enough to live on! You always rubbed my nose in it, how much you depended on me, how much you needed me. But I wanted something else out of life, and for once I wasn't about to let you leech it from me! Not feel guilty anymore about Francie, about you, about this life!" Defiant tears streamed, while the child inside her kicked and pounded in tempo with her throbbing temples.

Francie clouted the table a cracking blow with her cane, deliberately swept the sugar jug and creamer to crash on the floor. Doyce and Inez stood, stunned, as Francie grabbed both canes, surged to her feet. "You are *both* the most stubborn people I have *ever* met! There's right and wrong on both sides, but neither of you ever bother to listen to the full story. Where would you be without any wrongs to hug to you? Mayhap someday I'll tell you, if you'd both listen and not interrupt to salve your dignity. We're hardly poverty-

stricken when we're rich with reproaches." She flicked a
cane, sent a shattered piece of creamer skimming across the
planked floor. "But our poverty or wealth of emotions isn't
what we're supposed to be discussing right now, is it?" Her
cane tapped the table leg as a reminder, Doyce involuntarily
protecting her bottom as if she'd be whipped.

"Cuts right to the heart of things, doesn't she?" Khar
crept from under the table, checked to see how much the
creamer had held. **"No crying over spilt milk, but you can
lap it up. You might consider mending things."**

Sinking into her straight-backed chair, shaking her head,
Francie continued, "I believe we were discussing Davvy and
why he's here. Remember Davvy, nice little chap with
brown bangs hanging in his eyes and the ability to almost
look through you? Know what's going on inside your head?"

Turning the sugar jar lid between trembling, large-
knuckled fingers, Inez Marbon slumped on the bench.
"Doyce, we've got to talk, bury some things, bring others to
light. But Francie's right, that boy . . ." her lips creased in a
thin, bitter line, "he's a . . . he's one . . . of *them,* isn't he?
A . . ." the guttural sound trying to escape her lips alerted
her to her mistake and she corrected herself at excruciating
cost, "Resonant."

Nodding guardedly, Doyce leaned against the wall. Not
that it offered much comfort, but at least it was support, support of a kind her family seemed loath to offer.

**"You haven't given them a chance, slammed doors in
their faces before you fairly opened them."**

"Why not inspect the countryside with F'een?" she hinted
heavy-handedly, the ghatta's mental converse a distraction
she couldn't afford.

**"What? And leave you without a referee? Though I
think Francie has the makings of a sound one."** After an
ostentatiously long, deliberate—and delaying—stretch, the
ghatta ambled doorward, amber eyes surveying them all, impartial. **"But then who'd be present to make one of you
acknowledge the truth? Actually, a formal Truth Seeking
might be well advised. Of course, I'd never meddle in
family matters, except that I *am* family . . . when you remember it."**

"Oh, I remember . . . I remember." She scooped Khar up,
cradled her against the ledge of her belly, and staggered to

Francie, unceremoniously dumping Khar in her lap. "I believe Khar's claiming a neutral corner with you." Marching back to her mother she forced herself to meet her eyes, hazel eyes the twin of her own. And if her mother's eyes now sparked with yellow-green, no doubt her own matched. "You're right, Davvy is a Resonant. An orphan Resonant raised these past twelve years at the Research Hospice. He's a handful, but no more so than any spoiled boy his age."

Inez Marbon's hands came up, not in a warding gesture, but in acquiescence. "Strange. Strange what paths our lives take. You already so burned by what . . . *they* did to you, not once but twice. But the world changes faster than I can spin with it sometimes. Bad and good in every kind of people you meet. While he's a guest, he's one of our own. But he'd better behave." A smile cracked her face. "No antics! And he'd best leave the privy seat down where it belongs— haven't worried about that since your Da died, Francie and I've lost the habit of checking."

A titter of laughter, an unseemly sound, broke from Doyce, finally found voice in a full chuckle that cascaded into a helpless guffaw, mirth gone mad with memory. "Re . . . remember the time you thought Da gone for the night and you came scooting out without a candle? Nearly . . . fell in!"

"Should I be privy to this humor?" Khar sniffed, and Doyce began to hoot.

The three women continued laughing, holding their sides, wiping their tears, and soon other stories were shaken out of memory, dusted and polished and displayed, old and battered, frayed in spots, but still vital, still precious with love and sharing. How her days would pass here, whether she'd fall victim to the unspectacular pattern that comprised their lives, trapped in the amber of predictability, Doyce refused to judge. Wait till morning. Patterns could change. Still, she consoled herself, if I need relief, a break, I can always stay right here, yet join Matty and Kharm. A journey without boundaries within the confines of home. Home.

"Should I mention to your mother that you and Jenret haven't married yet?"

"Doors can slam on tails as well as in faces." But her threat was halfhearted, best ignore the ghatta's teasing. Yes,

home: trouble, spats, arguments, hurt feelings, love, respect, humor, belonging.

Faertom tossed his head, sweat droplets flying from his hair like a dog shaking after a sudden drenching. Borrowing Towbin's sturdy mount, he'd left Twink at camp, reluctant to subject either beast to the killing pace he planned to set. He couldn't bear to listen to Twink's groaning, blowing sounds, her valiant laboring to keep up as he lashed her with the reins, she who loved nothing more than a placid amble. He longed to set a breakneck pace, pounding impulses of hooves hammering away the truth that he'd been cast out. How he'd convinced Addawanna to ride he wasn't sure, but the Erakwan woman had ruminated and—amazingly enough—selected Jenret's black stallion Ophar as her mount, saddleless and bridleless. He'd expected her to be pitched headlong, but she stayed glued to his back, the stallion docile as a kitten. Some instinct told him she could have matched him without the horse, even beaten him to the capital if she'd so chosen.

Close enough to Gaernett—entering the outskirts but still beyond the wall, the night yawning, languishing toward dawn—that he'd risked a mindcall to Darl Allgood two kilometers back and the lack of response gnawed at him. He'd never dared it before with Darl, especially at such distance, half-convinced the man wrapped himself under so many shields of Normality that a late-night cry for help might pass unheeded. And so far it had. Still, Darl should be most receptive at night, sleeping mind uncluttered by his problems as High Conciliator—or thrashing in nightmare terrors from them. Please, he prayed, don't let Darl be too angry at me for this. Let him answer, not ignore me. Not someone else angry at him, abandoning him. Let him explain himself to Darl before he confronted the Monitor, told him of Jenret and the others held hostage, some willing, some less so, by the Resonants deep in the forest. Hostage to Resonant lives and the well-being of all innocent Canderisian citizens, Normal or not.

"You fool! Contacting me like that! You'd better have good reason!" As much as he'd longed for it, the belated

response took him by surprise. Every muscle in his body cramped reflexively, the horse under him veering in a half-circle, pounding back the way they'd come, not because of anything the horse could see or hear, but desperately attuned to Faertom's startlement. Addawanna kneed Ophar after him, grabbed his horse's bridle and brought them around. The hedge rustled as Darl Allgood stepped clear, heavily muffled against the night air and to disguise himself from prying eyes. *"If the Reapers find me consorting with you, I'm a marked man. Just the sort to make an example of. You've some safety as an avowed Resonant, but I've none."*

He patted the trembling horse, sidestepping and twitchy at Allgood's presence; its skin rippled under his hand. *"Come on, there's a woodshed back here. At least we'll be off the road."*

"Good," Addawanna wielded sarcasm like a knife, as if she'd actually heard their mindspeech. "Find us huddle-hidey in shed, no pretend lucky meetin on road. Much less s'picious."

"Madam," Darl managed with some dignity, "Reapers suspect anyone and anything, anywhere. But at least other innocent eyes won't notice us, won't mention our unorthodox meeting in passing as a curious incident enlivening their early-morning journey. Even if Faertom and I escape notice, Erakwa in the capital are novelties." His voice just above a whisper, he walked close to Addawanna's knee, guiding the horse.

After a seething but brief conversation, Allgood mounted and rode like fury for the center of the capital, barely waiting to see if the others followed in his wake. Never had Faertom been passed through the gates so expeditiously, the Guardians on duty apparently taking Allgood as a safe conduct for the others, although they scrutinized Addawanna and Faertom. Shivery and breathless, he returned their stares, head held high. More than mere gatekeepers, military police dealing with human and natural disasters, the Guardians had at last become what they were truly meant to be—soldiers on active duty, transformed by their war with Marchmont and the strange, troubling times around them. Did they know what he was and scorn it, despite their duty to protect all? Or did they vaguely remember him from his other trips through as a

Transitor? He could probe their minds for the answers but didn't want confirmation either way.

Darl led them to the rear of the Monitor's Hall and its living quarters as confidently as if it were his second home, drawn by the faint light at the windows. Elbowing a path through the crowded main kitchen, already pulsing with the day's quota of cooks, bakers, and scullery help, he escorted them into a smaller side kitchen, intimate and inviting, that reminded Faertom all too much of his mother's kitchen at home. His nose began to leak—the sudden heat after the cold, he told himself. The Monitor, fully dressed, and his wife, Marie, still in her robe, sat comfortably at the table, sipping cha.

Marie took one discreet but assessing look at them as they piled in silently, unannounced, poured additional mugs of cha and then left, kissing van Beieven on the top of his head.

Allgood filled in the Monitor as succinctly as possible and van Beieven's voice rasped early-morning hoarse, untested. "Hostage? Damn Wycherley for his stupidity!"

Faertom broke in. "He didn't *mean* to get taken hostage, sir!"

"A regular little stormy petrel, aren't you, Thomas, flapping here to bring me bad news, bad luck again?" Faertom's big knuckles cracked as he clutched the mug, stung by the unfairness. "And the rest of them, voluntarily allying themselves to give the Resonants more leverage! Pleased at least you," he nodded in Addawanna's direction, "had enough sense not to be a party to this."

"Erakwa don' make good hostages—no hold if don' wanna. So whad you gonna do?" she asked in return. "Send Guardians play hidey-seeky in woods, steal Jenret back? Or do somet'ing stop peoples bein' hurt?"

"I don't see how the blazes I can offer reassurances that no one, Resonants or Normals alike, will be hurt! Across all Canderis? Can you?" Mulishly aggrieved, he half-thrust himself across the table at Addawanna. "Well? Can you?"

"Neber easy makin liddle man big man, charge of all. Try grow big fast, support od'ers, od'ers fergit support him."

"Support?—ha!" The Monitor pressed the heels of his hands against his eyes as if to press his brains inside, gave a barked laugh without humor. "I know one job Resonants can have, if any are foolish enough to want it! I'd go back home in a flash!"

Was the Monitor serious about resigning? Who'd govern in his place—one of the High Conciliators? And if so, why not Allgood? Darl would know what to do! Faertom eagerly watched Darl Allgood's reaction from the corner of his eye, distrustful of attempting mindspeech given Addawanna's uncanny ability to sense what they'd said earlier. Was she one of them as well? But her power and endurance seemed bonded to the very earth itself, not a connection mind to mind. Nothing was certain anymore, not when his own kind spurned him, not when kin became enemies. He breathed hope on his original thought, burnished it in his heart until it shone—if Allgood were to become Monitor. . . .

Hands folded in an almost prayerful attitude on the table, Allgood addressed the Erakwan woman. "Put a minority in charge and they're still the minority. Gives the majority an even greater reason to rise against them."

"Phah! You bein' mi-nor'ty, too. Common sense always mi-nor'ty." Done slicing bread, Addawanna began spearing rashers of bacon between the slices, each stab viciously precise to Faertom's nervous view. "T'inking od ways so hard, can't t'ink new. Bedder be t'inking." She took a bite of the sandwich, chewing ravenously. "While you t'inking, Addawanna goin, findin way of savin Wycherley . . . mostly from himself." With that she marched out, sandwich still in hand, leaving the three remaining nonplussed, enmeshed in a dilemma of rising proportions.

Follow her—or stay? Faertom struggled like a fly caught in a spider web, unsure what to do, but trapped all the same. Darl's sickly color told him the High Conciliator felt equally trapped, but at least he retained hidden options, unpalatable as they might be. But Darl would never act on them, he realized with a sinking sensation, would never spring the trap to free himself. Well, he had options, too. The world might feel very empty, but it was up to Faertom to carve a place for himself in it, even if it did turn out he'd dug his own grave. Now, could he catch up with Addawanna?

❖

Gaily caparisoned horses, five carriages, and ten supply wagons, all loaded or nearly loaded, crammed the castle courtyard. Ezequiel Dunay counted under his breath, pencil

tickling the air as he tallied the conveyances. Too bad it
wasn't a magic wand—no under-counts or double-counts
then. If his list weren't accurate, his grandfather, the cham-
berlain, would have his head. Simple enough to account for
horses and wagons, the supplies being loaded, but checking
off the people accompanying the king's royal progress from
Marchmont to Canderis made for a nightmare of milling
confusion. No one held still! Without looking, Ezequiel
reached just above his knee and gave his hose a surreptitious
tug to smooth some of the wrinkles. Mayhap if he didn't
look so disheveled, he wouldn't act it either, could make
sense out of swarming activity. As impossible as counting
bees in a hive!

Easy to spot the neat ranks of Muscadeine's hundred soldiers hand-picked to accompany the royal entourage, aligned
on each side of the gates, ready to fall in in advance and behind the party when they departed. Furled banners would fly
free, boldly colored standards announcing the king and his
courtiers as they traveled. Well, the soldiers weren't his to
worry about, other than checking off their presence en
masse. But the rest, oh, the rest! Had he the eight ever-
welcoming arms of the Blessed Lady, it still wouldn't be
enough! His grandfather, Ignacio Lauzon, had charged him
with supplying the royal party, provisioning every man,
woman, child, soldier, and beast on the trip. If anything were
wrong, incomplete, missing, Ignacio would discover it, be
forced to improvise alterations, compensations for his grandson's mistakes. And Ezequiel would live in dread suspense,
wouldn't find out until later, because Ignacio would accompany King Eadwin and Arras Muscadeine and all the rest on
the grand tour, not him. No, *he* had to stay here, tend the
castle, ensure that Fabienne, the King's mother, wanted for
nothing as temporary regent, support her actions in the
king's absence and the absence of a goodly number of his
most loyal supporters. Important—yes. Crucial, even. But
hardly thrilling. Who else but he could court trouble at both
ends—home and abroad?

He tried again, crossing off names against his master list
as he spotted familiar faces. Except, once verified as present,
he couldn't guarantee the person wouldn't disappear on
some personal errand, wander off to retrieve something forgotten and judged too crucial to leave behind. What might
be left behind instead was that particular person. His head

whirled, ached from the strain, and he heartily wished he could tie everyone up once they'd been counted.

"Wouldn't do, you know," a voice sang out behind him, but he was already turning, alerted by the melodious chiming and chinking of bracelets, a multitude of narrow bangles rattling up and down each arm of . . . he concentrated, hoping one hand was visible. Dwyna! Yes, Dwyna Bannerjee, emerald flashing on her right hand, while her identical twin, Wyn, wore hers on the left.

"Could you give them an incredible urge to sit in the carriages, or mount up and stand ready once I've counted them off?" A forlorn hope, but he knew the answer, respected why she wouldn't employ coercive measures unless it were a crucial necessity. Resonants never toyed with minds needlessly—or heedlessly. He hurried on without waiting, "I didn't realize you were going."

A rueful grin sparked the turquoise eyes, so at odds with that dark complexion and the midnight black hair in a braid down her back. "Wyn threw a tantrum. Insisted I was the silly, sociable one, so I should go instead of her. Said I should represent the Public half of our office while she remained to attend to people's Weal." The twins were Resonant eumedicos who jointly shared the Ministration post of Public Weal Lord, responsible for people's health and well-being.

It didn't seem fair that he and his grandfather, who hated the whole outlandish idea of the tour, couldn't trade places as easily as the Bannerjees had. Dwyna peered over his shoulder, ran a finger under two more names on the list, then pointed. "Over there, on the shaded side. Now don't think they've gone missing, because they plan to go talk with Valeria Condorcet and her daughters. You've already counted them." So, no coercion, but a tad of forewarning from Dwyna Bannerjee.

Obedient, he touched pencil to list again, let the pencil point scribe the air as he searched for others. A party of fifty, including the King and Arras Muscadeine, plus other highly placed officials and important citizens, even a few with families, and at least half of them Resonants. Show the Canderisian citizenry firsthand that Resonants weren't ravening two-headed monsters, the careful inclusion of families'

reassurance they were harmless, with normal family lives
and relationships, just as everyone else had. He hoped it
worked. Hard to believe even his own meager Resonant
skills would arouse suspicion in Canderis. But then, hadn't
he and his own been taught to reflexively distrust and avoid
outsiders to keep the secret of their Resonant skills secure
from Canderis? Both seemed equally outmoded ideas now.
Why deny, ignore, constrain anyone with superior abilities?
Like insisting that musical talent should be concealed, not
nurtured and trained into a great singing voice or instrumen-
tal skill.

With a belated shout of dismay Ezequiel took off after a
child dashing across the gathering area—and one he'd already counted, at that—just as Eadwin and Arras
Muscadeine appeared, Hru'rul and Felix at their sides as
they moved informally amongst the throng. A rider on a
lathered horse had just entered the gates, shoving his way
through the crowd, waving a sealed envelope in one hand,
intent on attracting attention. The Monitor's device was em-
blazoned on his tabard, scarcely visible through the damp
caking of mud and sweat, and his eyes were narrowed and
searching in the midst of a face grimed by a long, hard ride.
Bending, he grabbed for a servant, tried to halt and question
him.

Arras noticed the commotion first and hailed the man,
who kicked free of his stirrups and came running over.
Thrusting out an envelope, he only tardily realized who
stood beside Muscadeine, made a sketchy bow, clearly un-
schooled in high formality. "Sir? Your Highness, sir? An urgent message from the Monitor, Kyril van Beieven. He
asked me to deliver it before you left, if possible. Made it
just in time." Another sketchy bow and he melted back to
grant them privacy.

Eadwin broke the seal, whistled low, and motioned for
Muscadeine to read over his shoulder. Arras's face darkened
as he scanned the message. *"So, Wycherley's being held hostage. I told you, Eadwin, this royal progress isn't wise in the
midst of Canderis's own personal turmoils. Our presence
would be equivalent to rubbing salt in their wounds. Thank
the Lady we received word in time. Surely the whole thing's
off now."* Inner relief wrestled with misgivings, one less
thing to worry about, and yet one more. How was Doyce
Marbon taking the news of her husband's capture? Worse, it

would be totally in character for Wycherley to attempt something foolish, strive to escape against overwhelming odds, get himself killed—and how would Doyce take that, especially in her condition?

Tucking the letter into his surcoat, Eadwin surveyed the courtyard, now stilling as people became aware of silence at the center of activity, assessing its import. *"Van Beieven hasn't canceled our visit. He simply wants us to be aware that the stakes have risen, and that if we decide against the trip, he'll understand."* He shook his head thoughtfully, staring into the distance. *"No, Arras, it's even more imperative that we go now. Their Resonants have given provocation by taking Wycherley and the others hostage, even if their motives are well-intentioned. It's possible we can defuse the situation there, perhaps reassure their own Resonants. It's up to us to alter the balance, make the two sides more nearly equal."*

"Fine, we create a stand-off—and what happens when we withdraw, return home?" Cursing under his breath, Arras savaged his mustache. Alter the balance of power, indeed! Even van Beieven lacked the political savvy or support to do that, his power eroding with every day as he tried to strike a balance, reach a compromise. This was a time to rule, not govern! And he, Arras Muscadeine, wanted to rush to Canderis, either to Doyce Marbon's side to comfort her, or to rescue Jenret Wycherley, if that would ensure her happiness. When had he become so noble—willing to give up the woman he loved to another? As big a romantic fool as Eadwin!

His duty to his king came first, not Doyce's happiness, not his own. Madness to go there now, sheer madness. Either that or Eadwin had grown more canny than he'd realized, envisioning a greater pattern, a greater potential than he could conceive. Fah! Greater potential for disaster, but even that had a reckless appeal. So—go they would, but with him damn near joined at the hip to Eadwin to keep him from harm, and Arras slapped his own hip for emphasis.

"It might be expedient to stop at the Research Hospice, bring Mahafny Annendahl along with us. After all, she is Wycherley's aunt by marriage." And then it hit with a knee-buckling shock and a wintery chill of foreboding. Mahafny! Did she know how Harrap and Parm fared in their quest after Hylan Crailford? Was everything all right? No recent

word had reached him, and he'd relegated the whole thing to the back of his mind, intent on Eadwin's "crusade," as he derisively called it to himself. If anything, that's where he'd anticipated trouble arising, a danger no one else acknowledged, rather than this twist to their problems.

She'd promised to send regular messages, regular reports twice an oct, every fourth day—when had they trailed off? Which meant that either all was well and he was being ridiculous, or that something had happened that even Mahafny and Saam weren't aware of yet. Had become equally distracted by their own multitudinous problems in analyzing how Resonant skills worked. Be damned how they worked! They did, and that was that, but the use of such power by untrained minds worried him. And whatever Hylan Crailford was or wasn't—and he had no idea what she was—something simmered deep and deadly inside her, ready to blow the proverbial lid off the pot when she came to a boil. Never had he sensed such unfocused malignancy in a human being, eating away at her inside. If it boiled over, who knew what could happen?

He registered Eadwin's concern at his long, abstracted silence. *"Maybe we'll be able to free Wycherley, convince our Canderisian brethren to release him to us."* Clear that Eadwin suspected his love for Doyce, was striving to commiserate without being too obvious. And he didn't have the heart to inform Eadwin of his greater, deeper fears. *"How far must we travel out of Sidonie before Hru'rul can 'speak Saam, let Mahafny know we're coming?"* Maybe that was it—Parm and Saam had reached the end of their mindspeaking range. How simple!

With a hundred questions rising to his lips at Muscadeine's chameleonic changes in expression, Eadwin selected one. *"Why not contact them directly? After all, there are Resonants at the Hospice."*

No time to explain, nor did he want to do so, despite Eadwin's logic. An excuse, and quickly. *"I don't know whom to trust—Yulyn Biddlecomb's off with Wycherley. Most of them respect Mahafny, but their loyalties have to be divided given everything happening around them at this point."* And most of all, he didn't want Eadwin to think he'd gotten panicky, although he suspected Hru'rul had some inkling of what his jumbled thoughts encompassed.

Eadwin consulted with the ghatt at his feet. *"Several*

days—at least. With a group like this we won't make good time, and I gather Saam still suffers from some residual mindspeech problems regarding distance, especially now that Nakum's left him to Mahafny."

Yes! That had to be it—Saam and Parm were too far apart! Eadwin had confirmed it. *"You wouldn't consider,"* he paused, not wanting his fears to shout out, alarm Eadwin, *"letting Hru'rul range ahead? Catch up with him later? I'm anxious for Mahafny to know she's coming with us, give her time to make plans."* A plausible reason on the surface. And if there were anything crucial to report, he'd know that much sooner, although so would Eadwin, since that's whom Hru'rul would mindspeak. Still, it was worth a try.

Parm's head hurt. Hurt astonishingly. He cracked open an eye, squinted at blurred suns setting. Shook his head, looked again—better. Only one sun, though there were many moons. Dusk? Already? Stretching each individual toe, he rubbed his muzzy head against the canvas. Canvas? Oh, yes, the canvas covering the goat cart. Been riding, I have, he decided as his head continued its annoying thump-thump-thumping. Hurt, but it didn't matter, so happy, so nicey-wicey, floaty-woaty ... happy. A little purr rippled and buzzed, oooh ... tickled.

He tried to gather his muddled thoughts, floating beneath the surface slippery as eel grass, sometimes as dangerously choking. Oh, yes, walked today, walked and rode, rode and walked, or was that road walked? No, the road didn't walk, but he had, he and Harrap, face creased with an absurdly happy grin, eyes spacily zigzagging across everything in sight, each thing a revelation. Blue feather on the roadway! Oh, glorious, he and Harrap scrabbling to claim it, scuffling over it, both giggling happily at the shared novelty. Such ... fun! Harrap lumbering along with the goat cart, galloping with it, sandals flippity-flopping, clippity-clopping, refusing to let Hylan help. Well, *he'd* helped, given Harrap something to chase, hopscotching along, hind legs springing his rump high into the air.

Funny, he reckoned Harrap had a headache but didn't mind either. How could you care about a minor hurt when you burst with happiness? Harrap had burst as well, a funny, falsetto sound yodel-lodel-lodeling from his mouth. So fortunate to be here, wrapped in each gold-tinted moment, the wonder and wondrousness of it all. Rapture!

And when he'd tired of running, chasing his tail, dancing ghatti gavottes across the roadway and up and down the slopes, Harrap had scooped him up, weak with laughter, and deposited him here on the top of the cart. Yes, lord of all he surveyed, and Harrap his humble servant. An absurd bow, Harrap's robe sweeping the dusty road, Hylan watching as if she didn't approve of their antics, but was somehow relieved, unable to resist them. Such ... fun!

So, they'd stopped for the night. And stopping meant it was almost dinnertime. And dinnertime ... meant, Parm licked his chops, yawned, heard Barnaby stir and whimper uneasily from under the cart. Dog didn't seem happy, poor, poor dog. Not happy dog, not happy as Parm was happy. Must ... cheer him up. But later, because stopping meant ... dinner. Perhaps, oh, perhaps, more of that lusciousness Hylan had sprinkled on their food last night. It had been last night, hadn't it? He didn't care as long as he received more, could read in Harrap's bumbling, fumbling thoughts that he yearned for more, craved it with every fiber of his being. A faint unease—not right, nice, to crave, to covet a thing so deeply, was it? To hunger and hope for something so much it consumed every bit of willpower, swept you away on a riptide of desire.

Parm scrabbled against the canvas, intent on making his legs work, and at last rose, dizzy with delight, head weaving. Yes, yes! Spin, world, spin and dance in kaleidoscopic colors and shapes and sounds and smells that trumpet the infinite glory of the whole creation! Yes, join in the dance with Harrap, but one small thing nagged at his mind. Something left to do, something left to be done? Something? What?

Something about dusk? Something about ... he squinched his face so tight he feared the orange right side might migrate to the black left side, his earring hoop bouncing, tickling his ear. Ears? Hears? Ouch, his head hurt! He pressed a paw between his eyes. Dog whining again, how could he love each particle in the world yet wish the terrier would shut his trap? Ears? Yes, something to do with ears, ears waiting to hear ... ? Scrambling upright, coasting down the canvas covered slope and tumbling off the cart, Parm landed in an undignified heap. The shock cleared his head a little. Didn't matter, but it did matter that he'd promised to report to Saam at dusk. Almost forgot, but almost wasn't the same as forgetting, he consoled himself, couldn't muster the energy to stay worried for long.

After nudging Harrap with his nose, he meandered away, weaving and looping. The big man leaned against a wheel, head tilted back and snoring, utterly limp, a little smile tickling his lips as he smacked after a particularly strident snore. Harrap happy, too! Bless his soul, and Harrap had assured him he had one, he was happy, too. A bobbing halt as he tried to stare at his stomach, finally see his soul inside, his whole being so light and translucent anything seemed possible. No, no soul, nothing remotely resembling a sandal or shoe, just fur . . . but Saam. Oh, yes, that was right, that was what he was supposed to be doing. Silly old serious ghatt, not to appreciate how wonderful everything was, always worrying.

Feet fickle as his brain, Parm haphazardly chose and discarded spots from which to broadcast his mindspeech, whoofling to check the wind direction against his whiskers. Wonderful, airy soft caress! Tantalizing smells! **"Oh, world . . . oh, world!"** he 'spoke with an excess of love. **"Oh, wonderful world that has a Saam ghatt in it!"**

"What's so bloody wonderful about it?" came the response after what seemed a languid, satin-soft pause. **"Where have you been? What have you been up to? I was concerned you'd forgotten to report tonight. It's dark now."**

Parm blinked. Surprise! So it was! When had the dark sifted down, the sun disappeared? Marvelous, like easing the wick of a lamp so slowly that even the flame barely noticed it'd been snuffed. **"Easy, Saam, easy! Such a wonderful day. . . ."**

"I know. You've told me that already—or was it a wonderful world you were babbling about. What's going on there? Anything we should know about?"

"No? Know?" Parm craned his head one way, then the other, tilting his muzzle high. Oooh—stars! **"Oh, no . . . nothing to know. Walking on, you know, no, you didn't know, I know unless I say so. Made good ground today. But the ground's always good, always wonder—"**

"Parm! I swear, what's gotten into you, you're raving like a lunatic!"

The words stung, but Parm shrugged them off. "Oh, by the way, you know what Hylan's carrying in her cart? Trees!" A touch of triumph that he'd remembered. For some reason he thought Saam would like to know.

Saam's 'speech shot back, stung like pellets. "I know she's transporting saplings, you've told me that. But what's she doing with them? Why is she carrying them?"

"Trees," he repeated solemnly, "little baby trees, twiglets, thirsty, always crying out for water, pointing to water."

"What kind of saplings, Parm?"

He yawned, couldn't help himself. "Hitch-hazel. Witch-wazel. Hitchy-witchy wazely-hazely."

"Parm! What's gotten into you?" Concern clear despite the distance. "Are you all right? Is Harrap all right?"

"Oh, of course," Parm ruffled himself, settled his fur with dignity. "Absolutely, of course. Couldn't be finer. Nothing much going on, but if you want us to stay with Hylan, fine. Wonderful walk, wondrous scenery. I wonder ... why we didn't do this before." His stomach growled. Blast Saam for yammering away when he was so ravenous, his very flesh and fur quivering with hunger. He nearly gave himself over to the hunger and yowled with dismay.

As if in reprieve, a distant shout floated to his ears, "Parm, supper!" The banging of spoon on pan for emphasis. Glorious noise, rapturous as the bells on a Bethel chiming! Or was he picking up Harrap's thoughts? "Really must go now, Saam. Oh, and by the way ..." He stood, trembling with longing, tasting the faint remains of that glorious seasoning from yesterday in his mouth, "I love you, old chap. Never fear, Parm's here, on the job, as always."

"But what's your course? What town are you approaching? You promised you'd—"

Town? The truth was ... he couldn't think of the truth ... or the town. Oh well, didn't matter, he would, always did. Oh, wait! "Dales and tales, wry tales, rye grows in the dale, you know, Saam, good old whatsis! You know." Ignoring Saam's demands, he broke the mindlink and dashed off, feet scrambling and tripping, drool threading his chin.

Could he smell it? Yes, yes! Oh, don't let Harrap have it all—save some! I'm coming!

And in the distance at the Research Hospice, Saam sat, perplexed, sorting through what he'd learned, assuming he'd learned anything at all. Parm *was* in one of his moods again, and when he was, it took effort to make heads or tails of what he'd said. But usually at least one nugget of information would be buried there somewhere, waiting to be panned. Dales and tales, wry tales? Rye in the dales? Ruysdael? Mayhap, mayhap not, knowing Parm. It just wasn't like him to be that flighty, as if he were in the grip of something greater than himself. Tell Mahafny everything Parm'd told him? No, not worth it, she only listened with half a mind these days, so intent on tinkering with that infernal machine she hadn't time for anything else. Parm's rhymes wouldn't amuse her. If only she did make time, he'd feel better about things.

The upriver trek in the midst of melting season lasted longer than Matty had liked, a constant foot-slogging battle against soggy snow sharp with splintered ice crystals, wading through clinging patches, jumping freezing freshets of runoff, and worst of all, the dragging, sucking mud when the sun came out and thawed the earth. Still, spring was nothing to sneeze at, though he did anyway, the residue of a cold. His boots squelched, always wet and beslimed, but barefoot season hadn't arrived, not unless he relished seeing his feet blue.

Worst of all, Kharm moaned and groaned piteously whenever he planted her on her own feet, lifting first one damp paw pad, then the other, balefully silent as she skittered from one dry spot to the next. Truth be known, there weren't many—had there been, he'd have fought temptation not to shove Kharm clear and clamor to dry land himself. In penance he'd carried the ghatta as often as possible, slung round his neck like a muffler, toted in his sack, or balanced on his shoulders, her long, curved claws digging through coat and shirt and sweater whenever he slipped or slithered. Blessed be the shepherd near the river who'd offered to trade him a cured sheepskin for three twists of copper wire (one blue, two yellow) and a silver coin, smallish, with the profile of a man with his hair knotted behind his head. Better yet, the man had helped cut a hole in the middle of the fleece to put his head through. Now, with it belted around his middle, he felt warm at last—overwarm, sometimes—and safe from Kharm's claws. The ghatta could cling without lacerating him, and they both rejoiced in it.

Today the sheepskin and all of his upper garments hung on a tilted, rotting fence post as Matty wiped his brow with his forearm and went back to swinging the mattock. Spring had progressed enough that folk could consider planting, and Matty had found a place on the outskirts of Waystown, or Waste-town, as it was nicknamed, helping the Widow Veltbrock till her fields. In build she reminded Matty of Mad Marg, though completely lucid, trenchant to a fault, sparing no more words than the situation warranted, grudgingly subtracted from her daily quota.

Skirts kilted, she labored ahead, leaning into the ox-drawn plow while he followed behind, breaking the clods the blade tossed aside, or running ahead to dig in front of the plow when she backed it after a clanging crunch that indicated she'd uncovered a stone too deep to turn with the blade. Those and other stones he hefted and carried to one side of the field or the other, stacking them for later wall-building. Rough work, his hands and arms stained red with the rich loam, feet and legs as well. Still, a repetitive peace to the effort, a battle slowly being won with each furrow.

Occasionally the Widow had let him spell her at the plow, and he'd realized how much bigger he'd grown, muscle to match the darker down decorating his upper lip, discovered one night in the sliver of mirror the Widow'd hung on the wall. He'd preened, admiring it without seeming to admire it, holding his hand across the down, quickly removing it to judge the contrast. As to the plowing, she'd allowed he'd managed credibly but that she still carried more bulk, the weight needed to drive the plow point deep and straight to match the other furrows.

She stopped now, dragging the reins from her neck and looping them around the plow handle, stretched extravagantly, bodice buttons close to popping. Squatting to work his hands around a particularly large and awkward rock, Matty thought she could almost blot out the sun. She grabbed for the water jug, tilted her head back, and drank so deeply he wondered how she breathed, then poured some over her head. Squinting down at his back and waist as he strained, she announced, "Pants. Tonight. Let'm out."

Thunderstruck, he dipped his head, faltered. "But I haven't got anything else to wear." His shirt didn't hang that long, oh, long enough, but the world was in for a sight if he bent over.

"Sack. Wrap yourself round. Bashful!"

By that evening the idea still lacked appeal as he huddled in a corner, burlap sack even skimpier than he'd realized when he'd cinched it round his waist. Kharm stared at him, candlelight reflecting in her eyes, inspecting him right below the waist, making him itchily self-conscious about the protuberance there. He wasn't, he reassured himself, attracted to the Widow like *that,* but it always reared its head when he least expected it these days.

Kharm had been acting coyly skittish lately, edgy and flirtatious, making outrageous murraowing sounds, arching her back and rubbing anything in sight. Now, as he stood on one foot, then the other, scratchy and bothered, praying the Widow would concentrate on her sewing fast as she could and toss his trousers back to him, Kharm abruptly let out a seductive coo and dipped her forequarters, hindquarters high and swaying. *"Kharm,"* he begged, *"stop acting the fool! Don't make her notice me any more than she has to!"*

But Kharm threw herself on the floor, arching, rolling on her back, digging in her shoulders, caught in some strange paroxysm of delight he couldn't fathom. She rilled and cooed again, began a dainty screech. To his everlasting shame, the Widow rubbed her eyes and speared him with an appraising glance. Blood rushed to his face, his body flaming hot all over. "Gets silly sometimes, she does," he allowed. "Sorry 'bout her antics."

"Sorry?" The Widow snorted. "Why sorry? Spring. Everyone, everything feels it. Wish old Reinholt was alive."

"What?" He clutched the sack closer, not sure he understood, left with a blank that needed filling in, expanding upon. Something he knew, or at least sensed but wasn't catching. Then, for no reason at all, he became scared. "Is there something wrong with her, something making her act like that?"

Sharp teeth bit the thread and his trousers sailed through the air at him, entangled on his head since he didn't dare let go of the sack to grab them. "Heat," the Widow's lips drew back, as if she'd nip him as she had the thread. When he still looked blank, she expanded, "In heat. Wanting a mate. Announcing she's ready. Larchcats aplenty coming courting, fighting and screaming to win her."

It dawned on him, sick certainty twisting his stomach, souring his mouth. Impossible to miss, so obvious! But not *his* little ghatten, his precious little one, his own. And now, now he'd lose her, she'd run off and mate, abandon him, revert to the wild, find one of her own to love. Just as it should be, just as it would have happened if he hadn't rescued her, tried to civilize her.

He slunk behind the storeroom door and, sheltered, pulled on his trousers, Kharm following and rubbing against the door, threatening to open it and expose his nakedness to the Widow. *"You're going to leave me,"* he accused. *"You won't want me any more, won't want to share my thoughts, won't have time for me."* Unprepared for what the loss of her would be like, the wrenching ache it would leave—until now. Would even miss her thoughts stealing into his, telling him truths he didn't want to know.

She rubbed and purred louder, stopped short. **"Leave you? Why leave? Love!"**

"You won't need me if you have a mate and ghatten. They'll take all your attention, nothing left to share with me. And that's the way it should be, the way nature intended it." It frightened him; he sounded too much like Granther. Was his wisdom born of such equal pain? But his grandmother had left for an ideal greater than love and family, deserting husband and son, Matty's father.

"No, no, no!" The ghatta wandered restlessly, paced, torn between the door outside and the room here with Matty. The Widow watched, attentive and aware, warmed by the wordless epic struggle of surging need. **"Don't want ghatten yet! Don't want to leave you! Help me not to leave you! Help me!"** Outside a hoarse merow racketed up and down the scale, a shivering, urgent wail, beckoningly seductive. The hair on the back of Matty's neck rose and prickled. **"Mine! You are mine, I am yours! So weak! Oh, that call! Help me!"**

Frightened eyes entreating the Widow, he begged silently, mouthing unformed words, desperate to ask but not sure what to ask for, how to ask. Like a statue come to life she rose, checked the outer door was latched, the two windows closed tight. "Don't want her pregnant, so young." She hesitated. "Only one thing to do."

"What?" Any hope, any hope at all he'd embrace, even the Widow—where had that thought come from? "Please, tell me. Is there something I can do? I don't think she wants to, but nature's awfully strong."

"Aye. Lock'er up." A deep breath as if girding herself, and she folded arms across her broad bosom to barricade herself inside. "Shed. Noisy, though."

"Lock her up," he repeated obediently, still hazy on the ramifications of her advice. "Lock her up in the shed."

"Aye. Day and night. Don't let her loose, no matter the racket inside or out. Should calm in an oct or so. May drive us mad screaming to get free. Your choice. Her choice. Lucky no neighbors close."

Bending, he stroked the quivering striped sides, hugged her to his knees, felt her pulling away against her will. *"Kharm? Your choice, not mine. I can lock you in the shed, bring you food and water, sit with you when I can. Or you can go free, go back to your own."*

She gave a scre— and jumped for his shoulders, and he cursed the ja— sheepskin. **"Do it! Now! Oh, Truth! I k— hat cries promise but don't want to — ss the urge. Must ignore it—just — I'm not like other ghatti, I am**

'd wrapped Kharm in his sheep-
is arm tingling all over, blood
low equally affected, licking
run her hand down his neck,
it away as if she'd been
door, shoved him and his
door propelling him, he
d and yellow eyes pul-
t, and deposited Kharm
ws, loose boards, the
lands over his ears to
to house. Found the
and alone.
s anguish. . . . As
carcerated for her
ever before, work-
oor would damp his own

bodily desires, block his thoughts, Kharm's cries savaging
his brain as she fought to conquer her body's biological
urges. Teeth clenched, temples throbbing, questioning everything he knew, Matty pried rocks free, rolled or carried them
into piles, worked the mattock so fiercely he almost chopped
his own toes numerous times. Throughout it all, the Widow
remained silent, but so, so achingly near that a carelessly
outstretched arm could graze breast or buttock as she hovered, watching him sweat and strain, still wordless, as if that
night's near-loquacity had bankrupted her of speech for the
following days. Nights were no better as he spread his pallet
in the shed to escape the Widow's earthy, salt-slicked scent,
her moistened lips, shared Kharm's imprisonment, sleep broken and fragmented as his randied thoughts.

Pausing, Matty wiped his hands on his trousers, wished
the Widow had shortened the legs the way Granther did
each spring, but he'd rolled them as best he could. Digging
fingers into the dirt, he burrowed to determine precisely
how far down this particular rock reached, dug deeper,
seeking the curve that would indicate he'd reached bottom,
could sink the pry bar and lever it free. It seemed to extend
forever, hiding deep in the ground, coupled with the planet's very core. Buried and obscured—hidden. What was
truth?

He gasped and dug harder, dirt flying. Was there
genuine, original truth lying in wait to be discover
putable? Were there different kinds of truth? And
Kharm possibly know them? How could she loca
people's minds when they didn't seem aware tha
them?

Indisputable, huh? He rammed his hand and
into the soil, fingers groping, snarling as a finge
Like $1 + 1 = 2$? Except Granther had explaine
sort of number code to him, numbers that form
basis for the computers, those strange, sentient
had made the spacecraft function. To those m
ther had said, $1 + 1 = 10$. Binary system? Ba
thing like that. If they were both true, did
different facets of the same truth, expres
ways? Binary—the Widow was binary. St
Think harder, puzzle it out!

Yes—at last, a bottom to the rock, dee
ever before encountered. Have to dig more

the pry bar, find something—another, smaller stone—for a fulcrum. Question: If a person says he's a coward—knows it from past experience, past actions—that's true, but does that truth always hold in the future? Once a coward, always a coward? Or was that a finite truth and future truth still to be written? How much could you change yourself, or were you always what you were inside? A true kernel of yourself that you never really became acquainted with. And did he want to? Maybe that was Naked Truth?

Worse than pulling a tooth, heaving this rock free from the middle of the field. Why bother? The Widow insisted it had always been there, that she plowed around it every year, just as her late husband had. Sunk too deep to remove. So why try?

And if there was truth, what was a lie? Did you always lie on purpose? Or could you lie through ignorance, misunderstanding? He rammed the pry bar home at an angle, sinking it deeper into the earth, boring toward what he believed was the bottom of the rock. But what he believed could be false—couldn't it? So did that make it a lie? What the Widow believed—that this rock would remain here for the ages—could be equally false. But what about those who lied on purpose? The Killanin boys'd throw a lie at you as readily as a rock. Different ways or kinds of lying? He sank in his heels, flexed his knees and began pulling the bar toward his chest. You could . . . umph! . . . distort, twist the truth. Umph! . . . evade it or . . . umph! . . . fabricate it. What was the expression, "made it up out of whole cloth"? Cut it to your fancy?

The muscles on his back and arms bulged as he swung around on top of the bar to put his shoulders into it, leaning his weight on it. Movement? Had the rock shifted, heaved a little before settling back? The strain ridged his neck, shot down through the muscles of his gut. Mis . . . represent? Conceal something, refuse to admit it? Or totally deny it to yourself? Everything swam before his eyes, black and red spots floating thick as midges, breath whistling in harsh, burning gasps from distended nostrils.

A squalling cry from the shed, a clawing and scratching at planks, desperate sounds. **"Truth is everywhere! If you want it, if you don't lie to yourself."** Another cry, coaxing, seductive. **"In the air, in the earth, in everything—not knowing, not acknowledging is blindness!"**

Yellow spangles wriggled like maggots, joined the black and red swarming dots. Blindness—not such a bad idea, mindblindness, that is. Simply Matty as Matty, not the vessel into which Kharm poured her knowledge of the world's perfidies. How did she do that? He spat on his hands, grabbed again, knuckles bulging white with strain, the cords on his neck popping. An unexpected bulk joined his on the pry bar and heaved with him, the Widow adding her considerable strength to his puny efforts. And with rising excitement he felt the rock yielding and shifting, reluctantly rising, erupting above the earth, tumbling on its side. Free at last, not immovable, permanently planted for the ages!

"Done it, boy! Ye had faith. Reinholt didn't, I didn't. Always trusted him. You didn't believe me without testing my words." She slapped him on the back; the blow stung his aching, moist flesh, made him tingle all over. Pride that he'd persevered, conquered something, even if only a stone.

"Conquered! Truth found!" Kharm's mindvoice plangent through the sticky afternoon air, ripe with unshed rain. **"Wanted to mate ... but wanted you more! Need you, and you need me!"**

The Widow shoved her personal water jug into his trembling hands, not making him traipse for his bucket and dipper, impossibly distant in the shade at the field's edge. He gasped as the sweet water poured into his mouth, down his throat, wondered if he could drink forever, throat working convulsively. The cold water hit his stomach fist-hard, cramping in shock. He lowered the jug, gasping, one arm clutched across his gut at the new pain. Straightening with care he returned the jug, and the Widow raised it in a little salute before she drank.

"I think," he dug toes into the cool, damp soil, peered into the gaping socket of earth where the stone had rested, "that we let the ox haul this. Don't think I can roll it to the side." He tried, experimentally, critical of his efforts, "But then, maybe I could. Just don't know." Truth was like trying—you couldn't know until you tried.

"Ox it is, boy. Set your mind to it, ye could. But lack the liniment you'd need." He grinned for the first time in days. Grinned harder as he realized that the yowls from the shed had tapered off, peace descending on his ears and in his brain. Kharm was sleeping, relaxed, lust slowly fading from her body. And the Widow just looked like a nice, large widow-lady, no longer an object of desire. "Aye, another day or so and she's safe to be let out."

PART
FOUR

Doyce squirmed to resettle her back pillows against the cedar bench tucked in the grape arbor behind the house. Most of the leaves were withered, crisped with autumn, and they clattered in the occasional breezes. A few small overripe bunches of unpicked grapes remained, shriveled and brown, but exuding a resinous, winy smell. Absently she plucked one, squeezed it between her fingers, licked at the oozing trickle of thick juice.

"Well?" Khar sniffed the grape, inspected it from all angles—feh, musky, not to her liking. **"How did it go? Did you enter Matty's and Kharm's world?"**

"Thought you'd know that. Weren't you monitoring me?" Had she been left to trespass alone through another age, cross invisible boundaries with Khar absent, not sharing the journey? She clutched the tattered diary, leather sticky against her hand's rising heat-fear, the grape juice. *"Weren't you?"*

"Of course," Khar soothed. **"But how much can you remember, how much do you remember? It's not a fantasy land to avoid the here and now."** A white paw grazed her knuckles. **"Besides, what I see and hear through you may not carry the same weight. I'm more tuned to Kharm than to Matty."**

Despite herself, Doyce winked at Khar. *"Sex, eh? Does it every time. The wanting, the longing . . ."* and stopped, physical longing for Jenret leaving her hollow with unfulfilled desire.

Huffy, the ghatta snapped, **"I've had enough of that recently, thank you very much. And so have you. Both of us from the looks of things."** A reminiscent look filtered her amber eyes. **"But it was nice, wasn't it?"** They both sat, silent, savoring the memories, theirs, rather than poor Kharm's unrequited longing and lust.

Gayle Greeno

"All right, I'll check the diary. See if I remember more details, more flavor than Matty's entries reveal. This second time should prove whether I'm succeeding on my own." Opening the diary she licked a finger, paged through until she found the right entry.

I think Kharm is louzing the urge two mate. She is so strong. But i m stronger two. I moved a rok that the Widder sayed couldn't be moved, but i didn't believe her. She wassnot li-ing but she did not no the truth. I found the truth. But it hurt. Thair r all kinds of truth and all kinds of lize. Well, not re-lee all kinds of truth, but different faces two it. Kharm iz helping me read behind the faces. $1 + 1 = 2$. $1 + 1 = 10$.

"Don't think I'll need it any more, do you? Our reaction proves it."

"Oh, oh," Khar warned, "I think another kind of truth is heading our way." Looking up, Doyce saw Francie approaching, canes probing ahead like an insect's feelers, testing and tasting the path she navigated. Her sewing basket was slung over her shoulder, strands of embroidery floss and gold thread spilling free, trailing behind.

"Want company?" she called and halted, waiting. In truth, Doyce didn't; that was why she and Khar had escaped to the grape arbor, hemmed in inside the compact house, new habits conflicting with ingrained ones, Davvy's and Cady's eager voices jumbling the dynamics of expectations, personalities. Best to be flexible, too much candor and frankness wouldn't help anyone right now, would dismantle what she so tentatively rebuilt with her family.

"Of course," she waved a welcome, slid along the bench to make room. Once Francie's cane wedged under a root, and Doyce controlled herself to not jump up, offer uninvited help. Francie had her pride and with good reason—she could function. But every time she focused on the withered hand and arm, the leg painfully stretched in its brace, it magnified her own remorse, her guilt.

"Guilt? We've been over that before," Khar reminded her.

"I know, I know. I know rationally. But you can't be sure, because it happened before your time. All you can see is what I've internalized." What she could do was unburden Francie, take the sewing box so her sister could maneuver onto the bench without the box bumping.

With a grimace of thanks, Francie possessively drew the worn wicker box to her as if its familiarity comforted, her identity concealed within it. Doyce craned to look inside as Francie opened it, hoping for a clue as to what her sister had become, beyond the label of "crippled." Everything so neatly organized, confident in its place, except for those few errant strands—Francie trying to escape the confines of her life? Francie had garnered local fame for embroidering intricately decorated trims and braids to be sewn on cuffs and collars, hems and waistlines. How she could bear the repetitious, meticulous details, the flying needle endlessly reworking itself in practically the same spot gave Doyce a panicky feeling of constraint. But that skill was Francie's contribution to the family's coffers, weaving trim on a small lap loom and then enhancing it with needlework. Having trained herself long ago to work left-handed, Francie began to ply her needle. It seemed it took forever to finish even a few centimeters of banding, color worked over color, finicking delicate stitches, demanding patterns that scrolled on, never-ending.

"Argh!" Exasperated, Doyce drove her fingers through her hair, gave the trim a tug to attract Francie's attention. "How do you find the patience? Over and over and over. Don't you have nightmares you'll never reach the end? Don't you get bored?"

Francie selected another color, began the diagonal overcast stitching. "Oh, there are minor compensations, though sometimes I'm the only one who appreciates them. Take a close look at the edging on Miz Swain's overvest sometime."

"What do you mean?" Doyce tried to picture it in her mind, remembering the woman who had bought two ells of fine-weave wool from her mother yesterday.

"Here." Francie smoothed a short length across Doyce's knee. "Couldn't resist a memento for myself."

Doyce examined it, held it near and far, turning it, angling it this way and that. A scrolling pattern of birds and foliage. Turned it sideways, flexed it to catch the light and gasped in glee. Subtle, very subtle, almost undetectable unless you hunted for it, but visible nonetheless. Minutely worked in the spacing, apparently part of the pattern, she could discern the shadow script, "Fat sow, fat sow," repeated over and over. "Does Mother know?"

Indignant, Francie snatched it back. "Of course not! And don't you dare tell her or Mother."

"But how can you enjoy it without sharing the joke with someone?"

"I just did, didn't I?" The laugh lines evaporated from Francie's face. "Doyce, there's something else I should share with you. It's been too long, and I'm not sure I fully realized when we were younger what it meant to you, did to you. Or to me—because accepting wasn't easy, either. Time you knew the truth, stopped miring yourself in guilt and fears. But you refused to listen before, ran crying when Mam or Da tried to tell you."

"Explain what?" She lobbed the words back like hostile missiles to defend herself against the opening skirmish, avoid confronting her sister or herself. "I don't need anything explained, rationalized after all these years, Francie! I know what happened, I was *there!*" Hard, so hard, to carry the humiliation, the shame for all these years. Oh, she'd repented, but lacked a way to expiate it, offer a penance capable of making a difference, changing a thing. The child within her kicked, drummed tiny feet and fists against her, butted in time with her agitation. Discomfort, but not as severe as what she faced each time she saw Francie.

"I know how you became paralyzed, Francie, it was all my fault! If I hadn't pushed you . . ." she covered her face with her hands. "Don't make me relive it again!"

But Francie continued to stitch, implacable, without removing her eyes from Doyce's face. "So tell me what happened," she challenged. "I want to know every detail you remember. Don't make up anything, don't gloss over anything. Relive it, if you dare," she taunted, "and I'm sure Khar will tell you if you stray from the truth. Am I right?"

Doyce rose, seething with resentment, almost downright

hatred, at herself, at Francie, for making her confront this. Couldn't the past stay the past, couldn't any of this be left alone, not prodded and picked to death? She grasped the arbor lattice with strained fingers, staring through it, beyond it. Finally leaned her forehead against it so that the lattice served as a kind of spectacles, framing and focusing her thoughts.

"Or blinkering your vision."

"End of winter," she began, coughed out the words. The pond lay on the other side of the knoll behind the house, and they'd spent much of the winter days outside, sliding on the sled their father had made them. Francie, the elder at seven, always steered, while Doyce, almost five, rode behind, arms locked around her sister's waist. Sometimes Francie stretched full-length on her stomach, knees bent, feet waving in the air, while Doyce piled on top, their faces rosy-cheeked with cold, chapped and wind-burned, hair sticking out from under their knit caps. Sailing, zooming down the hill, across the frozen, wind-swept pond, crashing into drifts, rolling in the snow. Shrieks of laughter, sharp and ice-bright in the air.

But that day had been different, the past few nights unseasonably warm, snow melting, pond ice rotting, refreezing each night to display a deceptive solid surface. Oh, they'd been warned not to venture on the pond, that it wasn't safe even for their minimal weight, and Francie had conscientiously steered the sled to one side or another as they glided downhill, ever-obedient, the responsible elder.

The last trip down something had happened; Doyce clenched her eyes shut, strove to see it, feel it. The sled slewing, the stoppage of motion—what? a runner worn through the snow down to the grass?—the abrupt halt, the sensation of flying, screaming with delight. And Doyce had landed on the icy pond, the cattail outcropping near shore, her sudden weight forcing little water geysers to spout around each stem where the ice had melted away.

Francie, still on land, rolled over and righted herself, shoving up her red knit cap where it had sunk over her eyes. "Doyce, get off there. Now!" she yelled from the bank, mittened hands sinking into the rotted, raddled snow as she struggled to her feet. The disapproving tone made Doyce laugh, giggle more wildly from where she lay on her back, dizzy with watching the clouds swirl above her, waving her arms in arcs, sweeping her legs back and forth, regaining her

breath after the breathless landing. Even the ice laughed
with her, little creaking, wheezing sounds, bubbling burps.
"Doyce, you're going to break through!"

Francie's hand on her ankle, tugging her toward shore,
and she fought and kicked, not ready to leave, digging mittened hands into any cracks and protrusions in the ice she
could find, faintly surprised when one mitten came back
sodden, soaked with water. Surprise gave way to dawning
recognition as a gush of water flowed up her back, her fanny
sinking as the ice beneath gave way. "Francie!" she'd
screamed. "Getting all wet!" Scared now, and cold, her coat
growing heavier and heavier.

But Francie continued pulling, Doyce helping now, not
fighting it, until at last Doyce lay safe on the bank. Rolling
onto her stomach, she saw her knit cap, a bright sunny yellow, forlorn on the ice. "Mama's going to be mad!" she'd
wailed, remembering all too well the fierce scolding three
days earlier when she'd mislaid the hat, thought it lost. Panicky, heedless of anything except her goal, Doyce began to
worm her way back across the ice.

Weight pinned, froze her in place as Francie lay atop her,
halting her, then dragged her back by one wrist, mitten and
coatsleeve parting company to expose the skinny extremity.
Francie swung with all her strength, let go and sent Doyce
stumbling toward the shore. Regaining her feet, angry beyond measure, she charged Francie, wool-covered fists
pounding and thudding, pushing. "That hurt, Francie! It
hurt!" Tears streaked her face, warmth burning against
chilled flesh.

Releasing the arbor, Doyce turned to face her sister, tears
streaming down her face. "I pushed you again, and you fell
backward, the ice gave. Slabs of it rising on either side of
you, the water splashing up, the slabs settling back down. I
pushed you in and then . . . you took fever from that, a burning fever that even the eumedico couldn't bring down before
it'd done its damage. If I hadn't pushed you, you wouldn't
have fallen through, taken sick, wouldn't be paralyzed."
Arms embracing her stomach, she moaned, swaying, hic-
cuping with the strain.

"Think about it," Khar advised, **"concentrate harder on
those last few images. You jumped to the end, left something out."** While Francie said, "Nonsense, almost right, but

not quite. What you wanted to do and what you did are two different things."

Head slumped, she tried to picture it, reenvision what had happened in those frenzied final moments. Why could she see Matty's and Kharm's lives so clearly but not this? **"Emotional involvement's not the same,"** Khar offered.

Emotional? A child's rage and fear bringing her to a white-hot boil, the world narrowed by her fury—at Francie for tossing her like that, hurting her, bossing her around, worry over the discarded hat, although that stood a distant second now. Lips peeled from pearly baby teeth, grimacing as she lunged at Francie, fists flailing, and . . . fell flat on her face, screaming with resentment, wailing for her cap. Francie had cautiously turned, judging the hat's position on the ice, debating whether she could reach it when her foot slipped and she crashed down, an incongruous look of surprise on her face as the ice split beneath her. The yellow knit cap sailed skyward, descended, and drifted like a flower petal on the now open water.

"I . . . didn't push you?" she appealed. "You were going after the cap even though . . . you knew better?"

"Oh, you wanted to shove me, right enough. Figured I'd redeem myself by rescuing the hat. Redeem myself with you—and with Mam if you tattled that I'd hurt you. Always had to be the good sister, the responsible one, keeping you out of trouble."

"In other words . . ." Doyce couldn't bring herself to say more, her sense of relief alien and unsettling.

"It was an accident. If you hadn't run back to the house to fetch Mam and Da, I would have drowned. You're not responsible, not for me falling in, not for me coming down with a brain fever, nothing." Francie jammed the needle through the unembroidered fabric, rolled the band around her useless hand, overlapping it to make it neat. "Easier to store this way."

And for the life of her Doyce didn't know what to do, how to react to this revised knowledge. Letting go of guilt and pain, remorse and sorrow, wasn't easy. What to replace them with? The potential of a new beginning for her and Francie, unclouded by the past, an adult relationship to be forged if she were brave enough. "I don't suppose I could order some special embroidered trim from you? Something with stylized ghatti on it?" She picked over the next words in her mind, discarding some, unsure which to choose. "And possibly something worked into it—a secret message, a secret reminder? What do you think—dunderhead, numbskull? Dumb cluck?"

"Dumb cluck is appealing, but that requires a chicken motif, not ghatti."

Although sorely tempted to toss a suitable rejoinder their way, Khar discovered a more pressing problem staring her in the face—through the lattice, to be precise—and Khar slipped around to confront it. F'een, with his odd, diamond-patched stripes, stood his ground, tail flicking, olivine eyes stubbornly determined. Khar conquered an overwhelming urge to administer a chastening swat for such bald-faced temerity. Instead, she sank her claws into the grass and set herself firmly so he couldn't brush past.

"**But we've just had word! She must be told immediately!**" he protested. "**You can't hide the truth from her—Jenret's been taken hostage!**"

"**I can and I will, if I think it necessary.**" How she disliked youth sometimes, so full of the importance of their new role as Seeker Bonds, brimming with innocent self-confidence after studying so hard, absorbing so much, certain everything ran exactly by the rules. Well, there were rules and there were rules.

"**If you don't tell her, I will, or I'll insist Cady do it. It's her right to know.**" The ghatt made ready to lunge by her. He might be younger, faster, but he wouldn't make it, not if she had to rip off half his ear, spit it in his face.

She exposed her fangs, snarled under her breath. "**And I heard the message as well. Koom on Mem'now's mindnet. Mind you, they've delayed in informing us, and the Seeker General didn't specifically say to inform Doyce. Koom simply said we should be aware of the situation. Tell her about Eadwin's royal progress if you're bound and determined to tell Doyce something, even though she's not your Bond.**"

The ghatt persisted. "**But why not tell her? How dare you keep secrets from her?**" He almost wailed his dismay, skinny tail lashing. "**I couldn't hide something so momentous from Cady! She trusts me!**"

The question was whether to lay down an edict—which she wouldn't hesitate to do, given her seniority, her height on the Spirals—or whether to explain her predicament, one that all knowledgeable ghatti would have deduced. Did he have enough sensitivity to understand, even lacking the experience? What did he—or Cady, for that matter—truly know of Doyce or herself? Oh, the tales, of course, the swashbuckling stories of heroism, their ability to conquer all foes. And of course F'een would blithely assume she and Doyce would dash to Jenret's rescue. That's what courageous champions did, after all.

"**One little thing,**" she grated, and flicked her whiskers in Doyce's direction. "**One little thing you haven't taken into account, have you? Think, simpleton! Try to see!**"

Itchy with impatience, the poor ghatt stared at Doyce sheltered by the arbor, wondering what he was supposed to see. "**Well, uh ... she's increasingly great with ... child,**" he finally mumbled.

"**Child?**" An ominous inflection convinced him he'd inadvertently slighted the truth, had better think harder.

The ghatt concentrated. "**Two? Doesn't happen often for them, does it? That's why she's so big.**"

"**Pregnant women are *not* identical to pregnant ghattas.**" She let that sink in. "**Those babies want to come early, and you'll increase the risk by telling her Jenret's been captured. She won't sit still for that, and I won't have her galloping around the countryside on Lokka without regard for the babies. I've never seen a human ghatten born, and I don't intend to see it alone in the midst of the forest with hostile Resonants or Reapers leaping out of the bushes. She'll have it properly—the way humans do!**"

"Oh." The ghatt's head bowed, and he licked a flank, glared his fractious tail into submission. Another, more perceptive, "Oh!" as enlightenment dawned. "**Truly—they don't just drop them?**" and shook himself in embarrassment. "**Of course, truly. I apologize.**"

"**Jenret can take care of himself for the time being. He and Rawn would insist if they thought Doyce would attempt anything foolish, imperil herself or the babies.**" She thought it was beginning to sink in, wash over the ghatt that experience counted far more than abstract learning.

"Cady and I could go instead, in your place." A certain hopefulness seized him, perked his ears.

"And your place is here, that's why you were sent—to protect Doyce and Davvy. After all, you and Cady scored first in self-defense, despite your size." She let the compliment meld with the comment about his slight build to take him down a peg, remind him of his duty and Cady's. "Now, can you convince Cady not to say anything?"

"I think ... yes." He paused. "We still have much to learn, don't we?"

There were moments when Khar'pern found herself desperately tired of teaching.

The old man held a steady, ground-devouring pace, not too fast but sure-footed. He laughed softly, these wooded, rolling hills as intimately known as the wrinkles on his face, old, familiar friends, a mapping of sorrows and joy. Same with the woods. Not much he didn't know about the southeast wedge of Canderis. Man and boy he'd hunted, fished and trapped this land when he wasn't on the road with Esmerelda, his donkey, drawing the cart with his knife-sharpening gear.

He'd shoved the cart into a hayrick at the edge of a deserted field, unharnessed Esmerelda, and slapped her butt to send her off safe. The sense of being followed had lain heavy on him for several days, eyes spying out of nowhere, rustlings where there should have been none. Nobody'd be out to hurt Uncle Billy, now, would they? Uncle Billy, as familiar a fixture as ever could be, traveling with Esmerelda, never staying overlong at any one place, but sharing gossip, listening, as he spun the circular whetstone into motion, hands steady setting steel to stone. Sparks flying, the grinding sound that set some people's teeth on edge but music to his ears, wrists cocked to hone just the merest edge, sharpen without wearing away too much. Yes, Uncle Billy's blades stayed sharp, and he stayed sharp and safe by never outwearing his welcome.

Well, be damned to them, that pack of teenage boys could follow all day and all night if they chose, and he'd lead them a merry chase. Exercise'd do them good, learn them a lesson. And that half-trained pack of hounds didn't frighten him a whit. He'd made friends with just about every dog in each town, a wise precaution. If that didn't suffice, he had his pepper packet handy but hated to use it. Wished he could fling it on the boys, he did, set them a-sneezing, coughing and choking, tripping over deadfalls as their eyes teared and watered. Dogs'd never been Uncle Billy's enemies. No, nor people, either. 'Specially if you let them see what they wanted to see. Hide in plain sight, and that's what he'd done ever since they'd massacred the Fifty, his cousin and brother amongst them. The Lady'd smiled on Uncle Billy, saved his foolish young hide that fateful day by giving him the green-apple quick-step, too busy scooting down the path that night to join them. No, acting standoffish, cowering, shrinking from normal, everyday contact made folk suspicious. But not of a fine, upstanding, outgoing citizen like Uncle Billy.

Stream ahead, and he squirreled up one of the maples, shifted from that into a long pin pine, and then another. Supreme faith and a harder scramble swung him from there into a beech that overhung the stream. Harder than it used to be, but he managed. Sat breathing a little heavier than he liked, straddling a branch, assessing his options as he unbuckled the belt from his waist, the one that wrapped round him twice, made people laugh. "Lost a lot of weight in my time," he'd joke when people teased. "My poor wife, may she rest in peace, was a terrible cook."

Wrapping the belt's end around the branch, its length snugged under the buckle, he readied himself to slide down, unlaced his boots, and slung them round his neck. Just drop easy into the stream. Wouldn't do now to sprain an ankle. Belt had to hold in place just long enough. Belike then he could twitch it free, bring it down to him. The leather burned his hands as he slid. Despite himself he winced as he sank knee-high into the water, icy cold on thin legs. Bedamn, winter coming fast, or was he so senile he'd forgotten how true cold stung and numbed?

He waded midstream for what felt like forever, slipping a few times, stone gashing a knee when he fell. Least the cold water kept the swelling and bleeding at bay. At last he reached the overhanging willow he remembered, pulled himself up its long, dangling shoots, and sat panting, shivering, massaging his blue-white toes, the pleached, puckered skin. Feeling returned eventually, always did, whether feeling to flesh or feeling to the heart, and he'd not let his heart feel the pain of the past for so long. Injustice, unfairness always turned him soft, vulnerable, when it should have hardened his heart. So the Fifty, his brother and cousin and all the rest, hadn't paid all, and he'd inherited their outstanding debt—with interest, no doubt. Come due today without warning. Mayhap pay them back in their own coin? Too dangerous unless he could make it look like an accident. How many others trapped in the same straits as he? Mayhap it was safer to be open about it, admit what you were. Then, at least, if anything happened to you, they'd know it for murder—and why. Didn't matter what edicts the Monitor and the High Conciliators set down. Dead was dead.

He jammed his boots back on, limping, slower now but still steady. Slower was fine since he'd gained a good lead. Those half-wit boys and their half-grown hounds couldn't track a plow in a snowstorm if they followed its path! Dusk soon, although the woods were hazed, that strange not-quite dark that turned a mounded berry bush into a lowering bear. Too bad it wasn't; a nice surprise for the boys if they'd managed to track him. Willed his heart to steady, ticked at himself for his false scare.

The sound of barking again, that sonorous baying that belled out of the hounds, bigger than they were, almost. Best move, double-time. Pick it up through the break in the elms over there, and on over hill and dale. And then he saw them, long, limber shapes running fast and furious, arrowing in on him. Not tracking hounds, but staghounds, their shoulders near as high as his waist, long, pointed muzzles, legs that devoured distance. They could lope forever and practically did sometimes, chasing elk or deer, running them down.

He ran anyway, refusing to give in. They'd stick to him like ticks wherever he chose to run, however long, could almost feel their breath, see the lolling tongues, the slashing teeth. Make friends with them? Douse them with pepper? Have to let them close in for that, and they seemed content to hang behind, drive him toward the gap in the trees. Until one drifted close, gave a nip at his heel, and he speeded up, frantic to regain his lead, sacrifice it on his terms. Fumbling with the pepper sack in his pocket, checking over his shoulder.

The ground disappeared beneath his feet, the woven vine net covered with moss, leaves, pine needles, grass sinking away under him, and he was falling, almost a swan dive,

frantic to bring his hands forward to break his fall. Pit drop!
The cunning little bastards had dug a pit drop—who would
have thought they had the brains, the savvy to drive him
ahead like this into a trap? The sharpened spikes pierced his
body, and he hung, writhing, gut-speared and chest-speared,
ground beyond the reach of dangling, lax fingers.

Two heads rose over the pit's edge like full moons.
"Thought'e was too canny by half, did Uncle Billy. Gullible
old fool."

"Aye, pity though. Nobody could sharpen a blade the way
Uncle Billy could, even if'e were a Gleaner. That be a
funny, I reckon. Gleaner should ha' a sharp blade."

"Yonk, you. Gleaners glean, sift the leftovers. That's why
we Reapers be better'n they."

Jenret sat on the ground, cuffed at ankles and wrists, his
right handcuff linked by a meter-long length of chain to his
left ankle, while a similar chain connected his opposite hand
and foot. The chains, in turn, passed under a wide leather
strap belted around his middle from behind. Sighing, he
drew his foot higher on his thigh to give his right hand more
play, shook the dice, and tossed them.

"You win." Sarrett threw two pinecones in his direction
while Towbin grudgingly passed along three. Although both
wore ankle shackles, their hands were free. If, Jenret observed bitterly to himself, you ignored the chains, it made
for a jolly little scene, a touch of friendly gambling over
lunch.

The chains proved utterly effective—if he wanted any
hand freedom, he found himself with his feet in his lap.
Choose to walk—forget about running—and he hunched
over, slamming into any tree that hove into view. Variations
on the theme of immobility were played when the Resonants
moved camp, something they did with numbingly constant
irregularity—sometimes twice a day, or once, or for three
blessed days, not at all. Moves meant a blindfold or hood,
hands behind back, leashed by a chain from the strap around
his waist. Towbin and Sarrett received more lenient treatment on moving days, though they both insisted on blind-
folds, more to make him feel less ill-treated than anything
else.

The only other woman besides Sarrett in their nomadic group, Yulyn Biddlecomb appeared subject to no strictures, or at least no physical ones. Scrupulously neutral, she left Towbin to his own devices, but showed no camaraderie toward their Resonant captors. Whether she mindspoke Towbin he wasn't sure, knew only that she rarely spoke aloud, and when she did, she conveyed brief apologies or explanations, all designed to cool his simmering temper. Even without her comments, the reason behind the constant camp moves was obvious: the Resonants showed caution in sequestering their hostages anywhere near loved ones, still hidden in the forest. Their nomadic movements also increased the difficulties any search parties would have locating them.

Once he'd thought he'd heard a woman's voice other than Sarrett's or Yulyn's—Faertom's mother Claudra, he was quite sure. Although he hadn't glimpsed Baen or any of the other Thomas men, it wouldn't surprise him if they'd joined Garvey's rotating group of guards, the family seemingly as hostile to Jenret as they were to Faertom. Garvey's scrutiny lately seemed destined to bore holes through him, as if he wanted to see inside Jenret, his usual phlegmatic personality giving way to a hectic intensity. Whatever shoe had dropped, Garvey seemed alert for the other to fall.

Giving up worrying about Garvey, Jenret anted four pinecones, tossed the three dice. Nine—triple three's. A perfect match by Sarrett or Towbin would win his cones; a combination of nine—say a two, a six, and a one—would earn the thrower half Jenret's bet. No match and Jenret won theirs. A stupid, petty game, and he played it relentlessly, bullying the others into playing.

To be honest, it afforded him a tenuous grip on sanity for the moment. Mayhap he should ask Garvey to join in, calm his nerves as well. He glowered at the dice, waiting for one or the other to scoop them up, rattle them for luck, shake, and toss. Even the muted clicking chipped at his nerves, likely to go stark raving mad if he didn't win his freedom soon, return to Doyce, find out all was well! The Monitor had to be doing something to quell anxiety, didn't he? Holding him hostage as surety against any harm befalling other Resonants or Normals was the slimmest thread of hope, didn't they see that? So slim nothing could be spun from it. Bound to be one idiot somewhere in Canderis, one malcontent—one? he snorted, only one?—who would never heed the Monitor's and the High Conciliators' proclamations, the laws protecting all citizens. Nor would he obey, he reflected, suddenly somber, if he believed Doyce and his unborn child threatened. His head ached, everything a muddle.

Reluctantly, Towbin's big hand scooped the dice, fingers spread to nip them between his fingers like extra, skeletal knuckle bones. Cradling the dice in his fist, crooning to them, Towbin cocked his wrist and released them, Jenret fulminating under his breath as the last one finally rolled to a stop. Six-Six-Six. Damn, a perfect double on his throw. He pushed the four cones across, added another four from his hoard, double winnings for a double match, face thunderous, scowl as black as his clothing.

"It's only a game," Rawn trotted into view, T'ss trailing behind. "And you devised the rules."

Jenret pulled both feet inward to sit cross-legged, raising his hands to run fingers through his hair. *"Find out anything?"* For whatever reason the Resonants couldn't monitor his conversations with Rawn, so he could 'speak him or T'ss, and thus Sarrett without resorting to audible speech. He'd sent the ghatti exploring as often as possible to pinpoint their location, whether anyone looked for them. The Resonants *had* to assume the ghatti had broadcast for help, that it was only a matter of time before it arrived.

"Does Doyce know yet?" he prodded Rawn. Would he feel better or worse if she did?

Rawn patted a pinecone, blinked as a prickly tip stabbed a toe pad. **"No, Khar knows, Koom assured me. She said she'd tell only if she had to. Otherwise she'd have to wind her in a fishing net and weigh her down to make her stay put."**

It almost made him smile. Sudden hands gripped his belt, jerked him to his feet, his legs unfolding to support himself and his chained wrists inexorably following downward till he bent at the waist, stared at his boots. Someone seized his hair and jerked his neck back until it cracked. A knife-blade glinted, disappeared to caress his throat, and Rawn erupted in a soaring black fury. Jenret grunted in satisfaction as the knife sailed clear, its wielder wrestling with twenty kilos of enraged ghatt, wrapped like a clawed, fanged limpet around wrist and arm, blood spattering. Collapsed on his knees, Jenret groaned as Somerset Garvey bodily slammed his be-

leaguered, encumbered arm against a tree trunk. A dull thud,
but Rawn twisted aside, most of the blow absorbed by Garvey's arm, although a minor growl indicated a pinched ghatt
paw. Without warning a white ghatt with shocking black
stripes draped himself over Garvey's head, half-hooding
him, front feet grabbing at eyes, hind feet digging behind
ears—T'ss, a fraction late from shock, had entered the fray.

Sarrett hurriedly hobbled after T'ss, stretching to pry him
loose, Towbin struggling to help. A long, thin shadow
whipped by Jenret's face, flash of metal on one side, and
smashed under his chin so hard he bit his tongue. An ax handle levering him backward, forcing him straight despite the
chains' pull. "Tell the beast to cut loose. You don't need a
voice to command him, and if you don't, I'll crush your
voice box so you can't speak." Faerbaen—Baen's voice—of
course he should have recollected who carried an ax as a
weapon.

"Rawn!" he 'spoke urgently, praying he could catch the
ghatt's attention through his boiling wrath. *"Rawn! Back
off, now—or I'm going to be strangled!"* The pressure
mounted, something in his throat cracked and protested at
the bruising, inexorable pain.

"We're all dead anyway!" Rawn snarled, teeth sunk into
Garvey's wrist as the man danced drunkenly, trying to batter
Rawn loose. **"A Resonant killed out Gilboa way!"**

"Dead?" Sarrett shrieked as she wrestled T'ss into submission. "Are you sure? Who was killed? How?" Her gilt
hair seemed haggard, grayed as she clumsily spun around,
gauging their expressions, finally comprehending their jeopardy. Even noble gestures had consequences. Pawns were
used, forfeited.

*"Everyone! Stop it! Wycherley, call off the ghatts, if you
can. Baen, release him. Calm the others, move them back!"*
The woman's mindvoice stung, snapped with a controlled
anger ready to spill at one more heedless move. He recognized that tone all too well, a tone mothers wielded when
driven to distraction by children of any age. The pressure on
his throat reluctantly eased and he leaned on his arms, gasping, trying to draw steady breaths. Had to get Rawn clear,
make him understand, but everything shimmered before his
eyes, two of Sarrett, two of Towbin—and that was a great
deal of Towbin. *"Rawn! Let up—now!"*

Rawn and his double both dropped free, two black ghatts

days, perhaps. But the old days would never return—
mutilated beyond recognition by Byrta's and P'wa's deaths.
The little girl, Lindy, distracted Bard from his disjointed
thoughts, and he'd been in no rush to return to Gaernett, deliver her over to Doyce. Time enough, if his calculations
were correct, for that. Better weather would be nice, but this
wasn't terrible for a season bending from fall into winter.
The increasingly early dusk each evening simply meant they
halted sooner, sometimes camping out, sometimes staying at
an inn or with a farmer, spent the time regaling each other
with stories. Lindy had a store of childish tales that echoed
his own at times, soothed him into occasionally recounting
stories from his and Byrta's childhood. Then, like a knife at
his heart, the pain would stab and he'd fall silent. She never
minded.

Rumors had it, confirmed by the broadside published each
Acht-dag, that the Marchmontian King and his entourage
were on their way to visit Canderis, tour the country. The
idea delighted Lindy no end as she'd stumblingly read
through the paper that night. "Oh, bet they wear gorgeous
jewels and crowns and all sorts of fancy satin and velvet
robes."

"Edged and lined with ermine, perhaps," he'd teased,
wondering from where this fanciful elaboration had sprung.
"But their jewelry isn't a whit nicer than your own," and
he'd tapped a finger at one of her ears. "Think they have
problems setting their crowns straight and level on their
heads?"

She'd crowed with laughter. "Even royalty have uneven
ears?"

"Sure," he'd confirmed. "Probably his crown rests on one
ear and doesn't even touch the other."

"Oh, I wish I could see a real King!"

"Well, mayhap, mayhap you can. Make a small detour."
Now the girl lay asleep, blanket over her and on top of that,
his tabard. He'd carried it out of habit, surprised at its bulky
weight when he wasn't wearing it. Stretching long legs toward the fire he wished he hadn't said anything about detours. Hated to promise the girl something, only to deny her.
Byrta wouldn't approve.

**"You don't want to meet more Marchmontians, do
you?"** M'wa tucked white front paws inward, roosted com-

pact, warm-breathing fur by his side. How could one presence remind him of another absence so much?

"No. No, not if I can help it. Even seeing Doyce and Jenret, Parse or Sarrett, is too close a reminder to ... to what. ..." he didn't bother to go on.

"Eadwin wasn't the enemy, nor Arras. Doyce and Jenret and the others even less so. They all just had the misfortune to be there, like you."

Misfortune! The word sounded far too benign, like a minor mishap. He clenched his eyes shut, as if that could block the vision of Byrta's severed head flying through the air, his mad dive to catch it, protect it, cradle it, kiss the still lips. Worse, in fact, with his eyes closed; everything engraved in his mind, impossible to obliterate. And all for him. Each always willing to sacrifice for the other, but they'd never counted on separation. A one-sided sacrifice they hadn't taken into account. A moan escaped, and he pressed his hand hard enough against his mouth to make his teeth saw through his inner lip. The pain a pleasure, just deserts for his dereliction. Why not just join Byrta, work up the courage to do it?

Claws struck the back of his hand so swiftly there was no evasion, scored the flesh with four parallel strokes. **"And abandon me? Leave me all alone—just as P'wa did? Deny our Bond?"**

Bard patterned the blood with a finger, connected the lines. *"We could go together."* A sense of hopefulness, *"The way Chak and Rolf did, so they wouldn't be parted."*

"Chak had no say in it, he died first. For all his love, he never would have beckoned Rolf down the path after him." Though neither had witnessed Rolf scooping up Chak's still-warm body and taking that final walk off the cliff just before The Shrouds, the high, echoing falls that separated Marchmont from Canderis, the shared image was vivid, passed along by Khar and the ghatti present. **"For our love, would you beckon me so?"**

"Only if you freely choose to come."

"And where does that leave the child?" M'wa sat hunched, head thrust forward, glaring.

Bard scrambled, breathless for words, couldn't find any. Finally controlled his breathing by sheer force of will. *"I didn't say it had to be this moment! Once we leave her with Doyce, that's another story. We're free again."*

"Leaving her to worry and mourn as she's mourned for Byrta? Unsure what happened or why, but suspecting she's responsible in some way? Haunted by nightmares of things she never saw but somehow sees?"

Unable to help himself, balked at every turn, he slapped the ghatt, a hard shoulder blow that spun him sideways. Ears pinned, M'wa reared and retaliated, claws unsheathed. Knuckles slashed, Bard slapped harder, M'wa's head wobbling as he connected, but then M'wa righted himself and sprang. And they collapsed in each other's arms, hugging close, whimpering, sobbing, desperate not to waken the child. *"All we have is each other, and I'm trying to destroy that!"*

"And Lindy, at least for a little while."

"We could go," he temporized, *"catch up with the royal progress, I remember the route the broadside listed. Rubberneck at royalty. Bound to be plenty of street entertainment at each stop, dancers, musicians, souvenir sellers. Lindy'd like that."*

M'wa hedged, wondering who else might be there—Reapers eager to kill the King or any other Resonants they found—or think they'd uncovered. And Bard's mindsharing with Byrta came perilously close to Resonant skills whether he acknowledged it or not. Still, who'd suspect a retired Seeker Bond-pair? "They're not all bad, you know. Eadwin and Muscadeine would have fought to the death to save Byrta and P'wa if they could."

Bard stretched out, M'wa layered on top of him from chin to hip as he fumbled a blanket over them. "You know, Doyce isn't in Gaernett right now," M'wa admitted.

Almost enough to make him sit up in shock. "What?" It burst out sharper than he'd meant, and aloud. Lindy stirred and mumbled, tucked the end of her braid against her lips for comfort and subsided. *"Where is she?"* he continued in mindspeech.

"You're retired, remember? Actually, any number of things have been happening, but I didn't think you retained any interest in that life." The tone caustic, meant to shame, and it did because it was true. "Doyce is visiting her mother and sister in Coventry, saddled with Davvy because the Seeker General thinks there's less risk for him away from the capital. And Jenret's been captured by

Resonants, held hostage to insure the safety of Resonants
still concealed in Canderis proper."

"That's a benighted plan if there ever was one!" He was
seething now. *"And I'm not sure any place is safe these days
if the wrong person suspects you're a Resonant."*

M'wa chuckled, well-pleased. **"Almost makes you wish
you could put things to rights, doesn't it?"**

"Go to sleep, M'wa." And Bard let his breathing slow,
knowing full well he wasn't fooling the ghatt. Kept his eyes
closed but imagined the stars wheeling overhead, knew their
patterns, and wondered what part he played in the pattern.
One twin above, one twin below. Wondered what his obliga-
tions now were—and why. Doyce was carrying twins, but
he'd not breathed it to a soul, the coincidence too hurtful.

Hru'rul the Magnificent, King's Bond, terror of the wild,
continued walking, fluid strides that effortlessly covered the
ground, veering to take shelter as needed, check for danger.
Yes, he was Hru'rul, entrusted with a mission, returned to
the wild, ruler of all he surveyed. Reach the Research Hospice or venture near enough to contact Saam, relay information about Harrap's and Parm's doings back to Eadwin and
Muscadeine.

Mostly he ignored the young man lagging behind, dark
auburn hair sweat-slicked, mouth ajar to suck in lungfuls of
air as the incline grew steeper. No, Hru'rul hadn't asked for
company, didn't require a guide or guard, and Ezequiel
Dunay was neither. Silly human constantly spinning in circles until he matched the disk with its floating needle to
their direction. Still, best keep an eye on him or Eadwin
would be angry, though not half as angry as the stork-leg
man would be.

Ezequiel chewed his lip, shifted the pack straps to a less
sore spot on his chafed shoulders, and checked how far his
hose had slipped. Pull them up now and they'd only slip
again—might as well wait until later when they'd dropped
as far as they could go. Just keep going because the ghatt
wasn't inclined to wait, taking paths and shortcuts he had no
hope of following. Thigh muscles burning, he bent and
straightened each leg, drove himself up the slope.

Well, it'd seemed an inspired idea at the time. Catching

the king's uneasiness at letting Hru'rul journey alone to the Hospice, Ezequiel had decided to accompany him, abandon his castle duties for a day or two and make sure the ghatt arrived safely, then skedaddle back across the border before anyone discovered his dereliction of duty. How was he to know the ghatt would disdain to ride with him, pick his own solitary way through mountain goat trails where a horse couldn't follow, secure in his own sense of direction?

A rock reared up in his path, a magnet attracting his weary toe—oouch! The flat black slippers he and his grandfather wore to unobtrusively slip around the castle were ruined, offered no protection or support, no purchase on rocks. He'd skidded and fallen more times than he could count, raw spots on knees and elbows, scabs itchy, breaking and oozing, his hose sticking to them. Everything he'd brought had been wrong: not enough sustaining food—who knew it would take this long or how ravenous he'd be?—too much cooking gear, the ghatt's combs, brushes and sleeping pillow, his own toiletries and dress clothes for their arrival at the Hospice. If he'd provisioned the royal progress as ineptly, he was in for it! In short, he was thoroughly miserable, and likely to be more so if his grandfather caught him at the Hospice—if they ever reached the Hospice.

They'd been traveling almost two full days now, Hru'rul and his laboring shadow, and Hru'rul sat suddenly, amused to see Ezequiel collapse with alacrity behind him. In truth, he felt footsore and weary. Ghatti didn't normally indulge in forced marches but traveled when and as they chose, seeking food, resting as the spirit moved them. And, oh, the spirit moved him to nap! Ah, ghatti did that *so* well, spent most of their time in some state of sleep, conserving themselves for lightning bolt spates of activity. His left hind paw-pad stung and he licked it thoroughly, biting at the long fur between his toes, licked some more, tongue a soothing balm. Oh, to sleep! His stomach rumbled piteously, reminding him of the other thing bothering him, though he'd tried to ignore it. The boy was down to a dozen nougats and two apples—not to his taste.

Truly, ghatti didn't *have* to eat as often as he did now, cosseted by Eadwin, no longer hunting for them both, too often resigned to passing his hard-won prey to Eadwin through the narrow window slit in the imprisoning tower. How often then had he gone hungry to ensure Eadwin ate?

Well, he'd had a huge breakfast the day they'd left, so much that his sides bulged, and he'd indulged himself with Ezequiel's tidbits while they lasted—smoked salmon, paté. Nothing today but a few unsatisfactory but crunchy mouthfuls of late crickets. He still bore the packet of trail mix Eadwin had lashed to him, a small canvas pouch that curved round his back, secured with leather thongs slipknotted at his chest where his teeth could pull it free. The more he fixated on it, the more the scents wafted from the pouch. Only trail mix, but even that sounded delicious. Share with Ezequiel? Or didn't humans like it? He hoped not.

How much farther? Eat now or wait? He heaved himself up, resolute, and glided ahead, favoring his sore foot, checking once to make sure Ezequiel followed. Contacting Saam wouldn't be easy; he'd tried several times but to no avail. Was Saam simply not listening, intent on searching out Parm's voice, or was he wrapped up in communication with Mahafny? A shame his mindvoice had faded, but better that than the nothingness, the speechlessness caused by hurt and anguish. Such emptiness, such aloneness, and knowing now what he himself had nearly missed with Eadwin, before they'd discovered true Bonding, Saam's loss pained him.

He worked upward from rock to rock, hesitating occasionally to reconnoiter. A thud, a slither, and another "ouch" told him Ezequiel still followed. Hard to concentrate with him banging and clanging like that, those pots and pans. Would the increased height enhance his mindspeech? From the pictures of the terrain he'd gathered from Muscadeine's mind, they must be close. He popped his head over the top of the ridge, cautious—eagles capable of carrying him away in their talons soared through these peaks, and claw-feet were the one thing he feared—and peered down, eyes sweeping the landscape, tufted ears swiveling, listening for danger. A puff of smoke, no—he sniffed, cracked his mouth to waft the scent across his palate—not smoke . . . so much as steam. A wind shift gusted the steam away and he saw it rising in the distance, the uncompromising white of the Research Hospice, its high, white central chimney.

End in sight, he worked at the slip knot, stepping free of the constraining leather thongs and nosing the pouch open, noisily crunching as he considered. Needed the energy. Ezequiel labored beside him and flopped on his stomach, spent, his pack rising like another insurmountable peak, weakly waved him away when Hru'rul dragged the pouch toward him. All his!—he crunched more, greedy, gulping some whole. Nosed for the final crumbs. Yes, he was Hru'rul, powerful and competent, ruler of all he surveyed. No way his mindvoice couldn't pierce that shell of a Hospice, rouse Saam with the clarion call of his mindspeech.

A deep breath as he concentrated, arrowed his mindspeech with the arching beauty of a shooting star. **"Saam! Hear me, Saam! I am Hru'rul, Bond of Eadwin. Hru'rul calls!"**

"Hru'rul?" The voice floated, gradually gaining focus as it groped for range. **"Why are *you* contacting me? In fact, where are you?"** Hru'rul ruffled at the suspicion in Saam's mindvoice. This was the gratitude he received for undertaking such a trek?

"Eadwin riding, be at Hospice late tomorrow. You tell white-coat lady ride with him. Also, word from Parm?" The words crowding his mind always snarled together when he 'spoke, so long had he been bereft of shared converse before his Bonding. In that, he was as crippled as Saam with his imperfect distance abilities.

Skittering caution, even at this range he sensed something askew, not as it should be. **"Where are you?"**

Patiently, Hru'rul described where he perched, the sun descending behind his back. Not happy to see him, not happy Eadwin coming? What?

"I'll have Mahafny send a horse and rider for you. Unless you'd like to leg it?"

The thought of riding sounded wonderful, a chance to nap, groom, ready himself for the meeting. In truth, he didn't know Saam well, the steel-gray ghatt keeping to himself, only comfortable around Doyce and Khar and, of course, Nakum, and now, Mahafny. **"Appreciate ride. You know Ezequiel? Here too, tired,"** he sent back. **"You hear Parm voice? Muscadeine worrying?"**

Again an awkward hesitancy. **"Yes, but . . . not exactly informative. He should be 'speaking me shortly, in fact he's overdue. Please, I should listen for him, not waste time 'speaking you."**

Ruff bristling, Hru'rul jerked as if slapped at the slight, raised himself higher on the ridge spine to hurl back a rejoinder. Eadwin was king and Hru'rul his messenger, worthy of respect, worthy of being heard. A dark shadow blotted the sky and a down draft smote him, dust flaring up, burning his eyes. **"Ware!"** "Look out!" gonged in his mind and ears, Saam and Ezequiel both shouting as the eagle dove, talons outstretched, beak a sharp-curved hook of a smile.

"No, no, no!" he flattened himself, mind exploding with another time he was too young to consciously remember but could only relive. Snatched from his nest in the tree crotch, bereft of mother and sibs before his eyes had opened, his tail clipped short by a cruel beak. No Eadwin now to drive off the bird, save him, salve his wounds.

A taloned foot sank into the loose skin at the back of his neck, the other foot searching out a grip lower down, near his tail. Air under him, not solid ground, and the thunderous beat of wings buffeting him senseless as the eagle strained aloft. He twisted, clawed at the feathered underbelly, bit the scaled leg, the taste bitter in his mouth, but not as bitter as his fear. **"No, no, no!"** Something whizzed by him, struck the eagle, more stones, one slamming a sensitive wing joint, and the bird screamed with pain, Hru'rul echoing it. Hands full of stones, Ezequiel clambered nearer, gaining one step for each two he slipped back. Squirming, biting, yowling, Hru'rul fought, the eagle sinking lower, wings mantling, scooping air, kicking up gravel and dust at Ezequiel.

Pack strap in one hand, Ezequiel swung the pack high, the other shoulder strap noosing the eagle's neck, the pack slamming his chest. Shocked, the bird loosened his grip and Hru'rul pulled free, a patch of his soon-to-be winter coat remaining behind. Shouting, Ezequiel lobbed his final stone, scored on the sensitive nasal area above the beak. With a long, drawn-out scream of protest at such ill-treatment from prospective dinners, the eagle flew off, pack bouncing against his chest, the rattle and clang of pots and pans drumming against him.

Hru'rul licked the boy's bare leg, the long hose completely ruckled around his ankles now, and felt thankful to be alive. **"Bravo! Did you snatch a feather for a souvenir?"** And Hru'rul couldn't think of a suitable rejoinder, so he retrieved a long, golden feather and presented it to Ezequiel.

❖

Humming, Doyce began setting up her mother's small loom for a weaving, warping the threads. Sunlight beat on her head and shoulders from the tall windows, bathing the room in brightness. This was the only part of weaving she actually enjoyed, making sure the threads ran true, unblemished by flaws, weren't twisted or kinked, their tension consistent. Orderly, dependable, logical, one following another in ordered ranks. Ever since she'd been a child she'd had a knack for this part of the task, the part her mother and sister considered deadly boring.

Well, hadn't lost her touch after all, had she? As if in mockery, a strand snapped, wrapped itself around her finger. And with that she went to pieces, something within her snapping as well. Damn, hateful, hateful, hateful when she overreacted like this, and the more she struggled for control, the worse she became. Another strand snapped as she brushed it, dangled there tickling her ear as she detached the first culprit.

"Easy, love," Khar stretched to bat at the offending strand. **"Don't make a spiderweb of it."**

Nuzzling the ghatta's neck, she blotted her eyes on Khar's shoulder. *"I just want to do something right, something Ma can appreciate, be proud of me for. I'm not sure she always understands—what I really do, I mean. What we really do. If I show her I can still do this . . ."* she trailed off, giggled, *"she'll still think there's a chance I ca be a weaver. Ugh!"*

"Perish the thought. You expect me to spend the rest of my life exhibiting self-control around so many potential toys dangling invitingly." Despite her best intentions, the ghatta's paw stole toward another strand. Only to touch, she told herself.

"Well, I've got to get this right." Doyce tried again, but even with her swing back to good humor, she was too intent about her task. Now everything she touched went subtly awry, a missed peg, an overlap, a twist. *"Damnation,'* she grumbled as she detached a mistake and tried again. *I used to be able to do this in my sleep. The only thing I could safely handle right now, not mangle, would be rope!"*

Chin on paws, the ghatta suggested, **"Can your fingers do one thing while your mind's doing something else?"**

"That's the idea. Supposedly this is so boring that you have time to think deep thoughts about solving the world's problems." A shaky laugh. *"I can't even convince Jenret to find time to marry me, let alone solve the world's problems. I wish he'd get back . . . before the baby's. . . ."* Doyce plumped down, head in hands, and commenced wailing in

earnest. *"And this blasted loom won't even cooperate so I
can think deep thoughts!"*

Khar half-rolled onto her back to regard her beloved.
**"Come on, love. Let's show your mother you haven't lost
your touch. Let your fingers go about their business
while we see what Matty and Kharm are doing."**

Dropping her hands, clearly aghast, Doyce snapped, *"Do
you want us both thinking about sex again?"*

**"It's another town, another day for Matty and Kharm.
I'm sure they can't think about sex all the time."**

"According to Jenret, that is *what boys Matty's age think
about all the time."* Leaning against the loom, she tried to
calm herself, slide into that other world, so like and yet so
unlike her own. Her hands began automatically warping the
threads.

Neu Bremen swarmed with commotion as Matty and
Kharm made their way down the road toward it. He'd heard
of places being called a beehive of activity, always thought
it fanciful, but from his vantage point overlooking the
spread-out town he could see why. People scurried along
dirt-packed streets, pouring toward the center of town, clot-
ting thicker and deeper as he watched. And all the time an
ominous buzzing floated toward him, the exact nasal hum an
angry hive makes when disturbed. The buzzing vibrations
set up a visceral unease deep within him.

He found a convenient rock and sat watching, wondering.
Might be wise to avoid Neu Bremen altogether. Kharm
stalked back and forth at his feet, clearly upset by the commotion, yet drawn to it. Ask her what was wrong and he'd
find out. Don't ask and he wouldn't know. Instead, he delayed his decision, eased a blistered heel free of the wooden
clogs he now wore, boots outgrown, far too short. They
rested in his sack, fit to be worn for dress, pinch-toed painful, but not for heavy walking. Heavy walking had been his
fare since leaving the Widow's farm in Waystown.

Absently he picked his woolen stocking away from the
blister, sucking in his breath as it stuck, then tore loose.
Winter, or near-winter, not the best time to be homeless and
on the road again, and if he didn't stay at Neu Bremen, find
odd jobs to support himself and Kharm, most likely he'd

move on north to Free Stead. But that, from what he'd heard, would be even less likely to offer jobs to tide him over the winter. What to do, where to go?

Life with the Widow hadn't been bad, indeed, had become almost too comfortable, which was why he'd determined to leave. Too easy to be trapped by complacency—his, not hers. Had seen her all too often in those nights after dinner casting sidelong glances at him as she mended, did the other thousand and one things to be done about the house. He'd be working at a task—carving a new tooth for the rake, harness mending, shaving an ax handle smooth—and they'd be chatting aimlessly or, more accurately, he'd be chattering, responding to the noncommittal sounds she uttered to soothe and smooth, occasionally tossing in a few words, sometimes several whole sentences.

She'd looked up one evening, hands bunched tight in the shirt she mended, "Like having Reinholt beside me again, having you here. Things only *we* knew, you seem to know. Find myself checking that he's still buried out back. Uncanny."

He'd shared a hot, complicitous look with Kharm, realizing he'd been the unwitting vessel into which Kharm had poured her knowledge of the Widow. Those trivial tidbits of thought, the vague, unspoken remembrances that aureate each person if one were sensitive enough to read it. Kharm hadn't actually read the Widow's mind, but those random thoughts hovered, ripe for the picking or, if not picking, absorption, just as dishclout soaks up water. As easy for him as for Kharm to gauge the Widow's mood by her expression, the set of her body, the number of words she chose to squander on any given subject. Not prying, but there for the asking, if one knew what to "ask."

That, and the fact that neighbors had been eyeing him, thoughts lurking lasciviously at whether he shared the Widow's bed yet. All too predictably comfortable—and disquieting—especially after he resolved a few thorny dilemmas for various neighbors. Reconciled them from what he'd absorbed from Kharm, not even realizing he was unraveling their problems, mediating their arguments, their disagreements. People began wondering at his insight, exhibited a faint discomfort in his presence, as if he'd eavesdropped on their lives, even the aspects they thought they'd suppressed. They had to admit he'd been impartial,

favoring no one over another, but even his endorsement of
their cause seemed to have violated their personhood.

Was there no place for him? Did the same reaction await
him in Neu Bremen? Did any place exist where it wouldn't?
And his loneliness for Granther and little Henryk and the
sweetly curved and padded Nelle, resourceful as she was
lovely, swept over him in a high tide of longing and emotion. "Kharm, what am I going to do?" he wailed aloud.
"What are *we* going to do? All I want is a home, a place to
settle down, be me. To belong!" His chest squeezed tight, his
sinuses flooding, the pressure building inside his head.

"I know, I know," the ghatta crooned. **"Own hearth,
own bed, own den to cuddle safe and warm. Miss it, too,
but I have you."** Wiping his eyes on Kharm's back, he
scrubbed his cheek against her whiskers, purposely trying to
scratch back with his softer and still limited facial hair. A
game they played. But the ghatta abruptly pulled away. **"Oh,
untruth! Wrongness!"**

The shouts and rumblings from below had intensified. Not
a disrupted hive now but worse, the growling sounds he'd
shivered at one winter night in Gilboa, the wolves hungry
enough to venture near, prowl the snow-packed streets,
eager to chase anything through the drifts if it represented
dinner. A keening hunger to these sounds as well, but a different sort of hunger, a rapacious desire for satiation no matter the need. Wolves hunted to assuage their hunger, not out
of a desire to kill for pleasure. He slammed his foot into his
clog, picked up the walking staff he'd carved, and straightened his sheepskin poncho.

"Can I do anything, can we do anything?" Please, let her
answer be no. No desire to enter that village, enmesh himself in their troubles, but he was Amyas Vandersma's grandson and responsibility always dogged him; if he could
somehow make things right, it was his duty to do so, or at
least try. One day he'd lose his nose from sticking it in
places it didn't belong. Why not be carefree, or at least uncaring like his father? A deep breath—too bad courage
couldn't be inhaled. "Kharm, what's the matter? Tell me
what's wrong."

And this time the surge as Kharm transmitted a multitude of
inner thoughts didn't swamp his senses, as if the ghatta herself
had learned to pick and choose, unbraid one strand before tugging another. One thought, an overwhelming one, raced from

mind to mind, left him grappling to shape it into coherence, the concept foreign to Kharm. "Rope?" No, it wasn't just rope. "Looped and knotted, around neck?" He stumbled, clogs unwieldy. "Noose. Kharm, it's a noose. To hang people by the neck, kill them. Sort of like how the Killanins trapped your mother."

A growl of anger and Kharm exploded down the dirt track toward the village, Matty rushing to keep up or at least not lose sight of her. Regardless, he guessed their destination: in almost every village or hamlet all roads converged at the village well, the nucleus for gatherings large and small, gossip, business, and plain daily converse. People poured out of alleyways between houses and shacks, tents, thronging the main streets, sweeping him along. No option but to ride the current, bobbing like a chip, and he didn't fight it, jostled harder to get there faster, push closer to the center.

Kharm belabored his mind with steady cautionary commentary, caution, the innate prudence of any wild creature. She'd already vanquished a pack of hungry-looking dogs, ill-kempt and ill-fed, who foraged around the village center for handouts, willingly given or snatched from unwitting hands, careless children balancing a slice of bread stacked with cheese or meat. Neu Bremen was huge in comparison to Waystown or Gilboa, especially Gilboa in the winter when most river boaters and traders had left for homes elsewhere. At least five hundred people, men, women and children, crammed the open area.

"There! Wagon on the east side," Kharm scrambled up a tree trunk so he could see her, tree limbs bending with their burden of youngsters like ripe fruit. "Climb up, see what's going on."

He shouldered his way through tight-packed bodies, grateful for increased strength housed in a barely noticeable cheeseparing of a body. Stand him sideways and he still wouldn't cast a shadow wider than a fence post. At times he strained to glimpse over heads, but someone always shifted, blocked his view. Not much room on the wagon, either, but he wedged a foot on a hub and propelled himself up, planted the other foot on the wheel's rim. A shove from behind and he tottered, toppled into a press of women and boys a few years younger than he who'd commandeered the wagon as their view site.

Trading shoves, he established his territory, elbowing ran-

domly to defend his space while he craned to see, giddy with
excitement, the crowd's overwrought mood contagious. Faint
disappointment, a letdown, as if he'd been primed for blood.
Whatever he'd anticipated, this wasn't it: a human chain of
ten people with arms linked, all men except for a diminutive
but sturdy woman at the center, penned in a desperate figure
at its core, a man so spackled with mud and refuse, splattered
eggs, rotted vegetables it was impossible to judge the color of
his clothes. The refuse piled at his feet, along with stones,
fragments of mud bricks, some still raining down. The crowd
heaved and thrust like a living thing, testing the human chain,
searching for a weak link, and Matty knew with a goose-
bumped surety that the link might snap not from physical
weakness, but from fear, cowardice. Taunts and jibes rained
on the man as well as refuse, despite a few overridden pleas
to better nature, common sense. So far, not a soul in the chain
had faltered, although they shifted, gaining and losing
ground, forcing themselves outward with grim determination
to press back the throng. A few weapons, mostly clubs and
cudgels, waved at the crowd's far edges, but so far no one
had employed them to sunder the joined arms or worse, batter
unprotected heads, jaws clenched in raw agony at the effort to
hold firm.

Something would tilt the balance—and soon—but he
couldn't imagine what. His stomach knotted at the impasse,
tightened with anticipation and fear, his own allegiance unclear. *"Kharm, what's this all about?"* If he couldn't make
sense of it, could she?

**"The man in the center, the dirty one, is Lorris
Stralforth."**

"But what's he done?" Stralforth looked a paltry figure, incapable of causing much trouble, although a sense of malcontent emanated from him, a soured view of the world and the
human condition. Hardly an unfounded view, given his current precarious situation, but Matty's nose wrinkled with dislike.

"They say he killed. But that's untruth," and Kharm's
mindspeech jittered to a halt as two men shouldered a coil of
rope through the crowd, dumping it with ostentatious show at
the feet of the woman padlocking the chain's center. He'd not
paid much heed before, other than wondering at her place in
the protective chain as he'd assessed possible weakness. Yet
everyone steered clear of her section. Brown hair straggling

from her bun, she kicked the coil of rope dismissively, her resolute expression never faltering, outstaring the men who'd dropped it there.

Two small children, a boy of perhaps two and a girl about four, choose that moment to worm their way through the crowd, rushing to clutch the woman's skirts, crying, "Mama! Mama!" They buried themselves in the folds, stricken with shyness and a dawning realization of wrongness, no longer the center of her universe, no hand to spare to stroke their heads, hug them safe in the depths of her skirts. The girl looked up at the faces staring down at her and veiled her face, wailing, "Mama! Bad men!"

The pair who'd thrown the rope at the woman's feet retreated as far as the crowd would let them, embarrassment and confusion flooding their faces. The woman chose that moment to speak. "No, Sissy. Not bad men. But men who don't know how to obey the laws they voted to govern them. Like the time you took it into your head to help Mama with the churning without asking and, much as you meant well, you made a mess Mama had to clean up, and you knew Mama'd said not to touch.

"From children I expect a lack of restraint, overzealousness even, but not from you, from adults." An intimate conversation with children meant to teach adults a lesson, and now her alto voice rose to reach the crowd's fringes, her poise impressive. "You know me, and well you should. You yourselves elected me, Rema Pelsaert, to serve as your Conciliator, ensure laws were obeyed, judge penalties when they weren't. And now you'd void the laws that bind us as a community, dissolve them in a fit of unreasoning anger without determining justice has been served."

A voice shot out from the crowd. "Horst Coornhert is dead."

"Yes, he is," she agreed sadly, "but no mob can bring him back."

"And we mean to punish who killed him," called another voice. "Clear enough!" "Rock all bloody in his hands when we found Horst." Indictments rang from various voices, though Matty could never attach a face to the voice, invisible accusations growing in strength because of their anonymity. "Clear as day Lorris killed him." "Always wanted to, always feeling cheated about everything in life. Said he'd like to see Horst dead in one day."

"It may be that Lorris Stralforth *is* guilty. I'm not arguing that possibility." The bedraggled man in the center sheltered his face with his arms as if to shield himself from the words. "But we don't know that for sure. We've not held a trial, heard the evidence. That's all I ask, that you not take the law into your own hands. That you don't deny him—and yourselves—the impartial treatment we so painstakingly established as a right to ensure no one is unfairly treated. Justice and honor mustn't discriminate amongst its citizens or none of us are safe."

Matty's stomach began to uncramp, the words convincing, heartfelt, reminding people of their better selves, the fact that they weren't animals. "Like murdering Horst was fair treatment?"

"What if it were you, Melville, cowering in the circle's center, no chance to defend yourself no matter how loudly you protested your innocence? Or you, Gelten?" She named every face confronting her from the front row, taking her time, allowing her plea to sink home. "All I ask is the chance to conduct a fair trial, hear any evidence pro and con, investigate further if it's warranted. If Lorris's guilt is proved, he'll get the rope. If he's judged innocent, you'll have to hang me first to reach him.

"Now, I suggest we confine him in his house, post guards to protect him and us, while we figure out what happened. Tomorrow? Can you wait until tomorrow for your fun?" Her lip curled with scorn at the word. "Deny yourselves for a day to see justice served? Or have the news spread that Neu Bremen's a lawless town where actions speak louder than words and emotions overrule truth, a town where justice is served by whomever can serve it first without considering right or wrong? Oh, yes, new settlers will flock to a town with a reputation like that, hordes of serious citizens to make it prosper. New hands eager to work that new sawmill, that new grist mill."

The crowd began to cluster and knot, its unity collapsing as it broke into segments of worried faces, whispered undertones. Not many, man or woman, with the courage to face down a writhing monster of a crowd, individuals sucked into a whirlwind of fermenting emotions, spinning faster from the mindless force it generated. Each knot or cluster disintegrated further, people streaming away shamefaced, others still muttering, whipsawed by frustration but unable to lash the frenzy

de la journée sur moi. Mon inquiétude gran-
dissait. Parfois, je bondissais hors de mon
fauteuil et, debout, je me mettais à scruter
le visage de Mia. J'approchais ma joue de sa
bouche, et son souffle était brûlant. Je voulais que le matin arrivât et qu'il fît culbuter
mes peurs. Et dans le même temps je crai-
gnais qu'il ne me rapprochât d'une issue
plus affreuse.

Ces jours-là ont passé, eux aussi.

Je ne me souviens plus de rien. Il y a Mia
partout. Je ne sais rien d'autre.

Je ne sais si le médecin revint. Boutros
était-il souvent près du lit ? J'entends, mais
comme dans une brume, la voix d'Om el
Kher : « Mon âme est avec toi », disait la
voix. Dans un coin du salon, des sanglots
étouffés, qui sont peut-être ceux d'Ammal ?
Et un jour, je crois qu'Abou Sliman m'ap-
porta un petit panier d'osier pour Mia, de
la part de l'aveugle. Je me souviens à peine
de tout cela. Je ne me souviens de rien
d'autre. Pourtant, les jours furent longs.

Le matin de ma vraie mort, Mia me regardait, et elle souriait, ce matin-là.

Je m'étais penchée pour prendre ce sou-
rire au coin de ses lèvres, quand elle se
retira de moi pour toujours.

* * *

Au bas de l'escalier, il y a les femmes du village. Elles restent l'une près de l'autre. Une masse noire et immobile. Au début, elles ont poussé des cris de deuil qui sont comme les hululements des chats-huants. Mais, depuis deux jours, elles se taisent et elles restent là, sur les quatre dernières marches, tout en bas. Si quelqu'un veut monter, elles se serrent un peu plus pour lui céder la place. Elles ne disent rien depuis deux jours. Elles ne se demandent même pas si je sais qu'elles sont là. Pourtant, elles restent au bas de l'escalier. Om el Kher, Zeinab, Ratiba et les autres n'ont pas bougé de toute la nuit. Elles ont pris du pain sec, de quoi les soutenir, et elles l'ont gardé sur leur poitrine, entre la robe et la peau. Le jour, elles sont assises, le menton dans les mains. La nuit, elles dorment sur les marches.

Une grande tache de silence au bas de l'escalier, elles gardent ma peine.

Et moi, je suis là-haut, dans la chambre de Mia. Sur une chaise. Un de mes bras passe par-dessus le dossier et pend. Personne n'a pu me faire bouger d'ici. Du salon, des voix me parviennent. Boutros reçoit les condoléances.

« C'est la volonté de Dieu », disent les religieuses. Elles ont passé deux nuits à veiller l'enfant mort.

« Qu'ai-je fait au Ciel ? dit Boutros. Je suis un homme juste.

— Il faut vous reposer, disent les employés. Cela ne sert à rien de perdre ses forces.

— C'était un ange ! disent les religieuses. Dieu la voulait pour lui.

— Moi, dit une voix de femme, moi aussi j'ai perdu un enfant ! Mais, depuis, Dieu m'a comblée. »

Sur les dernières marches, Om el Kher est silencieuse. Et Zeinab, et Ammal, et les autres sont silencieuses. Abou Sliman va parfois se pencher au-dessus de la rampe, pour prendre part, lui aussi, à ce silence.

« Qu'ai-je fait au Ciel ? répète Boutros. Je suis un homme juste, et il pleure bruyamment.

— Vous êtes chrétien, disent les religieuses. Que la volonté de Dieu soit faite !

— Mon fils aussi a eu la typhoïde, dit une voix. J'ai failli le perdre !

— Il faut du courage, dit quelqu'un à Boutros. Vous aurez besoin de toutes vos forces. »

Je chasse ce bruit de mes oreilles. Je répète : « Ma vie, ma petite vie... » Je répète : « Où es-tu, ma petite vie ? » Je ne sais plus ce que je dis.

Je suis seule dans la chambre où Mia n'est plus. Elle est immense, tout d'un coup, cette

231

chambre, et les pieds de ma chaise font des ombres maigres sur le plancher.

Encore ces voix autour de moi. On demande à me voir. Je dis « non ». Les voix sont toujours là. Elles remuent des souvenirs. Chacun a eu ses malades. Chacun a eu ses morts. Boutros explique combien l'air des villes est nocif aux enfants, et les voix l'approuvent. Est-ce que j'entends tout cela ? Je suis loin...

Et pourtant je ne suis pas seule.

Au bas des marches, il y a ces femmes qui gardent ma peine et qui ne prononcent pas un mot depuis deux jours.

XI

Je n'ai plus voulu vivre.

Était-ce la vie, que ces jours qui se suivaient sans but ? A présent, je souffrais bien plus que de l'ennui, et le sommeil ne pouvait m'apaiser.

Boutros portait un brassard noir. Lorsque j'essayais de parler de Mia, il se détournait d'un geste nerveux comme s'il voulait se préserver d'un souvenir pénible.

J'essayais de me raccrocher à mes moments de bonheur, de les rappeler, et en même temps j'éprouvais une espèce de crainte, comme si je faisais planer, par ma faute, un autre danger au-dessus de Mia. J'avais un cri de douleur en moi que rien ne calmait. Les jours venaient s'abattre les uns au-dessus des autres pour étouffer le passé, ils n'apportaient aucun répit. Mon mal ne cessait de brûler.

J'ai voulu en finir. Je savais où le fleuve était le plus profond.

C'était l'époque des récoltes, et Boutros rentrait tard. En fin d'après-midi, j'ai quitté la maison.

J'ai marché sur la route. La grand-route, celle qui borde le fleuve et qui mène à la ville. Le sol était d'abord poudreux et le ciel embrasé de plaques rouges. Je n'ai voulu penser à rien, ni à personne. J'ai rejeté de mon esprit Om el Kher et sa peine. J'ai rejeté Ammal que je trahissais. J'ai marché à la rencontre de ma mort. Plus je m'approchais, et plus elle me semblait familière, cette mort tant de fois haïe. Cette mort de ma mère si tôt enlevée, cette mort injuste de ma mère. Cette mort de Mia, cette insulte à la fraîcheur de Mia. Cette mort de l'homme qui a brûlé comme une torche. Toutes ces morts ! Oui, maintenant, cela devenait soudain simple et facile. Exaltant presque. Je répétais « Ammal, Ammal », comme si je voulais lui donner mon dernier souffle, et qu'il s'ajoutât à sa force. Je voulais qu'Ammal pût s'accomplir.

Quand le soleil décline, l'asphalte se refroidit et ne colle plus aux semelles. Chacun de mes pas se détachait avec un bruit distinct. J'ai marché au milieu de la route sans rencontrer d'autos. Sous le pont métallique, plus loin, à ma gauche, l'eau était la plus profonde.

J'allais de plus en plus vite et les tempes me battaient. J'ai couru sur la route et je croyais rejoindre toutes les routes du monde. J'entendais le claquement de mes talons sur l'asphalte. Le pont se teintait des dernières couleurs du soleil. J'entendais mes talons claquer sur l'asphalte, mais comme si c'étaient d'autres talons, qui n'appartenaient à personne et qui me poursuivaient de leur bruit. J'avais une rumeur dans la tête. La mort, ce n'était peut-être que cela, une rumeur très douce, comme celle qui tournait dans ma tête, et dans laquelle on n'aurait qu'à se jeter.

J'ai couru sur le pont, et je me suis arrêtée à l'endroit où l'eau était la plus profonde. Jaunâtre, avec de grandes rides qui s'effaçaient pour renaître. Je me suis accoudée sur le parapet pour mieux voir.

Je ne sais combien de temps cela a duré.

La nuit était tombée quand je me suis retrouvée sur le chemin de la maison.

Voici la route d'asphalte, la route poudreuse, le village, l'allée des bananiers et la maison blanche. Voici les escaliers, le

235

vestibule, la tenture de velours que j'écarte, et la voix de Boutros.

« Est-ce une heure pour rentrer ? Où étais-tu ? Mais où étais-tu donc ? »

J'ai répondu : « J'ai marché loin et j'ai oublié l'heure !

— Que cela ne se reproduise pas, reprit-il. Abou Sliman a dû réchauffer trois fois le plat. »

Son bras s'agitait en direction de la cuisine. Son brassard noir s'était usé et avait perdu de son luisant.

« Je t'ai acheté une montre, dit Boutros. Il n'y a pas de raison pour que tu sois en retard. » Il continuait : « Et puis, quel sens y a-t-il à traîner sur les routes ? Je t'ai déjà répété que je n'aimais pas te savoir en dehors de la maison après cinq heures. M'entends-tu ? »

J'ai répondu : « Oui, Boutros », mais je pensais à l'eau du fleuve. Elle était sombre, cette eau, elle vous entraînait très loin, n'importe où. Vers l'oubli, ou vers Dieu sait quelle rencontre ?

« Le riz est trop sec et c'est ta faute, disait Boutros. Jamais je n'ai mangé un riz aussi mauvais. »

Le fleuve s'en allait. Il traversait les villes et les campagnes avec votre corps. Le fleuve vous promenait entre les rives où marchent les femmes chargées de branchages ou de jarres. Parfois un ânon gris trotte tout seul. Les saules pleureurs gaspillent une existence à se mirer dans l'eau. Le fleuve vous entraînait sous les ponts, vous découvriez l'envers des barques. Votre mort et celle du fleuve allaient se mêler, bientôt, au fond des mers.

« Om el Kher nous a apporté trois pots de miel, disait Boutros. Tu me feras servir de ce miel tous les matins, mélangé à de la crème fraîche. »

Le fleuve ne voulait pas de moi. Il ne voulait pas de la morte que j'aurais pu être. Il ne s'arrête pour personne, il continue sa route. Pour qu'il vous emporte, il faut courir après le fleuve ; sinon, il vous abandonne sur la berge. Il vous laisse à votre mort, à votre petite mort solitaire et sèche.

Entre ma douleur et la honte de n'avoir jamais rien accompli, je m'empoisonnais lentement. Chacun de ceux qui m'entouraient s'alourdissait de symboles, et prenait à mes yeux une importance démesurée.

L'image de Boutros dépassait Boutros. Je le faisais semblable au méchant dans les rêves d'enfants. Je le chargeais de ma souffrance et de celle du monde. Boutros était laid et sans amour. Il tuait l'élan du cœur, il priait des lèvres et il vous emmurait dans ses calculs. Sa voix, son corps massif étaient dans chaque souvenir, entre moi et les autres, entre moi et la vie, écrasant la joie la plus délicate. Boutros était mon étouffement ; et ma crainte de lui me gardait muette.

L'image de Boutros s'amplifiait, se mêlait à l'image de mon père qui n'avait jamais su se pencher que sur lui-même ; se confondait à l'image de mes frères qui ne respectaient que l'argent. La misère était partout, Boutros lui opposait son indifférence. Il devenait, à lui seul, tous ceux qui vivent de principes aussi desséchés que leurs âmes. A la pensée de tout ceci, je l'ai haï plus d'une fois.

J'étais seule. Ma raison de vivre, arrachée. Devant un mur qui rejetait ou déformait ma propre voix. Il faut me comprendre. J'avais trente ans à peine, et quel espoir me restait-il ? Un horizon bouché. D'autres, comme moi, ont dû sentir leur vie s'effriter au long d'une existence sans amour. Celles-là me comprendront. Si je crie, je crie un peu pour elles. Et s'il n'y en a qu'une seule qui me comprenne, c'est pour celle-là que je crie, que je crie au fond de moi, aussi fort que je le peux.

Mais bientôt, même pour les cris, il sera trop tard. Tout deviendra inutile. Bientôt, il ne restera plus qu'à faire le vide autour de soi, et à se terrer.

* *
*

J'ai commencé par éloigner Om el Kher. Les images de Mia s'accrochaient à elle, traînaient sur ses robes. Je ne pouvais plus le supporter. Om el Kher revenait pourtant avec fidélité, mais j'évitais sa présence.

Pour les mêmes raisons, j'évitais Ammal, je ne pouvais plus rien pour elle ! Je voulais le vide, le silence. Je refusais tout. Même le souvenir de Mia, je le refusais.

Souvent, avant de dormir, je sentais Mia auprès de moi. Ses bras autour de mon cou, ses picds se blottissant entre mes jambes. Je me retournais entre mes draps. J'enfouissais ma tête dans l'oreiller. Je répétais : « Non. Je ne veux pas. » Le souvenir de Mia était tenace.

Une nuit, j'aperçus un visage collé à la vitre et qui me regardait. Qu'elle s'en aille, Mia ! Je m'étais levée brusquement pour tirer les rideaux. Sur le chemin blanchi par la lune, l'aveugle marchait. Je le reconnus à son turban très clair. Qu'il s'en aille, lui aussi ! J'étais debout près de la fenêtre, Mia ne s'y trouvait plus. Mais soudain, je la vis, montée sur l'épaule droite de l'aveugle. Ils me tournaient le dos et ils partaient tous les deux... Qu'ils s'en aillent ! Qu'ils s'en aillent tous ! J'ai tiré sur les cordons des rideaux, pour être dans le noir.

Le lendemain, je ne pouvais plus bouger de mon lit. Mes jambes étaient complètement inertes. J'en avais chassé la vie.

*
* *

Boutros se frappait le front : « Que vais-je devenir ? répétait-il. Que vais-je devenir ? »

Tout d'abord, il essaya de me persuader que je n'avais rien. Il arracha mes couvertures. « Marche ! » me dit-il. Mes jambes n'obéissaient pas.

« Que vais-je devenir ? » se lamentait Boutros.

Il se mit ensuite à m'insulter et à se plaindre de tout ce qu'il avait subi jusque-là, à cause de moi. De nouveau, il me rendit responsable de la mort de Mia : « C'est à cause de cette promenade en ville, c'est là qu'elle a attrapé sa maladie ! » ajouta-t-il.

Lorsque le médecin arriva, Boutros s'inquiéta de savoir si j'étais contagieuse.

« Non, dit le médecin. Mais elle ne pourra pas bouger. Elle ne pourra s'occuper de rien pendant longtemps. Pourtant, à son âge, ça devrait passer. »

Boutros s'effondra dans le fauteuil et laissa ses bras pendre de chaque côté des accoudoirs. « Quel malheur m'arrive », répétait-il.

Le médecin s'était assis au pied de mon lit, il sortit de sa serviette de cuir jaune les feuilles d'ordonnance et tira son stylo de sa poche.

« Je ne l'ai pas oublié, cette fois », me dit-il.

Il écrivit sans se presser, et il ajouta au bas de la page une signature illisible.

« Vous ne pourrez pas bouger pendant longtemps », me dit-il. Puis, se retournant vers Boutros, il continua : « Les malheurs arrivent tous à la fois ! Cela fait à peine quatre mois, n'est-ce pas ?

— Six mois », dit Boutros, et il soupira.

Le médecin secoua lentement la tête. Puis il se leva, s'approcha de Boutros et lui mit la main sur l'épaule.

« Courage, lui dit-il, c'est comme cela. Les malheurs arrivent tous à la fois. »

Abou Sliman venait de rentrer. Il portait, sur un plateau laqué noir, trois verres d'eau et trois tasses de café. Le médecin se rassit dans l'autre fauteuil, près de Boutros. Tous deux buvaient le café, je n'avais pas voulu le mien. J'étais étendue et je regardais les deux hommes.

Je ne bougeais plus jamais. Je ne le voulais pas d'ailleurs. Ah, si je pouvais chasser aussi ce qui remuait dans ma tête. Je me répétais, sans cesse, que j'avais été faite pour autre chose. Je me répétais qu'une action seule aurait pu me libérer et que j'en avais été incapable.

*
* *

Boutros ne tarda pas à faire appel à Rachida. Il écrivit la lettre sur la table ronde et je l'aperçus, par la porte entrebâillée, qui cherchait ses mots. Rachida ne tarda pas à lui répondre. Boutros larmoyait en parcourant ses lignes : « C'est comme si on venait de m'ôter un poids », dit-il.

Boutros ne revenait à la maison qu'à l'heure des repas, et Abou Sliman s'habitua très vite à m'asseoir tous les matins dans le fauteuil au grand dossier, qu'il poussait ensuite jusqu'au salon. J'y restais sans rien demander, excepté qu'on fermât les volets. La pénombre, parce qu'elle mettait du sommeil autour de l'agitation et des choses, permettait de fermer les yeux et d'oublier.

Le jour de l'arrivée de Rachida, Boutros ne cacha pas son impatience. Dès la fin du déjeuner, il partit avec Abou Sliman, pour ramener sa sœur de la gare.

C'était l'hiver et la nuit baissait vite. J'allumai la lampe à pétrole déposée sur une table à côté de moi. J'avais l'impression de savourer mes derniers instants de solitude. Bientôt Rachida sera là, et ses pas seront partout.

J'aperçus tout d'abord une ombre. J'avais dû somnoler car je n'avais entendu aucun bruit. L'ombre s'allongeait sur le tapis et se heurtait au coin du mur. Elle était étroite avec un visage en larmes. Puis je sentis le baiser de Rachida sur mon front.

« Qu'est-il encore arrivé à mon pauvre Boutros ? » dit-elle.

Rachida s'installa dans la maison, ou plutôt, elle reprit la place qui lui avait été gardée. Je sus vite à quel point chaque objet ici l'attendait. Il flotte autour d'un objet quelque chose qui appartient à celui qui l'a choisi. Quelque chose d'impalpable et qui ne s'efface pas. Près des immortelles, du meuble foncé chargé de bibelots et des rideaux opaques, Rachida était à sa place. C'est elle qui avait voulu la couleur grise du mur, avec ces impressions vers le bas qui imitaient le marbre.

Rachida donnait des ordres à Abou Sliman d'une voix cassante :

« Va chercher mes valises, et ne traîne pas. Tu sais que je n'aime pas attendre. »

Tandis qu'Abou Sliman descendait de son pas fatigué, Rachida allait et venait dans la maison. Elle avait ôté ses chaussures pour mettre ses pantoufles de feutre bleu qu'elle venait de tirer d'un large sac. Elle ne me prêta aucune attention. Elle se sentait soudain rajeunie, ces seize années n'avaient pas compté, elle se retrouvait, comme jadis, partageant la vie de son frère. Elle parcourait une chambre, puis l'autre, elle examinait chaque meuble. A présent, elle ouvrait mon armoire.

« J'enlève tes robes, disait-elle. Dans l'état où tu es, à quoi peuvent-elles servir ? Elles seront mieux dans ma valise. »

Elle s'était mise à décrocher mes robes et les jetait l'une sur l'autre. Abou Sliman remontait. Il portait d'une main une grosse valise bardée de lanières de cuir, sous l'aisselle il avait placé une valise plus petite entourée de cordes. Sur son dos, un énorme sac en toile verte. Il avançait péniblement.

« Enfin te voilà », dit Rachida, l'apercevant dans l'encadrement de la porte.

Elle sortait maintenant mes manteaux, mes lainages. « Tout cela doit être rangé autrement », disait-elle. Mes vêtements gisaient partout sur les fauteuils, sur les

244

tables, quelques-uns avaient glissé sur le sol. « Il faudra nettoyer les armoires, reprit Rachida. Abou Sliman, va m'apporter ce qu'il faut. »

Abou Sliman partait, revenait avec une cuvette pleine d'eau savonneuse et une brosse. Rachida vidait ses valises. Il y avait du désordre partout.

Rachida s'installa. Elle ne m'accorda pas plus d'importance qu'à un objet encombrant qu'il fallait subir.

Deux années, je crois, s'écoulèrent ainsi.

Au début de ma maladie, c'était à moi qu'Ammal remettait le fromage de son oncle Abou Mansour. Elle avait les yeux pleins de larmes quand elle me regardait. Rachida ne tarda pas à lui défendre l'accès du salon. Elle n'aimait pas Ammal et trouvait que je me donnais en spectacle.

La dernière fois que je vis Ammal, je trouvai la force de lui reparler de ses statuettes, et elle me promit de ne jamais les abandonner. « Je te le promets ! » me répondit-elle avec une passion soudaine. La seule lueur de volonté qui me restait était tendue vers elle. Je me disais que, si Ammal était sauvée, ma vie aurait eu un sens.

Des jours. Encore des jours à l'ombre des volets clos.

Parfois, j'entendais la voix d'Om el Kher près de la cuisine. Elle demandait de mes nouvelles. On lui répondait que les visites me fatiguaient. Et c'étaient de nouveau les pas de Rachida, les plaintes de Rachida, l'ombre de Rachida sur les murs, qui tissaient autour de moi une prison.

Ma présence ne gênait plus Rachida et Boutros. Ils parlaient de moi comme si je n'étais pas là. Au réveil, Rachida omettait de me dire bonjour. Mais Boutros, lui, n'oubliait pas ce baiser qu'il me donnait sur le front chaque soir, un rite dont il ne pouvait se défaire. Bientôt, toutes les pensées de ma journée viendraient se concentrer autour de cet instant où je sentirais le contact de ses lèvres sur ma peau.

Mes derniers sursauts de révolte se fixaient autour de ces minutes : la porte s'ouvrait et j'attendais, crispée, que les lèvres brunes me touchent le front. Un jour, je ne pourrai plus y tenir, je le sens bien.

Qu'est-ce que je dis ? Qu'est-ce que je viens de dire ? Les choses se mêlent terriblement. Une rumeur incessante dans ma tête. Tout s'embrouille. Et cette autre rumeur ? Qu'est-ce que c'est ?...

On dirait qu'on crie mon nom, qu'on crie

le nom de Boutros. C'est de plus en plus pro-
che. Que s'est-il passé ?

Des pas montent et se pressent dans les
escaliers. Je ne sais plus, je ne veux plus
rien savoir. Je n'ai plus peur de rien. Qu'ils
montent avec leurs pas et leurs cris ! Qu'ils
soient partout dans la chambre, tous !

Je suis morte à cette histoire, et tout se
tait en moi.

XII

Dans le vestibule, tout près de la tenture de velours qui a été arrachée par la foule, Ammal se dresse sur la pointe des pieds pour essayer d'apercevoir Samya.

Hussein est entré le premier, et il a tout vu malgré ses yeux malades. Les cris des autres se croisent comme des bâtons que l'on cogne. Rachida parle très haut. Barsoum sent une chaleur lui monter dans les bras : « Qu'on la jette hors de son fauteuil, qu'on la tue ! » crie-t-il. Les femmes se donnent des coups du plat de la main sur la poitrine et poussent ce même hululement de chat-huant. Om el Kher, le poing à moitié enfoncé dans la bouche, retient ses larmes, voudrait oublier, ne pas regarder Samya, ne pas regarder l'homme mort.

Peut-être qu'on tuera la femme là, sur

249

place ? Farid s'approche, la peau de son visage jaune et tendue : « On te piétinera ! » hurle-t-il. De grosses gouttes de sueur glissent le long de ses tempes.

Mais Samya est loin. Elle ne semble même pas respirer. Seule sa façon de se tenir, le buste droit, les mains sur les bras du fauteuil et les coudes légèrement surélevés, comme si elle était sur le point de se dresser sur ses jambes, laisse supposer qu'elle est encore en vie. Ammal l'aperçoit, mais seulement de profil. Elle la regarde de tous ses yeux.

« Tu seras sauvée, Ammal ! » Ce visage mort avait-il dit cela ? Il est si blanc maintenant, le visage de Samya, on dirait de la pierre. Ammal entend ses paroles muettes. Ammal sent tellement de choses qu'elle pourrait tout crier à la fois. Mais quels mots emploierait-elle ?

Rachida, elle, trouve tous ses mots. Au long des jours qui viennent, elle dira tout ! Quand elle parle, ses sourcils se rejoignent et deux sillons de chaque côté de sa lèvre inférieure tirent sa bouche vers le bas. Sa voix grince, on dirait le bruit d'une lime sur du bronze. On fait cercle autour de Rachida, on crie avec elle.

Mais, l'arrivée soudaine du Maamour[1] fait

1. Chef de la police.

taire les voix et la foule s'écarte. Puis c'est
le pas lourd des policiers sur les marches.
Ils montent chercher la femme pour la prendre, et la mettre dans la voiture cellulaire
qui attend dans la ruelle. Le Maamour veut
qu'on fasse vite ; il veut être chez lui pour
le repas du soir. Il y a près d'un mois il a
épousé Fatma, une fille de quatorze ans,
belle comme un fruit.

Fatma !... Le Maamour la voit comme si elle
était là, assise, les mains sur les cuisses, dans
la robe verte qu'il lui a choisie. Quand il entre,
elle se lève pour lui céder l'unique fauteuil.

Le Maamour a fait chasser la foule hors
de la chambre. Il ne reste que les quatre
hommes qui porteront le fauteuil. Ils se
baissent, ils la soulèvent, et la femme ne
bouge pas. Elle semble si étrangère à tout
cela que le Maamour n'a même pas songé à
lui poser de questions.

Les porteurs traversent le vestibule. Un
instant Ammal est tentée de crier : « Je suis
là ! » mais Samya n'entendrait pas. Et si elle
se jetait contre la foule, toute seule, pour la
lui arracher ? Que ferait-elle ensuite de cette
Samya de pierre ?

Les quatre hommes descendent péniblement les marches. Un des policiers les pré-
cède ; à chaque pas, il se retourne pour dire :
« Plus à droite », ou : « Plus à gauche ».

Personne sur les escaliers, excepté Fakhia, le visage troué de variole. Le menton sur la rampe, elle épie avec son œil de chouette. « On descend la meurtrière ! » crie-t-elle. Tous se précipitent alors pour escalader les marches en secouant leurs poings. Les policiers menacent de leurs bâtons.

« Jetez-la, qu'on la piétine ! » hurle la foule.

La femme n'entend rien, elle ne voit rien non plus. Même pas l'aveugle qui parvient, malgré les remous, à se maintenir à sa place ; la tête si haute que son turban blanc domine.

« Jetez-la par terre, le démon est en elle ! »

La main de l'aveugle se crispe. Il sent la terre qui cède sous son bâton. Il frappe de plus en plus fort. Il imprime sa silencieuse colère dans le sol pour qu'elle ne le quitte plus.

***

Dans le vestibule, il n'y a plus qu'Ammal.

Il faut partir d'ici. Avec des êtres qui naissent de vos doigts, plus semblables aux vivants qu'eux-mêmes ne le seront jamais, on n'est pas seule. Il faut partir. Loin de ce qui étouffe et de cette pourriture que devient la peur.

252

Ammal va jusqu'aux marches, et elle les regarde.

Elle remonte sa robe un peu au-dessus des genoux et la tient dans chaque main.

Elle attend encore, pour recueillir tout son souffle. Puis elle se met à courir.

Ammal court.

« C'est Ammal, elle court ! crie Fakhia.

— Elle a pris peur ! »

A ce cri, l'aveugle a cessé de creuser le sol.

« Elle court, Ammal ! »

Le dos au mur, l'aveugle respire en paix.

Comme elle court, Ammal ! Comme elle court !

Littérature

Cette collection est d'abord marquée par sa diversité : classiques, grands romans contemporains ou même des livres d'auteurs réputés plus difficiles, comme Borges, Soupault. En fait, c'est tout le roman qui est proposé ici, Henri Troyat, Bernard Clavel, Guy des Cars, Frison-Roche, Djan mais aussi des écrivains étrangers tels que Colleen McCullough ou Konsalik.

Les classiques tels que Stendhal, Maupassant, Flaubert, Zola, Balzac, etc. sont publiés en texte intégral au prix le plus bas de toute l'édition. Chaque volume est complété par un cahier photos illustrant la biographie de l'auteur.

2636

Impression Brodard et Taupin
à La Flèche (Sarthe) le 11 janvier 1990
1077C-5 Dépôt légal janvier 1990
ISBN 2-277-22636-X
1er dépôt légal dans la collection : juillet 1989
Imprimé en France
Editions J'ai lu
27, rue Cassette, 75006 Paris
diffusion France et étranger : Flammarion

to its previous peak. The wagon bed gradually cleared as various women and boys departed, returning to the tasks so gladly abandoned for a mindless stimulus.

At last, with an audible groan of relief the human chain unlinked, flexing arms and shoulders, legs shaking, weak pillars that had withstood the storm. Two men held Lorris Stralforth's arms, not unkindly, almost supportive as the shaken man was hurried to a hut and thrust inside, men assuming posts around it.

Sinking to her knees, shoving tendrils of hair off her forehead with an impatient arm, Rema Pelsaert at last embraced her children, shushing them against her shoulder, rhythmically rubbing small backs. Matty jumped from the wagon, walked slowly toward her, allowing her time to assess him. Kharm reappeared at his feet, only to move away, bridging the gap between herself and the little girl, squirming against her mother's shoulder, blue eyes wide.

Matty squatted, hands resting on his thighs, to bring himself eye-level with Rema Pelsaert. "My name's Matty Vandersma. This is my ghatta Kharm. I'm not sure, but I think I might be able to help."

No point in saying precisely how or why, that Kharm could discern the truth, determine who lied or not. Not that easy for someone to grasp—or believe. "Why? Why should you? Why involve yourself, stranger?"

That ice-chilled word again, "stranger." Frozen outside, someone who didn't belong, had no stake in the proceedings, no rights. But that might serve his purpose. "Because being a stranger means I'm not biased, not partial to either side, able to examine the facts as I find them. Besides, it's not just which questions you ask but how you ask, which answers you accept at face value and those that conceal something beneath the surface, even when the surface seems firm."

She sounded weary, longing to be left in peace. "I'll repeat it, why involve yourself? Why not trudge along to the next town? Leave our problems behind you, like shaking the dust from your feet." She studied him, trying to determine his motivation, but she hadn't that kind of skill, always surprised when people weren't as straightforward as she. Kind and decisive as well, and brave but troubled. That and more he'd learned about her, both from his own observation and Kharm's clear liking. "Vandersma? Not related to Manuel Vandersma?"

Matty's head jerked at the unexpected identification with Manuel Vandersma, his father. Whether absent or present, Manuel Vandersma would haunt him, the very name a scathing contradiction of the characteristics Matty strove to epitomize. Unfair, given that he hadn't laid eyes on his father in ten years, a weak man who gave the lie to everything his own father, Amyas, represented. Some of the first generation born on Canderis had rebelled at the loss of a future, gone weak, sunk into despair, or worse. What reputation Manuel had here and now, he could well imagine and hardly supposed it worth bragging about—it never was. A guarded nod served as his answer.

"Which means you're Amyas Vandersma's grandson. Neither's a bad relationship to claim." The little girl waggled stretched fingers at Kharm, while Rema nervously tugged her daughter's arm away. "What is that beast? You haven't tamed one of the larchcats, have you?"

"No," Matty laughed as Kharm slipped closer and the girl's hand reached toward the long, tantalizing flow of fur that begged to be petted. The tiny hand stroked, Kharm smoothly reversing herself to remove her tail from temptation. "But she's doing her best to tame and train me. Complains at the effort all the time." He paused. "Have you seen my father lately?"

She rose, decisive, two-year-old balanced on hip, the girl still tethered by one hand, face pouty at leaving the ghatta. "Yes. Why don't we talk further? Back at my house. Dinner for tonight if you'd like, a place to stay for a few days if you want . . . if I want. We've much to discuss."

He followed, obedient, wondering if this bordered on acceptance, but starkly aware how quickly, like grains of sand sifting between suddenly parted fingers, acceptance could drain away. A start, at least, and a chance to discover his father's whereabouts, other things as well. If he could prove his worth, carve out a place for himself, belong.

Sun high and hot on his head, squinting at the glare, Matty knelt in the center of the square, townsfolk ringed around him, while Rema Pelsaert sat on a stool behind him. Kendall Coornhert, the deceased's brother, the plea-bringer in the case paced around a stool at Matty's right, while the defendant, Lorris Stralforth, sat tensely on a chair to the left, arms tied behind the chair's back. Wetting his lips, he rehearsed everything he, Rema, and her husband Flaven had feverishly discussed through the night and this morning. Spacer's doom, he couldn't keep it straight, make the order right! How to handle this, make himself accepted, trusted as an outsider?

Flaven had stressed the need for ritual, even if only the beginnings of one, a solemn ceremoniality that carried beyond the familiar businesslike hearings Rema conducted, conferred greater assurance and accord to those who listened. It was he who'd loaned the old ceremonial sword belonging to his Spacer grandfather, and Rema who'd quickly stitched a black tabard to replace the sheepskin he wore. It made him feel mature, almost confident, investing him with a certain gravity, a dignity and seriousness of purpose suitable to the task he'd undertaken. Made him conspicuous as the neutral observer officiating over the questioning. What it didn't do was cancel the pinch of his too-small boots, freshly polished, constricting cramped toes wishing heartily for release.

Kharm sat facing him, sleekly striped, whiskers widespread and inquisitive, ears tracking the crowd's sounds. No one had any idea of her importance, how he depended on her. Hinting at it to Rema and Flaven, alluding to her abilities had gotten him nowhere, Rema distracted and fondly grumbling as she swept up the sawdust that showered out of Flaven's cuffs and boots, even his pockets, Flaven apologizing for not having brushed himself outside but protesting that at least he wasn't late for dinner. "Late for dinner and you brought me mud instead of sawdust last night," Rema'd teased. Mayhap he'd chosen that moment on purpose, hoping no one would pay attention, fearing it would thwart his acceptance, adjudged mad or worse. Like father, like son, they'd think.

Rema came behind him, placed both hands on his shoulders. "I name Matthias Vandersma, son of Manuel Vandersma and grandson of Amyas Vandersma, as our interlocutor to question, seek after the truth." That his father's name carried weight continued to puzzle him; Rema had refused to explain, saying it wasn't her place to do so, but if he continued on his travels, he might learn soon enough. "He knows us not, nor has he formed an opinion of us, of who is right and who is wrong. Who speaks truth and who speaks lies. Given the town's partisanship in this case, fairness demands the selection of an outsider to ask the questions, determine the veracity of accuser and accused. And only I, as your duly elected Conciliator, can pass judgment at the end. Do you object?"

Mutterings from the crowd, but no outright dissent, a certain breathless relief in trusting a neutral outsider. One who would quickly, without doubt, validate their claims of Lorris Stralforth's guilt. At least the rope wasn't in sight.

He switched his level gaze from Stralforth to Coornhert, unhurried, forcing them to meet his eye, while he strove to check his own emotions. "Be this your Choice or do ye Choose to await another neutral hearer?" Rema intoned.

"Get on with it," growled Kendall Coornhert, while Lorris Stralforth swallowed a lump, eyes darting, assessing the potential for escape, his chest rising shallow and fast like a frightened bird. All the nervous reactions of guilt.

Laying the sword horizontally in front of him like a barrier, Matty jerked it partway from its scabbard, amused at the crowd's quick intake of breath, the palpable silence. Let them interpret it as they would. Flaven had the right of it—a ritualistic action often assumes a deeper hidden meaning. Obscured even from him, sometimes. Let them believe he'd lop off their heads for lying—better than confessing to the fidgets.

"I call the first witness, Datrian Ballou." Reluctant, Ballou stepped forward. "Tell us what you found, sir, on the afternoon two days past."

"Herded the cows down to drink before taking them back to milk. Stream's on Coornhert property, Horst and Kendall inherited from their father, but they've given me leave to water there."

"Grazing rights?" Matty queried.

"Nay, not graze, though." A slight squirm of his dark spade beard, as if it independently protested.

"Not without payment," Kharm 'spoke Matty. "Ballou's offered several times, more than he paid their father, but not enough to satisfy the Coornherts. They'd rather leave the field wild than settle for what they consider less than a fair price."

He pondered that. So the Coornhert sons were greedy and stubborn, capable of flaunting their wealth, turning Ballou's offer into an insult. *"Both of them, Kharm?"* he mindspoke, nervous at distracting himself with unimportant background while Ballou waited, beard twitching, to reveal what he'd found.

"Both, but Horst was more obvious about it."

He forced himself to concentrate. "And what did you find there at the stream that afternoon, Mr. Ballou?"

"Found Horst half-in, half-out, head bashed in, water running bloody." Tiny bright eyes peeped between the bushy beard and a thatch of wild, dark hair, saucy as wrens in a shrub, flickering with enjoyment as he dragged out his revelation. "And Stralforth straddling the body, hefting a dripping rock, ready to bash him again in case once hadn't been enough."

"What makes you so sure he planned to hit him?" A near slip, he'd almost followed Ballou's lead and said "hit him again"—tacit agreement that Stralforth had struck the first blow.

Belligerently, "What else was he going to do with it?"

"He believes what he's saying, and Horst was dead when he arrived. Ask how Lorris looked, what the ground was like. He's stored details in his head, hasn't analyzed them."

Wonderful, what was he supposed to ask? "Was Stralforth wet?" A nod from Ballou. "How wet?"

"What do you mean how wet?"

"Was he splashed, soaked?"

A narrowed look as he dredged his brain. "No . . . no, just his hands and shirt cuffs." A pause for recollection. "A few drip splotches on his pants from picking up the wet rock."

"Wouldn't it be reasonable that Horst Coornhert's body would have heavily splashed him when it fell into the stream? Or when the rock landed there? Was the bank churned wet and muddy as if there'd been a struggle?"

A reluctant "Aye."

"Ask him what he did when Lorris picked up the rock and he saw Horst's body in the stream."

Matty relayed the question as if it were his own, throttled a burgeoning impatience. Why didn't Kharm simply *tell* him, not make him circle and circle for the scent of truth? But if he learned the truth without leading his listeners to it, he'd appear to have been touched by a revelation from on high—worse yet, be taken for a meddling Resonant.

"Shouted, of course. Yelled at him not to hit Horst again, and came running."

"You said the bank was muddy. Any footprints by the body or near it?"

"What kind of footprints?" Kharm interjected and Matty saw Stralforth wore clogs that termites had apparently snacked on.

"What do you mean? O'course there was footprints. Horst's and Lorris's. Added my own when I shoved Lorris aside and dragged Horst clear of the water."

"And Lorris didn't run while you rescued Horst?"

"No," a tiny acknowledgment issued from Ballou's beard. "Tried to help me drag him up on the verge."

Matty turned, whispered to Rema, "Have many people visited the site since Horst died?"

"I don't ... know," she sounded thoughtful. "I suppose enough to carry Horst back. What do you mean?"

"How close to the stream would the curious venture? Would any original prints still show?"

Her hands squeezed his shoulders, but her voice sounded calm. "Possibly. Shall we go look?"

"No, send someone who can track well, preferably several sure of Lorris's guilt."

The wait seemed to expand, swallow him until he feared he'd sink under the pressure of silent eyes, but worth it in the end. Two jumbled sets of boot prints marred the stream bank, small rocks in the water disarranged, rolled clean side up. A set of clog prints angled toward where Horst's body had lain, and moccasin prints overlaid some of these as well as the boot prints beside the ruts Horst's boots had carved when Ballou dragged him clear.

"So someone else was with Horst late that afternoon?" his voice invited the crowd to participate, learn along with him. "And that someone wore boots, not clogs, like Lorris here, or our moccasined dairyman, Mr. Ballou." He left that niggling seed of doubt to root, began to question Kendall Coornhert. "Mr. Coornhert, you admit you didn't witness Horst's death, but you're convinced Lorris Stralforth killed him. Why so?"

In a hardscrabble, make-do world, Kendall Coornhert radiated sleek complacency, too well-fed, too well-dressed, someone who always collected the lion's share while the rest contented themselves with scraps. Whether his prosperity was justified, his business acumen a cut above the average citizen's, wasn't the issue, but he fascinated Matty, the man so unlike his father Manuel. "Because he's hated us, been jealous from the very beginning. Always wanting what he hasn't got but lacking the guts to do what it takes to get it." Well, that answered part of Matty's internal question. "Be it work hard for it, pay the price asked, whatever's needful to obtain something. Everything he touches goes bad, turns sour. Ballou even had to turn him off from the dairy, Lorris spoiled so much milk." The crowd laughed dutifully.

"What would he gain from killing Horst?"

It struck Matty as curious as well; Kendall's dismissal of Lorris's ineffectualness almost enough to clear him. "What does your brother's death gain him?"

"Don't know for sure. Doubt if he needed a reason, malcontent that he is." Kendall shifted weightily from foot to foot, imprinting himself on the earth. Polished boots without a stain of wet or muck. "'Course Horst made some personal loans on the side, never spoke much about them, but I'm checking his records to see no one escapes a Coornhert debt." A barking cough split the air, and a voice that carried, "Never have and never will." Kendall swung at the words, a condemnatory, level stare. "If you owe, you owe. And you pay—with interest." Not a threat but an implacable fact; Matty didn't need Kharm to tell him that.

"The Coornhert brothers aren't well-liked. In fact, they didn't even like each other," Kharm contributed.

"Then why is everyone so upset he's dead?"

"Because it upsets things as they know it. They're used to being under Horst's thumb, afraid Kendall's may prove even heavier." The sophistication of her analysis surprised him, an ability to unravel human nuances whether she fully comprehended them or not. Nor was he convinced he comprehended them any better, but he *was* beginning to understand, like it or not. **"And everyone disliked Lorris because he constantly grumbled, threw their dependence on Horst in their faces whenever they tried to forget. And for all that, he was no better at escaping it than they were."** Khar twisted to wash the base of her tail. **"Why are humans so bitter?"**

He didn't know, couldn't dredge an answer to satisfy himself, let alone her. *"Did the brothers dislike each other*

enough for Kendall to kill Horst?" The thought brightened
in his mind, beckoning irresistibly, the solution so simple.

"He might have liked to, but he didn't," Kharm sighed
a wispy regret. **"And you won't like the truth, either. Nor
will the townfolk. I'm sorry."**

"Well then, who killed him?" Matty's patience wore thin.
*"Tell me, now! Otherwise I have to keep asking Kendall
questions."*

**"It's not just uncovering the truth, it's convincing ev-
eryone it's the truth, yourself included."** The ghatta
spared a glance at Rema, continued grooming. *"Talk with
Lorris for a while."*

"Mr. Stralforth?" The man's meandering eyes gradually
focused on him. His pasty complexion reminded Matty of
bread dough, soft, yielding, yet ready to expand with a desperate bravado, a morbid pleasure in making himself disliked. "Why were you at the stream?"

Stralforth rocked against his bonds, slumped back. "Why
not? Nothing wrong with traveling across it. If we had to
avoid trespassing on every bit of owned land, we'd be in for
some mighty big detours."

Matty sighed. "Had you planned to meet Horst Coornhert
there?"

"Absolutely not. No desire to see him if I could help it."

"Why were you holding the rock?"

Stralforth's features screwed tight. "Didn't look
properlike, rock on his head, him half-draped in the stream
like a discarded sack. Mayhap I've more respect for the dead
than for the living, but didn't like seeing him that way."

Spacer's glory! The man actually exhibited a minor sympathy, fellow feeling for another human. "Was there anything odd about the scene, out of place?"

"Other than Horst kissing the stream?" Well, so much for
sympathy; Stralforth had rekindled the crowd's displeasure,
needful as mother's milk to him.

"Stream bank had a dusting of raw sawdust, fresh, coarse
wood chips. Didn't look like anything'd been sawn or chopped nearby." A shallow grin stretched the scab by the corner
of his mouth where he'd been hit by a brick fragment.
"Who'd dare on Coornhert land? Cutting through he *might*
allow, cutting down—never."

One of the volunteer trackers, Dunbar, who'd been sent to
check by the stream, waved for recognition. It took Matty a

moment to notice, something about the man so self-effacing that he blended into the background. Not a bad trait when hunting. He gestured for him to speak. "Sawdust and rough grindings there was. Still there, ground-in and soggy now, but still fresh and bright-colored, not gray and crumbling." A hesitant apology in his voice, Matty couldn't judge why.

And then, though he couldn't see it, he felt it against his back, a wary tension radiating from Rema. As if she'd gone stiff with apprehension. It made him shiver through the black tabard, a presentiment that maddeningly refused to rise to his consciousness, and Kharm remained stubbornly silent. "Mr. Dunbar, how many men in town work at the sawmill?"

"Ah," his throat constricted, Dunbar cast a pleading look skyward, unwilling to meet anyone's eyes. "Ah, it's Flaven Pelsaert's mill, runs it with two hired hands, Twyser brothers. Trees enough to saw, demand for lumber's greater than Flav can fill—that's why Coornherts planned on building a bigger mill." Duty done, he sought camouflage amongst his neighbors.

A tingling enthusiasm, impatience. Now he was on the trail of something, something that would explain everything! "Are the Twyser brothers present?" So obvious, once he had the clues in hand! Even Rema had discerned where this would lead before he had. Two young men of perhaps twenty eased forward, both large and awkward at the attention, big hands twining in front of them, broad, empty faces confused. Matty stiffled a groan. Hardly a coherent brain between them, both simpleminded but strong enough to do what Flaven needed.

The larger of the two smiled, sweet and pure as a child, tugged his brother's belt as he crept forward to examine Kharm. "I be Gilly, and this be m'brother, Nils. I be older, 'sponsible for him." How much could he pry out of them? And how much would be reliable? Only Kharm could judge and, so far, she continued to leave him on his own. Must mean she trusted his judgment.

"So you work at the sawmill with Flaven Pelsaert?" Take it step by step, see what transpired.

Gilly nodded with a grave enthusiasm. "Yup. Seven days each oct, one day off. Go in when the sun's a hand-span off the 'rizon, quit when it's a hand-span from setting. Flav taught us that so we'd know when to come." He held his hand in front of his face to demonstrate.

"Can you remember two days ago? Not yesterday, but the day before?"

Gilly and Nils conferred, Nils whispering in his brother's ear. "'Course we can!"

If either of the Twyser brothers had murdered Coornhert, it had to have been an accident, Matty was convinced. They wouldn't hang a simpleminded man for an accident, would they? Dismayed when Matty didn't continue, Nil rushed to share his information. "Remember 'cause it was different that afternoon. Flav left with us at quitting time. We like Flav, good man to work for." He scanned the crowd, anxious, wanting them to know how much they liked Flaven Pelsaert.

He didn't want to know, didn't want to think what was coming, but he had to, no choice. And mayhap he was wrong, their information totally innocent, but knowledge was building inside him. "And Flaven usually didn't leave with you?"

Gilly was jigging up and down, "No, we sweep up and leave'n he stays on, sharpens the saws. Leaving early, thought he meant to walk with us, pleasant. People are nice to us when Flav's around."

"Did Flaven walk home with you?"

Gilly's mouth drooped. "No. Said he had to see a man about a horse."

The crowd tittered and Nils rounded on his brother, shouting "Did not, Gilly! Said he hada see a man, Horst. You're making 'em laugh at us!"

Kharm's mindvoice came soft, almost remorseful. **"Do you remember Flaven's and Rema's conversation last night?"** He reached blindly, gripped the sword, knuckles whitening. Sawdust inside the house, Flaven saying at least he wasn't late for dinner as he'd been last night. And mud, not sawdust tracked that night. No, please, no! **"Ask her, you have to confirm it."**

Face averted, he struggled, a plea in his voice. "Was Flaven later than usual for dinner the night before last? Did he say where he'd been?"

An inarticulate groan of disbelief from behind him, he sensed Rema battling with herself. But before she could answer, Flaven stepped to her side, and Matty pivoted, though he couldn't bear to look up at their faces. "I won't have you lie for me, Rema, pervert what you hold dear, what you represent as Conciliator." She sobbed now against Flaven's chest. "Can't live easy with myself either, though I thought I could. I was ready to go under one way or the other, either the mill'd fail or this."

The crowd hung on his words and Flaven pressed on with his confession. "Aye, I killed Horst Coornhert. We'd agreed to meet at the stream, somehow didn't want people to know I was groveling to Horst—don't know why, we all have one time or another. Tried to convince Horst to partner me at my sawmill, expand what I already had. Why build a whole new mill except to run me into the ground? He handed me a rock, said that was as much as he'd invest in my rattle-trap old mill, and laughed at me. I . . . I could have gone it alone, tried to compete with him, but that laughter drove me crazy. I hit him with the rock before I knew what I was doing. Heard Lorris coming and I ran."

Kneeling alone, forgotten, Flaven the center of attention, bile burned Matty's throat, tears stung his eyes. Not Flaven!

"Yes, Flaven. I'm sorry, beloved. I told you the truth would hurt."

More words glossed over his fevered thoughts and he tried to listen, only to be sorry he had. From a depth of strength he hadn't conceived possible, Rema stood, clutching her husband's hand. "The penalty for manslaughter is death, those are our laws. You will hang by the neck until dead. So be it, Neu Bremeners?"

The crowd's reaction was nothing like the other day's when a mindless lust for justice had swept over them. Reluctant, eyes averted, faces grim at unexpected, suddenly unwanted justice, they brought the rope. The crowd parted to let Flaven and Rema Pelsaert and the rope bearers pass.

Stomach heaving, Matty staggered to his feet, barely missed throwing up on his too-tight boots. As if invisible, and he was, the crowd caring nothing for him now, he limped and ran to Rema's house, hastily gathered his belongings. The only minor relief granted him was stripping off his boots, throwing them away, and shoving his feet into the clogs, and then he and Kharm were walking fast, faster, escaping before they were noticed. His shoulders ached, anticipating thrown stones. In the distance the crowd gave a collective gasp, and he froze, finally began walking again.

Almost to the last street, almost to the roadway, and a hand caught his shoulder, jerked him to a halt. He spun, afraid he'd be hit, ready to dodge. The blow he received wasn't physical, but it struck with an equal force. Rema Pelsaert, eyes sunken, face a mask of pain, stood there, studying him as if he were an insect. "May I never see you again," she whispered. "You did what you had to do, it's not your fault, but I hate the very sight of you and that strange larchcat at your heels. Here!" And she thrust Flaven's boots at him, still supple, still faintly warm with a life that was no more. A gift of hatred: to walk in a dead man's boots. He clutched them, arms spasming so hard he couldn't release them, and turned and ran, anywhere, anyplace to escape that face of sorrow, the vengeance he'd brought down on them all.

"Doyce, finished with the loom? Supper's 'bout ready and the light must be near gone in there. Can't see what you're doing any longer."

The voice, so familiar yet unfamiliar, fragmented her vision of despair, Matty's anguished face crumpling in her mind. *"Oh, Khar,"* Doyce's voice shook at the enormity of the agony she'd participated in. *"Poor Matty, poor, poor Rema! Such a harsh world he's wandering in, no arms to welcome him."*

"Remember, he has Kharm." The ghatta's ears had perked at the mention of supper. **"You're finished, aren't you? And it's time to eat."**

"Finished? No, I'm not finished—I have to find out what happened! I can't leave Matty alone like that, inconsolable with grief."

"Doyce, I'm not calling again. Supper's ready," Inez warned.

Stretching one hind leg, then the other, Khar moseyed toward the kitchen. **"The loom's finished, beloved. And you need to eat, let Matty's pain pass from you. You can't bear it for him. He did as he was bidden—discovered the truth."**

Reluctance plain in every dragging step, Doyce crossed the room, lost somewhere between the here and now, the then and there. *"I have to make sure he's all right. Could I . . . could we . . . ?"*

"After supper."

And wonder of wonders, Doyce found she was starving. But then, Matty'd had no lunch that day, after all.

Hylan tramped beside the goat cart, shimmering cloak of rich amber velvet flowing from her shoulders, gift from a believer in the last village. Lushly opulent, fit for a king, but damned impractical, especially when the fall rains came, and they would. Also too noticeable, and that she didn't like. At least not yet. A glance over her shoulder revealed her admirers, the converted, still trailing in her wake, vying for the honor of drawing the goat cart if Harrap should falter or fail. The man possessed the strength and docility of an ox with the drug still coursing through his system. He seemed oblivious to their followers, adrift in his own private world, humming and smiling vaguely. Have to do something about his sandals, though, they'd nearly worn through. He was limping but completely insensible to the fact. Time enough to repair it tonight.

And at each village or hamlet more fervent believers joined the throng, no matter how she begged them to stay at home and wait, wait for the summons, the burning satisfaction that she'd fought and conquered, overcome the enemy. This, this ... parade an unseemly charade of thanksgiving, the frenzied clashing of bells, a drum heralding her arrival at the crossroad for Beechcroft. What next, psalms of celebration? A promising beginning, but too early, too soon for evil to be vanquished. They formed two neat lines behind her and marched, though some capered and danced, ecstatic with relief at what she offered—hope. Safety from Gleaners. Well, if one undertook a pilgrimage, one had to have pilgrims. At this rate she wouldn't reach Ruysdael and the next witch hazel planting for five or six days. Worrisome, that, the crowd had lost its sense of urgency, become a stately procession.

The ghatt snored atop the cart, sprawled like a dead thing, its absurd black and orange and white splotchings dull and rumpled, although the ghatt's stupor didn't deter Harrap's cheery chatter. His one-sided senseless conversation grated on her. Barnaby rode beside the ghatt, ears pricked, his stubby body blocking the ghatt if he started to slide. The dog acted despondent lately, cringing in her presence, whining,

drawing away from her. That hurt. But hurt, betrayal was to
be expected, welcomed. Perhaps tonight she'd be able to
elude her stalwart followers, slip off and pray, do what must
be done, regain the humility that slipped away when she was
least looking for it to disappear. But it felt so good to be
needed. Ah, to scourge herself in penance. Let this throng
see her do that, and she'd invoke mass frenzy, communal
whipping in blissful confidence that atonement united them,
amplified their worthiness.

When would the Guardians, the Seekers, the Chief Conciliators in each town connect her visit with the disappearance
of certain of its citizenry? In fact, when would they notice
the puzzling absences? Time, at least, ran on her side: those
she ferreted out, forked witch hazel wand unerring, were
canny and reticent, difficult to trap, willing to risk much to
maintain their mask.

She risked another glance at her followers, some marching
with a military precision, expressions neutral, eyes watchful.
As frightening in their own way as the other faces radiating
a glowing, soul-deep intensity that increased her unease,
fearful they mirrored her own expression. Touched her cheek
warily to see if she could feel it bursting through. The
marchers didn't resemble the other followers, singing and
dancing in innocent pleasure, as if her preachings, her very
presence lofted them heavenward, brought them closer to the
perfect, promised land secure from Resonant predations.

No, these others, the ones adorned with silver sickles
pinned over a wheat shaft, Reapers, they named themselves,
instilled order in the masses, did her bidding yet somehow
distanced her from the believers. Still, they did whatever she
asked with no demur, the instruments she'd been given, so
they must serve a purpose she didn't yet understand. Let
them play their part, she wouldn't deny them so long as their
plans coincided. Yet they vanished at any sign of authority,
lingered on the outskirts of towns until she'd passed
through, caught up with her on the other side. Then she
could shoo the dancers and musicians away, let them find
food and drink, spread her word, a discreet hint here, an offhand question there. And so she subtly checked the pulse
and temperature of each place, the villagers' eyes, their
walk, their whole demeanor as they passed by her, even their
degree of silence, enabled her to test fertile ground, fertile
minds. Her covert business came later, beyond township

boundaries when they sought her out, hesitant, needy, and she the poltice to draw their pain, assuage it. For that she was always ready, she and the witch hazel rod.

When the sacrificial lambs would reveal themselves, she had no idea. Too soon to worry—all would come in good time. She rubbed at the knife sheathed at her hip, hidden by the cloak. That would be the sign that she'd attained goodness, truly favored. Perhaps they wouldn't show themselves until the end, but to have two pure, unblemished souls to freely offer, that would be the final absolution. Perhaps they were Harrap and Parm, but she thought not, despite their goodness. They had a role in this, and might be sacrificed, but not the ultimate sacrifice. Best not to think about it, yearn for them, she herself wasn't sanctified enough to deserve them yet. Perhaps by the last town, Roermond, the last tree planted, they would come. She'd know them, no doubt about that. If only it could be sooner.

Cape flowing about her, incongruously crowned by a dusty face, hair wiring in all directions, Hylan Crailford waved her arm in encouragement, prodded Harrap with her witch hazel wand to goad him along. He broke into a ragged trot, and she was transfixed by a trail of blood on the ground where his feet had trod. Yes, blood to drag them along, fertilize the earth, make it yield. And yes, she really had to patch that sandal for him. Or mayhap Tadj could do it tonight. How had she, when had she come to depend on him so much? Always there, hair sleeked back, neat, eager to please, he and his sickle friends, orderly, organized. A crutch, mayhap, but one she couldn't always resist leaning upon.

He punched the awl through the tough leather, laid it aside, and worked the curved needle through. The heavy thread didn't want to pull smoothly, so he stopped, hunted out a nubbin of beeswax, and ran it along the thread. All this for a drug-mazed Shepherd. Tadj examined his handiwork, less than satisfied. No matter where he shifted the candle stub, his hands still cast shadows over his work. He used his nail to pluck at the stitch, see if it were tight. He'd never played cobbler before, but his previous work for the tailor had taught him to appreciate good quality.

"I've been wondering ... you know so much more than I," he looked through lowered lashes at Hylan, sitting across the fire from him, yet as distant as if she inhabited another world—or would like to. Rubbing his thumb over the mended leather, he decided to find a suede patch in his kit, use it as an overlay to smooth the repair. Whatever else might be said about Harrap, Tadj had to admit he had the loveliest feet he'd ever seen, the arches' curves breathtaking. No sculptor had even carved better. "About the Spacers, I mean," he clarified as Hylan finally looked up, rejoined their world. "Will they really return, do you think?"

She nodded magisterially. "They'll be called back, oh, yes. They're being called even now, so close. Just be thankful that our time isn't theirs. I saw the evidence, you know." Saw his puzzlement as he wrapped an overlay of suede around the sandal strap. Good, she didn't want Harrap bleeding again, not yet. "The stabilizer fin—in the heartwood," as if that explained everything.

It didn't, but he decided not to press. "I'm worried."

"Why?" That seemed to capture her attention. "Everyone sees the connection. Else they wouldn't be here." She flung an arm to indicate the surrounding camp fires.

"Between Gleaners and Spacers, you mean?" She'd gone to check Harrap, tucked his hand under the blanket as if he were a child, drew it close.

"Yes, exactly. And, well, I'd hate for them to lose faith in you." He jabbed the awl through the heavy sole, wriggling it until it popped through. Deceptive, the amount of force needed when it pierced so easily at first. "Most people aren't good at leaps of faith."

She studied him, covert and shy, taken by his blond good looks, the sharp, chiseled features so prominent in light and shadow. Reminded her of someone, but then everyone seemed to remind her of someone these days. He'd been so helpful, so solicitous. Was it wrong, sinful, to have someone to lean on? But oh, the loneliness of her burden despite her believers. "They follow me, they believe in me," she said, suddenly sullen. "They have faith in me," as if to imply *And you don't?* Ah, she'd dealt with disappointment before.

His mouth was tight with effort, his hand clutching the awl's knobbed end, bearing down with his full strength. "They have ... umph! ... faith that you can identify Gleaners, Resonants."

"And if I do that, if they do their part in destroying them, there won't be any contact with the Spacers." Patience, like lecturing a child to learn his logic.

"I know." He sounded peevish, put out. "I know and you know. But they need something more immediate, can't relate to a future threat that to their minds may never come."

"If not in this life, perhaps another, as Harrap would say. Don't fret, it will come sooner than that." She was touched that Harrap had begun to envision her as the Lady, Her representative in the physical world. Mayhap it was sinful to style herself as such, but she relished the compliment.

He fiddled with the sandal, not entirely pleased with his handiwork. "I just don't want to see your followers taking you and your mission for granted. Their immediate concern, their immediate panic involves Gleaners—"

"Scourge them from the land. I point my rod and divine who may pass and who may not! So sad that I must sacrifice them, but I must." The gray eyes had come alive, lustrous, her body tense, shoulders hunched, and she gave a pleasurable shiver. Scourge, yes . . . would Tadj share that with her, increase his own worthiness? She could feel the worthiness within him yearning to break free, its blinders removed. Ah, Barnaby ran now when he saw the switches. From a sound sleep the terrier's head jerked up; he looked at her and subsided with a whimpering moan, laid his head on the ghatt.

"Will you listen, please?" He managed to turn it from a command into a plea. "I want to help so badly. Beliefs—and believers—can falter, fade away if they can't truly envision the end goal. Without your believers to dispatch the Gleaners, what good will it do to identify them? What you need— what we need—is a middle, create true believers step by step. You have a beginning and an end, but the end's too far distant for most to fear, perceive as clearly as you do." A deep, earnest breath, "Most people are concerned with Now. Few are farsighted enough to think or care much beyond tomorrow, the end of an oct or octant at most. They lack the vision, the strength of purpose I'm beginning to have because of your tutelage."

"A middle?" He was groping toward something, but Hylan wasn't sure what. Perhaps she groped as well, was at fault for not seeing clearly? Always she fixated on the end, their world ruined. Had she jumped too fast, too far— ignored the road she must travel to arrive there? So many people lining the road, would they make the full journey with her? They must!

"Something to tie together their genuine fear of Gleaners here and now with the Future, the Spacers returning, laying waste to our land once again with their technology. The Past, the Then that you invoke is as far distant as Future to them." He could see her thinking, trying to understand an average mindset. "You know what would be the perfect knot to tie it together?" and didn't wait for a response, too eager now. "Eadwin, King of Marchmont, is visiting Canderis. He, if anyone, has the power to call to the skies, call the Spacers."

She froze, a beatific expression on her face, so open and joyous she looked almost beautiful. And he had created that look, he alone. "King of the Resonants! He comes Now!"

"Yes. If we could just figure out how to—"

Swaying on her knees, she hugged herself. "The sacrifice! The sacrifice will bring him to me—to us!" Hylan stilled, stretched to touch the blanket covering Harrap. "But is he the right one? It has to be right, you know."

"Mayhap we'll find the right one, have it revealed to us." It struck him then, to whom exactly did Hylan plan to make her sacrifice? She was hardly a strong believer in the Lady, but her followers were. And Harrap seemed to consider Hylan a surrogate for the Lady. He felt spent, drained. There was so much to think about, work through. He'd brought her this far; if the sacrifice would bring her the rest of the way, so be it. If only Baz were here to guide him, direct him. But he wasn't, and Tadj was expected to guide and mold Hylan to their needs.

Molding beauty wasn't easy at all—no wonder Baz so ruthlessly discarded or destroyed flawed glass, even when the flaw was practically imperceptible to the eye. Hylan was becoming a thing of beauty in his eyes, and he'd reform her, remold her until he attained perfection. Perfection created by his hands and mind, perfection to astonish Baz, exalt Tadj in his eyes. Something to glory in, expunge the mortification, the shame those sailors, no, not sailors but Gleaners, had inflicted on his mind and body and soul. Beauty could inspire, but inspiration could breed beauty. His inspiration.

Hylan stood straight and proud, arms rigid at her sides, face turned toward the stars, his sword of retribution. All he had to do was wield it for Baz. Not a sickle but a sword, a human sword. "I must ... you'll excuse me ... but I ..."

She strode from the fires, beyond sleeping figures hedging the cart at a distance, and Tadj could hear a strange, eager swishing beneath her cloak, as if she repetitiously slapped her thigh, harder and harder and harder.

Davvy shuffled backward, edging from side to side, desperate to avoid presenting a target. No, don't retreat, he gritted his teeth. Float until you gain an advantage, an opening to do damage. But the crudely-drawn circle's perimeter loomed at his heels. Touch it, cross it, and you forfeited. Best make his move soon. Something else Cady had drummed into him: don't wait forever for the perfect moment. It might not come, no matter how long you waited.

Fluid as smoke Cady drifted after him, almost ignoring him, as if he weren't worthy of notice, as if she were engrossed by something beyond him. Not going to fall for that! A tentative grab and she eluded him, his fingers closing on nothingness. Sweat itched and trickled under his collar, around his waist, his shoes too tight and clumsy, feet trapped by the unyielding leather. It sparked an idea. Waiting until they closed again, he left himself vulnerable, confident she'd let him practice breaking the hold. She lunged and he half-freed his foot, kicked his shoe in the air behind her head. Catching the motion out of the corner of her eye, Cady half-turned and Davvy pressed home his advantage, both hands locking on her wrist as he dipped under her arm and straightened behind her, a hairsbreadth from pinning her arm between her shoulder blades. Limber as a willow she bent and twisted, looped free and sent him sailing across the ring.

He landed hard on his back, panting, rubbing his aching hip. Smerdle—it hurt! Kangsnarging woman'd tossed him like a rag doll, and with her bad arm, too. He wished she'd let him see the scar, like a badge of honor for protecting the old lady from the Reapers at the Elder Hostel. Smerdle! He couldn't protect himself, let alone anyone else if he didn't practice harder. She'd successfully fought men larger than she, so shouldn't he be able to handle her?

Cady's self-defense lessons were serious but fun, took his mind off things, gave him something to do. He was comfortable being around adults, indulged and petted; that had been the norm at the Research Hospice, but not here. He'd played his share of childish games, but always with adults, allowed to win, seldom having to truly test his mettle against his peers. Doyce and her mother and sister were nice but strict, didn't let him have his way like Swan did. No one to boss around here, not even Cady, who wasn't *that* much older. No one to charm or cajole, almost as if they'd been immunized against him.

Well, what was he supposed to be? Not allowed to be a little boy any longer, but not conferred adult responsibilities, either—confusing. As if he were a little old man trapped in an ungainly twelve-year-old body. Always too aware of adults and what they expected of him—without ever having to read their minds. Always overconcerned with doing right, being good—or being bad because he could get away with it, though that lessened the savor of it. Now this. Cady was tall but bony, couldn't weigh that much more because he was solid, chunky from all of Nana Cookie's good baking. And Cady wasn't going to let him win, not unless he'd earned it.

Ignoring her outstretched hand, he heaved himself up, then bent so his hands touched the ground and stretched some of the kinks from his protesting body. F'een watched from outside the circle, olive eyes eager, quivering as if he wanted to join in. He probably couldn't toss even the ghatt outside the circle. Adults *always* expected too much of him, and the inequity of it all left him flushed and angry. Swan expecting too much of him, and hadn't he been nursing her to make up for her being hurt because of him? A self-pitying tear trickled down his cheek. Honest—he hadn't meant to dash off like that in the midst of battle, banner in hand, loud huzzahs bursting from him. And he hadn't meant for her to be wounded when she tried to retrieve him! It was so unfair! And just when he thought she'd begun to forgive him, what did she do? Send him away like an unwanted parcel. With Doyce, no less, who acted as if she inhabited another world half the time lately. He didn't dare disturb the babies now, other than to tickle them lightly, reassure himself they were fine despite Doyce's moodiness. Away here in the country with no one else the least like him, no other Resonants near.

And even if there were, nobody else liked Resonants or trusted them; people made fear signs when they passed, Faertom had told him. Francie and Doyce's mother didn't make fear signs, but he sensed a niggling distrust held under tight wraps. All he wanted was to be like everyone else, accepted for his flaws and strengths. How could anyone not like him? He kicked at the dirt with his shoed foot, face screwed in an agony of thought. Pawed at the ground again, building up courage to launch himself at Cady, waiting as if she had nothing else in the world to do. Fine thing, indulging herself by thrashing him! Treat him like that, would they? Well, he could beat Cady, could beat anyone who stood in his way.

Use what you've been given, isn't that what Cady had admonished? Use your size, your weight, your brains, even your weak points to draw out the opposition, lure them along, then use what you're best at. Use what you've been given. Well, he'd kept his best skill under wraps, something Cady lacked, couldn't imagine.

"Going to sulk all day, Davvy?" she taunted, hands on hips. "If you are, put on your coat or you'll catch cold, standing around all hot and sweaty." She looked as coolly fresh as mint. Hand scrubbing under his nose to hide his scowl, he began to bob and weave, setting up a pattern, following through, mind ahead of body, body ahead of mind, mentally stepping back to watch himself, watch her. Feint, feint, jab. Don't worry about missing, that was the plan. Feint, feint, fake, pretend you've lost your nerve.

Did what he'd been cautioned against from the beginning, let his eyes shift, his stance fractionally reveal his intended move. The giveaway signs she'd been teaching him to read in an opponent. Yes, set it up, let her assume he wouldn't deviate, couldn't deviate, didn't know he'd given himself away. Give her an opening. And watch, watch—not only her eyes, her body to judge if she'd take the lure, but watch her mind, listen in, then beat her to the punch when she least expected it. Do it! Do it, because he was tired of being little, of being thwarted. And he wanted his own way. Now!

Letting down his guard, he sketched an eager, amateurish charge as she counteracted his previous clumsy move. Yes, he could hear her mind sketching her attack pattern, how hard to hit him to teach him a lesson. Not conscious thought, but exploding colors, synapses sparking and connecting that drew lines clear as a map. Well, no more lessons. Now it was time for him to teach!

"Davvy! Cady!" As the cry carried, his concentration broke, distracted him from what he'd overheard in Cady's mind. The next thing he knew he went cartwheeling across the circle as Cady jammed a hand under his armpit, used his own momentum to propel him up and over. Even in the middle of this interruption she hadn't allowed her own concentration to break.

He landed facedown, protecting his face with an arm as he skidded practically to Francie's feet. "Are you all right?" Francie asked, head cocked to examine the minor furrow he'd plowed with his chin. Gulping, spitting dirt, he blinked rapidly to show that he was. Hoped he was, but wasn't sure yet. She waved a broadside in his face, the air current grazing his overheated skin, ruffling hair off his sticky forehead. "You've both got to hear this! It's so exciting!" A shake of the paper. "The King of Marchmont is making a royal progress through Canderis, the first in history! Isn't that something! Imagine that, royalty here—and as close as Ruysdael. And special royalty at that." A wink in Davvy's direction at the shared secret, one that was never said aloud here.

Working himself onto hands and knees, Davvy let his head hang, still whipped. This time he let Cady haul him upright, glad for the help. "I ... saw ..." he worked to even his breathing, "the king ... before. Talked with him, even. And lots of the others." He left that ambiguous on purpose. Mostly he'd been ignored in that hastily organized camp for the wounded, the border spot where negotiations between Marchmont and Canderis had begun.

"Is he handsome, Davvy?" Francie's eyes twinkled, and for a moment Davvy forgot how old she was, the way her eyes lit up. Be almost pretty if she weren't gimpy on one side.

"Oh, yes," he took her arm, tucked his free arm into Cady's so that he stood between them, confident they hung on his every word. "Though I don't know if handsome's quite right. Nice open face, sensitive but worried looking behind that beard, as if he knew he'd have too much to deal with too soon. I told him, 'King Eadwin, don't fret. You're a Resonant and a Bondmate.' He bonded with one of the biggest, furriest, wildest ghatts you can imagine. Well, I said, 'King Eadwin, you can succeed at anything ...' "

A whisper pierced his brain. F'een sat, rigid with disapproval, glaring, boring him through. **"Don't you dare try to cheat on Cady like that again!"**

"Cheat?" He projected wounded innocence, hoping neither woman would notice his pause. It must be the ghatt 'speaking

him, had to be. No other Resonants around. But the ghatti wouldn't 'speak just anyone. *"I wouldn't cheat. Cady said to use what I had, what I did best to win."*

"Cheat you did. Took unfair advantage. Now do you see why people are afraid of Resonants?" F'een's words hissed and sizzled. **"And lie as well! King's friend, indeed! He spoke with you once. Remember what he said?"** Davvy winced; how could the ghatt know? **"He said, 'You're a brave lad, though a foolish one. You'll outgrow that, I trust.' Well, you haven't yet, have you? Just added dishonesty to foolishness."**

"But what's the matter with spinning a little story they'll both enjoy? So what if it isn't true?" He drew himself up, clutching the women's arms, deriving strength and innocent support from them. Oh, smerdling bandersnees—was F'een telling Cady everything? *"I did see the king, after all. I just didn't really . . . he didn't really have time . . ."* He ground to a halt.

"Davvy, tell us more," Francie cajoled. And Cady looked interested, impressed. It hurt, it really did. He wanted to be the center of attention, have everyone like him, respect him.

He swallowed hard, managed a weak grin. "Didn't really talk with the king, you know. Just teasing. Though I did see him a fair number of times, sometimes even up close." He searched for another subject to pursue. "As to handsome, you should see that Chevalier Capitain Arras Muscadeine with his bold mustache, those gaudy shirts, him that's now Defense Lord. Ask Doyce, let her tell you. She thought him mighty handsome."

A minor surge of triumph, let Doyce wriggle out of that if she could, let her do the telling, the denying, let her walk the path of truth without trampling its margins. Ought to make for an interesting supper tonight.

"I don't like you very much," came F'een's parting shot. **"Nor will Khar either, when I tell her."**

He ignored the ghatt, or tried to do so. "Do you think we could go see the king? Is Ruysdael very near here?" A scary but prideful thought to have the king acknowledge him as a Resonant, no more hiding, pretending. But it couldn't, shouldn't be known—wasn't that why Swan had banished him here, for safety's sake? If he were acknowledged for what he was, would that put Doyce and the babies, her mother and sister, even Cady in danger? He shrugged, uncomfortable with his thoughts. Time enough to decide later—if they ever went to Ruysdael. Mayhap he'd go, and mayhap he wouldn't, though no one would realize the sacrifice he'd be making to protect them all by staying home.

Grim behind her desk, Mahafny burrowed her hands inside her sleeves, heartily wishing the desk were a real barricade. A brick wall would be better, blockade her from the controversy besieging her from across the desk. She felt as if the Research Hospice had been overrun, and indeed it had been—Eadwin's royal entourage and his soldiers, not to mention the matching Guardian complement who'd hastily escorted the Monitor north after receiving word of Eadwin's unscheduled stop at the Hospice rather than proceeding directly to Gaernett.

Nigh on to three hundred people swarmed inside and outside the Hospice, tents erected in the yards, the stables full, every room in the Hospice crammed. *"We're not a bloody inn, you know,"* she 'spoke Saam, stretched on the windowsill behind her.

"So much for peace and solitude, the tranquillity of research," he yawned, whiskers spreading and flattening through a grimace. Actually, the commotion rather pleased him because it forced Mahafny to tear her mind away from that infernal contraption she'd liberated from the cellars. Now draped in an old sheet it sat on the table against the wall by the door, perfectly innocuous and innocent-looking. Just thinking about it made his fur rise, his skin itch, though not with the same anticipatory delight Mr. Farnham experienced. The machine had been taken apart and put together again, dusted and polished, the glass plates lovingly cleaned until they sparkled. Endowed with a mechanical aptitude they hadn't expected, old Farnham had done every bit himself. Of course, and Saam wrapped his tail over his eyes, the reason behind Farnham's assiduousness had come clear once the device was reassembled, and Mr. Farnham had gestured Mahafny to the crank, imploring "Do me again, ma'am!" Mahafny, aghast, had snapped, "Absolutely not!"

Well, the machine's safely under wraps, so stop thinking about it, he decided as he peered cautiously over his tail. Entirely too many strong personalities jammed the room,

Mahafny's not the least of them. Resplendent in black with crimson- and yellow-slashed sleeves certain to make a redwinged blackbird look dowdy, Arras Muscadeine spoke in vehement undertones with the Monitor. Eadwin, King of Marchmont, in cream and sky blue, hardly flashy but quietly elegant, wandered, confident Muscadeine pressed his case for him. The Monitor, Kyril van Beieven, looked the worse for wear and with good reason; it had been an exhausting ride on short notice to reach the Hospice. Fine for seasoned soldiers like the Guardians, but not so fine for a middle-aged man more used to sitting and paperwork. The farther he strayed from the capital, the more the Monitor worried what transpired in his absence. And Mahafny Annendahl, beleaguered behind her desk, appealed to by one man or another, clearly simmering at their interruption.

"**Are things always this ... vibrant ... in Marchmont?**" he inquired of the ghatt padding around to inspect the room, sticking his nose here and there. The ghatt sported several shaved patches along his back and neck, the fur clipped close to his skin a pale cream in contrast to the longer guard hairs of caramel and gray and buff. To ensure that Hru'rul's wounds were properly cleansed and sutured, the ghatt had suffered the indignity of having his fur shaved so they could treat the claw marks. A dark threading of stitches showed in two places.

Hru'rul appeared unalarmed by the interplay of personalities, a connoisseur of the textures and flavors of their interactions. Jumping on an adjacent window ledge, the ghatt twisted to lick at a wound. "**When Muscadeine with Eadwin, yes. Even sitting silent, mindtalking. Makes me tired, wanting nap. Mighty Hru'rul conserving strength.**"

"**Yes, well, it's not a bad idea. And we ghatti can sleep anywhere, despite the din.**" The steel-gray ghatt compacted himself on the sill, yellow eyes observant. "**Nap if you like, but I think I'll listen. Lick your wounds for you later if you want. Hard to reach, I know.**"

"But the plan had you advancing directly to Gaernett. It's not only the capital but our largest city," Kyril van Beieven bobbed in Eadwin's wake. "I can't have you wandering from town to town willy-nilly. I have to send proper escorts."

"Protection, you mean," Arras Muscadeine broke in. "It's all about protection, van Beieven. I won't have my king in any danger if I can help it. We've our own soldiers, but the populace will be more amenable to obeying your Guardians, their own."

Eadwin's mouth quirked, although he didn't pause, nearly lost van Beieven as he executed a sharp right turn and banked beside Mahafny's desk. Mahafny rolled her eyes at him, clearly displeased he'd breeched her refuge. "I'm not planning on wandering willy-nilly, as you call it. We agreed on the route. The route remains the same—it's merely the order we're altering, commencing the royal circuit here and concluding by visiting your fair capital."

The Monitor sputtered and Muscadeine's mouth thinned under his mustache as Eadwin continued. "Firstly, as you're so well aware, Jenet Wycherley is being held hostage by the Resonants. I take it he's not been located yet?"

"Well, of course I've had Guardians out trying to locate him," the Monitors's face was mottled, and he pressed a fist against his breastbone. "Indigestion," he muttered.

"What about Seekers, Kyril?" Mahafny spoke at last. "Wouldn't that make sense? Surely the ghatti could contact Rawn or T'ss, discover their location."

"I don't command the Seekers Veritas, as well you know."

"I know you don't," Mahafny laid both hands flat on the desk, studying their backs. "But I can't believe Swan would deny two of her own, Jenret and Sarrett. She's been known to borrow Sergeant Balthazar Lamb to solve problems of that sort before."

The Monitor swung, arm outstretched to point at Saam. "Ask him. Mayhap you'll receive a less convoluted answer than the one I got from Swan."

Saam's nose twitched and he studied the window ledge as the silence grew. **"From what I can gather through Mem'now and the mindnet, the ghatti do know where Rawn and T'ss are. However, Rawn feels it might be ..."** he hesitated, hoped Mahafny retained a modicum of humor regarding her nephew, **"salutary for Jenret to cool his heels a bit. An opportunity to master alternate ways to cope with problems, the mind over physical action. A chance to form a link with the Resonants. Consequently, none of the ghatti will reveal their location."**

Its springs creaking as she rocked back in her chair, Mahafny regarded the ghatt and waved her hands in a hopeless gesture. "I apologize, Kyril. I underestimated Swan as well. The ghatti know, but they're not telling." She shook her head in embarrassment. "They think Jenret and the Resonants should get to know one another, come to trust each other."

From behind her shoulder Eadwin spoke. "Not so unreasonable. He *is* a Resonant, but he isn't one of theirs, someone they're comfortable with, someone who's shared their adversities. If only I could find them, talk with them! You know, van Beieven, from what you've indicated, they must be in the vicinity, somewhere here on the edges of the Tetonords. That's part of my reason for starting the circuit out of sequence. If we can assuage your citizens' fears in this part of Canderis, mayhap the Resonants would feel safer in revealing themselves."

"That's not the only problem facing us, Marchmont and Canderis alike. There's something else you've forgotten, Kyril." Arras Muscadeine leaned against the wall, hand toying with the sheet draped over the machine, fingers tweaking and pleating it. Van Beieven stalked over, stood practically nose to nose with him. "Not just you, but Mahafny as well, I suspect," he placated.

"And what's that?" Their protests overrode and tangled with each other, truculence on the Monitor's part, patent surprise and discomfort on Mahafny's.

"Do we know," he pounded fist against palm, softly hammering home his words, "where Parm and Harrap are? What Hylan Crailford is doing?"

"Oh, that?" The Monitor shrugged, dismissive, faintly scornful. "I tell you there's nothing to worry about from that woman, not when I've more serious problems—like Reapers willing to murder anyone they suspect is a Resonant." He would *not* relive that night with Darl and Alyse, the dark streets closing in on him, the Reapers crowding forward.

"Mahafny?"

Eyes shut, she shook her head, shame creeping over her. How could she have shunted them out of her mind so easily? "I don't think I've been paying much attention to what Saam's found out lately, been somewhat distracted. But with good and justifiable reason," she added. "I've something important to show you."

"Later, Mahafny. We've things to settle here and now." Muscadeine hitched his hip on the table, nudging the draped machine aside. "That's why we sent Hru'rul ahead to contact Saam, find out what was happening. According to

Saam—and he'll correct me if I'm wrong, I'm sure—Parm's making even less sense than usual. Rambling, almost as if he's drunk."

"Ghatti don't drink," Mahafny snapped, and it was clear she was simultaneously and furiously 'speaking Saam. "But he could be . . . drugged."

"Yes, and if he's been drugged, then isn't it likely that Harrap's been drugged as well? I can't envision Harrap letting anyone hurt Parm; the only way that could happen is if he were incapacitated as well. The source must be Hylan, and if she's drugging them both, it must be because she's hiding something from them. Something a Seeker and a Shepherd wouldn't approve of." Eadwin laid a hand on Mahafny's shoulder, calming, protective. "Arras and I talked it through as we rode here. I've 'spoken Saam about it."

"Well, where are they, then?" Van Beieven pressed at his chest again, cheeks bulging as he suppressed a belch. "We can send Guardians to extricate Harrap and Parm from Hylan Crailford's company, though I still don't have any grounds to arrest or detain her, not until we have evidence they've been unwillingly drugged or coerced in some manner." Almost bitterly, "Unless there's more you haven't told me?"

"According to Saam, it sounds as if they're heading to Ruysdael," Eadwin placated. "And that just happens to be where I think we should make our first official stop on the royal circuit. Ceremonies, civilities, bowing and scraping and polite discussions do just so much good, but if we can convince Canderis that we Resonants are useful, helpful, so much the better. If we can rescue Harrap, control Hylan Crailford, perhaps even rescue Jenret Wycherley and his friends, they'll see we have a role to play!"

"Beyond the reason you've got Dwyna Bannerjee peering around my Research Hospice, you mean?" Mahafny snapped her sleeves down, curious why Kyril looked both apprehensive and smugly satisfied at the mention of Dwyna's name, like a schoolboy relieved of tattling because someone had beaten him to it. What was he keeping from her now? "It might just work, all of it, bit by bit, accretion by accretion. Unless you're staking your all on one incredibly melodramatic climax to proclaim your worth?" Eadwin had the grace to color slightly, but Muscadeine's eyebrows gave her a sardonic salute of amusement.

"Go to Ruysdael, go anywhere you damn choose, I don't know if I'm in charge here anymore or not." Van Beieven stalked toward the door, complexion ashy with fatigue.

"Kyril, wait!" Mahafny hurried around the desk, tugged his arm, almost hectically animated. After all, this was what he'd been browbeating her for for so long. "Don't you want to see my surprise? It's something you've been at me to do—a way to discover who is and who isn't a Resonant. Or at least I think it is." Their collective startlement soothed her vanity, but the muted hope Kyril radiated made her wince in sympathy for the burdens he carried.

With a flourish she tossed back the sheet to reveal the mechanical device beneath, Saam bounding out of the room, Hru'rul tight on his heels a scant moment later. **"I am *not* staying anywhere near that thing if you propose to crank it up again,"** she heard him say as he and Hru'rul dashed into the hall.

"Scaredy-cat," she informed the tip of his tail as it disappeared down the stairs. "At any rate, gentlemen, behold!"

They crowded the table, gingerly poking at it, touching the metal rods and wires, tracing the two curved arms tipped with metal balls, almost the way an ox's horns are capped. The circular glass plates gleamed from Mr. Farnham's zealous cleaning. "What does it do? How does it work?" Eadwin laid a hesitant hand on the handle but didn't turn it.

"I should warn you—Eadwin, Arras—that the reaction you feel won't harm you but may surprise you. It's, ah," she searched for the words, decided she was a blunt old eumedico, mixed company or not, "when it stops, there's almost a sensation of sexual relief involved, the satiation or repletion one feels after orgasm. So please don't entertain any ideas, because I'm entirely too old for such nonsense."

"Hardly nonsense when we've an attractive, elegant woman sharing the room with us," Arras bowed, gallantly flirtatious. "But, as gentlemen, I can assure you we'll control ourselves."

Removing Eadwin's hand from the crank, she began to turn it, slowly at first, then faster, the belts humming and thrumming, the glass plates spinning against each other in opposite directions, blue-white sparks beginning to flash, fly between the balls. Van Beieven stood, puzzled, feeling nothing, unsure what to make of the other men's reactions, their grimaces, the strange contortions their limbs made. "Kyril, I

have to speak to you about—" and he belatedly realized that
Darl Allgood had burst into the room, stumbling to a halt as
the peculiar effect overtook him as well, dropping him to his
knees.

Shocked, Mahafny let go of the crank as if it burned, the
plates gradually spinning slower and stopping, Allgood
seized by the same intense relief and release flooding
Eadwin and Muscadeine. "Oh, Blessed Lady, not you, too,
Darl?" the Monitor whispered and fainted dead away.

The days and nights lagged for Jenret, his near-brush with
death evidence he was doomed, the "when" only a matter of
time. Never had he felt such an impotent sense of inevitabil-
ity, doom. Win free, reach Doyce, be with her when the baby
came—the tasks mocked him, and he cudgeled his brain for
a way to accomplish them. His mind clenched tight, ready to
explode with all the thoughts he yearned to 'speak, but if he
so much as attempted a phrase of mindspeech, Garvey or
one of the others cuffed down his words, lashed back without mercy. Oh, he couldn't exactly blame them, or at least
didn't when his thinking was clear, reasonably pragmatic.
Garvey was retaliating both for being balked at killing
Jenret, justifiably so in his eyes, and for Rawn's and T'ss's
attack. His face resembled nothing so much as a patchwork
quilt, seamed with scratches, his arm swollen and hot-
looking.

Jenret's headache throbbed harder, almost constant now,
no surcease. Wonderful, those low-grade constant headaches
when his Resonant skills were awakening in Marchmont,
and headaches now because they were trapped inside, not allowed free play. Well, lose hope, lose all, so he husbanded
himself for one incredible soaring mindcry, a plea for help if
everyone else were simultaneously distracted. Worse still,
his moodiness estranged him from Sarrett, Towbin, even
Yulyn, she most of all who should have understood his pain.

Mostly he sat in stony silence, arms wrapped around
knees, watching yet not watching everything around him,
sunk in despair, even refusing to gamble. When he did rouse
himself, he taunted his captors in viciously subtle ways that
niggled under their skins. Easy enough to do, given his reputation as supercilious, condescending, arrogant—why try to

live it down now? Someone had taken pity on him the other night, allotted him a dipperful of wine with dinner. Much as he'd craved the wine, the relaxation it might offer, he'd raised the gourd to his lips, taken a sip and spat it in a fine spray, mouth curling as he muttered "vinegar" just loud enough to be heard. Laying the dipper aside, saying, "Thank you, but not to my taste. Palate's too well-educated. Best you drink it and enjoy it." Yes, small but transitory victories.

Sometimes when grief and rage flamed too hot, threatened to consume him, he hectored them for being a ragtag band of cowards, not brave enough to face the world, wrestle the respect they deserved from it. But his haranguing apparently fell on deaf ears, although in retrospect he could gauge its effectiveness by his treatment on changing camps. Whether care was taken to guide him over exposed roots or rocks with the hood in place on his head, or whether he was left to trip and fall, right himself as best he could. Or worst of all, once, when he'd been deserted—or so it seemed—hood cinched tight around his neck, hands locked behind him, ankles manacled. Left to stumble in darkness, material steamy with his breath, clinging to mouth and nostrils as he inhaled, clueless where he was, where he was going, whether anyone else lingered near, the silence deafening except for Rawn's worried directions. He'd finally stopped, dropped to his knees and waited. Either they'd drag him along with them or they wouldn't, and if they didn't, Rawn would free him somehow. But that, he suspected, was far too much to hope for. Any annoyances he visited on them revisited him tenfold.

As to where they camped now, he had no idea. Sometimes they climbed higher into the mountains until he thought they finally planned to cross into Marchmont, sometimes they sought lower ground. Could have been circle-dancing, but weren't; Rawn had assured him.

Tonight he sat as distant from the fire as they'd allow, arms embracing his knees, idly kicking his heel into the ground, not even realizing it. Rawn sat beside him, but at last stretched lazily and joined T'ss by the fire. Even Rawn found his company lacking these days. Worth it to ask T'ss and Rawn to play mindtricks, let their ghatti humor have full sway? Damn Resonants acted so sober-sided serious it might do them some good, make them lighten up a little. Question was, would Rawn indulge him? T'ss might, curiosity piqued until Sarrett chastised him. Oh, Rawn'd do it if it'd help them escape, but he lacked the temperament to tease, bedevil for the sake of it. Except for bedeviling him, his Bondmate.

Jenret ground his heel harder and took conscious note of his compulsion. Well, well, nervous tics now. Ran his right hand down his leg, holding the chain left-handed so it wouldn't rattle, and prodded at the dirt he'd disturbed. Burrowing like a mole. If only he could burrow away, escape them that easily. Digging in his fingers, he touched something hard and smooth, one finger slipping into a gap, an interstice where the earth wasn't so tightly packed. Interested despite himself he dug deeper, furtively checking if anyone noticed. Dark over here, and his dark clothing obscured the mound of dirt rapidly accumulating under his leg. In turn, that meant he lacked light enough to see clearly, dependent on his sense of touch.

Felt like, felt like . . . he worked his way farther, elongating the trench carved by his heel so it ran toward him, sheltered by his bent leg. Felt like . . . bone? Short and thin, tiny bits of knob between them. Changed hands, reached beneath his leg and placed his left hand palm down in the opening, revulsion rising as the bits and pieces organized themselves in his mind, matched the flesh overlay. A skeletal human hand! Gah! His neck hairs rose and he shivered. Did they plan to bury him here, too?

But at that moment something sharp slashed his thumb. Damn, felt as if it'd sliced to the bone. He jerked clear, sucked the dirty, bleeding thumb. *"Rawn,"* he 'spoke, urgent to share the puzzle, *"come here, tell me what you see."*

Reluctant at abandoning the fire, Rawn sauntered over, sniffing the scent of turned earth, a trailing whiff of blood. He hunkered by the trench, stuck his nose in, sniffing audibly, dirt particles dusting whiskers and muzzle. **"Hand. Human,"** he announced with a sneeze. **"Something near it, not sure what."**

"I know." Mounting excitement, a mystery, an unknown to shatter the numbing dullness. And mayhap more than that. Of course, he grinned, smothered it against his knee, I've dug up a skeleton key! *"Can you dig for it? Careful—it's sharp. Look!"* He thrust his thumb under the ghatt's nose to prove the damage. *"Just don't dig too vigorously, disturb things too badly. Don't want them to notice what we're up to, and we'll have to cover it come morning."*

"**It's got a hilt, I think.**" Rawn dug, working away from the spot where Jenret's blood scented the dirt. He dipped a paw with slow patience, scooted it along the object's side, not over it. "**Wait, think I can get it, if I . . .**" Tongue protruding in concentration, he fished with his claws, hooked them under the edge and dragged it forth. "**Like so. There!**" Satisfied, he flipped the thing clear of the trench so Jenret could grasp it.

A knife! Dirt-encrusted, but the shape felt solidly reassuring beneath his grip. Guilty as a grave robber, he laid it down, flicked fingers against it to dislodge the dirt, tapped it against his boot heel to knock off more. *"I wonder how it got here? Who that is—er, was."* Slipping the knife under his thigh to shield it, he began to shovel dirt back into the hole. *"Best get this covered up. Help me, Rawn."*

With Rawn's help, he refilled the trench, Jenret packing it in with the heel of his hand, trying to tamp it with his foot without being obvious. *"There,"* a triumphant glow warmed him inside, *"that should do it."*

"**Not quite.**" Rawn scratched at leaves and pine needles, Jenret helping rake them over the disturbed earth.

Traces mostly obliterated, he felt secure enough to examine his treasure, but only after risking a long, surveying glance to make sure his warders slept. Delicately fingering the knife to gauge its size, its heft and grip, he was amazed it had remained so sharp and unblemished. Eyes closed, he let his fingers analyze it—completely whole and all of a piece, its grip a continuation of the blade, no wood or leather wrapping to it. No, not eaten away by dirt, the hilt fit his palm comfortably, and he could feel, when he scratched his nails across it, cross-hatching to improve the grip.

"Can't have been buried too long," he remarked and shivered, remembering the bony hand. What would he have found if he'd dug further? *"Wasn't buried that deeply either."*

Rawn's whiskers grazed his hand as the ghatt conducted his own investigation. "**I don't agree. A scent of great age clings to it. It's possible that nature's pared away the earth over the grave, ice scraping across it, water flow, I'm not sure.**"

Hoarding the knife to himself, faintly jealous of Rawn's interest, he worked the blade against his ankle chain, rubbing the blade against a link. Might as well polish it a bit, it deserved better care than it had received. To his infinite surprise the blade peeled a thin sprig of metal with it, easy as paring a butter curl. A little harder, a little more force, and a larger paring spiraled free, the blade sliding along the link and nicking the next one before he could stop his motion.

"Rawn," his breath stopped, made him almost light-headed with delight, *"I think it's arborfer! It cuts like a dream!"*

"Must be an old Erakwan grave, then."

"But it can't be that old," he protested, unconvinced.

"Has to be. Arborfer hasn't grown this far south in years. Addawanna and Nakum and the Erakwa use steel knives like ours. This must be a relic from the past when it was plentiful enough that you'd bury it with someone because more was readily available."

With a stifled grumble, Jenret acquiesced. As usual, Rawn made sense and, frankly, he'd no desire to argue the knife's provenance, as long as he had it. Hope blossomed, though he refused to force it to full-bloom—a weapon, a way to defend himself, perhaps even escape!

"Think it through, think it through," Rawn nipped his joy in the bud. **"You can't just burst out of camp, stabbing Resonants left and right to escape, can you? What about Towbin and Sarrett and Yulyn? Would you desert them? Or do you think you can protect yourself and them with one little, though very sharp, knife?"**

"I don't know, Rawn, I don't know yet." Rawn's comments pricked his pride, his sense of honor. Could he kill a fellow Resonant—even Somerset Garvey?—slink up on him and slash his throat? Could he cold-bloodedly kill anyone, Resonant or Normal? And the answer drumming at the front of his brain was a resounding "Yes!" If he had to, if he lacked any other choice. After all, what option had they given him? His building, righteous rage felt good, gave him a purpose, a justification.

Except ... except ... however desperate he might be, they had even greater justification for their despair. Despite his black mood he couldn't envision them killing him unless hope was a long-forgotten memory. They had no stomach for killing—cooler heads had prevailed, even during the incident with Garvey. And Garvey, Towbin had whispered to him that night, didn't know where his sons were, if they survived, was half-mad with grief. They didn't want to kill him and he didn't want to kill them. His mind wavered, yearned to regain that dangerous, ugly edge, justify any action—would he do anything, anything at all to return to Doyce? Abandon the others? Knew he could not, although it was shamefully close, regret slashing as sharp as the arborfer blade.

Rawn continued his vigil, black-furred implacability, awaiting his answer, trusting him to search his heart. Sinking the knife into the dirt so it stood upright, he scratched Rawn's ears. *"Embarrassing to have two better halves—you and Doyce. Should make me whole, perfect, but it doesn't seem to, does it?"*

"I am not your conscience, nor is Doyce, but neither of us minds prodding you a bit."

"And damn well enjoy it," Jenret groused. *"Always trying to get my goat."*

Rawn's head swung round, consternation furrowing his brow. **"Why would I want your goat? You don't have one—and even if you did, why would I want it?"**

"Figure of speech, my friend, and an old one at that."

"If they don't let you shave soon, I'd be able to tug you by your chin whiskers just like a goat." Rawn bit down on the back of Jenret's hand. **"Now, what do you plan to do with the knife?"**

Cradling it against his boot, he thought. *"Well, there's nothing wrong with being prepared to escape—if the right opportunity comes along. First, I'm going to shave these links as thin as I can without making them look as if I've tampered with them. Get them thin enough and I should be able to snap them if the time's ripe. At least I'll be ready if an opportunity comes my way."*

Rawn made an aheming sound in his throat, a polite cough. **"I've another ancient saying for you. You could turn the tables on them, seize one of them as a hostage, although how and why you'd turn a table on someone, I don't understand."**

"An admirable thought, my favorite ghatt, an audaciously admirable thought that I'll bear in mind." And with that Jenret set to work, painstakingly shaving the inside of each link, working by touch, stifling his impatience now that he had a goal in mind.

Rawn watched, impatient with himself and with Jenret.

How many opportunities would his Bond squander? Escape,
avoid, elude—all things that Jenret did without conscious
thought, a preservative instinct to avoid a commitment that
might bind his heart and soul. At first Rawn had convinced
himself Jenret's captivity would provide an opportunity for
him to really learn what Resonants and their lives were like.
Garvey's actions had temporarily shaken but not dissuaded
the ghatt. If only Jenret would reach beyond himself, his
own needs. Another wasted opportunity, just as his relationship with Doyce boded that. And should Khar suspect he
thought that, she'd flay him alive. What would it take to
change Jenret?

Despite her intentions, Doyce found it was several days
before she dared return to Matty's world, see how he fared.
Each time she thought of him driven out of Neu Bremen, re-
viled for discerning the truth, it made her question anew everything she'd taken for granted about the Seekers' place in
society. A hard-won place. And questioning wasn't a wise
idea—the last time she'd sustained a crisis of faith she'd
been expelled from the eumedicos.

**"I understand the ceremony's quite impressive, reeks
of solemn disdain and disappointment."** Khar's eye
whiskers jutted forward.

She'd been holding a skein of yarn between her hands,
obediently dipping one, then the other as her mother re-
wound it into balls. Inez didn't harbor her own dislike of
knitting, and Doyce suspected she'd be seeing baby sweaters
speedily tumbling from the needles. By the time she'd manage to finish anything, the baby would have outgrown it. She
tried to ignore Khar but found she couldn't, not in the restless, doubtful mood she'd been indulging in. *"Have you actually witnessed one?"* For the life of her she'd never
encountered the ceremony, knew she wouldn't have forgotten if a person had been barred from the Seekers.

"First," Khar intoned with relish, **"they divest you of
your earrings. Then the miscreant hands over his tabard,
and they shred it before your eyes. Then—"**

"You're making it up! Don't scare me like that!" Always
the fear that she was responsible—not just for her duties, but
for some greater, unnamed charge she was bound to fail.

"**Then share a story with me—or I'll help with the yarn.**" Not an idle threat the way Khar's head moved back and forth, synchronized with each loop that unwound from Doyce's trapped hands. Grab for the ghatta and she'd wreath her with the skein, very possibly what Khar intended to happen. "**Action, adventure, death-defying heroics ... I promise.**"

"And the ending? Happy or sad?" What had happened to Matty, how could she have waited so long? Because she couldn't bear any more hurt for him or for herself.

"**Some of both. But if you don't dare it, you'll never know for sure.**"

She made a face, smoothed it into an insincere smile when her mother looked at her, only to shake her head and keep winding.

Heartsick, dazed, Matty wandered aimlessly, trapped in a nightmare of self-recrimination that disrupted distance, direction, time. Again and again he berated himself for so blithely believing he should reveal the unvarnished truth, his unwitting innocence and eagerness resulting in a man's death. So this was what his pride in discerning the truth accomplished? Berating Kharm might remove some of the onus from him, but she'd done precisely what he'd asked—sought out the truth. And the truth was an insupportable burden, crushing his heart and soul and mind.

He shuffled through frosted, rotting leaves, ran into trees on occasion, tripped and sprawled while his mind worked furiously, chewing over his responsibility. This time when he fell, his hands slithered, gouged dark tracks. Shaking his hair from his eyes, he realized the world was slowly growing white, a sleety, granular snow sifting from the sky, eddying around him, stinging his bare hands and face, burrowing into creases of his clothing. Damn it all, he was so incredibly tired of life, of everything! Kharm licked at the tears leaking down the snow-dusted face. "**Truth *is*—you have to accept it, you can't change it.**"

He slammed his hands over his ears, as if that would extinguish her mindvoice. "I don't want to know the truth! Never, ever again! I want to die!" With the rusty movements of an old man, he pushed himself to his knees and thrust his arms toward the leaden sky, snow crusting his shoulders, damp face upturned toward the heavy clouds. "I want to die!" he screamed, but the wind swallowed his words, swirled them in mockery. "Die—ie—ie!"

Rearing on hind legs, Kharm placed her paws on his shoulders, nose icy, then warm-moist against the soft skin under his chin. **"Selfish. Unreason, untruth. You do *not* want to die! Now, will you listen to reason?"**

With a grudging acknowledgment that the Lady refused to strike him dead, end his agony, Matty lowered his arms and embraced the ghatta, both of them quivering with cold. "Why did it have to be Flaven? He was basically a good man, a good husband to Rema. Why?"

"Would you have traded his life for Lorris Stralforth's?" The question took Matty aback. **"Is one death more acceptable than another? The death of an innocent but unpleasant man for the death of a guilty man who was basically good?"**

Matty shuddered. "But I'm responsible, without me . . . without you . . ." he trailed off. Too easy to accuse another when he himself was to blame.

"Could you, in good conscience, have ignored the evidence that exonerated Lorris and pointed the finger of guilt at him?" The ghatta pushed inexorably.

He jerked to relieve the tightness in his chest. "No. . . . It's just that life's so unfair sometimes."

"It is. But even more unfair if someone, someone like you doesn't search for the truth, make people understand and accept it. Do you wish me not to share these truths anymore?" The ghatta's nose nearly touched his, yellow-green eyes fixed on dark blue ones, stormy with shame. **"It will cripple me and it will cripple you, but if you wish, I'll stop."**

"Yes. No. I don't know. I just don't see where or how I became responsible for spreading the truth."

"You aren't—unless you make it your responsibility, your role in life."

A strangled laugh exploded into a hiccup. "It won't do much for my popularity, will it?"

"Well, we don't have to tell everybody the truth about everything—only to prevent an injustice. How's that?"

He hugged her close, snow melting between his cheek and her fur. "Mayhap I could live with that." Gently releasing her, he forced himself onto his feet, still clad in their wooden clogs, Flaven's work boots in his sack, a silent reminder, a constant reproach. They'd have to be worn someday, but not yet, not now. "And speaking about living or dying, we'll freeze to death if we stay out here in the snow. Like it or not, winter's setting in." He circled in place, considering, trying to determine his bearings, the likelihood of shelter. And food, his stomach rumbled with anticipation, he couldn't remember when he'd last eaten. "Where are we, anyway?" How long since he'd paid attention to where he walked, which direction the sun rose, the time of day, the day itself? Led them into the middle of nowhere and lost them both.

Kharm stood on his clogs, escaping the mounting snow that whistled around them. **"We've been moving mostly north. There's some sort of settlement ahead. I can smell it."** Her nose wrinkled to indicate the smell was less than pleasant, although he could scent nothing but cold dampness overriding woods odors.

"Could we have reached Free Stead?" If so, the farthest reach of the River Kuelper was west of him, the Taglias to the east. Mountainous, densely wooded lands, but nothing so bad as what he'd heard of the Tetonords on the other side of the Kuelper. "Have we come that far?" He'd not intended to winter at Free Stead, but at the moment any place appealed. "Can you find the settlement, Kharm?"

"Of course." With a bound she led off, Matty trailing behind, slipping, leaning into the wind, hair and eyebrows stiff with snow.

And thus Matty and Kharm found themselves about to winter at Free Stead. His first glimpse of the enclosed community did little to welcome him: the stockade reared defensively and almost invisibly, a sensation of bulky presence, slivers of timber and bark striating the coating of wind-driven snow like an animal's fur changing for winter camouflage. The gates stood firmly closed and showed no sign of recent opening, the snow pristine in front of them. Given the timbers' size, a knock wouldn't penetrate. Mayhap pound with a rock? Scuffing deep, praying the clogs would protect his numb toes, he hunted for something to beat against the door. Before he succeeded, dark figures armed with bows and arrows crowned the stockade top. "Halt!" and he obeyed. What other choice did he have? "What do you want?"

"Shelter from the storm, at least." Start with that, see how it went.

"For how many?"

Stupid—didn't the men have eyes? Did they think a horde of people hid in the woods, awaiting an invitation for shelter? "For myself and my animal," he shouted, afraid the storm had whipped his words away, so he gestured toward himself and Kharm.

"They *do* wonder if others are with us. They're suspicious, and with good reason. They've been attacked before."

If this were Free Stead, their caution held a certain wisdom, hard-gained, according to Kharm. This heavily guarded hamlet held the dubious distinction of being Canderis's most northerly outpost, although how civilized remained to be seen.

Bleary with cold, he tried to collect the bits and pieces he knew, anything to keep his mind working. A hunting and trapping post in the mountains' shadows, and in the mountains lived the Marauders, those men and women unable to abide by the laws each village voted on. Men and women with a brittle, urgent recklessness, and the conviction that since their world had cheated them, its dreamed-of bounty snatched away by the Plumbs, by the spaceships' desertion, it entitled them to survive on the backs of their brethren, plundering and stealing, killing if necessary. Yes—the world owed them a living—and more. Cold as he was, the memories made Matty colder, then hot with shame.

As children, the planet's firstborn after space colonization, they'd accepted life's luxuries as their due until they abruptly disappeared, replaced by hazy recollections of technological marvels, of plenty grown mythic in memory now that it had vanished. For some who reached maturity, the daily danger of Plumbs, the change from comfort to hardscrabble existence had turned them aimless, alienated. Life was barely worth living: all efforts at survival doomed, nothing worth the attempt. Why build, why plant, why care when random devastation struck, and once simple tasks took on monumental proportions, where eumedicos could no longer protect against simple illness or accident? For others more determined, the desolate mindview crystallized into a

flaming, self-righteous creed of entitlement, immediate gratification of any need or desire. This second group turned
dangerous, became Marauders, while Matty's father,
Manuel, drifted aimlessly between the two extremes, never
one to plunder and kill, but never able to concentrate on
anything useful, from raising a crop to raising a son. It was
all too, too much effort. Others could and did make such efforts, but not he.

Most Marauders lived here in the unsettled north, beyond
the haphazard efforts of a civilization they sneered at as a
paltry shadow of past splendors. Ravaging offered easier
plucking than anything else their world offered. By now the
second generation swelled their ranks, children younger and
older than Matty, themselves breeding more new citizens de-
void of conscience, respect, or ideals.

"Do they think I'm a Marauder?" It struck him as ludicrous as he swayed in the cold, slapping his hands against
his arms, stamping his feet, but for them it was no laughing
matter. *"That they'll take me in and I'll unbar the gates in
the dead of night, let in others to attack?"* He fidgeted, miserable and exhausted. Patience, let them talk amongst themselves, decide, Granther'd be equally wary. *"Pitiful
Marauder I'd make!"* and felt distinctly sorry for himself.

At last a deep voice thundered a command. "Toss your
sack over the stockade." He hesitated; all his worldly possessions, so few, inside, give them up and he'd have no
chance of survival. Mayhap *they* were Marauders, out to
pluck him clean. Wary, he ventured as close as he dared,
measured the trajectory, and began circling his arm to build
momentum. The sack flew free, slammed against the palisades and dropped, burying itself in the drifts, a jeering
laugh following it. A surge of heat ran through him, frustration and exertion, and he ran to reclaim it, backed off, and
tried again. This time it sailed clear with room to spare.
Now, nothing to do but wait, pray they wouldn't keep his
sack and its contents and leave him barricaded outside in the
storm.

A smaller segment of the main gate cracked free and a
disembodied arm beckoned. "Come on, then." As he and
Kharm rushed inside, blissful at the thought of shelter, Matty
found himself flung to embrace the wall, arms jerked upward, legs kicked apart while cold, rough hands efficiently
roamed his body. "Knife. Only a knife," a voice behind him

announced. "Can't expect anyone to travel without a knife. But nothing more. Probably safe enough long as we watch him."

Indignant, he lowered his arms and turned to confront the voices, working his jacket into place, tugging the sheepskin down over that. His jacket had parted company from his trousers during the search, his waist swathed with the full brunt of the cold. "Who be you, lad? Making your pelts trot along with you before skinning them?" A joke, he guessed, though Kharm didn't appear amused.

Stiff mouth cracked at the corners from windburn and leaked tears, he sputtered, "M . . . m . . . Mat . . . ty . . . V . . . van . . . d . . . der . . . sm . . . ma." He tried again. "Vandersma."

Someone thrust a mug of broth in his hands, and he laced grateful fingers around it, lifted it to thaw first one cheek, then the other, would have hugged it if it had been big enough. "Vandersma, hey? Well, if you was making up a name, that likely wouldn't be one you'd choose, so I'm thinking you're real." Hard to judge the man who spoke, wrapped in furs and leather, an earflapped cap of wolf fur low on his forehead, flaps snugged under his chin. Clutching one mitted hand in the other, the man dragged a hand free, bare flesh outthrust for Matty to shake. "I'm Elion Udemans, head man here. If you want to stay, best be willing to earn your keep."

"'Course I can!" Overpowering exhaustion swamped indignation as Matty slumped down the wall into a heap. Hands lifted him, carried him through the starry havens to the delight of a fire, piled furs over him, and he slept, relieved and relaxed for the first time in many days. Kharm purred as she burrowed underneath to nestle against his stomach.

Shoving his sleeves to his elbows, Matty began to scrape the hide, removing the last bits of fat and fiber, careful not to tear it. Stretch the hide too tightly when pegging it and spots thinned, vulnerable to rips or gashes. When done, he'd rub in a mixture of ash and clarified fat to keep the skin supple. He whistled under his breath, stepped back, and admired his handiwork.

Kharm had an assignment as well, sniffing through hides prepared earlier: fox, marten, wolf, rolapin, deer, and even a few elk, so much larger than the rest that Matty had to stand on a chunk of wood to reach his work. The ghatta determined which, if any, hadn't been properly treated, a spot overlooked. Her sensitive nose detected spoilage, made him appear more competent to the other hunters and trappers. His task was to prepare the pelts, enhance their trading value. They'd tried him at trapping, but he'd quickly discovered he now lacked the stomach for it—animals writhing in steel traps or snares, Kharm's mindmoans resounding through him as she relived her mother's death. Straightforward hunting he could manage, except that his archery skills were pitiful, his arrows possessed by their own sense of destiny, not his.

About thirty men lived in Free Stead, their winter numbers higher than in summer. Some resided year-round, grizzled veterans of the woods averse to human contact, content keeping themselves to themselves. Others made Free Stead their winter home to help support their families. These men tended to be more comradely and talkative, the winter octants offering an interlude of sorts from the responsibilities of home and family. A lark, but a dead serious one at that. Men froze to death in the wilderness, risked being killed by Marauders.

He'd thought Gilboa had been bad, but this was the most ferocious winter Matty could remember. True, he'd been raised in a more southerly part of Canderis, but Udemans and the others assured him this winter was a killer. Blizzard upon blizzard lashed them, with only a day or two between to clear the accumulated snow from the interconnected paths inside the stockade. They'd run out of space to shovel the snow and now packed it down on the paths, rolling a gravel-filled barrel to flatten it. As the paths rose higher, the huts grew shorter, doors once at normal height a menace to the unwary head.

Worst of all, the snow constantly drifted, piled halfway up or higher against the stockade's sides, and Udemans implacably decreed it be shoveled clear, hauled away. Since each wall ran thirty-five meters long, it wasn't a speedy task; a day's backbreaking effort could be obliterated by a night's mocking wind. Shoveling was one of Matty's prime duties, unskilled brute labor on command. Frankly, he felt as if he'd moved half the snow in Canderis at one time or another, probably some of it twice.

And necessary it was, for Udemans's peace of mind, because if the snow settled and hardened in place, it provided Marauders with a ramp up the palisades. Matty and any others not on trapline duty struggled through short daylight hours, crude wooden shovels swinging, dragging the snow away on crude sledges to dump in the river or pile on its frozen banks. Plying his shovel in steady rhythm, indistinguishable from the other hard-bitten men, cloaked and covered in layers of fur, his efforts had earned him his clothes, food and lodging, but little more. Still, he was alive, and if he hadn't found welcome at Free Stead, he and Kharm would have wandered lost until they froze to death.

Ducking his head outside the curing house, Matty gauged the sun's level. Sinking fast and swimming in overcast, its light diffuse, another storm due soon. He could smell it, the air heavy and sodden. As if to taunt him, a large snowflake pirouetted past his nose, insolently chased by its mates. Antoon, Pieck, and Govaerts had led out their trapping parties three days ago; Antoon's might be back tonight if they'd made a good start before the blizzard struck. If not, they'd have to camp rough again, rise out of their snow holes at dawn to fight their way back, sense of direction muted and baffled by the storm. Roiker's hunting party had left just this morning—whether they'd turn back or press on, he couldn't say. That left, he counted under his breath, sixteen men in the stockade. Assuming the storm struck soon, Udemans would rotate guard shifts often tonight, four men at a time, one to cover each wall. Not much sleep for anyone tonight.

Despite his lack of a jacket or hat, he lingered, watched his breath steam, varied his puffs to create cloud patterns in the air, like blowing smoke rings, when Kharm crested a snowbank, stripes dark against stark white. " **'Ware! Danger!**" An overpowering scream fractured the icy air as Mogens toppled off the narrow walkway that rimmed the inside of the palisade, an arrow lodged in his chest. Running before he even thought about it, unencumbered by his winter outer gear, still inside the curing shed, he loped toward the stockade entrance.

"Marauders?" he gasped. It made sense, a perfect sickening sense. Attack while they were shorthanded to defend the stockade—easy pickings if the Marauders had forces and

desperation in abundance. And when hadn't a Marauder been desperate enough to claim anything that wasn't his, that he hadn't worked to earn?

Others ran after him as well, pulling on outer gear, crude pikes and bows in hand. A quick headcount and he breathed a sigh of relief, no one outside shoveling. **"Weapon?"** Kharm prompted, and Matty realized he brandished the small scraping knife. Cursing himself for his stupidity, he detoured into the communal meal hut and snatched a hatchet from the kindling, grabbed a long carving knife. Better, but not much. It meant they had to be within reach before he could inflict any damage—and if he could, so could they. So don't think about it. He charged back outside, not noticing the cold goosebumping his shirtsleeved flesh as he clambered up the ladder to the walkway over the gates.

Udemans, back from his trapline yesterday, shouted orders, deployed men. "Two with bows on each far wall to watch for attack! You rest, stand firm by the entrance." With Mogens down, sprawled dead in the pathway, blood obscenely scrolled red across the whiteness, that left fifteen to fight—six in fixed positions on the far walls. Nine including himself to break the main attack. Sticking his head over the palisade before Udemans could thrust him down, Matty strained to tally how many Marauders they faced.

Twenty fur-clad figures scattered across the snow just at the edge of the woods, well beyond bowshot; over several summers Udemans had painstaking cleared trees to remove hiding places too near the stockade. Some clustered together, others moving forward on snowshoes and skis, seeking cover behind drifts. Yells from the east and west walls warned of more groups working their way around the sides of the stockade. Two men would be spread thin to defend each wall but could do it as long as their arrows held out.

Udemans cursed, laughed. "Could be worse, could be worse," he yelled to his men. "More of them outside, fewer of us inside, but we're behind strong walls, and they aren't. 'Less we let them take the walls or break down the gates, they can't hurt us much. Could sit tight until spring thaw if we have to."

The snow continued swirling, gusting sideways, upward, before falling back down in clinging, wet flakes. Pity for the men exposed to the elements surged through Matty until he realized he was more exposed, body quivering in regular waves. "Go get your gear on," Udemans barked, slapping his shoulder with a damp leather mitt. "Not high summer in the Sunderlies here." Grateful to scurry back to shelter, Matty dragged on his outerwear, bulky and furry as a bear. Back outside, the wait began.

As the night deepened, Matty busied himself passing hot soup to the men. A night with no stars, no moons hanging full and heavy, only oyster-gray swirls, squalls buffeting them, making them huddle behind the palisades. But if they suffered from the storm, the Marauders were fully exposed. Beyond arrowshot bonfires burned and leaped, flames streaming sideways, changing direction, precarious warmth at best.

Teeth chattering, he squatted next to Udemans's bulk to block the wind. "How long can they wait like that?" He held the mug under his chin, letting the steam lave his face. "I didn't think Marauders had much patience, more slash and grab, not sit and wait." Siege wasn't the Marauders' style and Udemans knew it; Kharm slipping his worries into Matty's brain.

"Aye, that's what's bothering me, boy." Slitting his eyes against the driving snow, Udemans paused before confiding his thoughts. "Weather's not to their liking, nor the lack of shelter. Doesn't make sense. I don't think it's a matter of waiting them out, but that they're waiting for something."

"What?" What would Marauders be waiting for? "They outnumber us—all they have to do is breach the walls, scale them on ladders."

"First into the breach, first over the walls are the first to die." Udemans spat, ducked as the wind sailed it back at him. "Marauders don't much like dying, just killing others. Not about to make a sacrifice, even for their fellows."

"You think they have something planned?"

"'Course. Just that I don't know what."

Kharm scrabbled up, claws digging into bark, leaped to Matty's shoulders, whole body straining into the wind. **"There! More by the fire!"** her tailed whipped as she fought for balance. **"Not theirs, but ours, one of the hunting parties—captured and bound!"**

Matty strained to match his vision to hers, but all the figures appeared alike at that distance. Paying no attention to what he assumed were the ghatta's usual antics, Udemans looked inward, not outward, checking his postings on the walls. Jerking his arm, Matty pointed, almost sizzling with excitement. "By the fire, there! They've got Antoon, Donner, and Braldt! Look, they're carrying torches, maybe they want to parley!"

Udemans thrust the flapped hat back from his forehead, face snow-caked against the dark wolf fur. "Marauders don't generally parley," but he waved the others onto the walls, ready with drawn bows. "Bless them, they're stark naked!"

And so they were, the prisoners that is—Antoon, Donner, and Braldt stripped to the skin, arms lashed behind them as they were prodded ahead, human shields. At a shout that barely carried above the wind, stout stakes were pounded through the snow crust, the blows sounding like distant, rumbling thunder, the prisoners tied to them. Four figures bent against the wind, toiled closer within hailing distance of the stockade. "Don't shoot, don't shoot!" Udemans commanded, desperate that everyone obey as he watched the Marauders' slow progress.

"Yo! Udemans!" The wind whipped the words at them, slashed their faces with the icy tones. "Found a few of yours out here, nasty weather to be out. Wondered if you wanted them back."

Hands around his mouth, Udemans shouted, "'Course we do! With or without clothes."

"Then surrender the stockade and everything in it to us."

At first Matty thought the growls were Kharm's, only to realize that the noise issued from the men crowded on either side of him. Anger and anguish in equal measure ululated from their throats; anger at seeing their friends as pinioned, naked pawns, and anguish at yielding what they'd toiled for all winter.

Udemans pounded at the top of the stockade with a mitted fist, as if he'd drive the pilings into the ground. The others cast sidelong glances at him as they watched their companions standing naked in the cold. Not a man of them, Matty knew from Kharm's thoughts, would abandon the others if he possibly could. Now Kharm had homed in on the Marauders' thoughts, transmitting them to his mind, and what he heard, he didn't like.

As Udemans opened his mouth, ready to capitulate, Matty blurted, "No! It's a trap! Whatever we do, the men are dead. They'll die if we refuse, and we'll die with them if we surrender!" He fought not to cry, sickened at such casual depravity.

Profoundly relieved at having the matter taken out of his hands, the stark truth spoken by someone other than himself, Udemans spat once more. "Boy's right. Ever known Marauders to honor the terms of a surrender?"

"But we can't leave them there like that!" Shrill panic in Casten's voice, for Casten was Donner's cousin.

"Well, Udemans?" the shout from outside invaded their thoughts.

"No! No deal, no compromise! Come get us—if you can!" Udeman's words were almost drowned out by stamping feet, jeers, growls. "Come . . . get . . . us!"

But their exhilaration snuffed like a candle flame as two men leaped to restrain Casten from vaulting the top of the stockade, running to fight with his bare hands if necessary. Kicking, screaming, Casten fought to break free, then slumped as he realized the futility of it all. The hopelessness of the situation chilled the others as well, though they struggled not to show it. "We've got to free them somehow! Can't we make a sortie?"

Conscious of the discord, the possibility not so much of insurrection but of a wanton waste of lives in an impossible gesture, Udemans turned helplessly, striving to regain command, his voice unexpectedly gentle. "Too many of them and not enough of us. We'd be throwing our lives away if we do. I don't mind, but I want a fair share of theirs thrown away, too."

"Tell them! Tell them!" Kharm urged inside Matty's head. **"The one they call Roiker and his party are sheltered nearby, they turned back when the storm struck. Too few of them to fight the Marauders, and they can't cross through the Marauders to make it back to the stockade."**

Diffident, unsure how to convince them, Matty slapped mitted hands together, the sharp sound of leather smacking leather. "Right, Roiker and his crew aren't far, I spotted him. That's three more of us, and them at the Marauders' backsides for surprise value if we can come up with a plan!"

"You sure?"

" 'Course I'm sure! He gave me the high sign from behind the outbuilding while you were all watching Donner and the others." A lie, but the truth of Kharm's knowledge bolstered him. Stubborn now, assured by the ghatta's counsel, Matty's mind desperately worked. The only structure separate from the stockade was a small outbuilding used for summer storage, sleds and sledges, odds and ends, nothing of value or they wouldn't have been left there. He'd been inside only once, but suspected Kharm's usual inquisitive nature had led her to investigate it before it had become completely buried by snow. He nodded, gulped, trying to look reassuring. "Sure. What've you stored inside the shed?" Maybe it contained something suitable for a distraction—if he could reach Roiker and his men. But that, his face fell, meant having Kharm contact them directly, and her alien touch would scare them witless.

Inventorying on his fingers, Udemans ticked off the shed's contents. "Couple broken-down sledges, good enough for light loads but not much more, 'bout ready to crack in half with anything too heavy. Some bear traps we had out earlier and some extra snow shovels. A few empty kegs." His face screwed up at the effort of recollection, "Crock of lamp oil I forgot to move inside for the winter, maybe a jug of turps for the traplines when we clean them over the summer."

Silence then, until a shamed voice finally chimed in, "And two kegs of apfeljack, Elion. Guess we fergot to mention that, saving it for a surprise-like."

"What's apfeljack?" Matty wanted to know.

"Hard cider, and then some," Udemans almost grinned. "Wish I had some now. Fill a barrel or crock with hard cider and leave it to freeze. Water part turns to ice, but the alcohol stays liquid. It's intense because it's not diluted with water. Throw away the ice and you've a powerful drink."

The germ of a plan began in Matty's brain or, more accurately, his brain and Kharm's humming as one. "Does apfeljack burn?" And inside his mind Kharm asked. **"Rolling kegs. Wouldn't that be nice?"**

"Think it would," Udemans sounded hesitant. "What you planning on doing?"

"Won't know yet till I get there," was the best Matty could offer.

"You can't go out, they'll kill you!" Udemans exploded.

Enjoying being the voice of sweet reason, Matty countered, "I'm likely to get killed if I stay in or if I go out. Besides, I'm the only one who knows precisely where Roiker and the others have holed up, Kharm and I," he amended.

"I'm not much of a fighter, but I *am* a good planner. It's my life to save or throw away."

As strong hands held the rope, Matty maneuvered himself down the stockade's north wall, revolving like a plumb bob on the end of a line, swinging sideways when a gust of wind snatched at him. What if he landed right in the enemy's waiting arms? Was this what a spider felt like when he dropped on his tether line, only to discover he'd lowered himself to the center of an occupied dinner table? To create a distraction Kharm had streaked over the east wall, hoots, shouts, and the sounds of muffled pursuit receded in the distance as Marauders chased after her, unsure what she represented but unwilling to let any of the stockade's residents escape, even an animal.

The wind whipped, pendulumed him again as his feet finally dragged on the ground, midriff strung with parcels. He wore the lightest, warmest clothes the others could contribute, overlaid with loose trousers and a hooded shirt hastily stitched from an old bed sheet, once white, now dingy gray from less-than-fastidious launderings. Still, it provided some cover against the snow; anything dark and moving would attract attention and arrows.

His plan was rudimentary, the best they could cobble together on such short notice, but all agreed any plan, any action, beat passively waiting for Antoon, Donner, and Braldt to be tortured, killed. Assuming they didn't freeze to death first, a sweeter death than the Marauders promised. *"Kharm?"* Matty 'spoke, reconnoitering on each side, snow melting and glazing his cheeks. *"Safe for me to move yet?"*

"Be patient." Although nowhere in sight, her mindvoice chimed brittle-bright with glee, **"Let me distract them a little more, just a little further. It's necessary—and it's fun."** He waited, tried to be patient, not to shiver. Excitement or cold, he wasn't sure which. Again he fumbled with the hammer, chisel, and crowbar strapped around his waist under the white shirt, fearful they'd clank and betray him. His fingers itched to check the pottery container shaped rather like a miniature clog, with its plug at the neck and its tiny air hole. Three glowing coals nestled inside amongst moss and punk to provide sustenance, keep them glowing.

What if he'd blocked the air hole, smothered them? **"Head there now!"** he heard at last, discerned what passed for a ghatti-giggle. A dark shape capered and darted off, shadowy figures he hadn't noticed rising out of nowhere and following in hot pursuit, away from the outbuilding.

Crawling, slithering on his stomach when necessary, he made his way through the snow to the deserted outbuilding. Although if Kharm had done her job right, Roiker and his mates now occupied it, overwhelmed by the need to seek it out, hide in its close safety like hibernating animals, the ghatta having planted the suggestion in their minds.

The snowbank and the path beside it almost unidentifiable as such, resculpted by drifting snow, Matty guessed at their location from the soft hollow and the sharp overhang of the drift at right angles to a low mound. The blizzard had altered all the landmarks. With a quick glance around, he rolled into the hollow and sank into the powder as if it were a featherbed. Half-floundering, half-swimming toward the mound, relief flooded him as he picked out shallow depressions—footprints filling in, Roiker's and his companions', he hoped. An outstretched arm glided under the snow surface, made contact with something unyielding. Squinting through eyelashes frosted with snow he saw the rough outlines of the door, already recoated with blowing snow like spun sugar. This was the tricky part: Roiker and the others fearful and jumpy, ready to fight anyone who forced a way inside. "Roiker?" he whispered, fearful the wind would snatch his words. A faint stirring inside, then absolute silence. "Roiker?" The wind grabbed the name, knotted it into a growling, grumbling complaint. "It's me, Matty! Let me in!"

"Who else I got with me?" Suspicion, more than a touch of fear and raw anger, the hibernating animal awaking, realizing its den has been broached. "Name'm!"

The cold seeped through Matty's knees, crept upward. "Teiguid and Wensell. Wensell got a marten skin last time out. I'm doing a good job curing it, should be worth a lot—" The door cracked open and Matty tumbled inside. He landed hard, scrambled to push Teiguid and Roiker away, make them leave the door open just a crack. "Wait, just a little," he pleaded, a heart-pounding eternity until Kharm slipped inside, chirping a greeting merow as she shook her coat, began to groom damp fur. Jamming the door behind her so fast he almost nipped her tail, he heard more than saw Teiguid bar it again in the darkness. He sat, panting with relief, hugging his knees, one hand possessively gripping the clay container in his pocket, hoarding the warmth.

"What are you doing out here, boy?" Roiker whispered at his ear, his face and beard a dim gray blur while Matty's eyes slowly adjusted. "Any way to get us inside?"

He shook his head, realized they couldn't see that. "No. Need us here more. Marauders have got Antoon, Donner, and Braldt staked out naked in the storm, planning on torturing them if we don't surrender." A deep breath. "Thing is, they're going to kill them anyway—and us, too, if we surrender." A strangled curse from Wensell, a strapping man with a temper hot-blooded enough to turn the hut tropical. "Udemans figured we'd best try something, anything."

Tinged with spruce gum, Teiguid's breath puffed soft against Matty's face. "Better to go down trying and dying than just dying. But what we gonna do?"

And quickly, heads together, Matty outlined his plan, and they started to work.

At length, everything was ready, the scent of apfeljack, strong and heady inside the enclosed hut, mingled with an overpowering aroma equally engendered by hard work and dread. Matty leaned against Teiguid's shoulder, waiting, counting off the time, praying for a soft knock at the door to tell them Roiker and Wensell had returned safe from their mission. With an almost demented glee Wensell had claimed the right to plant the bear traps just behind Marauder lines, a dicey task for the two to crawl close unseen, set the two traps, maws wide and waiting. It might prove a worthless effort, a menace to them all, but Wensell and Roiker swore it had a chance, the traps silent, waiting, quickly covered by a thin layer of snow, invisible to anyone who didn't know they were there. Now if they could only spook the Marauders to run that way, crest the hard-packed drifts, and slide down into their jaws.

"They're coming," Kharm announced, "and well pleased. I'll guarantee someone runs in the right direction, chasing after me."

"*Kharm! No!*" he grabbed the ghatta onto his lap, held her tight, Teiguid stroking her as well, glad for her warmth. "*You might get hurt, have the trap snap on you!*" The idea terrified him.

"Well, I planned to jump over before it snapped at me."

"*You'd better!*" And with that, Roiker and Wensell

crowded into the hut, blowing on their hands, shifting uncomfortably in the small space, even more cramped with the two sledges lying ready, repaired as best Matty and Teiguid could. Beside each sledge stood a keg of apfeljack, potent alcohol sloshing within. They'd painstakingly drained it from barrels still lined with fruity ice. Matty absently chipped a sliver and sucked on it, sharply intense with the essence of apple. Hard to secure the lids without pounding and banging, and Matty hoped they fit tight, that the few small holes he'd bored would vent them enough.

Without further speech, the four rolled the barrels onto the sledges and lashed them loosely in place, then began dragging them from the hut, checking nervously at every shadow, every sound. As promised, Udemans and the men massed on the front wall, letting off wild shots, yelling, shouting invectives, promises, threats, anything to distract their attention. Bodily lifting the sledges from the path and over the snowdrifts, they slipped away, hauling their cargo, sinking and sliding, praying the sledges wouldn't fly out of control. Back, back, back around and up the slope to the rise of the treeline.

Now Matty crouched low, loosely braided wicks of oil-soaked rags in hand, thrusting them into the holes on the lid, prying open his clay container and blowing on the coals until they sprang to life. Roiker coated the kegs with the turpentine and lamp oil they'd mixed together, thick like syrup in the cold, as Matty pressed the coals to the wicks, waiting patiently, sheltering behind the others' bodies until they caught. Then down the line to repeat the process with the other laden sledge. A cautious wave, barely able to be seen, and Teiguid slipped smoldering rags under the lashing holding his keg to the sledge while Matty did the same to his.

Teiguid and Wensell put their shoulders to the sledge and began to push it downslope, while Matty joined Roiker behind his sledge, gasping and slipping, leaning into it as hard as he could. And suddenly they coasted free, both sledges sailing toward the Marauders' rear line, silent and sleek as they swooped down the snowy incline, tiny flares of red winking and bobbing. A blinding flash and the turp coating Teiguid's and Wensell's barrel burst into flame, swathing it in fire, scarlet bright against the night. Another flash, and the other barrel caught.

At the flaring signal, the stockade gates opened and Udemans and his men poured out in a densely packed wedge, swords and pikes at the ready, the four men still on the walls making every arrow count. Roiker rose with a roar and began chasing the sledges, their packed trails offering easier footing, and the others followed, attacking from the rear, sowing confusion and dismay, their small number multiplied by their unexpectedness.

The right-hand sledge hit an ice patch, spun and overturned. Etched with its skin of fire, the keg broke its moorings, catapulted into the air as if an invisible giant hand had launched it, then plummeting like a shooting star, exploding as the fire reached the alcohol. Barrel stave splinters pierced the night, random but deadly as arrows. Matty ran, waving a short sword, and tripped over a Marauder sunk on the ground, a jagged splinter of wood through his neck, blood pulsing black on the snow. Out of the corner of his eye he caught Kharm enticing a man to chase her, halting just out of reach, taunting him, springing away. Screaming with frustration, determined a mere animal would never best him, the Marauder plowed after her, Kharm corkscrewing in midair, twisting clear at the last moment as he bumbled heavy-footed into the bear trap. A high-pitched scream pierced the air.

Abandoning the sledge tracks, Matty, Roiker, Teiguid, and Wensell waded toward the prisoners and began slashing their bonds, the three bodies hanging limp against the stakes. Intent on freeing Donner, Wensell never noticed the Marauder skiing down on him, and Matty flailed backhanded with his sword as he tried to swung round to face the enemy, cover Wensell's back. An elbow in his chest drove him aside, his sword stroke falling wide, carving an arc in the snow. The Marauder's sword drove into Wensell's back, and Matty scrambled up and lunged, swinging the sword with both hands at ankle-level as if he chopped at a tree. The man toppled on Wensell and rolled off, Matty hacking again and again, working his way upward until his blade took the Marauder through the throat. He sank the point in the snow, hands shaking on the hilt, and began vomiting, unable to fight any more, no matter who attacked him. At last he sank to his knees, head bent, refusing to look up.

Abruptly it was over, Udemans and the Free Steaders in control, some dead, some wounded, but the Marauders captured and contained or driven back into the blizzard. As Udemans hauled him to his feet, Matty watched the others calmly finishing off any Marauders who remained, even those who'd surrendered. He vomited again, nothing left to throw up, but unable to stop the spasms. "Treat them as they'd treat you." Udemans surveyed the scene of carnage, rubbed absently at the side of his head, his right earflap missing, as well as a piece of the ear itself. "Nothing else to do with them out here. Finishing them off's a kindness of sorts. Can't hold them and try them. It's rough justice, but justice all the same."

Matty nodded blearily, eyes and nose streaming from the strain of his exploding belly. This *was* justice, without his aid or Kharm's, although Udemans didn't realize how Kharm had helped bolster the odds by sharing the truth. In this case truth was truth, pure and uncomplex, and he felt a certain repugnant relief at that.

Kharm sniffed at the Marauder Matty had dispatched, and from what he could see, he looked like a man, a normal man, the guise of the enemy, the Marauder fading with death. **"Better to kill by your own hand or to reveal the truth and sit back, task done, and let someone else determine the punishment? Does it make your hands any cleaner?"**

He shivered, wondered if Udemans viewed him as a coward for his babylike response to violence. No matter which way he did it, he was responsible for death. Whether by his own hand here or by seeking the truth that sent Flaven Pelsaert to his death at the end of a rope. Truth was, he didn't like either way very much.

Truth was, she didn't like either way very much either. She compulsively drew her boots back under the chair as far as she could to avoid the vomit and bloodstains invisibly crowding her feet. Shaking her head only increased her queasiness, and Doyce discovered she wielded a crochet hook in one hand, had already shell-stitched three long rows with a blush apricot yarn. What had she absentmindedly acquiesced to while invisibly battling in the snow at Matty's side?

"Oooh, that bear trap!" Khar gave a delicious shiver that rippled from ears to tailtip. **"And wasn't Matty resourceful and brave?"**

"Yes. It's no easy task being brave when you're afraid and unsure." She wrapped the yarn around the hook, looped it in

and out. *"But dead is dead, Khar. I feel as if death's their third companion—invisible but always with them."* Not a good omen, but at least the hostages had been rescued.

"So it is with everyone; death shadows us all." She'd turned Khar pensive as well.

Death shadows us all—don't think about that, don't think about how closely it shadows Swan, don't think about how she's doing because you're too far away to make a difference. *"But it practically rides on Matty's shoulder. In all our years of Seeking we've never heard a murder case. Jenret and Rawn have, Rolf and Chak heard two, I know."* Her hook froze. *"But I have killed, just as Matty did, in that old stable in Sidonie."* She began pulling the shell-stitching apart, unraveling it with a vicious tug, much to her mother's startlement. "I hooked into the wrong spot, figured I'd undo it and try again," she temporized, not meeting her mother's eyes.

"Well, Free Stead was better for Matty than Neu Bremen, you have to agree. Mayhap things will be even better after Free Stead." It was Doyce's decision about when she'd explore Matty's life, but Khar couldn't resist dangling a lure. Doyce *had* to persevere, see it through, or all Khar's efforts and, by extension, the ghatti's efforts with the Elders would be a waste. And the future, what would the future be like if Doyce refused to learn from the past? The world she'd bequeath to her ghatten, the world Doyce's babies would inherit.

"I'm willing to wait. Here and now seems good to me." And to her mother's surprise, Doyce got up and kissed her, unprovoked. "I'm going to put on the kettle for cha." Mayhap that would wash the bitter taste from her mouth. Here and now was more than enough to cope with.

Addawanna rested a knuckle against her lips, hummed tunelessly against it. The only movement she'd make all morning now that she'd settled into place, surveying the Resonant encampment that held Jenret Wycherley and his friends. Unless *they* moved, and then, as always, she'd follow or arrive ahead of them, since she knew their own minds more intimately than they did. Or rather, she knew the land and its hazards, conversing with it at will, so attuned to its slow tides of love, longing and lament that every fiber of her body experienced it, pulsations pouring into the soles of her feet, her hand as she touched the earth, brushing it as lovingly as a mother ruffling a beloved child's hair.

This morning, long before the sun had risen, she'd chosen the old long pin pine as her vantage point, scrambled up it like a squirrel until she reached its forked crotch and settled in. Few pines boasted a crotch, but this one's crowning spire had been blasted young, two subsidiary points struggling for ascendency, each racing skyward. She knew because the tree told her so, grumbling about past trials for supremacy in whisper thin voices like its long needles, richly resinous. Indeed, even now they tried to lay claim to her, pitch clinging to her long, gray braid.

She'd informed the Monitor, Kyril van Beieven, that she would rescue Jenret and the others with or without his help, because never before had she witnessed a man so burdened, bowed down by sorrow and fear, coated with indecisiveness like a hardwood tree encrusted with ice. Dangerous, that, because he wouldn't bend but would shatter suddenly instead. Were he a tree, ice-encrusted branches would snap, a sharp retort splitting the frozen air as a healthy branch reluctantly detached itself and fell. In a human the mind would snap in much the same way, she suspected. A shame. She would ease his worries if she could, but the time had not yet come. The earth told her that, counseled for patience. And that she had in abundance, though she wasn't as sure about Jenret. The others with him, the young woman with hair like a beckoning pale candle flame and a name like a sigh, the earnest woman who spoke with her mind, and her loyal husband, they strove for restraint. But Jenret, like the Monitor, was liable to crack. Knowing that Doyce was alone, pregnant, she could understand his impetuosity—except that he was always impetuous. His mother's grace but not her tolerance in abiding with the bad times.

After spending yet another day in watching, what would she return to but another young cub, wearing his pain and disgrace the way moss weaves itself into bark, the bark itself becoming almost invisible? Worst of all, he wanted to help so desperately, but was well-nigh useless at the narrow, covert watching she desired, motionless and content, absorbing everything until it was time. Faertom had promised not to leave their camp, but to tend it and wait for messages. Not that any messages came, but she'd impressed on him the importance of being available. And when she returned each night for a brief respite before the evening watch, he inundated her with a storm of words, worries, fears, apprehensions, a pounding hail of emotion. Still, Faertom was a good young man, adrift from all he held dear, but not half the man her grandson Nakum was. An unfair comparison since Faertom hadn't been gifted with an earth-bond.

At that instant her own earth-bond pulsated, and she clasped the waist pouch to still it. Power in that pouch, more power than the children of usurpers, children of the silver birds that had landed so many years ago, could ever imagine. In that power an enduring strength, a will to survive that succored the Erakwa despite the changes in their world. The earth informed her of travelers, travelers across the land, not one or two but many, several hundred at least. Not an army, for the earth did not protest their passage but noted it with surprise, grumpy at being shaken so thoroughly this late in the season when it was ready to sleep. The earth rumbled itself like a bear trying to hibernate, disturbed by a flea. Interesting. She suspected who some of the travelers were, would know for certain shortly. But this, this might be what she waited for, a way to free her friends without loss of face on either side.

Smoke assailed her nose, the first of the morning fires sending up a thin, twisty plume, a finger pointing to the last shadow circles of the moons before they drowned in daylight, their ghost shadows always in the sky if one knew where—and how—to look. The distant fire gave a tiny pop, a snap, not a good omen given her previous thoughts, but she decided to ignore it. At last the one they called Gar-by— Gar-vey, she carefully corrected herself, hearing Nakum's gentle teasing inside her head—made his way, sleepy and shambling, beyond the guard ring so he could urinate in peace.

A little cloud of steam rose off cold stone as Garvey streamed urine on it, and he grimaced with effort, emptying his bladder. With his free hand he rubbed his eyes, knuckled the corners to wedge out the gluey sleep deposits. A shake, and he began to tuck himself together. It was then he spied the old Erakwan woman standing just left of the rock he'd peed on, and he nearly shied backward in surprise. How, in the name of the Blessed Lady, had she gotten here, and more accurately, when? Had he practically peed on her? What if he'd mistaken her for the rock? He buttoned his trousers, unable to meet her face. Except, guiltily, he wondered what *she* was looking at, embarrassing if she were. Mayhap it wasn't a woman at all, but some sort of will-o'-the-wisp, the tattered remains of his dreams.

"Morning, m'am." He brought his head up, leveled his eyes. How could something look so insubstantial yet solid at the same time? What if she didn't speak? "Can I help you with something? We're not real partial to strangers 'round our camp, so if there's nothing you need, best be on your way."

Her eyes were jet black with silvery spangles, like the polished hulls of sunflower seeds, or the liquid dance of streaming rain across polished marble. No, he wasn't scared, not yet; if he were, help was a mindshout away. For that matter, best take a peek in her mind, determine if she represented a danger. He smiled reassuringly, cast his thoughts to encompass hers, gentle and coaxing as he'd scoop up a new-hatched chick in both hands. But a heavy solidity loomed in front of him as if a door had slammed shut on well-oiled hinges a fraction ahead of his nose. He shook his head, shocked. Either she could block Resonant readings—and certainly he'd no right or permission to read her mind—or she *was* a spirit, some sort of ghost, without a mind to be read. When had she seized him by the wrist?

"No widout axing, Garby." She smiled, her cheeks like plump little crab apples, the top of her head barely reaching his shoulder. "An wha you mean, 'your camp'? Dis our land, camp on it mean it our camp."

"I . . . well, I . . . apologize if we're trespassing. But I . . . we . . . got the impression like, that you all didn't mind us . . . Gleaners, er Resonants, taking shelter." Anger smoldered despite himself. Was even this miniscule bit of safety, sanctuary, to be snatched from them now? They'd tried to be unobtrusive with their camps, but scarcely hide nor hair of an Erakwan had they seen. Was the land not big enough to share? To be driven off, driven away yet again, unbearable.

Hand tucked in the crook of his arm, she walked him unresisting further from camp. Reminded him of his mother Shoshana, she did, dragging him to view her garden patch when he was bone-tired and dusty from the quarry. "Ah, you bein' trex-passing, Erakwa be trex-passing, least 'cordin to

Canderis ideas. Land no big nuff hold us or you. Silly, how own wha you can't use? How own land an'way? Land let deer trex-pass, all od'er creatures, why not us?"

"Doubt any place'd welcome us. Least that's what it feels like most times." Why tell her this, confide in her? He still couldn't decide if she were a ghost or not, though she bumped solid and warm against his side, her hand wrinkling his sleeve, her fingers tickling a bit. But where was she taking him, why was he walking so obediently, as if he had no will of his own? He tried to hang back, found his feet refused, and it frightened him. Her sacklike doeskin dress looked real enough, the tattered blanket shawl as well. Mayhap he still dreamed, only thought he'd gotten up to urinate. But the sky was lightening, the birds commencing their early chirping, everything except him awakening if it were a dream.

"Hard bein' dif'rent, lookin' same outside, dif'rent inside." All he could see of her face was the part in her hair, the tip of her nose. He'd not realized what a nice, sort of burnished coppery color she was. Coppery? Or bronzy? How Wim would love to carve her shape in granite with a few simple, suggestive curves to hint at her power. And at the thought of Wim, dead, lost, he wasn't sure, his heart clutched. Wim and Waite, were they safe, just too far distant to reach? Or entombed under a slab in their own quarry—he'd not thought of that. Do to the sons what they thought they'd done to the father.

"Dey be safe. But Addawanna don know 'bout rock shaped like her. Weight her spirits down." She dragged against his arm to demonstrate, soft laughter bubbling.

How could she sense, have any idea what he thought? Erakwa weren't Gleaners as far as he knew. He strained to free his arm but she remained attached. "How do you know they're safe?" He wanted to howl at her, but his throat wouldn't oblige with more than a harsh whisper.

"Earth tell me. Earth tell me many t'ings. Feel." Dead serious, she crushed his fingers around a pouch that hung at her waist. The sensation reminded him of the time as a child that he'd trapped a bumbling, fat bee in a jar, the same vibrations transmitted through glass to his tingling palm. But with that he'd felt vexatious anger, and with this, nothing of the sort, just a peculiar, prickling energy. "Need be axing you somet'ing, Gar-vey man."

He tried to concentrate, still enveloped by the emanations from the pouch. "What?"

"I t'inking wise man like you, man who know hurt when loved ones lost, no wan 'flict dat on od'ers."

A jay's raucous cries shattered the air, an acorn whizzed by his head. Ah, they'd invaded someone else's sanctuary. The scolding cries upset him, made him want to hurl something back. Always an interloper. Damn all, he hadn't meant to invade the jay's territory, but he got blamed for everything. "I'd inflict pain on those who inflicted pain on me."

"Den why you keep Wycherley priz-ner? He, de od'ers hurt you, yours?" Another flying acorn grazed his ear, stung. For a crazed moment he wondered if she'd instructed the jay to torment him? Or did he merely torment himself? "Jenret got woman he love, woman great with child don' know where her man be."

He rubbed his ear, rubbed at his eyes to erase the sight of her. She'd released his arm, stood in front of him, wrists on hips, her hands turning out like the tips of a bird's wings. "I can't let him go. Don't you see? He and the others are the only bargaining chip we have left. At least to protect those of us here in the forest."

"An did I say gib him up to his own? You t'ink his own be dem od'ers who hurt you. Your kind his own. Gib him to highest of your own. Dat one from Marchmont, one dey call king comin soon. Let king decide wha do wid him. King keep you safe, make bridge to your world."

"I don't . . . know. Wouldn't the king punish us for seizing Wycherley?" But any punishment meted out by a Resonant who understood the direness of their straits couldn't be as severe as outsiders would be. "I don't know. I'll think about it, but I can't promise anything. Don't want to lie to you."

"Oh, you no lie to Addawanna." A beckoning motion, and Rawn strolled from behind an oak, stretched with a cocky, insolent strength. "My friend tell me dat."

The big ghatt made Garvey uneasy, his mostly healed scratches twinging with remembrance. Still, neither ghatt had offered him harm since that one night, and despite himself he couldn't blame their reactions. You fought for your friends, your loved ones. And Wycherley and Sarrett and Yulyn and Towbin were fighting to help them, their own kind in Wycherley's and Yulyn's case, even if no friendship had been offered in return.

"I said I'll think about it." How had they gotten so deep
in the woods? He couldn't see or smell the morning campfires any longer, hear any sound of human habitation other
than their own hushed voices.

"Don t'ink too long. King comin soon, prob'be by time
sun jes past high." She pointed behind her. "Dis way to
highway, case you ferget. I goin now. See you der in liddle
while, you and friends."

He turned toward what he hoped was the direction of
camp, the black ghatt pacing him. "You," he said, "don't
you be tattling on me to Wycherley, hear me?"

An acorn stung the back of his neck, and he spun to see
Addawanna, still solid and real. "Ya! Dat one I t'rew, jes
mind you no ferget."

Faertom sat, moping, on a log in front of the fire. He'd already gathered four loads of windblow wood and stacked it,
sand-scoured their breakfast dishes beside the trickle that
Addawanna deemed a stream, chopped fresh spruce for their
beds, rebuilt the fire, and swept up with a pine branch.
Proper little stay-at-home housewife he'd become while
Addawanna roamed out there somewhere. And the sun
wasn't even high yet.

He didn't understand how the Erakwan woman could be
content simply sitting and waiting, watching, not doing anything. Or was she? Hard to know what went on in her mind,
not that he'd dare try his Resonant skills on her, but her
bland face gave away nothing each time she returned to
camp to rest and eat before leaving him again. So he stayed
put, impatience brewing stronger than an unstrained pot of
day-old cha. There was nothing else to do, nowhere else to
go. Oh, he could go back to the capital, he supposed, stay
with Darl. More distractions there, but the things he'd see
and hear would only upset him more—the recriminations,
the roiling fears about Resonants. So he sat, in stasis of
sorts, useless here, useless there. Useless pretty well described his plight. He let his hands dangle between his
knees. Worthless. Couldn't help anybody, let alone himself.
All his thoughts running around inside his head and no one
to hear. No one who wanted to hear.

"Faeralleyn." The call resonated in his brain, made him

nearly fall backward off the log as he looked around wildly, a trickle of hope no larger than their private stream flowing through him. A trick, it had to be. Listen hard enough and you'll hear what you want to hear. Or he was going mad.

"Faeralleyn, over here!" And at length he made out her face, pale against the shadows where the cedar hung lacy.

"Mother?" Blessed Lady, he'd known in his heart she'd come to him! How could a mother deny a child of her heart, her flesh? No more than he could deny her—and that gave him pause. What if she asked him to give this up, called it a fool's errand, insisted he return home. Except they had no home, nor did he, only the surety of her love as shelter. She was prideful, but so was he, now that he had something to be proud about. He watched, bursting with barely contained emotions, as she picked her way to him, sat a calculated distance away on a rock on the fire's far side. *"How are you, Mother?"* Not Mama, Mam, not any of the things he usually called her.

"Alleyn." The diminutive his family used, a necessity, or one would spend half one's life calling for Faerbaen or Faerclough or Faeraday or Faeralleyn. Only outsiders knew him as Faertom, though he liked it. She waited until he snapped out of the reverie the litany of names induced. *"Alleyn, I had to come, had to see you—"*

"Of course," he interrupted, knew he was beaming foolishly, lovingly. How he basked in her presence, like the sun's radiance beating down on him, warming him.

Stubbornly, she plowed ahead, and with an effort of will he forced himself to be Faertom, not Alleyn, suddenly cold. *"I felt you should know that Wycherley and his friends are going to be released into the custody of the King of Marchmont. So you wouldn't worry any more about them. And . . ."* She studied her hands folded in her lap. Rare to see them still, not flying about the daily tasks of home and hearth. *"I'm trying to convince your father and brothers to return home. With the king's protection it may be possible."*

"Back to the island, you mean?" Faertom was up now, pacing. *"The king can't be everywhere, protect everyone. And he won't be here forever, whatever brought him here."*

"I'm well aware of that." She sounded tart as a green apple. *"I'm too old—"* he made a gesture of horrified denial, but she pressed on, *"to completely start over again, but I'm willing to try in small ways—try to make friends with women*

in town, share what we have in common about raising a family, running a home—surely we have that that unites us." A wry raising of her eyebrows, *"Do you have any idea how frustrating it is to be completely surrounded by men all the time?"*

"But what about Father, Baen, Clough? Will they agree?"

"Oh, eventually. With the proper persuasion." She looked at him as if he had two heads, six legs, was incapable of comprehending the obvious. *"Familiarity's a powerful lure. They like change even less than I. Sooner or later they'll realize the island's safer—and more comfortable—than hiding in the woods. That they have to stand up for what's theirs. Besides, they know there's no gainsaying me when I set my mind to something. I'm rather like you that way."*

He worked at wedging his toe under the log, wondered if he could flip it, anything to concentrate on, let him muster his strength to resist her. *"So why did you come here to tell me this?"* There—it was out in the open now.

"I didn't come here to demand you come home with us." He hung his head, hurt surging anew—still unwanted! *"I came to tell you your friends will be safe. And that you should go, join the king's party as well. Alleyn, your father was too hasty in shunning you. We need people like you, people who know how our world works, what our rules are, and how the outside world works, someone who can bridge both worlds. So few of us have had dealings with outsiders, but you count some of them as friends. Don't you understand? I'm proud of you."*

"Sure," he echoed dully, *"friends. Respected and admired by all who know me—except for my own kind."* Her pride eased some of the ache but couldn't banish all of it. Mothers always forgave, approved—but the rest, never. In truth, what else did he have, what other hope but to cast his lot with that other world? And at least it would be something to do.

"Alleyn? Who's that over there? Is that Addawanna? I never heard a thing."

Even at this distance he could read the compassion in Addawanna's eyes and didn't want any part of it. Was this what the rest of his life was to be like—everyone looking at him with compassion as if he were crippled in some way? *"You'd best go, get back to the others. Give Jenret my regards, if you can. Tell him I'll see him later."* He wanted so badly to hug her, denied himself the comfort, standing there woodenly. Undeterred by his expression, she circled the fire and embraced him. It would be so easy to fool himself that all was well, that this simple embrace made it all right. The island would never be home to him again despite his mother's welcoming arms. Not with his father there. He didn't want to see King Eadwin again or the others, but if one world were destroyed, he'd have to build a new and stronger one from the rubble and remnants. Except he wasn't sure he had the strength or the stamina anymore.

Addawanna clapped her hands once, his mother hugged him harder, reluctantly released him. "All in good time, Addawanna. All in good time," his mother warned the doeskin-clad figure. "And I take it it's time. Watch over him for me."

Addawanna shook her head regretfully, almost apologetically. "His life nod in your hands, my hands no more. In his own."

Claudra's mouth quirked wryly. "I know. They grow up." Head held high, she walked away, back straight.

"No got all day! Busy time ahead. Some t'ings change for bedder, od'ers not. Scurry, Faertom!" She flicked her hands at him, scowled. "Hab come allaway back fer you, den allaway back again. Bones be tired."

Despite himself Faertom grinned. The day her bones were tired, weary, his grandchildren would be old. If he ever had grandchildren, that is.

As he shuffled along, ankle chains rattling, the ground turned level and firm under his feet. Almost like . . . no, it couldn't be . . . a roadway? He scuffed his boot sole, swept it sideways to test his discovery, cautious not to stress the chain too much. Nothing made sense, they never changed camp at midday, just before lunch; transfers always happened early in the morning or at late afternoon to allow setup before dark. Something was up, and damned if he knew what. Not for the first time he cursed the sack muffling his head. Hearing and smell as well as vision were obscured, the flour-dusty closeness mixing with the moisture of his breath, his sweat, coating him with a thin layer of paste when the sack was removed. *"Rawn, where are we headed this time?"* The highway beneath his feet gave hope, as did

the knowledge his chains had been pared thin, the arborfer
knife secure in his boottop.

"And if it slips, slices your foot, don't blame me."
Rawn sounded testy, impatience ratchetted another notch
tighter. Interesting sign—but of what? **"As to where we're
going, you'll see."**

*"And wouldn't I love to, though. Next time you can tie the
sack round* your *head."* Patience of the Disciples, he hated
it when the ghatt went all snippy, then slid into evasiveness.

Rough hands grabbed at the binding around his throat and
Jenret Wycherley balked, panicky at the intrusion. The sack
came off, none too gently, and he stood blinking, squinting
at the expanse of smooth road unraveling before him. In the
distance, two figures, one far smaller than the other, waved
and a tethered black stallion gave a gladsome whicker of
welcome, pawed at the ground. Ophar! And . . . he slitted his
eyes, his long, dark lashes like a shading hedge . . . Faertom
and Addawanna?

A sweeping glance revealed Sarrett and T'ss, Yulyn and
Towbin, bound as he was but staring raptly ahead. Garvey's
bulky presence and broken face loomed at his shoulder, but
he ignored him. Just the five of them, or did other Resonants
hide close by? "What am I? Bait to trap another trusting
traveler?" He wiped his cheek against his shoulder, depositing a white smudge on the black sheepskin tabard, an excuse
to examine Garvey without directly confronting him. Now,
now! his heart sang. Snap the chains, slip the knife between
Garvey's ribs, and they could escape, run like the wind
along the road. Surely they'd find a house, a village, another
traveler along the way. Freedom beckoned, heady as the finest wine, leaving him drunk with desire.

Not paying any heed, Garvey grunted with effort as he
sawed through Sarrett's bonds, moved to free Towbin. Neither Addawanna nor Faertom made any effort to venture
closer. Indeed, Faertom now stood facing away, oak-sturdy,
head back-tilted as if he quested the way a hound searches
a scent. Jenret fought the urge; attempt mindspeech and
Garvey'd bowl him over. His momentary exultation evaporated at the uncanny stillness around him. "Boy's good,"
Garvey remarked as he unlocked Jenret's wrist manacles.
"Learn that at the Research Hospice, did he?"

A breeze stirred the crispness, fluttered bits of debris
along the road's shoulder, swept it toward them. With it

swept the sound of horns, strident blasts unheard since
Marchmont. Had Arras Muscadeine invaded Canderis?
Brought an armed party across the border? Had Marchmont
and Canderis's new relationships faltered since his capture?
**"Ahem. Look as far ahead as you can, where the road
bends. A gladsome sight."** Rising on his hind legs, Rawn's
long black sleekness emphasized an unvoiced exclamation.

Bits of color tantalized his eye, exotic swaths against the
grays and browns and ochers of autumn. White and lavender
snapping in the breeze, pale ice-gray with a vivid green zig-
zagged line so that the green almost writhed. The flags of
Marchmont and Canderis! And carrying those flags, Guardians in their crested helmets and leather half-armor, maroon
cloaks flaring behind them; Marchmontian soldiers as well,
a cacophony of colors, reds and purples, yellows and blues,
greens and oranges, sashes and slashed full sleeves rippling
in the breeze, their armor polished and blued, sunlight exploding against it.

Horses cantered on, more soldiers and Guardians ranging
into view, protectively clustered around highborn riders and
several closed coaches. He'd dreamed of rescue, but nothing
like this, and Jenret couldn't fathom its significance, over-
awed despite himself.

Equally overcome, Garvey elbowed Jenret, forced him to
abandon the vision, his dislike swelling as Garvey's damaged face begged for reassurance. "We've had our differences, belike, but what in all the wide havens do ye say to
a king?"

"King?" Jenret parroted the word, eyes drifting back as
the procession inexorably neared, breaking and rising like
seafoam. "King! Do you mean Eadwin's with them? And the
Monitor's flag? Is he here, too?"

"But what do ye say to a king? How do I address him?
What do I call him? I want to do right by him, he's not just
King of Marchmont, I'd guess he's King of the Resonants as
well." He clutched Jenret's tabard. "Mayhap they didn't treat
us well in the past, but they're more kin to us than most of
Canderis. What do I say?" Each tug at the tabard tilted
Jenret precariously off-balance.

"He's a pleasant, easygoing man, a bit younger than I."
He rescued his tabard from Garvey's grip. The man looked
petrified, and it pleased him no end. "Doesn't stand on ceremony. Blessed Lady, Garvey, don't fawn, just be polite."

Absurd to deliver lessons in etiquette in the midst of this . . .
this . . . whatever it was.

"Royal progress," Rawn contributed. **"One of Doyce's
ideas in your absence. To show Canderis there's nothing
to fear from Resonants, that they're as nicely normal as
Normals, except for their mindpowers."** He'd settled on
his haunches now and commenced washing his face. **"I wish
you could wash your face—looks as if someone spread
paste over you. Don't blame me if Arras Muscadeine
smirks when he sees you. Clever of Doyce, wasn't it?"**

A quick finger-lick and a touch to his forehead convinced
Jenret that Rawn was right, but nothing could be done to
rectify it. As he watched, Addawanna and Faertom separated, each stepping to the shoulder to let the riders sweep
through. Behind him the others whispered, fidgeting with
pent-up excitement. With overwhelming certainty, he knew
how young Davvy had felt that day as battle was joined, the
swirling flags, the rising noise and pulsing anticipation,
dreams of derring-do and heroism enflaming a boyish heart
until he'd rushed heedlessly between the opposing forces.
He was almost ready to enlist himself, and saw Garvey'd
been similarly affected.

"Stand your ground," he ordered. Let them surround him,
sweep over him like waves crashing on the shore, tumble
Garvey away, unable to torment him any longer. *"I'm coming, Doyce,"* he shouted, and damn Garvey if he tried to
crash his mindvoice, cripple its wings! *"I'm coming, Doyce,
I love you!"* The horses swerved around them, engulfing
them in the rich, ripe smell of horseflesh, leather saddles, armor polish, and a host of other odors. They rode so tall in
the saddles that they blocked the very sun, an animate forest
of men. Beside him Garvey shook, vibrating like a tuning
fork.

Three horses drew up in front of them: Arras Muscadeine
on his battle stallion, Eadwin on a caparisoned gray and, on
his left, diffident but comfortable, the honest, forthright face
of Darl Allgood, receding hairline and all.

"Somerset Garvey, I presume?" The king's gray dance-
stepped, Garvey visibly wilting but holding his ground. "I'm
told you've agreed to cede me something, or more accurately, someone? For the good of Resonants and Normals
alike? A knotty choice but an honorable decision, I might
add." Despite his commanding position atop the gray,

Eadwin appeared anything but regal, and his mouth quirked above his short beard. "I'm always pleased to meet a distant cousin from lands so long estranged. We've much to teach each other before you find your own road."

"Sir, your kingliness, you," Garvey sputtered to a halt and Jenret almost felt pity for him. "Past is past, but I want a future for us Resonants in this land that we love. If ye can aid us in that, I'd be much obliged." He seemed to draw himself together, gain strength and humor. "And I'd be much obliged if you'd take this folly off my hands, Jenret Wycherley and his mates, sir. Their hearts were in the right places, but I've learned you can't make others hostage to your fate. Will you relieve me of them, keep them safe? This one here," he nudged Jenret, "has a powerful urge to return to his loved ones."

For a moment Jenret's ire overflowed. "I'm not a package, a parcel to be passed from one person to another!" Much as it galled him, he appealed to Arras Muscadeine. "Arras, I've got to get back to Gaernett, Doyce must be due any time now!"

Muscadeine fondled his mustache, hiding his mouth. "I'm sorry, Wycherley, but you've been remanded to the king's charge to ensure nothing else untoward happens to you. Isn't that correct, your highness?" he appealed to Eadwin, intent on petting Hru'rul, perched on his gold-tasseled pommel platform. "Alas, we won't reach Gaernett for some time. Indeed, it's our final stop on this tour of your fair land."

"Well, fine! Ophar's over there. Surely there's no reason I can't ride to Gaernett. Sarrett and the others can go with you or come with me as they like, but Rawn and I are going!"

"Wycherley, Wycherley, what *are* we going to do with you? And you look so pale, almost pasty." By the Lady Above, how he disliked Muscadeine and his mincing, foreign ways! "Don't you understand? The Monitor's agreed you should remain in our care. You'll go with us, like it or not."

"Darl!" Desperate, Jenret swung on Darl Allgood. "Where *is* the Monitor? I saw his flag, where is he?"

"I'll explain later, Jenret, but I'm temporarily acting on his behalf." He massaged the bridge of his nose, grimaced, and finally took pity on the man. "Stop teasing him, it's cruel. Jenret, Doyce is in Coventry with her family. We're heading to Ruysdael first, and Ruysdael's not far from Coventry. Best you go with us."

Before he knew it, he was mounted on Ophar. Faertom and Garvey mounted as well but maintaining a calculated distance and disinterest between each other until the king gestured Garvey to ride beside him. Sarrett, Yulyn, and Towbin had chosen the carriages. "Where's Addawanna? I've something she should see," he whispered to Faertom.

"Oh, don't worry. She said she's bored with riding, too slow, so she'll see us in Ruysdael." The proximity of so many new Resonants left Faertom overwhelmed but happy, as if he'd cautiously determined a place might be found for him. In quick fragments he began filling in Jenret on what had transpired during his absence, Allgood on his other side, interjecting and expanding as necessary.

News exhausted, Faertom left Jenret alone with his thoughts, until a mindvoice politely intruded. *"Wycherley, I've a confession to make. Best you should hear now, not be surprised or shocked later."* For the life of him Jenret couldn't identify the voice though it sounded familiar, couldn't judge from where it emanated, yet it felt intimately close. Ezequiel or Ignacio? He'd seen them riding near at hand, had waved. Commerce Lord Lysenko Boersma as well, who possessed at least minimal Resonant skills, and others whose names he'd temporarily forgotten, too distracted to wrack his memory. *"Never ignore the obvious, Jenret. It's me, Darl Allgood. High Conciliator, loyal Canderisian citizen, and closeted Resonant—until now. Though I'm not sure I'd have chosen to reveal myself if it weren't for your aunt."*

"Aunt? Mahafny?" What in the blazes had she been up to now?

"Yes, Jenret. Mahafny's discovered a machine that reveals which people are Resonants, which people have the talent buried deep inside them. I'm afraid I was her first discovery, though. The shock caused Kyril to suffer a mild heart attack, or so we think. Once Mahafny has him settled in Gaernett with Marie, she'll be along to join us. She and her marvelous machine."

Sarcasm on the "marvelous"? Jenret wasn't sure. Mockery perhaps, and self-mockery at that. What *had* his aunt discovered, and what did she plan to do with it? To voluntarily identify oneself as a Resonant was one thing, another to be

involuntarily exposed, especially now, with things so unsettled. No doubt Mahafny saw it as a eumedico paradox—the
need to hurt before one could help. And a part of him wondered what the machine, Mahafny's marvelous device,
would reveal about Doyce? Did it matter, would he love her
more if she truly possessed such skills, love her less if she
didn't? Never! She was Doyce, his second heart, and
uniquely what she was. But the nagging curiosity continued.

Cross-legged on the old horse blanket, Davvy opened the
sketch pad, planted it in his lap. He fumbled through the
nubs and pieces of colored chalk left over from Doyce's and
Francie's childhood, more intent on keeping a covert eye on
Doyce than searching out any particular color. Didn't matter,
he couldn't draw very well anyway. Brown it was. Good, he
could do leafless trees, scraggly lines off a thicker vertical
base line. Francie had patiently pointed out that each type of
tree boasted a distinctive shape, that they could be identified
even without their leaves. A branch was a branch to him.

Besides, he wanted to see if Doyce were going to do it
again, there in the arbor. Go all distant and blank as if she
inhabited another world. Mayhap there was nothing to worry
about. After all, Khar was with her, and Khar wouldn't let
anything happen to her. He rubbed the chalk sideways,
smeared it with his thumb, not so much to make his art im-
itate nature but because he enjoyed messing around. Could
make good clouds, no, great clouds that way. Clouds were
his specialty.

Another side glance. Yes, there she went—was doing it
again, whatever it was. Would it hurt the babies? Should he
check? She looked the same and yet so different when she
got that way. He groped for another piece of chalk, decided
to try drawing the arbor—doing crossed lines that made di-
amonds was easy. And it was easier to watch her watching
whatever it was she watched in her head. Did Khar watch
with her? Impossible to read any of the ghatti, they always
looked totally innocent or totally guilty.

❖

Matty hitched the roll of furs higher on his hip and whistled to Kharm to attract her attention, the ghatta transfixed by a meandering, pale yellow butterfly that lacked the courtesy to remain still while she sniffed it. It floated erratically, Kharm following, rearing on her haunches, batting at empty air. **"Won't stay put! I just want to smell it."**

"It's not a flower. Come on, there'll be others," he promised. *"Look, you can see more all along the road. Maybe another will cooperate."* Lined with some sort of spindly but exuberant weed, or maybe it wasn't a weed, with tiny, densely yellow blossoms the color of egg yolks, the roadway was packed smooth, the winter's ruts filled, high spots graded. Impressive, all in all, as were the tended fields on each side, some already green with crops, others in the process of being planted. Workers of both sexes and all ages spared the time for an occasional wave or hallo in his direction, courteous but busy.

Six silver fox pelts remained from his share of the Free Stead trapping, a far more generous bounty than he'd expected. Udemans had told him to save the fox pelts for a buyer in Roermond, someone who'd asked specifically for them last fall. The rest of the furs he'd traded as he traveled from Free Stead toward Roermond, crossing the Kuelper's upper reaches, although now he headed west and south. South it might be, but he still journeyed fairly far to the north, indeed not far distant from the Tetonords. Where he'd go after Roermond he wasn't sure. At least in his recent wanderings Kharm's peculiar skills at Truth-Seeking hadn't been necessary. A relief, that.

The countryside looked incredibly rich, almost alluvial. Apparently the Spray had once curved through here long ago, before slicing a loop to straighten itself farther north. Oddly enough, no houses dotted the fields.

"They're all up ahead." Kharm danced along, hoping for a butterfly who wouldn't object to a questing nose.

The sun high overhead made Matty think longingly of lunch, the food in his pack less than appealing if there were a chance for fresh bread, perhaps some early greens. Greens in Free Stead had meant spruce cha. He pattered along barefoot, no need for Flaven's boots or the wooden clogs on this smooth roadway. Besides, best start toughening his feet for summer.

At last, scattered houses began to appear, built closer and closer together as he reached the heart of the village. All in all, a prosperous, contented place from its looks, not as large as Neu Bremen but somehow more house-proud, more community-oriented. Each house, unique as it might be in its recycled construction materials, looked tidy and well-built, effort taken. Many had been whitewashed, affording a uniformity their eclectic building methods and materials couldn't provide. But the little touches, shutters on windows, careful plantings of flowers in boxes, made him feel as if he'd landed in a pretend place, existing as it was *supposed* to, not the scrambling survival that sapped hope and joy and initiative in his accustomed world-view. Either the Roermonders thumbed their noses at any Plumbs that might explode or constantly rebuilt with renewed determination not to let the land conquer their spirits or their community.

Despite the sun's indication of lunchtime, not many people were about, mostly children. A young fellow about his age planed planks set between two sawhorses, the growing pile of wood curls indicating he'd been hard at work for some time. A group of children clustered around a rain barrel set at the corner of a house. They shoved, jostled for position, shrieking and yelling, jumping back, elbowing closer, the center of their attention a boy of about nine. He wielded a wooden paddle with both hands, the kind usually used for doing laundry, for punching and stirring clothes after scalding water had been added to the big tubs. The paddle lifted, then lowered, the boy intent on sinking something deep into the barrel, swishing the paddle from side to side. They looked as if they were having fun, and Matty thought of the childish games he'd played with Henryk, the sillinesses they'd devised, mimicking adult work.

Without warning, Kharm erupted in an earsplitting shriek and rushed toward the children, wedging between bare legs, upsetting the youngest child, who plopped straight-legged on its fanny. A fretful wail emanated from the child, boy or girl, Matty wasn't sure. The young man momentarily stopped planing and glanced over, only to shrug resignedly at the racket. Matty caught his eye as he dropped the fur roll and ran to retrieve Kharm.

"**Help me!**" Kharm cried as she leaped to the rain barrel, precariously balancing on its rim. A hiss and glare at the blond boy with the paddle made him retreat the length of the handle, but he stubbornly retained his grip, the paddle itself still submerged. She hissed again, made an unsteady grab for it, claws extended as she fished for the blade.

"What's the matter, what's going on?" The children squirmed as he broached their circle as best he could, picking up a four-year-old and redepositing her behind him, tickling a larger boy until he writhed out of reach. A terrible consciousness of his status, an outsider, a stranger invading children's territory haunted his every move. Not that he'd harm a child, but they couldn't know that—nor would their parents. A delicate situation fraught with potential misunderstandings, to say the least. *"Kharm, they're just children, having fun,"* he protested. *"What harm are they doing?"*

The ghatta's claws sank into the paddle, almost dragged it clear of the water. The boy on the other end fought to retain control, ram the paddle into the barrel's depths. **"These sweet little humans,"** she hissed, **"are drowning a ghatten!"** Her snarling expression indicated she was ready to scramble up the handle, lash at the boy.

Alarmed, Matty leaned over more heads, grasped the boy's wrist with one hand, the paddle with the other. "Let go there. Let's see what we've got." The boy refused to yield and Matty squeezed harder—better than slowly prying loose fingers one by one. "Come on, hand it over, that's a good fellow." The "good fellow" was not obliging, a snarl to match Kharm's most ferocious distracted Matty as a bare heel lashed his shin, tried to hook itself behind his knee. The handle's knobbed end swooped periously near the bridge of his nose, threatened to smash it as they struggled. Embarrassing to not be able to overpower a child this size, but he didn't dare use excessive force. Finally relinquishing his grip on the handle, Matty swept an arm around the boy's waist, hoisted him clear.

The dripping paddle rose as well, until the boy dropped it back into the barrel. "Take it, Roddy!" he screamed at a friend. "Hold it down till the bubbles stop!" He thrashed in Matty's arms, hands flailing, yanking his hair. "Jaak!" his high-pitched squeal nearly deafened at close range and, defeated, the young man who'd been planing finally gave up and came over.

"What's the matter here? Put Quint down, at least! If you don't, he's liable to bite your ear off. Bad habit, that."

"Pull the paddle clear first," Matty panted, trying to immobilize Quint while the boy crabbed and clawed and kicked. "I think they're drowning something, a baby larchcat." Depositing Quint was almost impossible since the boy's feet and legs wouldn't stay still. Tail and rear pointing skyward, Kharm fished in the barrel, stretching inside as far as she could reach, her lamentations filling his mind while Quint's cohort, Roddy, vigorously stirred, water splashing. "Hurry, I don't think it can take much more!" he implored Jaak.

Good humored but slightly exasperated at the fuss, the fellow called Jaak commandeered the paddle, pulled it free of the barrel. Something resembling a half-drowned black rodent, streaming water, clung to the blade-end. It opened its tiny mouth, gasped and gagged, produced a strangulated cry. Touched by its plight, Jaak worked to detach it from the paddle, miniature claws like burrs in the wood. Its head turned and it spat, then sank sharp baby teeth into Jaak's thumb to defend itself. Matty held his breath, convinced Jaak would plunge the little beast back underwater, complete its drowning, until a strange look filtered across his face.

"**I told him how to Bond,**" Kharm whispered, "**I had to save his life.**" She sprang from the barrel's rim and stretched up Jaak's leg to nose at the ghatten. It appeared totally black, just a hint of white at its chest, a patch no bigger than a thumbprint.

Jaak gawped, brown eyes widening to the size of chestnuts as he nestled the ghatten under his chin, water streaking his dusty workshirt. "It's . . . walking around . . . inside . . . my mind. . . ." He ran a hand through wispy hair the color of walnut shells, tried to push it off his forehead as if the action might clear his mind, erase the voice. "Astounding. . . ."

"They do that, you know," Matty offered, Quint still locked in his arms. At least the boy had ceased struggling, surveying the scene with interest. Safe to set him down at last. "It's perfectly natural, you'll get used to it." And that's what the Spacers said about the exploding Plumbs, no doubt. Regardless of Kharm's penchant for truth, sometimes a charitable lie was best.

Jaak bore the glazed look of someone lightning-struck. "It has a name, it keeps telling me its name. Tah'm, Tah'm." He rounded on Quint, furious and protective, "How could you try to drown Tah'm? Now be off with you all, now!" The children scattered like leaves, Jaak and Matty left face-to-face. "Does she," he nodded down at Kharm, finally stooped and let the ghatta nuzzle Tah'm, "do that with you? Walk inside your head?"

"Yes, although you're the first person I've ever actually told that. Didn't think anyone else would believe me."

"Phew! I can see why!" He managed a high-pitched laugh, slowly shaking his head in apparent disbelief. As if struck by sudden inspiration, Jaak stuck out a hand. "Jaak Campaan. I think we'd best talk, must talk. I'll make up the work later."

And talk they did, through the daylight hours and into the night when Jaak brought him home with him for dinner. And what amazed Matty most of all was that when Jaak told his parents and his sisters and brothers what had happened, they believed him. Believed even more strongly after Jaak demonstrated Tah'm's fledgling powers of mindspeaking. Then Matty and Kharm, first hesitantly, then more excitedly, demonstrated it more fully.

"Would she walk in my head as well?" Jaak asked. "There are questions I'd like to ask, things you may not know the answers to."

"I'm not sure. She's never done it with anyone else, I mean not directly spoken with them." A rising jealousy gnawed at Matty. "We've always been afraid it would frighten people, make them think they were mad."

Tah'm asleep on his lap, Jaak bent toward Kharm, but she stalked to Matty's side. **"I'm always yours,"** Kharm rubbed one side of her chin, then the other against his knee. **"Marked you—mine! Tah'm has Jaak, I have you."** A superior smile curved her face. **"Though we'll see how long before Jaak tires of ghatten-talk."**

Settling himself into the straw he'd carted from the barn to pile into the corner of the grape arbor, Davvy leaned back against the upturned bench, guardedly checked toward the house, the workshop where he and Cady slept. Cold gusts of wind slapped at him; yesterday'd been warm in comparison. But here, with the bench overturned to provide a windbreak, he felt marginally comfortable. He rummaged inside a coat pocket, retrieved an apple, investigated the other one until he found the pocketknife Miz Marbon had given him. Doyce's father's, she'd told him. The sun sank, bright bands of deep rose, patches of copper, orange, and purple. He put the apple to his mouth but didn't bite, polished it once against his jacket and tucked it away with something akin to regret. Too close to suppertime. Adults always knew how to deny themselves pleasures, waited to savor them. Like Jenret putting duty first, ahead of Doyce.

Instead he opened the pocketknife, looked for something to carve. The underside of the bench was tempting, crying out for his initials. He tested the wood with the point of his knife, sighed, and scrambled until he found a bit of branch that last night's storm had stripped from the maple tree and tossed inside the arbor. Yes, whittling would do and, tongue between his teeth, began to scrape the bark from the branch, painstakingly avoiding the wood beneath. Hard to do with the wood so raw, unaged, the bark ripping, shredding, the knife catching too deeply sometimes before he could stop it.

Frankly, a man needed his solitude sometimes, especially after being so surrounded by women. Only other male around was F'een, and ghatts didn't indulge much in idle chatter, or at least not with him. Cady acted cross and grumpy lately, something worrying her. Even his fighting lessons had been curtailed the past few days and he thought he knew why. Whatever was bothering Cady left her distracted, upset, her concentration shot. He should know; he'd nearly succeeded in legitimately throwing her twice because she wasn't paying attention. All fair and square and aboveboard. Nothing F'een could yell at him about, scold him for because he'd used his growing skills, nothing more. Enough to make him glow with pride, except he wanted to do it really, really right, show Cady he'd stopped playing around and had applied what he'd learned.

Instead, he'd hung around Francie and Miz Marbon in the house, and that, too, had begun to pall. Cranziliation, what was it with women? Cooing and smirking and crying with joy, tiny baby clothes being unpacked from old trunks and drawers, new ones flourished. If he held one more skein of yarn between his hands for Miz Marbon—Auntie Inez, she insisted he call her—he'd go out of his mind! Francie wasn't quite so bad, but even she got caught up in the whirl of things. And Doyce, well, she alternated from amusement and bemusement to abstracted silences, face pleasant but distant as if she weren't even there while the other two women rat-

tled away. Did it right in the house sometimes, didn't wait to
reach the privacy of the arbor.

Eyes inspecting every lattice of the arbor to see if he
could see what she saw, he tried again to figure out what she
saw. Nothing special here that he could judge. Perplexing.
Mayhap she missed, needed Jenret more than she'd let on.
Mayhap that's what she yearned after—the way he yearned
for Nana Cookie, for Swan. Things had been less complicated then. At least Doyce had seemed happier than she'd
been those other times when he'd waited breathless for her
to rejoin the world. He'd monitored the babies yesterday,
figured his worry canceled his promise not to, checking to
see how they fared. The babies acted as restless and irritable
as he felt, mewed up in the tiny kitchen with too many
women. Worst of all, he could sense how crowded, hemmed
in they felt, and he worried they'd grow impatient, arrive too
soon. How they were going to pop out of Doyce's belly button he couldn't imagine. The way he'd been told was silly—
what else was a belly button for?

Branch smoothed, he concentrated on diamond-notching
the green wood. Mayhap if he had some seasoned wood
from the workshop, he could carve toys for the babies. Have
to carve two, though, and that might give him away. Far as
he could tell, Doyce didn't have an inkling she was having
twins, boy and a girl, and the girl was the active one, crab-
bing her elbows, digging in her little heels, impatient as her
daddy. The boy seemed to take it in good stride, more placid
like Doyce, though Davvy had seen times when Doyce was
less than placid, easygoing.

Almost true dark now, he could barely see from his barricade behind the overturned bench so he worked by feel, almost peeled a knuckle when he heard Cady and F'een
hurrying by the arbor. Starting to get up and join them—
F'een sensed suppertime almost as well as Khar did—Davvy
folded the knife shut against his thigh, thunderstruck as
Cady wheeled round and stood over a throughly cowed
F'een.

"I can't believe you didn't tell me!" At least he could hear
half the conversation since she spoke aloud. "You've known
this long and you never said a word? To me, your
Bondmate?"

F'een's head tilted and he raised a paw as if to touch her
leg, pat her to calmness. "Jenret Wycherley held captive by

the Resonants and Doyce doesn't know a thing about it? She's going to be livid when she finds out. Livid with Khar and with the both of us, my fine furred friend, that we've kept it from her."

Davvy held on to his ankles, kept folded like the knife, wishing his ears could pivot like a ghatt's so as not to miss any words. Jenret Wycherley a prisoner? Captured by Resonants? It didn't make any sense. Jenret was a Resonant—why capture one of their own? Were these bad Resonants, like Prince Maurice and Jules Jampolis and the others who'd opposed Eadwin taking the throne? And Maurice had been mad, twisted, like Vesey had been there at the Research Hospice.

They moved on finally, Davvy scrambling on hands and knees, peering through the lattices, watching them out of sight, listening as hard as he could. Smerdlinsky! What he'd give to know what that was all about, but the last he heard was Cady saying, "Well, isn't someone trying to rescue him?" Her voice dropped as they approached the house, Cady switching to mindspeech now that the worst of her anger had been vented.

A rectangle of light as the door opened, Auntie Inez, silhouetted in it, calling, "Davvy, supper, get a move on, lad." Scrambling from the far side of the arbor under cover of darkness he dodged and wove his way behind the barn, then straightened and strolled along as if he'd just come from seeing Lokka. If Cady ever found out he'd been listening—and an honest, innocent overhearing it had been, not a hint of searching her mind, whatever F'een might suspect—he'd be in big trouble.

"Coming, Auntie," he called back. "Just let me wash up and I'll be in."

But all through supper Davvy worried the problem over in his mind, elbow on the table, head propped on hand, despite Cady's nudging rebukes. Jenret Wycherley captive, the babies due to burst any time now, more than ready for an excuse if Doyce found out the truth. His fork moved the food around the plate. Now suppose this piece of carrot was Jenret, surrounded by these tiny pearl onions he'd moved into position. How would you free him? His fork swooped and lifted the carrot to temporary safety before it disappeared in his mouth. Yes, the problem was the gravy from the chicken pot pie. The gravy represented the terrain, an unknown, because he had no idea where Jenret was being held. Made the whole problem particularly slippery. He plowed a piece of chicken through the gravy, scattered the onions.

"Davvy?" His head jerked up, mouth slightly open in shock. Francie held the plate of biscuits toward him. "Another?" He took the plate, thanked her as he selected one, and passed it on, belatedly remembering his manners. What else was Francie saying?

"Today's broadside says the king's rerouting the royal progress; he's going to Gaernett last, not first. In fact, he should be in Ruysdael late tomorrow afternoon." Her cheeks had a high color to them, as if she'd just come in from outdoors, and her eyes sparkled. "Oh, Doyce, can't we go, don't you think?"

Doyce grunted noncommittally, as if she really weren't there, and said "No, thank you," to nothing in particular.

"Doyce!" and Doyce shook herself, hazel eyes darting from one to another at the table, faintly embarrassed, unsure what was going on. "Can't we go see the royal progress? I'm dying to see that handsome Arras Muscadeine ride into Ruysdael, not to mention the king."

"It's not romantic, Francie, not something out of the storybooks. It's to show the world that Resonants and Normals can get along, work together, respect and value each other's abilities. They have work to do in Ruysdael, and at each town they stop at along the way, talk to people, convince them there's nothing to fear. We know that already, don't we?"

Francie's lips were tight, her mouth downcast, and Davvy felt a welling pity for her. Doyce didn't have to be so darn self-righteous and serious about it. 'Course it would be fun, something different. Everyone needed something different and exciting sometimes, change their old routines. And Francie, as far as he could judge, had a more routine life than most, few highs, few lows, just a steady, daily sameness, the way he'd had growing up at the Hospice. But Francie didn't get indulged the way he did—indulged in the things he wanted. They treated her like a child sometimes, indulged themselves, not her, as if being crippled meant she'd never grow up, never know what was best for her. No wonder she reared up against such treatment, though he didn't think she'd do it now.

"Besides," Doyce continued, "I want to stay here, not go

gallivanting around. Jenret's bound to come soon—what if I were in Ruysdael when he arrives here? What if I missed him altogether?"

It struck him then—the king, and nearly at Ruysdael! The king and Muscadeine would know how to rescue Jenret. All he had to do was go to Ruysdael and alert the king. Mayhap it should be up to the Monitor and the Guardians to rescue Jenret, but if they'd been trying, so far they hadn't done a very good job. But the king and Muscadeine were Resonants, could seek out Jenret's Resonant mind, locate him easy as pie! He snapped his fingers in excitement.

Abruptly aware that every eye was on him, he smiled until he thought his cheeks would crack. "I think you should go to Ruysdael. Don't think old Jenret is going to get around to coming tomorrow, just can feel it somehow." To his surprise, Cady nodded, backed him up, but gave him an odd look. Wasn't half so bad as the sour pickle look that came from F'een on the windowsill. *"Did not!"* he protested mentally. *"Check me and you'll see I'm telling the truth."*

"I just don't want to go," Doyce protested. "It's going to be crowded and busy, people milling around, a regular circus of the curious and the titillated, enjoying the idea of tempting fate by even looking at a Resonant. Besides, I'll never be able to find a privy when I need it!"

"No reason we can't take a chamber pot with us, leave it in the wagon." Inez got into the spirit of things. "Did it often enough when you were little and we went to the wool market. Couldn't always find enough trees to hide one or the other of you behind."

Francie and Doyce both pointed at each other, exclaiming, "It was always her!"

"Oh, I don't know. We'll see," Doyce grumped.

And with that, Davvy excused himself, let himself out and went to bed in the workshop, mind working furiously. Would they go—or wouldn't they? Can't wait on women to make a decision, he told himself. Rise at first light, saddle Lokka, and ride to Ruysdael. Make sure he knew what the town was like, how best to reach the king. Mayhap he couldn't save Jenret himself, but he had a mission, and if it would keep those babies quiet and peaceful inside their pods a little bit longer, it was worth it. Jenret had to be here when the babies were born or Doyce was going to be sooo upset.

Mahafny handled the reins roughly, mind still on her conversation with Swan. The black pacer whinnied a protest, but she ignored him, the high, two-wheeled gig taking the mostly deserted streets of Gaernett a little too fast for Saam's liking. He worried, too, about how much she could actually feel the reins, her hands cramping worse each day, numb at times, but he saw she'd looped them around her wrists.

"It may be late, but there are still a few people out," he pointed out. "Best not run them over, have the Guardians after you for reckless driving. After all, they know that eumedicos are generally the only ones who drive this sort of rig, and it won't take them long to check at the Hospice and see who signed one out tonight."

"I'll attempt not to leave a trail of mangled bodies in my wake," she snapped and meant it in utter seriousness, he judged, no subtle humor to her tone. Saam braced himself as best he could and tried not to think about what would happen when they left Gaernett and hit the straightaway. He hoped as well that the bundle in back was securely packed and tied down. Then again, it might be better if it weren't—if it got tossed out, shattered, and broke. At least it would deter Mahafny for a time. Swan's cautions hadn't had much effect, either.

The harder Mahafny tried to push Swan from her mind, the more her jaw clenched, the more erratic her handling of the reins, the horse edgy at her indecisiveness, the contradictory commands. Stop it, she scolded herself, it's not the poor horse's fault. With the Monitor entrusted to his beloved Marie's ministrations—the victim of stress and exhaustion, not a heart attack, thankfully—Mahafny had hurried to see her cousin before joining Eadwin and Muscadeine in Ruysdael. Harrap and Parm unaccounted for, Jenret and the others still missing, her growing hope that her strange machine could prove who was or wasn't a Resonant, all were enough to occupy her mind. Except she hadn't allowed her mind to think that Swan might have grown much worse since she'd last seen her.

"Won't be much longer, Mahafny," and she'd lain there in bed, so gaunt that her hip bones raised the bedclothes, her skin translucent and papery-thin. "It's time, past time, really. I'm not quite ready to go, wish I didn't have to, but I do, and I've accepted it." Koom lifted his head from where he stretched beside her on the bed, and even the ruddy ghatt looked thin and unkempt, as if he were fading as well.

"No," Mahafny had protested, "All we have to do is try another, a different medication, work on improving your breathing. And besides," she cajoled, "I've discovered something you'll find fascinating. What I've been searching for all this time, a way to tell who is and isn't a Resonant."

Swan's eyebrows arched, the effort of a smile more than she could muster. "For someone in a profession with a hundred percent mortality rate, you do seem to deny the obvious sometimes." Her voice was so faint that Mahafny had to bend to hear her. "But go ahead, tweak my curiosity if you must. I suppose that that, if anything, will be the last thing about me to die."

Shaken, Mahafny launched into her description of the machine, the strange reaction it engendered in Resonants—and to a lesser extent, in the ghatti—and only in Resonants. "Don't you see, we'll be able to determine who is and who isn't, very possibly even tell who has latent or dormant skills," she'd concluded, exhilarated by the idea, swept by the warm glow of accomplishment that comes from the solving of a demanding puzzle. A neat answer to a knotty problem.

But Swan's reaction took her completely aback. "Destroy it!" she'd shouted as she struggled upright in bed, Koom hovering helplessly nearby. "What right have we to determine such a thing? Bad enough to conclusively identify those who truly are Resonants but fear such exposure, and you want to determine who might, just possibly might have latent skills? People who consider themselves Normal and are happy being who and what they are? People with no desire for mindspeech. What right do you have to disrupt their worlds, make family and friends look askance at them?"

"But to know, to truly know. . . ." Mahafny trailed to a halt, amazed how anyone could ignore true knowledge. It would be tantamount to ignoring the truth, and Swan of all people, Seeker General of the Seekers Veritas, couldn't ignore the truth.

"But is your world ready for this truth?" Koom straddled Swan's body protectively. **"Truth always has two**

edges and both are sharp. If the world were perfect, perhaps this knowledge might be good, but it's not a perfect
world. How can you stigmatize people whose skill may
never ripen? What if they're ostracized? What of those
who know they're skilled but chose not to use it, content
to be no more or less than anyone else?"

"But . . . but Doyce, for example," desperate, she sought
for a way to convince them both. "Is Doyce a Resonant or
not? Don't you think she'd like to know?"

"Does it matter?" Swan's lips formed the words, but she
barely had the breath to utter them. She forced harder. "She
is what she is. Mayhap she'll develop in time, mayhap not.
Will Jenret love her any the less if she isn't?"

"But to have a literal meeting of the minds—"

"The day those two have a meeting of the minds, given
their personalities, I'd like to see it!" Swan scoffed.

"Don't try to push it away by joking!" Damn all, why
couldn't Swan see, agree with her? It hurt to have her cousin
so unalterably opposed, not able to share her vision.

"But Koom's vision is much more likely," Saam added.

"Please, Mahafny, think about it, think about it more
deeply, with your heart, not just your mind. Think about it
and destroy the machine. It's the last thing I'll ever ask of
you, I promise."

"I will," she'd vowed, and she was still pondering it as
they drove along, eyes suspiciously damp. Blasted torchères
were too damn bright after the side streets, she told herself
as she rubbed a sleeve against her eyes.

Saam stiffened beside her. **"Look out!"** The horse turned
skittish as she jerked the reins, and the gig swung wide
around the corner, wheels skidding on the pavement.

A thud and an irate shout, "You bloody fool driver!" And
an internal cry, **"Don't care if I've been invited to
mindspeak you or not! Mahafny, you wretch! How dare
you knock down Parse like that? Saam, stop her so I can
give her a piece of my mind!"**

She fought the gig to a halt, jumped down. "Parse, are
you all right?"

"Mahafny?" He sprawled on the pavement, desperately
scrabbling for his crutches. "What? It's not enough you half-
crippled me by amputating my leg? Now you want to finish
the job?" He pushed himself up. "Ouch!" Per'la stalked to
Mahafny, peridot eyes flashing sparks, tail ribbon snapping.

Better assuage the ghatta first from the looks of things, because Mahafny suspected she didn't have a prayer that Saam'd come to her defense. **"That's right,"** he commented as he sauntered over, sniffed at Parse, **"Apologies and patchwork, right up your alley—or patchwork, anyway. I'd suggest you work very hard on the apology, though."**

Retrieving the crutch beyond his grasp, she handed it to Parse. "I'll be happy to apologize once I'm sure you're not seriously hurt. If you are, medical attention comes first, apologies second."

He waved the crutch at her. "Breath knocked out of me, a few scrapes and bruises. Was in a brown study myself, mulling over some awfully interesting things and not looking where I was going. I'll live." He looked more closely at his crutch, "But this seems to have sustained a greenstick fracture. And you nearly scared Per'la witless."

She drew herself to rigid attention, intoned, "I am a careless, egocentric wretch of a eumedico, with too much on her mind, convinced that nothing but her problems are important." Per'la's fur fluffed, and she preened. "I humbly beg both your pardons and to make amends, ask if you'd be interested in traveling to Ruysdael with me. The king should be there late tomorrow, so we should arrive just about in time." Assuming they changed horses along the way, and assuming she and Parse shared the driving while the other slept as best as possible. And besides, with his love of puzzles and gadgets and gizmos, mechanical thingamabobbies, Parse was the perfect person to have along. He could make sketches of it in case she wanted more made.

"Ruysdael's near Coventry, isn't it?" Both crutches in one hand, Parse came upright before she could help. "That's what I was mulling over when we collided. I've some peculiar news for Doyce. Sort of present history replicating past history—oh, not desperately past, but fifty years ago, at least. We'll go, with pleasure."

Unable to restrain himself, Parse launched into his tale as soon as he'd boosted himself into the gig. "You know, I've been seeing a great deal of Maize Bartolotti lately," he confided, "and she's just fascinating."

"Who?" Was Parse becoming fickle, using Sarrett's absence to romance another woman? Well, none of her business.

He shook his head in surprise, tucked his arm around Per'la as the gig picked up speed. "Oh, I guess you've never met her. No reason you should, I guess I've been so wrapped up in her stories that I assumed everyone knew her. She's 103—used to be a Seeker, though for a very short time."

Don't burst out laughing, she instructed herself, transformed a chuckle into a throat-clearing. "And still has all her wits about her?" she ventured.

"Oh, definitely. She's become the hit of Myllard's Inn since the Elder Hostel burned, a regular fixture, house granny, so to speak. But it's not that she's wrapped up in the past, you know. Takes a lively interest in the present, astute about observing the world around her, drawing parallels between now and then."

"Such as . . .?" Couldn't he come to the point? She ached to tell him about the machine, her precious device, see what he thought. Surely he'd support her, given his love of winkling out solutions, solving riddles.

"Well, do you know what we were talking about tonight?" No, of course she didn't know, she wasn't a Resonant, was she? A tiny growl of frustration escaped her, but luckily Parse didn't hear as he pressed on. "Reapers, no less. They're the ones who burned the Elder Hostel. She said it reminded her of something that happened fifty years ago when a group of farmers banded together and massacred a gathering of Gleaners. Apparently they used various farm implements, shovels, rakes, sickles, scythes to kill the Gleaners, because those were the weapons they had at hand." An inward, swinging motion of his hand, "You see? Sickles, like those little silver crescents the Reapers wear on their collars?"

"Interesting, not exactly original, though." They'd be outside the city shortly and she could let the horse have his full stride, pacing the distance with tireless precision.

But Parse didn't notice her perfunctory response. "The farmer who organized the attack was named Hosea Bazelon. He and some of the others were convicted of murder, exiled to the Sunderlies."

"Odd name, Bazelon, don't think I've heard it before."

"Maize said his family went with him, and the few other relatives remaining in Canderis legally petitioned to have their names changed."

"With good reason, I suppose." An experimental flick of the whip to hide her irritation. She had nothing to contribute to this, and if she let him run on without interruption, he'd finish all the faster.

"Except I met someone named Bazelon the other day, Bazelon Foy. Right here in Canderis. I was going into the High Conciliators' offices when he bumped into me. Almost sent me sprawling, like you, but at least he didn't do it with a gig!" He was bouncing now, not in rhythm with the gig, but completely opposite, jarring it, jarring her. "Do you think he could be a relative, a grandson or nephew or something? Someone come back from the Sunderlies, just as relatives have the right to do. Planning to take revenge after so many years, prove Hosea Bazelon was right, finish off the job he started!"

"It sounds too much of a coincidence to me, that you're weaving together unrelated threads based on a chance circumstance of similar names." Best nip his fancies in the bud, bring him back to reality.

"There might be truth in the connections he's made. If she wasn't such a stubborn, single-minded—"

"Per'la!" Saam warned. "She's already said she's sorry."

"But he might be right!"

"Fine, then. I promise to let you tell me the whole story if you'll let Mahafny talk with Parse and get something off her mind. It's important as well."

❖

PART
FIVE

❖

PART
FIVE

Eeling his spine, digging in his shoulders, Parm waved all four feet in the air; his toes curling as he sank into even deeper sleep. Nicey-wicey, Ni— Ooof! A ball of ice rammed his slitted eye, and he twisted away, swinging a foreleg up to shield his face. A giant, slurping slab of raw, chilled liver draped itself across his muzzle, caressed it damply. **"Bar . . . na . . . by, go'way!"** And the wetness receded. **"Goo' dog!"** he mumbled, already sinking into the blessed wooliness of sleep as the cold nose worked its way to Parm's nether end and planted icy nostrils on a part of the ghatt's anatomy that only his nearest and dearest should touch. Yeow! Parm was upright now, at least marginally, trying to determine top from bottom when it came to planting his legs. He already knew where his bottom was, thanks to Barnaby.

Still, he couldn't stay mad at the terrier, couldn't stay mad at anyone for long. Sooo happy! he crooned to himself as he finally managed to stick his head under Harrap's blanket preparatory to burrowing underneath. Poor doggy, whining, pleading little moans in his ear. Poor, poor Barnaby. He tried to express the thought, but it wasn't always simple to converse with canines, so many of them spoke a shorthand doggerel, and Parm giggled to himself. *"Worry-hurry"* came from Barnaby's brain, singsonging like a squeaky hinge, *"worry-hurry."*

Cracking open an eye, he focused on the dog, bouncing on its neat little feet, his whiplike tail wagging encouragement. *"Come, come, head hum-thrum bad."* Dogs just couldn't concentrate on having a decent conversation, always becoming distracted, needing to water a tree, investigate an enticing aroma, roll in it. The icy nose poked him again, imploring, the dog's head dipping in supplication, springing away as if to entice him to follow. *"Please, please, need steady heady. Need your help."*

With a yawn, Parm slithered back into the night air, squinted in shock. When had all the people come, or was he seeing double or triple again? Where? How? Abruptly he sat, went to scratch his chin with a hind foot and missed, burped, the residual taste of that lovely seasoning Hylan gave them flooding his mouth, a hint of memory, past glory. Except now it tasted vile. Cock-eyed he examined the terrier, the white so sharp against the night, the brown ears almost invisible. **"Don't feel very well,"** he confessed.

"I know so, I know." The words came fast as the tail wags, blurred, as was the tail. *"Come, come, come. Barnaby fix icky-icks, sicky-icks. Then Parm help Barnaby? Warnaby helping Barnaby?"* Darting off, he dashed back again, back and forth, back and forth, making Parm dizzy as he stood and staggered off, anything to shorten Barnaby's dashes or at least head him in one direction. Head pounding, stomach roiling, he placed each foot carefully, as if he were a million years old.

They traversed two meadows filled with tents, wagons, people wrapped in bedrolls and blankets. Most slept, but there were plenty still awake, lanterns festive like fireflies, fires winking, a chattering, buzzing filling the air. It reminded Parm of the time years ago when he'd seen a field of locusts, the air thick with their wingbeats, the chewing sounds, the cracking buzz of their scraping legs. Catching them had been ridiculously easy—simply put a paw down and trap one or two underneath. He'd gorged himself, crunching away, swallowing still-kicking legs, beating wings, until he was sick.

Don't think about it, he commanded himself as Barnaby nosed him one way, then another, guiding him away from the worst of the crowds, a destination in mind that Parm couldn't decipher. **"Where did all the people come from?"** Mayhap if he thought about something else he wouldn't feel so ill. Yes, people had been following Hylan, following behind Harrap and the goat cart, more each day, but the numbers couldn't have swelled so high, could they?

"King thing," the dog whined. *"King thing, Hylan bring. Kill-he will-she. Not good. 'Splain later."*

King thing? Thing king? He squinted tight to keep the moon above from dancing gold-sphered pregnant overhead, multiplying each time he glanced skyward, dizzying him. Thinking was what he should be doing, but why did it seem so hard? King? The only king he knew of resided in Marchmont? Wasn't any reason for the king to come here. Hru'rul? Nice, bouncy Hru'rul. And Hru'rul's Bondmate was Eadwin, King of Marchmont and ... a Resonant. Hylan didn't like Resonants, did she? Why did he think that?

Was the dog going to walk him forever? As far as he could tell, they'd traversed the length of both meadows, had reached a stone wall. The dog bounded, scrabbled over and gave a pleading whine from the other side. Stretching as far as he could, Parm jumped, teetered on the top and toppled headfirst, twisted desperately and landed on his back, wind knocked out of him. He lay bordering the remains of a summer garden that stretched beyond a farm house. Empty mounds of dirt stretched before him in rows, shocks of dried cornstalks rustled, traded secrets with the dried gourd vines that wound through a wide, wire mesh fencing stapled between posts. Late cabbages over there, he could smell them, rank in his nose.

Barnaby, Barnaby the indefatigable, pushed him again, boosted him along to the southern side of the stone wall. There, tight against the stone, protected by the mounded side of the garden, grass still grew greenly. *"Eat, sweet eat,"* Barnaby urged, nipping a few blades himself. Parm took a tentative bite, and the fresh taste of grass flooded his mouth. Plucking the blades, sawing at them with teeth not meant for grazing, he gulped the grass. And the next thing he knew he was retching, heaving, turning himself inside out. He huddled there, miserable, exhausted. So weak, his head still pounding, but he could almost think, string together a coherent thought ... watched it drift away. Oh, dear, could Barnaby fetch it for him?

Nose to ground, Barnaby coursed the garden, the overgrown area at the far end, then pounced, forefeet frantically digging. The snap of jaws, a tremendous backward tug, and Barnaby shook his head, dirt flying from a long, whiplike tap root. He trotted back, dropped his treasure in front of Parm's nose. Wretched weed had an awful, reeking smell that made him sick all over again. *"Chew poo-phooey weed, chew,"* Barnaby exhorted him.

"Bleh!" Parm closed his eyes, turned his head away. Jaws gripped the back of his neck tight, pushed his face against the noxious weed.

He let go, panted, *"Helped whelp. Puppy Barnaby bad*

once," he sounded shamed. *"Greedy for seasoning weedy. Lurp, slurp, gulp, gulp—so happy!"* He rolled crazily on his back, tongue lolling, miming the past pleasure, then sprang up. *"Hylan catch, slash, lash. Thrust poo-phooey weed down hatch. Oh, Barnaby borribly horribly sicky-ick. After, head clear, never go near."*

It was too long and convoluted a speech for Parm to follow, but he registered the gist of it. Wrinkled his nose, chomped down on the offensive weed, sure the cure was worse than what ailed him. He ate more, eyes watering, stomach burning, and lay there gasping. Slowly his head became clearer, his limbs more responsive. Had enough strength to wonder what it was that had had him in its thrall.

"Poison? Is that seasoning a poison? Is Hylan trying to kill us, drug us?" The dog whined unhappy confirmation, backing away anxiously as if afraid Parm would take it out on him. Hoarse barking, basso deep and profoundly angry at discovering trespassers on its property, split the night air and a dark shape came hurtling over the wall.

Frozen in shock, Parm crouched, unable to make his legs work, fear, the aftereffects of the drug paralyzing him. The foe looked the size and shape of a mastiff, and the thought of its huge, slavering jaws made his spine ice. *"Hurry-worry!"* Barnaby's shrill barking pierced his brain as the terrier spun in circles around the larger dog, bearing down on him like an enraged bull. *"Dumb crumb, big but dumb! Hurry, hurry!"* Suddenly Parm's legs were churning, digging divots from the earth as he brought his paws under control, aimed them all in the same direction. *"Run toward gourds!"*

Tearing across the garden, the huge dog in his wake, trailed by a furiously bounding terrier, Parm dashed for the gourd trellis. Except for the few snakelike vines woven through, the space between each post appeared vacant, empty, but Parm cursed himself. He'd seen the wire fencing when they'd passed by it by. Throw himself at that and he'd come out in nice neat cubes on the other side. Minced ghatti. Gak! *"Duck! Dive!"* Barnaby yelped, and with no other choice before him, Parm did. The wire scraped his back but he slithered under. Wonder dog, wondrous Barnaby, percipient terrier terror! Barnaby had seen that the fencing didn't touch the ground, bare room enough for a terrified ghatt to squeeze under!

Convinced that if the ghatt could go through, that he could

as well, the black dog never checked his stride, sure another surge would let him snap at Parm's neck. With a "ka-wang!" and a "sprong!" the dog flew backward, the staples in the fence posts groaning at the impact. Barnaby took his time to neatly trot around the end of the fencing and join Parm.

They both leaped the stone wall without turning to look back, but Parm immediately stopped on the other side. **"Now tell me everything. What's Hylan up to? What do I do to get Harrap off this drug?"**

"No hurt Hylan? Help Hylan?" The terrier rolled on its back, presenting its vulnerable belly and throat to Parm. *"Hylan not same since burning bush flaming, naming ..."*

"Burning bush?" Parm echoed his words.

"Witch-switch hazel," the dog looked uncomfortable. *"Witch-switch hazel naming, her taming what it names."*

Parm's head began to ache again. Bushes that spoke, what next? Vegetation didn't speak. **"I must find Harrap, check on him. Explain to me on the way."**

Tadj moved stiffly, back stinging, throbbing. His shirt clung to the long, oozing slashes, impossible to remove if he didn't strip it off before the blood dried. Damn Hylan for importuning him, insisting they scourge each other with those long, limber switches! But tonight, tonight, he'd had no choice but to agree. She craved proof of her worthiness to gird herself for the ceremonies tomorrow—no, today. The sun would be rising soon. A sleepless night but not a switchless one. The thought was almost enough to make him crack a smile, but he didn't. This was serious, deadly serious, and he'd do whatever it took to have Hylan primed for the ceremony. Soon, soon, the King of Marchmont, the King of Resonants, would be dead! And Baz would applaud the part Tadj had played in accomplishing that feat. He tossed the well-worn switches on top of the goat cart, stretched, wished he hadn't.

Hylan, looking the same as always except for a blissful smile, peered under the cart. It was then that Tadj abruptly recognized the sawing, rasping undercurrent that punctuated his thoughts, Harrap's stertorous breathing. Hylan shook the Shepherd's shoulder, "Harrap, Harrap? Are you all right?" She shook harder, pushed at him, and a ripple coursed through his body, his flesh jiggling with her efforts, not from his response to her. "Harrap?" A genuine tenderness and distress enveloped that one tremulous word.

The next thing Tadj knew she'd sunk her fingers into the front of his heavy brocade overvest, practically lifting him off the ground. "Did you give him any at supper?" Her face pressed close to his, her matte gray eyes pebble hard, smile long gone.

"Yes, of course." He hated it, the vest's pull under his arms, dragging against the long, cross-hatched slashes on his back. Hated, most of all, the sensation of losing control and he didn't know how or why. "You were busy speaking with—"

"I'd already given him some, he was too eager to wait any longer for supper." She let go as if the feel of him sullied her, and Tadj unruffled himself, pulled the overvest down, wincing, wondering why the ground had fallen out from under him.

"Oh." He wasn't sure what else to say and she appeared to be ignoring him, all her energy and effort concentrated on Harrap, hand on his brow.

Abstracted, she tried to explain, "The doses have to be smaller now, they have a cumulative effect on the system." The dangerous flat look in her eyes had abated slightly. "You wouldn't have known, but you should have asked before—"

The dawning broke rapidly, both in the sky and in Tadj's mind. "Oh, Blessed Lady, what about the ceremony?" he gasped as the full magnitude of his innocent act sank in. They needed Harrap, more accurately, Hylan needed and wanted him for the ceremony tonight. Fouled up, he'd fouled up, one little, unthinking act and he'd jeopardized everything he and Baz—not to mention Hylan—had worked so hard to achieve. She *should* scourge him for that, just as the sailors had beaten him for admiring their beauty. Not a creator but a destroyer, destroying the rigorously pure, simple beauty of the plan!

"He's cold as death," Hylan rubbed Harrap's hand between her own.

How could they recover from his foolish slip, a minor error with such major consequences? What could he do to make it right? "Let's take him to my tent, strip him, rub him down, pile blankets over him. Will it help, will sleeping it off help?" He'd wrap Harrap in his arms, warm his body with his own if it would help. Would Hylan go ahead with the ceremony if Harrap weren't a part of it?

Hylan rubbed her lower lip across her teeth, dubious. "He's going to be impossible to move. He's a mountain of a man, Tadj. Even between us, I doubt we can manage. He's dead weight."

He closed his ears to the word "dead," frantically unlacing the canvas from the top of the cart, exposing the precious saplings. Hylan winced at their vulnerable slimness, so like her switches but not yet as strong. She'd plant one here at Ruysdael, protect them. "If we roll him onto the canvas, we can drag him there," he assured her, wished for assurance himself. He'd drag a chain of anvils behind him if it would make things right. If the loss of Harrap made her doubt herself, he was doomed.

They worked, desperate not to disturb the sleeping faithful camped around them, finally reached Tadj's tidy little tent. Breath coming in gasps, Tadj decided it would have been easier to move Harrap just enough and then dismantle the tent, pitch it over him. Next time he'd know. Not that there'd ever be a next time, never again. Hylan was busy stripping off Harrap's robe, rubbing him down. "See that his robe's washed, Tadj. It's filthy."

He nodded humbly, bundled it under his arm, nose crinkling at the smell, not just sweat and dirt but somehow the scent of Hylan's seasoning had permeated it as well. "I'll find someone." Easy enough to do, any of the faithful would be honored by even such a menial task as this. "Does that mean you think he'll recover for the ceremony?" If she didn't have her sacrifice, he wasn't sure what would happen.

"The Lady will provide." Her voice was clear and confident. Her response thrilled him, showed that all his work, his delicate insinuations about invoking the Lady's name in the ceremony hadn't been in vain. "The Lady will provide, I always have and I always will. Only I can shoulder the burden."

He froze, tried to decipher what she meant. It sounded askew. Had she taken to heart Harrap's drugged belief that she, Hylan, exemplified the Lady here in the world? He slowly exhaled, breath hissing between his teeth, inhaled. Did it matter? If not Harrap, then, most likely she'd provide her own sacrificial lambs. Just so long as it wasn't him!

"Have you seen Barnaby?" Her shift to the prosaic startled him, made him realize the terrier was nowhere around, nor the ghatt. He started to mention it but was cut off. "He'll be back. He always runs and hides when I get out the switches."

The summer in Roermond proved a godsend for Matty and Kharm, the community's quiet toleration of his difference a marvel, and the growing rapport with Jaak and Tah'm something sorely desired after so long a solitude. Yet with the harvest gathered, wanderlust compelled Matty to move on, try another town. Though he hated to admit it, he feared wearing out his welcome, that somehow one day the scales would drop from Roermonder eyes and they'd see him and Kharm for what they truly were.

"But they already see us for what we are, and they don't mind." As far as Kharm was concerned, facts were the first cousins of truth.

Indecisive, he stood admiring the valley that held Roermond and felt as if he relinquished a second home. "This isn't the real world here, it can't be. If it were, it would have seduced me long ago." What drove him onward like this? Restless, yearning both to be on his way and to stay, Kharm's swaying tail alerted him to her own inner questions. "Do you really want to go?" Any excuse and he'd seize it.

"Wherever you go I'll follow, unless you'd like me to lead the way?" Then why was the ghatta starting back down the path? Was she leading him back to Roermond? **"Company. Whatever you're seeking, we'll find it together."** And with that, that black imp of a ghatten, Tah'm, popped up the path, bounding almost like a rolapin. Kharm still outweighed him, although he'd grown nearly as large as she. With a chirrup of glee, he piled on top of her, wrestling her to the ground with mock growls and nips to the neck and throat.

"Come on, come on!" a voice boomed around the curve of the trail. "Stop brooding like a lover who's lost his lass. Start looking and you'll find one even more fair." Basket pack on his back, Jaak toiled into view. "Besides, I don't see why you and Kharm should be so selfish about sharing adventures. Roermond's in my heart, but no reason I can't experience other places before I formally declare my love. Which direction shall we head?"

Matty slapped his shoulder, unable to say anything. A compatriot, a companion, almost a brother. Come to think of it, a rather absurd looking brother, the basket pack tumpline creasing his forehead, making his thin hair stick up in clumps, his neck muscles bulging. Like Matty, he exuded a slight lanolin scent, courtesy of his new sheepskin poncho. But the greatest surprise, the most dramatic change was that Jaak now sported earrings, a gold ball on a post in his right ear and a hoop in his left. **"How handsome,"** a fleeting envy flooded Kharm. **"Look how they contrast with his black fur."**

"Huh?" He swiveled toward Tah'm, high spirits momentarily quelled, coat dusty from Kharm's drubbing. The ghatt sported earrings as well. "Didn't it hurt, Jaak? Didn't Tah'm mind? And why?"

Backing against a boulder so he could rest his pack, Jaak eased a thumb under the tumpline. "Struck me as a good idea. Traveling like this, strangers have no idea that Tah'm and Kharm are allied with us, that they belong with us. If they see a larchcat, of course they'll think it's a wild beast, possibly try to kill it. Figured if they saw earrings on an animal, they'd think twice. The matching pairs show we belong to each other." Tah'm generated deep, rumbling purrs of agreement. If he grew to match his purr, he'd be a very large ghatt.

"Oh, yes, big and clever and handsome." A certain proprietary tone to Kharm's mindspeech, and Matty wondered just how the ghatta viewed Tah'm. Ghatten he might now be, but not ghatten forever. **"I don't suppose we could have earrings, too?"** she wheedled, broadening her 'speech to include Jaak.

He spoke aloud for Jaak's benefit. "Kharm, Jaak's a friend, but it's not polite to root in his mind without permission. Isn't it enough that Tah'm's gamboling around in there?" Kharm looked only slightly abashed and Jaak more than a little amused. "Well? I wouldn't enter another's house without knocking, even a good friend's house. Everyone deserves a certain amount of privacy until you're sure you're wanted. If Jaak wants to ask you into his mind, he will."

"Jaak doesn't mind, do you?"

Jaak's twinkling eyes gave the lie to the solemn expression he'd pasted on his face with such care. "Well, sometimes it *does* get a little crowded with both you and Tah'm inside together," he allowed, "but then, I've enough brothers and sisters that I'm used to it." An almost imperceptible headshake from Matty reminded Jaak that discipline wasn't one of his strongest suits.

"How about if . . ." Matty paused for effect, appeared to consider, ". . . if Jaak invites you to 'speak? If we settle on a phrase that we always use so you know you're welcome? And the same applies to me inviting Tah'm." A staccato handclap denoted inspiration. "How about . . . 'Mindwalk if ye will'? Moments of privacy are as important as sharing."

"Except for Jaak I don't talk to other humans! I already promised because you said it upsets them. Not unless it's an emergency. Sometimes I prowl inside their minds, but I *never* 'speak them." Wavering between self-righteousness and sullenness, Kharm dipped her head for a peremptory lick at her chest to indicate submission without actually saying so. Gold earrings dancing, Tah'm nosed her, fretful at her discomfort.

"Mindwalk if ye will," Jaak squatted and scratched her ears.

Pushing her head into his hand she rubbed against his thumb, nibbled on a finger. **"Can you convince Matty we need earrings?"**

"Better than that. I brought a set for you both." Pinching a velvet-petaled ear he warned, "But it *does* hurt. Ask Tah'm."

Chin high, Tah'm swiveled his ears to indicate disdain. **"Bee sting. I am Tah'm, bravest of ghatts. I'll lick the pain away."**

Rising, Jaak dusted the knees of his pantaloons. "Well, that's settled, Matty. Assuming you trust me with the piercing at some point along the way?"

"Some point?" Matty fingered his own earlobes, suppressed a shudder. "Ouch!" The thought of a needle piercing through his flesh left him faint and dizzy.

"Coward, are you?" Jack mocked, already starting up the trail, the ghatti bounding ahead, assuming the lead, their dust plumes sifting down at him. "But where are we going?" he implored the receding backs. "I hadn't decided yet myself."

"Hadn't you?" Jaak swung around, the basket's weight

swinging him even further. "I saw how you looked any time Manuel Vandersma's name was mentioned in passing. You never asked any questions, but your ears practically flapped. That's why we have to pin them down. He's in Alkmaar, so, of course, that's where we're going."

Matty hurried, paired his stride with Jaak's. "I don't understand what he's doing there. Whatever it is, though, everyone utters his name with a certain respect." How to admit that respect and Manuel Vandersma seldom went hand-in-hand. Did he want to find the father he knew, the passive, indecisive wastrel? Or this alien new person his father had become? Known or unknown? Which to choose. "We don't *have* to go there," he emphasized. "No reason he should know me, probably'll barely remember me."

Jaak puffed along, neck muscles straining as Tah'm dove off a boulder and landed in the basket pack, a surprise delivery of nearly ten extra kilos. "Did it ever occur to you that word travels in all directions? That if you've recently heard about him he may have heard about you?"

With a noncommittal grunt, Matty continued. And so they traveled together, winding up and down the increasingly steep trails tracing the foothills of the Tetonords, the mountains majestically rearing purple at their backs as they swung southwest.

By the seventh day Matty found himself almost unable to speak, racked with apprehension the closer they came to Alkmaar. Odd, at last he had mates, Jaak and Tah'm, who accepted him and Kharm for what they were, and he couldn't exchange a word with them, explain what bothered him. Or tell Kharm for that matter. Instead he studied the rise and fall of his feet, thoughts pinwheeling and crashing. He didn't need a father; he had Granther, and a better father he'd been to Matty than his own. That was the truth, plain and simple.

As they spied the village of Alkmaar poking out of the mountainside like a mushroom, Kharm finally interrupted his churning thoughts. **"Must I wait for you to say 'Mindwalk if ye will'? I'm lonely."** She planted herself in his path, an immovable fur-covered stone. **"If you step around and don't speak, I'll scratch."**

"Sorry, beloved." He ordered his tired feet to halt, forced himself to see her—was struck anew, overwhelmed, admiring the exquisite stripes, the green eyes with a hint of gold

today, devouring him with their fierce devotion. His alone, no one else's. *"I've had thinking to do. Didn't mean to exclude you. Guess I assumed you followed along inside, even if you didn't 'speak much."*

"You didn't leave me any room to 'speak. Besides, you untangle truths pretty well yourself." A lightning paw cast a pebble at him, Tah'm chasing after it as if it were alive. **"You're slow—but thorough. There's something you should know. Your father, Manuel, is up there, waiting. I don't know how he knows, but he does, I can feel it. He's happy you're coming."**

His throat hurt when he swallowed, but the pain in his chest marginally eased. *"I guess I am, too."* Turning, he discovered Jaak and Tah'm had paused behind him, patient. "Jaak, would you mind if I went up alone?"

"Not alone! With me!" Kharm protested.

"I think of us as one," he reassured before calling back, "You could camp here for the night, join us in the morning."

Jaak laughed, shrugged out of his pack. The tumpline had creased his brow—not to mention leaving an untanned white strip. "Another forlorn night without an ale? Surely I'll perish." He caught up with Matty, hefted the backpack off his friend's shoulders. "You'll range ahead faster without it. Besides, you've got the cheese. Scoot along, then, both of you. Happy reunion."

Moments later, unencumbered, relieved at the loss of one burden—physical, if not mental—he and Kharm negotiated the steep trail leading to Alkmaar. Mineshaft openings dotted the landscape, and terraced, level spots grew greenly vigorous, marching up the slant of a wide valley where sheep and goats grazed, distant specks below him.

Autumn sun pounded on his head, soaked the hair on the back of his neck into rat tails, his eyes stinging with sweat, dazzled by light reflecting off quartz and mica studding the sheer path carved into the stone. It was like climbing into an aerie when he reached the top, panting, hoping that a more serviceable—and level—road existed on the other side of the village. If this were the back door, so to speak, only the most hardy would attempt bringing supplies or trade goods up and down it.

Kharm had already reached the final rough-hewn step, fur glistening as she basked in the sun, her eyes level with a set of toes protruding from worn sandals. Shoulders hunched, head bent to watch his footing, Matty's field of vision wasn't much wider, only slightly extending the figure to include solid ankles, the coarse hem of a wheat-colored robe. Were the feet in scale to the rest of the body, he was about to meet a very formidable woman. He straightened, back aching, pushed damp hair off his forehead, blinked to make the glittering spots stop quivering, a bright blue sky outlining the figure shimmering in his vision.

"Excuse me, m'am. My name's Matthias Vandersma, and I'm looking for Manuel Vandersma. I've heard he's residing here in—" Strong arms bodily dragged him up the remaining steps, crushed him close.

"Matty," a voice roared, a voice he'd never heard so strong and full of life before. "Oh, Matty!" His father's face, but a face suffused with glowing purpose, dark blue eyes clear and peaceful, almost farseeing in their contentment. His skin was creased and lined, but as if he'd earned each mark, not passively let fate write its script on his face. Matty gulped in surprise, though, at the razor-nicked bald crown surrounded by neatly-trimmed hair. He clung to that oddity, desperate to incorporate it in his mind, a singular symbol of a totally new man.

But before he could assimilate it, the strong voice turned hesitant, faintly diffident. "By the Blessed Lady, Matty, why's a larchcat sniffing my toes?" An intake of breath and the hands tightened on his arms, "It licked me! It's tasting me!" Despite himself Matty began to giggle, giggles turning to teary hiccups. "That's my Bondmate Kharm. She's a ghatta. They don't usually lick people, but when they do, their tongues are awfully rough. Say hello, or she'll think you're monopolizing me."

The rest of the day whirled by Matty as he and Manuel shyly constructed a new relationship built on who they both were now or were in the process of becoming. Like every other structure in Canderis, some of the beams from the past had to be reused, even if weak, for they supported part of the original framework of kinship. As night fell, they walked to the low limestone building that Manuel called a Bethel which housed the eight-armed statue of a compassionate-looking woman set above a stone-slabbed altar.

Matty sat through the service his father had conducted, disquieted but curious, desperately taking his cues from the six women and three men who'd filed in and sat cross-legged in front of the altar. Solemn but with a gladsome anticipation—and he had no idea himself what to expect, squirming uneasily, the stone floor unyielding under his buttocks. Several of the people had looked back at him, smiled as if happy at his presence—he, a complete stranger, welcomed. He'd left Kharm outside, unsure of her welcome, but knew she followed in his mind.

A dawning realization that light came not simply from the setting sun's rays through the long, narrow windows, but from the gentle-faced, eight-armed Lady, a continuously burning lamp in the statue's lap. Manuel entered and bowed to the statue, then to the people present. "Tonight is for the sixth Disciple's welcome at its half-fullness." They nodded approvingly as he addressed the statue. "As our lives wax and wane around us, so does Your love burn ever-brighter for us."

"Ever-bright, never-changing, ever-changing," his listeners intoned as he lit candles in six of the eight outstretched hands of the statue, forming a three-quarter arc of flickering light around the larger central lamp. The scent of warming beeswax trembled sweet on the air.

Manuel knelt in front of the altar, hands above his head, palms pressed together at right angles, thumbs interlocked and folded inward, his eight fingers spread. Not unlike the statue's arms, Matty realized. "In Thy blessed firmament are many havens for us now and in times to come. Other ways, other lives, ever-changing to aspire to Thy never-changing glory." Manuel continued, his listeners sometimes echoing a phrase or responding with a phrase of their own. It was strangely touching, moving, although Matty wasn't sure why. As if everyone knew he or she belonged, had a place, the repetitions giving comfort and surety. The world might change around them, but this, this would not. Matty lost himself in the rest of the service, not always understanding but content to let its love and warmth, its acceptance embrace him.

"But I still don't understand what you've become," Matty linked arms with his father, pensive after the ceremony. "Though I like it, I think." Five of the satellite moons around the unchanging moon hung full, the sixth half-visible. When the final two satellites reached ripeness, it would mark the change of another year, slightly over two years since he'd left Coventry, home. "What *is* a Shepherd?

I saw what you did, heard what you said, but what does it mean? Why the robe, the half-shaved head?"

His father laughed, ran an unself-conscious hand over the shaved portion of his head. "I'm not clear on that part myself. But as a visible reminder of the humility we strive for, I think."

Matty perched on a protruding tree root, picked at the bark. "But who's we?"

"It's a long story, Matty," Manuel warned. "I'm not one of the very first, but I'm one of many who've come to believe, want to spread the word." He held his hand in a shushing gesture, forestalling Matty's questions. "Come to believe that the life I led was worthless—as you and your granther well know. And out of unbelief must come belief if you want to change your life."

"But worshiping the moon and the satellite moons? Pretending your Lady is the moon, or the moon's a lady, whichever. That's not the truth." For a moment a wave of censorious superiority swept over him, and it troubled him.

"Then don't be so quick to judge." Kharm strolled in and out of moonlight shadows, flickering silver and black and white.

"Yes and no. We all require something larger than ourselves—our own finite existence, the daily drudgery of staying alive—to believe in. The moon and her satellites are symbols, reminding us that some things are immutable, others not—change and changelessness. Why we've come to believe it's a Lady in the moon and her eight Apostles instead of a man in the moon, I can't say.

"So many things in Canderis are leftovers from a previous life, or at least our previous way of life. Our beliefs are leftovers of a sort as well, bits of various archaic religious beliefs that the spacers brought with them like so much excess baggage, but which comfort in times of need. We Shepherds represent an amalgam of beliefs so we can reach out to everyone. I guess what we believe most strongly is the need we have to better ourselves, improve ourselves and our world—though not at another's expense. And betterment doesn't necessarily mean material things. After all, if not in this life, perhaps in another. If you've tried your best and failed, you've still tried, perhaps improved one little thing. And that little thing, be it kindness, an act of mercy, or a better water system may be the stepping stone for someone else's betterment."

"But some swear the moon and its satellite phases cause the Plumbs to explode! If that's true, how can you worship that?"

"According to your granther, that's doubtful. And how arrogant of us to lay blame on some outside source, refuse to take responsibility for our own actions. Your granther and the other explorers sited each Plumb in good faith, but had no idea the components would finally react as they did in a strange soil. But the phases of the satellite moons, our Apostles, *can* change us, remind us that we wax and wane, while the Lady Moon reminds us we can be bigger, better than we are. That's no mean accomplishment." His smile was the one thing Matty truly remembered, and it broadened now. "Though perhaps we've incorporated a bit of destruction into our Lady Moon. Remember me saying we took the best of the leftovers? Well, certainly She includes a touch of the Catholic Virgin Mary and Her Son and his disciples, not to mention the Hindu Shiva with his eight arms of destruction, pieces of the Buddha, and more."

Hands clasped around his knee, Matty stared up at the golden globed moons. The names were as exotic and alien to Matty as the ceremony had been. Perhaps not knowing what those names meant didn't matter if he could pin down an overriding concept behind the names. "So you have to *believe* in something bigger than yourself?"

"Yes, but first you have to believe in yourself." Manuel played with his hempen belt, finally laughed. "And I certainly had trouble with that! If you think you're nothing, worthless, then how can something bigger than you sustain you without crushing what little spirit you have—that feeble part crying, 'I am, aren't I?' But most of all, belief binds you into a community, a part of the whole, no matter how different you may feel or be in other ways, gives us a commonality and community of spirit and experience." Yes, he'd seen it, felt it inside, Manuel and his listeners had been as one, the repetitions, the patterns, binding them together.

His words rushed like a suddenly undammed stream. "But I *don't* belong. I don't fit in anywhere! The only one who wants me is Kharm!" Self-pity swamped him, threatened to drown him. He was sinking, gasping for air, but didn't know if he dared confess the worst. His father would cast him aside, deny him. "Kharm speaks in my mind, she mindspeaks me! She understands everything I think and can understand what other people think, what's really the truth." He flinched against the tree, waiting for denial, castigation.

"Truly? Then what does she think of me?" Manuel sounded curious. "I believe you, but I'd dearly love to meet someone or something, human or animal, who could judge the truth. And I suppose the question is, what do you do with the truth when you find it? Does truth always make things better or does it ever make things worse?"

Was his father mocking him, mocking his predicament? Or didn't he—Matty—believe in himself strongly enough? Matty could no longer see Kharm, could barely discern his father's face. Why had Kharm been so silent, so unsupportive, letting him grapple with this alone? The only confidence he had came from her. With shock he saw Manuel's shadowy figure go rigid, face upcast to the moons and the stars, mouth open in quiet ecstasy. Communing with his Blessed Lady, no doubt.

"Well, I'm sorry, but I didn't think he knew the rule about saying 'Mindwalk if ye will.' He's nice, and most of what he says and believes is true. The few misguided parts are working their way toward truth, though he has a distance to go and knows it. But your father relishes a challenge."

"Heavenly Lady, that's a ticklish sensation!" Manuel's smile beamed as broad as the moons. "But absolutely delightful, almost revelatory. You should have brought your friends Jaak and Tah'm up with you as well."

Friends? They *were* his friends, he hadn't really thought of them as that before, only as companions, the most he deserved. At least he belonged to Kharm, to them as well.

His father acted as if he, too, could read thoughts—or Kharm had revealed more than Matty had realized. "You have the nucleus of belonging, of making your own family. That's assuming you've outgrown your granther and Henryk and me—or if you simply want to build on it. You have to make your community, seek it out, find others like-minded in their beliefs. Don't just feel sorry for yourself as I did for so long."

It struck him so hard the tree itself might have fallen on him. Seek out others, seek out the truth. Believe and give them something to believe in, a consistency, a dependable sameness. That was betterment. The search might be long and arduous, but profitable, and if so, he would belong at last.

The air hung thin and bracing, the sky pinking, reflecting off hoarfrost like spun sugar on the grass edging the worn path. Khar wreathing her ankles, anxious for the back door to be opened, Doyce took a deep breath, wrapped the shawl tight around her shoulders and rushed into the cold air. *"Ah!"* she winced as she scurried along the path to the privy, *"almost makes you decide against it!"* A sharpening breeze molded her nightdress against her bulging form, tented it behind her, the breeze trickling up the backs of her legs, making her buttock muscles clench.

"Not likely! Couldn't have waited another moment." Khar had veered off the path, unable to rush any farther than the edge of the frost-killed garden, digging industriously. **"You're not the only one suffering from overcrowding."** Her sides had ballooned, stripes expanding into wide ribbons. Dirt damp against her white paws, she waited for the subdued shriek that heralded Doyce's enthronement on the cold seat, usually covered with a thin film of condensation this early in the morning. As usual, Doyce had forgotten to wipe it dry.

Their return more sedate than their leaving, Doyce busied herself reviving the coals in the stove, putting on the kettle while Khar completed her morning's ablutions. This early, no one else in the little house stirred, although Khar judged Inez was wakeful. The old required less sleep and despite her recent illness, Inez didn't appear the sort to linger in bed. Briefly Khar considered joining her there for the warmth, but at last the stove began to shed heat. Inez seemed to understand her younger daughter's need for solitude, had ceded her kitchen during the early mornings when Doyce found herself too uncomfortable to sleep any longer. Last night had been a particularly awkward, uncomfortable one for them both until Doyce had finally stilled herself by mentally journeying to Alkmaar with Matty and Kharm.

"It's humbling to see the beginnings of the Seeker ceremony, the Bethel service. They're different now, but seeing their origins makes them seem even more powerful. Strange

how much power rituals have over us." Too easy to let rituals become rote actions. *"And I'm so glad Matty found his father,"* she smiled at Khar, *"just as I've rediscovered my mother."* Spreading her papers on the table, Doyce set to work. The Seekers Veritas history filled the early dawns; she generally reserved her mental excursions with Matty and Kharm for later in the day when the closeness, both literal and figurative, of family life intruded. *"Well, I didn't have much choice last night. Wasn't fair to Francie for me to keep tossing and turning."*

She opened Parse's latest packet, scanned it to see what his research had unearthed, not to mention what gossip he'd heard. Parse had been amazing at winkling further tidbits out of Maize Bartolotti concerning Seeker Veritas life in the past, the sort of details that added color and flavor to the dry chronicling of history. And clearly Parse found her a delightful diversion. Funny, though, he hadn't mentioned Sarrett in any letters lately, as if her very name were embargoed. The kettle whistled and she grabbed it before it could protest too much, wake Francie or her mother.

Letting the cha steep, she went back to his letter. An exuberant ink splash there, several punctures and rips in the edge of the paper. She held it to the light to see what'd been written beneath the blotch. Looked like a "Jen" slightly darker than the ink smear covering it, and then another word or two. No, couldn't be, or Parse would simply have rewritten it and continued. Amazing how she could be so sure anything and everything pertained to Jenret. *"Silly, aren't I?"* she asked, waiting for the familiar bantering.

"Absolutely," Khar stretched uncomfortably, hoping to change the subject. **"Nutter-butter? Cheese with nutter-butter? Please?"** And as Doyce moved to the pantry, Khar snagged the letter, buried it under the other papers. Close, too close. Per'la had warned through the mindnet about Parse's absentminded mention of the Guardians still unsuccessfully searching for Jenret and Sarrett. Per'la had bumped the inkwell, snatched at the paper while chastising him for his stupidity.

Doyce shuffled her notes, integrating Parse's new information into the proper chapters, scribbling in the margins. A bit more effort and this section could be fair copied. She mumbled, "Good morning," as Inez slipped into the kitchen, poured and sat at the window, rocking and staring out, sipping. Not much later Francie appeared, took up her embroidery as Inez quietly set about making breakfast. Against the backdrop of homey sounds Doyce finished the chapter and laid the pages in a folder with a pleased "There!" as Cady, rubbing her eyes, made her way toward the house from the workshop.

Cady stopped midway of the path and commenced a complex set of stretching and bending exercises that made Khar flinch, while F'een essayed furious dashes punctuated by sharp turns, dissimulated changes in direction that revealed his intensity regarding his training. A zealous ghatt, anxious to shine at his assignment, overcompensating for his slight stature, F'een constantly harped on the textbook "rightness" of things until he set her teeth on edge. Too bad she'd flaunted his size in his face, but he'd deserved it.

Rosy-cheeked but not in the least breathless, Cady brought a gust of cold air in with her, sniffing appreciatively at the smell of baking biscuits. "All for me, I presume? I've worked up an appetite." It had become a joke, despite marathon bouts of eating, Cady never gained weight.

Inez peered inside the oven. "No, Doyce and Francie and I've laid claim to this batch. You and Davvy'll have to wait for the next pan since you've been such sleepyheads." Reaching for a potholder to pull the tray out, "'Course I hope we don't run out of honey by then."

Cady snatched a biscuit. "Consider this a loan," tossing it in the air to cool and asking, "Isn't Davvy here? I overslept a bit, but he was up and out when I got up. Thought he was probably annoying you."

"Wandering a bit before breakfast?" Francie hazarded as she laid her embroidery aside. "Probably poking around down by the pond. He does that sometimes."

Amber eyes locked on F'een, Khar watched the ghatt squirm once, then turn to stone. Interesting, he acted remarkably guilty, as if he'd done something or knew something, and she narrowed her stare accordingly to press him. Hmph! Remarkably reluctant to back down, his conviction of righteousness working overtime. Seniority and experience be damned. Look how she'd had to cow him not to tell Doyce about Jenret's capture, and it still rankled him. She stalked in his direction, bottle-brushing her tail for emphasis. **"What is it? Tell me, F'een. What do you know? And I want it right now."**

Backed tight against the door, he looked for an escape, head snaking. "Well? I'm waiting." And still he remained stubbornly silent, right side practically imprinting the door, left forepaw raised as if to ward her off.

"Gone," he squeaked, triumphant.

"Where?" She narrowed the space between them, weightily ominous, ghatta avengeant. "When, F'een? And where? You know more than you're letting on, you little—"

"Not telling!" he spat in her face. "Could tell, but won't!"

Francie's shocked inhalation drew their attention to the silent confrontation too late. Without warning Khar had launched herself on F'een, jaws pincering the back of his neck, her superior size and weight pinning him in place. Might not be as lithe and supple as he right now, but she'd struck the first blow, would squash the breath out of him! So much for fancy fighting tricks. She slipped sideward without loosening her grip, shook him soundly. He pummeled her back with all four feet, his claws sheathed, but she had no such compunctions and swatted hard, ripped a clump of fur. Knew she'd scored the skin beneath it.

"Khar!" Doyce shouted and Cady waded in, cursing, trying to separate knotted bodies. But Inez was faster, cha kettle in hand, tilting it ominously

"I won't have caterwauling and wrestling like that in my house, good-natured or ill-natured. You hear?" The kettle's angle increased, a drop poised at the end of the spout. F'een squinched his eyes, body contracting in anticipation of the hot, streaming deluge. "You, Missy Khar'pern, let him go. Mayhap he's deserving of a thrashing, but not in my house. I can switch your behind just as I used to Doyce's. In fact I'll switch both your furry little behinds for fighting in the house—no favorites."

"I'll tell, I'll tell," F'een sobbed with pain. "Just let me up, Khar." Reluctantly she relaxed her jaw muscles, rolled clear.

Cady scooped up F'een, hand under his chin to force him to meet her eye. *"Ghatti don't lie. Do you know something we should know about where Davvy is? Do you?"* She shook him slightly. *" 'Fess up, F'een."*

"I went for a run early this morning, saw him take Lokka out," he confessed in a rush as Doyce scowled.

"Rode for Ruysdael." No call to say he'd 'spoken the boy, wished him well, envious despite himself.

"Ruysdael!" At Doyce's exclamation Francie and Inez turned to look at her. *"What else do you 'think', F'een?"*

Writhing in Cady's arms, he blurted it out in a rush. **"He's going to beg a boon of the Marchmont king, ask him to rescue Jenret!"** There, let Khar try to stop him from telling the truth now! He hated keeping secrets!

"You scrawny, flea-bitten excuse for a ghatt," Khar snarled, practically hissing her dismay, **"you swore you wouldn't tell her!"**

"Rescue Jenret from what?" Doyce had sat, very pale, clutching her stomach. Too much bother to repeat the ghatt's words for her mother and sister, so she contented herself by making sure they at least heard her side of the conversation. "Has he been captured? By whom? And Khar, what do you know about this?"

Khar licked at her soft white underbelly, pretending to lose herself in its expansiveness. **"Some of the Resonants Jenret was searching for captured him. They're holding him hostage to ensure the safety of other Resonants and Normals, make the Reapers stop killing."** A sigh. **"Sarrett and Yulyn and Towbin Biddlecomb offered themselves as hostages as well. It's really not that bad, you know, or Rawn would have told me."**

"Did you two know about this?" she pivoted on the chair to confront her mother and sister, but they mutely shook their heads. "Cady, how did Davvy find out?"

The Novice Seeker only shrugged. "I didn't tell him, honestly. Unless he overheard me arguing last night with F'een about telling you. I agreed with Khar's reasoning, though F'een didn't."

"Which was?" Lady bless, did she have to extract every word?

"That you shouldn't be worried so close to your due date, that you'd rush off to rescue him, put yourself and the baby in danger."

"Well, at least that's one thing she can't do," Inez interjected, anxiously folding the potholder between her hands. "Davvy's got Lokka, so she's not likely to ride off."

"But what can Davvy hope to accomplish by seeing the king?" Francie added.

Cady stared hard at F'een, then answered, "He believes

the king and Arras Muscadeine can rescue Jenret, bring him back to Doyce. F'een apparently agreed with Davvy's reasoning."

Blast Davvy and blast Jenret! Both them and their chivalry and idealism as well! And if she were in a rational state, they'd all be better served! Find a solution, she ordered herself, the baby inside her jumping and racketing like popping corn inside a lidded iron kettle. *"Khar? Jenret is all right, isn't he? And the others? Truly? You wouldn't hide that from me, would you?"*

"They're fine, I promise. But what about Davvy?"

Inez echoed Khar's thought. "Doyce, if Jenret's been captive this long, a little longer won't hurt. But what about Davvy? I don't like the idea of him alone in Ruysdael ... being what he is, mind you." The word refused to pass her lips.

Davvy alone amongst a host of strangers? How would the town react to the royal progress—sullen and shuttered? Wary and unwelcoming, with spying eyes peering from behind curtains? Secret gatherings to plot? Or would there be a host of gawkers, inquisitive and curious, the novelty of seeing a king outweighing the fact he was a Resonant? Or did that add a special fillip, a frisson of illicit excitement to the momentous event? She'd argued for the latter last night, but feared the former was a more realistic assessment. Pessimistic but realistic.

"Francie?" she asked, helpless to know for sure. "I've been away too long. How will the town react to the king's visit? I'm afraid Davvy will be suspect, a stranger wandering there alone."

Francie chewed at a thumbnail, considering. "Well, you know the attitude of most Canderisians—don't provoke a beast, don't jab a sharp stick in its eye, and it's most likely it'll leave you alone." Inez chortled despite herself, then pursed her lips. "What I mean is, there are some out there, obviously, who'd do anything they could to thwart or kill Resonants, that's clear. But most people are more cautious, not quite willing to judge, though one side of the scale is heavily weighted with rumor and gossip. Put the king and his court on the other side of the scale and we'll see how it balances.

"And have you forgotten what the date is, Doyce?" she smiled forgivingly at her sister. "You *have* been away too

long. This is the last open air market of the season, a final
chance for people to have a fling, some fun before winter
sets in in earnest. A chance to show off, celebrate. I'll bet
people are coming from even farther than usual to catch the
royal progress—it's enough to enliven a whole winter's
worth of debates, pro and con."

Doyce stood, straining the shawl around her shoulders,
hands buried in its ends to hide her nerves. "Cady, get the
horses harnessed and the surrey ready. You wanted to see the
royal progress, Francie. Here's your chance. You and
Mother, scoot and get dressed."

Inez wagged a finger under her nose. "You're not going to
Ruysdael, Doyce. The excitement won't be good for you.
Best stay right here. We'll find Davvy and come right home.
You stay put."

"As Davvy would say, 'Smerdle!' " She captured and
stilled her mother's hand. "Better I have a nice half-day's
ride in a surrey than set off alone cross-country to find
Jenret, isn't it, dear?"

"Then you'd best get some clothes on as well—no child
of mine goes on rescues in her nightshift!"

An explosive crack, a dragged-out, protesting screech and
Doyce found herself jolted out of her thoughts and nearly
out of the surrey. Good leg grimly braced against the seat
back, Francie thrust her cane across Doyce and she clung to
halt her slide along a suddenly canted seat threatening to
chute her out the surrey's listing side. "Bloody damn, damn
bloody, misbegotten wheel!" Inez roared as Cady frantically
reined in the team. Her mother's language shocked Doyce
but didn't begin to do justice to the situation. But then, Inez
ever tended toward moderation, just as her daughters normally did.

A rumbling thud alerted her that Khar had rolled like a
barrel across the floor boards and now attempted to right
herself. **"If you'd prefer stronger language, don't worry
about my delicate ears—or your sister's,"** the ghatta
sounded distinctly put out, and Doyce could sense the sore-
ness of bruised ribs, the blow to the stretched flesh surrounding the unborn ghatten. **"Don't you humans have
some sort of saying about bad luck coming in threes?"**

F'een regarded them over the back of the seat, saved from a tumble by Inez's strong, skinny arms. **"Isn't this three, then?"** His whiskers twitched as he enumerated, **"Jenret's capture, Davvy's running away, and now this? What if there's more?"** Given Khar's baleful expression, he subsided, pretended to enjoy Inez's jittery stroking as Cady jumped down to inspect the damage.

"Axle broke." Her announcement surprised no one, though Doyce clambered down to inspect it. "It's all my fault, shouldn't have pushed the horses so fast." Cady walked a few stiff paces, spun back, mouth blade-narrow, eyes bleak. "What are we going to do? Davvy's out there by himself."

Sliding along her seat, Inez stepped from the tilted carriage, prepared to steady Francie's dismount. Stung by their forgetfulness, Cady and Doyce rushed to help, lock her leg brace, locate her other cane. "What you're going to do, my dear, is unhitch one of the horses and ride for help, rent another wagon." Hair disarrayed, Inez repaired it, as if its very untidiness affronted her thoughts. "And I'd suggest you snap to it before one or the other of my daughters seizes on the idea. They both tend to be resourceful that way. Often don't even wait to be told—unlike yourself."

Flushed with purpose, Cady hurried to unharness the horses, improvise reins. "See if you can't use a strap, stuff your tabard under it, make a pad for F'een," Doyce suggested as she walked around the surrey, stared into the distance. Lady give her strength! Better yet, Lady give her something to do, to occupy her mind because anything was better than sitting and waiting, worry winding through her head, strangling her thoughts. Jenret captured. And Davvy blithely flinging himself into the heart of a drama beyond him, an innocent stranger at large in a suspicious land already swamped by misconceptions about Resonants. Should he say something to the wrong person, the consequences could be beyond their wildest imaginings. Do something, do something, she screamed inside. I can't let my world collapse!

Khar limped to her side. *"Did you hurt your leg, love? Is it serious?"* Selfish!—she'd not spared a jot of worry for Khar. **"It'll loosen up if I walk for a bit. Why not settle your mother and sister on the blankets, then walk with me."**

She hurriedly reassured, **"Oh, we'll stay in sight, of course. But you could use the exercise as well."**

Once Cady and F'een had trotted off, Doyce made sure Francie and Inez were comfortable, sheltered from the wind, and walked slowly with Khar. Head bowed, hands clasped behind her back, she studied the ground as she trudged. Above her a skein of geese mourned their exodus. *"Khar, I don't think I can handle much more. Everything's building up inside, churning. I'm trying to keep my fears at bay or I'll be no good for anything."* She kicked a stone, followed after it, edging it ahead with the side of her boot. *"All I keep thinking of are What Ifs, and the harder I chase them the quicker they circle back on me."*

"What if you thought of something to take your mind off things?" The ghatta leaped on a tree stump, circled as if she'd settle, thus enticing Doyce to it. All ghatti knew that if they even considered napping in a favorite chair, a human would immediately covet it.

"Any suggestions for a pleasant distraction?" She rewrapped her cloak, flipped back the hem so Khar could shelter beneath it.

A familiar weight draped across her feet. **"That's easy. What town is Matty due to visit?"**

She considered. *"He's been in Alkmaar with his father, so I think it's ... Ruysdael next. I peeked ahead in the diary. Don't need it, but I couldn't resist. Funny coincidence, isn't it, Khar? Ruysdael? A good omen, I hope. Matty and Kharm going there, you and I as well, though I hope they had better luck reaching it than we've been having."* At least nothing horrible had happened in Roermond or Alkmaar. Far from it.

It caught Khar unawares with the force of a blow. Ruysdael? Had she not remembered, not known? What good were the Elders if not to guard them from predicaments like this? And worst of all, she couldn't remember what awaited Matty and Kharm in Ruysdael—impossible, because no ghatti would forget a Major Tale. She prickled with a peculiar premonition that the episode wasn't pleasant. But Doyce had already slipped into that state between being and not-being, hovering between worlds like a gull on an updraft. Nothing for Khar to do but guiltily follow, trail her as if she were a thief, steal into her mind for the journey.

❖

Everyone except Manuel was footsore that evening as they reached Ruysdael's outskirts, especially Tah'm, who'd collapsed into deep slumber inside Jaak's basket pack. Typical of a ghatten to squander every bit of energy and exuberance, husband nothing, and then tumble into limp, exhausted sleep.

"Well, at least he's not climbing every tree to see what's at the top," Kharm sniffed in a superior way. **"I was *never* that bad."**

"Which means Jaak doesn't have to climb up and rescue him every other tree." Matty stumbled in the dark, stubbed the same toe he'd abused not twenty paces back. *"I wish you ghatti'd learn that what goes up must come down."*

Doubtful Kharm considered it. **"Then he should jump, land on Jaak's head?"**

Ahead, Manuel gave a swooping wave to draw them after him. "Look, Ruysdael! Late for so many lights, and all in one spot—as if they're holding a meeting." Distinctly unfair to have a father, someone so much older, capable of such zesty energy after a five-day walk from Alkmaar, much of it on winding, down-slanted trails that made the backs of one's legs scream with strain, the effort of not pitching forward. And Manuel accomplished it in worn, flapping sandals, robe kirtled high, bare legs flashing like a mountain goat's. Getting used to a father wearing a robe, clothed in women's garb, still flustered Matty. But then this Manuel wasn't the old one, had metamorphosed into something different, better, surely, even if Matty couldn't fully grasp his motivations. The Lady's worship had given him a focus, a worthwhile partnership on which to expend his energies.

Jaak caught up, panting but cheery. It was a given about Jaak for which Matty was deeply grateful, although there were moments when his sunny disposition grated on his nerves. Well nigh impossible to wallow in a good sulk, a fit of depression, a doubt with Jaak there to dispel it. "Late for this many lights. Looks as if we've a welcoming committee."

"I don't think so, although they may be glad to see us." A dawning surety grew, the scene uncannily reminiscent— the season, the central fire ringed by torches—but he'd needed time to examine it from his new perspective, aloof from it, not part of it. "I think they're holding a conciliation meeting. If they were celebrating, there'd be movement, flow, laughter, but everyone's still, as if they're all listening." A mate to that meeting in Coventry when Miz Killanin attempted to expel Mad Marg, covetous of her house. The thought of Granther, Henryk, Nelle, even Mad Marg, loyal friend in her own way, made his eyes sting. Ruysdael wasn't *that* far from Coventry—should he go home and visit, bring Manuel—prodigal lamb returned as Shepherd?

Manuel was tramping down the track, walking staff spearing the ground. He had no need of support, but liked the heft of it, Matty decided, especially when flourished as an exuberant extension of his marching stride. "Doesn't he *ever* slow down?" Jaak moaned. "He's a bad influence, Matty, a bad influence, making us work all too hard. Were there flowers, we'd have no time to smell them."

"Well, come on, come on," Manuel's words drifted back, "if you're Seekers after truth, mayhap there's some truth that needs finding in Ruysdael. Not to mention people who might listen to a simple Shepherd spread Our Lady's word. Fallow ground, lads, fallow ground, so let's cultivate it."

Despite themselves Matty and Jaak grinned, shook their heads in admiring despair as they plunged after him. "Do you think they might need us in Ruysdael? I'd like to see you and Kharm at work, especially now that Tah'm's old enough to appreciate it." Jaak gave his basket a thump with his fist. "If I can wake him up."

"You saw us seeking in Roermond. Did a little yourself," Matty protested.

"But I knew everyone there, friends, neighbors, relatives. I want to see you two in action when I don't know anyone involved, where I don't fall back on my own suspicions and prejudices, no matter how hard Tah'm tries to disabuse me of them." His gait spraddled as he slowed, swung back, "You know, someplace where I'm a total stranger."

Those final words struck a dissonance in Matty, a hunger to belong, a yearning to lay claim to something, someone beyond himself, but "We'll see," was all he said. Ruysdael. He'd been there once as a child; it had been where he'd seen the little piglet. Ruysdael, bigger than Coventry, but smaller he guessed, than Jaak's beloved Roermond. And, as Granther had so often bemoaned, populated with suspicious, surly individuals, all faintly soured on life. Not total malcontents, but grouchy, grumpy, not just at the surface, but deep inside. He shrugged.

"Why are they grouchy?" Kharm wanted to know.

"I don't know exactly," he tried to remember what Granther had said, *"though at the beginning they did suffer more from the Plumbs than other areas. But sourness is ... sort of contagious. Be around a sour person who doesn't respond to cheerfulness, and you're bound to turn sour in self-defense."*

"Not a good place for Jaak and Tah'm to settle, then. They might be convicted of cheerfulness." They were closing the distance to the lights, and Kharm stayed near, as she always did when they entered a new town. He liked the earrings they both now wore, a badge showing they belonged to each other. Jaak's ear-piercing abilities left something to be desired; he cautiously touched his right earlobe, hot and puffy to the touch. Was Kharm enough, though? **"Can you cure sourness?"**

"I'm not sure," he confessed, wished the ghatta weren't so profoundly curious, at least when he was so tired. *"The eumedicos used to have injections and pills that cured all sorts of things, according to Granther."*

"Well, if we can't dose them with cheerfulness, we can dose them with truth."

Except all too often truth was a bitter potion. At his joyous shout Matty looked, realized Manuel had run ahead, legs flashing birch white, and a man broke from the center of the gathering. Manuel embraced the man, almost toppling him, but the man finally set himself solidly and bear-hugged the Shepherd, hosting him into the air. "Matty, Jaak! Move yourselves." Manuel sounded short of breath but happy. "I want you meet Samson Denellen, Denny."

"A greeting like that and my back'll crack like kindling," Jaak laughed. "Not sure I'll relish shaking hands, either." He pantomimed a crushed, boneless hand.

The enthusiastic hug surprised Matty, nothing begrudging about it, outgoing, not gloomy. Had Ruysdael changed since he'd been away, or had Samson "Denny" Denellen cured it of its sourness? He approached diffidently, hating to interrupt the outpouring between the two men. "Matty, come on!" How he was beginning to dislike that command, feeling sour as one of Ruysdael's finest. "It's the Blessed Lady's in-

tercession! Denny's Ruysdael's Conciliator—from a half-
hearted, half-wit Marauder to this! Surely the Lady swayed
his heart. And he'd welcome your talents."

As Denny explained, Matty's brain shrieked for deafness,
his body shrinking with revulsion, not at the man himself
but at the injustice he related. Just like Neu Bremen, the
problem was ensuring the guilty was punished. But Matty
experienced a gut-clenching desire for vengeance, longed
not merely to right a tragic wrong, but to punish it as well.
Only the Conciliator determined punishment, but Matty
ached with Ruysdael's citizens to take matters into their own
hands. A compact, no-nonsense sort of man, Denny's brown
eyes flooded with pain as he admitted he couldn't clearly determine the guilty party. His normally merry face tinged
green, Jaak looked sick.

"But do you believe that Kharm and I can truly uncover
the truth?" It was crucial that Denny trust him—and, more
importantly, trust Kharm.

"Your father says you can and I believe him." Denny
rubbed a bald spot, the natural counterpart to Manuel's tonsure. "He's developed some peculiar ideas and beliefs of
late, but they're not all bad, not by a long shot. Just different, hard to grasp. Many things exist in this world that I
don't understand because I don't think deep enough, but that
doesn't stop them from being right, being true."

"But will the townspeople accept Kharm and me? Will
they believe as you do?"

Denny polished his head more urgently. "Believing in
mindspeech is a strange thing, even more so with an animal.
You see, they've lived beside Resonants here—we've a few
leftovers, offspring of those not invited to Marchmont.
They're weak, but stronger than the paltry mindtrances
eumedicos offer, not that I blame eumedicos for doing the
best they can. Swear it's easier having an artist live next to
a Resonant than it is having an artist live next to a technician
most times, less squabbling, less tiffs. Resonants keep themselves to themselves for the most part. No, mindspeech's not
a problem if you're tactful in its use—it's an animal having
it that's downright odd."

His eyes implored Manuel for guidance. "But that
larchcat, that . . . what? Ghatta's a female, you say? Mayhap
if we present it as a special gift conferred by the very planet
itself . . . something we're privileged to share . . . well, it's

worth a try. Even acts of faith can confer relief. Between your father and old Denny, here, we'll convince them."

And convince them they apparently had, Matty decided as they hurriedly finished eating, although no one had much appetite, given the wrongdoing to be judged. Now Matty found himself ushered through tight-packed bodies that contracted as they caught sight of Kharm. Wonder, curiosity, controlled longing greeted them, but neither sensed any hostility. **"They're desperate. Willing to chance anything different, anything to find the truth. This case gnaws at their hearts and souls, and they'd welcome sharing the burden. Too hard-headed, though, to passively accept persuasion without proof, and proof's not easily found."**

By now the rituals he'd devised in Neu Bremen with Rema and Flaven Pelsaert were almost second nature, and he appreciated their importance even more after seeing his father's Bethel service. A ritual was like a river carving a channel for the faithful to follow. Tabard in place, Matty settled himself, laid the sword in position and drew it a handspan from its sheath. Manuel handed him his staff, exhorting, "Remember you walk in the Lady's footsteps." Behind him, Denny cleared his throat, spoke the words that invoked his presence. Not identical to Rema's but close enough. Comfort and discomfort at hearing them, knowing he and Kharm were on trial as well.

A night wind flickered intermittently, laying its death-chill finger across vulnerable necks, making the torches flare in long streamers before snapping straight. It drove before it a sprinkle of rain and a crow cawed, raucous at the disturbance. Abruptly hostility engulfed him, his heart incensed that such vileness had revealed its face in Ruysdael, and he stared at those he'd search for the truth, grimly determined that justice would not elude him. But justice seemed a paltry term.

"Never seek the truth in anger, never prejudge, even in your own mind." Kharm looked not at him but at the circle of faces, and he forced himself to recover his poise, a calm dispassion. But to molest a young girl! The thought screamed through his brain. Why would a man force himself on someone who didn't want him, a mere child at that?

"Seeker Vandersma," Samson Denellen moved beside a girl of perhaps eleven, willowy thin but budding, a hint of small, ripening breasts, curving hips a promise of future lushness. Dark blue eyes investigated nothingness, as if she were present in body but not in spirit, black hair curtaining her downturned face. "This is Priyani Vlaendren, and her grandmother, Mother Vlaen, we all call her." Denny briefly touched the child's head, as if to make her look up and acknowledge Matty; her body flinched, but nothing in her eyes changed. "She doesn't ... she can't seem to speak any longer." Denny jerked his hand away as if her pain burned him, took a step back. "It's as if she left her body untenanted, went somewhere else to live.

"On your right is the plea-bringer, Bernard Osterkamp, nephew of Mother Vlaen, and first cousin once-removed of Priyani, or Yani as we call her. He accuses Aron Reyphin of raping the child, causing grievous bodily and mental harm. Further, he insists Mother Vlaen is not a fit custodian for the child, and that Yani should be placed in his care."

There was time, there was time, Matty assured himself. Take it slowly, get it right. Kharm would untangle the truth, but he had to discern the how and why of it, convince the others beyond doubt. Each needed the other to uncover the truth, resurrect it from its premature burial of silence and lies, restore it to life.

"Mother Vlaen," he kept his voice neutral, uninflected, "since I'm a stranger here, could you tell me as best you can what happened to Yani, and when, please?" Mother Vlaen looked about his granther's age, although life apparently had treated her more harshly. One of the original spacers, clearly, but all her superior training and knowledge from another world had handicapped her for this one, any sustaining grace destroyed, beaten down long ago by the pressures of daily life, her body wasted, white hair thin across her scalp. But the dark blue eyes showed more life than Yani's, fire-bright with helpless rage as she restrained her granddaughter's fluttering hand, aimless as a butterfly.

"Three days past I sent Yani to fetch water from the stream, just as she always does each day. 'Twas near dark—latest I'd send her out alone—but we needed it for supper, for cha first thing the next morning." Yani had leaned into her grandmother, and Mother Vlaen wrapped her arms around her, cradled her close to still her rocking. "Scared of the dark, she is, and didn't come back, worry winding me tighter as night fell. Stood outside and called, but no answer. Finally couldn't stand it any longer, got a torch and started looking."

She hugged Yani harder, "This world's a dangerous place for children, but I never suspected that kind of danger. Thought we'd left such sickness behind. She'd been on her way back, that much was clear, the bucket beside her, the earth wet where it spilled. And she lay there, lay there—"

"Where was she lying, Mother Vlaen?" he interrupted to give her a moment to collect herself, and because he genuinely needed to know where the path ran, who lived near whom.

"Just at the far edge of Aron Reyphin's garden. He came running when I cried for help. She was sprawled there, her clothes half-ripped off, blood between her thighs, bruises and bite marks all over her body. Bad bruise on her head as well, where she'd been hit, her shirttail ripped off and stuffed in her mouth. Someone raped my baby, the only one I've left in this world!" Her eyes were large, black with pain, pleading with her nephew, Bernard Osterkamp, "And I'll not let you snatch her from me! No matter what you say, I've raised her well, done the best I could, but no one could have expected this to happen."

"Kharm, can you see anything in Yani's mind?" How could he obtain any direct evidence from the girl if she were mute? To ask them to believe Kharm could read her thoughts was asking a great deal, and everyone around her could say anything without fear of contradiction.

"Poor little child, poor baby. Why do humans do things like that?" Kharm soft-footed to Yani, let her tail caress Yani's wrist. Despite her grandmother's soothing, the girl's arms were bent at the elbows, fisted hands protruding in puny defense, as if this time she'd fend off her attacker. A blink, the first obvious one he'd seen her make, and she focused on the ghatta, a quiver of a smile, followed by blankness again. Fingers unclenched to encircle the tail. **"She's built a wall between herself and the truth, and she doesn't want it touched, doesn't want to remember. I can break it down, but it will hurt, destroy the fragile peace she's found."** Kharm sat abruptly, her tail slipping from the girl's fingers. **"It's as if someone's helped her find a precarious peace, a foundation to build on before knocking down the walls holding the truth at bay. Can you humans do that?"**

It took him unawares. *"Mayhap Manuel could. I'm beginning to believe he can do things I never thought about, that his faith confers a special strength. But generally, no, not that I know of—at least not any more."* He spoke aloud now, something to break the silence, reassure them he understood. "And the girl—" he stopped himself. She wasn't an inanimate object, a thing, she possessed a name. "Yani can't name her attacker or point him out, may not even remember who attacked her, correct?" He switched back to Kharm, hoped that Tah'm was telling Jaak what was happening. A few more raindrops pelted, then stopped. *"How are we going to find out who attacked her? Have you read the minds of every male in Ruysdael over the age of eight to determine the truth? And that doesn't account for the possibility of an outsider passing through."*

"We've plenty of ways to find out. That's why you're smart and I'm even smarter. If one person doesn't tell you what you need to know, we've others to ask. Don't be so impatient." She relented, but not by much. **"And in case you wondered, Mother Vlaen doesn't know who did it, either. According to her mind, if she did, that man would be nutless by now."** Puzzlement overwhelmed the ghatta, **"Why would she steal his nuts? Why would he have nuts, he's not a squirrel?"**

"Not that kind!" Matty exploded internally, heard Jaak give a belated hoot that he hastily smothered. He explained, quickly and succinctly, what the expression meant and the ghatta's eyes widened. Kharm might know his mind inside-out, but apparently that was one expression she'd never encountered. From the corner of his eye he caught Jaak whispering to Manuel, saw his father's grim head shake of agreement.

"Bernard Osterkamp, as plea-bringer in this case, would you enlighten me as to why you believe Aron Reyphin guilty?"

Osterkamp resembled his granther's description of a sour, churlish Ruysdaeler—so apparently they hadn't all changed, despite Samson Denellen's efforts. Grizzled red hair cut short so it bristled pugnaciously, eyes popping with suspicions, voiced and unvoiced, and an abundance of chest and arm hair that messily spilled from the front of his unbuttoned shirt and rolled-back sleeves. Odd, despite the cold, for him to be so uncovered, unconscious of the weather, the rain that occasionally stung. He radiated displeasure like an oven, the rain nearly sizzling as it struck him. Despite his size, his voice was high-pitched and whiny, relentless as a buzzing fly. "Aron Reyphin's always had a yen for the child. Spends as much time or more with her than he does with his own brood. Catch his face when he didn't know you saw and he'd be mooning over her as she played with the other children, practically leching after her."

"Did you observe this frequently, Osterkamp? How did you happen to be there often enough to notice?"

"I'm in and out, doing chores, fixing this or that for Auntie Vlaen." He cloaked himself with a long-suffering, put-upon expression, wearing his duty for all to see. "Someone has to take care of her and the little girl. I'm the only other family she's got." And not quite masked by his concern was the thought he could well do without that part of the family.

"Just the old woman, not the girl." And Kharm said nothing further.

"Are you sure those looks Aron Reyphin cast in Yani's direction were truly lustful? Or was he simply a father with enough love in his own heart to encompass another child in need of affection?" How did Osterkamp know so much about lustful looks?

"Then ask Auntie Vlaen, ask him what he's been doing over there practically day and night since Yani was hurt! Holding her close, whispering in her ear, stroking her. Got himself in the perfect position to take her whenever he wants now. And the old lady's aiding and abetting him!" Bits of spittal exploded from his mouth, the pop eyes ablaze with something closely akin to jealousy. "You know what he is, don't you? Beyond being a child molester, I mean. Thought we'd gotten rid of them all, but no, we've been holding a whole nest of them to our bosoms right here in Ruysdael. Reyphin and his whole family are Resonants!"

Ejaculations and jeers from the crowd, but whether directed at Reyphin or Osterkamp, Matty was unsure. The mutterings died quickly as Denellen moved through, restoring order. *"It's him, isn't it, Kharm? Osterkamp, I mean. You haven't said so, but somehow I can sense it. As if he were a rutting bull pawing the ground, desperate to get where the heifers are."* He recognized that lust a little, could acknowledge a touch of it as he remembered Kharm going into heat when he'd been staying with the Widow. Kharm had gone into heat again in Roermond, but it hadn't been as bad; he'd been prepared for its effect on him, and she seemed to have taken her confinement better as well. Rather as if she knew it was worth the wait for Tah'm to mature. *"He's dragging in Resonants to cloud the issue."*

"Yes, and he's not going to confess. He feels no remorse, only wants it again and again and again. That's why he wants to take Yani from Mother Vlaen. Have her at his beck and call, in his bed whenever he wants, and in the state she's in, she won't make much protest." The ghatta was poised to spring at Osterkamp, her tail thrashing, ears laid tight, claws shredding the earth. **"Help me, Matty! We have to prove it's him beyond a shadow of doubt. Proving Reyphin innocent isn't enough because he'll still be out there, lurking, taking her or other children."**

Osterkamp smirked, a triumphant grin that highlighted a gap just behind the eye tooth on the upper right side. Somehow its lack made his expression even more leeringly wanton. "You *do* know what Resonants are, don't you, Vandersma? Ought to, boy, your grandmother was one. Ask your father if you don't believe me. Least she had the good sense to move to Marchmont, even if your grandfather stayed behind. 'Course, in all fairness to old Amyas, I don't think he is one—no doubt his wife warped his mind into believing he loved her."

"I don't think my heritage is at issue here, Osterkamp. Yes, I know a little of what Resonants are, but that's past history."

"Thought you might, especially if you think to make us believe that larchcat can read minds, discern the truth." Matty found himself fixated by the gap in his teeth, losing the thread of the conversation. "No doubt you've a touch of it yourself, like Reyphin and his brood here. Weren't good enough to make the cut, go to Marchmont. Not real, true Resonants, but Gleaners, just able to glean bits and pieces out of peoples' minds. Bothersome, troublesome, but not dead-dangerous like the others. Sure, Resonants could harvest a mind clean if they chose; you, you're just after the leavings. Want to use that oversized cat as a front, fine with me, as long as you find Reyphin's guilty."

Matty fought the urge to spit in Osterkamp's face, at last turned toward Aron Reyphin, afraid his disgust still showed. The man, despite his own cares, looked back sympathetically, as if he sensed how Matty felt, wished he could ease the burden. "Mr. Reyphin, you've been spending a great deal of time with Yani and her grandmother since the incident took place?"

Reyphin divested himself of six youngsters, piled on his lap, clinging to his legs, or draped over his shoulders, all as darkly intense and small as their father. His wife shared the likeness, equally petite, though with lighter hair and a more strictly pretty face. Reyphin and his offspring looked foxy and chipper, the children like tumbling kits. "Yes. I've known Priyani since she was a toddler and came to live with her grandmother. Always room for one more to play at our house—who'd notice? Wife told me to go, do what I could that night, anything that would ease the pain. Anything," he emphasized.

"No, I'm not a Resonant—really. Bernard calling me a Gleaner isn't a half-bad description. I can unravel care in a human mind—though not the way my father could—distract pain until body, soul, and mind reach a stage where they can cope, but that's all—and it's not much. Sort of a poultice for the mind. Nothing as to what a full-fledged eumedico can do—but they're few and far between these days. With time and love and someone to share her problems, Yani'll heal. I hope I'm there to help her."

"Did you rape her, Mr. Reyphin?" The question had to be asked, the man given the right to deny it, proclaim his innocence.

A slow, emphatic head shake. "No, I'd cut off my own balls before I'd take advantage of a child like that, let alone one I consider as a daughter." His wife chimed in, "And if he didn't, I'd do it myself to begin the punishment a man like that deserves!"

"Do you know who did do it?"

A concise head bob this time, chin jutting. "I think so," he spread his hands to emphasize his everlasting regret, "but I've no proof. And to accuse a man without proof smacks of malice or worse, but I would if I thought it would do any good. If your larchcat—ghatta! She told me so, tweaked my mind—can judge truth, so be it. But you and all of us need evidence as well."

"And you won't speak the man's name without evidence? Even if it would protect other children from being treated thusly?" Matty couldn't decide if he respected Reyphin's reticence or not.

"Didn't say I wouldn't keep real tight watch over that man until such time as Priyani can accuse him herself. Why do you think I've been spending so much time with her and Mother Vlaen since then? And I've enough children to play hide and seek with the best, canny as wee foxes at watching and not being seen. It's a game they play, trailing each. Oh, one way or another a Reyphin will be tailing him, passing word if he makes a move he shouldn't. 'Tisn't what I'd like, but it's the best I can do."

"Even the littlest can trail, and she's but three. They'll worry him like a burr, but not so close he can inflict the same hurt on them." Kharm acted charmed by the whole brood, not to mention Reyphin. **"He's testing, trying to 'speak me, but isn't sure how. Can't quite figure it out, though he'd love time to try. And yes, he knows Osterkamp raped Yani. The first night he was furious enough to kill him, but his wife dissuaded him."**

"Well, then, Mr. Osterkamp, Mr. Reyphin, what we really need is some evidence that will point to the guilt of one person, be it Reyphin or someone else. Yani isn't able to speak, but she can still help." The wind cuffed the torches again, nearly guttering them, their light glowering across the crowd's dubious expressions. He wasn't a conjurer to mystify by sleight-of-hand, make their minds believe what their eyes thought they saw. But if the truth were there, incontrovertible for the eye to see? What could he prove? How? Osterkamp grinned again with savage smugness. Yes!

"Oh, yes, I like it. So clever, my Matty's so clever! Kharm knows truth, but Matty unshrouds it." Relaxing her previous attack stance, Kharm almost capered with joy, encircling the girl. **"They may not be as distinct as they were, it's been three days now,"** she warned, **"but it's a chance."**

He rose and moved to Yani, close, but not too close, achingly aware of her reaction when Denellen had touched her. Doubtful any man other than Reyphin could do so without causing her to flinch, withdraw even further. Kneeling, he willed the girl to look at him, but her hair still curtained her face. Kharm stretched against her, rubbed her head under her chin, forced the still face up. Not as blank as before, but he could sense something banked inside, protected, as she hadn't been protected that nightmarish night. "Yani, I need you to help us, help us find the man who hurt you, so he'll never hurt you or any other children again. You don't have to say anything, do anything, really, but I have to ask you for a favor."

"Can't you leave her be?" her grandmother protested.

Matty felt he'd aged a hundred years, dirty and soiled with a knowledge he didn't want, a view of sex as perversion, he who'd never yet managed to experience it except through Kharm's vivid but equally innocent emotions of want. "You said that Yani was bitten and bruised? Are any of the bites still visible?"

"Visible? You can practically see each individual tooth mark!" Her fingers were sunk into Yani's clothes, practically daring him to rip them off. "You can't expect her to flaunt them in public, parade them for everyone to see? Are you sick?"

"Yani," he addressed her instead of her grandmother, refused to forget she was there, a being, a person, listening and comprehending on some level, deserving of being consulted. "Yani, if I asked that only women surround you—no men, no men anywhere near. I'll move them out and away from the light, if you want—would you remove your clothes so the women can examine you? And my larchcat, my ghatta, Kharm, who's a girl just like you. Little black Tah'm over there with my friend Jaak, is a boy, so I wouldn't even let him look. Could you do that? And then put your clothes on quick as you can."

"What good's it going to do you if you can't see the bite marks, Vandersma?" Osterkamp hooted at his back.

He looked over his shoulder, smiled, made sure he raised his upper lip to bare his incisors, as if he were an animal, and to reveal that his were intact, no gaps. "I'm sure Kharm can give me an accurate description, and of course the women can back her up."

"So, bite marks are bite marks. We've all got teeth, haven't we? Or most of us have. Begging your pardon, Auntie Vlaen." Clear that Osterkamp hadn't figured it out yet, and Matty craved seeing his expression then. But everything revolved around whether Yani would agree.

"Priyani," he coaxed, "it's not just your own hurt at stake here. Some say Aron hurt you. If they think he did, you won't be able to see your friend any more. If you can't help yourself, can you help Aron, so his wife and family won't lose him?"

Her chin jerked tremulously as she fumbled under her grandmother's arms, working at her buttons while her legs kicked and thrashed to make him go away. He backed up rapidly as the women of the town surrounded her, layers of protective encirclement to bar men's prying eyes. But Kharm would see.

After a time the circle broke, Yani and her grandmother returning into view, the girl nestled under her arm, half-hidden behind her but distinctly involved at some level. Her eyes followed Kharm as the ghatta trotted to Matty's side. **"Just as you suspected, my most clever, beloved Bond."**

"Gentlewomen of Ruysdael, do the bite marks show a gap at one point, a gap on the upper right side," he pointed a finger at his own teeth. "As if someone were missing a tooth . . . about here?" Nods and murmurings from the women. "Do you good people happen to know anyone who lacks a tooth there?"

Despite himself, Aron Reyphin grinned broadly, displaying an intact set of even white teeth. "Smile for us, Osterkamp," he crowed, striding forward, a bantam confronting a large, red rooster of a man.

The citizens took up the cry, "Smile for us, Osterkamp! Smile!" Grim satisfaction buoyed their voices, made them bell like hounds running down their prey as they crowded round, hands reaching to grip him.

"Is that proof enough, Denellen?" Matty asked. "If so, you'd better intervene before he's missing any more teeth."

Samson Denellen stood beside him, arms folded across his chest. "Laws and obedience to the laws are crucial, but what Ruysdael needs more is catharsis, cleansing. Manuel's tried to convince me there are higher laws, laws beyond human laws. Think he has, though mayhap not the way he intended." He turned his back to the mob overwhelming Osterkamp. "An abomination of that sort doesn't follow our laws, doesn't deserve to be punished by them." He raised his face to the skies, voice ringing in the night, the rain finally falling in earnest as he shouted. "Quick and neat, folks. No torture or torment. Don't sink to his level."

The crowd parted, Reyphin walking briskly away from the crumpled figure on the ground and presenting a bloodied knife to Denellen. "If you'd be kind enough to dispose of this, Denny?" and handed him the knife butt-end first. "I'm afraid I slipped, fell where the ground's muddy. Osterkamp apparently was in the way."

"No, 'twas me, Denny," Mother Vlaen called. "Clumsy in old age, eyesight bad, shouldn't even be allowed to carry a knife." "No, must have been me." "No, me!" The shouts rose from one person, then another—unified guilt, collective justice. Matty forced himself to look at the body, rolled it over, revulsed by the feel of the slack flesh slicked with rain, arm hair springy and rough against his fingers. As he suspected, only one knife wound showed, not multiple stabs. Crude compassion of a sort, he supposed; more than he would have exhibited, his fingers itching for the knife. So did one mercy-kill a rogue animal.

"Then you don't mind Osterkamp's fate?" A sniff of surprise from the ghatta, followed by a damp sneeze. **"That this ending, this death was just and right?"**

"I don't know, mayhap I'm becoming bloodthirsty in my old age. A part of me's sorry that I didn't wield the knife." He walked away as his father came and knelt by the body, rain pattering on the tonsured, bowed head, beading brows and lashes, clasped hands. *"But some acts are righteous, just in a way I'd never envisioned. What would you have done?"*

"Ghatti claws are very sharp. And ghatti sometimes torment their kills." That was the last they said about the matter.

"Doyce! Doyce!" Francie's voice echoed sharp as flint as she beckoned with her cane. "Come on, hurry! Cady's back."

Shaking her head to clear it, Doyce concentrated on the scene around her, still blinded by the night torches of Ruysdael past, the snarls of the crowd as they flung themselves on Osterkamp. Child molester. Brazen as could be until he'd been caught out. What sort of human being could so torture a child? Mouth dry, hands trembling, she gathered her cloak around her as she rose, Khar tumbling free of the folds.

"Might have warned me," she groused as she tongue-licked fur into place. **"I was just as lost in the past as you. Astute of our Matty to solve the case. Truth almost al-**

ways leaves a tangible trail, doesn't it? Once you know
where and how to look for it." But Doyce, she realized,
hadn't heard a word, walking with grave deliberation toward
the broken surrey, her face a rigid mask of grief. "What,
love, what? What is it, what's the matter?"

*"Why did it happen in Ruysdael? Why did it have to in-
volve a child scarcely younger than Davvy?"* Jaw clenched,
she began to hurry, leaving Khar to catch up at a roly-poly
lope. *"I'm so scared about Davvy, as if something terrible's
about to happen to him. Silly, I know."* She manufactured a
little laugh and Khar shivered at its falsity. An afterimage of
Yani floated in Doyce's mind, blonde instead of black-
haired, her hand reaching out ... to Matty? ... to Davvy?
Khar blinked. What in the name of the Elders was Doyce
obsessing over now?

"Do you think it some sort of premonition, an omen?"
This part of the human mind no ghatti had ever been able to
comprehend, the ability to believe a totally different and distinct thing had attributes capable of influencing a completely
separate incident. That that was, was. And that that is Now
is distinctly itself, for good or for ill. The ghatti way made
much more sense. Khar stopped short, sank to her haunches.
Then why, by the Elders, why did she think that Doyce
would benefit from learning about the past, might find links
between Then and Now to serve as signposts toward the Future? Because of the Spirals, the circling up and up, Past
coiling by Present, Future coiling alongside Past, the Spiral
turning? If only Saam or Rawn were here to ask, or Terl.
Hoisting herself up, she ran after Doyce, bewildered but
thinking furiously.

Cady set the brake on the most dilapidated hay wagon
Doyce had ever encountered, and pulled, surprisingly
enough, by a pair of white mules. She started to scratch one
under the chin, but F'een planted himself in front of her,
fixed her with an imploring stare. "Wouldn't touch, if I
were you. They're the most nasty, ill-tempered brutes
I've ever met. Likely to snap a finger off. They kick, they
stamp, they bite—then deafen you by braying."

"Was this the best you could do?" Snatching her hand
clear, she heard the critical sting in her voice, reproach at
being jerked into the present.

Cady's nostrils tightened as she gathered her hair behind
her head, let it fall free, her expression constricting as if to

absorb a blow without flinching. "I stopped at every house and farm along the road, took every side road if I could see a house in the distance. No one home. Apparently everyone's decided to make a day of it, go to Ruysdael."

"Except Mr. Adderson." Inez gave the right-hand mule a stinging swat on the nose and it looked at her tenderly, nuzzled her while she scratched its ears. "Only one I know anywhere near who keeps white mules. Aren't nearly as ill-tempered as he is."

"Sorry I didn't make his acquaintance, but meeting his mules was pleasure enough." Cady was shifting gear from the surrey to the wagon—the food hamper, a few blankets and pillows, and Inez's carry-all, crammed with who knew what. From the past Doyce remembered hard candies, ointments, bandage rolls, extra buttons and pins. Always prepared, that was Inez. "I finally gave up, left a note and took the wagon and mules. Threw in as much straw as I could because we can't all fit on the seat."

"Did well, girl. Did fine." Inez made her way around the wagon, inspecting it. "Pretty is as pretty does, and as long as it does get us there, this is fine."

Francie clung to the wagon's high, slatted side, only her face and hands visible. "I'd best stay with the surrey and the team then. Don't think I can climb into this." No pity, simply a matter-of-fact assessment of the situation, all too commonplace in her straitened circumstances. Being left out, shunted to the side, was second nature to her.

But Cady swung athletically into the wagonbed, fumbling under the straw. "Thought of that. Someone drop the tailgate?" and Doyce awkwardly obeyed before her mother or Francie could try. A broad plank snake-tongued out. "Knew it would be hard for Miz Marbon as well as you, and Doyce's not all that graceful herself at the moment. If you can't climb the slant with me steadying, I borrowed some sacking as well. Sit on it, and I'll scoot you up."

"Thank you!" Francie's face glowed, and Doyce wondered how often she'd been left behind before. "I want to claim my fair share of scolding when we find Davvy."

"Then can we get on with it, please?" Her disquiet built, all patience eroded no matter how she tried to control it. And the two childish figures in her mind bravely walked toward some indistinct fate, and she was unable to move, run after them and save them. Her actual body felt equally

weighted, rooted, and she realized the baby had sunk downward like a stone. At least for the moment it wasn't kicking,
but the weight was a foreboding sign, and with good reason.
A horrible suspicion that labor impended, and sooner rather
than later. *"Just stay put, stay steady, little one,"* she mentally begged the unborn child. *"You're important to me, but
so's Davvy, and we can't let him down, can we?"* Damn
Jenret for not being here to help find Davvy, be with her
when she needed him! Not that he'd meant to be captured,
but why did he have to be so damned inconsiderate! She
kicked the wagon wheel, grabbed a handful of straw, and
knotted it. So there, take that!

**"If you've gotten that out of your system, we're ready
to go. There's time—if you don't let your fears conquer
you."** Khar peered over the wagon's side. **"Want to march
up the plank or have Cady boost you to the seat?"** The
ghatta read the twinges and shifts in Doyce's body and commenced a prayer to the Elders.

With as much dignity as she could muster, Doyce marched
to the wagon's front and climbed aboard. Someday it would
be nice to see her feet again, and someday was approaching
sooner than planned.

Cady slapped the reins on the mules' backs and they
brayed with displeasure as they took off. "Doyce," Inez
knelt behind Cady and Doyce, steadying herself on their
shoulders. "Did ye remember the chamber pot from under
the back seat of the surrey?"

"No, Mother, I did not." Each evenly spaced word
sounded a reproach. "There are more important things on
my mind right now."

"Like whether Davvy's safe and sound. I know." Inez
sighed. "Oh, I know. But you won't find him any faster with
the press of a full bladder. Any rate, I made sure I stuck it
in the corner."

"Thank you, Mother." But all her frantic thoughts
wheeled around lurid visions of Davvy hurt, lost, in
danger—from what she didn't know, but it grew stronger,
dread coming to fruition, ready to burst. Oh, reason enough
to be worried, but the black mood was growing, overwhelming her vision, as if her fears for her unborn child had transferred themselves to Davvy. *"Oh, please, Blessed Lady, let
him be safe!"* Whom could he be walking hand in hand
with? The girl in her fading vision wasn't Priyani.

"Be dark by the time we reach Ruysdael," Inez muttered thoughtfully and sank back beside Francie.

Violet, pink, turquoise. Apricot, apple green, buttercup yellow. Stretched on tiptoes, swaying in time to the globed paper lanterns that decorated trees, upper story railings, eaves, torchère posts, Lindy searched for more hues, upturned face bathed in soft pastels. There—that one, orange as a pumpkin! And over there, lonely amongst the richer purple cluster, a pale mint. The candle flames pulsated, the colors veering, colliding. Gorgeous, a fairyland fit for a king. More lanterns pearled the dark as it thickened, a myriad of food scents perfuming the air, reminding her she was hungry. She pressed a hand against her stomach to quell its protest but didn't rub—that would be unladylike, and tonight she'd be a perfect lady awaiting the King of Marchmont's arrival.

A festival, a carnival, a living fairy tale unfolded here in Ruysdael, and she, Lindy Marlin, a part of it. Hugging herself hard to make sure it was real, she pirouetted, coat belling out around her. Although Ruysdael was tight-packed with the curious from surrounding towns, Bard had found lodging with an innkeep he'd known from his Seeker days, accommodations so cramped Bard had slept in the kitchen and Lindy'd been relegated to share with the innkeeper's grandchildren, four to a bed just like home. But best of all, Miz Rooke had seen she'd had a proper bath and washed her hair. For some reason she'd refused to rebraid it, letting the long blonde tresses flow free, except for a barrette that gathered the hair around her temples behind her head. "O'course," Miz Rooke had said, pleased with her handiwork, "that way your lovely earrings'll show, dear." And then Miz Rooke had rummaged in a trunk, pulled out the dearest coat of aquamarine velvet with a navy velvet collar and cuffs, piping. "Kara outgrew it almost before she wore it. Try it on." It fit as if it had been tailored for her, the bodice formfitting, then swelling into a long, bell-shaped skirt.

All through the late afternoon and evening Bard had treated her with gentlemanly courtesy, never dragging her by the hand when the crowds became thick but decorously inviting her to take his arm. The crowds made him nervous, she'd decided, especially when a Guardian squad marched through, breaking up knots of Reapers, sullen at the polite refusal to let them congregate.

She felt mature, at least twelve, yes, perhaps even thirteen, on the verge of young womanhood. And Bard—where was Bard? Or M'wa? Scanning as much of the throng as she could, she discovered she was alone, or not precisely alone, since she stood in the midst of hundreds of people. Oh, well, it had happened before. Hardly anything to worry about. She'd meant to stay put, had promised she would while Bard ran a private errand, but there was always something just beyond that enticed her. Well, this time she simply *would* stay put and Bard or M'wa would find her shortly. Schooling herself to patience, she looked for something to occupy her wait—no, that's what had gotten her into trouble in the first place—discovered she stood in front of an impromptu stage with a midnight blue backdrop spangled with tiny silver stars and crescent moons. A man, dressed all in black with long, flowing sleeves lined with gold, stepped onto the platform with three brands in his hands. He was darkly, sleekly handsome, with a pouty red mouth and wavy hair. Not as handsome as Bard though, she decided loyally.

Curious, she clasped the stage for balance against the people milling closer for a good view, wondered what performance she'd see. Strange, he smelled almost smoky, the brands in his hands sooty looking. Well, hadn't she seen other wonders today? An acrobat walking a tightrope, magicians, dancers, musicians, a man with a Sunderlies macaque like a wee fur-suited human. A woman so scantily clad in gauzy gold veilings that Lindy shivered carried a brazier heaped with throbbing red coals, placed it stage left, then energetically pumped red leather bellows to make the coals spring into flame. Applause for that, appreciative whistles. Lindy thought it excessive. Anyone could do that.

The man in black rolled back his sleeves to reveal smooth, olive-tinted forearms and began juggling the brands, gradually moving closer to the brazier until at last each brand spun through the flames and ignited. The fiery torches danced in a never-ending circle until they formed a glowing loop, soaring arcs of fire blossoms that burned their afterimages on her eyes even when she blinked, dazzled. Without warning the man let one flaming brand remain in his right hand, his left hand still casually keeping the other two aloft.

Head bent back, he thrust the blazing torch into his mouth, almost down his throat while Lindy gasped, mesmerized by the stream of fire that shot from his mouth to light a new brand held by his assistant. The man ate another mouthful of fire, almost contemplatively and fountained it back into the air.

"I could do that, easy," a voice beside her informed her.

Without taking her eyes from the stage, she countered, "I bet not." As braggy as her brother Harry. The performance continued, the fire-eater and his assistant willingly consuming fiery morsels, flames coruscating in the night, bathing their faces in its red-orange glow. At last, one by one, the brands winked out and Lindy sighed in awed appreciation and turned to look at her new companion. "That was splendid! I wonder how they do it?"

"Oh, they gargle with something special beforehand to make sure they don't get burned," the boy reassured her. "Then, long as they're steady, don't hesitate, everything's fine." He looked like a nice boy, she decided, mayhap thirteen, a bit stocky, but with merry dark eyes and a heavy fringe of bangs. "Here, my name's Davvy. Want to walk a bit, see what else is doing? I gotta be someplace shortly, it's important, but I've a little time." Perhaps he wouldn't attract so many stares if he were with someone, wouldn't have people asking if he were lost, taking an interest in him. He wasn't used to crowds, cities; Gaernett might be bigger, but he'd barely seen any of it, had stayed close to Swan's bedside.

Shocked, Lindy realized that neither Bard nor M'wa had located her, and the faintest worry began to nag. "I'm Lindy. I don't think I'd better. I've misplaced my friends." She liked that, the adult "misplaced," not saying she was lost. "They ought to be along soon—mayhap you've seen them?"

"How'd you expect me to notice anyone in this crowd?" he waved a hand at the throng. "Less there's something special to make your friends noticeable—like those with silver sickles on their collars, lurking around." He scowled, cocked a brow, or at least she thought he did, since it vanished beneath his bangs.

"If I could get on the stage, I might be able to spot them." She tried to match actions to words, but couldn't manage, not and remain ladylike. "I'm not as tall as you, can't see as far. Of course M'wa's shorter than I am."

"M'wa? Who're you looking for? A Seeker? Wait."
Hands grabbed her waist and her feet left the ground, back
scraping against the edge of the stage until he finally hoisted
her high enough to sit. Davvy panted, rubbed at a shoulder.

"You're awfully strong," and put her hand on his shoulder
to make it feel better.

"I've been practicing unarmed combat. You've got to be
strong for that—and quick and clever, too. Sorry I didn't get
you up there more gracefullike, but I'm used to throwing
people, not lifting them polite and neat."

More boasting? She wasn't sure but didn't think so, or at
least not all of it. "How'd you know I'm looking for a
Seeker?"

He leaned on the stage, fingers toying with the piping on
her cuff, not quite meeting her eyes. " 'Cause if one of your
friends is named M'wa," he tossed his head back, eyes
closed, hand pressed against his brow in a dramatic gesture,
"then I see ... I see a man, tall and dark-honey colored, a
man called Bard!" The merry eyes popped open, awaiting
her reaction.

Lindy clapped, delighted. "You must be a Resonant, to
know that!" and Davvy's face slackened with shock, eyes
darting to see who stood near him. The backdrop rustled,
stilled.

"No, no, I'm a fortune-teller, can see into your future.
Want me to read your palm?" His hand, grasping hers, was
sweaty with fear as he tried to recover. "Actually, no, not
that either. It's just that I've met a black-and-white ghatt
called M'wa and his Bond is Bard. Listen, is he truly here?
I could use his help."

Tell, not tell? Davvy was torn. Could Bard help him gain
admittance to the king when the royal party arrived? Guarantee that he spoke true about Jenret Wycherley's capture by
Resonants? Or would Bard simply have M'wa contact F'een
and Cady, tell them his whereabouts, ignominiously pack
him off before he could complete his mission? Bard was a
friend of both Doyce and Jenret, wasn't he? Still, mayhap it
was prudent to trust no one, do it completely on his own.
Heroes couldn't depend on someone smoothing the way for
them, could they? He didn't know this girl, this Lindy, at all,
though she was nice, even kinda cute ... for a girl. But
she'd hit too close to home with her comment about Resonants, best be careful around her. He'd only stopped because

he'd been on the move all day, bone weary, desperate for
companionship, fearful the Reapers might sense him, snatch
him if he were alone.

But Lindy hadn't heard the last of what Davvy had asked,
was standing on tiptoe, craning in all directions. "I can't
wait to see the king—I've never seen one before, have you?"

He almost answered in the affirmative but stopped himself. Don't give too much away, be cautious, be canny. And
on top of that, he didn't dare lie again, even though, with
F'een so far distant, he'd never be caught out. Still, heroes
don't lie. But without waiting for an answer, Lindy caught
her breath. "Oooh, that woman over there—can you see her?
The one in the long amber cloak, satin amber, I think. Are
they here already, the royal party, I mean? She looks like a
queen, or a princess at least."

Scrambling beside her, Davvy followed her pointing finger, frowned. How could you dislike a woman you'd never
met, a stranger who stood six booths away? But he did, with
a visceral terror that made him want to cut and run, dragging
Lindy after him. Breathing through his mouth, he examined
her more closely. Yes, the cloak was rich, elegant—or had
been once. The rest was less impressive—gray-blonde hair
that stuck out like a wire brush, eyes that reminded him of
dull chips of slate, hands worn, almost dirty looking at a distance. Yet something about her chilled the marrow of his
bones. Worse feeling than mingling with the Reapers, passing them on the streets here, barely daring to breathe. Worse
yet, she'd caught sight of them, posed like actors on a stage,
and was working toward them through the crowd.

"Good evening, young lady, young sir. How fare you this
fine evening?" Her voice was rich but hoarse, the flat eyes
glittered now, widened as if they'd witnessed a miracle, a
holy vision of the Lady. To his utter astonishment, Lindy
dropped a curtsey and, loath to respond, Davvy jerked stiffly
at the waist. Don't, don't bend so deeply you can't watch
her, something inside him warned. He rammed a hand under
Lindy's arm, brought her upright.

"Are you royalty? You're royalty, aren't you? A queen, a
princess?" Davvy cringed at Lindy's words. "The king's arrived, then?" Absolutely impossible, Davvy knew it with every fiber of his being. There would have been fanfares,
fireworks, crowds parting to let the royal party pass. Horses
and plumes, gilded saddles and bridles, decorated carriages.

And guards, most of all, guards, Guardians and Muscadeine's soldiers. They couldn't have arrived, not with everyone still wandering around, eating, dancing, jesting, singing, entertained by and entertaining each other. Besides, he would have felt something if that many Resonants were near, that near-electric hum that shivered the air when they mindspoke. He'd felt it gradually intensifying through the evening, knew the royal party advanced, the way you anticipate an approaching thunderstorm, but they weren't here yet.

The cloaked woman staggered backward, almost as if struck, but recovered herself, her eyes never leaving their faces. "Why, yes, yes, of course. I am Princess Hylan, royal cousin to the king." Oh, yes, yes, it didn't matter what she said, how she babbled, she'd found them! Yes, the sacrificial lambs delivered to her hands to appease the Lady, offer them in tribute and of course the king would fall to her! One black lamb, oh, she knew that without even taking the forked witch hazel rod from her belt. And one white, pure and innocent, so sad to sacrifice her but so necessary. "Would you like to meet King Eadwin, my royal cousin?"

"Oh, yes!" pale with excitement, Lindy gathered herself, stopped in regret, "but I can't. I've misplaced my friends, mayhap you've seen them, the Seeker Bard and his Bondmate M'wa?"

"Ah, the gentleman with the ghatt? Of course. They were walking over that way just a little while ago, looking for you." A Seeker—that she didn't need! Best get these two under wraps. Indeed, she heard a fight breaking out in the next street over, sure to bring the Guardians at a trot. Had Tadj done something foolish? Doubtful, he was so circumspect, so organized. She pointed wildly in the direction of the goat cart and its sapling cargo. "Why don't we surprise him, bring him along when we find him?"

"Lindy," Davvy hissed, tugging at her arm, "I don't think you should go. Best wait here, let Bard catch up with you." At least he'd managed to drag her a step or two farther from Princess Hylan, and if she were a princess, he was King of Canderis!

Tugging impatiently until he bent his head, Lindy whispered, "Her ears aren't even! Bard was right!" Nonsense, gibberish, he decided. "Let's go with her, Davvy. I know Bard'll be worried, and this way we'll set his mind at ease.

Won't he be surprised?" Her hand clutched his fingers and he wasn't sure whose were icier.

"No," he scuffed mulishly, heard the hollowness of the stage. "Don't go, Lindy. Look, I've something important to do real soon. Matter of life and death, almost." Tell her the king hadn't arrived? Would she believe him? Not likely, given her infatuation with Princess Hylan. "Please, I think it's best you stay."

She dropped his hand, her mouth pouting. "Well, I'm going, Mr. Davvy whoever-you-are. This is my one chance to meet a king. Mayhap you have lots of chances, but I don't." And with that she skipped to the stage's lip, Hylan reaching to lift her down. He watched them go off, the turquoise coat with its navy velvet collar beside the taller exclamation mark of the amber cloak. The cloak was stained and dirty at the hem, as if its owner had walked long and far on dusty roads.

Follow her or stay? Stay or follow? Farfel and smerdle! He had a mission to accomplish, didn't he? The king had called him foolish once, said that he'd grow out of it. Well, wasn't saving Jenret serious, wasn't passing on word of his capture serious? And respecting your mission, sticking with it, meant avoiding childish distractions, not chasing after a new fancy. He'd already scouted a position for himself, a spot where he could observe the king's procession when it passed, mindspeak the king or Arras Muscadeine, pass the word. Except . . . except. . . . Indecision twitched his feet.

Except he didn't like or trust that Princess Hylan, she scared him, scared him so much he hadn't even considered trying to read her mind, afraid of what he'd find there. And Lindy, she was nice, he shouldn't have let her go like that. Bard'd skin him alive if he found out. Mayhap he could do both, keep track of Lindy's whereabouts and find Bard and M'wa, get back in time for the king's arrival. He concentrated, letting the emanations in the air brush against him, gauging them. Closer, definitely. But there was still time, especially if he acted quickly. He'd fix that Princess Hylan if she tried anything with Lindy. He knew self-defense, unarmed combat, after all! Mop the floor with the old hag!

He hopped down, began trailing after, hiding himself in the mass of moving people, edging closer but not too close. Smerdle, where were they headed? What was Princess Hylan doing, taking her on a tour of the meadows where everyone had camped last night? Anxious, he worked closer, still unseen, dodging and darting, taking cover as he could.

Hylan smiled to herself, smiled down at the girl. Yes, the boy was following, she was sure. The witch hazel rod hummed and vibrated against her ribs underneath the cloak. Yes, black lamb and white lamb.

Bazelon Foy stepped from behind the stage curtain, fastidiously unrolling and smoothing his sleeves. Enough gold and three quick lessons could make anyone a fire-eater for a day. That and the determination to succeed—nothing was impossible. Tadj had promised him the woman Hylan would be here in Ruysdael, primed with purpose and passion. Now that he'd seen her he thought her a flawed vessel, but even flawed vessels served. If she broke, had to be discarded after this, so be it. But if she could kill the king . . . he let the thought dangle deliciously, tempting. Why not let her try? Best go find Tadj now, let him know he was here.

❖

Fleet, yes, fleet as the wind! Parm raced toward camp, Barnaby pounding behind him, claws scrabbling on stones, tearing up grass, doggy panting delight steaming the air. Ecstatic at having escaped the guard dog, they giggled and wriggled, jumped sleeping bodies in sheer delight as they wove between wagons and tents and early risers. Glorious sunrise! Parm's head still pounded, but he didn't care, he could think again! Phew! Not as fleet as the wind after all, and his legs trembled, spasmed in reminder that the drug wouldn't relinquish its hold on him all that easily, despite Barnaby's antidote. All the way back he'd been calling to Harrap at intervals, waiting to hear the beloved mindvoice welcoming him.

But no mindvoice came and despite Barnaby's eager, crowding presence, he felt utterly bereft, alone, as they reached the goat cart. Why, oh why wouldn't Harrap 'speak him? He claw-carefully tugged at the coarse blanket draped over Harrap's form, Barnaby pushing behind him, whimpering. Parm staggered backward, tumbled and righted himself, bristling in shock. Tadj slept under the blanket, not Harrap! Where was he?

"Harrap! Harrap!" His mindvoice sounded sluggish to his ears. Try again—never had Harrap ignored him before, even when they were both deliriously happy from Hylan's special seasoning. **"Harrap, where are you? 'Speak me, Harrap!"** Silence. Had Barnaby's poo-phooey weed done something to his mindspeech?

Tadj stirred, groaned as he rolled onto his back and fell asleep again, but Parm skittered clear, arching his back. Best get away before Tadj awoke. There was nothing for him here, no beloved Harrap. If his mindspeech wouldn't work, he couldn't search Hylan's and Tadj's minds for an answer to explain Harrap's disappearance. **"Harrap!"** he wailed again. Still nothing.

Desperate, he commanded, **"Barnaby, find Harrap. Seek!"** There was more than one way to Seek, and he'd depend on Barnaby's nose.

Anxious, eager, Barnaby planted his nose to the ground, snuffling, nostrils flaring as he trotted back and forth. Returned, nose moist with exertion, sniffed sadly behind Parm's ear. *"Seek bleak. Scent weak. Scent spent."*

"Keep trying," he begged, but the dog sat, stubborn.

"No scent!" he repeated emphatically.

"Please, Barnaby. Barnaby good dog." Barnaby grinned his approval. Parm hated himself for it but drew himself up, looked as imposing as his bedraggled state would allow. **"Parm will whip Barnaby if Barnaby doesn't find Harrap."**

The dog cringed, tail wagging from side to side, low and appeasing. *"Parm rails, flails? Flail Barnaby for his failings? No find in your mind?"*

"No, I need you." His whiskers trembled. **"I'd never whip you. I'm sorry, Barnaby. Barnaby's a friend."**

"Barnaby find," the terrier reassured him, brow wrinkling. He began to quarter the camp, ranging wider and wider, Parm limping in his wake, head hanging, banging. By the Elders, he was beginning to sound like Barnaby! But by the Elders and the Lady that Harrap held dear, he'd make Hylan pay for this!

By the time the sun had risen high in the sky, Parm had had to concede Barnaby was right. *"No scent."* Barnaby sank his muzzle into a bucket of water by someone's wagon, splashed and bubbled and slurped, flopped wearily in the wagon's shade. *"Harrap's feet no beat path. No scent."*

"No scent," Parm agreed. No scent, no mindvoice. **"But he can't have flown away like a bird."** He heaved himself

up. **"Let's go back to the goat cart, check."** It was the only
place Harrap knew, the only place Parm knew where they
should expect to find each other. **"Barnaby's a loyal
friend."** The smell of frying sausage assailed his nose, his
stomach, although Barnaby's tail began a slow wag, his
tongue hanging out. Someone had returned from the festivities for lunch, pinching pennies, not buying food from the
street vendors. He wished he could cajole the person into
giving Barnaby a sausage. It seemed important to show his
thanks.

A baby cried from the wagon, its cry a bolt of inspiration.
He winked at Barnaby, directed him into a crouch behind the
wagon wheel, and marched around the wagon rowling,
weaving himself around the woman's ankles. "My, you're a
big kitty cat," she said, turning the sausages as the baby
cried again. Parm perked up his ears at the cry, jumped into
the wagon, pretending to investigate. Many women were uneasy having cats around infants, and this one was no exception, chasing after him. Parm came scooting out, a flash of
orange and black and white fur, hooked a sausage from the
skillet and tossed it to Barnaby. The dog snapped it in midair, gulped it. *"Phew! Hot-a-lot! But good!"*
"Come on, Barnaby, back to the cart!"
But the goat cart was deserted, Hylan and Tadj elsewhere,
and no sign of Harrap. Barnaby jumped on the dropped tailgate and onto the canvas covering, started to curl up, then
sniffed and sneezed. *"Harrap! Harrap layer-up here!"* He
bounced stiff-legged. *"Harrap not fly—lie! Lie on canvas—
drag saggy mass!"* With that he shot off.

Not entirely understanding, not daring to hope, Parm followed after. Barnaby seemed confident, which was more
than he was. He tried to puzzle it through: Harrap on the
canvas? Why? Drag sag mass? Panic as it clicked into
place—Harrap's body had been dragged somewhere on the
canvas. Was he dead—ill? **"Harrap! Hear me! 'Speak
me!"**

Barnaby was trotting faster now, nose to ground, confident, tail gaining speed. They dodged between tents, some
of canvas, others improvised from blankets, quilts. This was
where Hylan's faithful camped, Parm thought. Looping
around a tent, Barnaby came to a halt. *"Harrap canvas
scent, canvas scent tent,"* he announced proudly. *"Harrap*

nap." With a trembling paw, Parm hooked back the tent flap. And inside was Harrap.

With the gentlest of questing nose flickers, Parm sniffed along Harrap's face, breathed in his ear, touched eyelids, moved down to test at nose and mouth, practically reeling from the stench, the scent of Hylan's seasoning exuding from his breath, his very sweat, a miasma of it.

Abruptly Barnaby sat, dug a hind foot behind a brown ear, his whole head shaking, jowls flopping. *"Wake make?"* he inquired, shifting his foot behind a shoulder blade. *"Make wake? No wake?"*

"No wake," Parm agreed sadly. **"I can't make him wake up, he's even worse than I was."**

"No sick trick, make head less thick?"

"I can't make him sick if I can't wake him up." His body rumbled with purrs and he willed the vibrations to stop. He could never understand how or why the ghatti purred when they were hurt or afraid; it seemed contrary to such a state of distress.

In turn and in tandem the dog and ghatt spent the afternoon fruitlessly attempting to rouse Harrap to consciousness. Even Barnaby's chill nose had little effect, other than to elicit an occasional moan or quiver from Harrap. Barnaby at last threw himself across Harrap's shins, exhausted. *"Mind find?"* he yawned.

"It doesn't work any more. It's not me, but Harrap's got too much of the drug in him to hear me, I think." He settled on Harrap's chest, disconsolate.

"More again," Barnaby urged. *"Mind roar, can't ignore. Try,"* he cajoled. *"Barnaby tried. Barnaby found."*

More to avoid disappointing the terrier than from any hope of success, Parm tried again. **"Harrap! Harrap, my beloved Bond, listen to me!"** A slight movement gave him hope. **"Listen to me, I need you. It's important!"**

Harrap's head made little searching circling motions, tousling his sweaty hair. "Oh, wonder . . . wondrous, wonderful raptures," he whispered aloud, "the very world . . . speaks to me now that . . . Our Lady has spoken. Oh, Blessed Lady to have . . . revealed all this to me, her humble servant!" He fumbled at his chest for his golden Lady's Medallion, seemed to gain strength. "Oh, Blessed Lady, let your Disciples speak to me, let the whole world speak to me now that I have ears to hear."

"It isn't the ..." Parm almost stumbled, said "bloody," **"Blessed Lady or her world you're hearing, it's me— Parm."** Indignation raised him practically on tiptoe as he shoved and jammed his head under Harrap's chin. **"I've been 'speaking you for a long time now, how could you mistake me?"** And why did such maunderings as wonder, wondrous, wonderful raptures have a faint, embarrassing echo in his own brain? Damn Hylan and her seasonings, those drugs that had robbed them both of their will and reason!

"Reason-seasoning," Barnaby whined almost guiltily.

"Parm?" the switch to Harrap's mindvoice was as rusty and tentative as a speaker testing a foreign language learned long ago and unused for years. *"Nice Parm, nice ghatti."*

"Ghatt, Harrap, there's only one of me." Well, at least Harrap had the name straight. **"Listen to me. Hylan's been drugging you, drugging us. She's up to something she doesn't want us to know about. We've got to get away, report to Saam."**

"No, oh, no," Harrap's head thrashed on the pillow. "Hylan is the reincarnation of the Lady, I know that now, though I don't know how ... I could have been so blind. Whatever She does is for the good of us all, Her beneficence shines ... on us like the sun and rain make the flowers ... grow. Lady Hylan, Lady Hylan," he sang and the booming, joyous baritone that Parm loved so well was cracked and husky, barely there. Harrap's eyes flickered closed again.

"Harrap, I cannot lie, I 'speak truth, you know that. I am ghatti and we 'speak the truth. You can't have forgotten that, can you?" Parm felt as if the world were spinning under him, ready to throw him aside, unable to hang on any longer.

From wherever he'd been, Harrap painfully climbed back. "Oh, you 'speak the little ... truths, the truths of the earth, but Our Lady Hylan speaks the truth of the universe, the immutable, unchanging glorious verity of Her existence, Her care over Her children! My head resounds with the glory of it all. Resounds ..." breathless, he sank into unconsciousness again.

Unable to bear any more, Parm skittered out of the tent, desperate to lose himself in the dark, find a private place to think things through. The running felt good, made him temporarily forget that Harrap had cast him off in favor of

Hylan—or was he abandoning Harrap by running like this? Barnaby scurried after him, twiglike legs and dainty paws a blur. It struck him then and he blurted, **"Saam, I've got to contact Saam! He'll know what to do, he can ask Mahafny. Why didn't I think of it before?"** But he'd been so muddled with apprehension and fear, the residual effects of the drug leaching out of his system, that the obvious, the logical, hadn't pertained.

"Who Saam?" Barnaby panted plaintively. *"Saam who? Better-getter, better companion than Barnaby?"*

"No, Barnaby, you're a good friend, best, best friend." For a moment he feared the terrier would roll with joy. **"But Saam's clever, thinks from afar, thinks of things Barnaby and Parm can't because we're busy worrying about Harrap"**

"And Hylan," Barnaby insisted.

With a scramble Parm shot up an elm, the best vantage point he could find, leaving Barnaby below, leaping and snapping in frustration. He steadied his heaving sides, oriented himself to the north toward the lavender mountains in the distance, and cast his mind out. Again and again he cast, but there was nothing. Had Saam left the Hospice? He swung wider, searching for any trace of the mindnet, but unless Mem'now and the others were 'speaking in this direction, it would be almost impossible to alert them to his need. Nothing. His head sank on the branch, so limp with woe that he almost blended with the bark. Then he sat up with a scrabble and grab that barely retained his place.

Fool, fool, a thousand times fool! With this many people gathering in Ruysdael, there must be at least one Seeker Bond-pair somewhere near. Even without a gathering of this sort—was the king truly coming?—Ruysdael was a regular stop on Seeker circuits. Usually a pair passed through every other day. He began to comb the surrounding area, every fiber of his being alert, trilling out a general distress call, invoking the Elders to strengthen him and come to his aid.

Bard shouldered his way between stalls and booths, up and down streets, ceaselessly searching. M'wa prowled a quick, efficient path along the next packed aisle. That way they could cover twice as much ground. The colored lanterns bobbed, cast their eerie glows like a magic spell, transmuted the familiar into the unfamiliar, changing faces and forms into surreal, gyrating shapes. *"Any sign?"* He was increasingly nervous.

"No, nothing."

He veered back to the ribbon booth where he'd left Lindy after extracting her solemn promise to stay put, wait for him. He'd thought she'd find enough to admire there, be content waiting, but obviously something else had captivated her and she'd drifted away. He'd spied the gold chain with the cat pendant at a booth they'd passed earlier, had made careful note of it. The cat was chunky, broader than it ought to be, inadvertently ghattilike, which made it even more perfect. Touching his breast pocket, he could hear the tissue rustle, feel the lump of the pendant under his finger.

The crowds were more restless now, harder and harder to move logically, methodically through them, but he tried, asking as he went. "Have you seen . . . ?" "Have you seen . . . ?" And each time the answer was no. No, they hadn't, or no, they didn't remember, it wasn't always clear. *"M'wa? Anything?"*

"No. I think she was over here by this raised stage. I can almost catch her scent." The ghatt sounded harried, as flustered and frustrated as he felt. "But there's no one here to ask." And by that Bard knew that M'wa meant mindspeak, ready to enter a strangers's brain uninvited if it would aid in finding Lindy.

"Wait!" He could feel M'wa's shock, his intensity of focus as if the ghatt were beside him.

"You've found her?" Joy, relief flooded him. And an overpowering desire to paddle her fanny for disobeying him.

"No. Parm just 'spoke me! There's trouble. Harrap's here and Parm's terrified, thinks Harrap's dying. He wants us to come."

Bard scowled, frightening two elderly women with his savagely warped expression. *"But we have to find Lindy!"* How could he desert Lindy? She'd be waiting for him somewhere, more and more frightened because he and M'wa weren't there. And when it dawned on her that she was alone, adrift, she'd panic.

"We will, we will, but she'll have to amuse herself without us a little longer." M'wa pressed harder. "Would you deny Harrap, let him die?"

"M'wa, it's Parm saying that—Parm. Think about it, it can't be that bad. You know he always exaggerates, embroiders a tale to death." Death, why had he said that word?

"He's not exaggerating, and even when he does, he 'speaks truth—must! If you won't come, I'll go alone."

"All right, all right, I'm coming!" He shouldered himself around, oriented toward M'wa's mindvoice. Naturally it meant he was traveling against crowds streaming toward the city limits to welcome the king.

"Parm says bring salt!"

"Salt?" There, proof-positive Parm wasn't making sense.

"Yes, as an emetic. Harrap's been poisoned."

Poisoned? Bard saw an opening and plowed through the temporary gap, searched for the next one, gave up, and rammed his way ahead. Where was he going to find salt? Not to mention Lindy?

♣

"She's *not* a princess! I was wrong." Wrists tied to the cart's wheel rim, Lindy sat cross-legged, rested her head against the wheel. Davvy knelt opposite her, similarly bound, restlessly bouncing his hands between two spokes. His jacket shoulder was ripped, and a dirt-encrusted scrape glowed a raw, ugly red over his right eyebrow.

"It's all right," he reassured her in hushed tones, glancing toward where Tadj and Hylan sat in front of the fire. "Anybody from the country would have thought that. Not everyone's seen them like I have." Grabbing a spoke, he tested it at hub and rim, but it was tight. Pitch-dark now, but the moons' glow on her hair gilded it with strands of starlight. " 'Sides, you were awful brave to bite that old Hylan when she wouldn't let go of you to come help me. Smerdle, you should've seen her face!"

"Smerdle?" She tilted her head so the moonlight caught her brow, "What's smerdle mean? Sounds like one of the words my pa'd cane Jo for using."

"That's the beauty of it. Doesn't mean a thing, but it sounds bad. Sometimes a man's gotta let out his frustrations, but a gentleman wouldn't use improper words in front of—umph!—a lady." The spoke below showed no more sign of budging than the one above.

"That's what that man, that Tadj, should have said when

you threw him after he grabbed you! 'Stead of what he did."
Her giggle formed a trailer of mist in the cold night air.

"Well, I'da had him fair and square, but then, trying to get
that old Hylan separated from you, I didn't watch my back.
Stupid. You've got to watch everything, not get distracted."

"Know what's funny?" She tapped his foot with hers. "I
think I've met you in my dreams. Not you, exactly, but
someone who knows you, is looking for you. A pregnant
woman and a stripped ghatta, she's pregnant, too. They're
both going to have twins. She's been calling for you, looking worried." He cocked his head to one side, a fixed, wary
regard in his eyes. "That's why, when I heard your name, I
knew you must be nice." She shrugged. "Of course, I dream
a lot, and since I'm to help a woman who's having a baby
soon, I suppose it's not unusual. Bard's taking me to her."

"Is her name Doyce Marbon?"

An excited head bob. "Yes, do you know her? You must
know *everybody*."

"What's she look like in your dream, the dream-Doyce?"
How could Lindy know Doyce was having twins? He'd
hoarded that bit of information, shared it with no one. Would
Bard know? Being as he was a twin perhaps it was possible,
but had he told Lindy?

Frowning, she tried to describe the dream woman. "Not
real big, not a lot taller than you. Not plain, but not gorgeous, could be prettier if she tried. Brown hair that's fairly
short with reddish highlights in it. Nice hazel eyes, shrewd
but funny. And the ghatta's lovely, stripes almost like a
bull's-eye, a pink nose against the white." She looked
through Davvy, not at him, "I think I'll like them. I hope
that's what they look like, because Bard isn't good at de-
scribing people."

"Hush!" he kicked her calf to bring her back to herself,
mimed silence as best he could. "Someone's come."

They heard Tadj's exclamation of delight, the thumping
slaps that men make when they embrace. "You came, after
all."

The other voice was richly melodious, the kind you'd
trust. "When your note reached me, I had to. And this, I take
it, is Hylan Crailford. Madam, I'm at your service, in your
debt." Davvy strained to see, but they'd moved so the only
thing visible was three pairs of legs.

A sound like someone kissing air, and he could see Hylan

step backward, a disgusted grunt bursting from her. "Who are you?" she snapped. "I can barely see you in this light. Strangers trying to kiss my hands. I don't insist the faithful do that."

"My name's not important, my lady. Just my devotion."

Hylan shuffled uneasily. "Tadj, I'm going now. I'll leave the lambs in your charge, bring them along a little later."

The makeshift campgrounds were nearly deserted, the majority of the people off in the city proper, jostling for places to see the royal progress. But perhaps a hundred or more, Davvy couldn't be sure how many, flowed after Hylan as she stalked away from the cart, flowed after her like water coursing downstream, their faces rapturous at being permitted to follow. He didn't know what to make of it. What was it about that old Hylan, wrapped in her cloak, her hair straggly, that gave her such a profound authority, an ability to hold people in her sway? Left him with a queasy feeling in the pit of his stomach, though it might have been the sausage he'd eaten earlier. Something enormously wrong about her, and not just that her mind twisted different from most people's. Not evil, exactly, he grappled with the thought, but warped, distorted. It might be bad, but that was the last thing she meant to be, too earnest for that. And that odd tune she was humming as she strode away, "DA-de-Da DA-de-Da . . ."

Tadj waited until Hylan was out of sight. "Well, Baz, what do you think of her?"

"I'm not sure," the stranger replied. "Not entirely what I expected or envisioned. But if you're right, this is too precious a moment to miss, not at least share it as part of the crowd."

"Then you don't mind—"

"That I'll not be personally responsible for it?" the other voice finished for Tadj. "No, not in the least. You've helped instigate it, and you're one of my prime tools, one of my best Reapers, aren't you?" Embarrassed, inarticulate sounds of gratitude from Tadj. "If Hylan succeeds, she and her followers will distract attention from us, and no one will know which way to turn. Relations will be broken off with Marchmont, very possibly the Monitor thrown out of power. And we Reapers will toil in the midst of chaos to finish our task and restore the natural order."

"I tried to think how you'd do it, what would please you, Baz."

"By the way, what are the children for? Those two you've trussed to the wheel like a pair of hens."

Tadj made an apologetic sound. "Hylan has her heart set on it, her black lamb and her white lamb. Think of it as an opening act before the finale. She needed something, especially after her pet Shepherd became drug-mazed. I nearly brought the whole plan crashing down with that."

"Ah, the dancing bear? You'll have to tell me about that later. Isn't it about time, Tadj? Hylan should be beginning to work up her followers to the proper pitch. Shall we bring Hylan her lambs, let them gambol at our heels?"

"What lambs?" Lindy whispered so close that Davvy could feel her breath on his cheek. "They don't mean us, do they?"

The rising sound of trumpets sliced the air with silver and gold, cheers rising, a few boos and catcalls intermingled with them in the night air. The sound of hooves. He had to do it, do what he wasn't supposed to do, especially out like this in public. He let his mind insinuate itself, soft and cautious, quickly scanning Tadj's thoughts and the thoughts of the one called Baz. His head jerked upward, features screwed tight to contain his cry of terror, check his tears. His body shook and strained as he tried to break his bonds, flee from the blackness he'd encountered. They meant to kill the king! And even worse, he and Lindy were to be slaughtered like sacrificial lambs!

"Davvy, are you all right?" She'd pressed tight against the wheel so she could wrap her warm hands around his icy ones. So alive, but she wouldn't be for long—and neither would he!

He focused on the distant sounds, tried to gauge his mindpath, not let it blunder wide, though he'd do that if he had to, sweep every mind to find who he wanted. *"Eadwin! King Eadwin, sir! It's me, Davvy McNaught. Not a man yet, but working on it. Oh, be careful, sir. Don't get near a woman called Hylan, crazed flat gray eyes and an amber cloak, elegant once but ratty now. And look out for two men, one called Tadj and the other Baz. They want you dead, too!"* He'd encountered another mind, a receptive mind, he could tell, from the way the warmth swept round him. Confident and strong, a bit flashy, even. He smiled, bit his lip. Must be Arras Muscadeine, had to be.

"Davvy, you imp. What have you gotten yourself into?" Except, except Muscadeine didn't seem to be taking him seriously, dismissing it as a joke.

"They want to kill the king, rid the world of Resonants. They're going to sacrifice me and Lindy first. And that's not fair, 'cause she's not a Resonant. She's special, I think, but not that. If you don't believe me, ask Hru'rul to home in on my 'sending, judge the truth of what I'm saying!" Footsteps crunched around the cart, coming closer.

"Don't think Hru'rul knows you well enough. Will Rawn do? And if you're teasing, Jenret will tan your hide."

A hand slapped him, slammed his face into the wheel's metal rim, blood trickling as his skin split. "What are you doing, boy?" the one called Baz asked. "Staring up and away like that as if you were communing in the distance. The girl was right before, calling you a Resonant." It was the fire-eater! Another slap drove him harder against the wheel, and Davvy shut his eyes, gritted his teeth, kept sending. *"Rawn! Hurry, tell them to hurry! I don't want to die, don't want Lindy or the king to die! Don't let the king come anywhere near . . ."* The next blow knocked him out cold.

"Well, come on, Tadj. Let's get them untied." Lindy shrank back from the silver crescent blade that flashed at the ropes. Even in the uncertain light she recognized his face, wondered how she could ever have thrilled to his act. Davvy had been doing something, she wasn't sure what, but she had a suspicion from their earlier conversation. She thought furiously. If she heard and saw real people in her dreams, could she make them dream her? She began to concentrate with all her might on the pregnant woman she'd dreamed of before. After all, if she were already looking for Davvy, mayhap she wouldn't mind looking for her as well.

She walked docilely all the way, both wrists locked in Tadj's hard hands, her bones feeling as if they were being ground to powder, while the one called Baz tossed Davvy over his shoulder and followed along, whistling. She wished M'wa would come, M'wa would fix that man so he never whistled so jauntily again. And Bard, what he'd do to them . . . ! Well, they couldn't seem to find her, so she'd count on the dream-lady, the dream-Doyce. After all, she needed Lindy. She was going to have her hands full with twins.

Jog-trotting after M'wa, content for him to lead the way, Bard barely glanced where he was going, distracted by thoughts of Lindy, where she was, how she fared. He knew he traversed a forest of tents, all too reminiscent of the impromptu field hospice set up after the battle between Marchmont and Canderis. And with that, thoughts of Byrta, dead, dead. Not Lindy, too!

He almost overran M'wa, did step on his tail as the ghatt abruptly halted to avoid a barking terrier in their path. M'wa acted distinctly put out, both at being trod upon and at being accosted by a canine. **"Parm's new messenger,"** he sniffed. **"Conversing with a dog is limiting. But Parm's having problems keeping Harrap under control. The best I got out of ..."** a certain distaste as he uttered the name, **"Barnaby was 'Harrap sprawl, crawl, drug-thrall.'"** And he rushed after the dog.

The dog wriggled between canvas tent flaps, M'wa following. Bard lifted a flap, not sure what to expect but horrified to see Harrap sprawled naked on the ground, Parm trying to drag a blanket over him. Breathing raggedly, the Shepherd heaved himself on all fours, began to crawl toward the open flap, his shoulder butting Bard's leg. "Harrap," he squatted, forced the Shepherd's shoulders back until Harrap finally raised his head to see the obstruction, his pupils pinprick-sized. "Harrap, what's the matter? How can I help?" He shook the massive shoulders, "Harrap, it's me, Bard." The tent's walls entrapped a scent he'd never encountered, rank, sickly-sweet, densely pungent. It made his stomach churn; it churned worse when he realized the odor emanated from Harrap, could smell it on his hand after touching the sweat-glazed shoulder.

Despite the length of their separation, Parm didn't wait for an invitation to mindwalk. Guilt and exhaustion edged his 'speech. **"He's babbling about the cart where Hylan keeps the drug. He's knocked me over three times. I've scratched him once."** Striking a lucifer and lighting a lantern on the tent pole, Bard saw the livid scratches across Harrap's forearm.

"Parm, you had to stop him," he said absently. "Harrap, it's Bard, do you remember me? Blessed Lady, but you're a mess."

Mumbling, Harrap plucked at his Lady's Medallion, but it slipped through lax fingers. "Lady bless ... Blessed Lady. Lady Hylan must bless me again. Sacred ... sacred. Lady Hylan takes on all forms." He clung to Bard's knee, wheedling, cajoling. "Bless me, Lady?" He slid down and Bard carefully disentangled his foot.

M'wa stalked around the tent, glaring at Barnaby, who followed at his heels. **"Best heat some water to mix with the salt."**

He'd wondered why he'd been ordered to bring salt, had been forced to snatch a salt box off a grill stand as he plunged through the crowds. *"What's the salt supposed to do?"*

"Make him throw up. It's what Barnaby had me do, it helps." Parm lay beside Harrap, head between his paws, body limp.

"When did he last have the drug?"

Parm lifted his head to Barnaby, clearly asking for guidance. **"Before supper last night."**

"Then it won't do any good to make him throw up, there's nothing in his stomach to get rid of, it's all in his system." Bard yearned to pace like M'wa but lacked enough room. His head was aching, his own stomach heaving. *"We'd best find a eumedico."* The problem seemed too complex, he wasn't sure where to begin. He couldn't even find Lindy, let alone help Harrap!

Drawing back to avoid Barnaby's nose, M'wa began dissecting the problem. **"We either have to get him to a eumedico or bring a eumedico to him. I vote we get him there—faster than searching one out, then returning with him. Find Harrap some clothes. Heat water while you're looking, make cha."**

"Do you think it'll help Harrap?" He was grasping at straws now. Oh, how he wanted to help, have something turn right. He'd lost Byrta, lost Lindy, lost Harrap.

"I don't know about Harrap, but you need it. You haven't eaten since that mid-morning snack."

Bard left the cramped tent, relieved to act rather than think. He kicked a campfire to life, swung the kettle over it, and began rifling through strangers' belongings, looking for something large enough for Harrap. Without a doubt M'wa was right, he couldn't transport a blanket-wrapped man through the streets, and a different attire would at least make Harrap less immediately recognizable as a Shepherd, especially if Lady Hylan, whoever she was, should see them. After much rummaging he found a pair of outsized pantaloons and a sagging brown sweater that looked as if it would stretch. Good, a watch cap to hide his tonsure. Hastily he brewed cha, liberated sugar, and spooned it in with a liberal hand, poured two mugs.

Surprisingly, Harrap drank it, and Bard struggled to dress him. Barefoot would have to do, he decided as he fruitlessly searched for Harrap's sandals. **"Look out,"** he heard M'wa and Parm shout, and turned to see Harrap duck between the tent flaps.

Knees pumping high, Harrap sprinted through the maze of tents, intent on escape. For the life of him Bard couldn't imagine where he'd gotten the energy to run but suspected that the drug had commandeered Harrap's body. He caught up, grabbed Harrap's arm and dug in his heels, felt himself dragged along. "Harrap, damn it, stop! It's Bard. Tell me where you want to go, and we'll go together. No need for running." He didn't care what he promised, doubted it mattered, wasn't sure what words lodged in Harrap's brain.

The Shepherd slowed momentarily, focused a cockeyed, gladsome smile on him. "Bard! Dear Bard, how's Byrta, where is she?" Doubling over as if he'd sustained a blow, Bard retched the half-cup of cha he'd gulped down.

"Damn it, Harrap," he roared savagely and raced after him, anger making his vision blur red. "Damn it, Harrap, she's dead. You said the prayers over her!" Huffing, chuffing, mouth slack, Harrap ran toward the silent siren call. Again Bard grabbed him, tried to halt him, but Harrap's strength seemed almost superhuman.

The ghatti and dog had caught up, springing around Harrap, trying to trip him, bring him down. **"Hit him,"** Parm sobbed, gasping for breath. **"Hit him. Knock him out. If he finds Hylan's cart he'll kill himself if she isn't there to measure it out."**

Letting go of Harrap's sweater, Bard ran ahead and cut in front of him, set himself. Knew Harrap couldn't help it, couldn't remember Byrta was dead, but to be reminded of it like that made his world crash anew. He swung upward with

everything he had and slammed his fist into Harrap's jaw.
Harrap rocked back on his heels, then crumpled forward.

**"Best get your shoulder under him while you can.
You'll never be able to lift him off the ground,"** M'wa advised.

The weight was awkward, incredibly heavy, more than
he'd ever carried before. But rage engendered by Byrta's
death fueled his strength, as did thoughts of Lindy, alone and
missing, thoughts of a dear friend enslaved, ravaged by his
compulsion.

❖

"Do you think they'll bow? I think they'll bow." Eadwin
rode with Arras Muscadeine on his right and Ruysdael's
mayor on his left; to Muscadeine's right, Darl Allgood, and
to Talley Remaire's, the mayor's left, Jenret Wycherley.
Jenret had hastily sponge-bathed at a brief stop just before
Ruysdael and was now attired in a spare shirt of Arras's,
orange-crimson with black slashes on the sleeve. Over it he
wore his black sheepskin tabard for warmth and to make
himself immediately identifiable as a Seeker and a fellow
Canderisian.

**"You look like an overblown poppy, smell like one too
from that pomade. What was it?"** Earrings flickering,
Rawn sat tall and supercilious on the pommel platform. **"At
least they'll recognize me if they don't recognize you in
that getup."**

Guardians lined each side of the roadway to ensure that
the throng stayed in place, while a line of Muscadeine's soldiers served as a buffer between the Guardians and the king,
other mounted soldiers strung behind them, overseeing the
rest of the procession and their supplies. Harder at night, and
Jenret didn't envy either Guardians or Muscadeine's forces
their task of protecting the king and other Marchmontian
worthies. Too easy to mistake an innocent gesture in the
dark and shadows, the harsh torchlight; equally easy to miss
a threat.

*"Well, Wycherley, do I take Eadwin's bet or not? Deprive
him of his money, puncture his pride?"* It seemed almost unfair to Jenret, impolite, deceitful to converse in mindspeech
like this, thoughts flying over poor Remaire's unsuspecting

head while they smiled, waved at the people. Especially when the thoughts were faintly condescending, insulting.

"And we two have never done that?" A high, arching stretch and Rawn subsided.

"But people always know we talk to each other. With Resonants they aren't sure whether the words will issue from their mouths or connect mind-to-mind without warning. They really don't understand the proper protocol for Resonants to 'speak Normals—it's something we'll have to work to explain. And enforce," he added belatedly.

"Wycherley," Arras growled, *"do I wager or not? Do you want a piece of it with me? Make Eadwin deed the castle to us when he loses."*

Ophar dance-stepped, nudged the mayor's mare, nearly butting her into Eadwin's white stallion and sandwiching the mayor in the middle. He smiled nervously at Jenret and fought to control his horse. "Sorry," he told the mayor, "Ophar's a bit fractious because we've been separated." Best string together some trivial chatter with Remaire so he wouldn't feel outnumbered—although, havens knew, the poor man assumed he had Darl Allgood, High Conciliator, as an ally, a Normal. He spared a moment to answer Muscadeine. *"Before you wager, what instructions have Ignacio and Ezequiel been imparting to the welcoming committee regarding proper protocol for meeting a king?"*

"Damn all, Eadwin, I'll take the bet, but if you've tricked—"

A crow of mindlaughter as—in unison—the town's notables bent at the waist precisely fifteen degrees off stiff perpendicular and shot bolt upright again, nervous smiles pasted on their lips. (*"They bowed!" "That wasn't a bow, that was a nod!"*) They waited, Jenret judged, just beyond the city limits. He recognized Ruysdael's Chief Conciliator, Will Smith, could tell the All-Shepherd of the Flock from his robe and pectoral, the resident eumedico by her white coat, and recognized at least some of the other men and women of substance—merchanters, manufacturers, farmers. Eadwin halted and dismounted, waited for the other four to join him, and walked forward, hand outstretched.

Introductions, stilted pleasantries, pomp and circumstance as they warily mingled, conversing in fits and starts as a band of children, literally a band, stridently mangled various marches on a collection of trumpets, slide horns, fifes, drums, and a set of dented, dimpled brass cymbals. *"Will they ever run out of air, out of strength?"* Muscadeine's teeth flashed whitely under the sweeping mustache, and the youngest trumpet player gave a shriek and took off, running.

Darl Allgood strenuously pumped hands, talking as quickly and as loudly as he could to put everyone at ease, though he lapsed into mindspeech as he caught and comforted the child. *"Not a good start, Muscadeine, intimidating children. Parents up in arms before you know it."*

Instantly contrite, Muscadeine dropped to his knee before a girl clutching lavender and white mums, Marchmont's colors, and held his hands to his breast, then opened them suppliantly to receive the flowers. The little girl leaped away, used the bouquet to fetch Muscadeine a long-armed blow on the head, and indignantly jerked the flowers out of reach. *"They're meant for the king, Muscadeine,"* Jenret advised. *"Don't steal her shining moment."*

People laughed at the scene, Normal and Resonant alike, giddy with relief that the initial contact had gone off without mishap. And by mishap, all knew that they meant something far worse, far more unspeakable than an overenthusiastic if unmusical band, a child nearly deprived of her moment of glory.

As if to make up for that, Eadwin stood still, unassumingly regal yet elegant in trim salmon trousers, a dove gray coat topped by a short, darker gray cape lined in lavender with white facings. His thin gold circlet glinted in the torchlight as he beckoned the girl to him. "My daughter," whispered Remaire, clutching Muscadeine's arm, radiating a sunbeamish pride. Like the mayor, she was equally blocky and plump, dark blonde hair skinned tight in two matching plaits with pink bows that Per'la would have died for, Jenret judged. Crinolines flew as she bowed, offering the crowd behind her an unexpected perspective, and presented the bouquet to Eadwin, her round face solemn and adoring.

Eadwin sniffed them appreciatively and bowed back, plucked one flower from the bouquet and returned it to the girl, but not before kissing her hand and the flower. "Something to press in your scrapbook to commemorate this historic event. I hope you'll hold in your heart my devotion to you and to your land."

But Jenret didn't hear what else Eadwin said, although he feared the girl might melt at his feet, her doting father following suit on Muscadeine's arm. Muscadeine stood rigid, head canted skyward, his original smile fading as he concentrated harder. Then, *"Let me borrow Rawn, Wycherley. I need his help."*

Rawn? One didn't exactly borrow one of the ghatti like a cup of sugar or an extra egg, and he was about to protest, except that Rawn was already at Muscadeine's side. His green eyes widened and his head bobbed once, one foot poised in the air as if set to run, then his head jerked in the other direction.

Jenret's did as well, as some argument or commotion broke out behind the wall of Guardians who separated the town dignitaries and royal participants from the common folk. A ghatt's voice soared out of the blue, totally unexpected. **"Jenret, it's M'wa! Make them let us through, it's an emergency."** And tumbling over and through that plea, another familiar voice, **"Well, you see, but then mayhap I didn't mention, by the way, Wycherley, Harrap and I've had the most horrible—"**

Trying to work his way through without annoying or alarming anyone, Jenret found the knot of Guardians doing their best to halt a maniac intent on breaking through their lines by using another man as a battering ram. His face obscured by the man slung over his shoulder in a fireman's carry, he threw himself at the line again, slamming them with the solid and ample posterior of the man being carried. Perplexed by the strange assault, the Guardians were doing a creditable job of blocking the blows, feinting with their pikes, slamming interlocked shields at ground level to keep two ghatti from breaking through. Tired of the charade, M'wa launched himself over their heads and slammed onto Jenret's shoulders, and Jenret took two quick steps to steady himself. *"Hullo, M'wa, back in the thick of things, eh?"*

"Make them clear Bard and Harrap through, it's crucial." The question of including Parm didn't arise as Parm himself levitated overhead, a somersaulting tricolored flash of fur that landed with a thump at their feet.

"Harrap needs help! Get a eumedico!" A quick shake and he groomed his shoulder vigorously, too overcome to say more.

His tap on a sergeant's shoulder nearly swept Jenret into

the fray, the Guardian assuming he was being attacked from behind. "I'm Seeker Veritas Jenret Wycherley!" he shouted, finally managed to call attention to his tabard. "You're holding back a fellow Seeker, Bard Ambwasali, and a Seeker-Shepherd, Harrap." If Harrap had a last name, he realized with a sudden pain, he didn't know it, somehow thought it had been relinquished with other worldly possessions upon becoming a Shepherd. It seemed important to know, now more than ever. A little dog yapped ferociously, darting at the Guardians' feet, nipping and snapping.

"Don't look like none such to me, but if you'll vouch for them as your friends, I'll let them pass." As Bard staggered through with Harrap, Jenret had to admit the Guardian was right. Kneeling, Bard gently deposited Harrap at Jenret's feet, folded the Shepherd's hands across his breast, then abruptly rose. Bard's tabard was absent; he bore a crusted, bloody nose, the swollen beginnings of a black eye, and other marks of battle. Worst of all was an explosively lethal expression that Jenret gauged as just a step short of his berserker mode, when all evidence of compassion and civility fled to escape a cold, killing fury. He'd last seen it when Bard and Byrta had fought for their lives.

He grabbed Bard by the shoulders, shook him hard—at his own peril, he knew—and then hugged him tight, as if he could force sanity back into him. But Bard didn't erupt, marginally relaxed and focused on Jenret's face, nodded once and stepped out of the embrace. "Harrap's been drugged, damn near poisoned to death. And when I find the person responsible for addicting him . . ." his voice broke and he coughed.

Harrap, face greenish-white and an odd sweet-sour smell clinging to him, moaned and stirred, eyes half-opening before they rolled back in his head. The carefully folded hands began to twitch and pluck at nothing while Parm huddled miserably at his side. Shocked beyond belief at Harrap's wan, dissipated looked, Jenret urgently mindspoke Dwyna Bannerjee's help, blessed her comforting reply.

But Muscadeine's mindvoice crowded his brain with an equally sharp urgency. *"Wycherley, I need you. There's an emergency. It could mean danger for Eadwin."* Promotion to Defense Lord from Chevalier Capitain had made Muscadeine no less arrogant or demanding, especially when it involved his king. He'd made his way close enough to speak aloud now, and did, after recognizing Bard, finally registering Harrap's supine figure with growing dismay. "You've called Dwyna, haven't you? Good." Urgency overrode compassion. "Don't want to say much aloud, not here. But you all should know, a child's been kidnapped—"

"Have you had word, have you found Lindy?" Bard burst in, hands locked into Muscadeine's flowing sleeves as if he'd rip them free. "The poor little girl's—"

"Girl? Jenret, what's he talking about? I've had word from Davvy McNaught that he's in danger, and Eadwin as well, possible assassination by our old friend Hylan Crailford." He swung on Bard. "What happened between Harrap and Hylan? Has he been able to say anything, give any indication? Do you have any idea where she is right now?"

Jenret stood-stock still, torn by conflicting loyalties. Damn all, there was no question—Harrap looked at death's door, while Muscadeine worried that a rumor might knock at Eadwin's. Rawn trotted up, greet-sniffed Parm and M'wa. **"Let me sort out the facts because you're facing interconnecting problems here, puzzles that are part of larger puzzles. Davvy's been kidnapped, along with a little girl he called Lindy."**

Bard marginally brightened at learning someone knew her whereabouts. Danger he could cope with, but not danger in disguise—a missing child, a drug-mazed friend. He hoped Dwyna Bannerjee, the cinnamon-tinted woman in the white coat who now bent over the Shepherd could bring back the Harrap he knew.

"Apparently Hylan coaxed Lindy along with her and Davvy followed, then was seized himself. From what Davvy's overheard, Hylan plans to kill the King of the Resonants, Eadwin, as she refers to him. I was able to get a fix on Davvy's mindvoice before he was knocked out, so that's where we'll have to start."

Relaying the information to Muscadeine did nothing to improve his mood. He slapped his riding gloves against his palm, emotions chasing across his face. "Wycherley, I don't have the right to command my forces in your land except in protection of my king. So we'll have to use your Guardian forces, some of them at least."

"But you've no right to give them orders."

A wolfish smile, the same one that had momentarily terrified the little musician. "No, but Darl Allgood undoubtedly can, he's acting for the Monitor. I've called him and Faertom and that fellow—the one that brought you in—Garvey, is it? Three Resonants who look and dress like ordinary Canderisians, which is exactly what they are. I've got Yulyn Biddlecomb doing a mindscan for Davvy since she knows him best of all." He stood, feet apart, radiating confidence, though Jenret sensed the torment buffeting his mind.

"Most of all, I don't want Eadwin or anyone else to know of the possible danger, especially if we can thwart it. I've a plan, but you must understand, I *have* to remain with Eadwin, that's my duty. He can know about the children being kidnapped, but nothing more—and only that if it's absolutely necessary. Wycherley, I ask you as an upstanding Canderisian citizen to remain with me to guard the king. Besides, I know you want to stay with Harrap. I understand, commend you for it." He caught Bard's eye. "Stay or go? You've reason to go, the child needs finding."

Rousing at the sound of his name, Harrap lifted his head, brushed feebly at Dwyna Bannerjee as she tried to set an injection into a vein in his arm. "Hylan—goat cart," he wheezed. "Cart at campground," and his arm flailed, knocking Dwyna away. "Not hurt children! Parm, go! Show them where!" Dwyna slipped the needle in and pushed the plunger and Harrap's sense melted away again.

"What is it? Do you know what he took?" Bard whispered.

She swung her black braid angrily, her bracelets jangling. "I've no idea yet. I was planning on asking you. If I only had a sample I could tell more, decide what might counteract it. All I'm trying to do is strengthen and steady his heart right now."

"Mayhap we can get you one," Muscadeine mused, "if it's stored at that cart Harrap mentioned. Have a Guardian bring some back."

Faertom and Darl Allgood came together, Garvey from a different direction, nearly veering away when he caught sight of Faertom and Jenret. "Good, you're all here. Now let me outline the problem. And the plan. I want Eadwin safely moved into town to the central square where the festivities are to take place and we can reinforce the protective quadrant around him. By the way, Wycherley, do any of your people know any quaint country folk dancing? Something

entertaining that doesn't involve children and trumpets? I
want anything I can get to distract Eadwin."

While the roads out of Coventry had been deserted, the
roads leading into Ruysdael were crammed with wagons and
carriages, riders, and those afoot, all funneling into the city.
Traffic had slowed to a crawl or worse as people stopped to
picnic, gossip with old friends. No rush, no real rush, this
was a day and a night to come of tentative celebration, or at
least a time to witness a scene of epic proportions and importance. More than once the white mules had proved fractious as the afternoon wore on, backing in their traces,
lunging and snapping at jostling neighboring teams. Tired
and drawn, Cady constantly strove to anticipate and head off
the mules' stubbornness as twilight fell.

" 'Bout as patient and forbearing as their owner, Mr.
Adderson," Inez sniffed, wedging her way between Cady
and Doyce on the seat. "Good thing I'm small." An age-
spotted hand clamped down on Doyce's left hand, dragged it
away from her mouth. "And don't go chewing your nails
'cause it doesn't gain us a thing. Now get back with Francie
and let me show Cady how to drive. Mostly, where to
drive." Gathering the reins, she chirruped to the mules and
began inexorably easing them right, forcing an adjacent carriage to yield. "They'll close off the main road soon to clear
the way for the king. Can't get in the front door, try the
back. Brickyard Pond Road."

Unwilling, indeed, unable to argue, Doyce swung around
and slipped into the wagon bed, leaned against Francie, eyes
unseeing. Damn Ruysdael, damn it! Invading her brain like
that. All she could think of was the past in Ruysdael, children in danger. Not just Davvy, but a little girl as well, so
like yet unlike Priyani. And what would happen to her
would be a quicker end than Priyani's but equally perverse.
She blinked hard, snuggled against Francie, and ordered her
mind to think about Now. Jenret, what he was doing, where
he was, how he fared. Usually a good, righteous bout of anger at Jenret would snap her out of her funk. Her back ached
and she was so tired, but she didn't dare sleep. Her whole
body felt as if it were clenching and unclenching, and she
flexed her hands in time to it. Lady bless, she'd skin Davvy

alive when she got her hands on him, even if his intentions
had been good.

She sighed, dozed as they picked up speed, the road narrowed and hummocky but at least traffic-free. The rhythm
rocked like a cradle and she slept. Two children, hand in
hand, lost alone in a pit, cried piteously to her in the dream.

"What's that over there, that crowd of people?" Francie
asked her mother in hushed tones and Doyce awoke, picking
straw out of her hair. Khar's head popped out of the straw
where she'd nested.

They'd reached Ruysdael from the back, the section of
town where manufacturers and merchanters kept their ware-
houses, a mill on the pond, its wheel ghost-gray and still
against the night sky. Something was missing, although
Doyce couldn't think what. The people in the distance, at
least two hundred milling like ants, then somehow stilling,
reorganized into orderly ranks, some of them seemingly disappearing. The absence finally caught up with her. "I
thought the brickyard was there," she pointed at the winking
torches, harsh compared to the light of the stars and the
moons.

"Was," said Inez. "Burned down ten years past, built a
new one cross the pond. Only thing left here is the cellar
pit."

"Stop!" Impulsively, Doyce grabbed her mother from behind, hands over hers to control the reins. Cady turned and
looked at Doyce as if she'd lost her mind. "I want to see
what's going on."

Inez wriggled and bucked, Cady rescuing the reins as
mother and daughter tussled. "We're here to find Davvy,"
her mother reminded, "not go gallivanting around at anything that takes your fancy. If you'd been awake and listening, you'd have heard the cheers and yells and trumpets.
'Spect the king arrived not long ago."

"Meaning Davvy's likely in the thick of it," Cady
groaned.

"I don't care! I said stop." Why had this unreasonable
stubbornness swept over her, sweeping all else aside? "I
have to get down." Inspiration seized her. "Go to the bathroom."

"Use the pot, Doyce. That's why we brought it." Inez
wasn't about to brook any excuses.

With a cloaked, considering smile Francie swung her cane

to shift herself, and a cracking sound was heard. "Oh, dear, I think I knocked it over and broke it," she apologized, whispering, "You owe me, Doyce. I don't know what's up, but it had better be good. You've got a look about you that means trouble."

She kissed Francie and rolled off the tailgate as Cady pulled to a stop, Khar following after her. **"She's right, this had better be good. I sampled that dream, too. You're just getting crotchety and worried this far along in your term."** The two children had worried the ghatta as well, but she'd guessed they symbolized the boy and girl Doyce carried, still unaware there were twins. Vesey had manipulated Doyce's dreams and Khar had been unaware of it, but she'd never known anyone else with such an ability—or such a bent—to do so. Whatever Doyce had dreamed had been completely innocent—and true.

Dropping all pretense of finding a spot to relieve herself, Doyce marched straight toward the lights. Her whole abdomen felt tight and cramped, as if a giant hand squeezed her. The last thing she needed was this sort of tension and worry with the baby so near due. "I don't know what's going on there, Khar, but whatever it is is wrong somehow."

Khar shivered as she trotted beside Doyce. Something *was* wrong, she was just beginning to register it. What scared her most was that Doyce had discovered it long before she had. She strained for Davvy's mindvoice; even when he didn't use it there was a faint vibration to him. No use. The air was abuzz with mindvoice emanations, flowing and crackling like sheet lightning. What did she expect? If Eadwin had arrived, there'd be Resonants aplenty in the vicinity. The thought of Eadwin brought Hru'rul to mind, and she debated contacting the ghatt, letting them know they were here. No, best wait, whatever happened she needed all her concentration on Doyce right now, and it was hard, because the ghatten shoved and heaved inside her, her flanks expanding and contracting. **"Not now,"** she scolded. **"Wait,"** and they quieted as she purred to them.

They'd arrived at the outermost torch ring, but no one seemed to pay them any heed, all eyes fixed inward and downward, people swaying, craning for a better view. Few noticed when Doyce tapped them on the shoulder, asked what was happening or if they'd move, but they parted docilely enough, distracted but vaguely realizing a pregnant woman required passage through. Khar scrambled after her, wary of kicks to her bulging sides, all too aware of what the unexpected feel of fur against legs could engender.

The cellar pit no longer had any defined dimensions; its burned-out walls had partially collapsed, shifting outward to create a rubbled incline of dirt and stone that sloped down to what had once been the cellar floor. Spectators sat or stood along the slopes, the cellar pit almost like a natural amphitheater. The light of the torches from below was dazzling, cast up and outward onto the rapt faces of the audience, enthralled by the drama unfolding below. Leaning backward to avoid skidding, Doyce squinted, trying to pick out the figures.

Hell was a nebulous concept to Doyce's mind because the Lady's religion didn't allow for it. Still, it was a word and a concept that had journeyed with the Spacers. Hell was a pit of writhing flames, tormented bodies, an eternity of damnation. But the Lady never damned anyone, offered infinite opportunities for all to improve and refine their belief in Her; if not in this life, perhaps in another. She shifted uncomfortably, pain wrapping her pelvic girdle, squeezing inward until she wondered if she could draw breath. Then it eased and her knees went weak in relief. Amazing what fear could do to you.

Clad in a long cloak that captured the light, reflected it back in honey-bronze tones tipped with orange, a woman appeared in the center of the pit, positioned herself beside a stub-toothed pillar fragment, and warmed her hands over the battered iron brazier beside it as she inhaled the steam rising from a shallow copper bowl atop the coals. She turned deliberately, the cloak swirling around her, and allowed her gaze to rise, at last deigning to notice her audience. Large eyes dominated her face as she engulfed them with her stare, silently inviting them to partake of her private ritual. Her upraised right hand held something Doyce couldn't identify. It looked thin and forked. Toasting fork? Fish spear? An odd thing to wave, but she revised her opinion as the crowd moaned its approval.

From the woman's right, a knot of people separated to reveal a man struggling to drag two children, girl and boy, in his wake. Her breath came tight, moaning as the crowd's, but with dismay, not approbation. The girl battled, fought against the man, tried to bite his wrist before he jerked her arms over her head. The boy seemed to stagger, feet not fully obedient, his expression slack. Davvy—it was Davvy! And a girl a bit younger with long blonde hair and a perfect oval face, graceful as a bulrush next to Davvy's slightly chunky figure. Watching premonition become reality, Doyce's knees gave and she sat hard, hiding her eyes.

"Well, this is Hylan's goat cart." Bard tossed back the canvas, began throwing its contents on the ground as if he'd discover Lindy hiding beneath them. Giving a particularly vicious toss to the last sapling, he rounded on Parm. *"In what sort of container does Hylan store her seasoning?"* He snarled the euphemism.

Parm started forward, froze as the anticipatory longing seized him. Even at this distance the scent turned him weak with desire. I won't be like poor Harrap, I won't! Must be strong for him. **"Little stoneware jar with a cork."** Saliva flowing, he swallowed. **"Barnaby can show you."** He nudged Barnaby, and the dog jumped into the cart, giving M'wa a wide berth. Rooting around he unearthed the jar and Bard seized it, and threw it to a passing Guardian who hurried off with it.

Reassured that task had been accomplished, Darl gestured to the sergeant. "Have the men check the campgrounds, every tent and wagon, every nook and cranny. Remember, they're children, and scared children can jam themselves into impossibly small and unexpected spaces." The sergeant gave a brisk salute and he and his men fanned out at orderly intervals to search. Faertom made as if to join them, but Darl held him back. *"No, they know their jobs."*

"Feels sort of like the last time we rescued Davvy," Faertom ventured, shifting from foot to foot as he watched Bard searching all around the goat cart.

"Would that it were as easy as last time." Darl smiled despite himself. *"All we needed was a fast horse and the stupidity to hurl ourselves between opposing armies and drag Davvy to safety."*

"This is more complicated than that. I know." Faertom looked suddenly older. *"Somehow this is tied together with whether we gain acceptance as Resonants here in Canderis, isn't it?"* He blurted out the next part, *"Killing the king I can*

see—from their point of view. Cut off the serpent's head, they think, and the body'll die. But why take children?" Bard's futile search, more and more frantic, grated on Faertom's nerves. The man looked on the selvage edge of control, his normally golden skin the shallow, dun color of dried mud. Jenret had hurriedly warned of Bard's potential to snap, turn crazed in moments of true stress. All he could hope was that M'wa exercised some control over his Bond.

Darl watched Bard as well, fingers caressing the bald spots that receded from his temples, his center crest of hair rumpled. *"I doubt he can bear to lose someone again. He feels responsible for the girl, to lose her would be to lose a part of the legacy Byrta left him."*

Garvey trotted up, hand cradling something small. Not a young man, he bore his weariness with quiet expertise, not letting it completely drain him. "Is this something?" he opened his hand to show a small barrette. "Found it on the path that leads toward the back of town, I'd guess. Reason I thought it might is that it was dead center of the path, not crushed and trampled. Whoever dropped it was one of the last to leave. Course they could have been heading the other way."

"Bard," Darl called. "Do you recognize this?"

Bard came at a run, snatching roughly at Garvey's hand, managing a brief grimace of apology. "Lindy was given it to wear for the festivities today. Which way?" As Garvey mutely pointed, he raced away. But M'wa was already ahead of him, following a white and brown terrier with flashing legs, nose to the ground, yipping encouragement over his shoulder.

Parm made to follow, but the pace was too much, and he reluctantly dropped back, his skin crawling with longing. Just a taste, a taste to give him strength, let him keep up! No, never again! **"Harrap, I'm no good to them, I'm too weak. Not much better than you are."** He'd 'spoken Harrap all the way, not that it did much good, but it made him feel better. On occasion he'd feel the flutter of Harrap's mindspeech, disjointed, meandering, locked in battle with the demons in his system. Harrap had deserted him, even Barnaby had left him behind. He felt Faertom beside him, stroking away his loneliness and dismay. It almost helped.

"Damnation!" Darl spun to see where the Guardians were, spun back. *"We should have thought of that! The dog's*

Hylan's—knows her scent. We've got to reassemble the Guardians to go after them. Can we gather them in time? They're spread beyond hailing range, and Bard will be out of sight soon if we don't follow."

Garvey settled his belt more comfortably around his canvas smock. *"Are you gentlemen game?"* And to Faertom the words were a taunt, a challenge. *"Wouldn't leave a child, Resonant or Normal, in Reaper hands, and that's who has to have them. For once the hunted can be the hunter."*

But before Faertom could respond to the verbal gauntlet Garvey'd tossed at him, a mindvoice reached him, a mindvoice unlike any he'd ever heard before. **"Carry me, I'm sooo tired. We can bring the Guardians with us. M'wa can follow Barnaby, and I'll stay in touch with M'wa, find out where they're heading. Please, for Harrap if not for me."**

"'Fraid not, Garvey." Faertom hated the thought of not rushing after but knew Parm was right. If only he didn't appear to be cowardly! *"Some eager hunters forget the prey may be bigger, more deadly than they are. Best always to have ..."* he hesitated, *"trusted friends as backup. Parm and I will round up the Guardians, come after you."* Garvey nodded once, began running after Bard.

It took Darl longer than he wanted to catch up, pounding along at Garvey's heels. *"This is insane, you know,"* he saved his breath for running, not for speech. *"Faertom's right. There are logical ways to rescue the children, endanger as few as possible."*

"Mayhap so, in your world, the one you used to inhabit exclusively." Garvey's years of quarry work had left him hard and strong, not necessarily fast, but able to maintain a ground-devouring pace without setting his heart pounding, and Darl envied him that. *"But those of us who've lived as Gleaners, Resonants, trust ourselves to each other, not outsiders. I'll welcome the Guardians when they come, but I won't depend on them or Faertom."*

And Darl Allgood couldn't bring himself to argue with that, not given what he'd seen, what he knew from the past year.

❧

Addawanna slipped through Ruysdael, scarcely noticed by the few who remained instead of joining the crowds greeting the king's arrival. She'd wondered if city earth sounds would offer different news, if city streets had other information to share. With her incredible endurance she'd covered the distance to Ruysdael well ahead of the royal party and had spent the time wandering in the woods, the fields, and now the streets. Most of what she'd needed, she'd found effortlessly, the earth whispering the sites to her, but even it had forgotten the location of one thing.

So she'd searched on her own, found it. She patted the bark packet. Always there'd be some woman who grew it, knew its virtues. An unassuming plant with heart-shaped leaves and bulging, petalless flowers depending from its almost vinelike stem, each one resembling a pregnant uterus and cervix. Late in the season for flowers, but she'd found two withered blossoms, hoped they'd suffice. She might not need them at all.

The earth was telling her too many things, as if it couldn't make up its mind. And if it couldn't, how could she? Strange to be so drawn to these offspring of people from a different world, but then, so had her grandmother, Callis, been. And wasn't her grandson Nakum a part of them himself—cousin to Eadwin the king through her own long-ago liaison with Queen Wilhelmina's younger brother, Ludo? For better or worse these people were on this world, even gradually becoming a part of it. The earth told her that.

Strange, too, that she and Khar had found a bridge to let Erakwa and ghatti communicate, had shared their needs to help save Doyce from Vesey. Never before had ghatti and Erakwa spoken, the ghatti curious but the Erakwa feeling no need, not with the fullness of the earth's powers to sustain them. She touched her earth-bond, ran her fingers over the beading. Inside, along with her bond, revealed to no one because each Erakwan's was individual and distinct, was a clump of Khar's fur. The little Pern-khatt was always with her.

The earth sounds were converging, each one generating its own ripples with it. Soon the ripples would collide, make waves, crash down on one another. She'd headed off one rippling collision by placing Jenret in Eadwin's custody. Yes, tampering, but somehow it had seemed only right and proper. After all, wasn't Eadwin kin of a sort, hers as well as

Nakum's? Oh, not by blood, but by love, by knowing he shared Callis's care and concern for the arborfer. She hoped, but would not ask, that Jenret would give her the arborfer knife he'd found. She could ask, but it had to be given freely. Her earth-bond might suffice to key the herbs she'd gathered, release their full potency, but the knife gave better assurance.

Bored by the streets she moved outward, seen if she chose to be, unseen if she chose not. Yes, the earth spoke of big changes tonight, and she'd best hurry if she wanted to see it. See what these people truly were made of.

With Tadj's help Hylan seated the children on the pillar's base, struggling to chain their wrists to a rusted iron ring protruding from the pillar. The girl screamed, kicked, landed a solid blow to Hylan's shin. She forced herself not to react. Then the boy erupted as well until Tadj cuffed him into submission. A hand on each of their heads she looked at her audience and finally spoke. "Two children, both young, both innocent, both pure . . . or so you think. But let me be the judge of that." She lofted the forked stick with both hands. "I am a diviner, this my divining rod. A special rod because it, too, has known suffering, suffering that made it stronger and more sure of seeking out the source of its pain.

"Some four years past I was given a sign, a warning that those who came from the skies would come again. They who deserted us, abandoned us on this planet, *will* return, wreak destruction on a scale to dwarf our past sufferings! Think what Plumbs did to us in the past—what they or even worse evils could do now?" The crowd murmured, but not as much as she'd hoped when she'd dreamed of this moment. "And who will call to the stars, guide these strangers down into our midst?" Silence. Were they waiting for her—or did they truly not see? Well, she would lead them. "Why the children, of course. The offspring of Resonants who infested our planet from its very first days, Resonants who spoke mind-to-mind from one ship to another. Like calling to like, above and below.

"Our salvation is in knowing them. They cannot hide their faces from us any longer, cloud our minds with their powers." She flourished the rod, its forked ends gripped in each hand. "The witch hazel tells me the true from the false, the fair from the foul, no matter how outwardly fair!" The divining rod poised near Davvy's chest, Hylan fought to control it as it began to weave a pattern, end whipping the air. "You see," she screamed triumphantly. "Now watch." Fighting for control of the rod she jerked it in Lindy's direction and it instantly stilled, remained immobile. "Both must be sacrificed to the Lady to show Her we are earnest in our need." The word warmed her heart. "Sacrifice!"

But where, where was the answering roar of approval she'd heard in her dreams? Where was the response, sibilant and soft, whispered from two hundred pairs of lips, "Sacrifice, sacrifice!"?

Instead, murmurs, coughs, uncertain foot shufflings. Again she tried, voice trembling, cracking. "We *must* sacrifice them to avert the Spacers' return, avoid our destruction!"

A man, bolder than the rest, called back, "Lady Hylan, it's not right to hurt children, even a Resonant child."

Her lips trembled as she cast a pleading glance at Tadj, stationed behind the pillar to guard the children. "What do I do? Why won't they understand?" she whispered, a cold sweat on her upper lip. Why were his eyes boring holes in her like that? What had she forgotten?

His lips barely moved, didn't disturb the fixed smile on his face. "Resonants, Hylan. Resonants, Now, Today—not Tomorrow. Tell them what," a minute chin thrust in Davvy's direction, "he's done to the girl, made her bad. Bad girl, Hylan."

Strange how those words echoed, rippled in her mind, because Hylan had been a bad girl, deserved the whippings, yes, she had! Bad Terra, too, trying to corrupt little Hylan. DA-de-Da DA-de-Da. . . . Her silence had gone on too long, the crowd increasingly edgy, perturbed. No, not Past, but the Present, Now, Today. Forget her Past. Tadj knew, Tadj was right.

A deep, sustaining breath. "Yes, sacrifice, I say. And both of them, the foul and the fair!" She raised her hand to forestall them, quell their dismay. "Because that one," she pointed the quivering rod at Davvy, "has already begun to corrupt the fair," and the rod now jerked at Lindy. And lo, even she could feel the rod's tentative, hesitant stirrings— how had she missed it before? Oh, not as strongly, no, but questing, seeking. With a communal intake of breath, the crowd noted it as well. She was inspired now. "Just as in the short time that he has been with her her corruption has begun . . ." she looked around deliberately, catching the uneasy expressions, "so it will be with your *own* loved ones, *your* children! If the Resonants gain a place in society, they will corrupt *your* children, *corrupt us all!"*

She could feel them following her now, slowly merging with her, a fusion of minds and belief. "We must expunge them from the earth! Kill their Resonant King!" Yes, this was what they wanted to hear. If they could only grasp Today, so be it. If the Resonants were slaughtered, there'd be no worry about Tomorrow—for who'd remain to call the Spacers down? "Shall I sacrifice them?" And this time the affirmation roared back gratifyingly. Yes, ignore the few who slipped away, always the faint of heart, cowards lacking courage for the ultimate challenge.

"And when we've proved ourselves worthy, will not our Lady deliver to us the *ultimate* monster, the foul *beast* that controls them all, their King? Will She not say *crush* the serpent's head, cut it off? For a serpent without a head cannot control his followers, and they will be ripe for our reaping! And reap we shall!" Hylan reveled in the sound of her words, blessed Tadj for forming them, molding her inarticulate thoughts into transforming power. How she'd scourged herself, hoping the power would come, but it had been Tadj who'd shaped her raw longings. The crowd was hers now, hers alone.

Like a lumbering insect, Doyce scooted down the packed dirt slope on her fanny, people so mesmerized by Hylan's words her passage went unnoticed. Easier to shift unthinkingly than tear their attention away from the figure in the center. *"Khar, what are we going to do?"* She'd never felt such deep, physical dread, constricting, practically paralyzing her body.

Khar skidded, sank in her claws for traction. **"Try to reveal the truth to them, but I'm not sure truth will count for much in the face of mass hysteria."** So few minds around her ready to accept truth, the rest shuttered, closed from accepting anything that did not feed their needs. A hunger here, a desperate longing, like with like, no discord allowed or tolerated. **"Perhaps the best we can do is buy time."** How, she didn't know, but she would, somehow. There must be other ghatti in the vicinity, there had to be!

Hru'rul, if Eadwin had arrived, at least one Bond-pair nearby, either as Seeker Veritas representatives at the ceremonies or simply as part of their circuit. How could she have overlooked that? She dared not take her mind off Doyce, but she risked a quick, frantic shout to F'een. **"F'een, raise every ghatti you can reach! Get help!"**

She hurried after Doyce, who'd reached the cellar floor, rolling onto hands and knees to rise. At first no one noticed the bulging figure as Doyce made her way toward the triangle of Hylan, the children at the pillar, and the brazier with its steaming copper bowl. *"What can you find in this woman's mind, Khar? Any leverage, even her own untruths,"* she begged.

She stood, hands clasped behind her back, casting a jutting shadow that wavered in the torches' light. "Excuse me," and Hylan whirled, cloak flaring, its hem scything the children's faces.

"Ah, the faithful crowd closer, believing!" she smiled, love in her heart. "Don't fear, my child, you'll bring your baby into a safe world, a world free of Resonants, my promise to you." She raised the witch hazel rod in blessing and Khar shivered, but it remained perfectly still. It should have reacted to the babies Doyce carried. But then, wasn't it Hylan who truly made it react, based on some primitive, subliminal instinct? But in this instance the instinct was faulty, had been lulled, somehow. Khar had no time to feel relief as Hylan thrust the rod into her belt, but continued delving in Hylan's mind, urgently seeking a clue.

"Oh, I'm not afraid," Doyce forced her voice to carry, enfold the crowd above her, "but I *am* curious."

"The Fifty!" Khar threw the information like a lifeline. **"She was a child, the Fifty-first, their good luck charm, so she thought. Taken along that night of the massacre. May once have exhibited some latent or residual skills herself, but she's scourged them into submission."**

"Yes, curious," Doyce continued, open hands placatory. "You see, I don't know. How are you going to sacrifice them? With a scythe, a sickle?" Hylan backed away, a hand at her throat. **"Terra!"** Khar interrupted. "Like Terra that night so long ago? The scythe sweeping into her ribs," she was repeating Khar's words now, "like Wim and all the rest?"

"Terra?" Hylan's mouth formed the words. "No, no, not like Terra!" She shook her head frantically, conquered the memories, all but a nagging, DA-de-Da DA-de-Da. "Won't the Lady do it?" Hylan looked wildly for support, but everyone was still, even Tadj had a stricken expression on his face. "No, not blood," she elaborated, wanting this woman to understand, a woman blessed with what she'd never had, what Terra'd never had the chance to have. But Terra was bad, didn't deserve it, didn't deserve to live. "I'll mark him," she nodded in Davvy's direction, the girl huddled close. "He shouldn't go to the Lady without being marked for what he is. Then She'll know. The girl as well, don't you think?"

"Like the medallions the Fifty had? Such a special gift from Corneil, weren't they? How you wanted one." Hands pressed against her temples, Hylan reeled at Doyce's words.

"But a medallion can be removed," she protested, "hidden." She held her hands over the steaming bowl as if to cleanse them, then reached for the iron rod thrust deep into the brazier's coals, waved it to show Doyce. "Just a little burn, a little crescent shape. It won't wash off, can't be hidden. You shouldn't send something like that," she spat in the children's direction, "to the Lady without a reminder, should you?" she appealed to Doyce.

"You're depending on the Lady a great deal, aren't you? That She'll accept your sacrifice and then send you the king?"

Hylan nodded eagerly. "Oh, She will, She will! She transforms all, gives everything another chance. Just as water turns to steam, then air. Or earth turns to coal, then fire."

"Will you sully your hands with the Resonant King's death, or must She do that for you as well?"

A lone ghatt mindvoice rode the night, seeking, searching, worried beyond measure but not letting his Bond sense his fear. **"Hello? Hello, I am F'een, Bond of Cady Brandt. I seek one called Hru'rul, Hru'rul the Magnificent."**

He perched on the wagon seat, oblivious to Cady's constant pacing, indecision racking her. Distraction would hamper the contact. Khar had entrusted him with finding help, and what he'd read in her mind had been dire. Find the one called Hru'rul, likely to be closest. F'een knew the direction; if he had no luck there, he'd broaden his search, sweep through the quadrants, send his mind as far as he could until someone answered.

Besides, truth be told, he hero-worshiped Hru'rul. Stories already circulated amongst ghatti in training about the magnificent Hru'rul. His astounding looks—his thick ruff, tufted ears, and large furred feet, his stub of a tail, sacrificed to a hawk before his eyes were open. His devotion and loyalty to Eadwin—sharing his hard-caught food, going hungry himself—and all this before they had even truly Bonded!

He owed it to Davvy, too, felt guilty about letting him go like that. Davvy had wanted to contact Eadwin, so the next best thing F'een could do would be to contact Hru'rul, the king's Bond. He took a wispy breath, cold night air stinging his nostrils, and pressed harder, upward and outward just as Mem'now had instructed. **"Hru'rul? Are you there? You are needed. Help me, please."**

"Who you?" the voice 'spoke, almost flattened F'een with its powerful eagerness, like a good-natured cuff. **"What be wanting?"**

"I be ..." he broke off, corrected himself, the ghatt's compressed dialect contagious, **"I'm F'een, Bondmate of Cady Brandt. We've been assigned to protect Davvy McNaught, Doyce Marbon, and Khar'pern from danger. But the danger's more all-encompassing than we anticipated. Your Bond is in danger as well. Will you send help? Are other ghatti near?"**

"The beautious Khar? The sweet Doyce? In danger?" F'een quailed at the mindgrowls that reached him. **"Me tell Eadwin, tell Rawn and Jenret, everyone. We come. Already looking for Davvy."**

"Rawn?" F'een went rigid, wondered if his stripes had paled. **"Rawn and Jenret, are they with you, are they all right?"**

"Being fine but grumpy. Drop mindvoice short, other ghatti being close to you, too, namely Parm and M'wa. You know?"

He knew *of* M'wa, but had never really 'spoken him. As for Parm, he'd heard of him as well, the jester ghatt and his unprecedented second Bonding. **"Thank you! Hurry!"** He let his mindvoice sail high and wide in a shout of jubilation and relief.

Not far away Per'la jolted upright on the gig's bench, hackles rising. **"Saam, wake up!"** she nudged the steel-gray ghatt, poked at his face. **"Can you hear it?"** But it had faded, and she wasn't sure who had 'spoken, couldn't get a fix on it again. Waving a handwritten pass from the Monitor, Mahafny and Parse were arguing with a Guardian to let them through the cordon into Ruysdael.

Cady paced the length of the wagon, back again, caught on the horns of a monstrous dilemma. Doyce hadn't come back, and now F'een had informed her that Davvy was in the cellar as well. Every moment F'een spent searching for the other ghatti delayed her, delayed her duty. But what was her duty? To protect Davvy and Doyce—but how could she leave Inez and Francie alone?

As F'een blinked she made her decision. *"Come on, we're going after them!"*

"But wait, I haven't finished—"

"I don't care what you haven't finished! Come on!" "I'm going after Doyce," she announced and tossed her sword to Inez, who laid it across her lap.

" 'Bout time, girl. I've told you you need to make faster decisions."

Easy for Inez to say, but Cady wore the Novie green trim on her tabard. Still a beginner, still learning. No way to respond to Inez's remark, so she shrugged, went loping off before she was offered any more advice. "Always choose your terrain for a fight," her instructor had drilled into them. *"F'een, which side should we try?"* She suspected Doyce had descended the western slope, the one with the gentlest slant, as if it had been used to bring drays up from the cellar when workmen had removed anything salvageable after the fire. The other three sides were steeper, precarious to traverse, although they were all equally crowded with people. A fighter on the upgrade had the advantage over a downhill opponent, but once she started down, others would have the advantage over her. Well, steeper meant quicker as well, so the south slope in front of her it would be, and she plunged over the edge.

"Cady, we can wait, we don't have to—" But F'een realized Cady wasn't really listening to him, didn't care that he'd managed to contact M'wa as he ran at her side, knew that others were coming, Guardians as well. A roar rose from the pit—"Sacrifice!"—and Cady started to shove her way down, F'een tight behind her, exasperated yet exhilarated. After all it was his job to guard Cady, mindwarn her of danger, protect her back. And if she wouldn't listen to him, he'd have a great deal of protecting to do.

The same cry that sent Cady plunging to the rescue transfixed Inez and Francie at the wagon. "What does it mean?" Francie whispered as Inez clicked the sword hilt free of its sheath.

"Don't know yet, child, but suspect it's not good." And at the sound of running feet Inez drew the sword clear while Francie brought her cane up in her good hand. "Mayhap they'll not notice, run right by. Now hush."

A small white dog veered in their direction and bounced a frenzied greeting, springing beside the mules. A kick in his direction and he yapped his dismay, tumbled clear, crashed into a black and white ghatt who'd been following in his wake.

A voice snarled, "Damn, I knew we should never have followed that dog! First a rolapin, now this! Parm was mad to think the dog could lead us to Hylan."

M'wa washed his face, chagrined. Barnaby had been right and he'd refused to listen, had ignored Parm's entreaties to trust Barnaby, pulled them all offtrack instead by bullying the dog. If it hadn't been for F'een's mindshout, they'd still be running wide.

"Who be ye?" Inez shrilled, standing in the wagon bed, waving the sword. "What ye want? Speak quick or I'll skewer ye!"

"I could ask," a puffing sound, "you the same . . . question, ma'am," another panting gasp, "though we don't plan on skewering you. I'm Darl Allgood, High Conciliator for Wexler." And Inez realized that two other men approached the wagon from different directions, hemming them in. He watched the older woman whisper something quickly to the younger one, saw her head swing round, searching, then shake her head in the negative.

"What're ye doing with a ghatt? Don't see no Seeker garb amongst ye." The sword was trembling in her hand. "My Doyce always wears her tabard, excepting for now when it won't fit."

"Are you Doyce Marbon's mother?" The lithe, honey-gold man had slipped closer, eyes pleading. "Is Doyce truly down there with the children? Where are they, where's Lindy, have you seen her?"

"Don't know about any Lindy, son, but Doyce's looking for a little boy, Davvy McNaught by name." He'd pressed closer as she'd spoken, the ghatt by his side, and she could tell he meant her no harm, appeared to labor in the grip of strong emotion.

"Well, then, what are we doing up here?" A squarish, ugly man had joined them. "I'm Garvey, ma'am. If they're down there, that's where we should be."

"And isn't that what I've been thinking? I don't know you gentlemen, but you're just the perfect escort to get me and Francie down there." An imperious finger crook in All-good's direction. "You, sir. Unharness those mules. Me'n Francie should be able to ride down the slope unless you'd like to piggyback us."

"If you'll just be patient a bit, ma'am, we've got Guardians coming right after us. They may be enough to make a difference, we're not."

Inez whacked the wagon's side with the flat of her sword. "Would you leave your baby down there on her lonesome if you heard people chanting 'Sacrifice'? Cady and F'een are on their way down, and I plan to be there, too. Right, Francie?"

Garvey shot Darl a condescending look. "Let Faertom bring the Guardians down. No reason we can't invite ourselves to the party early."

Arras Muscadeine waved to the fiddlers to begin another reel, and breathless dancers re-formed their patterns. He'd not been joking to Wycherley about quaint folk dances, and he'd prevailed on the mayor, Remaire, to invite a few of the town's young people into the heavily-guarded central square where the evening's final festivities were taking place after the formal welcome at the city limits. He'd hurried Eadwin and the rest through with no dawdling, Eadwin faintly puzzled by his hand on the bridle, urging the royal mount along. Now he'd formed a defensive square, each of the four sides double-layered and dependent on Guardians for the outer wall. Whatever might happen—or not—he felt more confident in the city itself, not vulnerable to charges down the roadways or across the fields. Besides, any danger must pass through citizens still reveling in the streets outside the fortified square.

A messenger thrust a note at him and he read it impatiently, asked for a description. Yes, a red-haired, garrulous fellow, missing his right leg. Fine then, it was Parse, not an imposter, someone holding Mahafny hostage to get inside the defenses. He couldn't be too careful. "Bring them in." A deep relief that Mahafny had arrived, perhaps she'd know what to do about Harrap. He'd tried to shrug it off—things happened in war and this was perhaps another sort of war—but he felt an abiding guilt about having made Mahafny send the Shepherd after Hylan.

"Your aunt's just arrived. And Darl and the Guardians have reached the goat cart and are searching for the children," he told Wycherley.

Jenret ignored the second half of the report, having heard precisely the same thing from Faertom. But the first part was a relief to hear. He'd left Harrap in the hospice, Dwyna and the resident eumedicos poring through herbals, pharmacopoeias. If only Mahafny knew something that would help. Arms folded across his chest, hands practically lost in the billowing folds of the orange-red sleeves, he tapped his foot impatiently in time to the music. How Davvy had gotten himself into this fix, he'd love to know. Not to mention what Bard was doing in the company of a little girl. He concentrated on watching, searching for danger.

Eadwin hurled past him, a slightly bemused smile on his face, and was snapped back into the arms of his partner, a more than energetic and muscular young Ruysdael woman. Rather like one of those snail-curled paper whistles that children played with—blow on them and they unfurled themselves, only to snap tight again. The young dancers had lured some of the Marchmontians to join in the dance. Lysenko Boersma skipped, nimble as a flea, while Valeria Condorcet and her daughters seriously copied the patterns taught them. Ezequiel, auburn hair swinging like a girl's, capered by, arms intricately knotted with a young woman's who teased him about his drooping hosen. It all looked so innocent and merry.

The music came to a halt, the signal for dinner, trestle tables being set up in the square for various dignitaries. Muscadeine gestured Jenret to follow with a select few to the mayor's substantial, two-story red brick house for a private dinner. Ministration Lords Boersma and Condorcet, Muscadeine, Eadwin, and himself, plus anyone from Ruysdael whom Remaire thought deserving of the honor. Or those exceptionally unflappable about breaking bread with Resonants. Ignacio and Ezequiel hurried to help direct the servants.

Once inside the door and away from prying eyes, Eadwin stumbled, almost dropped in a faint. "I'm not feeling well," he apologized, "it must be all the excitement."

To Jenret's eyes the mayor looked paler than Eadwin. "But he hadn't even eaten yet!" Remaire blurted. "It can't be poison!"

Hand on sword, Muscadeine rounded on him. "And were you planning to poison him?" "No, no!" the mayor kept gibbering away.

"Easy, Arras. Call for Dwyna." Jenret took pity on the mayor, eased him away. "Have you a room we can use?" And following Remaire's quaking directions, Jenret and Muscadeine eased Eadwin up the stairs while the remaining Marchmontians soothed the other appalled, outraged Canderisian guests.

Once safely inside the room, Eadwin stopped short. "Precisely what have you been keeping from me, Arras?" There was no brooking his tone, a ruler to one of his subjects. "Hru'rul's been telling me about some extraordinary goings-on. I've a right to know."

Arras straightened, arms rigid at his sides, as if on report. "About what, sire?"

"About the fact that two children are missing and possibly in jeopardy?"

"That's correct, sire. We're taking measures to rescue them. Nothing to concern yourself about, the situation's under control or will be shortly. Won't it, Wycherley?" he appealed.

Before he could answer, Eadwin looked at him with pity. "There's more, Jenret. Hru'rul says Doyce is here as well."

But Rawn was running toward him, 'speaking as he came, confirming Eadwin's tidings. **"Faertom and the others haven't found the children yet, but Doyce has! She and Khar are with them, trying to convince Hylan Crailford**

not to sacrifice them." He skidded to a stop. **"Coming, or do I have to do this by myself?"**

Grabbing blindly at Arras and Eadwin, he tried to push by. "Doyce found them, but now they're all in danger! Let me go!"

Eadwin locked onto his arm, slowing him down. "What better trade for two children and a pregnant Seeker than a king, don't you agree, Wycherley? My Lord Muscadeine? That was the other little thing—the plot on my life—you neglected to mention, wasn't it?"

"Sire, I forbid you to go—"

A snap like steel, "You forbid me nothing, Muscadeine. Now do you plan to tag along, or do you want to stay here while Jenret and I go rescue Doyce and the children? I'm sure the dancing will start again," the quirked smile flashed. "You'll enjoy it."

"Sire, you can't!" But Eadwin and Jenret had already slipped down the back stairs toward the servants' quarters, grabbing cloaks from pegs and donning them for disguise.

Muscadeine stood immobile at the top of the landing, face suffused. Eadwin 'spoke back, *"Either come along, Arras, or reconcile yourself to breaking in a new king. I doubt Nakum will prove any more biddable than I. You'll be up there cooling your heels and more on that icy mountaintop trying to grow arborfer!"*

With a growl, Muscadeine rushed after them, joined, just outside the door, by Dwyna Bannerjee. Her bracelets tinkled as she sleeked back her hair, swung her braid over her shoulder. "You never know when you're going to need a eumedico until you need one," she murmured. "Best insurance not to is to have one around. There's nothing more I can do right now for Harrap. Mahafny's with him double-checking everything."

Mind in a whirl, Jenret shoved them out the back door before a startled servant realized what was happening. Doyce, so close! *"Oh, please, listen for me, darling. I'm coming, don't worry!"* He doubted his message would do any good, but he so craved to reassure her that he was here, was coming. The baby—of course, he could contact the baby!

"You wouldn't dare after last time, would you?"

But Jenret was already reaching, seeking the consolation of that little mindvoice—voices? he still wasn't clear about that—hoping it, they, would calm Doyce, allay at least some of her fears. He had the strangest vision in his mind of two tiny bodies, curled tight and compact as lima beans, heads pointed downward, constricted beyond belief. Was Doyce carrying wrongly, what was it? He probed and tried to cajole them into speech, but they were silent, the pressure increasing.

"Leave off! Don't get them started now!"

The pain clamped around her, bore down on her, and she gritted her teeth, rode it through. No more, she ordered herself, hold off, you have to hold off. Do you want to deliver in public like this? A man with burnished blond hair darted toward Hylan, both of them eyeing her with unconcealed dislike.

"Tell me it's false labor," she begged Khar as the crushing pain faded and she began the count under her breath.

"If it were, we'd all be happier. Your timing's exquisite," Khar paced, and to Doyce's eyes, still blurred with pain, it seemed as if her stripes jounced. **"Just pant and puff at Hylan and mayhap you'll scare her away. Try 'whooo! whooo!' and she'll think you're possessed."**

Most of all the ghatta didn't dare reveal that Jenret was near, approaching quickly. If Doyce lost her concentration, the situation would spin out of control. Damn Jenret anyway for interrupting like this! And what, in the name of the Elders, was Cady Brandt doing pushing her way down the slope? Didn't F'een have better sense?

Once clear of the house, Eadwin, Jenret, Muscadeine, and Dwyna Bannerjee slipped into the mayor's stables, Eadwin chuckling softly when he realized that Muscadeine's defensive square included part of the long, brick stable on one side—no soldiers or Guardians stationed behind it. Commandeering horses, they rode swiftly through the empty heart of Ruysdael.

Striped stole trailing behind her, Dwyna nudged her horse against Jenret's. "Do we know where we're going?"

"Yes, in a way. Hru'rul and Rawn pinpointed F'een's location, took different bearings on it, too, so they crossed.

They've relayed the information to Parm and M'wa as well."
He smote his thigh, his voice anguished, "It's almost mad,
as if we've all been playing blindman's bluff, never realizing
others were near enough to touch. I should have known
Doyce would find her way into the midst of trouble, Davvy
as well. As for Bard and Harrap, trouble seems to have
found them."

"It happens," Dwyna said gently.

"Oh, I'm often guilty of acting first, then thinking, but I
swear it's become contagious." He rode in silence for a
moment, then confessed, "I even 'spoke my unborn child,
children, before I considered the consequences."

"How far along is Doyce?" Dwyna asked, her profes-
sional interest piqued.

"She must be due very, very soon. The babies looked all
crowded and tight, upside down."

"You *are* a fool. I hope you haven't upset them. This
close to time you can induce labor if you excite them too
much." Dwyna gave him a disgusted look. "I've never yet
met a man who understood what it's like to give birth."

The audience had grown increasingly restless, the spell
dissipating as nothing happened. Coughs, murmurs, foot
shufflings, the desire to be swept up in the glory again, to be
made a part of the whole still existed, but for now they were
slowly separating. A scuffle just at the top of the west wall
was distracting attention, people milling, some striving to
get clear, some wanting to be closer. Do something! Tadj
told himself. Hylan had to seize control again. Worst of all,
he couldn't see where Baz was any longer.

He tugged at Hylan's arm, whispered hoarsely in her ear.
"Do something, Hylan! Make the king come to us, we can't
continue waiting like this. We're losing the faithful, their
minds are drifting! Don't you understand? I don't know who
this woman is, but I don't like it, she's distracting them."
And distracting Hylan as well, throwing her off course, confusing her, making niggling doubts surface like slow bubbles
rising in mud. Baz was still here, watching, waiting, wasn't
he? This was his chance to make an impression on Baz, and
it could so easily fall to pieces in an instant.

"But . . . ?" Hylan's face puckered with thought. "The

Lady will take the children to Her, won't She? Not refuse an offering of this magnitude?"

"She'll take them," he promised. She'd take them if he had to Reap them himself! So proud, honored by the small-scale silver sickle Baz had made with his own hands, presented it to him just before he'd brought the children out. He'd secreted it behind the pillar, ready if he needed it. The children were the key to attracting the king. "Hylan," his voice soothing, exhorting her, bolstering her determination. "The children are our staked lambs. Make them bleat, make them draw the king to us. Make the boy, especially, bleat his little heart out. Brand him," he urged. That should do it, if not, killing him certainly would, his dying mindcries carrying to the king.

Arm wrapped around her lower abdomen, Doyce watched and waited, praying her head would stay clear, her body obey. There was no way she could rescue the children and run, not in the midst of two hundred people. **"Just buy time. Every distraction buys more time."** Khar advised, then winced. **"Cady just manhandled someone in her path a little too strenuously. His friends are objecting to his treatment. Oh, dear, she and F'een are in for it now."**

"Cady?" Grimacing, Doyce waited as another pain gathered itself, then halted. *"She should be up there protecting Mother and Francie! Not down here!"* Don't think about it, don't. Other things to think about. *"Well, what I don't have at the moment is time."* She exhaled in relief as the pain momentarily ebbed. *"Unless you think having the baby here and now ranks as a monumental distraction. The idea's been suggesting itself with increasing regularity. Besides, who'll rescue us—besides Cady?"*

"Well, it's not the cavalry, but it's a start." She nosed Doyce. **"And F'een says a Guardian squad is on its way, should be here soon."**

She realized she heard the clop of hooves, the shuffle of bodies cautiously descending the sloped side of the brickyard cellar. A moan trickled through her lips—cavalry it was not. Bard—where had *he* come from, what was he doing here?—though she thrilled to see him and M'wa. Behind them, the white mules bore her mother and Francie, towering above—oh, dear Lady, was she hallucinating?—Darl Allgood and a man with a smashed-looking face she didn't recognize, leading the mules. A terrier dashed ahead of them, then froze and let loose a howl of woe. Nothing to do but pinch herself, wake herself from one outrageous dream, and slip back into the nightmare she inhabited on the cellar floor.

M'wa sounded gruff. **"Thought you might enjoy company. Is the little girl all right?"**

Khar answered back, **"If I'd known you were near, I'd certainly have invited you. The girl's fine for the moment, how long, we'll see. Same could be said for the rest of us."** The party had reached the floor by now and stood still, gauging the situation.

Hylan's eyes darted, agitated, unable to determine what it all meant. And in desperation Tadj found inspiration. "The Lady's Disciples, the Apostle moons are taking human form to judge if our plans are worthy, Hylan." He pointed excitedly, "Look, five already! When all eight appear, She'll accept our sacrifice, bring us the king so we can stop the Spacers." He crooned now, intimate and low, "Brand the boy, Hylan, brand him so the Lady will know he comes!"

Tadj *believed,* he believed if no one else did! Not like that pregnant woman, questioning, questioning, making Hylan question herself, making Hylan lose her audience's attention. It didn't matter—one true believer like Tadj was enough. How could she have been so sinful, so prideful to want more? Bad Hylan, greedy Hylan, always wanting what others had, never satisfied. But Tadj was hers, deservedly so, earned through scourging and penance!

Eyes wide and blank with exaltation, Hylan pulled the poker from the fire, its tip glowing a dull red, and brandished it at the boy. "Now just a moment there," a voice insisted, and Inez Marbon dismounted into the arms of the broken-faced man beside her mule. "I want to be crystal clear what's going on. Lady knows, it's best not to have mix-ups, misunderstandings. Wouldn't begrudge someone that, would you?" She navigated the broken flooring, elbows sticking out from her sides as she trotted along. Gave Doyce a surreptitious pat in passing, whispering, "Grit your teeth and hold on, we're trying."

Awed by this manifestation of an Apostle, Hylan swept into a curtsey and Inez stopped, nonplussed. "We must mark the boy, show he's a Resonant, so that Our Lady knows, doesn't mistake our need. You'll intercede for me, for us," she indicated Tadj, "won't you?"

"Our Blessed Lady never misunderstands." Inez was beside Hylan now, staring at the poker. "Here, give me that thing," and reached confidently for it. Tadj tried to grab it back, but Inez fended him off with the glowing end. Pulling it back, practically under her nose, she examined it. "So, being marked by this makes you a Resonant?" She slapped the heated point against the fleshy heel of her palm, held it there without flinching, lips clenched. "Oh, dear, must mean I'm one as well." The poker swung outward, and Hylan raised her hands, but not quickly enough to ward it off. "Oh, my, must mean you're one as well."

Hylan whimpered, cradling the burn to her lips. The pregnant woman gave her a look of compassion. "You never had a medallion from Corneil, but now you have this to remember them by." No, no medallion, no Terra. DA-de-Da DA-de-Da.

Inez's actions had been so surprising, beyond the pale, that no one had been able to move, stunned, unsure what would happen next. Too, moving would have broken the spell, the pattern that Inez had created. At last, legs cramping, body throbbing, Doyce started forward, as did Bard, Darl, and the rough-hewn stranger.

But before they could reach their goal, the pillar with the chained children, Tadj pushed Hylan aside. High and shrill as a whistle, his voice stopped them cold, "Lady, Blessed Lady, I send to You these children," and pulled Davvy's head back, flourishing a small silver sickle at Davvy's throat. The boy screamed then froze as the blade touched his flesh. Baz? Where was Baz? Would the Resonant King appear?

"No need of that, surely." A cloaked and hooded man stood at the top of the cellar foundation, threw back his hood so the torchlight reflected on the narrow circlet of gold around his forehead. "Not when the Resonant King has come to offer himself in exchange."

"Yes! Welcome!" Tadj exulted, shooting both arms high in the air, brandishing the sickle. It had worked, oh, it had worked! Yes, let all eyes see Eadwin in his Resonant splendor, fair yet foul, revel in the anticipation of his death! Baz would be so proud. Where *was* Baz, he hadn't left, deserted Tadj in his moment of triumph? His euphoria dimmed. No, so hard to judge what was happening, the king arrived at last, yet some of the faithful fleeing, rushing to avoid trouble; others watching, avid and unmoving. And some, yes, some, rushing down the slopes to the floor, eager to help, eager to partake! Yes, there was Baz, striding toward him, gesturing to other Reapers to follow!

"Shall I come down to you? I'll be pleased to—once the children are released."

Tadj nodded magnanimously. After all, the children had been Hylan's fetish, not his. Her with her mystical notions of outer space, danger from without. All he wished to do was cleanse the land of Resonants any way he was able. The children, especially the boy, could be dealt with later, when they swept up the remnants.

A noise intruded behind Tadj, an orderly "hut, hut, hut," and he managed a glance back to catch a horrific vision of Guardians cresting the lip of the pit, struggling to maintain a wedge formation as they traversed the steep north slope, slowing and dividing the scrambling crowd. They were led by a tawny-haired lion of a young man in civilian dress and carrying a tricolored ghatt. The young lion put the ghatt down and raced toward the pillar, shouting as he came. Tadj had a horrible, sick feeling of certainty that there were other cries he wasn't hearing as the craggy-faced man wheeled and started in his direction. He should *never* have relinquished his grip on the boy! A hand at his elbow brought him back to sanity. Baz! Baz had come, wouldn't fail him, wouldn't let them fail!

Bard, Faertom, and Darl struggled to release Davvy and Lindy, until at last Darl pushed the others aside to concentrate on the chains. Holding Lindy close, Bard heard her say, "Don't let them hurt the king! Did you see, Bard, his crown's lopsided." Sobbing, she drew as far away from Hylan as the chain allowed. "Hylan lied—she wanted to hurt the king!" Faertom comforted Davvy, the boy whispering furiously in his ear, urgently pointing.

He was pointing, Tadj realized, not at Hylan or him, but at Baz. But now Baz slighted him, took note of nothing but the balding man working at the chains, deserting Tadj, walking forward as if in a trance.

"No!" Baz's agonized cry split the air. "No, Darl, no!
Don't help them, stand by me, it's not too late. Together we
can conquer them all!" Bazelon Foy rushed across the floor
to Darl Allgood's side. "Don't forsake me! Help me make
the land safe from these wretched Resonants."

Darl's hands never stopped working, though he cast a re-
gretful glance over his shoulder. "Baz, I'm sorry, but I'm
one of Them, a Resonant. If you hate them, you hate me.
Unless you can finally learn to stop hating."

"You're lying, Darl! Don't toy with me, test me like this!"
Baz pleaded.

❧

Unregarded, ignored at the center of the activity as if she
no longer had any relevance, Hylan plucked the divining rod
from her belt, hugged it to her breast, stroked it for solace.
It trembled like a live thing and she continued stroking, felt
its abrupt tug and surge in the direction of the balding man,
and she watched it as if the very hand and the rod belonged
to someone else, a stranger.

Face contorted with the dawning surety of betrayal, the
dark-haired man cried, "Darl, it *is* true! You *are!*" Strange,
she'd not really seen the dark-haired man's face in the
gloom by the goat cart, but now, in the torchlight. . . .

Hylan's mind dashed from one confused image to another,
past and present coalescing, shooting bright sparks, sparks
that illuminated, sparks that burned. Sparks burned through
the fabric of the past, and she stared through the charred
holes.

That night, that happy, celebratory night, Terranova and
Wim and Corneil and all the others. Then the terror, the
grief, the sorrow, her mind locking down on it. The evil had
been in the repression, not the remembering. Corneil had
been wrong to try to help her that way. Nor was she bad,
evil, just a confused child who'd never quite grown up.

Swaying, pressing the rod to her temples, she tried to separate it out, Then and Now, Now and Then. Sickles Then,
sickles Now—where had Tadj gotten it, didn't he know she
hated them, even a child-sized silver replica like his?

"Darl, you deluded me, made me think I was less than
you, less worthy, less good, when all the time you were the

deceiver! Oh, how you must have laughed to think you had Hosea Bazelon's grandson at your feet!" A knife in his hand now, raised high and menacing, torchlight bright on knife, on face.

The world slowed for Hylan, stretched before her. That face, that name! Hosea Bazelon! The man who'd tried to kiss her hand earlier in the evening, the one who'd talked with Tadj. How could she have not seen? Had sensed it in the recesses of her mind but refused to believe, to see. "HO-se-A BAZ-e-Lon, HO-se-A BAZ-e-Lon!" No, No!

Oh, Blessed Lady, and that young man, the one who'd stopped at her house, whom she'd sensed was a Resonant, the one who looked so much like Terra. Here he was, or was it Terra come back to guide her? If not in this life, perhaps in another? Were they all coming back? The burly man with the ravaged face wrestled with Bazelon now and he had eyes so much like Wim's. But he couldn't protect Terra any better than he had the first time. She watched the knife take him under the breastbone as he raised his hands desperately toward Bazelon's temples, saw his hands fall slack, his knees sag. No, she wouldn't fail Terra and the rest this time. Why was Terra pushing toward Hosea Bazelon as he closed the space between himself and the balding man? Couldn't Terra see Hosea had a knife, Hosea would hurt Terra! He'd already hurt Wim! It was all the same, it was all repeating itself, the night poised to turn blood-red again!

"Hosea Bazelon, you cannot!" she screamed and rushed toward him, jabbing the divining rod at his face, his eyes. Cursing, Bazelon grabbed at her wrist with his free hand and, straining with effort, flung her headlong at the pillar. Her feet stumbled, trying to catch up with her body, and she tripped on the pillar's base, falling between the children's upraised hands, the rusted iron ring bolt driving into her temple, into her brain. A dog howled in misery, rushed to her side, frantically licked at her face, her hands.

"Tadj! Help me! Get the other one—Darl is all mine!" Baz shouted as he tried to right himself after flinging Hylan away. Where had that damn ghatt come from, rolling and clawing at him, under his feet? He kicked, drove the point of his boot into the calico ghatt's ribs, lofted him clear. But Faertom was practically on top of him now, hands reaching toward the knife, ready to rip it away from him to protect

Darl. He backed slightly, trying to find an opening, feint around Faertom to reach his target, his goal. No longer could he be mocked, deluded! Yes, he'd go through the young man now, remove one more obstacle from his path, destroy it and everything, everyone else if necessary! "Tadj!" he screamed again. If he must do everything himself, he would, not brook defeat, have Darl snatched from his revenge, his sweet revenge for that betrayal. He brought the knife up hard, rammed it under the young man's chin, watched him falter and fall, even as Baz pulled the knife free. Another step backward, just to get clear of the obstruction, give himself space to maneuver. No one between him and Darl now, no way to escape.

The kick took him behind the knee with no warning. Where? What? The boy? The boy chained to the pillar had stretched clear as far as he could, had kicked him, his tear-streaked face a mask of concentration. Damnation! "You little wretch, little demon! Resonant spawn!" Knee buckling, off balance, he threw himself forward, uncaring. Darl, stupid Darl, holding out his arms to him as he stumbled, as if to catch him, embrace him. He drove the knife home in Darl's heart with a deep, abiding satisfaction at its rightness, the justification of it all as Darl slumped against him. Falling now, falling if he weren't careful, couldn't get his balance, so unfair when the balance was finally tipping in his favor, showing he was right. Darl's dead weight dragging him down, just as it had in the past, though he'd never realized it. Twist away, twist out from under that dead weight and he would rise, rise triumphant! And just as he rolled to the side to get clear of Darl's encumbering body, Tadj desperately, awkwardly swept the sickle sideways toward where Darl had stood just moments before.

Screaming a warning, unable to stop the sweep of his arm, Tadj watched the silver sickle caress Baz's beautiful throat, the throat like a smooth, olive-tinted column. Watched in fascinated horror, as if an alien hand wielded the blade. Oh, blood! Oh, Baz! his mind screamed silently as he fell to his knees, staring at his bloody hand, the dripping sickle. Beauty obliterated. Drop it! Let it go. Don't touch! Who to blame, oh, who to blame? He hadn't done this, not Tadj, no! Hylan dead, Darl dead, the one Hylan had called Terra dead as well. Blame? He looked up blankly, caught the boy's burning eyes on him, his triumphant glare. Oh, Hylan had the right of it, the child was evil. Baz had been right calling him a demon, Resonant spawn! All his fault, all his. If the spawn hadn't kicked Baz, none of this would have ever happened! Never!

But another part of his mind screamed for self-preservation, to run away as fast and as far as he could, away from the carnage, away from the boy's malign influence. Tadj scrambled away on hands and knees, not feeling the blows, the pain as he was kicked and shoved by passing feet.

❖

The cellar floor seemed to swim before her eyes, swarming figures, screams of rage and lamentations, exhortations. And in the mist of it all, Doyce Marbon collapsed to her knees, rolled onto her side, breath coming in harsh, short pants, her whole focus centered on the explosive pain of a baby demanding to be born. Now. *"I can't hold back anymore,"* she groaned to Khar, *"it's coming too fast."* Second pregnancies rarely followed the long, tortuous process of a first delivery, and she'd felt her water break longer ago than she wanted to remember.

A foot bruised her shoulder, but the pain was a mere distraction, a minor insect bite against the waves of pain that swept through her, but it made her shout aloud, "Jenret!" *"Jenret, dammit,"* she screamed in her mind, *"this is all your fault!"*

Miraculously, Bard was at her side, a serious-looking little girl in tow. "She's bad, far along," the child said, placing her hands on Doyce's stomach. "Coming faster than Mama ever came."

Bard tried to scoop her up, arm beneath her shoulders, the other beneath her knees. "We've got to get her out of here before we're all killed! Darl and Faertom and Garvey are already dead." The urgency of the unborn twins' tiny mindvoices was shaking him to the core, tearing at his heart and mind, making him sick with worry.

"Don't think you can move her now, no matter what." Lindy stripped off her coat, stuffed it under her head as Doyce arched back, teeth sunk into her lip.

Khar was stretched beside her, her own flanks heaving. **"Leave her be, there's something even greater being born."** Her head tilted in a silent cry that unnerved M'wa. **"Just find Jenret."** And M'wa nodded, sent out his mindcry and stood guard.

Standing behind Eadwin, sword drawn, Jenret heard Doyce's mindcry, knew Muscadeine, Eadwin, and Dwyna had faintly heard it as well. The cellar pit was being rapidly surrounded now; more Guardians and Marchmontian soldiers streaming in, much to Muscadeine's relief. He'd mindcalled for reinforcements as soon as they'd left the mayor's house, regardless of Eadwin's wishes. He gestured for them to let the people fleeing the pit through, drain some of the mayhem clear, like lancing a boil, but still a red-hot throb of activity surged at the center. Whether the crowd would dissipate quickly enough to ensure Eadwin's safety and help Doyce and the others, he wasn't sure.

"Dear Lady, she'll be trampled, the crowd's going wild, some fleeing, some fighting. Go to her, Jenret," Muscadeine urged, roughly shaking his shoulder. *"She's called for you, though I've heard sweeter love calls. Eadwin and I'll have the Guardian squad down there cordon her off from the fighting—there's enough of them for that but not for much else. Best they get used to taking orders mind-to-mind."*

Jenret plunged down the slope, Dwyna behind him, her eumedico satchel in hand. No way for him to see Muscadeine's wistful look, though Eadwin did. Yes, Doyce wanted Jenret, and rightly so, face the facts, man! She was never yours.

"Beloved," Khar implored. **"Soar with me, take the pain and soar with me through the Spirals."** It was the best she could offer as Doyce's pain became her own, as her own pain invaded Doyce. **"Concentrate, beloved!"**

And Doyce bore down, felt the pain tear through her, ripping and shredding her flesh and soul, tried to fly, not to flee it, but to ride on it. Soar? How could one soar on mangled, torn wings, but she pumped higher and higher, Khar cajoling, urging her on. Other voices encouraging her now, other ghatti, some she knew, some she didn't, and a dimly familiar voice feathering her brain, laughter chiming, bracelets chinking. Dwyna? Dwyna Bannerjee?

But she didn't have time for that, she labored upward,

bouyed by Khar's encouragement, mingled with Khar's pain. Yes, she would soar. *"Bear down now, that's right,"* Dwyna's voice encouraged, *"The next one will come easier."* Next one? Next pain? No—why could she hear the thin squall of a baby?

She seized control of her mind—after all, wasn't pain something the mind could control, override if it had to?—and with each downward thrust she let herself spiral higher, mind reaching eagerly out to survey everything it could see. Pain and exultation, touching on every mind around her, rippling out from that like waves, touching and touching and touching. . . .

So many minds, some known, some strangers to her. Past Jenret's with a whispered endearment, all she had time for, because he was beside her now, but only her body was there. Mahafny, near but not near enough, looking up from Harrap's bedside, her face touched with wonder, and Parse's with surprise. For a moment Harrap sensed her presence, felt the craving fade. Swan, in the distance, sinking closer to death, but still not giving up, smiling as she felt Doyce's mindtouch like a benediction. Her mother and sister, clinging to each other, the livid burn mark on Inez's hand turning pale, healing.

And with pain as her vehicle she drove it forward, intent on reaching her goal. "A boy this time," a child's voice cried out, but another voice interjected, *"She's started to hemorrhage, an artery's torn."*

The pains had eased but she was weakening, starting to drift off of course as Khar encouraged her, lofting her higher. Well, if her body couldn't keep up, her mind could, and she reveled in the joy of following after Khar, surging past and beyond her. **"Ah, beloved, not too high or you'll crash."**

And all around Doyce, around the laboring figure, people stopped short, Resonant and Normal alike, Reapers and Guardians and average citizens, all felt a touch of the mighty battle being waged in one woman's mind and body. The will to live and love as her body pumped its lifeblood on the already crimsoned ground. Some quaked in fear, praying a brave soul would live. Others stood cheering, urging her on, all of them caught in the same web of passion and pain, and it spread slowly all across Canderis as people stopped in

their tracks, looked upward at the night sky as if they could
see her soaring there.

"Hurry, Khar," she begged, gasping. "Don't leave me
now."

"I'm coming," she heard faintly from behind.

"Welcome," the voice said, others echoing it, "Wel ...
wel ... come ... come ... come ... come."

She smiled to herself. "So, Kharm, beloved of Matty, we
meet at last." Hands closed gently on hers, "And Matty as
well. Did you return to Coventry? I never read that far, I'm
sorry. Strange for us both to be from the same little town, yet
so many years apart."

"Yes, I did, but we can save that for later." She strained
to see him, see him in reality as she had seen him in her
mind, the straight, serious brows, the dark blue eyes, the
boyish face firming into a hard-won adulthood. "You came
seeking answers to questions, though I'm not sure you found
any answers to help. I'm sorry."

He was translucent, she was looking right through him,
but then, her hands seemed equally clear. "No, the journey
itself holds half the answer, at least. Your journey wasn't
easy, but you did it."

"Then you think you can help people come to terms with
each other, Normal and Resonant?"

"You managed to make them come to terms with the ghatti
and their powers," she persisted. "All I can do is try as hard
as you did."

"Time to return now," Kharm purred in her ear. "Poor
Khar'pern couldn't spiral all the way, but she does have
two of the loveliest little ghatten you've ever seen."

"Ah," a relief, that, to know that Khar was fine, "is it
easier going down?" Soar on broken wings, land on mangled feet. Falling faster now, faster and faster, no control, no
control at all! But she didn't care. Speed was needed.

❖

Jenret pressed his fingers against Doyce's carotid artery,
caressed her clammy brow with the other hand. "I'm losing
it, Dwyna," he warned. "It's weaker and weaker. Hurry, for
the Lady's sake!"

Arms blood-soaked to the elbows, Dwyna Bannerjee
worked between Doyce's thighs, probing inward and up-

ward. "I'm trying! I can see where it's bleeding, it's clear in my mind, but I can't get in to clamp it. Can't reach!"

"Try harder!" He would not lose Doyce, he would not—not after all this, not after he'd barely found her. She towered above him, beyond him in goodness and strength, and he needed her for his soul's completion.

Dwyna caught Eadwin's and Muscadeine's gazes from where they'd been shunted to the periphery with Bard, safe inside the Guardians' ring. Wincing, Muscadeine tucked his bloody sword behind him, silently cursed Eadwin again for abandoning the relative safety their forces offered at the top of the pit, insistent on dashing below to see if they could help. The young Seeker woman they'd nearly crashed into on the floor of the pit had been unarmed, but she'd been brilliant at hand-to-hand combat, had managed to snag the bridle of a braying, kicking white mule ridden by Doyce's sister, so he'd gathered. The mule hadn't been half-bad support either. It had a natural talent for letting its heels fly at an enemy, and Doyce's sister had sent two potential threats reeling with blows from her cane. Her handicap hadn't crippled her feisty spirit.

"Can you reach her mind-to-mind?" Dwyna begged Jenret.

He shook his head, "She's involved in a conversation beyond this life. I can't break through to her."

Arras whispered, "I think she's the strongest Resonant ever born."

Dwyna let out a groan. "It's no use! I can't put any pressure on it! I can't reach!"

"Mayhap I can. I've got smaller hands," Lindy crouched at Dwyna's elbow. She shook her long, blonde hair back, pushed up her sleeves.

"Absolutely not! Your hands are filthy. I can't risk infection on top of everything else." The girl rubbed her hands on her dress, looked imploringly at Bard. Stripping off his coat and wrapping it around his hands, Bard went to the brazier, removed the copper basin, its water still steaming. He knelt before Lindy and she winced, began methodically washing her hands, making little sounds of dismay at the water's penetrating heat.

"But you can't 'see' where to reach, only I can," Dwyna despaired. "She can't take much more fumbling around inside, I've done more than enough."

Davvy held Lindy's shoulders. "I can tell where it is, guide Lindy's hands through my mind."

Swiping her brow with a bloody forearm, uncaring, Dwyna wondered wearily when children had become eumedicos. She didn't care, anything was worth a try. "What you do when you reach it is—" she started to explain.

How the Erakwan woman had broached the defensive circle, Dwyna didn't know. She only saw Addawanna staring compellingly at Jenret, as if willing him to do something. Mouth agape in amazement, Jenret freed one hand and pulled a knife from his boot top; Dwyna stifled a scream of surprise. "I believe this belongs to you, your people. Forgive me, I forgot I had it."

Addawanna accepted the knife with a grateful smile, touched it reverently against a small birch bark packet. Suddenly the scent of growth, of the earth, filled the air. "Whad you do is press dis gainst it, hold it dere hard til Addawanna say 'nough."

Now Dwyna had had enough—ghatti 'speaking her, transmitting Mahafny's chivying advice, desperate suggestions, children interloping on her domain, and now this, this Erakwan woman with a smelly, disgusting handful of pulverized . . . something, she didn't even want to think what. Totally unsterile, unidentifiable, twigs and leaves to carry and hold infection. "Absolutely not!"

The black ghatt, Rawn, stared her down. **"Do it. Mahafny says trust Addawanna."**

And damn Mahafny for ordering her around like this from a distance—she wasn't on the scene, couldn't judge the gravity of the situation! She was a Resonant eumedico, surely knew better than a Canderisian eumedico dependent on physical, not mental talent. "I don't care what Mahafny wants!" With shock Dwyna realized that both Rawn and Hru'rul had bared their teeth, hissing a clear warning. Before she could muster further protest, Eadwin and Arras had dragged her clear. Chastened but still determined to exert at least a modicum of control, Dwyna nodded unwilling permission, and the girl seized the contents of the packet, plunged her hand inside Doyce. "Do I want to know what that is, Addawanna?"

"Neh. Mebbe someday Addawanna get round 'splaining to you. Eumedicos don' know ebry-t'ing."

The crimson tide pumping from between Doyce's thighs slowed, ebbed to a trickle, finally stopped.

"Dat be 'nough, Addawanna t'inking," and Lindy obediently pulled out her small hand. "No movin her fer while."

EPILOGUE

Doyce snugged the plaid lap robe closer and swung slippered feet onto the chair across from hers, looking guiltily to see if anyone would scold her. So many people had surrounded her, fussing and bustling for the past two octs, that she couldn't do a thing she wanted to do. But tonight she was almost blessedly alone—if you didn't count two infants content in their cradles and a ten-year-old nursemaid sound asleep on a couch. She might, just might, have time enough to finish the last chapter of the Bicentennial History of the Seekers Veritas. A wave of laughter came from downstairs, Jenret holding court with the last of the guests from the naming day celebration.

The babies roused and stirred, made eager little grunting sounds. *"Davvy, stop that this instant! The babies are settled and Lindy's exhausted."* Blast the boy! The infants recognized his mindvoice, reacted when they heard him "tweaking" them. It had taken her time to realize that that was why they'd often been so unsettled during her pregnancy when Davvy was anywhere near.

An unrepentant, *"Sorry!"* floated up to her.

"You're hardly alone when I'm here," came a muffled voice from the closet. **"These ghatten are insatiable, they never stop nursing."**

"When they fall asleep, come out and keep me company."

But the last few lines of the history eluded her, so she doodled instead. So wonderful to be back in their stone house on Headquarters grounds, she and Jenret and the babies.

"And your mother and Francie and Jenret's mother Damaris and Jacobia and Syndar Saffron and ... need I go on?" Khar sounded equally weary of visitors.

"Well, we had to invite everyone for the wedding and the naming day." She'd been moved back to Gaernett by slow,

easy stages an oct after the babies' births when Mahafny and
Dwyna were confident she wouldn't bleed again. At first
she'd feared Khar wouldn't return with her, the ghatten, eyes
still closed, too young to travel, but Sarrett and Per'la had
helped, taking zealous charge of a large wooden packing
crate stuffed with straw for Khar and the ghatten to nest in,
safe from prying eyes. The crate had been transferred to the
closet here, and it wasn't until earlier today that she'd been
privileged to see the ghatten.

She grinned. What a day, and what a night from the
sounds below. Parse's voice rose high and indignant, "I did
not lose the plans, Mahafny! I left them there on the table
for you while you and Jenret were outside hammering away,
pulverizing that device." "Well, they weren't there when I
came back." "I think I can remember how to redraw it,
though the ratios may be slightly off."

An insidious device that revealed Resonant powers
whether the person wished it revealed or not. A chill crept
up her spine—would she have wanted to know in advance of
her bursting forth, her powers surging high in the midst of
the contorting pain—hemorrhaging after labor, drained almost bloodless—and then sweeping through to fill the emptiness within her. No, and pray the Lady that the plans were
well and truly lost, hadn't fallen into the wrong hands. Not
while at least a tenuous reservoir of goodwill existed between Normals and Resonants, the deaths of Darl and
Faertom, Garvey, Hylan, and Bazelon Foy amongst others
serving as an all too grim reminder of what could happen,
had almost happened. Too bad the one that Lindy and Davvy
referred to as Tadj had escaped, but surely he was long gone
by now.

Goodwill had deepened as well between Marchmont and
Canderis, Eadwin and Muscadeine hastily canceling the
royal progress after Ruysdael and returning to Gaernett as
part of Doyce's anxious escort, surrounded by his soldiers
and Guardians. Eadwin and his people had been spending
long days with the recuperating Monitor and the High Conciliators, and she suspected the talks ranged from trade and
tariffs to the utilization of Resonant abilities. Certainly
Mahafny had looked abstracted of late, muttering to herself
about aptitudes, training periods, and testing.

As to her own skills, she wasn't sure where they would
lead her, content to take it "with all due, deliberate speed,"

as Arras had advised. Comfortable, safe, right to touch the
infants' minds, explore a whole new universe of closeness
with Jenret, or chastise Davvy, but there must be a happy
medium between those "simple" pleasures and touching every mind on Methuen! Well, it could be put off a bit longer.

Think of pleasanter things, she sternly ordered herself, because for once she *was* surrounded by happiness. The wedding this morning, Harrap unaccustomedly brief and totally
solemn. It hadn't seemed terribly necessary somehow, but
Harrap refused to name-bless the twins unless Doyce and
Jenret were joined in matrimony. "The Lady will bless them
whether I do or not," he'd said, "but no blessing from me
unless you commit yourselves." So they had, and Inez had
cried, and Francie had cried, and everyone else, herself included. Yet even that had been marred, some of her tears a
secret mourning for the burly, bouncy Harrap who once was,
replaced by a gaunt, gray soul still conquering the craving
for Hylan's special drug and the transcendent communion
with the Lady it had offered.

The only one missing today had been Swan, and for that
Doyce grieved. The Seeker General hovered at the twilight
borders now, no matter what Mahafny and the other
eumedicos did for her. Jenret and Bard had carried Doyce in
to see her, but Swan barely recognized her. Without Swan's
presence, something essential was lacking.

And then the naming day this afternoon. Damaris, so
much like Jenret with her dark hair and blue eyes, had con-
trived to whisper a warning before the ceremony. "Have you
talked about names with Jenret? You do understand that it's
family tradition to give the children names beginning with
J."

She thought it over, realized she'd missed the obvious.
Jadrian, Jenret's father; Jared, his dead brother; Jacobia, his
sister. And Damaris had had little choice but to name
Jacobia as she had, since it couldn't be revealed that Jadrian
was not her father, a shell of a man, a body with no brain after Jared had swept it clean. "I understand," she said, patting
Damaris's hand. Understand she did, but she didn't much
care for the idea.

Thus she'd been surprised when Jenret stood stiffly in
front of Harrap, Bard and Jacobia on his left, holding the girl
baby, and Arras and Francie on the right, with the boy.

"What do you name these children before the eyes of Our Lady and of your friends and relatives?" Harrap had asked.

He'd hesitated, longer than Doyce had thought possible, color sweeping up the back of his neck, burning his ears. Not from embarrassment, but laboring in the grip of strong emotions. At last he'd spoken. "All family traditions must expand and grow as families expand and grow. It's been tradition for all children of this Wycherley branch to bear names that begin with 'J,' and to honor that I name my daughter—our daughter," he caught Doyce's gaze, "Jenneth. But in honor of my wife, Doyce, and my mother, Damaris, I proclaim our son Diccon. With their mother's permission, of course." Diccon, Jenneth, two good, solid names.

As Damaris and Inez herded most of the guests from the room after the ceremony to start the party below, Khar's voice had issued from the closet. **"It's stuffy in here. We need fresh air. Rawn, Saam, if you please."**

In total abashment, tripping over each other and their own feet, the two ghatts had slunk into the closet. No one except Sarrett had laid eyes on the ghatten, and it dawned on Doyce that she'd never wormed out of Khar who the father was. *"You don't suppose . . . ?"* she asked Jenret.

Head held high, Khar marched out, amber eyes twinkling and triumphant. She looked thin as a rail, her suddenly slim sides saggy below. A surreptitious hand on her own abdomen, Doyce winced in agreement. Behind her came Rawn, careful and fussy as if he held an egg in his mouth, a coal black ghatten painted with almost circular gray-brown stripes, its tiny nose bright pink. After him came Saam, quizzical but capable, carrying a steel-gray ghatten, and again the ghatten boasted the heritage of its mother, the same circular striping.

Mahafny gasped, laughed nervously. "She didn't! I mean, I know it's possible, but . . ."

A slow parade of the room, the momentary laying of each ghatten in Doyce's hands, their tiny claws working, little faces scrunched as they butted blindly against her palm, and then the two ghatts returned their charges to the closet.

"If Jenret can honor past and present, then we have as well," Saam said, **"and Khar felt it was necessary to heal the past."**

"We three have shared much together," Rawn added, **"and Khar has let us share more."**

"You're making it damnably hard charts straight," Mahafny sputtered, rassed.

"Ghatti don't need genealogy S-curved around the closet door and s

"Well you bloody do, now!"

Remembering the earlier scene, Doy could hear Khar chuckling. "Don't blame known as Khar of the Loose Morals."

"Only puritanical humans could thi Didn't notice Harrap taking it amiss, d

The wind picked up outside, made D they'd have snow, but on looking outside s Disciple moons around the Lady moon were The turn of the year, a new year. She gaspe as a dark shadow brushed the window, regain she heard a plaintive scratching.

Bursting out of the closet, Khar rushed to **"Hurry, it's cold, and Koom's so tired,"** Doyce. The window stuck when she tried to p abdominal muscles too lax and weak, so she con the power she could muster in her shoulders, s ward so hard the window frame bit her hands.

"What's he doing here, why isn't he with Swan opened the window and the ghatt staggered inside, gan to toll. Once ruddy, now rust-colored and thi dragged himself onto her lap. **"I came to tell y** rasped, **"that Swan's dead."** Tears dripped down cheeks, pattered on Koom. **"Thought I could beat th tell you first."** He swallowed, licked his chops. **"You be the next Seeker General, Doyce. You and Kha what Swan wanted."**

"But, but . . . it's not what Swan wants, it's what the S ers decide, vote on! I'm not suitable Seeker General m rial, I've a family to raise."

"Would you refuse her wish, then?" His eyes search hers, looking for doubts, looking for strength, looking fo truth. **"You'll be voted in, never fear. After all, we ghatti *do* have a say in how our Bonds cast their votes."** He paused, eyes closing tiredly. **"You're the only one who can help knit Canderis together. You've done it unconsciously once, and now you must do it consciously, bit by bit, stitch by stitch. Swan knew that, prayed she could sur-**

Tad Williams

Memory, Sorrow and Thorn

THE DRAGONBONE CHAIR: Book 1
☐ **Hardcover Edition**   0-8099-003-3—$19.50
☐ **Paperback Edition**   UE2384—$5.99

A war fueled by the dark powers of sorcery is about to engulf the long-peaceful land of Osten Ard—as the Storm King, undead ruler of the elvishlike Sithi, seeks to regain his lost realm through a pact with one of human royal blood. And to Simon, a former castle scullion, will go the task of spearheading the quest that offers the only hope of salvation . . . a quest that will see him fleeing and facing enemies straight out of a legend-maker's worst nightmares!

STONE OF FAREWELL: Book 2
☐ **Hardcover Edition**   UE2435—$21.95
☐ **Paperback Edition**   UE2480—$5.99

As the dark magic and dread minions of the undead Sithi ruler spread their seemingly undefeatable evil across the land, the tattered remnants of a once-proud human army flee in search of a last sanctuary and rallying point, and the last survivors of the League of the Scroll seek to fulfill missions which will take them from the fallen citadels of humans to the secret heartland of the Sithi.

TO GREEN ANGEL TOWER: Book 3
☐ **Hardcover Edition**   UE2521—$25.00
☐ **Paperback Edition, Part I**   UE2598—$5.99
☐ **Paperback Edition, Part II**   UE2606—$5.99

In this concluding volume of the best-selling trilogy, the forces of Prince Josua march toward their final confrontation with the dread minions of the undead Storm King, while Simon, Miriamele, and Binabek embark on a desperate mission into evil's stronghold.
